FREE A[...]
PAR[...]

FREE AT LAST IN PARADISE

A historical novel on Sri Lanka

by

ANANDA W. P. GURUGE

ISBN 1-58500-136-8

1st Books-rev. 5/19/00

FREE AT LAST IN PARADISE is a historical novel on Sri Lanka. This Island nation of great antiquity had been known to the Greeks and the Romans as Taprobane, to the Arabs as Serendip, to the Portuguese as Ceilao and to the Dutch as Ceylaan. A British Colony from 1796 to 1948, it has been known as Ceylon until, as a republic in 1972, it reverted to its age-old nomenclature of Sri Lanka. Its rich culture as reflected by an astounding heritage of monuments, literature, art, religious traditions and social values has merited many scholarly works.

This is a pioneering work in that a reputed scholar-diplomat of Sri Lanka has chosen the medium of fiction to share the highlights of this heritage with the worldwide English-reading public. It is a fictography or a fictional biography which "draws aside curtains and allows the reader to enter a world to which other authors had not been privy - one of the central character growing to adulthood and death."

Portraying Sri Lanka's march to Independence over well nigh a century, the novel highlights the role of Colonel Henry Steel Olcott, Madame Blavatsky and other Theosophists of USA who spearheaded the struggle of this British Colony for liberation through the revival of Buddhism and nationalistic sentiments. The key characters are renowned proteges of Olcott, who continues to be hailed and honored as a foremost national leader.

"The book will be read with pleasure," says David Vickery of Britain, "by those who love Ceylon and introduce those who have no knowledge of the country to a fascinating society."

Leslie Grey M.D. of Denver, Colorado, USA, in his review published in the Journal of Theosophical History, says, "a *magnum opus,* a masterpiece from any angle. Elegant style, eloquent language, relentless tempo, exciting and almost galloping

Ceylon is really a Paradise of natural beauties for one who can appreciate them..

Ernst Haeckel (1882)

Ah! Lovely Lanka, Gem of the summer Seas, how doeth thy sweet image rise before me as I write the story of my experiences among thy dusky children, of my success in warming their hearts to revere their incomparable religion and its holiest Founder.. Happy the Karma which brought me to thy shores!

Colonel Henry Steel Olcott
(1899)

Map of Sri Lanka (Ceylon)

ACKNOWLEDGEMENTS

The author is deeply indebted to his wife Darshanika Guruge for her unfailing assistance and encouragement and to Mr. David J. Vickery of Langrick, Boston, Lincolnshire, Britain, who read the manuscript as it was written and made invaluable comments and suggestions on the basis of his excellent knowledge of the history and culture of Sri Lanka.

To Darshanika with love

Prologue

Thrice have I begun in earnest to write the story of my life and times. On each occasion, a formidable obstacle was the thought that so much was happening around me and I needed to be in touch with new developments. After almost a year since the last aborted or rather abandoned start, I am obsessed with a persisting urge to make one more attempt. At the ripe old age of ninety, I have no alternative. It is now or never.

Today, the fourth of February 1948, is a day of dual significance - one personal and the other national.

It is my ninetieth birthday. For a long time, my birthday has become an occasion for reflection rather than celebration. I recall the vicissitudes of a life through eventful times less for the joy of having survived them all but more for the confirmation that all phenomena, the good, the bad and the indifferent, are evanescent and impermanent. Life is but a sequence of fleeting images, voices and impressions.

Of far greater importance, however, is that today the land of my birth regains independence after centuries of foreign domination. It is the culmination of a persistently peaceful two-track process: one of national self-conscientization to become a modern nation with a proper appreciation of its cultural heritage and history; and another of progressive constitutional evolution based on agitation, consultation and negotiation and guided by a deep commitment to democracy.

I have had a ring-side seat in the national arena. It is true that for the most part I have been an interested, if not concerned, observer. But I also had the rare privilege of making a few humble contributions. For well nigh seven decades, less three decades of voluntary isolation, have I been active in one way or another to usher in this day of joy.

Therefore do I begin to dictate my memoirs with a sense of fulfillment, tinged though not tainted, I must frankly admit, by a feeling of pride and jubilation.

The island whose recent history I propose to recount in these pages has been home to many peoples over several millennia. Fascinating discoveries of its pre-historic past speak of cultures long forgotten. A megalithic dolmen and cave paintings, urn burials and stone age implements predate a recorded history of at least twenty-five centuries.

Legends and literature confirm the nation's antiquity. The *Ramayana*, the popular epic poem of the neighboring subcontinent, calls this island *Lanka* and describes its location off the southern tip of India accurately. The mythical demon-king Ravana of Lanka is portrayed as a villain who abducts the consort of Rama, a prince of Northern India. The line of tiny islands and sandbanks which dot the eighteen miles of the sea separating it from the mainland is believed to be the vestiges of a bridge or rather a causeway which Rama constructed to invade Lanka with his army of monkeys. The vanquished demon-king, however, continues to be celebrated in legends and poems of India as a scholar, poet, expert in medicine and inventor of the violin! Both the Jains and the Buddhists claim him as a pious adherent!! Buddhists of China, Korea and Japan believe that an important philosophical text which they hold in high veneration contains a sermon preached by the Buddha to this demon-king in Lanka. In their scriptures both Ravana and his brother Vibhisana are mentioned as pious adherents to the Greater Vehicle of Buddhism.

The country still bears the name *Lanka*, which, some scholars posit, means simply an island. About a thousand years ago, the prefix *Sri* had been added as an honorific. Thus came the usage *Sri Lanka*, meaning "The Resplendent Island". This name may still be unfamiliar to my readers who know our island home only as *Ceylon* or its other European equivalents *Ceylan, Ceylaan* and *Ceilao*.

Do we like any of these names? No one has really asked us.

My preference, of course, is for *Sri Lanka*.

Like Australia or New Zealand, it has only a geographical connotation. For the same reason, I would have even liked the ancient name by which Greeks and Romans knew it. *Taprobane* which Ptolemy in his map magnified to many times its size was called by us *Tamraparni* or *Tambapanni*. Signifying "Copper-coloured Palms" - palms of the hand and not the trees - it refers to the fertile soil of the Island's coastal plain.

Ceylon, on the contrary, has an ethnic sense like England, the land of the Angles or France, the land of the Franks. Ceylon comes via Latin, Persian and Arabic corruptions, *Singaldivi/Seren-Devi/Serendib*, of Sanskrit and Pali appellations *Sinhala-dipa /Sihalanam dipa* - the Island of the Sinhalas.

The Sinhalas of Northern Indian origin, speaking a language of the Indo-Aryan family of Indo-European languages, continue to be the majority. Yet, several other distinct ethnic groups claim as their home this charming island with its salubrious climate and breath-taking scenic beauty.

Book One

ALL TOO BRIEF A CHILDHOOD
AND
MENTORLESS MEANDERING

The pear-shaped Island rises to a triangular central massif which at the highest point is over eight thousand feet. Well-watered by both monsoons from southwest and northeast, three mighty rivers flow through the highlands carving out a medley of fertile valleys. They form ideal homelands for the rice-growing peasantry. Where the longest of these rivers cuts through a deep and noisy cataract for several miles is a historic hamlet.

Commemorating a royal grant of its rice fields to the Sangha (that is, the Buddhist Clergy), it was called the Sangha-Gem-Field. *Hanguranketa* protected by the mountainous terrain but yet accessible through the winding valleys of the Great Sand *Mahaveli* River, this hamlet had seen better days. The kings of Kandy, the last capital of the hilly kingdom, escaped to it when forced by the invading armies of the Portuguese, the Dutch and the British from the sixteenth to early nineteenth century.

A Buddhist temple reputed for its remarkable repository of invaluable palmleaf manuscripts and a Hindu temple with exceptional works of art in sculpture and mural paintings suggest an age when this sleepy hamlet was a centre of national culture.

On the fourth of February 1858, recorded in my horoscope as 1780 of the Saka Era, I was born in this hamlet. It is a date few people in the neighborhood had forgotten. In a freak landslide of gigantic scale, the hillock bearing our cottage of wattle and daub with cadjan or coconut frond roofing slid a quarter of a mile to settle on the meagre rice field on which the family subsisted. A good part of what was once our high land of mixed cultivation of exotic tropical fruit trees was washed down the Great Sand River in an unprecedented flood. I do not know how welcome my birth was.

With seven older children, my arrival would have normally meant an additional mouth to feed, at least till I was big enough to become economically active for the family unit. But the disaster which coincided with my birth - to the very minute, as the midwife never failed to remind me - left my position somewhat dubious.

Some blamed the catastrophe as a misfortune which I had brought with me to a family which deserved better. They commiserated with my father who had been a proud and independent cultivator of his own freehold. Now he was doomed to forego his dignity and become a hired hand or a share-cropper in other's fields. That applied to all his children too.

Others thought differently. They attributed to my luck the fact that our cottage alone survived the slide which had taken a toll of a dozen men and children in two similar cottages nearer the rice field. The midwife and two women who came to help her from these cottages were the only fortunate survivors.

The midwife who was a cousin of my mother had declared that I was born with an impressive destiny. Her proof was that I was nearly strangled by the umbilical cord which circled my neck. Even before she or any one else in the house was aware of the catastrophic landslide, she is said to have declared, "The baby brings a lot of merit from his previous births".

According to the prevailing belief of the Buddhists, one reaps in this world the reward or retribution for one's good or bad action from any number of previous births. Good action leads to the accumulation of merit. My mother and her maternal uncle who was the chief monk of the village temple were easily convinced by the midwife. Later, the monk confirmed his conviction with a horoscope which he wrote on an ivory-coloured palmleaf.

Hardly a day passed in my childhood without being reminded of the fateful night. Some children would refuse forthright to let me join their teams in competitive games. Others would beg me to join them, specially when luck had turned against them. I have often heard myself being called "black-eared". To be called black-eared is to be rated good-for-nothing. In our native idiom, a pun on this pejorative term also had the meaning of "devourer of time".

As disconcerting as being called names were equally frequent occasions when I was pointed out in a crowd by strangers who seem to be impressed by what they considered a miracle. It was worse when people asked me for details of the night's happenings and expected me to know all answers. The strict code of conduct which was ingrained in us by home, temple and community and, later school, required children to be always polite, obedient and obliging to adults. There were times when I wished I was never born. Few could attribute a miserable childhood to a natural disaster from which one escaped miraculously!

I have no idea when the family took the decision that I would be a monk. Perhaps it was a vow taken at the time of my birth or shortly afterward. If so, it could have been taken by my father. Mother had been in pain for almost the whole day and in shock for long hours after my birth.

2

As I came to know later from different accounts, it was an unusually dark night. Heavy unseasonable rains had lasted over three days and nights with intermittent thunder and lightning.

As was the custom, our neighbors had taken turns to bring us meals from the time mother was incapacitated. Father had asked a few of our closest relatives and friends to be in readiness to carry her to the house of the village physician if the midwife felt incompetent to handle any unexpected situation. The males huddled together in the leaking verandah around an imported chimney lamp whose flame threatened to blow out with every gust of wind. As the night grew and no encouraging news came from the women inside, someone suggested that they should chant a particular religious text. Associated with a ferocious bandit named Finger-Garland whom the Buddha converted to a saintly life, this short text is believed to be significantly efficacious in easing the pain of childbirth.

An elderly relative of mine who was a teacher by day and a astrologer/witch-doctor in his spare time used to describe most dramatically the events of that night which he remembered from his teens:

"That bout of lightning literally lasted hours. The clap of thunder which followed was the loudest. The lamp was about to blow out and I reached for it. But I failed and the glass broke into smithereens even as the oil on the unpaved earthen floor caught fire. I was stamping on it when my knees plopped. I felt as though I was in a boat shooting the rapids. I was groping in the dark for any available support when an eerie crushing and scraping noise deafened us. In the cacophony of voices, shrieks and wailing, the voice of uncle Big Banda was the loudest asking us to take cover from what he described as 'an enormous earthquake' and the next was the distinct cry of a new born baby from inside.

"Within minutes everything was calm. An oil lamp was found and lit. The joy of a new arrival made everybody oblivious of what had happened outside. Only the village headman who was among the adults who recited the sacred text worried that the roar of the river rose suddenly to a high pitch. 'This is very funny. I hear as if the river has come to our doorstep,' he said.

"My uncle's thoughts were elsewhere. He had expected to have a daughter after seven sons. He looked relieved but not happy. None of us dared to ask him how he felt."

I had heard this account in varying versions on all kinds of family occasions. As time went by, more and more embellishments came to be added. From the earliest moment of my life which I can recall, that is, from about the third or fourth year, I suffered inside with the impression that I was an unwanted child. My mother would always comfort me.

"You are born with a mission, a destiny. There are great things in store for you," she would tell me referring to predictions made in the horoscope which her own uncle, Chief Monk of the temple, had cast on my birth.

The monk himself repeated them as often as he could. He would stroke my head and say,

"You will bring so much fame to this hamlet that people from all over will come here."

I do not know how he was so sure. I also did not know what such fame meant to me or what benefit I would derive from it.

I would have been happier if I was not called names or pointed out as a wonder. As I grew up, I was less and less affected by either.

The extensive slab of granite which was exposed as the hillock with our cottage slid down to the rice fields had become the playground of the village children. The terrain suited our rural games such as 'dodging the bear" or "capturing the enemy." But I was hardly there. When children refused to play with me, which was more often than not, I would go to the temple where I found a lot of solace and fun in the company of young novices.

Novices in a Buddhist Monastery were not allowed to play. But when senior monks were not around, their boyish pranks could be as boisterous and noisy as those of their lay counterparts. They had a flare to return with baffling rapidity from such behaviour to perfect calmness and serenity. It was a game by itself. The senior monks felt flattered that their presence could instantly turn shouting brats into saintly hermits.

In the company of these novices, I learned almost seven hundred letter forms of the Sinhala alphabet with twenty vowels and thirty-four consonants from an illustrated palmleaf book and practised writing on a sandboard. It was an ingenious device. Letters were formed by writing on a thin layer of sand with the index finger. One could try over and over again until one mastered a letter with all its forms. My progress was apparently watched by the senior monks. One of them in his early twenties called me one day and led me to a nearby tree. Every shady tree seemed to have a few boulders carefully arranged to benefit from the shade of the tree right through the day. The monk spread a leather prayer mat and sat on a rock. I was asked to stand before him slightly to the right. From under his flowing yellow robe, he produced a slim palmleaf book with profusely illustrated wooden binders.

4

This was to be my first book. I was a bit disappointed. I remembered how at least two of my elder brothers were introduced to their first books. "Reading the first letters" was an elaborate ceremony. Milk rice, oil cakes and new clothes were indispensable to it. I felt cheated. But I had learned to expect the unusual - all because I was born with the landslide. The monk must have read my thoughts. He explained that there would be no such ceremony for me because I had already learned to read.

"You have read your first letters long before anyone could introduce them to you at an auspicious time with all the rites involved", he said.

I wondered whether I was being punished. I had been too eager to emulate my friends among the novices. And, worse still, I had pre-empted my parents from finding an astrologically auspicious time to get me to read my first letters.

"Was it a good thing?", some lurking superstition prompted me to ask. Any one with the slightest claim to an education, particularly monks and physicians, were expected to be well versed in astrology to answer such a question.

"There is no good thing or bad thing when it comes to learning. The earlier you learn anything the more time you will have to learn something else. Any way, learning the alphabet is a very boring thing. Now you can begin to read. That could be pleasanter and more rewarding."

He was correct. I felt elated as I read the list of place names in the palmleaf book. "Sagama" "Pasgama" "Arattana," I read aloud and the nodding head of my teacher confirmed that I was correct. I had read more than half the book before I met my first difficulty with the bane of pedantic complexity of written Sinhala - contorted single symbols for syllables like ksa, jna, jjha, nkti. Back to the sandboard.

For several weeks I looked forward daily to this hour-long session under the flowering ironwood tree. Then did my grand-uncle, Chief Monk, hear me out reading the entire text in one session. He stroked my head as he always did to express his affection or appreciation and produced from the refectory a plateful of the most delicious sweetmeats. So my sweets came at the end of my first book. It was typical of many things which happened in my life. Mine has always been a case of the cart before the horse.

With neither ceremony nor pre-warning, I was thus introduced to a traditional course of literacy and memory training. It was challenging but in no way threatening. Instruction was on a one to one basis. Repetitive drill and memorization were at one's own pace. The setting

5

was invariably informal: under a tree, on the doorstep or in a corner of the preaching hall. I could come to the temple any time in the afternoon. Any monk who was free would be my teacher for the day. I would read the text, which was in Sanskrit verse, along with the word-to-word Sinhala translation and recite the verses I had to memorize. The teacher would correct mistakes, if any, and set work for the next day. In less than an hour I would be back, unless, of course, novices were inclined to fool around.

I progressed from book to book. It was all rote learning. Some of the verses I had committed to memory provided material for reflection. They were meant to summarize for you the values and ideals upheld by society. Among them were beautiful verses in Sinhala in praise of learning:

What no thief could steal from wherever you keep,
What no flood of boundless water would ever wash away,
What no angry king or minister could ever snatch from you
That learning should one acquire for one's good in the future

Gnomes in Sanskrit verse embodied rare gems of wisdom:

Devoid of malice, sound in health and senses restrained,
Compassionate, forbearing and popular with all persons,
Generous, giving and free from fear and grief,
These ten qualities the learned do define.

The routine changed when I was eleven. One day I was given a tiny stylus and a polished palmleaf. I had seen other novices scratching letters on palmleaf. It required skill to hold the leaf between the thumb and index finger of the left hand and to cut circular letters with the fine point of the steel stylus, held firm with the right hand. The nail of the left thumb was used as the fulcrum for the stylus.

"Go home and practise all letters of the alphabet including conjunct letters" was all the instruction.

It must have been some form of promotion or graduation. My mother was thrilled to see my stylus. Father who was rarely demonstrative of any emotion was visibly pleased as he held me out as a model for several of my older brothers. Three of them had still to graduate to writing. They were slow learners and showed little enthusiasm. Of the other four, the eldest two had dropped out from studies and were helping the father in a project he had started by himself seven years ago.

Taking advantage of the sliding of our high land toward the river, he had been converting its lower reaches into terraced rice fields. Every year he added a few narrow ribbons of paddies. Watering them profusely to grow rice demanded ingenuity. Water was tapped from a stream flowing down a nearby hill slope to the river and diverted to his fields through a miniature aqueduct made of massive green bamboos slit into halves and mounted on a procession of tripods. This curious contraption which snaked along the slope of the two hillocks and spanned the tiny valley at the narrowest point provided gallons of water day and night to the highest terrace and filled in succession each paddy to the level determined by the break in the little dyke.

"I have never seen anything like this anywhere," said the village headman, who, apart from being a distant relative of my father, was a much loved friend of the family. "How ever did you think of it?"

"This chap's mighty brain", my father replied pointing to my eldest brother.

Both my eldest brothers who were rapidly lapsing to illiteracy had their own skills. They were wonderful with their hands. They could hoe and plough, saw and plane, and make things with wood and metal. They were helping father to convert our cottage of wattle and daub into a burnt brick structure with a roof of flat clay tiles. They knew a lot of the river and mountains on both banks.

I was their most fervent admirer. They took me out on some of their adventures. But all did not turn out well. Once we returned red and swollen from a honey gathering expedition.   When the parents remonstrated them for taking me on these wild escapades, they had a ready answer:

"The Tiny One is too involved with novices in the temple and is becoming too lazy. He should learn some things that are not in books."

By this they meant the plants and animals and the fantastic secrets of nature that an observant eye could unravel at every step in the lush vegetation of our environment. For some reason, which I never understood, my father endorsed their view. When mother stressed the need for safety and discouraged our excursions to the roaring river and the jungle of the mountain slopes, he would cut her short sternly,

"These children have to live their lives in this place."

Both parents and all my brothers were there when I brought home the stylus and the palmleaf.

"I must have been at least fourteen when I was taught writing", said my eldest brother.

"Then I must have been only thirteen because we began writing with the same stylus", said the next brother in a note which assumed that he had a claim to some additional respect. "But see the Tiny One. He is hardly eleven."

There was no doubt that I was a little hero that night. We had two special guests at dinner time. Eating in our home, as was the custom at that time, was a very private affair. Mother would cook a huge pot of rice and a number of curries in earthenware pans. Pumpkins both golden and silver, a variety of gourds of different sizes and tastes and all kinds of edible leaves went into these curries, besides such favourites as young jak fruit, purple taro leaves and tender shoots of the madu palm. Tiny cubes of dry fish, deep fried with onion were a special delicacy.

My mother's uncle, junior by twelve years to Chief Monk of the temple, had dropped in to consult my parents on a marriage proposal received from a nearby family for his daughter. My father's younger brother was a frequent visitor and this evening he had come as usual to spend a few leisurely moments with his nephews. Mother insisted that they should eat with us.

Deftly she filled large clay bowls which served as plates. Each found a quiet spot in the house and the verandah to deal with the mountain of rice and the selection of curries. Mother's cooking had quite a reputation in the village. Tonight the food was unusually good. She must have thought of asking her uncle to eat with us. She went in turn to each of us with seconds, which she served directly from the cooking pots. With everyone's attention directed to the food, she had a

8

silent audience. Whether this was by accident or design, I could never guess. That was the time when she would address the family on whatever she had in her mind. Tonight she was happy.

"The monks in the temple seem to think that our Tiny One is cut out to be a learned Buddhist monk," she began. "Our Chief Monk would like to have him in the temple as soon as possible. He spoke to me on the last fullmoon day also."

"Let the Tiny One enjoy his childhood," said my paternal uncle, whom we called Little Father.

He was about ten years older than my eldest brother. Yet, he played with us and confided in us his little secrets. He was once a candidate for monkhood. He was held up as a role model to the children who came to the temple for their education. Sometimes, he supervised their studies. But he never entered the Order. We wondered why he changed his mind. Now that he was well past twenty years of age, he could no longer be a novice. Will they admit him to the Order without the obligatory period of acolyte and novice? Perhaps, he did not see much fun in monastic life.

He continued in a gloomy tone,

"Times are changing. It is not like in olden times. What future is there for a monk? What future is there for Buddhism in this country? I wonder whether there will be enough Buddhists even to give a monk his single square meal for the day."

My seventh brother who was seated with me on the kitchen floor laughed and whispered,

"That's the best thing that can happen to you for all your gluttony. You go to the temple because the monks give you those nice things to eat, you gluttonous pig. You think that you can have the best of everything without working one bit, you lazy good-for-nothing. I will wait for the day you starve and come home begging for food."

A scuffle resulting from my throwing a handful of hot curry on his face distracted us for some time. In the semi-darkness of the kitchen lit by only a one-wick coconut oil lamp, no one saw us fighting. We also settle our quarrels very fast. That is something you learn in a household of eight boys. If a petty fight is not settled soon, it becomes a veritable melee.

Meanwhile, mother has gone on to elaborate her plans for me. I could only hear the last part.

"He is not even eleven. He has read all the 'Century Books'. Chief Monk tells me that he has memorized many verses in Sinhala, Pali and Sanskrit. Now he wants him to learn writing. In fact, he was given a stylus today."

9

"What an auspicious day I have chosen to come here," said my maternal grand-uncle. "So, we have another budding scholar in the family. We have to think of a successor to our brother Chief Monk some day. Maybe, that is what they are thinking of Tiny One."

"Me! To be Chief Monk of the temple! Not just any temple!! The Royal Monastery of Sangha-Gem-Field !!!" The very thought amused me. "Will the novices and even the other monks take me seriously?" But the prospect appeared a pleasant one. Perhaps, my brother was right. I had a fascination for the lazy life of comfort and luxury which I saw in the temple. Suddenly a cold shiver went down my spine.

"What will I do when all these adults, my parents, grandparents, uncles and aunts and even the village headman fall at my feet, worship me and await my benedictions?"

My reverie was broken by the grave voice of my father who said, " I think there is a lot of truth in what my younger brother says. One does not give one's son to the Order only to get merit. One looks forward to the prestige of the family. See how much we all gained in recognition by having someone from our family as Chief Monk here and as Abbot in my own village. But if Buddhism declines as all the present signs show, will there be temples? Will there be monks? It will be terrible to see the brightest child of the family leading a life useless to him and useless to society."

"That is what I thought, elder brother. I want to see what other avenues exist for a diligent and hard-working young man in an evolving society."

What followed was a long and intricate discussion among the three adults to which mother gave ear and contributed a few sporadic remarks. But the whole thing was beyond us.

One by one the eight boys got up, rinsed the clay bowls, drank a little water from the pitcher kept outside the house, placed the bowls upside down on the little bamboo platform for pots and pans and melted into the darkness of the compound. We formed little groups to while away the rest of the evening. There were many things we could do. We solved riddles and puzzles, narrated stories, sang carter's and boatman's working songs or committed to memory the verses set by our teachers in the temple. The last to join us was the eldest brother. He placed his hands on my shoulders and made a cryptic statement.

"You are going places, Tiny One. They are thinking of sending you to study in some far off place."

"When and where?" I asked him.

"I have no idea at all."

Reverend Thomas Blake was not a stranger in our village even though he lived in Bo-tree Plain a few miles down the hill track. The village was so named because an ancient Pipal (*Ficus Religiosa*) tree, renowned for its association with the enlightenment of the Buddha, was the centrepiece of the temple. The padre was seen frequently at the temple of Sangha-Gem-Field as he was a close friend of my grand-uncle, Chief Monk. Within days of his arrival in the area, he had called on the then Chief Monk and established good relations with monks and important supporters of the temple.

An enthusiastic evangelist and dedicated church-worker, he had since made it a point to come in contact with practically everyone from every walk of life in the neighbourhood.

"He is a gregarious go-getter by inclination or training or both," was the assessment of Chief Monk.

Reverend Blake whom the villagers called "White Padre" hailed from Hornby in Kent in England. He used to call it a sleepy town with only one claim to fame. From its bay one looked north onto an open sea which extended right up to the Arctic Circle. The harsh northern winds brought chill and snow. From there to warm sunny Ceylon was a trip to paradise.

As the second son of an affluent and influential land-owning family, he could have chosen any mission either in the British Isles or anywhere in the far-flung British Empire. He had selected Ceylon for several reasons. In his family library were several books on exotic foreign lands. Taking advantage of a break in his Divinity Studies at the nearby Canterbury Cathedral, he had read them avidly. Two books captured his imagination, he told me once. One was AN HISTORICAL RELATION OF CEYLON IN THE EAST-INDIES TOGETHER *with an ACCOUNT of the Detaining in Captivity the Author and divers other Englishmen now Living there, and of the Author's Miraculous ESACAPE by Robert Knox, A Captive there near Twenty Years, published in 1681.* It was a remarkable book which presented a comprehensive first hand account of the country and the people. No aspect of the life of the people went unmentioned.

The other published in 1837 in Ceylon in two volumes was *The Mahavamso in Roman Characters with the Translation subjoined and an Introductory Essay on Pali Buddhistical Literature by George Turnour.* This was Sri Lanka's non-stop epic or rather its first part of thirty-seven chapters. The Mahavamsa or the Great Chronicle has been described as non-stop because it was periodically prolonged to cover the entire history of the island from 543 Before Christ right up to 1815 of the Christian Era. Few countries in the world could boast of a long

11

history of over two millennia and fewer still would have it written down unbroken.

Young Blake was fascinated by not only the history and the culture which the epic described but also the unique role which Buddhism played in fashioning them. He longed to make a career in Ceylon.

It did not take too long to find that the Church Missionary Society was looking for men like him to open new missions in the central hills of Ceylon, which had become a part of the British Empire only a decade and a half ago. He was given a choice. He could assist a senior padre to set up a prestigious school in Kandy which until 1815 was the capital of the independent Sinhala Kingdom and engage in proselitizing boys from important Buddhist families. The importance of this project was explained to him as directly related to the future of Christianity in the Island and the stability of British rule.

"One boy from the Kandyan Sinhala aristocracy means to the Church more than a thousand peasants. Once he is Christian, his loyalty to the regime will be undivided."

Reverend Blake used to mention this statement from his initial briefing to emphasize what he missed by taking the second option, which was to come to a strange village, find friends and converts, set up a school and eventually build a church. In either case, he would receive the fullest support of the British administration. The British Governor, Robert Brownrigg, who was responsible for the annexation of the hill-country had gone on record with the statement,

"It is not necessary to dwell upon my sincere zeal for a wide extension of the Christian faith, as it were independent of other motives; *because it is inseparably connected with my political office.*"

Reverend Blake had asked for an assignment close to the area where Robert Knox was held captive by Royal-Lion the Second (1635-1687).

"I have a feel for this place because I have read Knox's book at least twice. Besides, the people there must have some familiarity with white foreigners," he had urged.

He was fully aware of the advantage of being accepted or at least unobstructed by the people for success in a foreign land. For some curious reason, Royal-Lion the Second had held captive at least a score of Europeans who were allowed to settle down and have families. Only Knox is recorded to have not taken that option and escaped from captivity.

As Reverend Blake had guessed, the people in our region had retained a vivid memory of these captives whose life style found

12

mention in our folk tales. In addition, there were their descendants distinguished by a lighter complexion, brownish hair and, in some rare instances, blue or brown eyes. The light and fair skin of practically all members of our family would suggest some connection with one or more captives of the king eight generations ago.

Elders remember the day Reverend Blake arrived in the village. That was eighteen years before I was born. They speak of an erect, handsome and confident young man with an imposing beard and whiskers who walked along the river bank with his belongings straddled on two donkeys. With a letter from the new British Administrator in Kandy, he met the village headman and was accommodated in a tent in his garden. Later a modest cottage was built at a spot he chose for his mission in the village of Bo-tree Plain. The land originally belonged to a family who, in terms of the traditional land tenure system, had received it as a royal grant in exchange for some services to be rendered to the Hindu Temple in our village dedicated to God Vishnu or Rama.

The British administration had declared all uncultivated land to be crown property and was thus able to allot a sizeable acreage to the Church Missionary Society on a nominal lease for ninety-nine years.

Within twenty years, Reverend Blake had established a school, a dispensary where an apothecary saw patients twice a week, and an orphanage for boys.The construction of a church was in progress. In comparison with the modest Buddhist temple, Reverend Blake's establishment was already a grand institution.

That was where I found myself in the company of my father and his youngest brother on the morning following the dinner where my mother raised the question of my future studies. We walked down meandering shortcuts and reached the school before it opened. This was not my first visit to this area. I had passed by the school several times when we visited our relatives.

There was something that made the church complex different from a Buddhist monastery. The imposing site on the slope of the hill commanded the view of the approaching traveller and presented an impression of grandeur. The white walls and red tiles, contrasted by dark green window shutters and door frames, were picturesque. Much thought had gone into landscaping the premises. Flowering and fruit-bearing trees of different sizes were planted at the right places. The rectangular school hall appeared to be more spacious than the square, pavilion-like preaching hall of a monastery. A brick-paved stairway led to a beautiful house at the highest point. Around it were beds of the most exquisite flowers I had seen anywhere. Most of them were exotic and could have been imported from abroad. The place was called the "Church School".

My two adult companions must have been equally impressed with what they saw. Little Father was full of praise.

"See, elder brother, this is what I keep on saying. Our monks at the temple, however, do not like what I say. They think I am disloyal to them. The moment you come to this place, you see that somebody cares; somebody knows that the environment conveys the very first impression of order, discipline and seriousness. Look at the trees, the flowers, the pathways. Don't you see how orderly they are? There isn't a speck of dirt. Don't you realize that White Padre means business and is doing it really right"

I could not discern whether my father agreed or not. His comment was not all that intelligible to me at that time.

"The White Padre has an advantage that our monks don't have. There's a lady who looks after these finer aspects. All that's beautiful here - the trees, the flowers and the garden - is definitely her work. I have seen her working with her own hands, weeding the flower beds and watering the plants. I must say that he was very lucky to get a kind and nice wife like her. Specially so because he knew nothing of her when he agreed to marry her."

"How was that?" asked Little Father who seemed not to know how the Blakes met.

"His friends in England were asked to send him a bride. But for several years, they couldn't find a girl with all the qualifications he has scrupulously listed. One day he heard that a lady who had come all the way from England was stranded in Kandy. The planter to whom she was bethrothed had started an affair with the daughter of a recently imported South Indian indentured labourer. White Padre went to Kandy to knock some good sense into the errant planter. In this he failed. But when the padre saw the lady, it was love at first sight for both of them. So they married then and there. What if she was of the wrong type? Or she didn't like the village? He was taking so many risks. But from what we see, they are getting on well."

"That's what most of the British planters are doing even today. Every horse-drawn state coach to Kandy from the coast brings a couple of brides from Great Britain betrothed to unseen suitors. White Padre, at least, had a choice. She did not come earmarked for him. It's not very different from our arranged marriages, is it?"

Little Father spoke very precisely. He made a distinction between England and Great Britain. I was keen to know how he acquired his wide knowledge of things so far away. My curiosity was satisfied within a few minutes. Reverend Blake stepped out of his house on the hill and saw us standing by the gate. He waved to us and the gesture was friendly. He was half way down the steps when he spoke to Little Father.

"Little Banda, you didn't tell me you were coming today. I thought you will be here as usual on Saturday."

So Little Father was no stranger to this place or to White Padre. My father was as surprised as I was. We had no reason to beleive that he met White Padre regularly on Saturdays.

We approached White Padre as he came to the foot of the steps and made our traditional salutation with clasped hands. None of us went on our knees as we would have done when saluting Buddhist monks. Little Father, however, was noticeably more deferential than my father.

The padre wore a black cassock with a clerical collar. An inch of white satin showed under his chin. He seemed to be more formal this morning. I had seen him in the village in riding breeches with only the clerical collar as a mark of his calling.

"This must be your famous nephew who brought the whole place down the night he was born," he said in perfect fluent, Sinhala. "I hear you are a fine student. Your uncles are very proud of you."

If the plural was meant to include Chief Monk, with whom White Father was known to have frequent and friendly visits, it was not quite accurate. That monk was my grand-uncle. Of course, the Abbot of this village who was a cousin of my father was an uncle.

"I am a good friend of your wife's uncle, Chief Monk of the Royal Monastery," he told my father. "I know your cousin who is the Abbot of the temple here but I must say that I haven't much to do with him."

The comment which by its tone suggested some sort of rivalry between the temple and the church was allowed to pass without a reply. Or rather, Little Father changed the subject swiftly.

"I brought my elder brother and Tiny One to get some advice on his education."

White Padre pulled a watch from a side pocket, read the time.

"Go up to my home. Take your seats in the verandah. I will speak to teachers and children at the school assembly and join you in a few minutes. If Mrs. Blake sees you, you will get something to drink."

15

III

"Am I going to be a student in this school?" I asked myself. If not, what is the advice that White Padre can give us. I have known my parents as well as all others in the family going to the temple for advice on any matter. This appeared to be a very strange situation.

The bell rang. About a hundred students formed three sides of a hollow square facing a flagpost. White Father and six teachers stood facing them. The tallest of the students came forward, said something which was inaudible from where we were and hoisted a flag. It intrigued me as I had not seen it before. It was not the Lion Flag of the Kandyan Kingdom - the flag we still used to decorate the temple on every special occasion. This strange flag was a medley of vertical, horizontal and diagonal lines in red, white and blue.

"That's the British Flag. They call it the 'Union Jack'. It is hoisted here because we are now a part of the British Empire. They rule us and their sovereign Queen Victoria is our Queen. When children and teachers salute the flag they express their allegiance to the Queen. On special days White Padre and his wife sing a song asking God to save the Queen, something like 'God save our Gracious Queen'," Little Father whispered.

This was the first time I had heard him say anything in English. "Could he be coming here to study English?" I wondered. How else could he use such expressions as "Union Jack' and "God save our Gracious Queen"?

What created in my throat a little lump was his reference to the loss of national independence. At my age, I had no idea what it meant to be ruled by the British or a king of our own. I had, however, heard enough from the elders and the monks to feel that something that the people were proud of was taken away from them when my grandfather was about my age or a little younger. I recalled a poem which a senior novice at the temple once taught me.

> "Luckier than we you little ants are
> There is still a king to govern you
> We indeed are the ones deprived
> Hence, alas, we weep in grief"

This was attributed to a woman who wailed as the British deposed the last king of Kandy and led him away a prisoner. I could not believe that my Little Father could so easily accept Queen Victoria as his sovereign.

"Little Father, you seem to be happy that Queen Victoria is your sovereign. Wouldn't you have preferred if we had our king in Kandy? We could at least see him once a while or even take a petition to him," I asked.

"The only thing I have in common with Queen Victoria is that she became Queen the same year I was born. That was in their calender 1837. You must ask White Padre. He has so much to tell you about England, the Queen, national leaders and the greatness of the British people."

"You come here often to meet him?" my father queried. "I thought you went to Kandy for two days a week to study indigenous medicine at the Flower Garden Monastery. When did you come here?"

"I gave up going to Kandy at least two years ago. I come here to join White Father in his work. He has promised to make me a teacher in the school when the time comes."

"Why didn't you tell anyone about your change of mind?"

"I do not want anyone to know I come here or that I help the padre to meet villagers in need of his assistance. Some people will be very upset as most of these villagers had given up Buddhism and become Christians."

The normally inscrutable face of my father half-hidden by his lush beard was red with anger. "You don't think that you are a traitor?"

What could have become an ugly incident was averted by the emergence from the dark interior of the house of an English lady, pale and slim to the point of being lean and emaciated but alert, agile and pleasant. I had seen her in our village on several occasions. Every time she wore identical clothes - a white dress which reached her ankles. Today there was a slight difference. She had covered her head with a white bonnet.

She was visibly pleased to see Little Father. After fifteen years at Bo-tree Plain, she spoke Sinhala as fluently as the padre with the same kind of English accent which conveyed a sense of child-like affability.

"Padre didn't tell me that Little Banda was coming today. Aren't you coming on Saturday? After your beautiful speech at Palm Branch Stream, two more families have agreed to be baptized. Padre thought that you should speak to the whole village. There will be a big crowd to see the baptism. That will be a rare opportunity to ...."

"I will come. But today I brought my nephew to get some advice from the Lord on his education. You may remember my elder brother." Little Father interjected even before Mrs. Blake had completed the sentence.

"Why not? The moment we heard of the landslide we came to your village with whatever food, clothes and blankets we had in the store. We were amazed at the miraculous escape. What a tragedy! How many people were buried alive that night? Weren't some bodies found way down the river? You lost your rice paddies, didn't you? The last time I was there, I saw that you have recovered more than half of your rice fields? What a clever idea to have terraced fields. They really look nice, don't they? So, this is your son who was born that night?"

She apparently knew the answers to all the questions. She didn't give my father any chance to reply.

Suddenly she turned. "Sit down. I will get you something to drink."

The school assembly was coming to a close. In a reverberating voice White Father was addressing not so much the students and the teachers but somebody up on the distant mountain towards whom he had raised both his hands in a begging or supplicating gesture.

"What's he saying?" I asked Little Father.

"He is praying to God for protection, support and guidance."

"Which God? Lord Vishnu or Lord Kataragama?"

I saw a slight resemblance in White Padre's gesture of supplication and that of the Gentleman Priest of the Vishnu Temple. The latter invoked God Vishnu several times a day on behalf of devotees who sought his help in times of sickness or anxiety. I imitated him to the novices who thought that my rendering of the invocation was quite funny.

"To none of them. But to a greater God. No, the one and only God. The most powerful. One who is everywhere. One who knows everything. Not even the feather of a sparrow falls without his knowledge. Those who worship Him rule the whole wide world. I will tell you more about Him when we get back." Little Father went on as in a trance.

I looked at my father. He looked agitated and confused. Was he annoyed or angry? He was not an educated man in any sense. He must have gone to the temple and had some early literacy training like my first and second brothers. He read with difficulty and explained it as due to both his failing eyesight and inadequate schooling. Being the husband of the niece of Chief Monk of a major temple and the cousin of another important monk in the neighbouring village, he was expected to be a man with an above average education. Perhaps he was. But he was conspicuously taciturn, proving in the process the truth of an aphorism I had memorized from a Sanskrit 'Century Book' - "As long as one remains silent in an assembly, he can pass off as a learned man."

18

Mrs. Blake brought us some unfermented palm sap. It was cold and delicious. "This is from our own Kitul palms on the hill," she said pointing to the hill above the shed-like structure which they called the Church. This local drink was very refreshing. She could see how much we liked it. She brought a small clay pitcher and handed it over to Little Father. We had several refills before White Padre returned to the house.

We stood up and saluted him as before. He said something in English to Little Father, who replied in a somewhat halting fashion. He looked very embarrassed and was relieved when White Padre focused his attention on me.

"What can I do for this bright young man?" he asked my father.

"It is my younger brother's idea that I should consult your reverence on his education. He is a good student. Since yesterday the monks are teaching him to write on palmleaf."

"Just as you all have done for thousands of years. No progress? You don't have to write on palmleaf anymore. What a primitive way in this modern age. Don't the monks use slates or paper?"

Father appeared to be non-plussed. He was yet not familiar with slates or paper. Nor was I? There were many thousands of palmleaf manuscripts in the temple chests. These were taken out once a year, aired and dried, blackened and polished with oil and soot. The palmleaf manuscript bound in painted, sculptured or inlaid wooden binders represented to me the state-of-the-art technology!

The padre turned toward me.

"How can you read all those jaw-breaking Sanskrit words which do not mean anything to you? To what Century Book have you read?"

How did a foreign Christian padre know about the series of books read in temples? I wondered. As each consisted on a hundred verses, they were called Century Books. They were graded in some way and the "Century Book on the Buddha" marked the pinnacle of the system.

"I have gone up to the Century Book on the Buddha," I replied.

"For an eleven year old that's very good. Your Little Father thinks that you will do very well in a modern school like ours. Would you like to study here?"

If White Padre expected me to answer this question, he did not know of the traditions which governed our relations with parents and elders. I replied meekly.

"I will do whatever my father wants me to do."

He looked at the father, who once again clasped his palms together in salutation and said,

"It is my wife and this younger brother of mine who think that this boy should have a better education than the temple can give him. I am an ordinary rural farmer and I do not understand these things very much. I know only one thing. On that stormy night when we thought that an earthquake heralded his birth, I vowed that he would be made a Buddhist monk. Will he be a better monk if he studies in this school?"

The padre lowered his head as if to take a careful look at his shoes and was in contemplation for quite some time before he spoke. I had no idea at that moment why he could not answer the question immediately. Yet I felt that White Padre was asked too difficult a question. After what appeared to be hours, he spoke.

"I have to be honest, Big Banda. When I see an intelligent young boy like this fellow, I must honestly tell you that he could benefit from all that this school can expose him to. It is, of course, only a little village school teaching in the vernacular. We teach only a period of English a day. Yet, we bring our children modern knowledge and we teach according to modern methods. You can send him in due course to a bigger school in Kandy, where he could study in English. With a good knowledge of English and a little arithmetic and general knowledge, he can qualify for job in a Government office. But teaching children for that purpose is not our main goal. Thousands of pious and dedicated people in Great Britain give my Society a lot of money to propagate Christianity in various nooks and corners of the Empire. They pay my salary, send us donations of clothes, books and other necessities and pay for all the buildings and activities here. We have to show them results in terms of numbers. Yes, numbers of people who have abandoned their traditional religion and embraced Christianity. That's my mission. That's also my wife's mission. We can teach your son. But whether that will make him a good Buddhist monk, I cannot say. I cannot say whether he will even want to be a Buddhist monk after we have given him a good education."

"Why, my lord?"

I could observe a note of confusion and concern from the way he emphasized the formal manner in which the padre was addressed. In Sinhala, a variety of honorifics are added before and after the name or title of all clergy, irrespective of the religion or the denomination. They are invariably called, "Lord" or 'Master". The greater the deference one wished to show a monk or a priest, the humbler one became in his formal address. Thus, in the case of a senior monk, one addressed not the person directly but "the shadow of the footwear of the lord" or "the shadow of the footwear of the foremost of the lords." Although the padre was simply called "my lord", father appeared in tone to be more deferential than to Chief Monk for whom he reserved the highest honorific.

20

"We will teach your son to be a good Christian. I am obliged to do this. We will, however, never force him to become one. It will have to be by his own free will. But, Big Banda, in nine out of ten cases ...."

Mrs. Blake came out to remind the padre of something he had to do at the dispensary. They had to attend to patients who had lined up along the path leading to the church. The apothecary was already there. As the white dress and the bonnet indicated, Mrs. Blake was the nurse in attendance. White Padre had something urgent to attend to at the dispensary. Without further elaborating his answer to my father's query, he told us,

"Go home. Think of what I told you. Get more information from Little Banda who is almost one of us. When you make up your mind bring the young fellow along. I will admit him to school. I can give him a place in the boarding house."

White Padre turned around to enter the living room. With an equally agile movement, he looked back and told us,

"One more thing for you to consider: the Government has decided to close down all temple schools. The law was passed a few years ago - in 1865. To be sure, they are going to implement it with vigor from next year. There will be only mission schools then."

According to etiquette, one has to visit one's closest relatives whenever one is in their village. More family squabbles are traceable to acts of omission in this regard than any other cause.

Bo-tree Plain was my father's native village and his parental home was not very far from the temple. The footpath from the school to the temple passed through well-kept gardens of snake, bottle and bitter gourds, fluted zucchini, ash and golden pumpkin and banana. Every other day caravans of bullock carts transported the sumptuous crops to the main market in the city of Kandy. Many of our relatives and friends had turned out to tend their plots.

It took us a long time to reach the village as the custom demanded both us and them to engage in a few moments of pleasant conversation: usually, a bit longer than "Hello" and "Goodbye". It was no doubt repetitive: May you live long! Going out? Any special purpose? In good health? Family? We'll go and return. May you live long! Our visit to the school and my possible admission would be known to everyone in the village by nightfall.

Finally, we descended to the valley where clusters of houses spanned a little stream. There was an air of prosperity in the village. People were well fed. They were clothed reasonably well. Most of the houses were in brick and had tile roofs. The village shop, owned by a

21

Muslim from Kandy, was well-stocked with white rice, lentils, spices, dried fish and coconuts as well as pots and pans, imported lamps with glass chimneys, webs of cloth and large multi-purpose kerchiefs. With the cash economy which had come to Bo-tree Plain on account of its sale of vegetables, this shop had things I had never seen in the far more modest shop an uncle of mine ran in our village.

Our ancestral home was at an higher elevation and commanded a view of the whole village. There my grandparents lived with two of their younger unmarried daughters. Again as etiquette demanded, we went there first to announce our arrival in the village. A few more rounds of sweet Kitul palm sap was followed by the inevitable invitation to lunch. Giving time to grandmother and aunts to prepare lunch, we visited my father's cousin, the Abbot of the temple.

Little Father summarized our conversation with Reverend Blake and told him of the new law on the closure of temple schools.

"That'll never be the end, Little Banda. Mark my word. These missionaries will pressurize the government in every possible way. They do it here. They get their supporters to do it in England. Their power has no limit. They will never rest until Buddhism is wiped out from our country. I don't know what to do any more."

"Is it not all your fault, venerable sir," Little Father asked. "For instance, what are you doing to preserve Buddhism? I hear a lot of people who blame White Padre for taking people away from their traditional religion. But none of them does anything for the village the way he does."

"Now. Now. Don't you stir me up. I will tell all that I hear about your role and what you get in return for betraying all that we hold near and dear to our heart." The monk was angry.

From bits and pieces of the day's conversations I could gather that Little Father was in some way involved with the activities of White Padre. At first, my father appeared to be confused and later angry when Mrs. Blake referred to his cooperation with the church in their proselitizing movement. Now the Abbot of the Bo-tree Plain temple lost his temper and threatened to divulge information which could have some adverse family or social consequences for Little Father.

What was he really up to? I had held him as my mentor with esteem and affection. I loved him for more than one reason. He was young, athletic and very handsome. He spoke nicely and showed how very fond he was of me and my brothers. We could talk to him freely. He spent more time at our home than at the grandparents'. He was cleverer and more devoted to studies than any of my elder brothers. Mother always held him up as a role model. So did Chief Monk.

Little Father had a prodigious memory. He could retrieve from memory verses in Sanskrit and Sinhala prescribing herbal medicines for all kinds of diseases. He already had a reputation for his decoctions which even Chief Monk considered more efficacious than those dispensed by his own brother - my maternal grandfather, the native physician of the village.

He was also a budding witch-doctor with hundreds of charms and incantations for all kinds of situations, from headaches and sleeplessness to snake-bites. My eldest brother never fails to narrate how an intolerable toothache was removed instantly by merely driving a nail into a door-frame to the accompaniment of incantations. A smooth and convincing speaker, he had answers to every question. Now he was speaking English, although hesitantly. My admiration for him was indeed very great. If he was in trouble I would be on his side.

I had never seen him lose his temper or shout back to anyone. This morning too he chose to be silent.

My father was a man of peace and did not want a quarrel to mar the visit. He waved Little Father to a side and asked for his venerable cousin's opinion on my pursuing formal studies in the church school. To my surprise, his answer was in the affirmative.

"It is a very good idea. Tiny One will benefit a lot. We have to admit that we have never been good at teaching lay students. But ......" He stammered and added, "Don't put him in that boarding house. He can either stay with the grandparents or else I can keep him here."

His answer intrigued me. Just a while ago he was accusing Little Father of betrayal and unholy alliance with White Padre. Now he was advocating my admission to church school. One more thing I do not understand about these adults, I told myself. How contradictory!

IV

Exactly five weeks later on a Monday morning, I was back in Bo-tree Plain.

I was told that the date was 17 September 1869. Little Father had given me a preliminary idea of the new calender that had come in to use. I knew, therefore, that 1869 was counted from the birth of Jesus Christ and was equivalent to 1791 of the Saka Era and 2412 of the Buddhist Era. Similarly, the English date represented the second or third day of the waning moon of the Ploughing Month in the Sinhala calendar. I was also told that the school would begin every day with an assembly by the flagstaff at 8.00 A. M., which again was a new way of saying six Sinhala hours from dawn.

"Eight A.M. on Monday the 17th of September 1869" on the school notice board did appear neat and simple in comparison to how Chief Monk gave me the astrologically auspicious time to leave home to go the school: "Three and a half hours from the break of dawn on Monday the Second day of the Waning Moon of the Ploughing Month of the Buddhist Era 2412 or Saka Era 1791." I made a mental note of the new calender as Change No. 2.

Change No. 1 was in my own appearance.

Many things happened since my last visit to White Padre's school. After prolonged discussions, the elders of the family decided in favour of my being given a modern education. Little Father extolled the virtue of an open mind and receptivity to advancement of knowledge and technology. He reinforced his argument with an oft-heard proverb pertaining to the fate of the frog in the well. It was in reference to a popular fable on a frog who thought that the entire universe consisted of the walls of the well and the bit of the sky he saw from the bottom.

The most emphatic voice in the affirmative came from Chief Monk who convinced the family with a parable from Buddhist lore:

There was once a group men who were bringing back to the village bundles of jute they had collected in the wilds. On the way, silver was being given away free. Several of the men threw away their bundles of jute and accepted as many bags of silver as they could carry. Further down the road, gold was being distributed and the same men discarded silver and accepted gold. But the men who refused to jettison the jute and take in its place silver or gold came home with only a lost opportunity to be happy and prosperous. The Buddha called conservative people who did not accept new opportunities the carriers of jute.

Whatever my father thought about this parable, he did not want to be called a frog in the well. I had no doubt in my mind that my mother, on her part, would never allow herself to be labelled a carrier of jute.

Little Father as the progenitor of the idea was indeed elated. To say that I was an indifferent spectator would be palpably false. But social decorum demanded that I should leave the decision to the elders and hide my excitement as far as possible. I woke up every morning with the relief that one more day of waiting was over.

Preparations for my departure were more complex than I had imagined. A visit to Kandy was needed to get my new outfits and a hair-cut. It was not easy to allow my lovely black locks to be cut. I had tended them with care. I reminded myself that I was expected to be a fully shaven monk. The only thing now was that it had happened earlier and for another reason.

As children we were clothed sparingly. Until five or six we went about the way we were born. Most of the time, after that, too, we wore nothing more than a loin cloth supported by a G-string which were permanently tied around our waists. For special occasions we draped a cloth round the waist and gathered the rear lower end between our legs to enclose them in some sort of baggy leggings. The Muslim traders wore striped sarongs, which were tubular skirts draped around one's waist. Being more practical than the cloth we wore, the sarong was steadily being adopted by men and boys. The long sleeved Portuguese chemise had gradually gained in popularity. Each of us had one of them. Only my eldest brother had a new one made for him from time to time. Others had to wear what became tight for the immediately older brother. Mine was about ten years old. I had never seen any child wear the sleeveless tunic which too was in imitation of the Portuguese attire. A few adults like my father owned a tunic.

White Padre had a strict dress code. Pupils of his school dressed like children in England with the exception that shoes and stockings were optional. A tailor recommended by him in a street near the Temple of the Sacred Tooth Relic turned out three sets of blue drill shorts and white short-sleeved shirts. They were purposely made two to three sizes bigger on the premise that I was growing up fast. As a result I was very comfortably attired. No one seemed to be bothered that I appeared have come in my eldest brother's clothing. But, of course, that did not include White Padre.

"Valour-Lion, you look very nice in this suit. A lot of food and exercise will help you to fill yourself into it soon.," he said after formal salutations to my father and Little Father. "Mrs. Blake will see to it as you stay with us."

Father tried to explain but words did not come readily. Little Father took over and murmured in an apologetic tone that the grandparents wanted to have me with them.

"He'll make better progress if he stays at the boarding house," the padre said and a faint tinge of disappointment was noticeable in his slight shrugging of shoulders.

"When he is a little bigger, we will keep him in the boarding house," father responded.

"That'll be very wise. I think you will have to send Valour-Lion to a bigger school in Kandy to study English. He must be civilized a bit before he goes there. We have to make him a little gentleman. He has to learn how to eat and drink, behave at a table and follow modern etiquette."

Even Little Father, whom I had reckoned by now to be a sycophant of White Padre, looked displeased with this statement. "Does he think that we live like uncivilized Veddahs?" was the thought that crossed my mind.

Veddahs are Sri Lanka's aborigines who continued to live a life of fruit-gatherers and hunters in the jungles and eschewed agriculture and the complex civilization which the Sinhalas and the Tamils had brought to the Island. But this was not the occasion to start a quarrel on issues of this nature.

Both Chief Monk and Little Father had it grilled to me that I should be ready for some denigration, ridicule and unjust criticism. Of course, they thought that new converts rather than White Padre and his wife would be the greater culprits. But to the surprise of both Little Father and me, father said,

"Yes, indeed, my lord."

For the second time, I found myself being called Valour-Lion. I was impatient to get an explanation. The opportunity came only when White Padre was called in by Mrs. Blake.

"Little Father, what is this? He keeps on calling me Valour-Lion. Why?"

"That's our family name, you see. We are called the family of the Chieftain Valour-Lion of Bo-tree Plain. Your full name is "Tiny Banda of the house of Chieftain Valour-Lion of Bo-tree Plain." White Padre

26

will call you T. B. Valour-Lion. That's the name by which you will be known in the future. But to us you will always be our Tiny One."

He patted my right shoulder and drew me to him. White Padre came out with a new proposal which he attributed to Mrs. Blake.

"There are some day pupils who eat in the boarding house. That way they get used to some table manners at least."

Little Father sensed that this was as far as they were prepared to go. Rather than risk being refused admission, he told my father that it was a good idea. Father would have to do a lot of explaining to his own mother. Yet, he agreed.

The rest of the formalities were to be taken care of by the Headmaster. He was a youngish man with a prominent moustache. He was darker in complexion than most of us and had his hair cut short, combed back and held in place with some creamy oil. Named Sam Silva, he hailed from a fishing village on the northwestern coast of the Island. His family name was arbitrarily given by the Portuguese scribes who prepared the first land registries of the maritime provinces which they ruled for nearly a hundred and fifty years. The first name was given by the church when he was baptized in his mid-teens.

Sam Silva represented the earliest wave of immigrants from the coast to the hill country. Apart from speaking the same language but with many borrowed words from Portuguese and Dutch, people like Sam Silva were culturally and spiritually as alienated from us as men from Mars.

He could have been in his thirties, but looked older. His smartly turned out grey English Tweed coat, white shirt, blue and black striped tie, socks and shoes belonged to the fashionable dress of the town elite I saw a couple of weeks ago in Kandy. The only difference was that the Europeans and some in government offices wore long trousers in matching colour and quality. Instead the headmaster wore a matching Tweed cloth which he draped around his lower body from waist to ankles. It resembled the calico or cambay cloth of women or the sarong of Muslim traders. A canvas belt with a prominent chrome-plated buckle held the cloth in place. His glamourous outfit included a pocket watch which was fastened to the flap of the coat with a gold or gold-plated chain, recently imported from England.

He was asked to take us to the school and to decide what class I had to be admitted to.

"Boy, what is your name?" he asked me in a rough and condescending tone. He was addressing me by terms that we would only use in instances of extreme anger. I was non-plussed.

27

Little Father came to my rescue. "In school we'll call him Bo-tree Plain Tiny Banda Valour-Lion or rather B. T. B. Valour-Lion."

"Age and proof thereof?"

"Eleven years seven months and thirteen days," my father replied. "We have his horoscope."

He handed to the headmaster the tiny roll of palm-leaf on which were two neatly drawn astrological charts and the basic information necessary for an astrologer to analyze character and future happenings. It seemed to satisfy the headmaster.

He turned his attention to me.

"Can you read this?" He handed to me a little paper book. I had seen paper books of different sizes. White Padre carried one bound in black leather and was seen reading it silently even at meetings. But this was the first time I touched one. All this while I have read only palmleaf books. I took the book with some trepidation. But when I opened it I was so relieved. The letters were large and clear and there were only about twenty words to a page. I began reading.

> *"This contains the five main prayers, the twelve articles of Christian belief and the ten commandments which our Lord declared from Heaven. Printed on behalf of the illustrious Company in the year 1737."*

I read the first page with ease and stopped.

"Continue."

> *"The prayer of our Lord Jesus Christ. Our Father who art in heaven. Hallowed be thy name. Thy kingdom come. Thy will be done in earth, as it is in heaven. Give us this day our daily bread. And forgive us our debts as we forgive our debtors. And lead us not into temptation, but deliver us from evil. For thine is the kingdom, and the power and the glory for ever. Amen"*

It was easy colloquial Sinhala and I could read it much faster than the tiny letters scratched on palmleaf. Headmaster nodded approvingly. But father looked very confused. So was I. What I read meant nothing to me - just as the jaw-breaking passages I read and memorized at the temple. But there was a difference. I knew almost every word. But still I had no idea what this passage was all about.

"Your reading is very good," complimented the Headmaster. "Can you count?" I nodded in the affirmative.

"Can you add and subtract?" I could do small sums mentally. I missed only one because it involved two additions and three subtractions and I was not careful enough. But his questions on multiplication and division were total disasters. I could not go beyond three times five and six into eighteen.

"We'll put you into grade three for the time being." It sounded more a threat than a welcome to the school. Yet there was one thing I liked. I was not wanted in school until next morning.

V

Within weeks, all excitement abated. I missed my brothers and our pranks and adventures. I longed to be held and hugged by my mother. I eagerly awaited father's periodical visits. I thought nostalgically of the afternoons at the temple playing with novices. Nevertheless, I had a very good time. Grandfather was my biggest support and saviour. No one could say anything against me. To him I was a boy away from home and had to be treated with gentleness and affection. Grandmother was sometimes quite strict. But the two aunties always found ways to make things a bit mischievous and exciting.

Little Father lived up to the nickname that grandfather had given him. He called him the "Comet". I loved the days when he stayed at Bo-tree Plain. He was my mentor. He was my role-model. I had a myriad things for him to explain to me. These ranged from my home work to unusual incidents in school and outside which had begun to make an impression on me.

As his visits home became infrequent, I made lists of questions to ask him. Later on, they looked funny to me. But when I wrote them, my keenness to have answers was genuine:

"White Padre hugs and kisses Mrs. Blake in front of any one every time he leaves home or he returns. Why doesn't father or grandfather do likewise to mother or grandmother?"

"In the church we sit on benches when we listen, kneel down to pray and stand up to sing. The change of posture keeps us from falling asleep. Why don't they do the same in the temple?"

"Marriage is a big affair for the newly converted Christians. Everything takes place in the church and White Padre conducts an impressive ceremony with song, prayer and sermon. The bride wears the European dress in pure white, covers her face with a veil, has flowers on her head and carries a beautiful bouquet of flowers. The bridegroom comes in dark Tweed coat and cloth. All their friends join in celebrations where they consume a lot of liquor and serve cake. Why do we have very simple family weddings and why don't our monks play any role in them?"

I do not recall how Little Father answered these or most other questions. But never did he caution me that I was developing an admiration for many aspects of the Christian life which the missionary was keen to instil in us. Instead he did encourage me to write more questions and to preserve my lists. I should still have them somewhere among my papers.

On one occasion, however, he took a firm stand. It was in my third week at the school.

I had my lunch daily with a dozen boarders and five day students. The eighteen of us sat at a long and narrow table. White Padre sat at the head of the table. Mrs. Blake sat facing him at the opposite end. My seat was to her left. To her right was a fifth grader from Thorn-tree Ford, a village close to Kandy.

Almost fourteen years old, he was boisterous and quarrelsome. He pried into everyone's affairs. We were seated close to Mrs. Blake as she was teaching us how to use fork and spoon at table. I had to learn from scratch. The fifth-grader had been at it for two terms. But he had not or would not master the skill. Once again, he was rebuked by her for being inattentive.

"This is the last time. Watch where my index finger is. It presses down the fork on the plate. On Friday when we eat with cutlery, I will fine you a rupee if you don't do it correctly."

We were expected to apologize on such occasions. "I am very sorry, Ma'am. I will do my best", would have been the standard answer. Instead he said,

"Can I ask you something? Yesterday, I was passing by the kitchen and you were outside holding a chicken between your knees. It was struggling and making a big noise. Is it not cruel to kill a bird that loves its life just as we do ours? How do you explain all your nice and kindly ways, your elegant and correct ways of eating, speaking and going about when you can be so wicked like a low caste butcher?"

I was shocked. Was it a blatant criticism of the missionaries? Perhaps, White Padre took it to be so. He stood up and drew our attention.

"Children, Golden Banda's question is answered in the Bible. Does anyone remember the passage?"

An eighth-grader seated to his right put his hand up and was duly recognized.

"Then God said," the student recited from memory. " 'let us make man in our image, in our likeness, and let them rule over the fish of the sea, and the birds of the air, over the livestock, over all the earth, and over all the creatures that move along the ground.' Genesis 1. 26. Again after the Flood, God told Noah, 'Every moving thing that lives shall be your food.' Genesis 9. 3"

"Very good, Sanctuary-Lion. God made all these for man to enjoy. There's no difference between a chicken and a cucumber. You have to cut both and cook before we can eat."

Not all were convinced. We came from village homes, where we had been told of aeons of suffering in one or more of eight hells if we take any life intentionally. We were not vegetarians. But we have not seen anyone killing an animal for our food. When young, my mother had seen a man fish in the river. She was so moved by the thrashing death pangs of the fish that she had abstained from eating even dry fish. But she did cook fish and on very rare occasions venison and wild boar flesh which forest folk brought to sell in villages. As regards beef there was a uncompromising taboo. It was believed that eating beef made one an outcaste.

Fortunately, we did not have to quarrel with the missionaries on that count. Our one rupee a month for lunch could not get a fare more luxurious or varied than a core meal of rice with lentils (called dahl as in India), potatoes (called artapal, derived from Dutch Aardappel) and dry fish and different kinds of broiled leaf. It was a joke among the boarders that their menu changed from "lentils, potatoes and dry fish for lunch" to "dry fish, potatoes and lentils for dinner". Not even the rich varieties of vegetables which the village sent to town markets ever figured on our plates.

I thought that the matter would end there. But Golden Banda stood up and with a defiant gesture said,

"Lord, I don't think that is what the Bible says. God wanted us all to be vegetarians. Genesis I, 29-31 says, 'Then God said, 'I give you every seed-bearing plant on the face of the whole earth and every tree that has fruit with seed in it . They will be yours for food. And to all the beasts of the earth and all the birds of the air and all the creatures that move on the ground - everything that has the breath of life in it - I give every green plant for food.' Lord, It is also said in Numbers 11, 33-34 that God smote the men who craved for meat. Is it said anywhere in the Bible that beasts and birds or even fish were created for man's enjoyment?"

Sanctuary-Banda stood up to answer.

White Padre was obviously angry. His blood-shot ear lobes were redder than the face. A slight, nevertheless, perceptible twitch of his moustache disclosed inner tension. He motioned Golden Banda to sit down but Mrs. Blake asked him to sit down.

"I will talk to you after lunch, Golden Banda. Don't you go away."

We finished the meal in silence and dispersed as soon as White Padre stood. Golden Banda did not budge from his seat. If he was

32

scared, he did not show it. If he was remorseful, that was not evident either.

For the next three days, the seat to the right of Mrs. Blake was empty. On Friday, it was assigned to a new boy admitted to the boarding house. Unable to keep my curiosity under control any longer, I asked Mrs. Blake what happened to Golden Banda.

"We have no place here for boys like that," she said. "You know, two good apples, two good apples; one good apple and one bad apple, two bad apples."

Although I had no idea what apples were, I understood what she wanted me to know. Golden Banda was expelled as he was considered a bad influence.

When Little Father made his next appearance at home, I related to him this incident in as much detail as I could recall. That was the time he told me what was happening in the country.

"Tiny One, you must be very careful. Specially so because Chief Monks of both our villages are our close family members. Don't you get into any argument with anyone and certainly not with White Padre and his wife. They are our friends. We must not hurt them. They are here to serve us the way they think fit. Whether they are right or wrong is not for us to judge. We must appreciate their motive. Do you understand what I say?"

"Yes, Little Father. They want us to study Christianity because they think that will give us a better guide to life than our own religion. So I should not hurt them."

"Quite right, Tiny One. Let us for argument's sake say that they are wrong. But that does not matter to us? You have been here barely a month. See how many things you have learned. You are a little gentleman in blue shorts and a pure white shirt. You can handle a slate pencil and write beautiful letters. Mrs. Silva tells me that you are very good in arithmetic. All of them agree that you are gentle and polite. Aren't all these positive results of coming to study in a missionary school."

"Yes, indeed, Little Father."

"And what's the price you pay? You have to study a bit of Christianity. Does that bother you?"

I had to admit that I enjoyed studying something new.

"You know, Little Father, I know by memory that book - the one printed in 1737 - from cover to cover. You like to hear."

I rattled through the five prayers, twelve articles of Christian belief and the Ten Commandments. It was not altogether parrot-like. I had been very attentive in the Bible class. Mrs. Silva was a good teacher. She narrated many stories. Some were similar to those that monks related in their sermons. I thought that there were similarities between the Ten Commandments and Five Precepts.

Little Father was impressed with my performance. But he did not compliment me. Instead he explained that the study of Christianity, however enriching and interesting, was not the real purpose of coming to this school.

"This is your doorway to a better future than we could have in the village. When you are bigger, we want to send you to an English school in Kandy. There you will learn not only the language but also the literature and the culture of the Europeans. They have made great strides in science, medicine and industry. They know better methods of agriculture. Their superiority politically, economically and even militarily is the result of new knowledge in different fields. What we have to do is to get access to this knowledge. White Padre's help is indispensable to get you to a good school. To that extent you must do all you can to win his heart. Better still, win the heart of Mrs. Blake also."

Little Father spoke clearly and convincingly. I had to be diligent in my Bible studies but that was not the end all and be all of my education.

"Have I to show that I am ready to be baptized?" I asked. "Last week, too, two children were baptized and their boarding fees were reduced by half."

New converts had many privileges. Both the headmaster and his wife more than even White Padre and Mrs. Blake treated them as very important people in the school community.

"No, we do not have to go that far. At least not for the moment."

When my father visited us that week-end, Little Father told him what we had discussed. He chose to do so while we had our evening meal together. It was grand-mother who had some really interesting news to share with us.

"You know that boy from Thorn-tree Ford? White Padre had sent a message to his parents to come to the school and remove him. Nothing was done for three or four days. Then his father had sent word through a carter demanding the padre to bring the boy. The padre was busy at that time. So one of the teachers accompanied him to Thorn-tree Ford. And what do you think had happened? Hundreds of monks and people from far off villages, even from Kandy and the City of the Elephant Rock, had gathered to receive the boy. He was taken in a procession on

34

the back of an elephant. The teacher got so scared when he saw the crowds that he ran for his dear life."

"How do you know?" we asked all together.

"The teacher himself was relating the story of his narrow escape to the Muslim shopkeeper and I was there to buy some lentils."

As soon as we finished dinner, Little Father called me out and we walked to the house of Peter Perera, the teacher in question. He was a younger brother of Mrs. Silva and as such the brother-in-law of the headmaster. We were not surprised to find White Padre and the headmaster along with their spouses. It was like a war council in session. Little Father beckoned me to stay outside. He cleared his throat aloud and coughed audibly as etiquette demanded. White Padre looked out and recognized Little Father.

"Come in. Come in. You are the man we want at this moment."

I sat on the step of the outer verandah and dozed off.

It must have been hours later that Little Father came out of the house. He half-carried me home. But by the time we reached home, I was fully awake. I became even more alert when grandmother yelled at Little Father with a string of rebukes. The gist was that he should not have taken me out at that ungodly hour.

Grandfather had guessed where we had been. He was curious. So Little Father started in the most matter-of-fact manner:

"We live up on these hills as frogs in a well. We know nothing that goes on elsewhere in our own country."

"Why? Are there riots again? Where?" asked grandfather. But before Little Father could reply, he added,

"I do hope never again. Never again."

With his inborn talent as a narrator, Little Father described the concerns of the White Padre and the tiny Christian population around the school. It made very little sense to me. Evidently, there was a background which I had to know before the night's happenings could be placed in a context within my grasp. In my little brain I formulated the questions to be posed as usual to Little Father. I was glad that the next day was a Saturday and there would be no school.

I woke up with a shudder. I could not believe my ears. The house was silent. It was an eerie kind of silence. Neither the reassuring low snoring of my aunts nor the cacophony of my grandfather's asthmatic breathing was to be heard. I felt as though I was abandoned in an empty house. It was pitch dark.

35

A cold shiver went down my spine. I recalled that my last thoughts on bed before sleeping were on the riots which had taken place ten years ago. Just as I was born on the night of the calamitous landslide, my second brother's birth had coincided with the execution of a neighbour of ours for treason. I had heard many conflicting versions of this incident but all had agreed that it was a travesty of justice. My thoughts went to Dingi Rala or Minor Functionary, as he was called in the village.

Dingi Rala had left our village in search of greener pastures long years ago. But when, in the wake of the riots of 1848, he was elected the subking of the Seven Sub-division District, he became an instant hero of the community. Men and women from their tree-huts in temporary slash and burn farms sang songs in his praise as they watched over their meagre crops of millet and hill-rice. The carters had their own version of songs which they sang to keep themselves awake as their caravans of bullock carts winded up the hill tracts. According to them, he was shot and his body was kept hanging for four days from the branch of a tree to serve as a deterrent to other "traitors".

"Has anyone heard our talk last night? Is it possible that some angry neighbour has reported us as traitors to the British?"

These chilling thoughts vanished when the morning breeze carried faint voices from the lower end of our garden. The two aunts were there. I joined them and was soon caught up in the mood of agitation that had gripped them.

"What? What happened?" I was almost in tears.

"Nothing, son. Nothing," they said in unison. But no explanation came immediately.

Even before the first crowing of cocks, the headmaster had come to our place and asked Little Father to get ready for a long journey with White Padre. They wanted to take the first caravan of carts taking vegetables to Kandy market. He knew nothing more. Of course, grandfather had protested. He was always very protective of the family. As regards Little Father he was even more protective. His close friendship and association with White Padre had made him a subject of comment in temples and many homes. The Abbot of Bo-tree Plain temple who was my father's first cousin had once called him a bat, meaning an opportunist.

The bat, in our folklore, changed his loyalties to and fro in the war of animals. When the birds were winning, he showed his wings and claimed to be a bird. When the tide turned in favour of the beasts, he

36

showed them his mouse-like face and teeth and sided with them. But at the end when peace returned, the bat was rejected by both.

Any mission with White Padre had to be more explicit, grandfather had insisted and I knew the reason. Little Father was adamant and I could understand that too. He could not let down his benevolent friend. Little Father had made a bundle of his clothes and was ready to go with the headmaster. Grandfather would not let him go until he could get more information from White Padre. Grandmother would not trust her husband's lack of tact. So she too had joined them. The two aunts were waiting for them to return.

The eastern sky was turning from the bright red of dawn to the brighter hue of a rainless day - a rarity in our area. Several neighbours passed us as they went up the hill to their vegetable plots. They wanted to know why we were out so early. They looked really concerned and the aunts reassured them.

Aunt Flower turned round to go into the house: "What's the use of hanging around here. I will go in and cook some milk-rice and keep some water to boil for coffee."

"Why did you get so late? What happened?" my aunts inquired when grandparents returned long after the sun had appeared over the hills. "Did our brother go with White Padre?"

"Yes, he did. We were not very happy. So we went to see your uncle the monk."

White Padre, headmaster and Little Father could not take the first caravan of bullock carts to Kandy. In fact, they would have missed the last one, too. There had been a heated argument between White Padre and grandfather. But grandmother had intervened as she thought that the request of the padre was reasonable.

"All he wanted to do was to go to Colombo and a few places on the coast and find out whether the incident at Thorn-tree Ford was connected with any Islandwide movement. Golden Banda can't be an isolated case. Someone must be fanning trouble for the missionaries. This was his view but he being a good man did not want to rush to any conclusion. He wanted your brother in this investigation because he knows both religions and does not take sides. He is impartial. He will tell what is right and wrong to any party. White Padre says that's the greatest quality of your brother."

"Yes," interrupted grandfather. "No wonder he is called a bat by everybody that I know. Neither party will have any faith in him at the end. See. He will have nobody to turn to."

He looked disgusted. He kept on a side the clay bowl with a sumptuous helping of milk rice, garnished with a red hot mixture of onions, chillies and condiments. That was his favourite breakfast but he seemed to have lost interest in it.

"This woman" he pointed at grandmother with an outstretched arm with the palm turned upwards; "She is the curse of the family. How much I tried to keep back the womb-sweeper?"

I knew that grandfather was upset. It was only on such occasions that he called Little Father by the pet name of "womb-sweeper" which literally meant that, as the last born, he had cleaned out the mother's womb.

After a while, grandfather launched on a soliloquy,

"I know what happened in the riots ten years ago. Even to see the new-born baby of my eldest son, I had to take the most circuitous route through the jungles. British soldiers gunned down every intelligent-looking young man they laid their eyes on. Even the forest-dwelling monk of Trunk-Fair was executed. What was the charge? Peliyagoda David also known as Banda of Bull-Kraal-Settlement, the self-styled king, visited the monk and worshipped him. He uttered the usual words of benediction. 'May you live long in happiness.'. Was it a crime? What else could the monk have done? A monk has to bless anyone who prostrates oneself before a him."

Once again, I noted with sadness that grandfather was drifting. But he gathered himself quickly and continued,

"If there are any riots in the maritime region, no White Padre can save him from soldiers. I kept on telling her. She wouldn't listen. To your brother going to places he had not been before is a great adventure. He looked forward to the excitement. So, he wouldn't listen either. I can think of nothing but the riots and how they dealt with them. Even that venerable old Chief of Woodapple-Lake was not spared. Not a single soldier was killed or hurt. Yet, thousands of our people were shot down mercilessly. I'll not sleep until I see the face of my little boy again."

Tears trickled down his cheeks.

If grandmother was penitent, she did not show it. She turned to me and said, "Go to the temple. The monk, your uncle, would like to talk to you."

I was relieved. I am used to tense situations at home. After all I come from a family of eight boys. But I hate when adults have to cry. It makes one feel very helpless. Perhaps, grand-mother sensed this. Or the monk had actually wanted to see me. Whatever be the case, I rinsed the bowl, washed my hand, drank some water and ran all the way to the temple.

The Abbot was seated at a low table and was writing something on a small sheet of paper with a feather pen which he dipped into a little glass bottle. He looked up and motioned me to sit on the mat in front of him.

"I am practising to write with pen and ink on paper." he said without raising his head. "It takes more than a little effort. There's a lot of things that we have to begin now. We on the mountains have hardly changed for centuries. People in the low-country had a three hundred year start with modern para-phernalia."

He shook his head and continued,

"There is a price to pay for having stayed free and independent. But it is worth it. We preserved our spiritual heritage and our culture - our traditional values more than everything else. That's what I am thinking as I learn to write again as I once did on the sandboard. It's not easy. The feather keeps slipping from your fingers and the ink smudges if you are not careful. How are you faring? Can you write with pen and ink, Tiny One?"

"I have not come to it yet. I do most of my written exercises and sums on a slate. When I use paper, which is very rarely, I write with a pencil."

"I wanted to see you, Tiny One. Tell me what Golden Banda did to be expelled from school."

I gave him a precise account of what happened. I could not repeat the Biblical texts word for word nor could I give the references. The monk listened to me attentively.

"How did the other children react?"

"There was pin-drop silence. I was gripped with some sort of fear. That's because Little Father had warned me from the very first day not to argue on any matter and not at all on religion. I think that's what all of us have been told by our elders. Even Golden Banda's best friend said later that it was foolish for him to have annoyed White Padre and his wife."

"What do you know of the reception given to Golden Banda by the people of Thorn-tree Ford?"

"Only what grandmother told us at dinner." The monk had already met her at daybreak and it was not necessary for me to elaborate.

"A whole lot of new things are taking place in the Island. We are back again in bad times."

"Are there riots again?" I asked. I had no idea what they were. But every time they were mentioned a gripping fear consumes the elders.

So, I thought that suddenly for no reason the British soldiers shot down local people in large numbers.

"No. Not exactly. At least, not yet. Maybe, something even more eventful."

He capped the bottle of ink, laid down the feather pen which was by now dry and showed his inclination to talk to me at length.

VI

"Tiny One, I have never been in favour of your going to the church school. But your Little Father was very persuasive. I don't want him to be your role model or mentor. But we all know that you are his pet and he is your hero. There's little I can do for you. I was hoping to get you here every evening and help you to complete the traditional education in which you fared so well. But I am told by none other than White Padre that any learning I impart in this temple would be a violation of a new law which abolishes all temple schools. I am prepared to go to jail if that's what he means. But I don't want to jeopardize your chances of success in the new system of education. Will it be all right if I ask you to come now and then like this to have a chat? That could help you to keep an open mind about your culture and religion."

"If it is all right with the elders, I will be only very happy."

I loved him as an uncle and venerated him as a saintly monk. More than that, I had a sneaking admiration for his unequivocal candour. He was convinced that he had a mission to fulfill in safeguarding the ancient religion of the Island. He brooked no opposition. His open antagonism to Little Father made him quite an enigma to me.

"Do you know that this Island of ours was thrice visited and blessed by the Buddha who prophesied that his religion would flourish and prosper here?" the monk asked me.

"I have heard it said in many sermons," I replied.

"Do you know that King Vijaya, the founder of the Aryan Sinhala Kingdom in this Island, landed on the same day that the Buddha passed into final Liberation in the Rose-Apple Continent two thousand four hundred and eleven years ago?"

"Yes, Venerable Sir, I have been reading the 'Genealogy of Kings' on the advice of Little Father. In fact, I read a bit of it aloud every night to grandmother and the two aunts."

"Your Little Father asked you to read it? After all, he may not be as bad as I think."

I was puzzled by the monk's comment. But I did not ask for clarification.

This modest book outlining the twenty-four century history of the Island in simple and lucid Sinhala was among the few palmleaf manuscripts which grandfather had inherited from his father. It was among the first books which the monks at the temple gave me to read when I had completed the third and fourth books of my course of studies.

41

Designed to help in the perfection of pronunciation and diction in reading, these texts were called "Prose of the Buddha" and "Refiner". As regards the latter, a Sinhala proverb highlighted its importance:

"The mouth that had not read 'Refiner' is the mouth of an anthill."

"So you have some idea of what I am going to tell you?" said the monk in approval of my acquaintance with this manual of the Island's history. "Have you read the part on the introduction of Buddhism?"

"Yes, Venerable Sir. I know about the arrival of the Great Saint Mahinda and the introduction of Buddhism. I also know of the Great Saint Sanghamitta, his sister, who brought a sapling of the Bo-tree under which the Buddha attained Enlightenment. One day I would like to go to another country and preach Buddhism."

"That's very encouraging to hear, Tiny One. Let us wish that this dream comes true. This is a further reason that you should be in touch with me."

"Venerable Sir, you really think that I could go to another country some day? I wasn't sure. I thought that the Great Saints Mahinda and Sanghamitta could do so because their father was the great emperor Asoka the Righteous. He was powerful and had a very large empire. I also thought that they were readily received by our king Tissa the Beloved of Gods because they were the children of a mighty emperor of the Rose-Apple Continent. How much I would like to go to Portugal, Holland and England!"

"And to preach Buddhism there?" A sly smile puckered the lips of the monk. "Why not? You'll see a whole new world. Who would have ever thought that our last king would spend his last days in Vellore and our controversial Chief Ehelepola would die in a little known island called Mauritius in the middle of nowhere? Why go so far? Your mother's granduncle was a monk in Siam. He went there in a Dutch ship. Monks travel freely to and from Burma and Siam. I don't know if any monk has still gone to Europe. But that will be only a matter of time."

If I let imagination run riot and dreamt of going as a missionary to Europe in a British sailing boat (what it looked like, I had no idea at all !), it was immediately noticed by the monk.

"Don't build castles in the air just yet, Tiny One. You have to do many first things first. Never forget the night you were born. Your family survived a landslide of three hundred fathoms down a steep incline. Nothing happened to your house or to any of the people in it. We have no doubt that you were saved because you have a mission to fulfil. Promise that you will see me at least once every week."

"Yes. I will, Venerable Sir," I said and prostrated myself to take leave of him. To the customary benedictions, he added,

"Continue to read the 'Genealogy of Kings' and be ready to tell me about the great king Gamini the Disobedient."

I returned home to find the family steeped in the gloom cast by the pre-dawn event. The morning's argument, which might have been inordinately prolonged, had left both my grandparents in utter exhaustion. The aunts leaned on the door jambs and looked vacantly. I wondered if they had received any bad news from the party that left in the early hours of the day to Kandy.

I was about to ask them when the grandfather jumped out of his seat suddenly and removed the kerchief from his shoulder. I looked behind. How relieved I was. My father had come along with Chief Monk of the Royal Monastery of Sangha-Gem-Field.

"We left as soon as we got your message," Chief Monk said after the customary formalities and salutations. "I was at the Flower Garden Monastery yesterday and came by the early evening caravan of carts. So I know something of what is happening. There's nothing alarming. At present there is nothing more than a few peaceful confrontations between Buddhists and Christians on public platforms in the low country. All such debates have been quite friendly. But one has to take precautions that these don't come to the hill country. Here there's too much distrust, fear and hatred as regards anything foreign. I don't like what happened at Thorn-tree Ford. It's like playing with gunpowder. There had been too many civil disturbances in recent times. And too many innocent lives lost."

"Will there be anything like the riots at the time my second son was born?" queried my father.

"I don't think so. For one thing, our people learned a big lesson. We can't match the well organized, well armed British army. It is true that our last king was tyrannical and made quick decisions in violent fits of temper. You must have heard of the fate of the family of Ehelepola - how his wife was forced to pound her baby in a mortar before she herself was drowned and the other children were beheaded."

Chief Monk looked at me as if to find out whether I knew the story. I nodded and he knew that I was aware of the second son of Ehelepola, Middle Banda, who stepped ahead of his sobbing elder brother, saying, " Fear not, Elder Brother. I will show you how to die."

Middle Banda has been my hero since I heard this story from my mother after my last visit to the Bo-tree Plain. Only she had the patience

43

to recount Ehelepola's role in ousting the last Nayakkar king of Kandy and the price his family had to pay.

The monk continued, "More complicated is the British legal system. There's a lot of show of justice. They say that all are equal under the eyes of the law. Days on end, the drama goes on - speeches in English, questions, counter questions, legal arguments - with great ceremony. The judge covers his head with horse hair and wears a black robe. One thinks that nothing but a carefully deliberated decision will be given. Now in the case of Trunk-Fair monk, what happened?"

He paused for a reply. Apparently none of us knew the answer or the elders thought the pause was merely for dramatic effect.

"Many lawyers - all of them British - protested when the Trunk-Fair monk was convicted in a military court. They said that it was not a fair trial. But what was the reply of the authorities in government?. The Governor in Colombo, who represents the Queen in England, says, 'By God, if all the proctors in the place said the man was innocent, he shall be shot tomorrow morning.' That's exactly what was done. To make matters worse, they chose to do it in front of the Temple of the Sacred Tooth."

Aunts Jasmine and Flower sobbed as the story was narrated. Perhaps, they were thinking of Dingi Rala, whose family lived close to our home in Sangha-Gem-Field.

The monk prepared for himself a chew of betel. He wrapped sliced arecanut with a betel leaf, applied a bit of burnt lime, picked a few cardamoms and cloves and began chewing. It was only after he had aimed several streams of red saliva into the spittoon that he resumed his narrative.

"The government also learned a big lesson. The British realized that they could never rule this country peacefully unless and until the religious and spiritual aspirations of the people were fully recognized and satisfied. That disturbance led to a series of major reforms and they were very good. As a result, the grievances of the people now are very different. Monks have no complaints. They have been exempted from poll tax which really was very demeaning in that monks in robes were compelled to do menial work as road and irrigation labourers."

Another stream of red saliva into the spittoon and a redeeming interruption.

What he said about poll tax of monks was beyond me. As usual, I made a mental note to ask for clarification when the Little Father returned. Suddenly, I felt a pang of sorrow as if a red hot stylus pierced my heart. It dawned on me that the visit of my father and my mother's uncle, Chief Monk, had a bearing on Little Father's decision to

44

accompany White Padre on what he called an investigation into the alleged confrontation of Buddhists and Christians. Why this strange and inexplicable foreboding of a calamity!

The monk continued, "The new British official is very different in attitude and outlook. The reason is simple. He is required to learn our languages and literature and pass qualifying examinations to be in service. The more they come to know our religion and culture, the more respectful and considerate they become to us. Some have taken to serious study and research. They are also very sympathetic to the plight of the people. I know several who are deeply interested in Buddhism, our literature, history and customs. So I don't think that the administration would let loose the army on the people the way it did on the last two occasions."

I made a further mental note of the reference to last two occasions. So far I had heard of only the riots which took place when my second brother was born. This was not the time for me to ask Chief Monk. There was protocol to be followed. Little children were not prevented from being present at family conversations and discussions. On occasions like this they were actually encouraged. But they were to be seen and not heard. We spoke only if and when we were spoken to. Perhaps, grandfather realized my curiosity or he thought of my two aunts also.

"I don't think these young ones know about the first rebellion."

Realizing that the two daughters would have to listen to Chief Monk for some time, grandmother clasped her hands in salutation to him and retired to the kitchen to prepare the mid-day meal which he had to take before noon. A monk fasted from noon to the dawn of next day. Guessing her intention, the monk called after her.

"I am not very well, Sister. Do not make any fried dishes. Just something simple like snake gourd with very little coconut milk." Aunt Flower rose to accompany the mother.

"No, Little Daughter. You sit here and listen to what I have to say. You must know the history our country. You will have to instruct your children some day. You know what the Buddha called the parents?"

"The first teachers." she replied in a soft voice.

He cleared his throat and spit out the wad of the betel chew into the spittoon.

"This country had an unbroken line of Sinhala kings from the day Prince Vijaya landed with his seven hundred followers. That's a history of two thousand four hundred years. To be exact, two thousand four hundred and eleven years and three and a half months. Even during brief periods when a South Indian invader occupied the throne at Anuradhapura or when the Cola Empire wrested the northern part of the

45

Island, there was some Sinhala leader ruling a part of the country and performing the royal duty of safeguarding the Buddhist Faith, guaranteeing the security of the Sacred Tooth Relic and sustaining the Sangha, the community of monks. But about one hundred and thirty years ago, the last Sinhala king who ruled in Kandy died without an heir.

"His queen was from a royal family in Southern India. Her brother was anointed king and thus arose the Nayakkar dynasty. The second and third kings were remarkable rulers. Fame-Resplendent-Royal-Lion (1747-1782) helped Refuge-Maker of Velivita to get the necessary quorum of monks from Siam to re-establish higher ordination and usher in a literary and cultural renaissance in the country. Later, he made this energetic and wise monk the King of the Sangha."

I had heard parts of this story before. Perhaps, I was nodding. As I heard my name being called called out, I raised my head and feared a sharp rebuke from the monk. Instead, he continued.

"The third king was a scholar and he wrote a beautiful poem on a popular story of a previous life of the Buddha. But the last king, Resplendent-Valour-Royal-Lion (1798-1815) was a disaster. To begin with he was the cause of what followed. He became king at a wrong time. The Dutch were in control of the maritime region which they took over from the Portuguese. As far as the Kandyan Kingdom was concerned, they had no political interest. Their sole preoccupation was with trade and profits. But the British who took over the maritime region from the Dutch had a different agenda. Do you know when this happened?"

He apparently read the eagerness on my face and asked me to answer the question. With what I had heard from Little Father, I could say correctly that the British replaced the Dutch two years before the last King of Kandy was crowned.

"That's right. The British were determined to be the masters of the whole Island. First they did what the Portuguese and the Dutch had tried unsuccessfully on numerous occasions - that is to capture the Kingdom by force. In every attempt they failed miserably, not because our men fought better or had better weapons but because the central massif was inaccessible and was protected by mountains, rivers and forests. Of course, our people knew the terrain better and therefore could entice the British army deep inside and turn on it when it were bereft of any defence."

This was another part of the story I knew in some detail as Little Father could describe war scenes vividly. He was fond of popular Sinhala ballads written on recent wars. It was remarkable that poets with minimum language skills still kept records of our wars with

46

foreign powers, he used to say. His favourite was the ballad on English wars.

Chief Monk was a consummate historian. Possibly all monks were. It was not surprising because history has been for centuries a major interest of the people. Yet not eleven, I was myself steeped in books like the "Genealogy of Kings," reading of kings and battles which had taken place thousands of years ago. The more recent history that the monk was presenting, however, had a sense of urgency as if it had a message for the immediate future. So despite occasional distractions, I tried to follow the trend of his discourse. For the second time, he called out my name as if to wake me from a reverie.

"So, Tiny One, the British had to find other ways of conquering our Kingdom. The last king's personality gave them a few ideas. He was scared, insecure, short-tempered and prone to suspect anybody and everybody. The British conspired with the Prime Minister, a stately leader named after his native village as Statue-Plain, to incite the king to commit unconscionable acts of cruelty and tyranny so as to make him unpopular with his subjects. The king obliged them.

"Statue-Plain was himself a victim of the king's cruelty. He aspired to become king and Resplendent-Valour-Royal-Lion pardoned him twice. But on the third occasion, he was executed.

"His nephew Ehelepola, named after his village, August-Fair, succeeded him as Prime Minister. He too plotted against the king. By now the king was quite deranged and lived a precarious life fearing his assassination at any moment. When Ehelepola was in the Gem Region, a rebellion took place and the king suspected him to have masterminded it. The king ordered him to return to Kandy. Instead of coming to Kandy he fled to Colombo in search of aid from the British. That was the time his family was tortured. We discussed that episode a while ago. Do you remember it?"

I nodded. So did the aunts.

"Were the British really going to make him king?" asked grandfather.

"That's what Ehelepola believed. He thought he was doing a service to the nation by having a tyrannical and inhumanly cruel king deposed. But the British had other plans. Why should they depose one king and place on the throne another? They had no reason to be specially partial to Ehelepola."

"Venerable sir, I have heard that there were some British officials in Colombo who favoured the idea of Ehelepola becoming king under British protection," added grandfather.

47

"Possibly that was one of the options discussed in the councils of state in Colombo. When the British planned its invasion of Kandy a few months later, Ehelepola was confident that he was to be made king because the British said so. The invasion was described as 'led by the invitation of the Chiefs and welcomed by the acclamations of the people'. It was also presented as being launched in response to 'unanimous and direct demand of the people of five Provinces, constituting more than one half of the Kandyan Kingdom, to be taken under British protection'. You see the key words were 'taken under British protection'.

"The propaganda backed by promises that they never intended to keep were so effective that our mature leaders, the Chiefs, had no doubt in their minds that the country was going to have a better future. The British administrators were so clever or shrewd that they agreed to protect the Buddhism and the worship of gods and perform all the royal duties to protect Buddhism. So they agreed to sign away their freedom in what is called the Kandyan Convention. It looked a good document between a proud and free people and the ruler of a mighty empire. If only it was not meant to be just a piece of paper with promises which were put in merely to deceive the people!"

Chief Monk looked angry. I have heard him shouting at the novices when they forgot themselves and behaved like boys. I have also heard him scolding Little Father for his unexplained absences. But the tone now was different. It was a different kind of anger. There was more than a tinge of frustration. What surfaced loud and clear was intense pain of mind.

For years in my adult life when the 2nd of March of 1815 was commemorated as a day of mourning in Kandy, I recalled the pain-stricken face of Chief Monk from whom I heard of this fateful day on the day Little Father accompanied White Father to Kandy.

"For two thousand three hundred and fifty-eight years, the independence of the country was maintained at least in some parts amidst invasions and rebellions. Now it was all over. Even the lowest British soldier on the street had more prestige than the highest of our Chiefs or, worse still, our leading prelates and learned scholar-monks.The promise to keep the religion inviolable was a clever disguise to fool the people.

"Right from the beginning they had a different idea of the religion. The Sinhala text covers both Buddhism and the worship of gods. The English text says nothing about the latter. The whole trouble was that the British were different from us in every way, race, language, religion,

48

customs, habits, modes of thinking. There could be no common interest between them and us. They are masters and we their humble and helpless subjects."

Grandmother came out of the kitchen to announce that the mid-day meal for the monk was ready and grandfather should arrange a place for it to be offered. A break in the story was thus demanded. All but me had something to do. I was left alone with the monk.

"Tiny One, I am telling this story specially for you," he told me as he beckoned me to come closer. He stroke my head. "I have a strong feeling that you will live to see the end of foreign rule. I even think that you will play a part in the national awakening of the country. All I want you is to study as hard as you can. There is no limit to knowledge. There's no knowledge that is useless. Learn everything you have an opportunity to learn."

I nodded in agreement. He continued.

"I hear you are doing well at the church school. Is it true that church attendance, prayer and Bible studies are compulsory? There's no harm in doing all these as long as you do not get carried away by the novelty of things. Learn everything diligently, just as you studied at the temple. When the time comes, I will tell you what you should and should not do."

He stopped long enough to signify that he would like me to say something. That was an excellent quality of this pious and learned monk. He wanted to listen to others. Even to an eleven-year old like me.

"Is Little Father in any trouble?" I asked him. I felt as if a great burden had been taken off my head. I had wanted to ask this question from my father or Chief Monk and up to now did not have an occasion.

He shook his head diagonally which in our body language meant that he had some doubts in his mind.

"I hope not. When I heard about his accompanying White Padre to Kandy, I felt like reading the horoscope. I don't know why? Now I don't like what it says. But I may be mistaken. I hope I am mistaken."

I, too, did hope that Chief Monk had read Little Father's horoscope incorrectly. The last thing I wanted was for Little Father to be in any trouble.

A special seat was prepared on the floor of the opposite inner verandah and covered with a white cloth. The monk sat cross-legged. He administered the five precepts, conducted briefly the relevant ceremonies connected with the offering of alms and partook of the meal that was offered in accordance with tradition. A special benediction was chanted for the safe return of Little Father. Then he discreetly left the house to walk in the shade of the trees in the garden so that the family could have their lunch.

I whispered to Aunt Flower what Chief Monk told me of Little Father's horoscope.

"Yes. We know it," she said sadly. "That's why we are all so worried. He has a bad time for seven years."

Father was huddled together with his parents. Though we did not hear a word of what they said, we knew that they had no other subject in their minds on this day. Their belief in astrology, coupled with what they had learned of the growing tensions between Buddhists and Christians and the pro-Christian leanings of Little Father, gave them little hope. I was beginning to understand why Chief Monk was unusually loquacious this morning. He wanted the family to be distracted and he chose recent history as the theme for this purpose.

Sipping the steaming coffee which father offered him, Chief Monk resumed the session.

"An indomitable nation which has learned to defend itself from foreign invasion for over three hundred years could not adjust itself to the massive changes which foreign domination demanded. The people had reacted to the tyranny and despotism of a errant ruler. But they were not ready to accept humiliation and oppression from an alien government in exchange for deposing that ruler. So within two years of the assumption of British rule, riots broke out. They started in Uva, where the mountains and the plains meet to the southeast." He waved his hand in the general direction.

"Soon the rebellion spread all over the Kingdom and was nearly successful. Keppetipola was an inspiring leader. So was Madugalle. They were Chiefs and deeply patriotic. Other Chiefs either encouraged the riots without assuming any roles of leadership or were mere spectators. Only Ehelepola declared himself a friend of the British. It was a pity that there wasn't enough unity among the leaders to whom the people looked up for vision, guidance and resources."

Once again, I detected the slight change of voice, which showed that this holy man whose control over emotions was near perfect, was crying inside.

Father sensed the monk's inner tension. His solutions to such situations were simple and direct. He stood up and reached for the mounted brass tray with ingredients for a chew of betel and offered it to

50

the monk. He reached out and spent the next few minutes silently to prepare the chew. Then he resumed.

"The British took no chances. They have had very bad experiences for nineteen years. They knew the power of will of the Kandyan peasant who rushed to the battlefield when summoned. So the British were merciless. They beheaded Keppetipola and Madugalle in front of the Temple of the Sacred Tooth. Even in death Chief Keppetipola was fearless as he had been in life. He walked to the block, chanted verses in worship and offered his neck to the executioner.

"You know the British were so impressed with that show of courage that his cranium was sent to a seat of higher learning in England for study. He was a remarkable man, a born leader."

I had been getting used to his eye contact with me whenever there was a point which he wanted me to note. I knew that he held out Keppetipola for me to admire as a national leader.

"The British distrusted everybody. Even Ehelepola who claimed to be their friend was arrested, imprisoned and later exiled to an island far away in the sea. The people themselves were harassed in every possible way. Many lost their lives. As usual they singled out the young, the healthy and the strong for brutal torture which invariably ended in death. Homes were burnt. Crops which were about to be harvested were destroyed. The worst of their misdeeds was to cut down fruit-bearing trees which had taken thirty or forty years to grow. They deprived the people of their sustenance. With such harsh punishment the rebellion hardly lasted two years. It was a catastrophe. The British took the upper hand. They made the rebellion an excuse to default on their promises in the Kandyan Convention. Things went from bad to worse."

Chief Monk seemed tired. Yet he continued the lucid presentation of what the British administration had done to undermine patriotism and wean people from the influence of the Buddhist temple. He said a lot about education and social services. He made a point with regard to English-educated Sinhalas whose alienation from national culture seemed to worry him. But most of these were too complicated for me. If only Little Father was here, I thought. There were many loose ends which only he would have the patience to tie up for me!

"Thing went from bad to worse," he repeated and concluded, "That's why in thirty years a second rebellion was inevitable."

What a treat it was! I wished that he would do this oftener. Whether by inclination or training or both, a Buddhist monk was an adept in communication with the spoken word. Among those I knew, Chief Monk was undoubtedly preeminent. Next to him was the Abbot of the Bo-tree Plain temple. To have met two of the most eloquent exponents our national history in one day made it a truly memorable day.

The elders discussed plans for the rest of the day. Chief Monk and father proposed that they should wait for some news which the carters would bring from Kandy and, if it was necessary, stay the night over.

Our long wait well past dusk was of no avail. The monk decided to go to the temple for the night and father stayed behind and had dinner with us. Perhaps, we were all too tired or else the anxiety was too strong for words. We ate in silence.

I lay on a mat to sleep. The elders remained in the inner verandah. They hardly spoke.

For the second morning in succession, I got up with a shock. But I was better prepared. I walked out of the house and looked for the others where I expected to find them. It was a repetition of the previous dawn's scene. The only difference was that my father was there instead of Little Father. Mr. Silva the Headmaster was gesticulating as he spoke exactly as on the day before. I joined the crowd in time to hear him say,

"No. They didn't tell me when they would return. I had to come back to run the school."

"Did my son have anything to tell us?" asked grandmother.

"No, Jewel. he appeared to be very happy to go anywhere that White Padre wanted him to go." It was the custom to address a woman of high social standing as "Jewel".

"So, they are going to tour the low-country. Not a bad idea. But not at this time." said grandfather. "There could be trouble."

"Don't worry." responded the headmaster. "If there is any trouble, it can only endanger White Padre. There are far too many ungrateful people in our wretched country who have no idea what great benefits the British and the kind people like our padre had brought to us. But let me tell you one thing. If any of these ingrates try to touch one little hair of White Padre, your son will save him even if it costs his own life. He is such a good man."

Leaving us stunned and incredulous, Mr. Sam Silva the newly converted Christian Headmaster of the Church Missionary Society's Sinhala Mixed School of Bo-tree Plain walked nonchalantly into the mist.

VII

Three years had passed almost to the day since the pre-dawn departure of Little Father with White Padre. The gloom which descended on the home of my grandparents that morning had hovered like a dark malevolent cloud. There had been no news of him.

The flickering hope that he was still among the living has been kept alive by a succession of astrologers who spoke of malefic planets which would affect his life for seven years.

"It is all Saturn, the remorseless planet," said my maternal grandfather, the physician, astrologer and witchdoctor of the family.

He had a rich repertoire of legends of kings and gods to prove his point. To everyone in the family, these frequent sessions with my mother's father was a source of infinite solace.

Chief Monk had more in his arsenal than astrology although he too upheld the same theory of Saturn and Moon being eight houses apart.

To me, however, these simple explanations had less and less meaning. Repeated condemnations of local beliefs and practices as superstition and meaningless magic by my teachers in the Church School had made a dent in my blind and submissive acceptance of this particular aspect of my cultural heritage. I scoffed at these beliefs and spoke of a rational attitude to life's problems, even though I had no concrete suggestions to offer. I was sometimes cornered by the Abbot of the Bo-tree Plain Temple, who listed similar beliefs and practices of the small but active population of Christians. He succeeded in convincing me that every popular religion had its own baggage of what a critical rationalist would consider to be superstitious.

The more I was drawn in to these discussions, the more I longed to be by Little Father. He would not preach to me or ridicule me as some did. He listened sympathetically. His patience was infinite. How well he would have explained whether or not a distant planet like Saturn transformed the life of a whole family or whether or not superstition and popular beliefs were the real criteria for assessing the efficacy of a particular religion! When this thought overwhelmed me and I missed him, it took quite some time before I realized that his disappearance was the very reason for all these theories and disputes. If he did not go with White Padre that morning or if he returned with him or shortly afterwards or if the family had some regular news about him, all these explanations and debates would not have been necessary.

On this last day of school for the year, I missed him most. Not only had I been close to him but he was the star to which all my hopes and aspirations were hitched. Without my mentor, the last three years had seen me meandering at a loss without guidance, encouragement and support. Now I needed them all and that, too, most urgently.

White Padre paid me an unusual tribute at the morning assembly by the flagstaff. He recounted my career in the school and complimented me on my rapid progress to the eighth grade covering five years of work in three years. He also announced that his Mission's English high school in Kandy had offered me a full scholarship for further education. I was beaming with pride and joy until White Padre recounted how I came to the school and the role which Little Father had played in it. He praised Little Father as a man of great wisdom and a rare intellectual who could see beyond narrow prejudices, petty jealousies and parochial misrepresentations. He concluded the talk with a prayer for Little Father's early return to the village.

Despite the gloom that the reference to Little Father caused, I was pleased with the prospect of going to Kandy. I had diligently followed Little Father's advice and made this my goal in all I did at the Church School. What should I do? As a child of fourteen years I had no choice. The elders would decide for me. But the person who would have been most concerned with my interests was no longer present to make his contribution. On the contrary, the circumstances leading to his disappearance could have a prejudicial impact as far as my grandparents and parents were concerned. The only one in whom I could rely on for support in pursuing further studies in Kandy was Chief Monk. How could I get to him before any one else could know? That was pure wishful thinking. By evening the whole village would know what White Padre said at the assembly and I would not go to Sangha-Gem-Field for two more days.

Mrs. Blake saw me thoughtful at the lunch table. This day, I was called to sit on her right.

"You are our guest of honour today", she told me in English.

"Thank you, Mrs. Blake. I am sad I will not be here next year," I responded somewhat haltingly.

"That's good, Tiny Banda. You speak English quite well. More and more practice is all you want."

"When I go to Sangha-Gem-Field ....." I began but she continued.

"There'll be no one to whom you can speak in English. I know. If you want, you can come here for a couple of days every week. In fact, it's better if you concentrate on your English before you go to Kandy."

How sure she was that I would go to Kandy to study in an English school!

I certainly knew my village. By the time I came home in the evening, grandparents and aunts had received verbatim reports of White Padre's announcement. Grandfather looked unhappy and thoughtful. He hardly noticed my entry. He was reclining on his easy chair and looking at the ceiling vacantly. I was worried. Aunt Flower assured me that he was all right but was unhappy that I might go to Kandy.

"Why is he worried?" I asked her in a whisper.

"He thinks the church will take you also away from us for good. See what happened to your Little Father? Three years and we don't know whether he's alive or dead." Tears welled in her eyes as she embraced me.

"You have been our only solace. Without you none of us would have survived the shock and the loss. We don't want to lose you, my precious little boy."

As I nibbled at the steamed millet-flour delicacy which she had specially made for me, I recalled the fateful morning of Little Father's departure with White Padre. The thought that I was not awake to wish him a safe journey gnawed at my conscience. My thoughts of our last meeting was his half-carrying me from the headmaster's house.

I remembered the day White Padre returned from his absence. He had been away for nearly three weeks. Apart from regular squabbles between grandparents as everyone in the family blamed grandmother for encouraging Little Father to go, there was no despair. As long as he was with White Padre, the assumption was that they would return together. It was another pre-dawn event. I heard him first as he called out grandfather's name from the pathway by our house. I was the first to go out and ask him to come in.

"I came here directly from the cart stand because I know how anxious you must be," he said as he saw grandfather.

"Where's he?"

He asked the question loud enough for the ladies who were still inside to rush out in panic.

"That's what I want to tell you," replied White Padre calmly. "First and foremost, he is well and well cared for. We did quite a long trip. He wanted to see more of the country and learn more of what was happening. My superior in Colombo liked him very much and gave him work. It will take him to places where the church encounters difficulties due to the new interest which the Buddhist monks are taking in their religion. He has a knack of speaking to people of all walks of life and getting valuable information."

"You mean that he has been engaged as a spy by the church to gather information from the people?" asked grandfather, staring not at the padre but bewildered grandmother who would not or could not comprehend what was taking place.

"It looks as if I am too tired and not tactful enough this early in the morning," said White Padre. "Your son is a big man. He is no small boy. We offered him a job and he accepted it. He could have refused it if he he didn't like it. Remember only one thing. He will return when he wants .... or if he wants."

He left us dazed.

As days became weeks, weeks became months and months became years, we asked ourselves collectively and severally why Little Father did not want to return home or at least inform us of his whereabouts. The elders were tenacious. Their efforts to get more information from White Padre failed dismally. On one occasion, he nearly drove grandfather and me out of his house, shouting, "Am I Little Banda's keeper?"

When they failed to get information from the living, they resorted to many an occult practice current among the people. A woman living near the Vishnu temple went into a trance. Speaking in an eerie otherworldly screech, she assured us that Little Father was fast a sleep on a bed in a room full of books and was covering himself with a white shawl.

"He is well and happy. That's why he is covering himself with a white shawl", explained the medium's mother who collected the fee of a few silver fanams wrapped in a betel leaf. Grandmother's questions "Where?" and "When will we see him again?" were conveniently glossed over. The woman awoke from the trance and smiled at us as if she was seeing us for the first time.

On another occasion, we climbed a steep hill to a cottage where a man claimed to be a light reader. On the back of a ceramic saucer was drawn a solid black circle with soot mixed in some oil. A coconut lamp with a single wick was placed a few inches in front of the circle. The flame reflected in the centre of the circle. A child, a year or two younger than I, sat gazing at the reflection.

"What do you see in the light of the Monkey-god?", the adult asked repeatedly. Every time the boy said "Nothing", the other broke into droning incantations which sounded gibberish. After what seemed hours, the boy said,

"I see a young man. He is dressed like a teacher in the church school. He is walking on the ridge of a rice field."

The boy's voice changes suddenly to a high pitch. He is agitated and screams,

" Now he is in a crowd. A lot of people. But different people. Not like those I have seen. He is speaking to them. He has climbed on to a rock. He is waving his hands. That's all. That's all. Now I see nothing. Nothing. It's pitch dark."

This time it was my father who wanted to have an interpretation of the scene described by the boy.

"That's exactly what he should be doing wherever he is" was all that the light reader could say. Questioning the boy on the topography or the vegetation of the place was of little use. His only reply was that he told us what he saw and after the light disappeared, he remembered nothing.

These were mind-boggling experiences. Members of the family, alone or with others, were engaged in some consultation of this kind in some place almost every other day. None gave any clues as to where he could be found. All ended with the hope that the answer to our persistent question was imminent.

I never missed an opportunity to attend such sessions. I, too, like the rest of the family clung on to the tiniest shred of hope these mysterious, nevertheless inconclusive, predictions gave us. The loss of Little Father had the most ponderous impact on me in so many different ways.

In my case, the hope of his imminent return motivated me to continue my lists of questions. Many of them sprung from the long discourse Chief Monk gave us on the day after Little Father's departure. The Abbot of the Bo-tree Plain whom I met twice or thrice a week on a regular basis to broaden my knowledge of Sinhala language and literature had contributed to a dozen or more questions. The rest came from my experiences and observations in school. White Padre and Mrs. Blake showed me immense kindness. She gave me private classes in English after school and the padre went out of his way to show how much he cared for my well-being. Their solicitude embarrassed me. I had a notion that, in some inexplicable way, they felt guilty for Little Father's absence and silence.

It had been three months and three days from Little Father's departure when I was sent for by White Padre.

"Tiny Banda, we have some bad news. I want to tell your grandparents myself. Please tell them I will come to your place this evening. But don't tell them that it is to give any bad news."

We were all at home when White Padre in a black cassock walked into the inner verandah. Braving the heavy downpour and endless lightning and thunder, he had waded ankle-deep in muddy water to keep his appointment. The family fussed over him for a while bringing a rag to wipe his shoes and hot water to soak his feet in. Sipping from a steaming cup of coffee which Aunt Flower offered him, he sat erect on grandfather's easy chair and said,

"This morning a carter brought a letter which my Superior in Colombo had sent through the Vicar in Kandy. It was all about your son."

"Is he all right?" asked all of us in one voice.

"I am sorry I cannot answer the question. Until about ten days ago, he was all right. But what he did after that is no compliment to him. He has really let me down and I am blamed by the Mission. That's, of course, a minor matter. Now you also will blame me. He has left the Mission service and gone away without giving any information about where he could be contacted. So, even I have no way of contacting him any more."

That was definitely bad news. All this while we thought that the church could have helped us to reach him if there was a legitimate reason. We were hopeful that the church would be more considerate. As regards the padre's theoretical position, we expected no change for he repeatedly stressed that an adult had a right to be isolated if that was his or her wish. Now this slender hope too was dashed.

For some reason, no one showed any keenness to find out what went wrong between him and the Mission. White Padre finished the cup of coffee and handed to me the empty cup. As another clap of loud and long thunder subsided, he resumed,

"I am not surprised that you don't want to know how Little Banda has got me into trouble. Are you still keeping a grudge because I was tactless when I last came to your house?"

It was grandmother who had the presence of mind to say,

"No, my lord. Not at all. We are dazed. We don't know whom to look up to. Please forgive us."

"Yes, Jewel. I can understand that. Litttle Banda had a good job at the Mission. He did what we call in England field research. He went about meeting people and asking them questions. He recorded their answers. The church was trying to find out what was going wrong, why so many new Christians were relapsing to their old religion, where there were pockets of poverty and destitution so that the church could help them and find new converts. All this was harmless and hurt nobody. He had done this work for me here and he knew how to do it without causing any trouble to anyone. During the first few weeks of work for the Mission, Litttle Banda had turned in some fantastic information. The Mission had many answers to their dilemmas.

"The Deputy Chief of the Mission was so impressed with the vision and output of Little Banda that he sent him to a village about twenty miles to the southeast of Colombo. It was a trouble spot for the church. The padre there was a bit overzealous. He was upset that the villagers who relied on the church for their education and welfare assistance did not readily agree to be converted. He tried to put too much pressure. The villagers who were normally very courteous and friendly to padres were openly hostile to them. Some acts of sabotage - but not all that serious - had taken place recently. I would have laughed at them as pranks of some hot-headed young men. But this padre had tried to take retaliatory measures. Things were not going well for the Mission.

"Little Banda was asked to find out what was going on. In a couple of days he had done a good job. He had really got a good dialogue going on between the padre and some of the more influential members of the community. You know that your son is very good at that. Then an unfortunate incident took place.

"He wanted to bring about some understanding between the padre and some people who were building a new Buddhist temple in the furthest corner of the village. A monk from the south of the Island had come with a mason, a carpenter and two workers and constructed a substantial shrine-room, preaching hall and a residence for monks. The tiles for all three buildings had been delivered at the foot of the hill. Hauling them to the building sites required more labour than the monk had at his disposal. So, this particular week-end, when Little Banda was scouting in the village, the whole village turned up to help the monk. He, too, joined them and hauled some tiles. In fact, he went there the second day also and gave a helping hand.

"In the night, Little Banda gave a full account of the activities to the padre and mentioned about the way I got on with the whole community here. This padre who is no friend of mine was furious and accused Little Banda on failure to keep Sabbath. When it was explained that he had no obligation to observe Sabbath as he was not a baptized Christian, the padre was further infuriated. He drove Little Banda out of the room that was allotted to him. Fearing bodily harm, he left the church premises. He had no place to go. So he went to the temple site where he and the monk slept in the work-shed.

"Next day, however, Little Banda returned to the church premises to see the padre. At that moment, the padre had lined up the students and was interrogating them. When he saw Little Banda, the padre had briefly apologized for what happened the night before and asked his aid to check whether the students were truthful. The question asked from them was whether and, if so, when each student had helped in the construction of the temple. Little Banda refused to have anything to do with the padre's inquiry. It was now Little Banda's turn to be infuriated.

"The padre had decided to punish every child who had had anything to do with the construction of the temple. But the punishment was not the same for all. Each baptized Christian child was fined a rupee a day. The others were expelled from the school. He was not concerned that the latter group was as much as two thirds of the school population. Little Banda had reacted angrily. He had once again made the mistake of praising me as a fair and unprejudiced padre. He had gone further and questioned some students for having lied to remain in the school. Between the padre and Little Banda the situation became so bad that parents came to the school and removed all children."

We could not believe our ears. We had never known Little Father to be angry and argumentative. Apparently he had been provoked. Grandfather was quick in telling that to White Padre.

"Don't I know your son?" was his sincere response. "Something really bad had taken place. It would have been sheer injustice. Little Banda has very high principles. I also know that all my colleagues are not free from prejudice, bigotry and fanaticism. So, I don't blame Little Banda for having got into an argument with the padre. If I were there I would have definitely done the same thing."

I was elated. This was exactly my estimate of Little Father. He admired all that Christian Padres brought by way of a new culture, knowledge base and norms of etiquette and behaviour. He was grateful to White Padre for having broadened his horizons. But he was not ready to abandon his native religion or traditions even when he was assured that becoming a Christian would bring him many privileges and gains. If he had praised White Padre, he had good reasons. With a little more than six months of close association with him and his wife, I would myself be generous in complimenting them for their tolerance and understanding.

I cannot remember who among us realized that the padre had not come to the end of the story and the break was only momentary. Some one asked what happened after the closure of the school.

"That night too, Little Banda had slept in the work-shed of the new temple. In the early hours of the morning someone had gone there and set fire to the shed. When the monk and Little Banda came out of the burning shed, a number of men had attacked them. They had been badly beaten. Fortunately neither suffered any cuts or fractures. Workmen, sleeping in an unfinished building, had come to their help and beaten

60

the attackers with whatever they could find in the dark. After the attackers fled, these workmen had taken the monk and Little Banda to a native physician. They were rubbed down with medicinal oil and given some herbs for a decoction."

"The gods have looked after them," reacted grandmother. "Did they find out who attacked them?"

"Yes and no", said the Padre. "Next morning, one of the attackers was found in a ditch nearby. He was very badly injured but was alive. A hard blow with a crowbar had smashed his left shoulder. There were a number of compound fractures and he had bled badly.

"Now, this was the problem. He was the grave-digger of the church and the villagers suspect that the attack was instigated by the padre. The village headman thinks so and his report to the Assistant Government Agent in charge of the District spells out the motive as Little Father's protest that morning."

"What do you think?" asked grandfather. He sounded a bit defiant.

"I really cannot say. In our system of justice, which is what we have introduced to this country, a person is innocent until he is found guilty. We need evidence. The injured man wouldn't tell who the other attackers were. He has no idea who hit him with a crowbar. To make the whole situation worse, Little Banda has taken his bag of belongings and left the village. No one had seen him since."

The loud wailing of grandmother and two aunts was spontaneous. I felt as though a red hot iron pierced my chest. Only grandfather had some control over his emotions to ask the padre,

"Does the disappearance of my son create any complications. For example, do the authorities think he hit the grave-digger with a crowbar?"

"Now that I have gone so far, let me go the whole way," said White Padre. "Not necessarily. But the young padre was over anxious to have the matter closed by putting the entire blame on Little Banda and advancing his disappearance as an admission of guilt. Someone in the District Office at Black-Haven did not agree and sent an officer to investigate the matter.

"The officer who came for the inquiry did a good job. He cleared Little Banda. He had told the padre in no uncertain terms that the evidence was more against him in that a church employee was found to be involved in trespass, arson and assault. Besides, a motive for the attack could be established. Several villagers testified that Little Banda was not strong enough to have wielded a heavy crowbar in a way to cause the injury. The monk also gave a statement to the effect that Little Banda was a peace-loving non-violent man with an incredible sense of fair play and tolerance.

"This is what I also wrote to my Superior who blames me for having recommended for employment a person who had not been baptized a Christian and, therefore, not tested for his undivided loyalty to the church. I said further that he was a better Christian than anyone I have found either in England or here among thousands who had gone through baptism for worldly gains."

"It's nice to hear that our little son has gained recognition for his good qualities. That's all a mother wants to hear," said grandmother.

I was smarting to ask him what happened to the padre who evidently instigated the attack and tried very hard to implicate Little Father as the villain. But, once again, my age was against me. I was near enough to Aunt Jasmine to whisper my question to her ears.

"Yes, Valour-Lion", White Father turned to me. "The Mission lost decades of work due to this hot-headed young padre. He has been recalled. Maybe, he will be sent back to England or even defrocked. The school is closed. The church is deserted. Converts have forsaken the Mission. We aren't sure if the Mission can go back to the village any more."

"Was it a white officer who came for the investigation?" asked grandfather.

"Yes. The padre used all his influence to get the highest officer in the District Office in the mistaken notion that the administration would support him without question. But the new civil servant is an impartial man with a sound head on his shoulders and cannot easily be fooled."

"That's a great relief, my lord," said grandmother.

Another cup of coffee and a long discussion followed on what Little Father would decide to do. How fertile the brains of the elders were when it came to creating different scenarios and pursuing them to logical conclusions! They ranged from the possible to the probable and the utterly impossible!

As grandfather and I set out to accompany White Padre to the church school with two torches, he saluted the three women with clasped hands in the traditional manner and told them,

"We'll continue to search for him. We'll never give up. He has been my best friend. I am your friend."

VIII

That was two years and nine months ago. White Father kept to his word. He wrote to all his friends. He contacted officials who could help him. He himself pursued some clues and went to faraway places. But to no avail.

Both White Padre and his wife extended to me and the two aunts every possible help. When Aunt Jasmine fell in love and married the landless son of a sharecropper, White Padre leased them a plot of land adjoining the school to have their own farm to grow vegetables for the market. They have prospered and have built their own tile-roofed brick house and had their first child, a beautiful baby girl. Aunt Flower was trained to work as an attendant in the church dispensary and encouraged to become a skilled midwife.

To me they were extraordinarily generous. They gave me their time and energy unstintingly. Mrs. Blake taught me English every day after school. We were three boys and two girls in this class and I was the only non-Christian. As I made steady progress, she arranged extra classes specially for me. White Padre would find time to talk to me in English. He introduced me to a technical vocabulary in Arithmetic, Geography and History. Their aim was to ensure that I could proceed to an English school in Kandy. I did some chores in the house and garden to show my gratitude. Always they dissuaded me saying,

"What we do for you is nothing when we consider what you personally lost by the absence of your Little Father. He was your hero and mentor? Wasn't he?"

Both of them had assumed a deep sense of guilt for his disappearance. They expressed it most eloquently when they exempted me from church attendance and encouraged me to continue my studies in the temple.

The special treatment they gave our family was not unnoticed. It became a subject for comment and criticism. The headmaster's wife was once reported to have complained that the Christian population was dissatisfied on account of our receiving privileges that were reserved for new converts. Her younger brother, the headmaster's brother-in-law, who escaped manhandling from the unruly crowd at Thorn-tree-Ford was more vocal.

He had told the Muslim trader that if the Mission instituted an inquiry against White Padre, he would not hesitate to give evidence against the padre. "He is a hidden pagan, a heretic" were the words this teacher had used. The trader, in turn, told the whole story to grandmother and I was asked to apprise the Blakes. I chose to tell that to Mrs. Blake during the private class she gave me. That was the theme of that day's class and it was indeed very instructive as she wanted me to say it in English. When I finished with her help in the search for the correct words, she made a long statement. I disturbed her only when I did not understand a word or an expression.

"Roman Catholicism came here with the Portuguese. For one hundred and fifty years their missionaries did everything possible to convert the people to that religion. Not all their methods were fair or kindly. When the Dutch came, they brought the religious disputes of Europe to this country. They persecuted the Catholics."

I interrupted her to find out what the the religious disputes of Europe were and what the word "persecute" meant. She explained half in English and half in Sinhala.

"The Kandyan Buddhist kings showed much greater qualities of tolerance and love to Catholics than the Dutch who also claimed to worship the same God and accept the same Saviour in Jesus." She continued, "After the British occupied the country, so many missionaries came here because they were invited to take over the school system. These days, all these missions are celebrating their Diamond and Golden Jubilees. But what do we see? Is Christianity advancing? I say yes. Our influence is widespread. We have influenced the life and thinking of the people. People in the low-country have changed a lot due to Christian influence.

"A decade or two ago, we thought that Christianity would replace all other religions in the Island with the exception of perhaps Islam. Most of us had no objection to Islam first because Muslims are only a very small minority in the population and, secondly, because they also believe in one single God. They were not idolators, I mean they don't worship statues and idols. They are not very superstitios either. But it was different with Buddhism and Hinduism. A well-known Sinhala scholar even predicted that Buddhism would soon disappear and Sinhala authors would invoke Father, Son and Holy Spirit in place of the Buddhist Trinity. But all these predictions have been proved wrong."

She paused for a while and resumed with a jab into the air in front of my face.

"Are we making converts? I say no. Really speaking, we are losing our flock daily. Conversion, baptism, confirmation and so forth are no guarantee that a person who calls oneself a Christian is not in fact a Buddhist or a Hindu at heart. Attendance at church services does not mean that they do not practice Buddhism or Hinduism secretly and support their temples."

This was nothing new to me. I met some of them in my grand-uncle's temple in Sangha-Gem-Field.

"Are you angry with them?" I asked. She did not answer my question directly.

"We are in a country where our service has to be different. That is what Reverend Blake and I try to achieve," she continued. "We want to set a Christian example and make our lives a testimony to Christian virtues. We are not in the numbers game."

"But are you not in some sort of trouble on account of this attitude?' I asked in Sinhala as my poor vocabulary would not permit the question to be posed elegantly.

"We could be. But Reverend Blake is a very courageous man - a man of conviction and high principles."

Two months prior to the day I was told of my admission to the high school in Kandy, I met an equally courageous man of conviction and high principles. It was no wonder that he was the closest friend of White Padre and belonged to the same Mission. Reverend Kenneth Saunders was on a visit to Bo-tree Plain. He was recovering from a long bout of malaria, then called simply jungle fever. With medical science still ignorant of the role which mosquitoes played in the spread of the parasites that caused shivering fever with bouts of deliria, the debilitating sickness was said to come from the foul air in wet swampy forests.

The circumstances under which we met appeared to be fortuitous. I was asked by Mrs. Blake to take a bowl of soup to his room. I had, however, a feeling that the meeting was arranged for a purpose. He knew all about me, my catastrophic birth, my temple studies, my relationship with the two most important Buddhist monks of the region, my mentor's disappearance and my possible future as a Buddhist monk.

Reverend Saunders was the very opposite of White Padre - short and stocky, paunchy belly, easy and hilarious laughter and a loud and gravelly voice which could be heard for hundreds of yards. He was expecting me to bring the soup.

"Hey! Young man!" he greeted me. "You are the one who brought down so many houses with your birth."

He gave a guffaw as if he had just said something sparklingly comic. To me who had heard a surfeit of jokes on the unfortunate circumstances attending my birth, it sounded macabre.

I felt touchy. One more stranger making fun of me for no fault of mine! I was about to leave the bowl of soup on a small table and beat a hasty retreat.

"Come here, come here," he said and his right hand was stretched in friendship. I took his hand and shook the way I had seen White Padre doing with his friends. If I was clumsy about it, Reverend Saunders did not say a word. Instead he asked me to sit at the foot of his bed. He adjusted his pillows, raised himself and chose a posture which would enable him to make eye contact with me and have an intimate conversation.

"Do you know why I am here?" he asked me.

" No," I said. "But I have heard that you were not well and White Padre was a very good friend of yours."

"But that was not enough reason to come here. I could have gone to any church in a hill station. I am here to kill two birds with one stone."

Something symapthetic and kindly in his tone encouraged me to speak in English with ease and confidence. So far I had no difficulty in understanding what he told me. But I had no idea what he meant by killing two birds with one stone. Perhaps he read the confusion on my face.

"I am here for two purposes. One to get back some strength after the horrible fever. The other to find out how to support a recommendation which Reverend Blake had made about you."

In spite of three years of education in the church school, my attitude to elders was exactly as was demanded by tradition. I would not ask what he had recommended about me. Perhaps, this time he read curiosity on my face.

"Reverend Blake says that the Mission owes you an English education. He has given many good reasons."

He paused for a full minute to take a few spoonfuls of soup. The thought that came to my mind was that White Padre had made another attempt to compensate me and perhaps my family for his assumed role in the disappearance of Little Father. Almost as a mind-reader with magic powers, he said,

"Doing something for you and the family on account of your paternal uncle is, however, the very last reason. Your relationship with the important Buddhist monks of the region is only mentioned in passing in his letter."

66

Again, he drank some of his soup, placed the bowl on the table and asked me with another loud laugh,

"Valour-Lion, are you as good as he says you are?"

The rest of the time was devoted almost entirely to my academic work. I found him increasing the level of language until I had to ask for the meaning of more and more words and expressions. He also posed several mental arithmetic sums. I felt that he was satisfied with my performance, even though he said nothing about it. He was so child-like and transparent. I liked him instantly and was pleased when I was asked to see him the next day around the same time.

Next day, too, I brought him his soup. He was seated at the table. I was asked to sit on the bed facing him. This day's conversation bordered on my knowledge of the Bible, prayers and Christian beliefs and practices. I could not answer some questions. But, on the whole, I felt that I acquitted myself creditably.

"You are very good, Valour-Lion. You really know your Christianity. Why didn't you want to be baptized a Christian?"

"May I answer this question in Sinhala?" I asked him and I was not surprised when he consented to it. A padre who was so sympathetic and understanding would certainly have mastered the Sinhala language and even some Pali, I surmised.

I told him of the question my father asked White Father on the day I was admitted to the church school. All in my extended family, with the exception of my paternal grandfather, expected me to be a Buddhist monk.

"With the education and training I have had from the family and the two temples from the earliest day I can recall, I am made to believe that I have a mission to fulfill and that is related to Buddhism in this country."

For a while I was frightened that Reverend Saunders was a secret agent of the Mission and I was being interrogated in an effort to find fault with the Blakes for being unusually generous and helpful to our family. Have I told him anything that I should not?

I had to live with this nagging fear a whole day until the routine was repeated. This time I had to carry him a whole meal in a tray. Reverend Saunders was on his feet. In fact, he was pacing about the room when I cleared my throat and coughed softly to announce my arrival. He laughed.

"What a good Sinhala technique. Very useful if your hands are full and you can't knock on the door."

67

He was bouyantly cheerful.

"My mind is made, young man. Congratulations."

What a simple sentence! Yet it meant nothing to me. I knew from the tone that I was expected to react with some form of elation. The word "congratulations" was totally unfamiliar. As regards his making up his mind, I was not sure on what. I presumed, however, that he had decided not to report against the Blakes because I showed enough interest in Christianity. Without really knowing why, I said,

"Thank you, Reverend Saunders. You are very kind. I am very glad for Reverend Blake and Mrs. Blake."

Reverend Saunders was amused.

"Hey, young man. What do you think? Do you think that I am here to hold an inquiry against the Blakes? Don't you see I am their guest."

I felt miserable. It was then he opened out giving his own ideas on how Christian padres should work in countries like ours.

"I am a friend of the Blakes because we think alike. We have a love for this country, for its people and their culture. We bring you a new religion, a new culture and a new heritage. We don't think that we should replace everything in your country with what we have brought with us. We are even convinced that we could never do so. It is nevertheless a pity that some firebrands among us missionaries are over zealous and make many mistakes."

I thought the reference was to the padre in the low-country on account of whose machinations Little Father was obliged to become a fugitive. But he seemed to think of a situation more widespread.

"We are in 1872. It is not like 1796 when we took over the maritime belt from the Dutch or 1815 when the Kingdom of Kandy was annexed. I went on furlough to England last year and what I saw there was very encouraging. We are liberating ourselves from the stranglehold of the church. Scientific discoveries and increasing knowledge of Asian religions, specially Buddhism, have put our faith in Christianity to the test."

His gestures and body language conveyed to me the sense of the words which I did not know. He described briefly in a mixture of English and Sinhala the anti-ecclesiastical socialist movement which had brought about significant policy changes in England.

"We can't have two policies - one in the British Isles and another in the Colonies. There aren't enough men of learning and courage among the missionaries in the Island to fight for a better deal for the people."

He looked very sad. He gave me the impression of a tired old man who was desperate to have his wishes fulfilled. But he was not that old. He could have been only a couple of years older than White Padre.

"Valour-Lion, don't you ever forget what we have spoken about in this room. People like the Blakes and me are far ahead of our times. We'll die before the right things are done. It is not because we do not try hard enough. It is because changes in society take a long time in coming. But you will be there to benefit from the great changes for the better that are taking place in Europe today. I hope you'll be a good monk. No! - - I want to do all I can to see that you become a good monk. Fifty years from now we will be happy if the monks of this country assess our services dispassionately and fairly and give us credit for what we have tried to do."

I was baffled by his wish.

He wished me good-bye. His handshake was firm. It seemed to mean that a permanent bond was established between us. If I felt within me that I was going to be in close touch with this great visionary, the feeling was more prophetic than wishful thinking. I was sad when I learned the next day that he had taken the early morning caravan of carts to Kandy.

IX

I woke up from my reverie when the icy cold hand of grandmother touched my right cheek.

"Tiny One, what are you doing with your sweet palm sap untouched and the leaf covering of your millet-flour delicacy only half open? How long have you been like this?

I was no doubt shaken. I had to return to normal behaviour as soon as I could and as convincingly as was possible. Otherwise, the next scene would have been sheer panic in the house and urgent summons to the witch-doctor.

Any out-of-the-normal behaviour was, as a rule, attributed to malefic intervention of demons and evil spirits. They were supposed to be everywhere and one could be a victim by just being at the wrong place at the wrong time! Witch-doctors had their own remedies. Some were simple and involved only applying a little "charmed" oil on the forehead. Others could be so elaborate as to eat up an year's revenue of a family for a single night of ceremonial chanting and dancing. Another moment of day-dreaming and inattentivenesss was all that was needed to get the family diving into ruination.

My recovery evidently was adequately convincing. Yet, to make it more effective, I told grandmother of the many thoughts that passed through my mind.

"I know, Tiny One. You always think of my womb-sweeper. What a wonderful thing it would have been if he was here to bless your plans for further studies."

I recalled how this aging woman of firm determination defied her husband and sent her youngest son to an uncertain destiny.

"She could be my ally," I thought. "Or will her support be contrary to my interests?"

Now that the matter was raised by her, I had no alternative but explore her reaction.

"Tiny One, I want you to go to Kandy. I think your father will agree. In any case Chief Monk, your grand-uncle, will have the last word."

How prophetic she was. The rural grapevine had taken only a few hours to bring news from Bo-tree Plain to Sangha-Gem-Field. On Sunday, I reached home a short while before father returned from a bath in the river to have his mid-day meal. He was glad to see me. He hugged me and kissed me on the head even before I went on my knees to touch his feet with clasped hands.

"I'm proud of you, my son. You have done well. You are a credit to the family."

From father, who was usually reticent, it was a lot. Mother reacted in a similar fashion. None of the brothers were at home.

"Till I get the meals ready, why don't the two of you go to the temple before the monks have their mid-day snooze?" mother proposed. It was a good idea specially as the timing ensured that it would be a brief meeting.

Chief Monk was out cleaning his teeth with a brush formed by chewing the end of a twig of a medicinal plant.

"Here comes our *gentleman*," he said with stress on the last word.

This word which originally meant "lofty-souled" was fast acquiring a new meaning in our language to signify an English educated person with a good standing in society. If I went to Kandy, did my studies well and made myself well established economically, I would have earned this designation of esteem. No further words were needed to convey his decision.

"Let us not confuse what happened to Little Banda with what we have to do for you," he said to me even though he meant it for my father. "If we are short-sighted, we are bound to regret it."

The tension caused by the disappearance of Little Father had taken a toll of the whole family and my usually docile father ventured to disagree with Chief Monk's observation.

"Aren't we regretting the leeway we gave my youngest brother to dabble with padres and church?"

"Yes and no. Yes, because we have gone through so much grief and anxiety due to his unexplained absence. No, because he will, in another three or four years, come out into the public smelling like a rose. Then we'll all rejoice."

Chief Monk was precise and forceful.

"I am very happy to hear that", said father. "Does this boy's horoscope predict any such calamity? The family will not be able to go through the same grief twice."

"Definitely not. Tiny One is going to be the star of the family. He already is."

His words were honey in my ears. Astrology, as my teachers in school never fail to denigrate, might be pure superstition. But what a problem-solver it could be in our credulous society! Once he had pronounced and invoked astrological reinforcement, none in the family would override him.

My going to Kandy was now a foregone conclusion. I pranced all the way home, stopping from time to time to catch up with father who walked slower than on other days.

Mother might have consulted her uncle or else she interpreted my buoyancy.

"So, he wants you to go to Kandy?" she asked but did not expect an answer.

A new routine developed over the next four weeks when the rest of the students were enjoying a care-free vacation. Every third day, I went to Bo-tree Plain. Spoken English with Mrs. Blake. Bible reading with White Padre. Chores for either of them while engaged in a lively conversation in English. Lunch as their guest. A chat with the Abbot of the temple. Dinner with grandparents. A trudge back to Sangha-Gem-Field the next morning. Christmas with the Blakes was a memorable treat. So was New Year.

On these festive days, I attended church service. I genuinely enjoyed the singing and White Padre's sermons. I joined in prayers not simply as I knew most of them by heart but because I enjoyed them as a spiritual experience. The question of faith was in no way involved. Even though I could cope with the gods and goddesses of polytheistic Hinduism which was a part of the central credo of a Buddhist of my background, the omniscient, omnipresent, omnipotent single creator God was beyond my grasp. White Padre, who understood my reservations, was quick to dissuade me. He said,

"Valour-Lion, you don't have to attend church service simply to please us. Be the good Buddhist you are. That will be our reward for whatever we do for you."

Having heard similar sentiments expressed by Reverend Kenneth Saunders, I was emboldened to ask him, "My lord, do all the padres of the Mission agree with you?"

"Increasingly they do. But don't forget we have our share of black sheep, not to speak of what our patrons and church leadership expect from us."

He had to switch on to Sinhala to explain who black sheep were and the discontinuity between what the church authorities and their financiers thought in England and the reality in the field. Then he continued in English,

"You wouldn't imagine what some of the more enlightened padres had done to promote Buddhist studies. There was Reverend D. J. Gogerly. He died about ten years ago. He translated a number of very interesting discourses of the Buddha into English. You know the advice he gave the Buddhists. He said something like, 'Educated Sinhalas in giving attention to English literature and learning had entirely overlooked their own.' In other words, he wanted them to study the Buddha's sermons and your own rich literature. Do you know the Buddha's sermon to a young man called Sigala?"

"Yes. Sigala who worshipped the six directions," I replied. Switching on to Sinhala, I asked whether he meant the discourse which the monks called "Lay Discipline".

"That's right. You recall what was told about the acquisition of wealth?"

I did. Chief Monk's sermon on the last Fullmoon Sabbath was on this particular subject. I said promptly,

"Divide your income into four parts. Use one part for your living expenses. Invest two parts in your business. Save the last part for a time of need."

"Very good, Valour-Lion. That discourse was Reverend Gogerly's favourite. I read it in his translation and liked it myself. I have never seen the proper relationships with such pairs like child and parent, wife and husband, teacher and pupil, religious teacher and disciple, master and servant and friend and friend explained with such precision and depth of understanding anywhere else. That is wisdom which has no boundaries in time or place."

He also spoke highly of an earlier padre named Reverend R. Spence Hardy.

"Much of the Buddhism I know I picked up from his two books. I have them here with me. Some day you must read them. I was very pleased when Chief Monk found that I understood some teachings quite well and complimented me. I had to offer my silent thanks to Reverend Hardy."

White Padre was an indefatigable teacher. He would go over the same topic in English and Sinhala, explain every new word, discuss the grammar of each sentence, parse every word in detail and end up by asking me to write down a gist of the conversation.

Even now at the age of ninety, I recall every new word or expression, he taught me. It is even more interesting that I have a mental picture of the time, place and circumstances under which I learnt some things from him.

Daily I felt more and more confident that I could fit into an English medium school in Kandy. Will they admit me to the ninth grade or ask me to repeat one or more grades? The question bothered me. I think I was my own worst slave-driver!!! I asked White Padre,

"Will I be able to proceed to grade nine with my present knowledge of English?"

"I thought you knew. Reverend Saunders considered your knowledge of English good enough to put you into grade nine and he would personally help you if you have problems of switch-over."

It was only then I came to know that Reverend Saunders was the second in command in the school. Only then did I know that I had been admitted on a full scholarship because the recommendation of White Padre was strongly supported by Reverend Saunders. I had, hitherto, been under the impression that Mrs. Blake obtained my services to take food to his room as I was conveniently available. Now some of the cryptic statements that he used to make about killing two birds with one stone became clearer. I was so thrilled.

The distance from church school to my home appeared unending due to my anxiety. I ran into my house shouting the good news about the grade and Reverend Saunders. I did not realize that there was no one at home and I was talking to myself. Mother came in from the garden minutes later to find me in a state of pure ecstasy.

"Son, you are beaming? Any more good news?"

"I know the padre who will take care of me in Kandy. He is a wonderful man. A twin brother of White Padre. Not literally."

Her muffled sigh of relief hinted how this bit of information was as important to her as it was to me.

Three years in the high school in Kandy passed too quickly. The first couple of months were difficult. Socially, I was a misfit in spite of what the Blakes had done to introduce me to the Western way of life. Much of my village shyness and crudity persisted until the peers removed them through their painful and sadistic pranks. Twice I went to Reverend Saunders and asked for his intervention. He pretended that I was hallucinating. On the third occasion I went with a bloody nose. His reaction was even more insensitive.

"Too bad for a Valour-Lion not to know what to do. Fight your own battles, son. More will be on the way."

That was good advice. I found time to join the boxing class. I took literally the Latin adage painted on one of the school walls: *Mens sana in corpore sano*.

The day a deftly delivered upper right sent the class bully reeling to the ground, I was accepted into the school community with full honours. Henceforth I was on my own. Reverend Saunders was the first to notice the change.

"Valour-Lion, (or shall I simply call you T.B.?), I was waiting for this day. That invisible umbilical cord that existed between you and me had to be severed for you to grow up and be a man."

I was determined to be a man. A man befitting the trust that so many people had reposed in me. Little Father, of course, led the list. I could see him in my mind's eye. Often, I felt that his spirit guided me. Whenever this feeling overcame me, I shuddered. Was he guiding me from "the other world"? I asked myself and soon added, "Hope not. He should be living to see me evolving into what he wanted me to be."

The academic programme presented no difficulty. From the third term in the new school, I was the unchallenged top scorer in practically every subject. My long walks between Bo-tree Plain and Sangha-Gem-Field had trained me to be an enduring long distance runner. Similarly acquired stamina earned me a place in the Junior Rugby Team.

One area in which I could have used my temple learning to the utmost advantage was not available to me. Sinhala was not a subject either taught or encouraged. In fact, it was positively discouraged. One ran the risk of being fined new five cents for every Sinhala word spoken in the class or the dormitory.

My attempt to get into the Debating Team was only partially successful. English had already become the home language of the upper class and the well-to-do. Children from such homes, naturally had a better command of the language. Yet three years in succession I won the open English essay competition.

At every prize-giving, I managed to win all class prizes and almost half of the open prizes. I was on the way to success. I was a favourite among teachers. Each had a different idea of what I should do in life. They were all very sincere. But I knew in my heart that mine was a destiny already cast out for me.

There were frequent incidents when my religious attitudes were subject to comment. The boys in the hostel thought I was unduly privileged in that I was exempted from church service. They were really envious. A walk up the hill to church in the chilly morning mist of Kandy on a Sunday morning was not everyone's cup of tea. Few had strong enough piety to motivate them to do so.

On my own initiative, I decided to attend the Biblical classes. I liked the Bible for its entrancing tales of human interest. White Padre had impressed on me that the King James version of the Bible, which the Mission used, was first class literature. The more I read the Bible, the more I appreciated the beauty of the English language. Invariably, however, I got dragged into some kind of controversy in these classes when either a newly converted teacher or student wittingly or otherwise denigrated some aspect of Buddhism or Sri Lankan culture. While using every opportunity to set the record straight and remove misconceptions or misunderstandings, I remained calm. I tried very hard to maintain the level of objectivity which I had seen in three of the people I most admired, namely Little Father, White Padre and Reverend Saunders. But just on one occasion, I failed.

The same bully who was instrumental in launching me on boxing taunted me one night in the hostel for having spent the previous weekend at the Flower Garden Monastery. It was an insulting remark which was as uncouth as it was provocative. To add insult to injury, he stood on my bed and urinated on the pillow. The rest of the boarders laughed at what he did and was urging me to retaliate. It was fun and excitement for them. But not for me. A well aimed blow to the exposed lower part of his body which was at eye level sent him unconscious to the floor resulting in a gash above his left ear. It was mayhem for a while. The assistant teacher in charge of our dormitory happened to pass by. With copious sprinkling of water, the bully revived. Only I was by him to own up what happened. The rest had disappeared to the study room beyond the dormitories.

Although more than enough evidence substantiated my grievance, the teacher accepted the bully's version. He alleged that I had lured him to bed for an unnatural act, tried to pull down his trousers in which I was said to have half-succeeded and finally pushed him down in anger because he refused to oblige me. The urine on the pillow was disregarded.

"I have waited long enough, you bloody B... bastard. You have it here better than any one of us. You'll see what I will do to you," shouted the teacher as he approached with an outstretched hand to slap me.

His reference to me as a bastard would not have upset me so much. We used such strong words of denigration as bloody, bastard, bugger, rascal, cad, s-o-b in everyday conversation both in play and in anger. But adding to it a reference to my faith must have done something to me. My reaction to his physical violence - those days, approved as corrective corporal punishment - was to bump him hard on his chest with my lowered head. Not only was he thrown off balance by the aborted slap but my hard blow sent him on his back to the ground wet with water and urine. A healthy athletic seventeen year village boy was no match to an emaciated malnourished man of mid-twenties who had never known a home as a child.

76

The teacher's version that I attacked him without provocation was readily corroborated by the bully just as the former expressed his readiness to accept the bully's version of his injury. That night I had no friend. Those who saw the beginning of the incident and even aggravated it lied that they were all in the study room. Quite unintentionally they gave some support to the bully's story about sexual advances.

I was hauled before a disciplinary committee of three teachers. They had been so chosen that none had been a class teacher or a subject teacher of either me or the bully. But the charge against me was that I assaulted a teacher and no fellow teacher would take kindly to such conduct. I told the committee what happened. The bully and the teacher stuck to their version and corroborated each other. The session ended with no doubt in my mind that I would be declared guilty and even expelled.

I recalled the fate of Golden Banda of Thorn-tree Ford. I made up my mind with regard to one thing. I would never allow myself to be used by anyone for any interreligious dissension. I owed so much to men of such fine qualities like the Blakes and Reverend Saunders, not to mention all my teachers in the high school.

I was very sad for the assistant teacher. I had heard about his background. An orphan brought up by the Mission in one of its children's homes near Colombo, Paul Ferdinando had neither family nor relatives. The Mission found him to be a good student and had him trained as a high school teacher. To enable him to save some money from his paltry salary, he was assigned as an assistant hostel master. Student discipline was his main responsibility. He was a loner, had no friends among the staff or the student body and was rated as a cantankerous man of no consequence. For once he was receiving some sympathy. After all, he was a teacher and an audacious student had violated his person!

He saw me outside the room after the inquiry.

"Pack your bloody bag, you good for nothing B... bastard. Go back to your village and buy yourself a plough with a buffalo. You deserve to be tied to the other end of the yoke," he kept ranting.

I moved away quickly. He was still calling me bad names which were becoming more and more related to my position as a member of the very small non-Christian population of the school, when the three members of the disciplinary team emerged and "caught him in the act."

They needed no further proof for my version of the incident. His long-winded scolding was adequately self-incriminating.

Watching the team members from over a hundred yards, I could discern what they planned to do. They went back to the room for further deliberation. I climbed to the hostel with a sense of satisfaction that justice would be done. Just as Little Father, I was confident that we could rely on the scrupulously principled persons produced by the new norms of social culture.

I was right. The bully was expelled from the hostel. The teacher was removed from his hostel duties. I received a severe warning that violence of any form and specially against a teacher would be dealt with seriously in the future.

The following Monday, all my friends had returned to me. Some congratulated me on having got rid of two bad apples in one go. Others apologized for their cowardice. That night I thought of the Blakes. I remembered what Mrs. Blake told me, "Two good apples, two good apples; one bad apple and one good apple, two bad apples"

X

On the home front every thing had been normal. My brothers joined the father in rice cultivation. With enough help, he could take over most of the land belonging to the temple for cultivation as a sharecropper. Two elder brothers moved into the homes of the girls they married. In the Kandyan legal system, which the British Administration continued to uphold in matters of person and property, two forms of marriages were recognized. One was *Deega* when the bride left her home and the other was *Binna*. In the case of my brothers, the *Binna* marriage was preferred as the girls' families had no sons of their own. My father had done likewise and the elders in the village joked about *Binna* marriages as endemic to our family!

I returned home only during the month long vacations at the end of each three-month term. I felt lonely and left out as my brothers worked in the fields most of the time and I was discouraged from joining them. "You are more an obstacle than a help," was their explanation. I understood it. How deftly, they managed the bulls and ploughed in a straight line! My attempt to guide the bulls was a near disaster. They sensed my incompetence and had no patience for me. Once, I nearly cut my toes when I used the hoe and on another occasion almost smashed the head of my immediate elder brother. With that accident averted due to the presence of mind of another brother, I agreed with them that I was beyond training in the noble profession of the family. Mother consoled me with her usual reminder of great things I was destined to do.

I was conscious of the gradual change in my behaviour at every vacation. I looked forward to the very first vacation. I felt a great relief to be at home with the family and to eat my meals seated anywhere in the house out of a clay bowl using my fingers. Sleeping on the folding camp-bed called a "donkey-bed" was a welcome change from the luxury of the dormitory. So was it to get into a sarong and a loose shirt and walk bare-footed on the ridges of the rice-fields. I put on my blue drill short trousers and white shirt only when I visited the Blakes in Bo-tree Plain. Then, too, I preferred to go bare-footed the way I had done in the past. By the seventh vacation, however, the change was complete.

I went about in my school uniform, long stockings and shoes included. I took them off hardly before bed-time. I had persuaded the parents to buy a dining table with six chairs and some modern furniture for the rooms. The bed I slept on was about the same as the one at the hostel. We ate from ceramic plates which grandfather had bought for us in Kandy. Through my persisting goading, to which the family grudgingly succumbed, our home was becoming urban or rather Western in style. An area was set in the inner verandah to receive visitors and appropriately furnished with a modern, though modest, sofa set bought in Kandy and transported all the way in a bullock cart. Only the Divisional Administrator, holding the traditional title of the 'Country Gentleman' and referred to deferentially by the abbreviation of his Sinhala title as R.M., was known to have been ahead of us in this matter.

The modernization of our home as a result of my exposure to a new life style was the subject of gossip in and around the village. If imitation and denunciation are outward signs of sneaking admiration, we certainly had much.

"T.B., you are making history in this area as the bearer of a new culture," commented White Padre during one of my visits.

My transformation from a rural ignoramus to someone different was already confirmed when the Blakes ceased to call me Tiny Banda or Valour-Lion. To call me T.B. was to show that I was someone close to them.

"I am trying to do something my Little Father taught me. He convinced me that I should make an effort to assimilate all that is good and worthwhile in Western culture without being prejudiced."

White Padre tapped me on the shoulder affectionately.

"Already using big words like *convinced*, *effort*, *assimilate*, *worthwhile* and *prejudiced*. Very good, my son. Keep it up."

My eighth vacation in August 1875 was memorable. The term ended a day before the great pageant of elephants, dancers and torches. Reverend Saunders permitted us to remain in the hostel for a few days provided the parents agreed. I had not only the required permission but also an additional bonus. Aunt flower would come to Kandy to witness the pageant and stay with some friends living not too far from the school. Since Aunt Jasmine married and began to tend her own family of a devoted husband and two lovely kids, Aunt Flower became my special friend and confidante.

The new postal system introduced to the village was a boon to us. For a few cents, we could write to each other and exchange news of the family and our friends, acquaintances and neighbours. In my Western or English background in school, writing to her was the only way that I could maintain my proficiency in Sinhala. We could be funny. We even wrote in verse. Once she imitated the handwriting of my eldest brother's wife's sister and wrote a moving love letter all in verse. I was duped until I received her next letter. If I had not been too busy with term tests, I would have reciprocated the sentiments in a similar letter in verse to my beautiful sister-in-law and got into serious trouble or become a laughing stock!

But what made the vacation memorable had something to do with this very symbol of charm. She was to accompany Aunt Flower. I pretended that I took this news as nothing extraordinary. Yet, inside me excitement and longing reigned supreme until I met them at the coach stand.

Slim-Jewel wore a pure white tight-fitting blouse with short sleeves and a matching cloth which reached from her gracefully thin waist to her ankles. The bare midriff with its glossy fair complexion appeared more like a broad waist-band of silk. She was bare-footed. But the silver anklets and a couple of toe rings adorned her shapely feet.

Tenets of modesty precluded us from eye contact. She looked down at her toes and the smile on her face was faint. A fifteen year old Kandyan belle bursting visibly into voluptuous womanhood was indeed a joy to behold. She saluted me with clasped hands and I reciprocated.

"You know why I brought her?" asked Aunt Flower.

Expecting her to be naughty, Slim-Jewel turned her face away. In that pose she looked prettier.

"Tiny One, you are fast becoming a book-worm, or should I say a book-lunatic? Worse still, the old codgers at home are waiting for the day when they could shave your head, don a yellow robe on you and let you rot in a monastery. And for what? Just to be sure that the bright young grand-nephew will inherit the temple and one day be the Chief Monk of the Great Royal Monastery of Sangha-Gem-Field."

The more explicit Aunt Flower tried to be about her motive for bringing Slim-Jewel to Kandy, the more embarrassed I became. In any case, the public coach stand in front of the new market was not the proper place to discuss my future or Aunt Flower's plans to design it differently. As soon as the little tin suitcase was unloaded, I led the way for them to follow.

How silly for me to go ahead of them, I told myself. After all, it was our custom. Men went ahead to ward off danger that may befall the weaker sex! The Western custom in whose favour I had a lot to say would have given me the opportunity to experience the ecstasy of watching her graceful walk. As I carried the heavy case, I could do nothing else than visualize her beauty and grace.

81

If Aunt flower expected a sudden rush of fervour and the two of us to fall in love at first sight and declare lasting affection and commitment, that did not happen.

"I must be a lousy matchmaker," Aunt Flower groused at the end of the second day of our visits to the Temple of the Sacred Tooth Relic, the four temples for Hindu deities, the major Monasteries of the Flower Garden and Horse Peak and a long and amply rewarding trudge to the River Monastery and the Double Rock Slit Temple with its exquisite murals.

Two brief moments of sheer joy marked the high water-mark of the day. I had to hold Slim-Jewel by both her hands to help her into the single-log dug-out canoe. The three standing passengers and the ferryman balanced themselves precariously as the canoe rolled by eddying waters of the Great Sand River at the Bloody Shore. Suddenly the canoe bounced and a frightened Slim-Jewel held my forearm to steady herself. Reacting to her fear, with no aforethought, I wrapped her with my other arm. It was the most delightful sensation I had ever experienced. I wished those minutes would last for ever. But that was not to be. We were soon discharged on the other shore. These moments, however, became only a pleasant memory.

I longed to touch her again. To do so under any excuse would have been a breach of social etiqutte. The nearest to a repetition of intimacy was when I had to steer my aunt and slim-Jewel out of the milling crowd of spectators after the second night of viewing the pageant. With train travel becoming more and more popular, the pageant attracted spectators from all corners of the Island. On this occasion I was too protective to savour the pleasure of having her so close to me.

Three of us returned to our village. In the coach, our eyes met several times.

There was a lot that I would have liked to tell her. I could have written a poem of many quatrains on what passed through my mind. Despite Aunt Flower's incessant encouragement, we reached our respective homes with nothing said, yet everything fully grasped and understood.

It was innocent love between two teenagers drawn together by nature's most charming design but nevertheless separated by centuries of tradition.

If the arousal of our desire for each other was the ultimate result of Slim-Jewel's trip to Kandy, what it meant for Aunt Flower was far more momentous. Whether the apothecary had planned it in advance was never too clear. But Aunt Flower met in the host's house a delightful young man who took an instant fancy to her. Before she left Kandy, her mind was set. Within the month she returned to Kandy to work in the new General Hospital, located a mile or so from the coach stand and the market.

Grandparents were naturally upset. With both daughters out of the house and the youngest son still untraced, the old couple was doomed to a lonely life with no one to help them with day-to-day chores which gradually became more and more difficult and cumbersome. Sooner or later, they would have to leave their favourite surroundings in Bo-tree Plain and reside in the house of the eldest son, my father.

I could understand grandparents' feeling of desolation and despondency. But the most cutting remarks on Aunt Flower's decision came from my own otherwise-reticent father.

"Where can we hide our faces? Why does she apply soot on our faces?" he muttered. Mother's efforts to becalm father proved to be of no avail.

To me the matter was very simple. Aunt Flower was an adult. She earned her own living. She had been a good daughter, a good sister and to me and my brothers and cousins a good aunt. She moved in a different circle of friends. Like Little Father and me, she had been exposed to a new culture and system of values. She has already passed the acceptable age of marriage and none in the village would propose to her both on account of her age and her refined life style. One of her friends had introduced to her a young man whose interests and tastes were compatible. They met in Kandy. They liked what they saw in each other. They planned a future according to their needs and aspirations.

Going to Kandy was logical. White Padre used his influence and obtained for her a job in the General Hospital. The couple had announced their intention to have a civil marriage conducted at the Governments Agent's Office. Why did my father berate her as though she streaked naked through the Sabbath crowd at the temple? I felt I was big and responsible enough to ask him. I did so softly and politely. Father's response was equally so.

"Three things, my son. The man she wants to marry is from the low country. He's a Christian. He belongs to a wrong caste - a low caste."

Enlightened, indoctrinated or brainwashed (the choice is left to my reader) by the Blakes, Reverend Saunders and my teachers in both schools, I could see nothing wrong with any of the three factors that my father listed. If my face showed scepticism, father was non-plussed.

"Are you also rejecting me as an ignoramus of the Coffee Era?"

83

We were in 1875 - sixty years from the fall of the Kingdom of Kandy, the annexation of this region to the mighty British Empire or the reunification of Sri Lanka under one administration. Whichever was one's choice of expression to describe the overarching event of 1815, the people of the hill-country have seen a sea change in everything around them.

One of the most significant was that in the economy. The British, through the infamous Waste Lands Policy, managed to get control over the uncultivated land or fallow fields which chiefs and temples owned under the ancient land tenure system. This land was sold away for a pittance to planters who would grow coffee - a booming cash crop with an expanding market in Europe. From the Governor and Government Agents of Provinces to other officials and immigrant entrepreneurs, the growing ranks of the European population took to coffee cultivation which was lucrative. Coffee reached its zenith by 1847.

Within a decade, disaster hit the crop. A blister blight of unknown origin wiped out the coffee estates. Cinchona was tried as an alternative. This pharmaceutically important crop had a limited market although Malaria was rampant and quinine was the most efficacious deterrent. Around 1867, tea was introduced. It had already proved to be an attractive alternative. The time when coffee was of paramount importance was long past. It was ancient history, as most people felt. Hence the derogatory expression for anything out-of-date and archaic as belonging to the Coffee Era.

When father asked me whether I considered him to be an ignoramus of the Coffee Era, he was most certainly expecting me to say no. It would have boosted his ego. I did not, however, reply him immediately. I tried to weigh the three disqualifications and ascertain whether any of them had any relevance and which of them was the most obnoxious from father's point of view. Perhaps, he listed them according to the weightage that he assigned to them.

We in the hill country had been long secluded. The only outsiders we had encountered were invaders. The Portuguese, the Dutch and the British came with their soldiers and mercenaries from their other colonies and from the maritime region of the Island itself. Invasions had been successfully repelled, each bolstering our image as the true custodian of national culture. Hardly any foreigners, with the notable exceptions of the human menagerie of King Royal-Lion the Second and Muslim traders with concentrations in a few places, settled down in the Kingdom. Since the British came and the country was reunified, it had been different.

White officials, missionaries and planters from the British Isles, police and security personnel from Malaya, coffee and later tea estate workers from South India and others of diverse nationalities and occupations like Muslim money lenders from Afghanistan, goldsmiths and financiers from Cochin and the Malabar Coast of South India and petty traders and entrepreneurs of diverse origins poured into the region. The villagers had no complaint as long as they were left alone to cultivate their rice fields and vegetable plots and preserve their age-old traditions and way of life.

One group of outsiders was, however, an open threat. They were the low country Sinhalas. Settled in the maritime regions, they mingled with foreigners easily. They were there to to receive the Greeks and the Romans who traded in Sri Lanka with merchants from East Asia.The Arab sailors dealt with them and Arab traders settled down in their midst. The low-country Sinhalas came under the direct cultural and spiritual influence of the Portuguese and the Dutch over a period of three centuries. Among them, the Roman Catholic Church made steady progress until it was checked by the Dutch Reformed Church. The language too underwent significant change. They used thousands of borrowed words from Portuguese and Dutch. These and many of their idioms were hardly intelligible to us. Even the British were there two decades longer than in the hill country.

These sophisticated low-country Sinhalas grabbed every opportunity for self-improvement. As coffee became plentiful, they undertook its transportation. Their caravans of several hundred carts criss-crossed the Kandyan region. They came as builders with newfangled architectural and structural designs. They established bakeries and popularized bread, cakes and pastries in a land which never knew them before. They came as teachers first in the missionary schools and later in the few schools which the government established. The padres had them as helpers in churches and medical facilities. To look the same, to speak more or less the same language and profess the same religion and yet be so clever, cunning and opportunistic made the low-country Sinhalas the subject of envy, fear, jealousy and, in some extreme cases, xenophobia.

The Kandyans did whatever they could to dissuade the low-country Sinhalas from intruding into their territory. Those measures hardly met with success. So the local humourists narrate how the makers of molasses added extra poundage to packets of molasses so as to "take the hell out of the low-country transporters"!

If father was xenophobic, he was not in a minority. I could guess his objection to Christianity. A shadow which hung over our family over the last six years had been the disappearance of Little Father, its smartest and most promising member. It was suspected that he was a victim of some Christian ploy. Inwardly, they blamed the Blakes even though they were grateful for whatever the missionaries were doing to give me a good education.

Our conversation took place while father was repairing the ploughshares. I was holding a plough firm as he nailed down loose metal facers. When one plough was done and he was reaching for the other, I asked,

"Father, why do you say that Uncle Victor is of a low caste? I think he is doing a good job in a government office. He speaks English fluently and wears European dress - long trousers, tie, coat and all. He looks a very decent man."

"That's the problem. Here, we know a person from what he does and what his parents and their parents did. With all the masks and disguises which foreigners had brought in, we can't do the same with these low-country intruders who do not even respect the religion into which they were born."

He was becoming more and more vituperative. I thought it wise to let him continue his tirade. Again, to my mind, nothing he said of caste as a firm, fixed and indelible stamp on a person made any sense. It was not only the Christian influence to which I had been subjected over the last six years. What I had learnt in the temple, too, militated against classifying human beings by birth.

Twice I was tempted to interrupt father and remind him of what the Buddha had said on the subject of caste: "One becomes a Brahman - that is, an high caste priest - or an outcaste not by birth but by action and action alone."

XI

I had to be silent as I was privy to another family secret. I had confided my feelings for Slim-Jewel to my third brother who walked with me a few days back to Bo-tree Plain. We were an incongruous pair. He in his brown and black striped sarong and worn-out and discoloured chemise and I in spotless blue drill shorts, white shirt, stockings and shoes. He compensated for his poor clothing with his tall, erect, and handsome figure and muscular limbs. Six years my senior in age, he was a successful sharecropper and was planning to acquire his own land.

"You little puppy, what girls for you?" he teased me. I expected him to go the whole hog and remind me of the family expectations. Instead, he became very serious.

"Tiny One, I have a different kind of problem and I don't know what to do or whom to turn to."

"The last is an easy question, brother. Mother is always the most understanding, whatever the problem be," I suggested.

"I have thought of it myself. I wonder whether Bo-tree Plain grandmother is not a better starting point."

I was getting curiouser and curiouser. His was a story with a charming historical parallel. On the other side of the river was a little village inhabited by handsome men and exquisitely pretty women. Of unknown origin, their traditional occupations ranged from butchery to scavenging. These occupations being ranked unclean and menial, they were a depressed community. They lived apart from the rest of the people and came to the village only on a very rare occasion when a rotten carcass or the corpse of a drowned person had to be handled. They were outcastes.

Their women went about without covering their upper bodies. This exhibition on the part of women who were exceptionally beautiful had tickled many a young man. Watching them across the river was a known pastime. Of course, my third brother had gone beyond feasting his eyes. He had actually met a girl and fallen in love. He pined for her and was anxious to marry her. At twenty-three, the world was crashing for him. Or, that was how we felt.

To say that the remaining fortnight of that August vacation was exciting and eventful would be an under-statement. I found more opportunities to see Slim-Jewel, even though her elder sister, my eldest brother's wife, was always present and did most of the talking. On my third visit, she had put whatever clues she had gathered by observing us and come to the conclusion that two young hearts were on fire! At least, that is what she said half in fun but definitely with ample wishful thinking.

"The Kandy Pageant had done something to both of you," she said. "Now don't say that I have no eyes."

Both Slim-Jewel and I blushed. The tell-tale redness of our clear fair complexion was unmistakable. It was funny in a way. I could summon the courage to visit her consecutively for three days. Yet I felt shy and missed the fourth day. The next day, my eldest brother took me home for dinner.

In the meantime, my third brother contrived an opportunity for me to meet his girl. She was a real beauty. Her statuesque body swayed gracefully as she trod lightly on the ridge of a rice field. Her mirthful laughter accentuated her chirpy voice as she related how she duped her mother and crossed the river to see us.

"She looks a divine damsel," I whispered to my brother's ears.

"You think I have any hope?" my brother asked after she made a hasty retreat back to her village. Despair and despondence sounded loud and clear.

"Don't give up, Elder brother. Our national hero, Gamini the Disobedient, had an only son. He was named Saliya. He, too, fell in love with a pretty girl from the same depressed caste. His love for her was so great and sincere that he gave up his right to the throne to make her his wife." I narrated in detail the story of Saliya and Asokamala, the most celebrated romance of our history.

"I have no throne or crown to renounce. But the feelings of my parents are very precious to me."

"Wouldn't that be the real test of love, elder brother?"

Our decision to consult the paternal grandmother was timely. It happened the day after father had visited her at Bo-tree Plain to seek her advice on the same matter. He had learned of it from a rumour that was floating in the marketplace.

"You know what I told your father?" she asked even before my third brother could tell her about his clandestine romance. Her pause was for effect. But it did make both of us very anxious.

"I said that Great Brahma engraves on everyone's forehead at birth the name of the spouse. There's nothing we could do to change that fate." Her reference to the Hindu creator-god was half in fun.

"Is that why you don't object to Aunt Flower's idea of marrying Uncle Victor?" I asked.

"In a way, yes," she said with what sounded like a suppressed chuckle. " Will anyone's objection make any difference? You think your grandfather or father is going to change her mind? When a woman decides, that's it. Never make a mistake."

"What are we doing here, elder brother?" I said half in fun. "If the girls make up their minds, that would be it."

"Exactly," agreed grandmother but in all seriousness.

That was her way of telling her adolescent grandsons that waiting was a virtue. We were both a bit abashed by the fact that we divulged our secrets to her. But we thought that they were safe with her. There was no reason to think otherwise.

Now that we were in Bo-tree Plain, I had to pay my regular courtesy call on the Blakes and the temple. I did it at least once a week during each vacation. Brother pointed to his less than presentable clothes and excused himself. Later he joined grandfather at his flourishing garden by the stream. His experiment in growing "English" vegetables had proved to be successful. Later in the day, we had each a heavy load of beets, carrots, leeks and cabbages to carry home. He carried a bag three times heavier and walked up the hilly trails twice faster than I. All my long distance track training and Rugby football was no match for native brawn.

I walked more slowly as I was dejected. The Blakes looked worse off than ever before. Mrs. Blake was always slim and now she looked skinny and very ill. Her pale face was baggy and ashen. Her drooping eyelids gave her a ghostly appearance. He hair was dishevelled. She seemed to have forced herself out of bed just to see me. She held on to a shelf by the door to steady herself and the prolonged cough sounded eerie. What a sprightly woman she had been! White Padre was visibly worried.

"Are you both all right?" I asked them.

"We wish we could say yes," replied White Padre, but proceeded no further.

Were both of them ill? Who was there to look after them? I wondered. I wished I could do something for them. They had done so much for me.

Grandmother's pronouncements on our romantic adventures were all forgotten by the time we reached home. Brother ran to the the river to get a glimpse of the apple of his eye. I made myself an uninvited -- nevertheless warmly received -- guest at dinner at Slim-Jewel's.

Neither my brother nor I had much to tell the other when we met at bed-time. Brother was thrilled that she waved to him across the river. In my case I was puzzled. Every time Slim-Jewel asked whether I needed any more rice, curry or water, she would address me emphatically as "elder brother".

"What do you think it means?" I asked my brother.

"Nothing. Nothing at all."

I did not understand his cryptic answer until he reminded me that mother often called father as "elder brother". It was just the old habit, he told me further.

From childhood, we call our elders by the same names that we call their age-cohorts in the family.

So, I still have hope, I told myself as I lay on my camp-bed with the fervent wish that all all my dreams be of Slim-Jewel.

Back at school for the concluding term of the year, I was conscious of the final examinations and numerous competitions for open prizes. I settled down to serious work. With effort, I converted recurring thoughts on Slim-Jewel to a source of inspiration rather than distraction. Thrice I wrote letters pouring out my heart, but never posted them. Will Slim-Jewel write? To come to think of it there was no understanding between us. I knew the intensity of my thoughts and feelings but had not told her. I did not know whether she had any special feelings for me. All I could say honestly was that we enjoyed the few moments we were together though never too far away from watchful eyes. We had made no commitment to each other.

On two week-ends, I went to visit Aunt Flower. She was fast becoming accustomed to town life. Uncle Victor was a kind man with a fine sense of humour. On both occasions, he took me to new eating places, generally referred to as 'hotels' even though they were nothing more than tea-rooms or restaurants. He spoiled me with cakes and Indian sweets - so different, colourful and delicious when compared with those we made as sweetmeats in the village.

"Don't go home when holidays are given." he told me. "We want to register our marriage and have a little party for our friends."

"Will you ask my parents and brothers to come?"

He really was a decent chap. He had already written to most of our relatives. He had asked father to fix the date.

"Father might want your horoscope."

I was not sure how he, as a new convert to Christianity, would react to our traditions.

"You wouldn't believe it, son. My parents had my horoscope. I have sent it to your father already."

For some unknown reason, I felt very happy for Aunt Flower. Maybe, I saw in Uncle Victor's words and deeds the true reflection of love.

This conversation was taking place in the outer verandah of the house in which Aunt Flower was a boarder or paying guest. From inside emerged a girl in a cream and beige outfit, better fitting than the dresses I had seen on wives of missionaries. She wore a tiny bonnet with a spray of roses. It took some time to realize that this lovely person was none other than Aunt Flower. I expressed my amazement and admiration.

"Tiny One, you have a chat with Uncle Victor and go back to school. I have night classes. I study English."

Uncle Victor filled in.

"You know, son. That's the only thing I asked of your aunt. Go to school, learn some English and take the examination as a trainee nurse. She has the knowledge and the experience. All she needs is English."

I thought of many persons in the village whose lives could change dramatically if they took advantage of an English education - my brothers, Slim-Jewel, some of the brighter novices in the temple, for example. But the traditions weigh too heavy.

In the village, Little Father was a misfit. His open-minded curiosity, his thirst for new knowledge and experience and readiness to try new things were not virtues. I was not without problems myself, even though two of the most important monks in the area backed me. They had unwavering confidence that I would not be lost to the village. Aunt Flower was the subject of malicious gossip.

I asked myself, "When will the Kandyan peasant recognize that life must change and that the old order must yield to the new."

"English very very difficult" she said in English with a childlike chuckle, waved to us gracefully and walked into the street.

91

This year I had more visitors at the school prize-giving. Reverend Saunders found a few extra tickets from boys whose families lived too far from Kandy. Uncle Victor was a great help. I had wanted my parents and as many of my brothers as possible to see me walking many times to the dais to receive a multitude of prizes. As usual, I had won all the class prizes and many open prizes. The most coveted was a new Scripture Prize of a hundred rupees.

I nearly lost the prize for English Literature. A boy from an English speaking home of Dutch origin - called Burghers in Sri Lanka - scored the same marks as I did. A toss of a coin decided it in my favour. But I insisted that the prize should be equally divided between us. The boy was very happy and the teacher praised me in class for what he called an admirable gesture.

To have my family to share my joy had always been my wish. But parents felt that they did not fit into the environment of a modern school.

"We don't like to apply soot on your face" was my mother's explanation.

Uncle Victor whose parents were also from a similar socioeconomic background understood the reason for their reluctance. This time, he took the initiative to buy them appropriate clothes. Mother looked gorgeous in the outfit he had chosen for her - nothing newfangled but only a more sophisticated version of what she wore in the village. Father, of course, had more problems. He rejected outright the suggestion that he cut his long hair. Brothers took haircuts and looked fine. At the end, we did not press father. Yet, he carried himself well in a Tweed coat and cloth, tie and shirt, socks and shoes - the emerging dress of the non-English speaking gentry. The prize-giving passed off well.

Uncle victor and Aunt Flower hosted a dinner at one of the 'hotels'. The food was delicious. It was a happy family occasion.

Uncle Victor had taken a few days' leave from office to give my parents and three brothers a grand tour of Kandy. He had taken them first to the Temple of the Sacred Tooth Relic, where my parents were impressed with his knowledge of the ritual. On the way down from the sanctum sanctorum, in the Drum Hall in front of the steps leading to the Octagon, father raised the delicate issue of Aunt Flower's religion.

"Now that you two have decided everything and none of us have any voice in the matter. Will you want my sister to change her religion?"

"That's her business. We have talked about it. I told her plainly that I would rather see her as a good practising Buddhist than a person without a religion."

"Aney sadhu!" said mother, using a Sinhala Buddhist expression of unreserved appreciation.

The visit was so successful that I expected not only my parents but also grandparents to be present at their wedding which was to be in two weeks. They made no promise. Before leaving Kandy, father blessed his sister and something gave me the impression of some finality in their relationship.

"You are on your own, dear sister," he seemed to imply.

I blamed myself for not having been a bit more perspicacious. I should have got grandmother for the prize-giving. She was the "man" in the family.

The wedding took place with me as the only representative of Aunt Flower's family. It did not look too bad as Uncle Victor's family could not make it either. The reception was well attended and ended with dancing to Portuguese music.

The music and the dance was called *Baila*. This lively music along with silly, funny and naughty songs, mostly adlibbed to include topical themes of humour as well as personal references, had just made its way to Kandy from the coast where it had been popular for over three centuries. One pranced, gyrated or fancifully moved hands and feet and made bodily contortions as the beat of the music prompted. It was a lot of fun.

The lavish flow of foreign and local liquor had something to do to the liveliness of the evening. The bride and the bridegroom did not dance. Nor did I. Aunt Flower in her white gown and veil, holding in her gloved hands a fancy bouquet of tube roses, was dazzling. She looked more English than the wives of the young British civil servants who were among the invitees!

It was just sixty years from the day the independent Kingdom of Kandy ceased to exist. Already, we were in the throes of a new culture with its own values and norms and forms of artistic expression.

Reverend Saunders drew my attention to it as he shook my hand and bid good night.

"See this crowd, T. B. Forget about the complexion and the hair. This could be a scene from any one of the colonies and dominions of the mighty British Empire over which the sun never sets. The dresses, the food, the band and music, the atmosphere and, of course, the language. I am pleased to see the Union Jack dominating the hall but a bit of your tender coconut leaf decorations would have done wonders."

Whom was he complimenting for this? I asked myself: Us for our malleability or himself and the like who were the bearers of this new culture? Or, and that was more likely from the last comment, was he being critical of our slavish mentality to ape the West?

Right through the ceremony and the reception, my thoughts went back frequently to Little Father. I thought that he would have known how to bridge the gap between the culture of the past and the new influences. How he and he alone of those I knew had a fantastic capacity to weave them together into a seamless web? He could have made Uncle Victor and Aunt Flower proud of each one's culture and guided them to derive wisdom and pleasure from their separate heritages.

Six years had passed from his departure from the village and subsequent disappearance. The optimism of the family that he would appear in another year or so had lasted with frequent reinforcement from all kinds of astrological and occult predictions.

XII

After the excitement of the prize-giving and the wedding, I was looking forward to returning to Sangha-Gem-Field. My thoughts were often on Slim-Jewel. Will she be wanting to see me as eagerly as I do? A doubt occurred from time to time. I brushed it off attributing it to my anxiety.

Another recent innovation in the transport system of Kandy was the rickshaw - a two-wheeled sedan chair drawn by a man. I got into one of them with my bag and bundle of books at my feet and went to the coach stand to make an early start.

When I came to Kandy six years ago to get my first haircut and to buy shorts and shirts, I travelled uncomfortably crouched in a covered bullock cart with a vaulted cadjan roof. It took eight hours on the rutty, bumpy dirt road. Several times on the way, the cart would get stuck in muddy stretches and the passengers helped the bulls to extricate the cart from the mire. Now, a horse-drawn coach on a macadamized or asphalt-treated road would take four hours. That really was progress.

Equally fascinating was the postal service. For a few cents to buy a stamp, it was now possible to be in contact with my family. I carried a notebook of addresses of teachers, classmates and friends with whom I planned to be in touch. How very quickly and easily we progressed from palmleaf to paper, from stylus to pen and pencil.

If I had not been from a remote village and had not been in it at regular intervals, I would never have appreciated the magnitude and the speed of the change.

My thoughts were interrupted by the sing-song recitation of a poem by an old man. He was selling for a few cents a long sheet of paper in which was printed his poem. He was author, publisher, advertizer and seller. He advertized his ware by reciting a few verses here and there in a craggy but yet melodious voice. The poem attracted my attention. It was on the public debate between the Christian and the Buddhist clergy which had taken place in 1873 in a coastal town called Panadura.

Although the event was two years old, the news was being diffused by this successor to the traditional balladeer only now. He read some funny verses:

> "Of this earth of ours we know a lot
> It's being scanned and mapped and studied in depth,
> But nowhere have we seen, Oh Sirs!
> The peak your books call Mount Meru."

Thus said the padre in a jeering tone
And all his followers chuckled and laughed.

Undaunted stood our courageous hero
As a lion on the head of a vanquished elephant.
Clearing his throat the Son of Bonito Plain,
Immortalizing his home in Secretary's Garden,
The Venerable Gunananda, a monk renowned, roared,
"I'll tell you, sir, where to find Mount Meru.
Take out your maps and ready your pencils.

Go ye, sir, to the Garden of Eden
Straight up to the Tree of Wisdom.
Eating its fruit your Adam and Eve became wise
They were all this while stark naked!
To the north of it is the branch with the apple
Which the Serpent did use to tempt dear Eve.
Climb ye, sir, to the top of this branch.
Look north, sir, and you'll see no doubt
The sun-clad peak of the Meru Mount."

Fathers, mothers, sisters, brothers, uncles, aunties,
All of you,
What a pity that you were here.
For You'd have heard
The laughter that shook
The earth all the way
To where the sea and the sky did meet
In yonder town of Panadura.

What a gift for my grandparents and parents! For six cents I bought two. The news-vending balladeer picked a few verses from the bottom of the sheet. He drawled in his craggy melodious voice. Someone in the crowd volunteered to sell the poem while the singing went on:

The Venerable Gunananda in a dazzling yellow robe
Stood with his right hand raised
Stabbing the air with his finger

"Tell me, sir, the proof you have
That I and all here are created by your God.
Whence your knowledge? Whence your revelation?

Night after night I read your Bible
But it leaves me still in the dark.
It says what you say,
'God in his infinite wisdom made man
In his own image and likeness.
Adam was made from the dust of the earth
And God's own breath.'

What was his purpose? Vain and simple pleasure?
Why else was Eve an afterthought?
And why from the rib of a man?
Didn't women deserve better?"

Laughter, my friends, the laughter.
The first of many a round.

"Or that's how he decreed for all time to come
A role secondary for women?"

Laughter, the Nemesis the padres dreaded!

"Say, good sir, God was wise and had other reason
To create for Adam a lovely companion.
What for? Sir? What for? Simply to look at?

Laughter, good friends, peels and peels of laughter.

The roaring monk was on to the next point:
"A wise and craftier Serpent it was
Who found the secret locked in a luscious apple
In the Tree of Knowledge.
It was Eve at first who learnt the Truth.
Here I agree, sir, for the Books of the Buddha say
'In many a matter, women are better'"

Laughter again, but only a flutter.

"What do they learn - dear Adam and Eve?
Nothing but the truth even an idiot knows
That man and woman are blessed to have children.
Here, my friends, your Bible keeps me wondering.
If Adam and Eve were made for this purpose

97

Why was it kept a secret?
To be taught by a jumping Serpent?
And, good sir! Why? Why punish them for ever?
The Serpent to crawl? Adam to plough?
And Eve to shriek at child-birth?"

Was it thunder heralding the monsoon?
No, dear friends, the applause of thousands!

The Venerable Gunananda steps forward on the dais
"Pray, tell me, good sir, tell me if I'm wrong.
In God's new farm to breed mankind,
Why did everything go wrong?
Adam and Eve, degraded, banished and punished
And yet very forgiving,
Continue their mission doomed from the start.
They breed two boys - A tragedy? A catastrophe?
Cain kills Abel and breeding must stop
A fact that every cowherd knows in the village."

Laughter, again. Uneasy whispers hum in the air
"How can we answer?" ask padres in despair.

The Venerable Gunananda runs post haste to victory.
"Silence, my friends. I have come to the end.
With just a simple question - one with many parts.
"Father, mother and son - The End of the Dynasty!!!
Did Cain dupe Eve like the daughters of Lot?
From whom had God to save ignoble Cain?
Whose rib made a woman for Cain?
No, my friends, you have no answers.
Your Book sure does, for it's quite fair.
It tells the truth that people were always there
Of many a tribe with normal lives,
Producing biologically this lovely race -
The human race which the Buddhas praise
Is rare beyond price.
With merit are you born in it.

A simple gesture with his up-raised hand.
The crowd burst forth "Sadhu! Sadhu!! Sadhu!!!

I had read the Bible and asked more or less the same questions, of course, with no frills from Reverend Blake in the Scripture class. I had accepted his explanation that ancient religious lore had to be read not as history or scientific documentation but in a spirit of grasping the spiritual fervour of the people who invented them. Yet, I thought it was clever for a monk to work on a simple Biblical story to win so many debating points. It flashed that Chief Monk and the Abbot of the Bo-tree Plain temple would like to read the poem. I bought two more copies and rolled all four. Then I bought a fifth to read on the way.

A fellow passenger in the coach was the son of R. M., the 'Country Gentleman', serving the British administration but retaining the traditional title. Claiming to be blood relatives of the erstwhile royalty of the Kingdom of Kandy, he was ranked an aristocrat, a clan apart, proud of their privileges and sometimes quite arrogant. He got the best seat and his servant sat in front of him.

As the coachman knew Chief Monk, he invited me to sit beside him. That was great. I had a guided tour along the Great Sand River by a man who knew much of the local folklore.

My plans to read the news sheet on the Great Controversy of Panadura of 1873 was duly aborted.

Once in Sangha-Gem-Field, things were different. My thoughts revolved on matters closer to me. Whether I returned to school in January 1876 depended on a decision to be made on extending my scholarship for higher education in Calcutta, India. There were no comparable facilities anywhere in Sri Lanka. As far as Reverend Saunders and many of my teachers were concerned, I was the obvious choice. The last meeting I had with the Principal, however, sounded more or less like a final farewell. Obviously the decision was being made elsewhere. As a Buddhist I was conditioned to expect the unexpected: "What is thought will not take place. What is not thought will take place" was a quote from the Buddha we had heard quite often. Fatalistic? No. Realistic? Yes.

Yet, I could not help visualizing different scenarios for my future. To Calcutta and to an unknown future in an ever-expanding horizon appeared adventurous and exciting. The more delectable was the possible alternative: becoming a teacher in the Church School, marrying Slim-Jewel, building a house by the road at a dreamy spot I had already identified and leading a quiet rural life.

I dreamt of the serenity of such a life: the house overlooking the winding road, the valley below, the receding ranges of mountains in the

99

distance and the graceful skyline in the form of a beautiful damsel reclining on her back!!!

A house full of noisy kids, each handsomer and prettier than the other, rushing out to greet the father, a veritable gentleman in a gleaming white suit !!!

Slim-Jewel watching over her brood like a protective hen !!!

Slim-Jewel who would have rushed out to greet her husband with a warm kiss if only all her years of indoctrination as a rural Sinhala girl had not made her so modest !!!

A familiar voice broke my reverie. It was my third brother who had seen me perched by the driver's seat as the coach approached the stand. He was beaming. Our reunion after three months, specially after the short vacation when we went on an emotional roller coaster together, would have been adequate reason for his happiness. Or could it be that his romance has prospered? In any case, I made a mental note to ask him what made him so contented.

Within minutes, I found my belongings. Gathering things together, we walked home. I carried the suitcase and brother the bulky bundle of books.

"You look quite contented, elder brother. I would say, even happy. That can't be just because I came home?"

"Your coming home is enough reason, Tiny One," he replied. "But how observant you are?"

"Anything happened about your affair?"

"A lot."

Once again, he was unusually reticent. There was something he was not ready to share with me. Every time I fell back to be abreast of him, he slid back a few steps. When this was deliberately repeated several times, I was about to burst out in frustration. This I was not able to do for I saw father stepping out of the tiny coffee kiosk overlooking the coach stand.

The coffee kiosk was a new institution in the village. Over the last few years it had become a club or meeting place for the villagers. That was where adults shared their gossip and commented on what went on around them.

I stopped for father to come down, greeted him according to tradition by falling on my knees and stepped aside for him to go ahead of me.

Someone shouted from the coffee kiosk.

"Elder brother, please tell that to Tiny One yourself."

100

My heartbeat quickened and I blushed. It was Slim-Jewel's father who wanted my father to tell me something personally.

"Yes, cousin. I will do that. Don't you worry," was father's reply.

Much had changed in my home over the last six years. Now we had a big enough table for half the family to have its meals the way I had learnt in the Church School. It was one of the many innovations I had introduced as a direct result to the new values which the missionaries had inculcated in me. The lunch for me was served at the table and father and mother joined me. I went into a room to change into a sarong and a banyan - another newfangled apparel which proved to be more convenient than the Portuguese chemise. In the meantime, the third brother had his lunch in the kitchen and left home in a hurry. I thought that he had his usual rendezvous on the river bank.

The conversation centred on what happened in school, the excitement of their experience at the prize-giving ceremony and how much they had missed me. Father whose economy for words was at times irritating was unusually vivacious. They were happy for me. They were happy that they could share a part of my colourful life as a celebrated pupil of a prestigious school in the city.

"Will the school send you to to the Rose-apple Continent?"

That was how they knew the land of the Buddha from books and sermons. The term meant specifically Northern India and distinguished it from the southern region from which more and more indentured labourers were being imported by the planters for work in the burgeoning tea plantations.

"I really don't know, father. Teachers and even Reverend Saunders sounded hopeful. The Principal spoke of uncertainties and advised me to take failures as pillars of success. My feeling is that the powers that be had decided against me and some others are appealing for reconsideration."

"Don't worry about whatever happens," intervened mother. "Everything happens for the best."

Having disposed of that subject, father cleared his throat, coughed a few times and looked at mother for support or approval.

"Tiny One, we had your horoscope read. It was really your eldest brother's father-in-law who first suggested it. He said that you are an up and coming young man and many families in the region will be interested in your future."

My heart pounded heavily and I wondered whether it was audible to my parents. Was grandmother the genius? Did they compare my horoscope with that of Slim-Jewel? If so, what had the stars pre-ordained for us?

"A couple of weeks ago, it was returned to us. Son, you are not destined to live the life of a householder. We knew it all the time. The four major houses of your horoscope are empty. There are no planets in any. In your case, it is very good. Very good only if you take to a religious life. You'll be a famous monk. Your family, your village and even the whole country will be proud of you."

Father reached out to a comb of bananas, took one, peeled it and ate it slowly.

I could not believe my ears. Is this the truth? Or has the horoscope become a convenient way of avoiding social embarrassment, family rifts or misunderstanding with an important neighbour? If Slim-Jewel's family did not like me for for whatever reason - and I could think of many - they could have simply said that my horoscope did not agree with hers. It had to be taken on face value. There could be no quarrel as the stars had pre-ordained it. Of course, my case was differently presented. No reference has been made to a possible marriage proposal. Yet, it was a decision without appeal. I cursed my fate. My birth coincided with the death of neighbours and years of economic struggle for the family. Lest my feelings be noticed, I wanted to excuse myself from the table and, if really possible, disappear into thin air.

"That's not all, son," started mother. "If you marry anyone even with a very strong horoscope, you are destined to be widowed very soon."

So that was it. Slim-Jewel's family had been really concerned. Who would ever want a daughter of theirs to die prematurely on account of an ill-fated marriage? Will I risk it? With all my incredulity nurtured by a modern Christian education, I did not have the courage even to suggest it. I treasured her as the sweetest person on whom my eyes had fallen. I would sacrifice anything if it was for her benefit. Yet, I was not prepared for what followed.

"But, Tiny One, Slim-Jewel's family is quite happy that she could be a part of our family any way."

"How come?" I asked impatiently. It had to be one of my five unmarried brothers. But which one? Not the third brother. He was far too entangled with the outcaste girl across the river.

Mother pushed the plate of bananas towards me and I took one reluctantly. She peeled one herself and began eating. I played with mine as if it was a dagger. Father watched me silently.

I could think of a hundred reasons why a brother of mine was preferred to me even if the horoscope played no part in the decision. My education had made me a misfit in the village. Any girl marrying me had to be ready to move to a city sooner or later. My dream of a house on the hill and a career in the Church School had many holes. Will White Padre have a free hand in offering me a job? Will my superior English education stand in the way of integration with its staff? Will I be required to change my religion?

All these things confirmed one thing. I have made myself a stranger in my own village. This in the eyes of Slim-Jewel's family could be my biggest disqualification. They would love to have their daughter nearer them even as the wife of a moderately successful farmer with good family connections.

"I wanted to tell you about his matter when we came to your school. But we found no occasion. The Middle One gave us a very anxious time. He had been enticed by an outcaste girl, you know, with their powerful black magic and charms. They almost succeeded in getting him to their settlement. If that happened, it would have been the end of all of us. We would have all lost our caste. You know how serious it is?"

I really did not know or care, but nodded my head.

"But the gods looked after us. Somebody had told in time the whole story to your grandmother at Bo-tree Plain and she told us exactly what to do."

Again, I could not fathom what was going on. It was my brother and I who confided in grandmother. We thought that she was the most reliable person to help us. What role had she played in the drama that was unfolding?

"Seven times seven days, I bathed in the river before dawn and went to the Rama Temple in my wet clothes," she continued. "I made every possible vow and pleaded with Lord Vishnu to save us. When nothing happened and I was getting frustrated, the Gentleman Priest of the Temple asked me to make a vow that I would cut and donate my long hair to be made into a broom to sweep the inner sanctorum."

I turned around to look at her hair. The lustreless dull hair of a wig she had used to tie her hair into a knot was a tell-tale sign that her vow was fulfilled.

"What happened, mother? You had to cut your hair?"

103

"It's nothing. I could have given Lord Vishnu my life if that was what he wanted."

Placating Hindu gods for worldly favours came naturally to our people. Here was the niece of Chief Monk of the Great Royal Monastery of Sangha-Gem-Field, the premier Buddhist temple of the region. She saw no contradiction between Buddhism which taught liberation through self-reliance and Hindu cults through which she sought solutions to her day-to-day problems. Her religious persuasions or the underlying discrepancies in her convictions and beliefs mattered little to her.

I was still curious about my third brother and his girl across the river for whom he was ready to offer his life just three months ago. Was it the reason that he was edgy from the moment I met him in the coach stand?

Mother took the unpeeled banana from my hands, peeled it and handed it back to me without a word. Suspense was killing me. After what looked hours, she continued,

"Tiny One, would you believe what happened? It was the third day after my vow. The village headman came in search of your third brother. The outcaste girl had disappeared. Her parents and relatives suspected that she had eloped with Middle One."

"Can't you tell all these stories later. Tiny One must be tired after his long journey," said father. But mother disregarded him and continued,

"As luck would have it, he was at home. He had not left home for three days even to go to the fields. He had a mysterious swelling on his leg and could hardly stand. Not only the headman but also some of the men across the river saw that your brother was too ill to have kidnapped their girl.

"To cut a long story short, the girl was found in another outcaste settlement nearer Kandy. She had eloped with a man she had met only a few days ago. Only Lord Vishnu could work such miracles."

"How did elder brother react?" I asked trying to sound as innocent and matter-of-fact as possible.

"He was probably quite upset and he ran a high temperature for several days. Even you grandmother in Bo-tree Plain came to see him. We don't know what she said or did. From that moment his temperature came down and he recovered rapidly. You know. She has all kinds of spells and charms. They work like magic."

"Today I thought that he looked quite happy but also very edgy. He wouldn't tell me why?" I said.

104

"He has reason to be happy", replied mother quite innocently. "It was about the time your horoscope was read. Not even a powerful horoscope like Slim-Jewel's would match with yours. You are not destined to marry and have a family. We compared hers with that of your brother. They matched perfectly."

I felt as though a red hot stylus pierced my heart. In our credulous society, an astrologer's word could change hearts, terminate relationships, sever loyalties and build new lives on the ashes of old ones. Yet, no one involved would feel the slightest of scruples, not a modicum of the guilt of betrayal. How easy it was to believe in a pre-ordained life in which one was just a pawn in the hand of destiny!

Slim-Jewel would have been told that a certain death awaited her if she were ever to marry me. She had no option but to accept it, even if it was the most painful thing to do. My brother would have thought that he was doing the correct thing in the emerging situation. Why let a lovely girl be married outside the family? I, too, was naturally expected to accept the ineluctability of fate.

If fatalism was an effective narcotic to numb my pain of mind and heart, why reject it and suffer unnecessarily? I had long ceased to hear what mother was saying. I stood up, washed and dried my hands and went to the room which I used during vacations.

XIII

I closed the door so as not to eavesdrop on the heated argument between my parents. They were engaged in a post mortem of their attempt to break the news to me.

"He would have come to know all this anyway. Why worry now?" was all I heard from father in a conciliatory tone.

I was glad that I heard this news from my parents. I felt a bit ashamed that I let my emotions be known. I have known disappointment. I could cope with the most blatant forms of emotional terrorism - something you learnt in an all-boys school. I had borne the grief of Little Father's disappearance. All this with what the British called "a stiff upper lip." But now I failed.

Was it because of Slim-Jewel? The girl I longed for was soon to be my elder brother's wife? Was it jealousy? Was it self-pity? Was it the feeling of sheer helplessness in the face of tradition and stupidity?

In our long isolated society, religion and magic, superstition and credulity built walls around individuals. No stone prison was so impregnable! All my education - all my smartness I thought I had gained from an exposure to the best education a boy of my age could have received only in the West - counted for nothing against the defence mechanisms of a simple Sinhala home. How all adults had contrived to refashion the fate of their young ones!

Rolling on bed, I thought of mother's tenacious belief in a Hindu god's ability to break her son's clandestine romance. What a severe penance she had undertaken! In the shivering wintry cold of misty mornings in the mountains, a moment's wetness was bad enough. To dip in the icy river waters every morning, to walk through windy rice fields for over half an hour and stay in wet clothes for hours for forty-nine days at a stretch! What faith! What determination!

What motivated her? The love for her child? The family honour? The fear of humiliation? The welfare of children yet to step into society? It could have been any or all of these. But how could she reconcile her beliefs and actions with the Buddhist faith? Faced with ultimate reality, she would affirm her faith that one had to succumb to one's fate resulting from one's good or bad actions in so many previous births. This she would call the ineluctable Law of Karma. She was unwavering in her belief in this law of action and reaction. But for forty-nine days she did penance to propitiate a non-Buddhsit deity to change her son's fate, her family's fate and, in consequence, a poor outcaste girl's fate! Mother was convinced that the girl's change of heart and her elopement with a man of her choice were doings of Vishnu, the benevolent Hindu god of sustenance. Were her parent's engaged in similar appeals to unknown powers?

What am I doing here? I asked myself - a product of as good a Western Christian education as only a baptized Christian boy could get? How was it that I was as irrational and credulous as any villager who had not seen the inside of a school? Was this what Little Father rebelled against? Was his disappointment with monks and lay Buddhists based on the heresies they nurtured?

Little Father admired the Buddha and his teachings. But he was appalled with what was in practice. He hoped to bring back to Buddhist life the tenets of rationalism of the Buddha's teachings. How he appeared an unwelcome critic to some Buddhists, including the Abbot of Bo-tree Plain temple! Did Little Father side too much with the Christians and become a victim of some fanatic somewhere? Or, did he get disappointed with the Christians he met elsewhere in the Island and lose his faith in both religions? Or, did he find the opportunity he sought for - the opportunity to revive Buddhism to its pristine glory? Did he fall a victim to someone's plot to dissuade him from such a role?

It was as usual. I could never spend a few quiet moments by myself without all these thoughts rushing into my head. Little Father and his disappearance! I slept with him in my thoughts. I woke up with him in my thoughts.

I woke up to find that I had slept at least four hours. The house was full. Brothers had all come to see me. The married ones had brought their families. Preparations were on for a big family dinner. With effort, I dispelled the dismal thoughts of the afternoon. I summoned enough magnanimity to congratulate the third brother on being betrothed to Slim-Jewel.

"I was only a second choice, you know." he said. I felt genuinely pleased. Was I, too, yielding to the belief in the inevitability of fate and the horoscope as its infallible decree?

It was a relatively cheerful evening. Happy as he appeared on the prospects of settling down in life, the third brother had not got over his feelings for the outcaste girl.

"I don't believe a thing about mother's vows and penances. It's all a plot. I think grandfather, father or eldest brother or all three of them used the headman to intimidate her family. You know, they are very innocent, harmless, timid people. So they had to do something."

"Did she tell you anything?"

"That's where fate comes in. For a week I could not get out of bed. There was such a painful swelling on my leg. I couldn't go to see her. I had no way to send her a message. She must have thought that I was a party to whatever the adults did. I feel betrayed. I also have betrayed her."

Brother was evidently suffering inside. If he was Slim-Jewel's second choice, she too was his second choice!

"So, you don't believe that she eloped with a man of her choice?"

"I'll never believe unless she tells me with her own lips." He choked and I realized how hard he tried to hide his emotions.

With such an unmistakable demonstration of sincerity, I was happy for both my brother and Slim-Jewel. They both needed solace. I was sure that each would provide it to the other.

Hardly had we finished our conversation that Slim-Jewel and her parents arrived. I had no idea that they too were invited. Perhaps, this evening's preparations were not exclusively to welcome me home! I greeted her parents in the traditional manner and she did likewise to me. She was as pretty as she was when I last met her. I was confused. But she broke the ice.

"Elder brother, how is Auntie Flower? Couldn't you persuade her to come with you this time?"

What did she mean. Was it a reminder of the wonderful time we had in Kandy coming to know each other. That was Aunt Flower's idea. I wondered whether she knew what happened during the last three months or more precisely last two weeks?

More visitors dropped in. Whether by design or otherwise, women disappeared into the kitchen and inner rooms. Men milled together in the central courtyard and the enclosing inner verandah. From time to time a male visitor would be surreptitiously led to the rear of the house, where a few pots of palm toddy had been hidden. To drink alcohol in public was a serious breach of etiquette. Yet, the guests did have enough of it. We, the younger ones, from whom this adult pastime was laboriously concealed, had fun in seeing adults emerging from the darkness still wiping the foam from their lips or moustaches. What hypocrisy! But that was our culture.

The evening passed pleasantly enough despite tensions and disappointments. Slim-Jewel served me a plate of rice and curries and handed it to me herself. She pressed my fingers as I held the plate. If that was done intentionally, it could have been her way of saying that the gnawing feeling of disappointment was mutual.

Her father spoke to me and assured me that I was their choice.

"But what can we do? We can't change what the stars have decreed or what we have brought from our previous lives."

Her mother, too, said something similar. Once again, I felt sad for both Slim-Jewel and my brother. I knew there was only one thing to do. My love for both them would demand that I distance myself from them and allow them to build a life out of the debris of their first and true loves.

I was up early morning. It had been a bad night. I lay awake for long hours in between spells of fitful sleep. I planned my future whenever I was awake. I got up with three options.

I drafted a letter to the Principal of the high school in Kandy. I wrote how important it was for me to proceed to Calcutta for higher education. I asked if the authorities concerned would give my candidature additional weightage if I agreed to be baptized a Christian and seek training for a Ministry abroad. I offered to serve in any country where the Mission had difficulties in sending qualified padres.

Then I worked on the draft of another letter to the same Principal. It was shorter and subtler. I said how much I benefited from my education for which I would always be grateful to the Mission. I thanked in particular the staff of the two schools and made a special reference to his kind guidance. I underscored how beneficial it was for me to have learnt in depth the Christian religion - a fact supported by my winning the coveted hundred-rupee prize for Scripture. With no reference whatsoever to the scholarship, I said that I was looking forward to receiving baptism in the very near future. I thought that the Principal would be more impressed with this letter. Of course, what I hoped for was that his hands would be strengthened to support my candidature. I needed so badly to go as far away as I could. Calcutta just fitted my specifications.

The third letter I prepared was addressed to the Vicar of Kandy through the Reverend Thomas Blake, alias White Padre. It was an application for a teaching post anywhere in his area of administration. In this, too, I added a sentence about looking forward to becoming a Christian in the near future.

I had to make a choice. In the absence of Little Father, I had no one to go to. After much thought, I decided to consult two persons in whose sincerity I had faith : One was Chief Monk, my mother's uncle, and the other was White Padre. I was confident that they would guide me if I told them my problem honestly. I chose to consult White Padre first.

My personal crisis had taken much of the joy of life. Yet, I dressed in the best suit to impress White Padre that I was worthy of the requests I was making. I wore long flannel trousers, a white shirt with a bow tie in school colours and the blue blazer coat with the Rugby colours stitched on the left breast pocket. I wore matching socks and a black pair of leather shoes. All these belonged to the city and had no place in the simple life of the village. But that did not bother me.

I trudged down to Bo-tree Plain with hardly a look at the breathtaking scenic beauty which normally held me bewitched. I passed several friends and acquaintances absent-mindedly. One of them scolded me roundly. I was at the church school around eight thirty in the morning.

I was surprised to see quite a crowd at the foot of the steps leading to White Padre's residence. I was further surprised to see a hastily refurbished palanquin at the door step and four able-bodied men to carry it. I went into the verandah of the house and found White Padre reading the Bible. Reclining on a couch nearby was Mrs. Blake. I stood at the door reverently. He concluded the reading with a soulful prayer for Mrs. Blake's recovery and return to the friends and family she knew in the village. Then he led her to the palanquin and saw to it that she was propped on pillows to be comfortable. The he turned round to me.

"T. B., Mrs. Blake is very ill. There's very little that can be done for her. She is to be admitted to the Sanatorium at Toddy Village. I too may have to join her there shortly. I am waiting until my successor is sent."

The mention of Toddy Village, not too far from Colombo, was adequate to know that both of them were suffering from acute tuberculosis. No effective cure was yet known for this dreaded disease. The disease itself was bad enough. But its social implications were grave and painful. It was a highly contagious disease. They would be shunned even by their closest friends.

A little procession accompanied the Blakes to the tarred road where a specially fitted cart awaited her. Made ingeniously comfortable for her to lie down, the cart was to take her to the Railway Station in Kandy. I touched her hand and wished her a speedy recovery. She could barely say "Thank you." The finality of the farewell struck me hard. What a kindly woman!

110

The stately, imposing, handsome and self-confident padre whom I had seen as a child riding through my village with his comely wife and under whose benign care I had grown was no longer recognizable. With intense pain - both physical and mental - suppressed with effort, he stood holding her hands, comforting her with prayer and assuring her that the All-mighty God who had been hitherto merciful would remain so to the very end. It was a tragic scene. The fall of a righteous, self-negating couple! The victory of all-conquering reality of impermanence and misery! Who are we but mere pawns of forces beyond our control!

The injustice of the situation hurt me. Here were two of the most decent people of selfless piety who had exiled themselves from their homeland to serve God. They chose their way of serving God. It was to travel to an unknown corner of a little Island-nation which they hardly knew. They gave the best years of their lives happily and generously to the poor and the destitute, the sick and the disadvantaged.

They sought no glory. Rewards for their sacrifices were few and far between: a smile from a mother whose child had recovered from an illness; a word of thanks from a school-leaving child; a minor gesture of homage from a fellow Christian. They looked up to God for courage and guidance. They accepted whatever came their way without question, without grumbling. That included the dreaded disease they had contracted from the very patients they had tried to comfort. Where was justice? Where was fair play?

I was emotionally too disturbed to continue my visit in Bo-tree Plain. I had a few words with the headmaster and the teachers who had come to see the Blakes off.

"It's all very sad," said the headmaster. "Reverend Blake is so weak that he may not last this strenuous trip. But he insists going. He wouldn't let me go with them. He wants me to keep the dispensary open right through the vacation."

"Who's there to help you?" I asked.

"Since your aunt left us, we have nobody. The apothecary comes as usual. He has to mix and dispense the medicine himself. He wants help badly."

"Can I help? Now that I am on vacation and I have no idea what happens next year, it may not be a bad idea."

The offer was spontaneous. I was surprised to hear my own words! Such a thing was not in any of the many scenarios I had worked on. For a moment I shuddered. Was I becoming suicidal? Was it a death wish?

Was I inviting a fate similar to that of the Blakes as an end to my misery?

"I'll have to ask the apothecary," he replied.

I was in no hurry. I walked slowly along the tarred road. All the time I was wondering how my fate cheated me. Here, I came to get advice on the three letters in my pocket. Already, one was obsolete. White Padre was in no position to help me fashion my future. Without his guide, I had no courage to send either of the other letters to the Principal of the high school. If I had the time to talk to White Padre, he would have told me as he had done once before that God never closed a door without opening another.

I was almost in Sangha-Gem-Field when the thought occurred to me that Chief Monk, my grand-uncle, was a patient listener and a wise counsellor. I recalled how he stood by Little Father and indirectly influenced me to be open-minded and pragmatic. I felt shy to tell him about the source of my grief and frustration. I felt even worse to divulge my plans to embrace Christianity simply as a means of distancing myself from the family. A dozen opening gambits were considered and rejected. Finally I decided to tell the truth with a slight bent which I thought was excusable.

It was not a proper time to go to a temple. Monks would be about to sit for their main meal which had to be taken before noon. Nor was the Western finery in which I was dressed the most appropriate. I was not considered an outsider. Hence I was not required to adhere to strict formalities. Chief Monk was seated under a shady tree with a palmleaf book on his lap and another on a rock beside him. I approached him, fell on my knees and saluted him with clasped hands.

"May you be happy," he said in Pali, the language of Buddhist Scriptures, and switching on to Sinhala continued, "How, my son, I heard you came yesterday. Did you hear what had happened to the Blakes?"

I told of him the shock and the grief I experienced in the morning when I went to see them just in time to wish her good-bye.

"That's Karma," he responded. It looked awkward to apply the Buddhist moral law of action and its reward or retribution and an individual's sole responsibility for one's destiny to a pair of Christians who would have derived a greater solace and comfort by attributing their misfortune to the will of God. Chief Monk continued,

"They are remarkable people. I don't see anyone like that among us in the Sangha. At least, not in the Kandyan region. We are too selfish, lazy and unconcerned. We speak a lot of loving kindness and compassion. But for the most part, this is confined to books and chantings. The padre and his wife are different. They slaved for the good of the people. We should take them as an example."

I was deeply touched by Chief Monk's appreciation of the missionaries whose express purpose in coming to our midst was to wean us away from the traditional religion. He judged them not for what they stood for but for what they did.

Once more I heard the story of the landslide on the night of my birth and how the Blakes were the first to rush to the village with provisions and blankets. He ended the account with a new piece of information.

"They were the first outsiders to hold you in their arms. They blessed you in their Christian way. And that was before anyone of us could bless you."

I took it as a convenient cue to say what I had in mind.

"I went to see them this morning on a very important matter," I said. "I am the best in my class in high school and the best boy is to be awarded a scholarship to proceed to Calcuttla for four or five years of higher education. I have a strong feeling that my religion could stand as an obstacle."

"Did anyone tell you that?"

"No. But the Principal prepared me for bad news."

"That could only mean that the final decision was in someone else's hands. Did he even hint that your embracing Christianity would help in the decision being favourable to you?"

"No. Never. No one had ever suggested that to me during my three years here and three years in Kandy."

"Did you know that White Padre had something to do about it?"

"I guessed, Venerable Sir."

"It is not a matter of guess. He told me himself. He got you the scholarship to Kandy strictly on that understanding."

I had always assessed White Padre to be an honest and magnanimous man of the highest calibre. My admiration for him soared.

I felt uneasy and fidgety. Chief Monk noticed it.

"Did you want to ask him to intervene on your behalf to get the scholarship to Calcutta?"

"Yes. In a way. Yes." I was hesitant to proceed.

113

"You went ready to tell him that you will agree to be baptized a Christian if that would help in getting the scholarship?"

Was he clairvoyant? My silence was long enough for him to form his own impression of my unproffered reply.

"Son, I don't blame you. Thousands have done it for immediate material gain ever since the Portuguese introduced Christianity. Not only that, the same people have moved from one denomination to another for the same purpose. There are yet others who are Christians by day and Buddhists at other times." He chuckled as if he saw the situation ludicrous.

"But tell me one thing," he said pointing his index finger right into my face. "Is there any other reason for you to be a Christian?"

Again, I took too long to reply. He did not insist on a reply.

"Son, I know what is happening to you? You are at an age when everything in life appears to be black or white. There are many shades of grey in life. Before I give you any advice, let me emphasize one thing. All of us, you elders, had similar crises in their lives at about the same age as you are. So there's nothing new in your situation."

Even as a little child, I admired Chief Monk's capacity to get one to speak freely with him. It was a very rare gift of affability. I wanted to tell him everything. I started at the beginning, as Little Father always said that it was the best place to start. I told him of Slim-Jewel's visit to Kandy and third brother's escapades with the girl across the river. A message came that the rest of the monks were waiting for him to commence pre-lunch ceremonies.

"Ask them to make the offerings to the Buddha," he ordered. It is usually a brief ceremony. An offering of small quantities of all the items of food was symbolically made to the Buddha, represented either by a statue or a relic casket. Monks and devotees recited verses in Pali in praise of the Buddha, his teachings and the community of the Sangha he founded. Each item was dedicated with an appropriate verse also in Pali. Chief Monk had still to tell me something and his estimate was that it could take less than ten minutes.

"So, you think that your brother and Slim-Jewel will live happily ever after if you leave your family for good, your village for good and your religion and culture for good?"

It was another of his dramatic pauses. Then he lost his temper.

"You fool," he scolded me. "It is you. Your selfish ego. Your uninhibited superiority complex. You can't stand what has happened. You want to punish yourself because you can't accept your fate. You are jealous of them, worse still, you are envious. Your brother and Slim-Jewel are simple rural folk. They don't have your newfangled

114

notions. They accept the situation as fate or destiny. That's it for them. They aren't mixed up like you."

I was smarting to retort. Chief Monk knew it.

"You think I am wrong? All right? Go ahead and tell me."

His challenge was so forceful that I lost courage. He softened his voice.

"Son, this is your first defeat in life," he beckoned me to come closer. I knelt down so that he could touch my head. "But it's not your last. Life is a series of defeats and victories. Only one victory is worthwhile because it's forever. Son, conquer your own self. I know you will."

I worshipped him touching his feet and he stroked my head as usual as he blessed me.

He stood up and walked toward the refectory and I followed him. He turned back and said casually,

"We are cleaning and polishing the palmleaf books. Join us from tomorrow."

XIV

"Hard work is the best medicine for all ailments of head and heart," teased a novice who was about my age and had been ordained two years ago.

For a week I had put in over ten hours a day of hard work along with the novices. It involved taking hundreds of palmleaf books out of huge chests, drying them in the sun to take the humidity away, rubbing a mixture of oil and soot on each leaf and polishing thoroughly until the page was clean and the scratched writing was black and legible. I had done this work before, though never so intensely.

I had an additional assignment. It was to check the titles, count the pages and make a list with name of the book and the author and the number of pages. It took a lot of time. Over the last six years, I had got used to neatly printed paper books and lost much of the ability to read palmleaf manuscript. A further factor interfered with speed. From time to time, I got interested in some passage and read several pages before resuming the routine job of cataloguing.

As the list grew in length, how impressed I was with what I was discovering! What a treasure! The whole of the Buddhist Canon, the Three Baskets in Pali, in forty-five volumes! Extensive commentaries on major works of the Canon, also in Pali, filling a chest of ten by six by four feet! Hundreds of volumes of Pali treatises with word-to-word Sinhala translations! As many Sinhala works in prose and verse!

One of them was a charming poem on a musician who challenged his ageing teacher for a contest. The lucid language, the fascinating imagery and the music of the meters were so irresistible that I took the book home to read at night. I also found a fair number of Sanskrit poems with word-to-word translations in Sinhala. Among them was a poem in the form of a message sent by a pining husband to his wife through a rain cloud. I was being transported to a world which I hardly thought ever existed.

The vacation month passed faster than I could imagine. The work in the library proved to be therapeutic. I had changed gradually and re-integrated myself in the environment of my birth and childhood.

"Now our little *Gentleman* has become a much *Greater Being*," Chief Monk joked, punning on the same word which we used in Sinhala for an English educated person and a respected personality of lofty soul. The change of meaning was conveyed subtly through slight accentuation of the second syllable.

Only then did I realize that I had shed my Western clothes and come barefooted to the temple in a sarong and a chemise. That was how

I came to the temple before I went to the high school in Kandy. I felt that this change in my exterior was important in my search for myself. As most adolescents of my age, I was passing through the difficult years of transition from boyhood to manhood. What was really hard was the absence of an identity. Boys rejected you as too old and even meddlesome. The adults refused to accept the maturity you wanted them to recognize. Girls made you uneasy even as you yearned for their company. Work, reading and discovery of new knowledge were ideal ways to minimize the trials and tribulations of trying to find out who you really were.

The letter I expected from school never arrived. The only conclusion I could draw was that I was not awarded the scholarship. It seemed not to bother me too much. To say that I was totally immune to the pangs of disappointment and frustration would be a blatant lie.

I wondered why Reverend Saunders was silent. Now that the Blakes were both confined to the Sanatorium at Toddy-Village and the news reaching the village was very disconcerting, he was my only link with my "other life." I needed guidance as to my immediate future.

Uncle Victor, at the instance of Aunt Flower, had written to me a long letter. It was to convince me that I should sit a competitive examination to become a government clerical officer, as he had done. He thought my chances would be very good as I could score enough marks in written papers to compensate for any difficulties I might have at the oral examination.

Once again, I missed Little Father, my guide and mentor. He pointed out to me a new direction in life and now I was lost in a maze.

I was writing a reply to Uncle Victor, when I received a letter with an unfamiliar stamp. It was from India, or more precisely, Calcutta. Reverend Saunders happened to be there on a church mission and had explored ways and means of getting me a place in a comparable college. He had succeeded in getting a partial scholarship which exempted me from tuition fees. He had given an account of the growing system of higher education in India and urged me to convince my parents to find the money for the train fare, board and lodging.

"With rupees thirty a month, you can live like a prince," he had written.

I took the letter to the temple in the afternoon to consult Chief Monk. If he agreed, he would convince my parents. With all the boys

117

being economically active, the family could afford the level of expenditure which Reverend Saunders had indicated.

Perhaps, it was an omen. Chief Monk was confined to his room after a spell of dizziness and vomiting just as he finished his mid-day meal. He was not to be disturbed. In any case, I would not dare do so. Even as I left the temple to go home for dinner, I stepped into his room to find him listless and groaning.

"What's happening to me?" I asked myself. "Everytime I need a particular person's counsel, he becomes unavailable to me. Tragedy befalls those I seek."

The news I brought home was received with consternation. Father and my maternal grandfather, along with a number of others whom they could round up, rushed to the temple. I joined them. So did several of my brothers.

Grandfather took control of the situation as he ordered everyone around him to bring or do certain things for his double-track treatment. He administered some pills and powder with the juice of garlic and ginger while performing an elaborate ceremony with oil and flowers to exorcize the evil spirits responsible for the illness. Within minutes, Chief Monk was soundly asleep.

Elders congratulated the physician-cum-witchdoctor. We returned home around midnight with a feeling of great relief.

The next morning began abnormally. Most of the family tried to catch some of the lost sleep. Mother was shouting from the kitchen that the rice gruel with medicinal herbs and leaves - our regular breakfast - was getting cold. After the third call to me, I got up. Still wiping my eyes with both hands, I stepped into the inner verandah. An acolyte from the temple bumped into me as he rushed into the house. I held him and steadied both of us who nearly fell down.

"Where's your father? Where's your grandfather?" he was shouting. I calmed him enough to find out what had happened.

Chief Monk had had a good night's sleep. He had got up a few minutes ago, gone to the toilet and was washing his face with water from a clay basin which a novice was holding. He had seen Chief Monk swaying to a side and, with remarkable presence of mind, dropped the basin and held the monk before he could fall. He was taken to his bed. The monks attending on him thought that his right limbs were paralyzed.

All of us who were at the temple the previous night were there back again. Grandfather proceeded to do what he had learned to do. Someone managed to contact the apothecary before he could go to Bo-tree Plain. My brothers and I ran all kinds of errands - gathering medicinal herbs, summoning people, purchasing oil and incense and so forth. I was assigned to do a trek to Bo-tree Plain to inform my paternal grandfather, the Abbot of the temple and several other people who were relatives of Chief Monk.

The sun was setting over the mountains when I returned to the temple with the Abbot of the Bo-tree Plain temple and grandfather. We entered Chief Monk's room silently and in single file. He was alert enough to notice my presence. He tried to say something. But no words came out of his mouth which opened vertically with every effort he made.

I went close to him and bent over him. With his left hand he reached for the end of his robe and tried to put it around my neck. It was a moving site. His gesture was deliberate and determined. The Abbot of Bo-tree temple was first to understand the significance of Chief Monk's gesture.

"Venerable Sir, I understand what you want us to do. It will be done. Tonight, if an auspicious time can be found. In any case, by early morning. The whole day tomorrow is very good."

Apparently, Chief Monk was pleased with what he heard. He put down his left hand and looked at me with tearful eyes which said a hundred things.

I knelt by the bed and worshipped him thrice the way I had seen novices soliciting admission to the Sangha.

Book Two

A WHITE MESSIAH

I

"If you say that you have just got out of jail, I will believe you, T.B.", said Reverend Saunders who met me in front of the Temple of the Sacred Tooth in Kandy. I must have looked so haggard. I was, of course, very tired. My shaven head and the yellow robe draped across my chest and balanced toga-like on my left shoulder might have added to my sorry appearance. It had been exactly two years and six months since I had been in Kandy and we had last seen each other. These had been very difficult and trying times for me.

Playing with novices, I had thought that the life as a monk was a bed of roses. But the reality was very different. Ordinarily, it had its many demands and responsibilities. In my case, however, everything was multiplied many times over.

"But, Lord, you look fine in spite of all I hear of your new responsibilities," I replied. "Congratulations."

He nearly patted me on the back and stopped suddenly when he realized that I was no longer a lay man.

A steady stream of devotees filed out of the Temple after the morning service on this most sacred of the holy days. It was the fullmoon day of the month of May. We called it a thrice blessed day as it marked the anniversary of the Buddha's Birth, Enlightenment and Demise.

Devotees from rural areas in particular were curious that an English padre and a Buddhist monk had not only met on this day in front of the Temple of the Sacred Tooth but were conversing in English. Some worshipped me in traditional style and were at a loss as to how they should greet the aimiable padre.

"Let's get out of here, Reverend Saunders", I suggested and beckoned to the driver of the buggy cart to approach us. I had been given Chief Monk's new vehicle for this special trip to the city. A trip that took a whole night by bullock cart or almost half a day by state coach could be done in a couple of hours in this light fast-moving passenger cart.

"It's nice to travel in one of these," said Reverend Saunders as he sat opposite me on the cushioned bench-like seat. "A double bullock buggy! All new! Didn't the Dutch bring this from Java where a still lighter version with no awning or canvas covers on the sides is used for racing?"

"I don't know. But it's possible. This cart was specially made in Galle for Chief Monk. When he recovered from his prolonged illness, he couldn't do his long walks. He needed something comfortable to travel in."

"I remember what you wrote about Chief Monk. It was a miraculous recovery. Is it really true that he got up one morning, stood up, steadied himself by holding to the bedpost and walked out of the room as if nothing had happened."

"Exactly so. Good merit from past lives, we say."

"May be. But I would rather give credit to his peasant heredity."

"Both, perhaps," I replied.

Reverend Saunders gave directions to the carter. We circled the Temple Square, turned eastwards past the Saint Paul's Church, with its prominent red tower, and rode in front of the Temple dedicated to Vishnu - a Hindu deity whom the Buddhists of Sri Lanka believe had been charged with the protection of their Faith in the Island.

In front of us was an impressive long building. It was old and somewhat quaint but well maintained and colour-washed in a light tint of yellow. The sprawling single-story building had a moulded facade with figures of the sun and the moon, which reflected on the still water of the moat in front of it. The thickly wooded hill of Upper Garden Jungle served it as an attractive verdant backdrop. Before the British came, it was the palace of the kings of the Kandyan Kingdom. Now it had become the official residence of the most senior British official who administered the Central Province.

On arrival, a uniformed valet received us and led us past a series of reception halls to a large office room. En route we were welcomed by a host of officers, mostly British. I was amused by the elaborate protocol and visualized how foreign ambassadors to the court could have proceeded in order from officer to officer to the monarch's majestic presence. It was an interminable but necessary series of receptions, small talk and an ineluctable reminder by each officer of the Government Agent's generosity and kindness in seeing us despite his enormous responsibilities and urgent engagements.

Finally, the Chief Interpreter, a burly Sinhala in a grotesque black attire complete with a knife-sized scabbard hanging under the left armpit, took us to a grand room where the laird of the mansion sat behind a table as large as my room in the temple.

He rose, stepped forward, greeted me in the traditional style by bringing his palms together and shook hands with Reverend Saunders.

Tall and handsome, confident and debonair, Ernest Dickinson had a winning smile.

"This young Bongyi needs no escort," he said with a friendly laugh, referring to me with an expression he had learned when he was a young civil servant stationed in the Chittagong Hill Tracts on the Burmese border. "I remember you, bongyi. Weren't you the best long distance runner and a mighty good rugby player?"

"That I was, Sir," I said, dwarfed by his charismatic presence. "You pinned on my Rugby colours."

"Oh! yes. You were in grey flannel longs, a pressed white shirt with a bow tie in school colours, white silk socks and shining brown Oxford shoes. And .. Your bushy hair was parted in the middle."

He was perfectly correct. Did I make such an impression that he remembered what I wore to the very last detail? I was about to congratulate him on his photographic memory when I saw the little mischievous glint on his eyes. He was teasing me. All of us in the upper classes were dressed alike and perhaps Dickinson, too, in his high school in Mill Hill in North London dressed similarly on special occasions. I responded to his comment with a broad grin. He laughed again. He waved away the Chief Interpreter for his attendance at this meeting was superfluous.

He turned to Reverend Saunders.

"You are always welcome here, Kenneth. Thank you for a clever draft." They both laughed heartily on what appeared to be a private joke between them.

"You must tell him about it, Sir," prompted Reverend Saunders.

I had to be in Kandy to make arrangements for my higher ordination. This was a special ceremony. One could enter the Buddhist Order at any age; some did when they were between seven and eleven. But for higher ordination, one had to be twenty years old. From a simple ceremony to reaffirm one's decision to remain in the Sangha or the Buddhist Order, it had become an elaborate social occasion.

The novice seeking higher ordination was disrobed and put in lay clothing. It was in lay clothes that one applied for higher ordination. The Buddha, in all probability, designed this feature in the ceremony to signify that one returned to the Sangha on one's own accord - an option exercised in maturity at twenty. But the brief spell as a lay man had given rise to the most pompous, irrelevant, contradictory and, above all, the most exorbitantly expensive part of the ceremony. It had become an occasion to show off the wealth and social importance of the temple and the family to which the candidate for higher ordination belonged.

My father and a senior monk representing Chief Monk had been in Kandy to make the necessary arrangements for the elephants, drummers and dancers for the procession and the princely raiments in which I would be decked. I had to come a few days earlier than the actual ceremony to tie up a few loose ends.

My higher ordination could have taken place at any time after the fourth of February 1878. But the annual higher ordination ceremony of the Flower Garden Monastery would normally take place towards the latter part of the year. Either I was very fortunate or Chief Monk, who had returned to his normal active self, was supremely resourceful. He had heard through the grapevine that the Monastery was in some sort of quandary as a result of having to oblige a foreign benefactor.

The Ambassador of Siam in England was a prince who was a close cousin of the King. On account of a misunderstanding, the prince had been recalled to the capital. Unsure of his future in the hands of an all-too-powerful autocratic ruler, he had decided to "jump ship" in Colombo and become a member of the Sangha. That would grant him an extraordinary sanctuary as the Siamese, being ardent Buddhists, held the Sangha in great veneration.

The quandary in which the Monastery found itself was twofold: The higher ordination of a Siamese prince had to be a very special occasion and the externa like processions, almsgivings, social receptions had to be appropriate to the status of a scion of the royal family. This branch of the royal family was particularly important to the Monastery as it had played a major role in sending monks to Sri Lanka for the revival of the Sangha in 1753.

Nothing, however, could be done openly with advance publicity as the prince's chances of escaping to Kandy could be jeopardized if the King had the slightest suspicion that his errant Ambassador was seeking refuge in the Sangha. The secrecy that had been requested by the prince was not to the liking of the prelate whom we called the "Great Leader." He liked to do grandiose things.

Being a member of the twenty-strong executive committee of the Chapter, Chief Monk was apprised of the dilemma. He consulted the Abbot of Bo-tree Plain. Together they made to the prelate of the Chapter an offer which he could hardly reject:

"Novice Pure-Wisdom is eligible for higher ordination since February. We'll arrange everything - processions, almsgivings, receptions and, above all, a public function in the city, chaired by no less a person than the British Government Agent himself. A few Christian dignitaries would also speak at the function. In all these functions, precedence will be given to the prince in view of his royal status and age."

The offer responded to all the needs of the prelate who wanted to mark the ordination of this particular Siamese prince as very special occasion. After all, the Fraternity whose two Chapters had the Flower Garden and Horse Peak Monasteries as their headquarters in Kandy was founded by a quorum of monks from Siam, headed by Elder Upali. The Fraternity itself had as its designation, "The Siamese Upali Fraternity". The prelate was confident that anything which Chief Monk arranged would be more than fitting for a prince. I was the beneficiary of this move in that I was to have this special ceremony just two days after the most sacred holiday of the Buddhists.

It was, nevertheless, an inconvenient day to travel out of Sangha-Gem-Field. Since I became a monk, my grandparents, parents and many members of the family had made it a point to have me administer the Eight Precepts on special Sabbath days. This day was the most important of them all and I made it a point to get my family an hour earlier than others and had the Precepts administered before I left. My parents were particularly touched and my mother said,

"Little Venerable Sir, for the third time on this thrice blessed day, I have have had my precepts administered by you, my own son. May we both have this fortune for long years to come."

Neither my austere discipline nor transformed exterior precluded me from a spontaneous public display of my emotions. I shed a few tears which I quickly wiped with my multi-purpose kerchief.

Chief Monk's cart, at a steady trot downhill, brought us to the Temple of the Sacred Tooth in time for the morning service. I was cordially received by the monks in attendance and given an extra robe to be donned in a special way before I could join them in the inner sanctum.

"The Great Agent is looking forward to seeing you today," said the seniormost monk in attendance after I had offered flowers to the casket containing the Sacred Tooth Relic of the Buddha.

"I know. But how do you happen to know it?" I was curious.

"You have a fine reputation among the young British officers who had either visited your temple and its library or asked for help from you for their studies and research. I hear that you did a fine job of classifying and cataloguing the palmleaf books."

"Yes. I continue to do it."

"The Great Agent will ask you to do something similar with regard to the library we have right here in the Octagon," he said pointing in the general direction. The Octagon was an imposing tower-like structure abutting the Temple of the Tooth. It was from there that the kings of Kandy gave their public audiences. The large esplanade in front of it would accommodate many thousands. Thus being more a part of the palace than of the Temple, it passed into the hands of the British Administration. The substantial library of palmleaf books it housed was, therefore, managed by the Government Agent, whom the people and specially the monks called "the great agent" in deference to the enormous powers vested in him.

My purpose in seeing him that morning was to make sure that he would preside over the social reception. I was a bit annoyed that he insisted that he could meet me only this morning. After what the monk in attendance at the inner sanctum of the Temple said, I was better disposed towards him and was looking forward to the meeting. I was glad that he took more than an ordinary interest in the library. I was happier still that he appreciated what I had done to make the library of the Sangha-Gem-Field Monastery more accessible and serviceable to scholars.

Whatever Ernest Dickinson and Reverend Saunders wanted to share with me was very funny. Neither could suppress their laughter long enough to start telling me the story. At last, the Government Agent started.

"You see, Bongyi, His Excellency the Governor has an annual levee. It's a big party to which every important official and private citizen is invited. When the Governor invites you, it is a command. No one can decline it unless, of course, one is literally dying. That was fixed for today."

A peon in a garish uniform with a red sash draped across the chest entered with some papers. He turned to attend to them and requested Reverend Saunders to continue.

"The Government Agent was very worried. He wanted to felicitate you in person even more than bamboozling the Siamese prince. If he went to Colombo, he would not be able to get back in time. After the levee, there are all kinds of meetings, conferences and consultations because all the senior administrators of the Island are in one place."

"So" joined in the Government Agent. "I asked for advice from my friend of the cloth here. Kenneth, your letter was simply marvellous. I shot it up without changing even a comma. The reply I got from the Governor is a gem."

He shuffled the papers on his table and pulled out an important looking letter on parchment paper. "Let me read it. It goes like this;

126

" 'Dear Ernest,

It is my fortune to have a colleague of your calibre in the administration of this Colony. None else had pointed out the political impropriety of my fixing the annual levee on the day which the Buddhists consider to be their most important holiday, the Vesak. After your letter, many have, with hind sight, come forward to say how serious a matter it would have been. They say that it would have fuelled criticism against me and the Government by the rapidly increasing cadre of Buddhist activists. Venerable Gunananda of Scribe's Garden in Bonito Plain would have had a field day. I am grateful to you for your timely advice. I am sure that your experience with Burmese and East Bengal Buddhists made you sensitive to Buddhist sentiments. You are indeed an asset to us specially in Kandy.'*

"The Governor goes on to say what he looks forward to accomplishing in our relations with the two Prelates of the Flower Garden and Horse Peak Monasteries and so forth."

Dickinson turned to the next page and scanned the letter.

"Here's what is more interesting:

*'I am even more grateful for showing me how my mistake could be taken advantage of. I sent for Venerable Sumangala to see me with Venerable Gunananda. I apologized to them that the powers that be had not yet agreed to making the Buddhist holy day a public and bank holiday. I expressed to them my disappointment and promised to pursue the issue until justice was done. In conclusion, I told them that, in deference to Buddhist sentiments, I was cancelling the annual levee. They were really very pleased.'"

Both Dickinson and Reverend Saunders were thrilled. They shook hands, patted each other and laughed. They were so engrossed in their celebration of the success of their secret ploy that I was virtually forgotten. After another round of laughter, the Government Agent walked to my end of the table.

"Bongyi, you have any idea why we are so amused?"

"Yes, Sir. I think I have. You had to be in Colombo today. But you did not wish to disappoint my Chief Monk. So you asked Reverend Saunders to find a way out. He did so by getting you to point out to the Governor that a big party by him on the Vesak night would hurt the feelings of the Buddhists. Now you haven't to go to Colombo. Yet, the

127

Governor is thanking you for helping him to get round the Sangha. Isn't that what happened?" I asked for my own clarification.

"Beware, Kenneth. Your Bongyi is quick on the uptake."

It was a good meeting. He asked me about my catalogue and what I had done over the last two years to help foreign scholars who wanted information.

"Do you remember the manuscripts you copied for one Rhys Davids? He was a civil servant here until 1872. Now he is active in England in the promotion of Buddhist Studies. I have a surprise for you from him. Do you know that he has become your publicity agent in London?"

I did remember the request of Thomas William Rhys Davids. His request which came through a young civil servant in the Provincial Office was very precise. He wanted a Pali text copied in Roman characters with diacritical marks to indicate the phonetic value of certain letters. He also wanted punctuation marks to be added to the text the way it was done in English. Only I could do it and I did it.

For a man who had almost absolute power over the Central Province, Ernest Dickinson was relaxed and humourous. He spoke of his experiences in Chiitagong where he had befriended many Chakma and Burmese monks. He had received some instruction in meditation and was hoping to learn more in Kandy. My heart sank when he said this, as I could hardly think of any monks of my acquaintance who were seriously engaged in meditation. Over two years as a novice, I had received no instruction whatsoever!

I offered to work on the palmleaf books in the Octagon. He saluted me as before. I thanked him for the trouble he had taken to be present at my higher ordination. As we left, he whispered something to Reverend Saunder's ears. I guessed that it was a request for a draft speech for the occasion.

"You made a good impression on the Government Agent, T.B.," said Reverend Saunders as we left the palace. "He is a fine man. He'll be your friend."

"I would certainly like to have him as a friend," I replied. "None has taken the place of the Blakes. And I have little hope of ever seeing Little Father again."

II

Back in Chief Monk's buggy cart, I was faced with a dilemma. Uncle Victor and Aunt Flower had invited me to the mid-day meal in their new residence at Royal Spout. "What if I invite Reverend Saunders?" Uncle Victor would be very happy. But they could also be embarrassed because I as a monk had to be treated differently. This was my first visit and the day was of very special significance. It was the first birthday of their son, Autumn-Moon. "Will they be able to serve me and Reverend Saunders at the same time? After all he, too, was a member of the clergy? If so, where should we sit? Get him to sit with me on the floor? Or, ask them to serve both of us at the table Western-style at the same time?"

I did not have to worry too long. Reverend Saunders had figured out what to do.

"Pure-wisdom, - no, T.B., your uncle invited me to lunch and we have ironed out the protocol! I am going there with you."

It was a relief. But what was the protocol?

Royal Spout was a lovely hamlet a mile or so from the eastern end of the Kandy Lake. The undulating hills covered with jak, mango and other fruit trees sloped to a vast extent of rice fields. A perennial stream which watered these fields fell a dozen feet down a granite boulder. From a stone spout cut out of the living rock issued a jet of icy cold water. Its force ensured a most stimulating shower. As the name suggested, this spout was reserved for the royalty who lived close by on the slope of a hill. The hill and the road leading to it were both called Malabar. This name signified the place of origin of the royal relatives in the western coast of South India.

In a matter of twenty minutes we were there to be surprised by the presence of the prelate himself, accompanied by his two senior deputies and another senior monk.

"This is as high as we can go by way of company," whispered Reverend Saunders.

Uncle Victor was washing the feet of the monks and drying them with a towel. He must have done this quite often before his conversion to Christianity. I was in a quandary.

"Do I submit to the tradition? Or, should I ask for exemption?"

I was embarrassed that my uncle should wash and dry my feet simply because I became a monk a little over two years ago. Again, the padre came to my aid.

"Let him have the fun, T.B. He doesn't get a chance to do this too often. When the vicar and his deputies come for dinner, we come in shoes."

It was a very formal occasion. The presence of the prelate of the Flower Garden Monastery and his most senior deputies made it special. There was the quorum of four monks with higher ordination for the purpose of making everything offered to us a gift to the entire Sangha. Such an almsgiving was considered the most meritorious. I was an extra and would not count until I had gone through the ceremony. We sat cross-legged on a row of cushions on the floor and leaned on the wall. As dictated by seniority I sat on the seat at the very end and was the last to be served.

While the conduct of Uncle Victor was not surprising in view of his youthful years in the village as a Buddhist, that of Reverend Saunders was baffling. He joined the family in serving us, removing used plates, bringing water and so forth. He knew what to do and did everything gracefully and with appropriate deference to the Prelate and his deputies. He took a keen interest in the sermons which followed.

The prelate felicitated Reverend Saunders on his promotion to the post of Principal of the high school and praised him for his tolerance and compassion. I figured in the sermon due to a variety of reasons. The hosts were my relatives. I was here to receive my higher ordination in a matter of three days. The fact that I was to be the successor to the Abbot of Sangha-Gem-Field Monastery with numerous titles and positions which went along with it was not lost sight of. I was embarrassed.

My mind flashed back to the fateful night when without a second thought I agreed to become a monk. I had no idea why I acquiesced so readily to the mute gesture of Chief Monk.

Was it the shock of his sudden illness and the fear of losing the last of the persons in whom I could confide and to whom I could go for counselling and guidance? Was I reacting to the inexorably cruel fate of the Blakes who were consigned to wait patiently for a slow, certain death as wages for a selfless life of dedication to humanity? Was this a delayed response to the unexplained disappearance of Little Father? Did my disappointment in my first-ever romantic experience play a part? Amidst these negative thoughts also arose memories of times when I fancied myself as a monk held in high esteem and veneration.

130

As a child it was my ambition - a life of plenty and luxury with apparently no work!

I collected my thoughts and regained mindfulness just in time to join in the chanting of sacred texts. Silently, I offered merit to all beings starting with those nearest and dearest to me. In that list were my brothers and their families right down to Moon-Beam, the six-month old baby girl of Slim-Jewel and my third brother.

The Siamese prince must have been in his early fifties. But he looked younger. Fair in complexion, short and stocky but erect, smart and smiling he was every inch a prince in his gorgeous costume of dazzling silk, embroidered with gold braids. He wore strands of gem-set necklaces and gold rings. It was the ceremonial dress of the Siamese court and the headdress was particularly attractive. In contrast, I looked more like a Kandyan dancer dressed in his elaborate costume for what was called a "Ves" dance - the most agile and fast-moving of the wide repertoire of Kandyan choreography. The only difference was that I wore a traditional, four-cornered, tasseled cap of a Kandyan chieftain.

We met in the inner sanctum of the Temple of the Sacred Tooth to make our offerings before proceeding to the venue of the higher ordination. In recognition not only of his royal birth but more of his age and status as a guest, he was accorded precedence in the ceremonies. But he was quick in having our plans changed.

"You may be in lay clothes now, my friend. But merely an hour ago when you were yet in a monk's robes I would have fallen at your feet and asked for your blessings."

The procession was stupendous. A hundred drummers beating tambours, tambourins, tambourines and double-faced kettle drums were followed by a line of trumpet and horn players whose plaintive melodies mingled with the martial notes of the drums. In teams of twenty to thirty, dancers displayed their distinctive dance forms which imitated the gait of various animals like the elephant, the horse, the hare and the snake. Songs to the accompaniment of cymbals described each dance.

Now that the prince had decided to ride behind me, I insisted that the caparisoned elephants carrying us should walk abreast. The procession circled the temple square and wended its way to the Flower Garden Monastery along the western bund of the Lake. An enormous crowd had come to witness the procession. There was no doubt that the Siamese prince becoming a monk to escape the wrath of his monarch was the main attraction.

Even as I rode majestically on the elephant, my mind wandered. I wondered when and by whom these elaborate ceremonies were evolved to distract a candidate for higher ordination in a manner that the glamour overshadowed the spiritual significance of returning to lay life. I have not had a moment by myself to ask myself the question which I was sure the Buddha expected me to answer: "Is it my considered decision as an adult to return to monastic life?" Now an answer either way was irrelevant. My higher ordination was a *fait accompli*.

The ceremony took place in the historic Chapter House of the monastery where the Siamese monks re-established higher ordination in the Island a hundred years ago. Practically all my relatives had come from Sangha-Gem-Field and Bo-tree Plain. Chief Monk and Abbot of Bo-tree Plain temple were to be my preceptor and teacher. The prelate presided over the ceremonies.

My knowledge of the teachings of the Buddha was tested mainly by ascertaining whether I had learnt by rote the "Book of Protection", an anthology of discourses used in ritual chanting and a text in verse from the Buddhist Canon. Called "the Path of Virtue", the latter is a delightful collection of utterances in verse of the Buddha. When the first line was prompted, I was expected to complete the quatrain.

The verses I was asked to recite were easy and happened to be among the ones I had considered to be most inspirational:

"*Hatred by hatred*" the examiner began and I completed,

"*Is never appeased.*
With love alone is hatred appeased.
This is the ancient law."

"*Ancient this is, Atula*" he chanted and I followed,

"*This is not something new.*
They blame one who speaks too much,
They blame one who speaks moderately,
They even blame the silent,
There's none who's not blamed in this world."

Finally, he recited the first line of the Buddha's joyous utterance on the occasion of his enlightenment: "*Many a life in this cycle of births*". I recited the rest:

I wandered seeking but not finding
The builder of the house.

132

Sorrowful is to be born again and again.
O House-builder, you are found out;
Not again will you build a house.
Your rafters are all broken.
Your ridge-pole is shattered.
My mind has attained the unconditioned.
Accomplished is the end of cravings."

"What does it mean?" asked the examiner.

I gave in brief the meaning as I had memorized. But he was not satisfied. He wanted me to comment on the imagery.

"Who is the house-buider? What is the unconditioned? What does it mean that the house shall not be built again?"

I gave the standard answers:

"House-builder is the insatiable craving which causes rebirth and redeath and hence the origin of all suffering, pain and distress. The unconditioned is the final bliss of Nibbana. Once one attains Nibbana there shall be no more rebecoming. That's what the simile of the house conveys."

He shook his head to indicate the acceptance of my answers.

He was about take me to the assembly when the monk who was similarly testing the prince's knowledge of the teachings requested my assistance as an interpreter.

"Please tell His Royal Highness that his knowledge of the 'Book of Protection' was astounding."

The prince smiled and replied,

"Please tell the Venerable Elder that when I returned from school in France, I had to be a novice in the main temple of Bangkok for three months. I still recall what I had learned then."

"Please ask His Royal Highness to comment on

"By your self alone has the striving to be done.
The Buddhas are but teachers.
Set in the Path and engaged in meditation
One frees oneself from bonds of death."

The prince apparently knew a little Pali. Yet, I translated the verse into English. His commentary on the verse had me stupefied. In very clear terms he explained how Buddhism was a do-it-yourself religion, that Buddhas were not saviours who led people by their hands to salvation, and that meditation and not prayer was the way to liberate

133

oneself from defilements and fetters. When I translated his commentary into Sinhala both examiners were impressed with the prince's command of the fundamentals of the Buddha's teachings.

I was to be presented to the assembly first. As I took leave of the examiners and the prince, the latter hugged me with affection. He said,

"Thank you, my friend. I will never forget this night. Do please be in touch with me, wherever I am. I will always be your friend."

"I am impressed, your Royal Highness, with your deep knowledge of the Buddha's teachings. If you learned all these during the three months you spent in the monastery, there's much to commend in temporary ordination."

"Yes. Indeed. Those three months made me a life-long student of our great religion."

I could not believe that I was the centrepiece in the enactment of a ritual which was as old as Buddhism. Months of rehearsal had prepared me to answer the rapid-fire questions which probed into my eligibility to be a monk. First related to my health, that is, whether I was suffering from diseases like leprosy, boils, eczema, consumption and epilepsy. The next "Are you a human being?" was followed by detailed queries to ascertain my freedom from bondage, indebtedness and any obligations to the government. My age was verified. So was the fact that I had my parental consent to seek higher ordination.

"Who is your preceptor?" I was asked. I gave the full name of Chief Monk with all his titles and honours.

Three times the assembly was asked if there was any objection to my being given higher ordination. With the consent of the Sangha so obtained, a longish homily advised me on the importance of a frugal life limited to the barest necessities of food, clothing, shelter and medicaments.

It was a relief when the ceremony was over and I could retire to an adjoining room until the Siamese prince was put through similar rites.

The next event was the almsgiving fixed for the fore-noon of the following day. Once again, the prince, now named Noble Son of Wisdom, was the star attraction. The prelates of both Chapters of the Siamese Upali Fraternity and their senior deputies were present. This by itself made it an extraordinarily prestigious occasion. In addition, as many as forty of the senior monks had come from different parts of the

Island. Chief Monk had made the list and had included the best known scholar-monks from the maritime Provinces.

A pavilion was specially constructed for the occasion. Many days had gone into its decoration with thousands of yards of colourful cloth in a typical Kandyan technique called "Wavy Bridges". I had not seen anything so elaborate and picturesque. The vaulted ceiling was covered with a row of red and yellow lotus-like circular arrangements from which radiated down each pillar gigantic tapering "arms" adorned with folded yardage of red and white cloth. As much love as effort had gone into its creation.

Monks were led from the Chapter House of the Flower Garden Monastery to this pavilion in a procession of drummers and dancers. They walked in single file carrying exquisitely embroidered ceremonial fans which signified each monk's eminence. Many spectators lined the route and the prince and I received their special attention. What a leveller the Sangha was! In contrast to the the previous night, we looked the same in the mendicant's robes for which we had exchanged his real and my imitation royal garb!

If there was nothing unusual as far as the offering of alms to the monks was concerned, the speeches which followed were significant. Both prelates spoke of the historical relations between Siam and Sri Lanka and the importance of Sangha-Gem-Field in the history of the Kingdom of Kandy. They highlighted its importance as a centre of culture and learning. I was asked to render their speeches into English for the benefit of the prince and many British officials who were present on invitation. The third in line to speak was a guest monk from Colombo.

Lean and slightly hunched, he had draped his robe in a way that both shoulders were covered. That alone made him more distinguished than the majority of the monks from Kandy who had the right shoulder bare. He wore spectacles with an iron frame. The crowd showed much enthusiasm when he was introduced as Venerable Sumangala of Learning Sword of the Southern Province, the Principal of the Learning-Awakening Oriental College of Palace Hill in Colombo and Abbot of the Temple of the Sacred Footprint on top of Adam's Peak. I wished it was mentioned that he was also the brain behind the silver tongue of Venerable Gunananda in the famous Buddhist-Christian controversies in places like Baddegama and Panadura.

The scholar-monk surveyed the audience with his shining eyes which looked larger through the glasses. He began in English slowly. I was disappointed that my services would not be required to interpret him.

135

"Noble Son of Wisdom, you are the latest in a magnificent line of royal princes and nobles who sought peace and security in the Sangha. Its founder, the Buddha, was himself a prince who chose the mendicant's robe in exchange for his royal regalia. He renounced all that power and wealth could confer on him. He was seeking a way to end suffering brought about by impermanence, on the one hand, and our deep-seated self-love and self-importance, on the other. I do not know what prompted you to become a monk. I do not believe that you would have chosen our noble company, if you were not convinced of the benefits you could derive from it for your eventual deliverance from the vale of suffering. Be diligent. Practise the Path."

The prince prostrated in the direction of the scholar-monk and worshipped him thrice.

"Pure-Wisdom, I know I could address you too in the same language. But let your preceptor and teacher know what special message I have for you"

Switching on to Sinhala, he came direct to the point.

"You are a rare person - what they call in Latin, *rara avis*, a rare bird. Your Western education is an asset which the Buddhists need very badly. I have heard of your services in the promotion of Buddhist research. But you are cut out for far greater things. I would urge your teacher to send you to my college in Colombo where you will not only master traditional learning but also play a role in the Buddhist renaissance which is taking place in the country. You are too valuable to be wasted in a rural temple, however important it is in the history of our culture."

He underscored his point with a faint criticism of the monks in the hill country for their narrow-minded parochialism. He outlined a global role for the Buddhists of Sri Lanka. He concluded his speech with the peroration,

"We in Sri Lanka have not only preserved Buddhism in its pristine purity but have played the most active role in its propagation in major parts of Asia. We are but custodians of this great spiritual and cultural heritage of the humankind. We have to share it with the world and now is the time to do it."

I recalled what I had asked the Abbot of Bo-tree Plain almost a decade ago about going out to the world to preach Buddhism. How wise he was when he encouraged me to pursue my dream! Now this highly venerated scholar-monk of Colombo had not merely a vision but a plan. He had the oratory to motivate even the most sluggish to action. I had found for myself a goal.

The afternoon's social reception was no less inspiring. With Ernest Dickinson and Reverend Kenneth Saunders as the main speakers, it was heavily loaded in my favour. They mentioned the prince only in passing. How very partial could my erstwhile teacher be! Though the voices were different, the substance and the language was his! I translated both speeches into Sinhala. It was hard to suppress my amusement when I had to refer to myself in the third person and render as accurately as possible the encomia showered on me. Once I was trounced for my modesty by Reverend Saunders who translated a part of the Government Agent's remarks. He was thanking me profusely for having helped several eminent international scholars.

"Reverend Pure-wisdom, you have unseen admirers in England and elsewhere. Young as you are, you have impressed a galaxy of renowned scholars of Pali and Buddhism. As a token of their gratitude, they have sent me three important publications. It is my pleasure and privilege to present them to you."

He gave a signal with his hand and a peon in uniform and red sash approached the dais with a brass tray laden with two substantial volumes and a slim book. I was puzzled. Do I walk up to the Government Agent and receive the books? That would be in keeping with the dignity of Dickinson's office but totally unbecoming of a monk. I need not have worried. With his experience with Buddhist monks in the Indo-Burmese border, he knew exactly what to do. He took the tray in his hands, walked across the dais to where I was seated and presented it to me in strict conformity with the local custom.

What a thrill it was to receive leather-bound copies of George Turnour's *Mahavamso*, Robert Childers' *Pali Dictionary* and T. W. Rhys Davids' new book "*Buddhism,*" published by the London Society for the Promotion of Christian Knowledge.

Noble Son of Wisdom spoke before me and offered thanks to the dignitaries who had gathered to honour both of us. He spoke of the growing interest in Buddhism in the Western world. In London where he had been the Siamese Ambassador he had heard that an eminent poet who was on the editorial staff of the Daily Telegraph was about to publish a poem on the Buddha.

"This poem when published will enlighten millions of English-speaking people on the noble and inspiring life of the Buddha and his teachings. It is bound to be the most sought after book during the next few decades."

What an accurate prediction he made of Edwin Arnold's *Light of Asia*, which as he envisaged was published in the following year! I was deeply touched by the princely monk's confidence expressed in my prospects as a missionary scholar-monk.

I spoke in both languages. It had to be a vote of thanks to numerous people and nothing profound could be said on the occasion. I ended my somewhat dull incantation with the hope:

"If only a minute fraction of what each one of the speakers had wished for me were to be fulfilled, I would consider my life well spent."

My poor performance did not go unnoticed. It was Reverend Saunders who told me at the end of the meeting:

"T. B., you must have been very tired after rendering all our speeches into one or the other language? Or, are you having second thoughts about the commitment you have made?"

How transparent I must have been? In spite of the heavy demand that the interpretation of others' speeches made, I had taken time to survey the audience from time to time and take note of the people present. Slim-Jewel was there with the baby on her lap. But my third brother was not to be seen.

In fact, he was the only member of the family who was absent. Instinctively I was in the grip of an inexplicable fear - not for myself but for Slim-Jewel and the baby. Something was not right.

III

The next few days were hectic. Chief Monk invited Noble Son of Wisdom to our temple. That was a full time assignment for me as I was the only one who could communicate with him. He was appreciative of my services and taught me many things that became very useful in later years. In a fortnight, I had to deliver my first ceremonial sermon. That again was a formal affair and elaborate arrangements were necessary.

I had given many sermons even as a novice. These were mostly on behalf of Chief Monk who was paralyzed and bed-ridden. That was one of the many responsibilities which I had to assume prematurely as the heir apparent to his position in the temple and the community. But as a monk who had recently received higher ordination, I had to conform to the tradition.

Noble Son of Wisdom helped me to design a new format for this sermon. The custom hitherto had been to deliver a sermon which lasted three to four hours to a partially and intermittently attentive audience in high flown classical Sinhala strewn generously with Pali quotations. From time to time, the preacher had to tell stories to sustain the sagging interest of the crowd. The only evidence that he had that the audience was not in deep sleep was that they intoned "Sadhu! Sadhu! " (the equivalent of 'Amen' in a way) every time the Buddha or the Nibbana, the sumnum bonum of the Buddha's Path of Deliverance, was mentioned. A quaint custom was also in operation to keep the preacher on the ball. A senior devotee seated right in front of the preacher's seat would punctuate every sentence with "Yes, venerable sir!". Some older and better read men were known to correct the preacher if he were to make a mistake.

Prince-Ambassador-turned-Monk wanted to do away with the entire tradition. He suggested that I speak standing, avoid Pali citations altogether, use the simple colloquial Sinhala which the villagers understood, engage the audience in a dialogue with questions and answers from both sides, limit the whole session to about an hour and a half and eliminate the the senior devotee's role.

"What of the audience response to the name of the Buddha and Nibbana with "Sadhu! Sadhu!"?" I asked him.

"Let's leave it to the people."

The usually liberal Chief Monk was adamant on two points: I should be seated as tradition demanded in a suitably adorned preacher's seat and my maternal grandfather had to play the role of the senior devotee. Noble Son of Wisdom did not give in easily. Their debate brought more publicity to the innovations I was supposed to introduce to the age-old tradition of preaching. I had a record crowd for what was technically my maiden sermon.

I was as excited as I was on the day I made my real maiden speech barely two months from the day I became a monk. It was on a very sad occasion. Mrs. Blake had died first and White Padre followed in a week. We were informed only after the funerals were held in a church not far from Toddy-Village. I attended the memorial service at the Bo-tree Plain church on the invitation of the new padre. Not only as the representative of Chief Monk but more importantly as a beneficiary of the many benevolent services of the Blakes, I spoke on them with gratitude and affection. My speech came directly from my heart and I was exceptionally eloquent. Words seemed to flow from an unknown source. I was never at a loss for one either in Sinhala or in English.

How much I wished the Blakes were alive and could be in the crowd to listen to my maiden sermon. To them I was their handiwork - their Pygmalion. They were proud of my achievements. Just a week before the death of Mrs. Blake I received a post card with their congratulations and best wishes on my becoming a Buddhist monk. What a magnanimous gesture!

We had not invited White Padre's successor to my ceremonial sermon. Perhaps, I was prejudiced from the moment I first met Reverend Percy Smith and his wife. It was at the memorial service. They appeared cold, formal, rigid and, above all, cynical. Just out of a Divinity School in Central England, they were in for a bad time. To succeed the Blakes would have been a hard act for anybody to follow. But for the Smiths the task was Himalayan.

They had come to a country they hardly knew and found themselves in a place of which they knew nothing. They came to civilize a dark colony and save the souls of wayward heathens. They had been persuaded to believe that the Blakes were cursed by God for being too tolerant to a pagan religion and for concentrating less on asserting the supremacy of Christianity. The Smiths had vowed to do God's work in the God's own way - which to them meant their own bigotted way! They were totally unprepared for what they saw and encountered in the Island.

Their culture shock found expression in aloofness which the people interpreted as disdain. They painted themselves to a corner and had no idea how to get out of it. Whereas White Padre and Mrs. Blake were the first to rush with humanitarian aid - as on the day of the landslide for which some still assigned blame to me - the Smiths hardly left the church premises. They were unhappy. So, as far as I could gather from my relatives and friends, was the dwindling Christian community.

The Smiths had a rare knack for antagonizing everybody. After every Sunday sermon which was delivered in English with a poor translation by a deacon, a few more Christians had reason to be offended and to leave the church.

One person who was admittedly very pleased with the new Christian leadership in the area was the Abbot of the Bo-tree Plain temple.

"All we should wish for are more and more Reverend Smiths until the Buddhists can organize themselves," he told Chief Monk when the question of inviting him was raised.

The decision not to invite them was unanimous:

"Why add to their misery and why clutter this place with a pair of disgruntled faces?" was the reason.

Reverend Saunders, if he came, would have represented the Christian community. But he was prevented from doing so on account of an earlier engagement. So the honour went to the R. M., the Divisional Administrator, as he was locally called.

Since the public reception with the Government Agent in the chair and the brilliant speech of Reverend Saunders, he had begun to show some interest in me. Until then, he had been more royal than the king. Now he admitted to seeing things differently.

He was keen to be associated with the temple and claim credit for what his ancestors had donated to the Monastery. His renewed interest in Buddhism could also be a reaction to Reverend Percy Smith's disregard of local customs and values. On this day the R. M. had agreed to present to me a framed testimonial in verse on behalf of the Christian community.

He had made it a point to appear in the traditional dress of a Kandyan chieftain. He looked majestic in his gold embroidered vest, shoes and hat. The forty yards of cloth wrapped around him made him appear prosperously rotund. The dagger with exquisitely carved gilt handle looked out of place in a preaching hall.

Seated on a large velvet-covered chair in a raised pavilion in the centre of the square Preaching Hall, I could see the distinguished invitees in front of me - the men and women to my left and right. Behind me were the monks seated in accordance with their seniority with the exception of Noble Son of Wisdom to whom a seat had been given close to the pavilion.

141

The unusually long preliminaries included speeches by Chief Monk and Abbot of Bo-tree Plain temple and the presentation of framed testimonials called "Praise Papers" by various individuals and organizations. Starting with a long eulogy written in bombastic prose, the document ended with a ten-line stanza, similar in some respects to a sonnet.. A representative of the organization read the paper and one of its more affluent or influential members presented it to me. There were at least a score of such eulogies which revelled in hyperbolic accounts of what my family and I had done for the community.

I was bored. I surveyed the crowd. I tried to recognize faces and remember names and relationships. I looked for members of my family. My mother's father was seated right in front of me. He was ready to play his role as the "respondent". The elders were clustered together in the front row on both sides. The young had found their peers. Partially hidden by her mother sat Slim-Jewel with Moon-Beam on her lap. I wondered where my third brother was. He was not to be seen anywhere. At first I thought that he could have been with younger men who loitered about in the compound. Then I remembered that he was absent on the day of the social reception in Kandy. A sense of foreboding overcame me. Once could be understood. But twice within a fortnight?

I nearly missed my cue to start the sermon by administering the Five Precepts. Noble Son of Wisdom whispered in my ears,

"Friend, now it's your turn to bore us."

My smile was spontaneous and the audience appeared very pleased. The text chosen by me for the sermon was on diligence:

Diligence is the path to immortality;
Heedlessness is the path to death;
The diligent do not die;
The heedless are like unto death.

In the third century before Christ, a novice converted the great Indian Emperor Asoka the Righteous with a sermon on this very quatrain. As Buddhism was introduced to Sri Lanka by the son and daughter of this emperor, I could preface my sermon with a brief history of this event. In honour of the Siamese prince, I added also a note on the contribution of his country to the revival of Buddhism.

The topic itself was elaborated with reference to the Buddhist system of spiritual training, with special emphasis on moral conduct, meditation and the realization of Wisdom. I made my sermon extremely simple. I paused to ask questions and the answers came mainly from women whose interest in the study of religion appeared to be

142

significantly higher. I encouraged people to ask questions and most of them came from my grandfather. He got me to relate in detail the circumstances under which the verse concerned was preached by the Buddha. The dialogue that ensued enlivened the session. It was with some effort that I brought the sermon to a close within an hour and a half.

Literally a mountain of gifts were offered to me. I concluded the thanks-giving or rather merit-offering part of the ceremony with a few words in English for Noble Son of Wisdom and the Divisional Administrator who claimed that English came to him more easily than Sinhala.

I was led from the preaching hall in a procession which took the longest possible route to my room. The family gathered to express their appreciation of the sermon. When it was Slim-Jewel's turn to worship me, I asked her where her husband was. She began to sob and cry. She was led away by my mother and hers. My question was not answered by any one. I was very upset.

The next day as early as I found it possible, I walked to Slim-Jewel's house. I hoped to be there before her parents and my brothers had gone to work in the fields. Due to late rains, the ploughing and levelling of the fields for the major season had been postponed. To catch up the lost time, the transferring of the rice plants from the nursery to the fields had to be done as each plot was ready. The latter task, called transplanting, was traditionally women's work. Not only did the tender plants need gentle handling but the women were patient and careful to place each plant at regular intervals. A transplanted field was a work of art. The lilting songs they sang to lighten the back-breaking work were haunting.

When I stood in front of the house without entering or making any noise as the monastic etiquette demanded, it was Slim-Jewel who noticed me and invited me inside. She was carrying the baby straddled on her hip and was looking for sand and gravel in a winnowing fan full of rice.

"Enter, Venerable Sir. There's none else in the house. Mother and sisters have gone to transplant rice. I remained behind because of the baby. I also have to get the mid-day meal ready for everyone."

"I came to find out what's happening between you and my brother. Why didn't I see him at either of the last two functions? Why did you sob and cry when I asked you about him?"

She thought for a while and said,

"I don't think it proper to discuss this matter with you. The elders are doing all they can. I have confidence in them."

143

With further persuasion, however, I managed to elicit some information. On the day of the social reception, he had taken Chief Monk's buggy cart saying that he had to get something urgently. He had returned in time to leave the buggy cart in front of the reception hall before the function was over. But he was missing. My mother had suspected that he could have gone to a village beyond Thorn-tree Ford in search of the outcaste girl with whom he was once in love. In this she was correct. The eldest brother who was married to Slim-Jewel's sister was told by two Muslim traders of the village that the cart was seen there at the time concerned. They could not have made a mistake because the cart was unique.

"Do you know where he is?"

"Yes. He has written me a letter asking me to forgive and forget him. I don't understand what it means or what I am expected to do."

"Can I see the letter?"

"No. It's with your father."

I was angry. Slim-Jewel did not deserve to be deserted. Nor was my brother fair to Moon-Beam, such a darling baby with curly hair and sharp blue eyes. She gave me a sweet smile and I regreted that as a monk I could not take her in my arms.

In the temple, I was missed. I had to see Chief Monk and offer my apologies for leaving the monastery without permission. I had to give him a full account of the conversation with Slim-Jewel.

"Who else was in the house when you spoke to Slim-Jewel?"

"Nobody but her baby."

"Do you know the rule of discipline which prohibits your talking to a woman other than in the presence of another person of discerning age?"

"Yes, Venerable Sir. But I was so disturbed by my third brother's behaviour that I forgot to observe the rule."

I expected him to be angry. Instead, he told me in a matter-of-fact tone,

"On the Full Moon day will be your very first confessional ceremony in the Chapter House. Remember to confess the transgression of the rule and ask for expiation from the Sangha present. We may decide whether any further action is necessary."

What a close-knit, rule-laden and discipline-bound society the Sangha was. This was to be my first experience. I have read the relevant books of the Buddhist Canon. Its first Basket or group of five substantial texts is devoted to the Rules of Discipline. As many as two hundred and twenty-seven rules are to be observed on a regular basis and violations are categorized according to the penal steps that would be taken by the Sangha. Mine was a minor offence and it would not affect my membership in the Sangha. Yet I had to face the consequences.

I worshipped Chief Monk and was about to take leave of him. He called me very formally as "The Little Name" - the standard nomenclature for a younger monk - and said sternly.

"Whatever is happening in you brother's home is no longer your business. You have renounced your lay life and that means your family as well. Do you understand?"

"Yes, Venerable Sir," I worshipped him thrice.

Though we had known each other for only about three weeks, Noble Son of Wisdom and I had developed a close friendship. I was with him all the time specially when he met senior monks for instruction. As a prince in Bangkok, he had been used to a life of luxury and pleasure. As the Ambassador of Siam in Great Britain, he had befriended many a world leader and acquired a deep understanding of the Western culture. As a monk in a rural temple in the mountains of Sri Lanka, he displayed a degree of adjustment which was remarkable. With his vast array of life experiences, he knew the correct answer to many of the questions I had posed.

Rebuked by Chief Monk, I sought solace in my friend. He was in the process of writing a letter to his family now in self-imposed exile in Kedah in the Malay Peninsula.

"They must be knowing all about me. But it is my duty to tell them myself."

"That's good," I said vaguely. " What was it that you feared at the hands of your monarch?"

"From an oriental despot anything can be expected. I have no idea what made him angry. For all I know, somebody who had interest in my post in London carried tales to him. The king believes the slanderer and there's little I can do to disabuse his mind."

"What would have happened, if you did not cut short your journey in Colombo and proceeded to Bangkok?"

"One of four things: I would have been arrested and after a mock trial in the court, he would have either had me executed by beheading or incarcerated for life. The third would have been to exile me to Siam-Burma border where every movement of mine will be watched by the king's henchmen. But the last of the four options, which in the eyes of the people would look very benign, could have been the most disastrous."

He laughed out aloud. I could not think of anything more disastrous than his deprivation of life or freedom. By now I was used to his sense of humour which often could border on the macabre.

"The king could have invited me to the court and in a great ceremony presented me one of his famous white elephants."

"And you say that's the worst punishment?"

"Yes, my friend, a white elephant is holy. Presented by the king, it has to treated like a king. No work for a white elephant. So it brings its owner nothing in return other than some vague prestige among the commoners which is cancelled by the message of royal displeasure given to the court. It has to be fed the best food and a whole army of keepers must be engaged to look after its every whim. In three to four years I would be reduced to a pauper. That could be living hell."

"Now that you have become a monk, do you worry about these matters? If so, what do you do about it?"

Noble Son of Wisdom put the pen down, closed the bottle of ink and signalled me to sit on his bed. I expected him to share with me some personal information. Instead, he said,

"Now! Now! My young friend, you don't want to know how I handle my worries. Something is worrying you and you want my mature advice. So why don't we talk about it?"

I made a clean breast of my problem starting from the first day I saw Slim-Jewel. I told him how much I loved her, how I dreamt of a home with lots of children and how our belief in horoscopes brought about the present situation. As regards the girl across the river, I described how my mother did Hindu penances to get her out of the scene. I explained why I felt in some way responsible for my brother's unfair treatment of Slim-Jewel. I concluded with a brief account of Chief Monk's rebuke. Noble Son of Wisdom listened to my story most attentively.

"Let's take the last problem first,"he said. "You violated a rule and you have to face the consequences. The Sangha, as you may know, is the world's longest lasting closed society. Even though admission to it is open to anybody, I call it a closed society because it's self-renewing, self-regulating and self-policing. One thing really great about it is that the process is one hundred per cent democratic. Its efficacy is best established by its survival. So. my friend, you are a first offender. Go through it and write it off to experience. You'll never regret it."

That was a bit of useful advice. It took away the pang of frustration. I had wanted Chief Monk and all other monks to have the best impression of me. It ached to have failed myself. But the ex-diplomat's point of view was worth considering. Having given me enough time to understand what he said, he proceeded.

146

"Your brother has written to his wife asking her to forgive and forget him. So, there is no doubt that he has started a life of his own with his first sweetheart. Is that not so?"

"Yes. It is quite clear."

"Now what's the real problem?"

I had no answer.

"I'll tell you what the real problem is and what you can do about it. You feel responsible for your brother's desertion of his wife. Why? Because with all your Western education you hadn't enough guts to defy the astrologers. Now you are upset that she is left alone with a baby to bring up. So ask yourself whether you are man enough to give up robes, marry your old heart throb and look after her and your brother's daughter."

I was shocked by his razor-sharp accuracy. Again, I had no answer. He continued.

"You see, my dear friend. Your problem is that your heart tells you what's right and your mind tells you what's correct. Your Chief Monk knows that you will not return to lay life because of your sense of dignity. You would do anything to avoid the stigma of an ex-monk. So go back to your room, take a sheet of paper, list all the pros and cons for each proposition, namely.........."

He paused expecting me to complete the sentence. It took some time for me to formulate the two propositions:

"To be man enough to leave the Order and take over the responsibilities of a family or to renounce worldly interests and continue as a monk?"

"Precisely, my friend. But don't be in a hurry. You have more than a week for the confessional ceremony."

IV

"Have you reached a verdict, my dear young friend?" Son of Noble Wisdom asked me when I joined him in the early morning chanting of the Book of Protection on the Full Moon day of the month of June. It was also a special day in the history of Buddhism in the country - 2185th anniversary of the introduction of Buddhism. Both my grandmothers had decided to observe the Eight Precepts and I conducted the brief ceremony for them.

"I did exactly as you advised. I also asked myself two additional questions: How much is my present consternation based on my selfish desire to repossess Slim-Jewel? Does she want to pick up the pieces of her life with mine? You see I never asked her and I have no way to ask her."

"That's good work, my friend. But do you want to ask her?"

"In a way I have an answer. When I met her alone, her first reaction was to tell me to mind my own business."

The confessional ceremony lasted two hours. It was solemn and full of archaic ritual. The two hundred and twenty-seven rules of discipline were recited. Each of the eleven monks asked the community, "Have you seen, heard or suspected that I had transgressed any of these Fundamental Rules?" It must have become a formal question over the millennia. But even the youngest monk present had the right to respond. It was my turn. I prefaced the question with a full confession of my encounter with Slim-Jewel. No excuses were presented. The guilt was admitted.

"Great," Noble Son of Wisdom whispered to my ear.

Outside the Chapter House, Chief Monk called me to a side.

"Little Name, next week you are going to Colombo. The Siamese Name will also go with you. We are accepting the invitation of Venerable Sumangala."

If that was punishment, it was very light indeed. To study in the newly established Learning-Awakening Oriental College under the guidance of its illustrious Principal and equally renowned staff would be a rare privilege. As far as Chief Monk was concerned, he was achieving two ends. He wanted his only pupil and therefore the heir apparent to his positions of influence and importance in the Sangha given the best available monastic education. At the same time, he wanted me out of the ugly domestic complications of my errant brother. The message was simple: what you renounced is renounced for ever.

Once again, I went to meet Noble Son of Wisdom. I had never found him idling. Every minute he found in between various monastic duties he utilized in some useful activity. He would write letters, summarize lesson notes, study Pali in Sinhala characters or read a book.

"In one thing you are so much like me. You do a lot of things in crevice time," I told him when I realized that he was memorizing Pali declensions.

"What's that? What's crevice time?"

"That's a great lesson I learnt from a saintly Christian Padre to whom I owe not merely my Western education but my entire social and cultural orientation."

I related the story of an extraordinary English lesson which White Padre gave during that busy vacation when he and Mrs. Blake were preparing me for high school.

"You see. He was a resourceful teacher. Very theatrical in approach. He came with a tin suitcase packed to the brim with various items of clothing and toiletry. He unpacked it carefully, teaching us the names of the things he took out. We were three in the class. He asked us to repack the case. Nobody could get the things fully into the case. I think I did the best. But I too left out most of his toiletries - brushes, shoe cremes, talcum powder. Then he packed the case showing us his secret. For every crevice in between folded clothing, he would find space for something. It was very clever indeed."

"That's fascinating. But what did that have to do with your crevice time?"

"That's right. That was the moral he drew from the exercise. He said, 'We all have twenty-four hours a day. Some fill in the unforgiving minute with more distance run than others do. How do they do it? They fit in bits and pieces of useful work in unutilized crevices - the time we waste by waiting for someone to come or something to happen.' "

"That's' a lovely story," said Noble Son of Wisdom. "I learnt my habit the hard way. When I was young, my father who was king then was very strict. He didn't want us to grow lazy. He believed in the discipline of the royal family as an example to the people. We had foreign governesses who were ordered to discipline us and teach us Western ways - punctuality, politeness, etiquette and that sort of stuff. I think time management was something we could learn from them."

For the umpteenth time, I realized that our conversations always began with some general discussion, however pressing the matter on which I needed his advice was. Was it something he learnt from his governesses? Or else, are all diplomats trained to wait for the other side to state the case?

Whatever be the reason , it was after an hour-long chat on several interesting themes that he opened the subject of our impending departure to Colombo.

"I have enjoyed having you as my ears and mouth, my friend. I have learnt so much of your nation's history and culture from you. I could myself benefit from a bit of formal education in the new oriental college."

"Was it your idea?"

"Good ideas never belong to an individual."

Nothing I had read in books or heard from travellers had prepared me for what I saw and felt as the train snaked down the historic Balana or Lookout Pass through so many tunnels and along tantalizingly precipitous ledges of granite. What a feat of engineering! I had heard of a prophesy that the independence of the Kingdom of Kandy would last until a road was constructed "bridging rivers and drilling rocks". It was ironical that the gleaming white tower in memory of the engineers of the British armed forces who built the first road to Kandy was located at a point bearing a militarily significant name: Sword-drawing Point.

"This place should now be renamed Sword-sheathing Point," I told my travelling companion. It needed a long commentary before he grasped what I was trying to tell.

"You are sad that the price for development was your national independence. Aren't you?"

"Indeed, Sir. It's too high a price."

If I suppressed the sigh that formed within me, it was due to the decorum that I had to maintain as a member of the Sangha.

This was my first train ride. All was sheer luxury. The roominess and the comfortable padded seats made it a veritable bungalow on wheels. The frequent tea service in bone china teapots and cups and glistening silver with scones had the air of a continuous party. Easy and instant friendship which the ability to talk in English brought us provided a pleasant social experience.

We were, of course, amused by the nosiness of at least one passenger, possibly a tea planter from up-country, who insisted that the ticket examiner should check whether we were travelling in the correct class! Engine drivers, guards and ticket examiners of Ceylon

150

Government Railway were drawn from the small Dutch Burgher community and looked European. They were deferential to European merchants and planters who usually travelled in higher class saloons.

Travelling second class was the idea of Noble Son of Wisdom.

"It's strictly the Buddhist thing to do, " he argued. "Avoid extremes: neither the self-indulgence of the snobbish first class nor the self-mortification of the crowded hard-seated third class!! So the Middle Path is second class!!!" He had a knack for making even a serious teaching of the Buddha a theme for a hearty laugh.

I have always been an avid admirer of the Island's scenic beauty. I was born and bred in an exceptional environment. Yet, the vast River Plain which spread below me to the horizon, dominated by the book-shaped granite block of Bible Rock, far exceeded in beauty what I had hitherto seen. I was glad that we had chosen window seats on the correct side of the carriage. The moving scene was enthralling.

I could visualize the precarious ascent of Portuguese, Dutch and English columns on their numerous unsuccessful invasions from the sixteenth to the nineteenth century through the lush vegetation on rocky slopes. How deadly could have been the huge boulders which the defenders of the Kingdom hurled down on the advancing intruders! No wonder the Kingdom of Kandy was declared impregnable due to rivers, forests and mountains.

Occasionally a curious European stopped to speak to us. Two Buddhist monks - one plainly recognizable as a foreigner - were not a common sight in a train. A stocky Englishman in Khaki shorts, white short-sleeved shirt and bowler hat was more curious than others,

"You wear a funny looking dress. Are you coming from or going to a fancy dress party?"

What a cue for Noble Son of Wisdom to have another good laugh! With a straight face, he described in impeccable English all the events connected with our higher ordination as a series of fancy dress parties. He was becoming funnier and funnier. Our interlocutor was taken as far as possible into a realm of pure imagination interlaced with magic, superstition and romance. We were not shaved, he insisted: each invitee was given the privilege of taking just one hair out with a tweezer and by morning we were both bald and many of the invitees were disappointed!!! We were having a fine time teasing the unsuspectingly gullible tea-maker when we had an unexpected visitor - Ernest Dickinson, the Government Agent of Central Province.

"Eh! you Bongies. I heard that two shaven headed yellow-robed thugs were having fun at the expense of my tea-making friend and I

151

came to rescue him," he said in mock seriousness. "I know both of you are called Wisdom. Who is Pure and who is Noble?"

In a rare moment of inspired wit, I replied,

"Sir, Nobility sticks with royalty!"

We had no idea that we had drawn quite a crowd with the yarn of my Siamese colleague. The courtesies extended to us by the Government Agent impressed them. When he led us to have lunch with him at the next stop, their esteem for us enhanced.

By the time we reached Colombo, our fellow travellers knew who we were, what we represented and why we were different. We had made several friends with whom we had exchanged our addresses.

My first impression of Colombo was that it was scorchingly hot and steamy. The mid-afternoon sun in a cloudless blue sky was in no way friendly to our shaven heads or exposed right shoulders. That meant there was one more comfort to renounce: the balmy, salubrious climate of the mountains.

"Not for me, my friend," said Noble Son of Wisdom. "In Bangkok the three seasons are hot, hotter and hottest! And this could be a nice mildly hot day!!"

A young monk had been sent by the College to receive us at the Station. Two porters followed us with our meagre belongings. Buddhist monks do really travel light. In the past, all their requisites, called the Eight Essentials, consisted of a set of three robes, kerchief, begging bowl, water strainer, razor and needle and thread and were carried on one's person. Writing and printing had added an additional burden in that the books once carried invisibly in one's head had also to be hauled now.

Within yards from the railway station there was ample evidence that Venerable Sumangala's effort to revive the ancient traditions of learning was remarkably successful. The streets were lined with bookshops of varying sizes and special stores which catered for the monastic needs of monks.

"It's becoming a small college town," explained the shop-keeper from whom we bought several sets of Eight Requisites to be presented to the leading monks of the institution. My Siamese colleague was impressed with the rapidity with which Buddhist and Sinhala classics were being printed and made available to the public at affordable prices. We were both taken up by a novel display device which a growing band of poet-publisher-advertizer-seller-enterpreneurs had adopted for what appeared to be a brisk business: the upturned umbrella. Their poems in simple colloquial Sinhala retold popular stories. A line drawing of the central event was block-printed on the cover.

"You fellows must be a book-loving, literate society," remarked Noble Son of Wisdom.

We were cordially received at the College. Imperceptibly, Noble Son of Wisdom became the centre of attraction. It was a relief for me. His age and experience, apart from his royal birth, made him more eligible for special attention. All this while I had been basking in the glory of my teacher, Chief Monk. Most of the deference shown to me reflected what a closed community expected me to be some day in the future rather than what I really was. I felt as though a great burden was lifted from my shoulders. I was no longer a thing or an office. I was a person. How wonderful it was to be free once again!

In a tiny modest cell at the far end of the College premises, I spent my first night more awake than asleep. Fatigue, excitement, unfamiliar surroundings, sagging bed and hard pillow could have contributed to my feeling of restlessness. But the dominating sensation as I rolled on my bed was that I was about to embark on something unthinkably extraordinary. This feeling was intensified when I got up in the middle of the night from a fitful spell of sleep during which I had an unusual dream. I remembered it vividly in every detail.

A tall young monk, dark as ebony in complexion, was standing by me in some sort of religious ceremony. Suddenly he turned toward me and called me by my name. I was surprised as he was altogether a stranger. Then he wanted to change places with me, apologizing for not having respected my seniority. I protested that I was so new as a confirmed member of the Sangha that I had not passed even a single rainy season.

In the Sangha, seniority and whatever privileges that went with it were determined by the number of rainy seasons of Lent and Retreat that one had passed from the date of higher ordination. He would not accept my explanation.

Other monks at the ceremony were curious to find out what we were so agitated about and gathered around us. As our argument became more intense, I noticed that the complexion of the monk was visibly changing. He was becoming fairer by the minute. The glistening white teeth which were prominent at the beginning ceased to glitter whereas his face reflected the sun and assumed a golden glow. That was not the only change. His features too underwent rapid transformation. Suddenly, and that was when I awoke, he was no longer a stranger. It was Little Father in the robes of a monk. He wore his robe the way the monks in the low-country did. That was with both shoulders covered.

153

Thoughts of Little Father kept me awake for the rest of the night. That ill-fated morning when he left the village with White Padre, the disturbing news of his disappearance a few months later, and the long period of anxiety and hope, sustained by clinging to folk cults and beliefs, presented themselves in my mind's eye like a recurring parade. I felt a sharp stab deep within my chest. I knew it for what it was - a deep feeling of guilt and shame that more recent preoccupations had contrived to relegate him to the background in my memory.

What did the dream mean? Did it portend that I would be soon rejoining him? Was he a monk like me? Was someone going to mistake me for him? Is that how we are destined to meet?

The Western educated product of the Age of Reason within me chided me for my childish enthusiasm. But the voice of the simple rural boy of the mountain fastnesses of the least developed part of the Island reasserted the right to believe in what was comfortable, pleasant and reassuring.

All my thoughts were not on Little Father. It was but natural that the whole of my life should reappear for review. Slim-Jewel, Moon-Beam, my errant brother and the lovely girl across the river all had a place in my thoughts. I visualized how two paragons of beauty could be so entwined with the life of a single man that one or the other had to suffer. What if all of them could be under one roof and no one be the loser?

The unsophisticated local customs would not bar it. The strict laws of monogamy, which Christian missionaries advocated and colonial powers upheld, had not begun to influence the Kandyan region yet. But what a chasm had society created between these two women - one held in high esteem and the other despised and down-trodden. Why? All due to a pure accident of birth! I thought wishfully of an ideal society in which everyone was equal and was judged on the basis of their actions and actions alone.

These thoughts must have calmed me enough to permit another spell of sleep. Again I woke up at the end of a dream in which the two women were engaged in pounding rice in a single mortar with two pestles. I laughed to myself. What phantasy? If centuries of Buddhism had not made us ready for such a rapprochement, what else could succeed? Love? Compassion? Tolerance?

I thought of the Buddha and his struggle against caste discrimination. How convincing he was in asserting the oneness of humanity. His own concept of an ideal society, as reflected in the constitution and organization of the Sangha, was that scavengers,

154

barbers, slaves and the like had equal status in it with those who claimed to be high born. But what an irony that his own clan of Sakyas was massacred on account of the caste prejudices of a member of the family!

Reverend Saunders referred frequently to a story from the Buddhist literature to illustrate that it was one thing for the founder of a religion to teach but something else for the teachings to make a dent in the behaviour of even the people closest to him:

> The king of the kingdom which abutted that of the Buddha's clan, the Sakyas, was keen to become a kinsman of the Buddha through marriage. Considering themselves to be superior in birth, the Sakyas offered him a bride who had a flaw in her lineage. She was a daughter of a cousin of the Buddha by a slave girl. She had a son who was named Vidudhabha and he was the heir apparent to the king's throne. One day the young prince visited the home of the maternal grandparents. He was well received and treated as a kinsman. But the Sakyas were conscious of the fact that his mother was a menial servant. When he was about to leave, his retinue overheard a servant in the house remark, "Wash with milk and water the seat on which the slave girl's son sat." Vidudhaba was angry that the Sakyas had tricked his father and also humuliated him. On ascending the throne, he marched against the Sakyas and almost exterminated the clan.

I tried to recall when and where I heard this story from Reverend Saunders for the first time. It was in a class on caste and class in the Island. How right he was about the hypocrisy which manifested itself in our society: maintaining a caste system, while praising the Buddha's principle of equality! promising not to kill, while eating flesh and meat! drinking alcoholic beverages in secrecy, while claiming to desist from drunkenness!

My thoughts dwelt on the incident of the boy from Thorn-tree Ford who entered into a dispute with White Padre. I remembered asking Reverend Saunders in that class whether the references made to the Bible by either party were correct and conclusive. It had long been perplexed how White Father who symbolized compassion in practice compared the cutting of a shrieking, struggling chicken to that of a cucumber. I wracked my brain in vain for the response I got from Reverend Saunders. All I could remember was that he quoted the Bible to the effect that what went into the mouth of a person did not make one unholy while what came out of it could make one unholy. It had to do something with intentions of the heart. He also referred to a Buddhist parallel. I made a mental note to check these references.

Tossing in bed while sleep eluded me, I thought again of my third brother and his infidelity. I realized that the reason for my presence in the dingy cell in a damp and humid valley in Colombo was the concern on the part of the elders that I would want to solve Slim-Jewel's problem in my way. Noble Son of Wisdom castigated me for not being man enough to do what I thought was right. Perhaps, he was correct. That I had made a greater commitment to a holy life was a lame excuse. Again, my conscience accused me of insensitivity and declared me to be a selfish, hypocritical fool.

It was a relief that the matinal bell rang at five in the morning. With the clear briefing on the previous day, I could find the facilities, don new robes and join the College community for the dawn chanting of the Book of Protection.

I was standing outside the shrine room when it happened.

"Pure, Pure, when did you come?" someone standing behind me asked.

I have been called by so many names. But no one had called me "Pure" and therefore I took no notice. Then the caller, who was a few rows of monks behind me, wormed himself through the crowd and touched me lightly on my bare right shoulder. With a shudder I turned my head. I recognized the face. He was the monk of a dark hue whom I saw in my dream.

"I am sorry," he said. "I made a mistake. You are so much like Venerable Pure-Intellect who was a student here a few years ago".

"Do you know from where he was?"

"No, that was the only funny thing about him. He never used the name of his village as we all did. He wanted to be known simply by his name."

"Do you know anything more about him?" I asked him.

"A lot. He was a great orator. He knew his English quite well and that made him very special among us. He was a fighter. He wanted to get back to some campaign to which he was committed. A remarkable man. I tell you. A very remarkable man. You know what he was telling us: 'There's no time to be memorizing all these musty books. There's much to be done to save our religion and culture. Don't waste your time in Colombo. Go back to the villages and teach what little you know to children and their parents' "

156

Our conversation was cut short by the arrival of the Principal, Venerable Sumangala along with his senior colleagues and Noble Son of Wisdom. The chanting began immediately. I could not even ask my interlocutor to see me later. Nor could I get his name or whereabouts. Even as I chanted the texts parrot-like, I wished as fervently as I could that my dream come true.

I called on Venerable Sumangala, presented a set of the Eight Requisites in the name of Chief Monk and worshipped him as tradition demanded.

"I am glad, Little Name, that you took my advice or rather your preceptor and teacher were prepared to release you. There's a lot you have to study. But more importantly, there's a lot that you should do. We are a nation with no future unless we raise our heads from despondency and assert our right to our culture, our religion and our way of life. With your Western education you are indispensable to our campaign. Do you understand me?"

"Yes, Venerable sir, I have discussed this matter at length with the Abbot of Bo-tree Plain temple."

"Yes, I know. Every day you must find time to deal with my English correspondence. The best time is when others take a snooze after their mid-day meal".

I was very pleased. To work with him on his correspondence would be to have a ring-side seat in the national arena. What a privilege! What an honour!

The first to congratulate me was Noble Son of Wisdom.

"For a young man there could be no better opportunity than to be working closely with a national figure," he said. "This will be the best education you can ever have".

We were strolling down the Palace Hill Road to the bookshops to buy the books and notebooks needed for our studies. We were to work together on a special programme in which the emphasis was on Pali, Sanskrit and Classical Sinhala and the medium of instruction would be English.

"What a remarkably innovative man this Principal is!" said Noble Son of Wisdom. "His College took nine years to materialize and it is hardly five years since it was founded. He is already planning to attract students from India, Burma, Siam and other Buddhist countries. The course he is developing for us is going to be the prototype for his international programme".

157

"We will be willing guinea pigs. Won't we?"

The street between the bookshops and the College grounds was being built up rapidly. A few lines of tenements had already come up. The Siamese monk's attention was drawn to several houses whose front door was covered with bamboo tats.

"Do you see what I see? At least half the houses in the street belong to Muslims". With his knowledge of Malay Peninsula, he showed how the bamboo tats and conspicuous shades of pink and green distinguished their homes.

"I must say that you are a very tolerant nation. A Muslim settlement around the foremost College of Buddhist leaning of the country!". It was not clear to me whether he was critical or appreciative.

V

It was on our way back laden with books that I told Noble Son of Wisdom of my hunch that the monk who mistook me for somebody like me could be referring to my long-lost Little Father.

"That would be wonderful if we can find him," he responded. "Why didn't you talk to him again?"

"I tried. But the monk who spoke to me was gone by the time I paid my courtesy call on the Principal. He was only an overnight visitor. Nobody could give me any further information about him."

"That's too bad. But not altogether hopeless. You have two strong clues: he was and most likely still is a monk and he was once a student here. Fortunately, this College had been in existence for only five years. Why not ask the Principal himself?"

Noble Son of Wisdom was delighted to play sleuth. His career in the service of his nation as a prince, culminating in his term as its Ambassador in the most powerful and prosperous country of the time, had given him a wide range of experience. For obvious reasons, it was easier for him to meet Venerable Sumangala and ask probing questions. I had to wait until I was sent for.

"You think that this Pure-Intellect could be your paternal uncle?" asked the venerable monk, who sent for me half an hour after Noble Son of Wisdom had seen him. "I think we can find him."

He spoke in English in recognition of the Siamese colleague's presence.

"Can I be allowed to postpone the commencement of studies until I found him?" I, too, spoke in English.

"We don't have an alternative? Do we? I can't start working with our Siamese friend until you are also there," he said.

It was explicit permission for both of us to play detective together. I thanked him for his understanding.

"Why don't you commence your investigation now?" he asked us. We were confused and looked at each other. With a gentle laugh, Venerable Sumangala added,

"Won't you like to find out what I might know on this Pure-Intellect".

Voluntarily, he told us what he recalled.

"I remember this young monk. He must have been in his late twenties. He was odd. He gave the impression of being excited or even agitated. He did not use the name of his village nor would he give us any information about his family or native village. We thought that he could be a fugitive. But he looked decent, well-behaved, respectful and helpful. He came on his own to register and I would not accept any young monk without the explicit permission of his preceptor or teacher. For several weeks he stalled saying that he had written to the teacher who ordained him. When nothing happened, I sent him back to come with the teacher. That's the last time I saw him. He never came back. But that was not unusual. More than half the students who registered at the beginning dropped out for a variety of reasons. Not everyone was ready for my concept of learning. Our traditional monastic education is for the tough and the persevering, you know.".

Our hopes were dashed. All we learnt was that an evasive monk named Pure-Intellect had been in Colombo five years ago.

We went to each teacher. They had no new information to give us. We were leaving the cell of the last teacher when a youngish monk approached us,

"You are inquiring about Pure-Intellect, aren't you? Any relation of yours? As far as I recall, he looked exactly like you. The same golden complexion. The same smile. He slept with me in my cell and offered to teach me English".

He took us to his cell and pulled out an old notebook.

"He wrote some sentences for me to memorize. Do you know his hand-writing?"

There was no doubt that we were on the correct track. The monk confirmed with a further piece of information.

"I think I remember something he told me about a scar on his shoulder. Somebody had beaten him because he helped a Buddhist monk who was building a new temple. Something to do with children of a missionary school transporting tiles and his protesting on the punishment meted out to them by a padre."

My excitement knew no bounds. This exercise was very different from that the family had gone through with all kinds of occult practices. We were receiving solid evidence.

"Did he ever tell you who his teacher was? Did he write to the teacher and wait for a reply? Now think carefully and try to recall anything that can connect him with someone you know." Noble Son of Wisdom framed the questions and the request and I translated them to the monk whose name we had by now learnt to be God-Protected.

God-Protected thought for a while.

"I don't think that he wrote to his teacher for permission. He went to all the classes for about two or three weeks. What he told me was that he was not sure whether any formal education was needed for him to continue the work he was doing. He was not happy with the programme of studies or the methods of teaching. He thought that the methods were as archaic as the contents. He wanted action and knowledge that would sustain action. He wanted to return to his work."

"Did he tell you what kind of work he did?"

"Not precisely. It had something to do with providing modern schooling to children in villages. He was vehement in his criticism of how education was abused for sectarian purposes by some of the Christian missionaries. Students used to draw him into controversies just to hear him berating all and sundry for every national ill. He was an ardent nationalist. He wanted to be an active agitator and not a passive scholar."

All this was encouraging information. But it left us with no new clue to pursue. It was the idea of Noble Son of Wisdom that we should go back to Venerable Sumangala.

"That's a bit of useful information," the venerable monk said. "To my knowledge there are two monks who are actively engaged in setting up Buddhist schools. Let us start with the one nearer to Colombo. Why don't you go to Mine Estate and meet Venerable Golden Lustre? He has been opening two or three schools every year. If he doesn't know anything about your uncle, you must go to Orange Island and meet Pleasant-Gem-Tissa."

We travelled south by train about twenty miles and took a cart to the new school at Mine Estate. It was a flourishing school and we wanted to know how it came to be established. Every bit of information tallied with what White Padre told us when he reported the disappearance of Little Father. It was here that the dispute on the transport of tiles had taken place. It was here that Little Father was mercilessly beaten.

We met Venerable Golden Lustre who gave us an additional piece of information.

"Your uncle was a very reasonable man. He talked of the importance of friendly interaction with missionaries. He thought that the missionaries would be the conduit through which we could have access to modern science and Western culture. He held a missionary friend of his in the highest esteem and most unrealistically thought that all foreign missionaries were equally enlightened and tolerant. The night he and a pupil of mine were nearly beaten to death, he swore that he would devote his whole life to save the Buddhist way of life in this country. But he had a serious problem. His family and specially a young nephew were beneficiaries of the missionary in his village. He wanted

161

to safeguard their interests. So he wanted to be totally incognito for the sake of his family."

"I am that nephew. We were very close. It was his idea that I should have a modern Western education."

I gave Noble Son of Wisdom a gist of what Golden Lustre said.

"Venerable Sir, so, you made him a monk? That's a perfect disguise?"

"No," replied Golden Lustre. "I sent him to Orange Island. I was only setting up village schools. Venerable Pleasant-Gem-Tissa had a wider and more varied programme in hand and he was short of dedicated manpower."

How perspicacious Venerable Sumangala was. He knew exactly where we should go. Back to the rail head and fifteen miles to the south along the beach in a train. I had been too preoccupied with the quest for Little Father that I had hardly taken note of the beautiful seascape through which we passed. Now that success appeared to be round the corner, both of us relaxed.

We enjoyed the evening breeze which was most welcome. The train steamed through an unending plantation of coconuts. What contortions the gracefully slender trunks of the coconut palms assumed as the lush crowns scrambled for sunlight! As ballerinas reaching up to heavens on their toes, they opened out their golden tender leaves to the cloudeless blue sky over the equally blue ocean.

Every now and then we saw a long line of fishermen dragging their fish-laden nets to shore. Even from the moving train, we could sense the excitement among the people on the beach as each net was drawn in.

The ebullient Noble Son of Wisdom picked up the rhythm of the fishermen's work song and repeated it with the excitement of a child, '*Odi helei helai laam*'. The day ended with a gorgeous sunset which left the western sky effulgent in ochre-red for minutes after the sun has dipped into the ocean.

The railway terminated at Black Ford. Overnight stay at the station was made a bit comfortable by a kindly railway employee who found us two camp beds. We slept in the Station Master's office between the two tablet machines which rang as every departing train had to be issued a metal tablet guaranteeing that the line was clear up to the next station. The rest of the journey of a little over thirty miles had to be done by stage coach. The same scenery of lush, waving coconut palms. The same activity on the beach. Refreshing water of the golden coconut at regular intervals. A sumptuous, if hot, lunch at a rest house. We reached Orange Island at dusk.

It was easy to identify the temple. Its white washed archways were visible from the coach station. We climbed the hundred steps and was received by a monk of unmistakable charisma in his early fifties.

"A crow told me to expect visitors and I was looking out to see if the state coach brought in any," he said with a pleasant laugh. We were welcomed with affection. A torch of coconut husk dipped in black oil shed an orangish light on us and extended our long shadows on the well-swept courtyard. In the faint light, he observed us and turning to Noble Son of Wisdom asked in halting English,

"You from Burma, Siam, Malaya?"

"Venerable Sir, You are very correct. I am from that region. We know Venerable Pure-Intellect. We came to see him," the cautious diplomat in robes replied.

"Everyone comes here to see him!" the other said in feigned disappointment. "He must be a very important person."

Again, he laughed. He gave us directions to the cell of Pure-Intellect and resumed a slow meditative walk in the courtyard.

We found the cell quite easily. There was no need to knock as the door was open. But, as custom demanded, I cleared my throat and coughed softly. The crouching figure poring over a document in the mellow light of a coconut oil lamp straightened itself and turned to face us. We were in the dark and he had no way of recognizing us.

"Please come in. What may I do for you?" he asked.

If there was still a slight shred of doubt about the identity of Pure-Intellect, that unmistakable voice removed it. I knelt on the floor, touched his feet and, with tears that I could not withhold, said,

"Little Father, I am Tiny One, your nephew".

If he was in any way moved emotionally as I was he did not show it.

"Tiny One, you are a monk! What happened?" He was surprised.

By now our eyes had got used to the dim light. The silhouette of Noble Son of Wisdom at the threshold reminded me that I should do the honours before starting a conversation with Little Father.

"Venerable Noble Son of Wisdom of Siam is here with me. I would like you to meet him. Without his help I could not have found you."

The Siamese monk stepped into the room, saying,

163

"That you know, my friend, is an exaggeration. I am nevertheless delighted that we found you, Venerable Pure-Intellect. I think the time for the two of you to meet was pre-ordained."

As expected, Little Father replied in English.

"Thank you very much, Venerable Sir. Maybe, your seniority demands that I should venerate you."

He was about to go on his knees and worship Noble Son of Wisdom, whom it was easy to mistake for a venerable elder.

"No, Sir. It has to be the other way about. I haven't passed even a single rainy season as a monk. I am even an hour junior to this brat!".

With salutations out of the way, we sat on his tiny bed.

"I have a lot to explain. I do not know how much you already know. You must have had enough clues to find me right here".

Noble Son of Wisdom said,

"As I did the brain work in our new career as private detectives, let me tell you the clues on which we worked. Then you can tell us the rest. All right?"

"Yes, indeed," my uncle replied.

"You left your village with White Father. You accepted a job in the Christian Mission. You were sent to Mine Estate to do some ground research. You fell out with the missionary running the school there. It had something to do with punishments meted out to children who transported tile to a new Buddhist temple. You were beaten by some unknown people in the night. You left Mine Estate and no one knew your whereabouts. All this was known within weeks of the happening. White Padre had reported these to your family."

"He did. He was always so precise".

"You had joined the Learning-Awakening College at Palace Hill in Colombo when it was opened five years ago. You were there for only a couple of weeks. You left with your room mate, God-Protected, a sample of your handwriting in both Sinhala and English. You also told him that you were not interested in any kind of traditional formal monastic education. You left to carry on your work, which he understood to be setting up modern schools for Buddhist children".

"How fascinating! All this while, I thought I have covered my trail," interjected Little Father.

"It's not that easy, my friend, when your beautiful island-home is blessed with such eminent scholars like Venerable Sumangala. It was he who knew exactly where we should go in search of you. We started with Mine Estate. Venerable Golden Lustre was most helpful. He sent us here".

Little Father looked amused as a child caught in a game of hide and seek.

"There's nothing for me to add than to say why I was forced to be so secretive," he said. "My mentor, friend, guide and philosopher during my formative years was that wonderful missionary from Kent, England, Reverend Thomas Blake. His wife played a similar role. He convinced me that Christianity as he preached and practised could make a big difference to the evolution of my country as a modern nation. I assumed that the missionaries would in due course introduce science and technology and enable us to benefit from their rich culture. I learnt so much about Western literature, music and philosophy from the Blakes. I thought every missionary was a Blake. They are all well educated and cultured people. When they went to poverty-ridden villages, chose the most disadvantaged families for assistance and in every possible way uplifted them economically and socially, I went with them. I was thrilled with the positive change they made in the life of these people. If the price was that they had to be baptized Christians, there was no harm, I thought. In any case, these people were not being cared for by our Buddhist Sangha. I blamed the Sangha for not being as active, dedicated and socially conscious as the Blakes were. I had often thought of embracing Christianity. So powerful was the spiritual message which they conveyed to me by their living testimony".

"I agree with you a hundred per cent," I added. "You know the Blakes died of consumption a little over two years ago? Both of them a week apart at the Sanatorium in Toddy-Village.".

He buried his face in his hands. Visibly he grieved for them. I should have known better and not been so blunt. With the discipline of a monk, however, he recovered soon and continued.

"What prevented me from going that far was the family. Our family had produced a number of eminent monks whose standing in the ecclesiastical life of the region was very high. I could not dishonour them. I thought the least I could do for the Blakes was to do as they advised. Accordingly, I agreed to be an employee of the Mission.

"I worked very hard. I produced good results. The Mission was happy that my analysis of problems in the field could smoothen their activities. For them, what I did was trouble-shooting. I was happy that I ensured the most deserving to benefit from the work of the Mission. They thought I could solve the problem in Mine Estate. Perhaps, I could have if the missionary in charge was not so stubborn and short-sighted."

"Do you think that the missionary had you beaten?" I asked him.

"To be fair and frank, I don't know. One of the assailants was the sexton of the church. A workman in the temple had hit him with a crowbar and he was very badly injured. I had a feeling that I would be framed as the assailant. I don't know why I felt so. I thought the best thing was to disappear. For many days I was a fugitive. I decided to become a monk only after the dust settled down and the Mission showed good sense in removing the missionary. During long hours of loneliness in various places arranged by Venerable Golden Lustre, I reflected on the incident at Mine Estate. That's how I made up my mind to dedicate myself to the revival of Buddhism and Buddhist way of life through the education of children".

I was keen to find out why he kept the family in the dark. A little post card was all that was needed. How much his parents suffered. What agony, anxiety and grief I had gone through! I was about to chide him for his insensitivity, when we were disturbed.

"Pure-Intellect, what are you doing for your visitors?" asked a voice from the darkness outside.

It was the same monk who received us on arrival. He entered the room with an acolyte carrying two cups of tea.

"They can use the rooms next to you. Dasa will have them cleaned and arranged for them".

"I am sorry, Venerable Sir. I hadn't thought of it myself. I am so intrigued how my nephew found me," said Little Father.

We stood up in deference to the senior monk and followed Little Father in paying our respects to him as monastic etiquette demanded. Little Father's seat was offered to him and we stood on a side. Introductions followed. Noble Son of Wisdom and I were elated that the monk we had already met was none other than Venerable Pleasant-Gem-Tissa, the doyen of monks engaged in a campaign to counter Christianity with Buddhist education. How wonderful that all our senior scholar-monks were so child-like and affable! Noble Son of Wisdom had an explanation:

"They are at peace with themselves and the world".

It was certainly the case with Venerable Pleasant-Gem-Tissa.

Tea was served to us and the senior monk, who disregarded the excuses offered by Little Father, turned to Noble Son of Wisdom.

"Last week, I had letter from chamberlain of King of Siam. King wants me to be on the look out for a prince coming here to become monk. If you know, I like to know who he is and where he can be?" Though somewhat halting, he communicated well in English.

166

"Yes, Venerable Sir. I know him very well. In fact, better than anybody else. He is right here now". With this he pointed to himself.

Venerable Pleasant-Gem-Tissa led Noble Son of Wisdom out of the room. Apparently they had some serious business to talk over. Little Father was relieved that we could let our non-existent hair down and talk more intimately. He knew that I was about to scold him for the pain he had given the family.

"Tiny One, all this while I thought I was doing it for you. Perhaps, I was correct. I wanted you to get all the help you could from the Blakes. Right from the time you came to his school, Reverend Blake had the idea of sending you to a high school in Kandy to get a good modern Western education in English. We even felt - and that was the conviction of Mrs. Blake - that you would win a scholarship to Calcutta for higher education. If the Mission knew what I was engaged in, you could have been penalized. In their eyes, my campaign for Buddhist education in areas where missionaries were influential was an act of hostility".

"In a way, you are right, Little Father. The Blakes did a lot for our family. Both Aunties Jasmine and Flower have a good life because of their kindness. In fact, they felt that they were responsible for what happened to you and did more than what they would have ordinarily done to help us. In their minds, it was some form of compensation. They even had trouble from the Mission for being more partial to us than to baptized Christian converts in the village".

We talked late into the night - long after Noble Son of Wisdom returned from his conversation with the scholar-monk and retired to his room next door. I gave Little Father a resume of the events that had taken place in Sangha-Gem-Field since his departure. It was not like those days when our age, relationship and experience created an insurmountable obstacle. He was my *Guru*, the Master, and I was his *Chela*, the obedient disciple. Now we talked like old friends.

I told him about my romance and its ill-fated denouement. "First round I get knocked down and I end up as a monk. The second time my discomfiture is repeated, I am banished to Colombo" was how I summarized my brief encounter with Slim-Jewel.

He asked me a hundred and one questions. The number of times the oil lamp had to be refilled indicated that we could have been engrossed in our review of the lost eight years well past midnight.

"Tomorrow I will write a long letter to Chief Monk asking him to read it to the family. I hope they will understand that I put them through so much anxiety all because I loved you".

167

Little Father filled the lamp again.

"Aren't you planning to sleep?" I asked.

"Not yet. I have a letter to translate".

Then only did I realize that we had interrupted some important work he was engaged in.

"Is it something that can wait till tomorrow morning?"

"No. Venerable Pleasant-Gem-Tissa and I plan to leave for Galle early in the morning and have this letter printed for distribution on the next fullmoon day. It's very important to what we are doing".

I was about to excuse myself when an idea flashed in his mind.

"Tiny One, wait a minute. From what you have said and from the way you speak, there's no doubt that your English is better than that of any one we can find in the neighbourhood. Why don't you sit up with me and finish this translation?"

I agreed. What unfolded was beyond imagination.

VI

All I knew of the Great Debate at Panadura of 26 - 27 August 1873 was the popular account I read in the ballad which I bought in multiple copies in Kandy. I remembered the witty and humorous interventions attributed to the hero of the day, Venerable Gunananda of Scribe's Garden in Bonito Plain. The documents which Little Father had with him showed that the encounter between the Buddhists and the Christians on this occasion was a very serious one.

Both parties were represented by scholarly heavy-weights. Reverend David Silva was a reputed scholar of Oriental languages. Practically every renowned scholar-monk of the Island was present to assist the silver tongue of Scribe's Garden, Venerable Gunananda. They discussed very important and serious issues like God, soul, causality. rebirth or reincarnation, eternal life, moral responsibility. Each party knew the literature of the opponent. In this matter, of course, the Buddhists were at an advantage as they had access to biblical criticism of such Western writers and speakers as Thomas Paine, Bishop John Colenso and Robert Green Ingersoll.

A very special person happened to visit Sri Lanka at the time of the Debate. He was Dr. J. M. Peebles, M.D., M.A., Ph.D. He described himself as "author, lecturer, USA Ex-Consul, Fellow of the Geographical Society, Washington D. C., Member of the Victoria Institute of London, Vice-President of Psycho-Therapeutic Society of London, Fellow of the Academy of Sciences, New Orleans, USA, Corresponding Member of the Oriental Society, Calcutta, India etc." In eight articles published in the oldest English newspaper of the island, The Times, he had given a gist of the interventions on each side as well as his own general impressions. These articles had been published in USA in book form under the title "*The Great Debate: Buddhism and Christianity Face to Face*". With the growing interest in Eastern religions in the New World, it reached a wide readership.

Among those who read it was a Colonel of the American Civil War, Henry Steel Olcott of Orange, New Jersey. In 1875 he along with a spiritualist of Russian origin, named Madame Helena Petrovna Blavatsky, had founded the Theosophical Society and was engaged in exploring alternatives to Christianity as a spiritual base for modern life. He was already familiar with the Hindu reform movement in India and established contact with its leading lights such as Dayananda Sarasvati of Arya Samaj.

It was a letter from Olcott to Pleasant-Gem-Tissa and the latter's reply to it of 15 June 1878 that Little Father was translating into Sinhala to be published in brochure form.

"You see, Tiny One, our people are mesmerized by whatever is said by a foreigner, specially a white foreigner. So our strategy is to use their writings in every possible way. We have already published the works of Bishop John Colenso. I refer a lot to Thomas Paine and Ingersoll in my speeches. Olcott is more vituperative than any of them. He apparently has a big grievance against the Christian clergy or else he is convinced that no religion which demands submission to any dogma is suitable for modern times."

He held Olcott's letter in his hand and waving it added,

"Missionaries will have a tough time once this reaches the people."

Little Father had translated the letter and I read it carefully comparing sentence by sentence with the original. It was fairly well done although I could make a number of suggestions to improve it.

Two more hours and another bottle of coconut oil burnt in the lamp, we had the texts ready for the printer.

"Could you take us to Galle with you?" I sked.

"I will ask Venerable Pleasant-Gem-Tissa."

Little Father had made the request on behalf of both Noble Son of Wisdom and me. The scholar-monk was delighted to take us with him specially as he was due to address a meeting on the way back in the afternoon. He wanted both of us "to say a few words". He could not have thought of anyone more willing and enthusiastic.

Noble Son of Wisdom was in high spirits. I had not met him since his meeting with the scholar-monk. Apparently, the request of the King of Siam was innocuous and was in no way threatening to him. I could also think of several other possibilities. I had come to know him well since our joint ordination. He was a consummate prankster. Apparently, he had got around the senior monk and was basking in the glory of another innocent conquest.

He had another reason to be very happy. Our double-bullock buggy cart was passing through clumps of sweet-smelling cinnamon and vast coconut groves. Coconut palms and the sea made him nostalgic for Southern Siam with which he was most familiar. It brought him memories of Little Ceylon and the Phuket Beach, the favourite haunts of his family when he was a kid and when his children were kids. He chattered incessantly, recalling incidents in his life or telling fascinating stories of monkeys trained to pluck coconuts and midnight hikes to dig up turtle eggs. Even the Dutch ramparts of Galle evoked memories of smaller but equally impressive fortresses he had seen in the Malay

Peninsula. He was still speaking of the wonders of a place called Malacca when we reached the printer to whom Little Father's "copy" was to be delivered.

While Pleasant-Gem-Tissa and Little Father attended to their business we had a tour of our own on the well-preserved, grass-carpeted ramparts of the huge Dutch fortification overlooking the large natural harbour of Galle. The sea, the gleaming white lighthouse and the quaint Dutch buildings with high roofs, large verandahs, ornamental timber railings and balustrades gave a surfeit of sensory perceptions of an order never experienced in the mountains of my native village. We were enthralled by the wooded promontory on the other side of the harbour. A foreman of a gang of coolies loading graphite into a barge took time off to relate an episode from the great Indian epic, the Ramayana.

"When Rama was wounded in battle in Lanka, a rare medicinal herb had to be brought from the Himalayas" he narrated. "Hanuman the monkey was sent there to bring it. Once in the Himalayas he forgot which herb to bring. Of course, he solved the problem by bringing the entire hill where it was supposed to be found. This is that hill. It is full of medicinal herbs even today."

"That's a lovely story" commented Noble Son of Wisdom.

The sun-kissed water of the deepest turquoise hue along the ramparts was so inviting. But we had not come with the wherewithal for a dip in the sea. That, of course, did not discourage the Siamese adventurer. Within minutes he found a little shop in the Fort where he could buy two lengths of yellow cloth, which served us amply as our bathing costumes. This was my first experience with the sea. As compared to the Great Sand River at Sangha-Gem-Field, the sea at this particular point was calm and docile.

"I must take you to a really rough spot one of these days. Let the monsoon come," teased my Siamese friend of long and varied experience.

We were still sporting in the sea when the elder scholar-monk and Little Father called us from the top of the ramparts. Noble Son of Wisdom offered to buy lengths of cloth for them to join us. The elder monk would not hear of it.

"This is not the sea. This water-hole is nothing but a kitchen tub - only a little bigger. You must bathe in the open sea riding on the crest of waves and feel what is to be rolled over and over again."

That unravelled another facet of this child-like scholar who really had not overlooked little things that gave some innocent pleasure in life.

The dip in the sea was a fitting prelude to the sumptuous lunch that was offered to us by a devotee in China Garden. Our Siamese companion was pleasantly surprised to see so many people in this part of Galle who shared with him typical Mongolian traits like flat noses, high cheekbones and narrow eyes.

"All these people look like my cousins," he said.

"They could be. Many of their ancestors were Chinese sailors and traders who settled down here over the centuries when the Maritime Silk Route from China to Europe had this island as the mid-way emporium" Pleasant-Gem-Tissa explained.

"You mean the Emporium Mediatrix of Cosmas Indicopleustes was Sri Lanka?" exclaimed Noble Son of Wisdom.

"Precisely though this is not the haven that he refers to."

The city of Galle was contained within the Dutch Fort. Old Dutch houses, renovated and white-washed were occupied by a flourishing British population. To be any one but a white in the city looked strange and out of place. Four Buddhist monks in a bullock cart in this transplanted Western urbia constituted the highest incongruity.

"I must call on the new Gentleman Cadet. He wrote me a letter on arrival, " said the elder monk. We found him in the Provincial Office not too far from the lighthouse.

"What an honour! What a pleasure!" the smart young man of twenty years in khaki shorts and white short-sleeved shirt kept on repeating as he rearranged the chairs in the room. That he was fresh from England was evident. He was still pale-faced. We sat facing him across his file-laden table.

"I was fascinated to see two yellow-robed monks sauntering on the ramparts and for one thing I knew they were foreigners".

"That's true, Mr. Williams. This is a prince from Siam and he is here as a monk until his little quarrel with the king is settled. I have become his self-appointed guard. This young monk is a nephew of Pure-Intellect and this is his first experience with the sea and low country. Two of them could be close cousins of Robert Knox whose book, you said, you had read."

"How nice, Venerable Sir. As I wrote to you, my teacher Professor Rhys Davids asked me to convey his best wishes to you".

Stanley Williams had come with a Bachelor of Arts Degree from Manchester University and one of his subjects had been Pali. He looked forward to further study though his immediate interest was in passing the efficiency bar examinations. He had to find a Pandit to coach him.

172

Orange Island within six miles from Galle would be the most convenient.

"I'll take you over myself. When I am not free, Pure-Intellect could help you".

"Thank you very much, Venerable Sir. I should have paid a visit to you and made this request in person with due respect."

"You have done better, Mr. Williams. You came all the way over oceans to this country to serve us. It's now our turn to see that you know us well enough to understand not only our needs but our aspirations".

"What would you say your aspirations are, Venerable Sir?"

"Mr. Williams, we are a proud nation with an ancient culture and a long recorded history. We have a way of life we cherish. We have a religion that we hold dear to us. We have a vast literature in at least three languages. We still read books written seven to eight centuries ago. But we are not a nation of diehard conservatives. From our Northern neighbour we borrowed thousands of Tamil words. From the Portuguese and the Dutch we did likewise. We accepted Islam, Roman Catholicism and the Dutch Reformed Church to enrich our spiritual heritage of Buddhism and Hinduism. We persecuted none. On the contrary, we gave refuge to Muslims when Christians persecuted them and to Catholics whom fellow Christians were persecuting. What could, Mr. Williams, the aspirations of such a nation be? Would it not be to have the freedom and power of self-determination to safeguard their lifestyle, culture and ideals of tolerance? Our aspiration is for a measure of Self-rule immediately and full independence eventually."

Though it sounded like a prepared speech, his halting delivery and frequent pauses in search of the correct word underscored that he spoke from his heart. He believed that the country deserved a better destiny.

"Venerable Sir, I know enough of Buddhism and what your country had done not merely to preserve it in its pristine glory but also to propagate it in Southeast Asia. I cannot agree with you more when you speak of your nation's greatness in many domains. But Self-rule and Independence are matters to which a whole lot of different criteria apply."

"I know, Mr. Williams. But whose criteria? Why had the American colonies to fight for their freedom a hundred years ago? Because in the eyes of your ancestors they did not meet the criteria. These same criteria. But what's the situation today? Isn't that a flourishing country - a democracy with full potential for world leadership? Who would now say that they were not ready for Self-rule or Independence?"

"You make a lot of sense, Venerable Sir. I look forward to a stimulating dialogue when I begin my studies with you ...."

173

"Starting with next Saturday. Say three-thirty in the afternoon".

Noble Son of Wisdom was astonished by Pleasant-Gem-Tissa's forthright frankness. Back in the cart he congratulated the scholar-monk.

"I wouldn't have ever believed that you were an undaunted freedom fighter".

"Aren't we all?" was the laconic reply of Pleasant-Gem-Tissa.

A large crowd had gathered under coconut palms near the estuary of Gin River. Seats for us were arranged on a dais made of coconut stumps and timber board. It was beautifully decorated with exquisite motifs of creamy coloured tender leaves of the coconut. The coconut fronds waving in the wafting breeze cast their moving shadows on the crowd. The setting sun in the crimson sky provided the most attractive backdrop. The towering scholar-monk stood up to address the meeting and his hundred-foot shadow danced on the heads of the vast audience in front of him.

Those were days without mechanical aids to public speaking. After every sentence he paused so that the strategically placed "amplifiers" repeated in series his statements to the surging crowd. It was comical at times. The more ardent "amplifiers" would add their own histrionics in tone and gesture.

What a powerful orator he was in Sinhala! His mastery over its idiom and vocabulary was unparalleled. He had the audience on the palm of his hand. He could sway it the way he wanted. His message was an illustrated elaboration of what he told Stanley Williams. In addition was a strong denunciation of the objectives, contents and methods of education in missionary schools. In all he said, he was logical, moderate and factually correct. He made no wild accusations. He attacked nobody.

"What our country needs," he shouted, "are first schools, second schools and third schools. Not just schools, my friends. But schools where our children learn to be proud of their national heritage and trained for national service. The missionaries won't give us those schools. The government won't give us those schools. We - we alone - must build them with our bare hands. Our own bare hands!"

He held out his outstretched hands to the crowd. The applause was thunderous.

Noble Son of Wisdom rose to the occasion and spoke of the glory of independence.

"My country Siam has been spared the humiliation of foreign domination. You know what it has done to us, to our people? We are proud of our heritage, our culture, our language and our religion. We are ready to die to protect our nation's freedom. We may make mistakes. But they are our mistakes".

He turned to some children close to the dais, bent forward and asked them,

"If some outsiders come into your home and say that they would cook for you a better meal than your mother and try to take her place in the home and ask you to do things in their way, what would you tell them?"

A bright young lad shouted back,

"Even with bad cooking, we want our mother to do things for us."

"That applies to one's country too. However good and benevolent a foreign power is, there is something obnoxious and demeaning to be a subject nation".

He made a very strong case in favour of national independence and all the time he spoke of his own country. But as he waxed eloquent, he was carried away. He was making statements which could with little effort be interpreted as seditious. As the translator of his speech into Sinhala, I felt apprehensive. I expected a posse of policemen to appear at any moment to take both of us into custody. I was relieved when his stirring speech ended without any incident.

When my turn came, I was in no mood to speak. But the presiding monk insisted that I say my few words. I made a few innocuous remarks. It was a plop. Fortunately, my lacklustre performance was written off as caused by fatigue.

Little Father wound up the meeting. He sounded in diction and content a perfect amalgam of Chief Monk and White Padre. He spoke of concrete action, of bricks and mortar, desks and benches and, above all, teachers with adequate professional training.

"We need new text-books and manuals and we are writing them. We need teacher trainers and we are appealing to the nationalist leadership of India to help us. We need funds to put up buildings, pay salaries to teachers and provide learning materials and books. We solicit all of you to give whatever you can afford, one cent or one handful of rice".

Volunteers spread out into the crowd to collect whatever the people were willing to give. The day ended with a little less than five hundred rupees added to the education fund. A few stepped forward to pledge larger donations mainly in kind.

"Not bad at all. Not bad at all," repeated a smiling Pleasant-Gem-Tissa. "Three more meetings like this and we'll have another school".

For me it was a mission accomplished. I had found Little Father. After all these years of worry and anxiety, I should have been elated. But I was not. Something was not all right within me.

Was it the explanation that he gave for his long silence - a silence that had brought untold misery to all members of the family? It was true that his discretion did help me. Did that not transfer the responsibly to me? Vicariously I had been the cause of everyone's suffering. I was sure that Little Father was in no way happy to have remained incognito. How much had he himself missed in life? Eight years in self-imposed exile! A fugitive! All because he loved me!

He had gone through much deprivation to ensure that I had a good education and perhaps a career in the Government with the indispensable help of the missionaries. I could not understand how he could be so contradictory. He made such a tremendous sacrifice to secure for me the benefits of the very system he now denounced and would readily dismantle. What made my case different? Was it the faith he had in the saintly qualities of the Blakes? Or was it sheer hypocrisy?

These were my thoughts as we rode in silence back to Orange Island. It had been a long and tiring day for all of us. Little Father and I were exhausted because we hardly had a wink of sleep the previous night. We returned to a crowded temple. The news had spread that a nephew of Venerable Pure-Intellect had come in search of him with a Siamese princely monk. The latter was once again the attraction.

Pleasant-Gem-Tissa got out of the cart, greeted some of the people who were close to him at the foot of steps and asked everyone to go quietly to the preaching hall. A young monk was instructed to arrange a meeting to welcome the two guests and to honour the Siamese princely monk on his speech on the value and indispensability of national independence. I could not help admiring a man who saw an opportunity in every incident to further his cause.

After a wash and a hot cup of plain tea with a plenty of sugar, the scholar monk led Little Father, Noble Son of Wisdom and me to the rostrum of the preaching hall. The deferential silence of the audience gave no indication of who among us caused the most curiosity.

It could have been an orderly meeting - a miniature of the evening's meeting. But that was not to be. We had unexpected visitors.

The Inspector of Police in blue turtle-neck tunic with brass buttons, long trousers and bowler hat could have been a young Englishman or a

176

Dutch Burgher, that is, a descendant of the Dutch who made Sri Lanka their home. The two barefooted constables in khaki shirt and shorts with woolen putties wrapped from knee to ankle and felt hat were unmistakably Malay.

"We have a warrant to arrest Pure-Wisdom of Bo-tree Plain on a charge of murder," the inspector announced.

I stepped forward to be identified. Pleasant-Gem-Tissa protested and demanded that the warrant be read to him. The officer was rude and angry. In a moment of uncontrolled fury, he committed the unpardonable crime of pushing the venerable monk aside. I held him to prevent him staggering to the floor. There was pandemonium. The crowd rose in unison and quietly circled the three policemen. Neither the uniform nor the baton evoked any fear in this particular crowd. What the surging mass did to them, we could not see. It moved around the three men as surreptitiously as a giant python would grab its prey. We were led out of the hall.

"We have had a very successful meeting, Pure-Wisdom," said Pleasant-Gem-Tissa. "This kind of aftermaths are not very rare. I am used to some harassment from our misguided lower rungs. But what is this charge of murder against you?"

"I have no idea whatsoever. I left Sangha-Gem-Field five days ago. I spent two nights in Palace Hill, Colombo and one night at Black Ford in the railway station and the last night here. Noble Son of Wisdom had been always with me", I replied.

"Let's write a letter to the Police Chief in Galle. I'll have it delivered tonight itself if possible. You take my buggy cart to Black Ford, board a train and proceed to Kandy as soon as possible. First thing in Kandy, see your friend the Government Agent and explain to him that I sent you to avoid a civil disturbance here".

How precise he was. He had planned everything in a jiffy.

"What happens here? I hope the police officers do not get hurt. That could lead us to further trouble," intervened Noble Son of Wisdom who had remained silent all this while.

"No, my friend. Not in this temple. Not by these people. All we show them by our non-violent response to their anger and rudeness is that a proud nation cannot be cowed down by silly-looking fancy dresses or two foot clubs. I'll rescue them in due course and give them some tea and sweets".

The grin on the face of Noble Son of Wisdom was inscrutable.

To cut a long story short, the three of us did exactly what we were asked to do. A steady trot brought us to Black Ford in time for the first train in the morning which enabled us to get the afternoon train to Kandy. We hired a horse carriage at the station and were at Royal Spout around nine in the night.

"How did you come? Don't you know what has happened?" asked Uncle Victor.

"I was about to be arrested for murder. Why? What has happened?"

In deference to the presence of Noble Son of Wisdom, we spoke in English. Aunt Flower joined us. She must have been crying for a long time. She was so distraught that she could not recognize her long-lost brother. Tacitly, we came to the conclusion that the celebration of the long-awaited family reunion had to be postponed to a better time.

It was a sad story that was unfolded. Three days ago, my middle brother's body was found on the bank of the river. It had been there for a couple of days. The village headman had reported to the Police and an investigation was conducted. My sudden departure from Sangha-Gem-Field was construed as evidence of knowledge or involvement. Chief Monk knew where I was and given my address in Palace Hill. The fact that I had left Palace Hill hurriedly made the Police even more suspicious. When I was not in Mine Estate, the suspicion had developed into full-fledged conviction that I was a fugitive. My swift disappearance from Orange Island was not going to make things easy.

"What evidence do they have? Why do they think that I have something to do with it?" I asked Uncle Victor.

"Nothing much as far as we know. Only a statement by Slim-Jewel to the effect that you saw her alone a few weeks back, that you were very angry for what your brother had done to her and that you said he should be taught a good lesson. Your mother, in all innocence, had said that you were in love with Slim-Jewel and that you became a monk as a result of your disappointment. The Police only wanted a statement from you. They thought initially that you could provide them some clues to work on. But now things are different."

Uncle Victor also thought that surrendering to the Government Agent would be a good idea. With his influence in the Provincial Office, redoubled by the personal intervention of Reverend Saunders whom I saw at dawn at the school, the meeting was arranged for early afternoon with enough time for me to be taken to the magistrate for necessary formalities. We met in the same room in the old palace. The Police Chief was present with the papers.

"Bongyi, what's this I hear of you? In the first place, you are criss-crossing the country with the speed your books ascribe to flying saints!

178

As if that's not enough, you are hobnobbing with all the heavy weights in the Sangha!"

I concealed nothing. From the day Slim-Jewel visited Kandy to the time I appeared before him, I gave a brief account of what I had done or said. I stressed on the amazing encounter with the monk who mistook me for my uncle and how with the blessings of Venerable Sumangala I set out in search of Little Father. The police officer took notes.

"Will your Siamese friend agree to give a corroborative statement?"

"He's outside and I could ask him."

"Maybe, we get a statement from your uncle as well," added the Chief of Police.

They both agreed and statements were recorded. After the police officer departed, Ernest Dickinson called all three of us together. From an imperious bureaucrat conducting a formal inquiry, he transformed himself to the friend he had shown he was. It was a great relief.

"I think the matter is solved. I am sorry for your family. Please convey to them and specially Chief Monk my condolences. Bongyi, present yourself to the magistrate and he will have the warrant cancelled."

He turned to Little Father.

"So you kept your family in the dark for so many years."

"I had to, Sir," Little Father replied. "My convictions and the actions in which I was involved would not have been to the best advantage of the family".

"You mean that your actions are outside the law, Bongyi?"

"Not at all, Sir. But law, as you know, is a relative concept".

"That's interesting. What makes you think so?"

Little Father outlined his experience with the missionary in Mine Estate and his near escape from death. He did not omit to praise the officer who could not be manipulated by the missionary.

"I am a free man because of your lofty ideals of British justice," he said in conclusion.

"I am glad you recognize it. Every morning I ask myself the question: What am I doing in this place? And I tell myself: 'Ernest, you are on a mission to help a great nation to regain its lost glory and return to its proud niche in history' ".

In a show of emotion which is hardly in conformity with our status as monks, all three of us spontaneously reached out for the right hand of the Government Agent to show our admiration and wish him strength.

179

VII

The next day all three of us went to Sangha-Gem-Field by the first stage coach of the morning. It stopped at every post office to deliver the mail. We were not expected. A telegram sent by Uncle Victor had not been delivered. None in the village had any idea of the dramatic events that we had gone through over the last few days. Chief Monk whose eye sight had been steadily deteriorating since the stroke could not recognize Little Father. Nor could any others in the temple. He had been long forgotten and, in some people's minds, given up for dead.

My parents and maternal grandparents had got word of his return as a monk. There was thus no element of surprise in their meeting. So was it when the relatives in Bo-tree Plain made their way to Sangha-Gem-Field toward evening. Of course, there was a great deal of rejoicing. Grandparents shed tears of joy on seeing their son after eight years. Aunt Jasmine started chirping like a bird. So many questions were asked almost simultaniously and so few could be answered. The joy which pervaded their reunion was shattered when reality dawned with the arrival of my eldest brother accompanied by his wife's parents and Slim-Jewel. A gloomy shadow was cast as we settled down to talk of the murder and its tragic implications to the family.

My encounter with the police in far off Orange Island and my overnight escape to Kandy evoked a momentary comic streak in a discussion replete with grief and dismay.

What little information the family had on the tragedy was exchanged. The body was found on our side of the river. He had several cut wounds inflicted with a curved pruning knife such as were used in coffee and tea plantations. The death was caused by a deep slit of the throat. He had been attacked from behind. It was not clear if more than one assailant was involved. His belt with the money pocket was missing and theft was not ruled out as a motive. But the police felt that the assailant could have been in a state of impassioned rage. The investigation was being carried out on the basis that the outcaste girl across the river could be in some way involved: *Cherchez la femme.*

"I am sorry that we could not welcome you under happier circumstances," Slim-Jewel's father told Little Father.

"What's important is that I am back in the family. What can I do to relieve the pain that all of you are going through?"

Noble Son of Wisdom had all this while been a passive spectator of a family grappling to comprehend and come to terms with a happy reunion with a long-lost member and a dastardly murder of another. I gave him a running commentary on what was being said. Suddenly he stopped me in mid-sentence.

"Pure, can we talk to Slim-Joy for a while?"

That was easily arranged.

"When did you last see Middle Banda?" began Noble son of Wisdom.

"The day before his body was discovered".

"At what time?"

"Around the time of the sun-set".

"Was he alone?"

"Yes".

"Were you alone?"

"There was no one else at home other than my baby".

"Did he tell you why he came?"

"Yes. He said he had trouble. He needed money".

"Did you give him any money?"

"Yes. I had fifty rupees hidden for an emergency. I gave it to him. I also gave him a pair of gold earrings which he had given me."

"Did he tell you what sort of trouble he was in?"

"No".

"Did you see anything unusual in the way he spoke or in the way he behaved?"

"He was uneasy and looking behind him all the time. He didn't want to enter the house. I asked him whether he was being chased by somebody because he gave me that impression".

"What were his last words?"

"He said something like 'See what happened to us all because of my foolishness. I can never forgive myself. Whatever happens to me, do please take the best care of our baby.' He touched the baby and stroked my cheek. Then he ran away into the darkness."

Noble Son of Wisdom sent Slim-Jewel away and turned to me.

"Pure, two things are clear. First, by no stretch of imagination can you be involved. Your brother was alive and was seen by Slim-Jewel precisely at the time we went to the Learning-Awakening College at Palace Hill. Second, your brother was in some trouble and what he wanted to get out of it was some money. One or more people who wanted money from him were on the lookout for him and he was apprehensive. Third, not only his money belt with at least fifty rupees but also a pair of gold earrings had been taken from him. Now add to it the nature of the injuries, one can surmise that his trouble had to be related to the girl in question. My guess is that either the husband of

181

that girl, if she was married, or a boy friend of some sort could be the prime suspect".

The news of Little Father's return had spread fast and relatives and friends came to see him. Among them was the Village Headman. Noble Son of Wisdom outlined his thinking on the crime and the petty official agreed with him.

"We have been going after the wrong people," he admitted. "I'll report to the Police and, maybe, they would want to talk to you".

When the visitors had left and we could return to the quiet privacy of our rooms, I asked Noble Son of Wisdom,

"Did you for a moment suspect that I could have been my brother's murderer?"

"What armour does a mortal man have to save himself when the overpowering passion for a woman makes him blind, ruthless and merciless?"

To say that I was shaken by his forthright question would have been a gross understatement.

Three days later Noble Son of Wisdom and I were back at Palace Hill. It had been a hectic week and I had not fully recovered from either the emotional drain or the physical fatigue. Venerable Sumangala listened attentively to our long account and our excuses.

"I am glad this week is behind you. You don't have to be detectives any longer. We commence your programme of studies from tomorrow".

Within days everything returned to normal. We had no distractions. Noble Son of Wisdom set his mind on learning Pali and he was relentless as a student - determined, systematic, curious, persevering and exceedingly modest. He would seek help from anyone whom he found handy. He was consequently very popular. To most of the students who were about the age of his eldest son he was an indispensable father figure. In this he was more successful than the learned scholar-monks on the staff whom he once described in affection as "men among children but children among men". What a fantastic influence he had on everyone in the College! When he offered to teach English and World Geography, the entire student body and the staff including Venerable Sumangala joined his class.

He continued to be my friend. To me he was a delightful combination of the affectionately inspiring mentor that was Little Father and compassionately serious shepard that was White Padre. Despite the gap in our ages, we developed between us a mutually rewarding relationship. Whenever we had a little time to spare, we walked

182

together, visited the new harbour where a relaxing boat-ride could be had for a few cents and discovered new and old curiosities in and around the Capital. At times, for fun we would try to converse in Pali especially when we were in a crowd.

In his new life of poverty and austerity, away from the cares and burdens of office and royal rank but deprived of the day-to-day joys of a family of a principal wife and a dozen concubines and many children, Noble Son of Wisdom was determined to make the best of a bad deal. But as months passed by, he saw purpose in his new status and visibly became less agitated and better settled in a life of study, meditation and social service. He was a great inspiration and role model to me.

I settled down to a daily routine. While others had a relaxing snooze after the mid-day meal, I attended to the correspondence of Venerable Sumangala. It was on a wide variety of subjects and ranged from abstruse scholarly and philosophical issues to secular matters in which the British administrators wished to have the opinion of an enlightened national leader of opinion. I marvelled at the diversity of his interests and the depth of his insights. The most rewarding experience to me was that he would accept more than two thirds of the draft replies I put up to him for approval.

I had also my own correspondence to deal with. The contacts I had made during the two years I reorganized the palmleaf manuscript library at Sangha-Gem-Field continued to be in touch with me. Although I could not be as thorough as I was on account of the distance, I was able to enlist the cooperation of two novices who had worked with me. They were good at identifying manuscripts and making fairly accurate copies on paper.

At Palace Hill, I had a further advantage. I also had access to several collections of palmleaf manuscripts which British officials had acquired either for their personal use or for despatch to the British Museum Library in London. They obliged me whenever I wanted to refer to them or copy them because I had helped them in identifying and cataloguing them. In addition, I had recourse to the expertise of several high-ranking scholar-monks in the premises. So, the foreign scholars who were in touch with me were pleased with what I could do for them. The most active among them, of course, was T. W. Rhys Davids who was planning to have the whole of the Buddhist Canon and the Commentaries in Pali published in Roman script and translated into English.

There were occasional respites in this otherwise relentless routine. On the day after the elaborate ceremonies which marked our first Rainy Season, spent strictly according to the Buddha's injunctions, Noble Son

183

of Wisdom took off for Kandy with the idea of proceeding to Sangha-Gem-Field.

"I want to find out how the investigation into your brother's murder had proceeded," he gave as the reason.

He did not return for ten days and Venerable Sumangala was quite annoyed that our classes in Pali were interrupted. But when he returned, I was grateful for his timely intervention which was providential.

The report of the Village Headman, based on the conclusions of the interrogation of Slim-Jewel by Noble Son of Wisdom, had been scoffed at by the Police. Their opinion was that an outcaste would never use violence against a person of a higher caste.

The Chief of Police had been surprised to find that the matter had been shelved at the level of a junior officer, whose conclusion was: "The outcastes don't kill with weapons. They use black magic".

With a little persuasion, Noble Son of Wisdom was able to have the two pawn brokers of the city interrogated on Slim-Jewel's earrings.

"At first they scoffed at my suggestion. It was pursued because they feared that I would go to the Government Agent. The Police were right. No one had brought a pair of gold earrings to them. But the second broker had a grievance. A number of illicit pawn-brokers had come into operation in the same street. Again, I insisted, they raid each of these shops. What booty they uncovered!"

The earrings were there. Slim-Jewel identified them and even gave their precise weight. Her sister corroborated with information on where they were bought. The jeweller remembered the purchaser.

The illicit pawn-broker had no records as he never expected them to be redeemed. One night in the police station with the threat of being booked as a suspect in a gruesome murder had a magic effect on his memory. The police worked with alacrity. The suspect was apprehended in his home across the river. The woman in question had gone to live with him. Enough evidence to incriminate him was uncovered: my brother's belt with the money pocket and, more importantly, the murder weapon.

"I wanted to be sure whether it was a crime of passion or premeditated" continued the proud detective in monastic robes. "You know what we found out. The police were correct about black magic. To punish your brother for having enticed this woman, this man and his friends had resorted to all kinds of black magic. But nothing had succeeded. We traced the mastermind behind the crime - an old man whose plan was that your brother should not be killed until every cent he could get by begging, borrowing or stealing had been collected".

184

The prince-ambassador-monk-detective was very pleased with his latest achievement. To my family it was a relief that the mystery was solved. Slim-Jewel wrote a letter of thanks and I translated it for him. I was personally grateful to him.

The furor it caused in the Sangha, however, was not anticipated. The ethical issue raised was that Noble Son of Wisdom had gone out his way to pursue an investigation which resulted in the execution of the convicted criminal and thus become a party to the killing of a man. Some took up the position that he was guilty of a major offence and hence lost his membership in the Sangha.

There are four offences which would oblige a monk to leave the Order and return to lay life. Described as "Defeat", these offences relate to sexual intercourse, homicide, theft and pretension of high spiritual attainments.

Equally learned exponents of the Rules of Discipline argued in his favour highlighting that intention was not to harm the person concerned but to uncover the perpetrator of a crime.

Students had a debate on the subject and it was almost a mock trial of Noble Son of Wisdom carried out according to the rules of monastic jurisprudence. Venerable Sumangala who presided over the meeting summed up wisely,

"We are here not to judge our venerable friend. However improper it was for him as a monk to have dabbled in a secular matter, he is no way responsible for the capital punishment to which the convicted was sentenced. So the question of "Defeat" does not arise. Let us all take a lesson out of this. The monks have renounced lay life. Leave lay matters to the laity. That's my advice".

As the statement of Venerable Sumangala came to be known in wider circles, the uproar subsided and both Noble Son of Wisdom and I heaved a sigh of relief.

A few days after the student debate, I was pleasantly surprised to find Little Father at the refectory.

" I came to get a special favour from you," he said as he saw me.

What special favour could I do for my resourceful uncle, I wondered. He had with him a sheaf of paper.

"You remember, I told you of Dr. Peeble's report on the Great Debate at Panadura . One of its readers was a Colonel of the army of the United States of America. I don't think you had time to read the correspondence which Venerable Pleasant-Gem-Tissa had with Colonel Henry Olcott. The day you had to leave Orange Island in a hurry, we went to Galle to get a brochure printed. You remember?"

Little Father reached for his bag and took out a pamphlet in a yellow cover.

"Now he has sent a wonderful reply to our elder monk's letter. We want to publish it with a translation. It can have a momentous impact on our people. Just the shot in the arm we have long awaited". He was bubbling with enthusiasm.

He handed over the sheaf of papers to me.

"We want the best possible translation. Our elder monk thinks that we have three indispensable assets in one place here. You will do the translation. Venerable Noble Son of Wisdom could help you if any word or expression needs elucidation. The final text can be checked by Venerable Sumangala who knows the readership best".

For a moment, I was amazed. Here we meet after a lapse of several months. No small talk. No inquiries about the family or my progress. It was as if nothing mattered in the world outside his campaign. What a perfect one-track mind!

"Little Father, many things happened since we last met. How is it that you show no interest or concern?'

"I am sorry, son. I am so preoccupied with what I do".

Once I started giving him news of the family, he showed more interest than I expected. He realized how much he missed through his self-imposed isolation when I gave accounts of the children, specially Moon-Beam and Autumn-Moon.

I was keen to know what happened to the police officers who were detained by the crowd on the night we fled from Orange Island. It was typical of Little Father's limited range of interests. He had forgotten all about it.

"You know I was not there. I left with you?'

"But weren't you curious to find out if the elder scholar-monk had any trouble as a result of the incident".

"If there was any trouble, somebody would have told me".

It took a couple of more months before my curiosity was satisfied by a visiting monk who was an eyewitness to Pleasant-Gem-Tissa's ingenuity. After we left Orange Island, the scholar-monk had returned to the preaching hall, dispersed the crowd and brought the three officers to his room in the temple. He had given them tea and sweets and requested them to await the arrival of an officer from Galle.

"Venerable Sir, Why did you contact the head office? This was a matter that we could have easily settled among us," the inspector had said solicitously.

"How could we, young man? You refused to show me the warrant and you violated my person".

For the next half hour the inspector had pleaded for mercy. He had begged the elder monk to accept his apology and not to report him to higher authorities. The only answer of Pleasant-Gem-Tissa had been,

"Now that I am alone, why don't you take me to custody for aiding and abetting a criminal to escape arrest?"

He had taunted the police officer several times with the same question. The narrator described the inspector's frustration with two colourful local similes: "He was like a mouse caught in the paws of a cat or an arecanut held firmly in a nutcracker".

Eventually, when the Headquarters Inspector representing the Chief of Police of Galle arrived on horseback, the monk had asked for the warrant. It was respectfully handed over to him. He read it slowly.

"We have had a little misunderstanding and I thought you'll be able to help us. Let me say how thankful I am to your Chief and to you for heeding to my request at dead of night", he had said very calmly. "I had a visiting monk whom the Kandy Police had wanted for questioning on the murder of his own brother. These officers came to take action as specified in the warrant".

He had paused for a moment to watch the reaction of the inspector and continued,

"Yes. To take action according to the letter of the warrant. That was to question the monk concerned, verify his identity and movements, check any alibi he could present and arrange to have him escorted to Kandy if a *prima facie* case of his involvement was established".

Pleasant-Gem-Tissa had again paused for what appeared to the inspector a very long time. The narrator had seen beads of perspiration trickling down his cheeks. After a few more minutes of silence, the elder monk had said.

"Unfortunately, there were too many people here to conduct such an investigation. So I did the best I could. I sent him in the custody of two monks to the Government Agent of Kandy. If everything goes as I planned, they will meet the Government Agent tomorrow. Have I done anything wrong?"

A visibly grateful inspector, to the amusement of his own subalterns, had almost shouted, "No. Venerable Sir, you did the best under the circumstances".

What an ingenious man Pleasant-Gem-Tissa was! More tea and sweets and the police officers had descended the steps of the Rock-Reflection Temple with a signed statement in which the monk had taken full responsibility for my actions.

187

Little Father was in a hurry. He gave me the neat copy which he had made of Colonel Olcott's letter of 29 August 1878, had the mid-day meal with us and left immediately.

"I have to be at Mine Estate in a couple of hours. Venerable Golden Lustre is opening his fourteenth school. I had been there for the start of each school since the day I was beaten in that village," was his excuse.

That afternoon, I gave priority to the letter from Henry Steel Olcott, President of the Theosophical Society, which had the sender's address as *The Theosophical Society, 64 Madison Avenue, New York.*"

"Very impressive!' I said to myself as I began translating it. My first hurdle: "*Theosophical*" ("pertaining to the love of God" ?!). I noted it for consultation with Noble Son of Wisdom and perhaps Venerable Sumangala.

Pleasant-Gem-Tissa had been addressed as "*Reverend Sir and Dear Brother in Faith*". His letter on 15 June 1878 was said to have filled Olcott's "*heart with real joy.*" He continued,

> "*It was the voice of a brother speaking comfort and encouragement to those who need them sadly - being surrounded by enemies who wish them ill and have done and would do them all possible harm. It fastens the other end of an unseen but sensitive thread of sympathy and unites our little corps of pioneers with the main body. Believe me, my brother, the hand of welcome you extend to us is most cordially, most warmly, grasped*".

He proceeded to give a few bits of information about his "*unworthy self*". He was an American by birth and was 46 years old. His family had been in the States since 1633 and fought against the British in the wars of 1776 and 1812.

> "*Until I assisted in laying the foundation of this society of ours as a the Brotherhood of Humanity, I was an intense patriot but now I am striving everyday to make myself feel that all nations are but one family, and all men but one Kindred*", he continued. "*I pass among the ignorant Western people as a thoroughly well informed man but in comparison with the learning possessed by my brothers in the oriental priesthoods, I am as ignorant as the last of their neophytes*".

188

I was not ready for what followed. I have for at least six years in my formative years heard exactly the opposite. I read the next two pages several times before I resumed translation.

> "What I call wisdom is the thorough knowledge of the real truth of the Cosmos and of Man. Where in Christendom can this be learnt? Where is the University? Where the professor? Where the books from which the hungry student may discover what lies behind the shell of physical natures? That divine knowledge is in the keeping of the temples and priests and ascetics of the East - of despised heathendom. There alone the way to purification, illumination, power, beatitude can be pointed out. At the West, a sensual clergy; a demoralizing theology; a forged book; a substitution of faith for merit; of words for deeds.

> "Physical Science is tearing down the barriers from behind which a fraudulent caste have so long entrenched themselves and ruled the consciences and destinies of the people, at the same time beclouding their perceptions of spiritual things. Christianity is losing its adherents by tens of thousands and the past vestiges of its ancient influence are almost even now swept away.

> "This is the state of things here: whither, then, shall we? Can we turn our eyes for the proofs of man's nature and destiny? The ancient writings have been falsely translated to us by missionaries and corrupt philologists. The maxims and precepts of the ancient sages have been misstated or withheld."

That was quite hard work. Not only were there many unfamiliar words but the concepts themselves could not be rendered into intelligible Sinhala. Hoping to return to the translation after the evening chanting, I attended to the correspondence of Venerable Sumangala.

For the next four afternoons and nights, Olcott's letter was my principal preoccupation. It was powerfully written and the underlying sincerity was patent. He appealed for help from the East.

> "To you and you must we turn, and say: 'Father, brother, the Western world is dying of brutal sensuality; come and

189

help; rescue it. Come as missionaries, as teachers, as disputants, preachers. Come prepared to be hated, opposed, threatened, perhaps maltreated. Come expecting nothing but determined to accomplish everything'. I tell you, my brother, the hour and the people are ready. If you have not travelled in spirit or body to Europe and America, you cannot imagine how the people need just that comfort and enlightenment that the Buddhist philosophy can give".

He quoted one Mr. Dana, the Editor of the New York Sun, to corroborate his view that Buddhism would have a receptive audience in America:

If you will persuade a good, pure, learned, eloquent Buddhist to come here and preach, you will sweep the country before you. People want to believe in their souls but how can they after their disgust with Christianity caused by the scientific reaction?"

The more I worked on this letter the more I came to see Olcott as a man of strong conviction with a vision which encompassed the whole world. He had brought together in his movement "*Jews, Rationalists, Spiritualists, Parsis, Buddhists, Brahmanists, Jains, Lamaists, to say nothing of nominal Christians of all shades of opinion who have the desire but not the courage to emancipate themselves from their older yokes*".

Of course, his vitriolic criticism of Christianity baffled me. He called his society "*a Brotherhood of Humanity*" but admitted "*that it is also a league of religions against the common enemy - Christianity*". What a contradiction, I thought. If it was to be a brotherhood of humanity, it certainly could not be against another segment of humanity. I was not altogether convinced of the reasons he gave for his opinion and action:

"*If we form a league against Christianity it is because that being aggressive is opposed to the best interest of mankind, because it is not willing to accept the divine precept of the Buddha that we should respect every man's faith, holding our own, nevertheless, in chief affection, but sets itself up to be the one true religion, bears the curse of the eternal damnation against all who deny its supremacy, and by cunning and violence aims to submit and corrupt the whole earth.*"

190

Olcott's Society had done in the States what the Buddhists tried in their public debates with Christian padres. I could now see why the Great Debate of Panadura impressed him.

> "*Recognizing this feature of Christianity, our young Society began by defying its priests to their faces denouncing their system as a fraud, repudiating the Bible and their saviour and proclaiming itself the ally and the defender of the Heathen*".

I could also see why Little Father and the leaders of the campaign for Buddhist education that he represented wanted to give the widest publicity to this letter. It was very partial to Buddhism. In one place he had said,

> "*With all my heart and soul I accept and profess the philosophy and try to act upto the precepts of Gautama Buddha. But as to the Church as it is, I know nothing, having had no means of observation. I ought or might feel called upon to make a public profession and enter its fold. I cannot say I understand the sublime doctrine of Sakya Muni. I see myself at the feet of his disciples as one of the humblest though most sincere disciples. In any debate between Buddhism and Christianity my place would be with you* ."

In passing a reference had been made to a book by the name of *Isis Unveiled* "*the great work from the pen*" of a H. P. Blavatsky who was described as the Corresponding Secretary of the Theosophical Society. Reminiscent of the notes I used to make as a boy on matters to be raised with Little Father, I wrote out several questions. They referred to H. P. Blavatsky, Arya Samaj, Pandit Dayanand Sarasvati, idolatrous Brahmanism and several other concepts which I was not familiar with. I would, of course, pose these questions to Noble Son of Wisdom whose wide reading and multicultural education were enviable assets. He was exceedingly helpful.

Three drafts had to be torn up and a fourth prepared before I felt that I had a text fit enough to be shown to Venerable Sumangala. He was brutally honest.

"Who will understand your high flown flowery language? You have got the meaning correct. Now rewrite for the man in the street. He is the one we want to convert".

191

With a plenty of instructive directions, I sat down to do a new document - an adaptation rather than a translation. I visualized Colonel Henry Steel Olcott standing in front of the Colombo Fort railway station and explaining the contents of his letter to the commuters. I was myself surprised how a new life could be given to my archaic phraseology. I had had another lesson.

When Little Father came to collect the document a few days later, he was very pleased. He brought me a copy of the second edition of Dr. J. M. Peeble's *Buddhism and Christianity Face to Face.*

"This is for you to keep, Tiny One. But if you can put it into Sinhala in the same style as Olcott's letter, it could be wonderful".

"You know what Colonel Olcott says about this book and its author?"

"Nothing very bad as far as I remember".

"All right. Please listen". I found the relevant paragraphs and read out to him:

> *"Its second edition has been getting handsome compliments by the press. Dr. Peebles has thus done a service to Buddhism. He is a kind and good man, though credulous as to the interviews with 'Angles' through 'mediums' and prove to choose Buddha, Jesus, Confucius, Pythagoras, Porphyry and all religious philosophers as 'mediums', in short, the slaves and tools of bhutas. He was formerly a Christian clergyman and that position is very hard to eradicate."*

Little Father was disturbed.

"We have to delete it from the letter when we publish it," he said. "If Dr. Peebles is branded an odd ball, his publication which is having an incredible impact on the educated Sri Lankans will be repudiated as worthless".

"I don't know, Little Father. I can offer you no advice. But a doctored document is not worth the paper on which it is printed".

Little Father left as hurriedly as he came. He was a very busy man indeed.

VIII

After the two interludes of tracking down my brother's murderer and the translation of Olcott's letter, life returned to normal for both Noble Son of Wisdom and me. We made good progress in Pali and were introduced to a basic grammar in Sanskrit. The Siamese colleague extended his classes in English and World Geography to include European History and Western Philosophy. I had settled down to be his interpreter. Perhaps, I derived the highest benefit from his erudition and critical acumen. He was a great teacher and what distinguished him from many other competent teachers was that he spoke from direct experience. His digressions and interpolations proved to be far more interesting and valuable than the subject under study.

"Watch my word. Keep your eyes and ears open." he would tell his classes every now and then. "The world will see in the next twenty-five years scientific and technological advances it had never seen before in any of the great civilizations. What we know of the universe and our planet will go through rapid revision. Every discovery will humble us. Each will demand our theories to be thrown overboard and our textbooks revised."

He once elaborated his thesis poignantly,

"What we have held as true, inviolable knowledge is already being questioned. A French Novelist called Jules Verne writes convincingly of a time when man will conquer the space, land on the moon, travel below the surface of the sea, circle the earth in eighty days and grow chicken as big as ostriches and a single crab to feed a village. Scientific fiction is already reaching out to hitherto unimagined frontiers. With new tools of investigation and research, both intellectual and physical, we are in for many surprises.

"The next century will dawn with a growing realization of the dominance of man over nature in every field. Already we hear the rumblings. Steam, electricity and fossil fuels are making it possible for man to overcome distance, handle weights and volumes beyond his physical capacity and reach the unreachable. Man will fly in machines similar to Ravana's Wooden Peacock of your legends.

"Individuals will travel at will wherever they want without the aid of beasts of burden. They will communicate rapidly between continents. The train and the telegraph in current use will appear primitive and inadequate as technology evolves more efficient and faster modes. Diseases will be better treated and even more amazingly prevented with precautionary measures.

"We will delve into the origin of life, workings of the human mind and the magnitude and secrets of the universe and come up with astounding insights. Are we ready for this new age?"

Even the teachers who were masters of ancient lore and literature listened to him attentively and participated in the discussions he promoted. Noble Son of Wisdom was our window to the modern world. He spoke with similar enthusiasm on current political events in the world. He compared the rate of development of his own country with the rest of the world and specially with British and French colonies.

"In 1689, King William III of England ascended the throne not by grace of God but by the will of the people expressed through the Parliament. In no enlightened society could a king claim a divine right to rule over fellow humans. It is far more incongruous and anachronistic to think that one nation has a right to dominate over another" he said on a class devoted to the Bill of Rights of England of 1688.

Students loved his forays into the contemporary political situation of the country. What we all appreciated most was his ingenuity in bringing conviction to his audience by introducing guest speakers. On this occasion, he had a young civil servant from the Office of the Colonial Secretary to speak to us on the the suffrage movements in England and the United States of America.

While thanking the speaker, he said, "We do hope that the enlightened leadership of England sees the injustice of disfranchising millions of people in their colonies".

1879 also brought its share of misfortune for both me and Noble Son of Wisdom. He had sad news of his mother and he spent a whole day in isolation, fasting and meditating. He also had news of the death of a close relative who was a consort of the King of Siam, Little Ornament, also known as Rama V. Her boat capsized and she was drowned in the Chao Phya River, right by the King's summer palace in Bang Pa-in. What was really tragic was that any one of the hundreds of people on either bank of the river could have saved her easily but for an immutable royal privilege or prerogative. No commoner could have, under pain of death, touched the person of a member of the royalty even to save her from drowning! My Siamese friend was as much in grief as in rage.

"This is outrageous. It is ridiculous. It is senseless. When will we ever enter the modern age?' he asked angrily.

It was ironical that he should ask this question. In an well-intentioned move to modernize his nation, this particular king had

194

recently decreed that the Siamese should desist from eating with their fingers or entering the capital other than in Western clothes!

During this same year I lost both my parents. The tragic events of the last few years pertaining to my third brother had taken a heavy toll of my mother's health. His murder was the last straw. She lost her will to live. She lost weight rapidly and within months she was nothing more than a breathing skeleton. I paid her two brief visits and on both occasions persuaded her to go the Sanatorium at Toddy-Village.

"What good did that do to White Padre and his wife?" she asked me and pleaded. "Let me die in peace in my own home".

Her uncle Chief Monk and my father agreed with her.

When I went for the funeral, I stayed behind for a week to participate in the ceremony of offering alms to monks on the seventh day of her death. It was a sad ceremony. The family had requested me to deliver the sermon on the eve of the almsgiving. Little Father who had come all the way from Orange Island helped to put my thoughts together. I took as my text the Buddha's definition of loving kindness which one should practise toward all creatures:

Just as a mother with her life
Would protect her only child - her son,
So should one feel for all beings without limit;
So should one extend loving kindness to all beings.

This time both Little Father and I did our very best to persuade father to seek medical assistance for shortness of breath and recurring chest pain. Uncle Victor was ready to make necessary arrangements to keep him at Royal Spout if he was reluctant to be admitted to hospital. He was as adamant as mother was.

"Now that she is gone what is the point in my trying to lag alone," he had told his sister Jasmine.

I believed this when she repeated it to me as I had known how much my parents loved each other.

I was again in Sangha-Gem-Field for the third month almsgiving in memory of mother. It coincided with the first anniversary of my third brother's death. Accordingly the almsgiving was to bestow merit on both. Father had over-exerted himself in organizing an elaborate ceremony - his last demonstration of his deep love for his indefatigable wife and unfortunate son.

On this occasion, too, I delivered the sermon on the eve of the almsgiving and Little Father gave the sermon at the almsgiving. Both were moving tributes to two members of the family whom we all loved.

The next morning Little Father and I were about to set out for Kandy to take the afternoon train to Colombo, when my eldest brother came running to the temple. Words were not necessary for us to know what had happened. We did not ask what or how. We simply asked when.

"We don't know. He passed away in his sleep".

The funeral and the seventh day almsgiving kept us in the village for another ten days. This time the sermon was delivered by Chief Monk.

A Buddhist monk, by training, concentrates on the inevitability of death and meditates regularly on impermanence and futility of life. I had sought to console others on many occasions. I had found the numerous statements in the scriptures on the need to accept and prepare for death very cogent in sermons and conversations. Yet, when death comes so swiftly to one's closest family, religion or philosophy gives but little consolation. I was devastated. I lay awake in the night, vacantly looking at the ceiling and repeating with little solace,

"Life is like a drop of dew on a blade of grass."

I felt compelled to see Slim-Jewel and her daughter before I left Sangha-Gem-Field. I felt in some way responsible for the triple tragedy of my family. Through some inexplicable logic, I had come to the conclusion that my love for Slim-Jewel brought about the misery.

Why did I fall in love with her? Was it not the reason for her family to think of giving her in marriage to our family? I cursed the stars which, in the eyes of elders, condemned me to a life of a recluse.

In an inner recess of my heart, there still were tender thoughts for the girl who kindled from concealed cinders a glowing fire of desire, made me conscious of the beauty and serenity of love and set me dreaming of the bliss and fulfillment of home life with a wife and children. Why was I not man enough to withstand the pressures of superstition and pursue the dictates of true love? The mocking question of Noble Son of Wisdom haunted me. I took responsibility for the love tangle of my third brother. Did I not encourage him? Did I not approve his choice? Did I not envy him for being loved by an exceptionally beautiful girl?

I tried in vain to salve my conscience with the thought that I was in no way responsible for my brother's infidelity.

196

"Am I my brother's keeper?" I asked myself. My mind said "No" but the response of the heart was different. How can one blame someone for returning to one's first love?

Over and over again, my lack of courage loomed as the cause of all that happened in the family. The least I could do to assuage my guilt would be to confess it to the one and only victim of the tragedy. Not only had she borne the heaviest share of grief, shame and despair but had to live with them.

I was alone. Neither of the two elders with whom I could have discussed my feelings freely were near at hand. Little Father left on the previous evening. Noble Son of Wisdom was at Palace Hill. It was not easy to discuss my innermost thoughts with Chief Monk. But I had no alternative. But in preparation for my meeting with him, I spent an hour in the shrine room in worship and meditation. I had to be sure of my feelings. I had to have a nagging question satisfactorily answered:

"Pure-Wisdom, are you ready to return to lay life for the sake of Slim-Jewel and her daughter Moon-Beam?" If this was the solution that Chief Monk in his dual capacity of an elder in the family and my spiritual mentor offered, what would be my answer?

Once again, Chief Monk surprised me. Scarcely had I straightened myself after prostrating before him in salutation that he asked,

"Little Number, shouldn't you talk to Slim-Jewel before you go back to Colombo? It could be of great help. One can say that there's nothing anybody could do in the face of one's Kamma. But some compassion and encouragement could go a long away."

As usual, he said a lot in his few words. I had to return to Colombo. But he felt that Slim-Jewel needed my moral support in her hour of need.

In order to prevent a repetition of the violation of monastic rules of discipline, I went to my eldest brother's home with a novice. Such a precaution was unnecessary as everyone was at home. The whole family was pleased that I visited them before leaving for Colombo. Tea was served and they sat on the floor before me. It was for me to deliver a formal sermon or to start a conversation. I thought that the elders would prefer a short sermon. I spoke to them of Kamma.

"To explain all our miseries as a result of our past actions and specially of unknown previous births could be very comforting," I said. "We can dismiss our responsibility for our destiny by placing trust in some kind of fatalism. That would in no way be different to saying, as

197

some do, that everything right up to the dropping of a sparrow's feather happens according to the will of God.

"We Buddhists have no such easy course of relief. Karma, when properly understood, re-emphasizes our responsibility for everything that happens to us. We form our Karma by willful intentional action. We shape our Karma every moment. We do so by mindful effort and ethically correct action. Every time some misery assails us we redouble our effort to overcome it. A true Buddhist does not pray to and seek the intervention of supernatural forces or powers. He steels himself to action as, in the words of the Buddha, one is one's own refuge, master or lord."

I narrated from the Birth Stories of the Buddha the story of the squirrel, who when her little ones were washed away by the sea did not despair but valiantly set to the task of emptying the sea with her bushy tail. At the end of the sermon, I lowered the round fan with which I had covered my face while speaking.

Slim-Jewel's father saluted me with clasped hands:

"Venerable Sir, our little squirrel is setting out to empty the sea." He pointed at Slim-Jewel. "She is going to Kandy. Flower had asked her to come there so that she could go to school, further her education and find employment. It was all Victor's idea. Though an outsider, he is a very kind man. Isn't that a good idea?"

"Where will Moon-Beam be?" I asked.

"For the time being, she will be with my parents. She is very fond of her Big Mother," replied Slim-Jewel.

"I think it's a good idea, Younger Sister. You have to start a new life and I know you have the courage and the strength to do it."

"That's what I thought myself. Aunt Flower stayed behind to go with me. It will be good for her too. They have only a small servant girl to look after Autumn-Moon when she goes to work. I am sure everything will work out well."

I admired her strength of character. The novice and I were invited to lunch which was offered in accordance with traditional ceremony. To wish success on Slim-Jewel's new life, the novice and I chanted the three discourses on Blessings, Jewels and Loving Kindness and followed up with a number of texts invoking health, success and happiness.

It was a memorable morning. Whatever it meant to the family I counselled, it was therapeutic to me. I returned to the temple a free man.

Nothing was irreparable when indomitable courage went hand in hand with vision. It was a solace to know that Slim-Jewel was ready to face the world and spare no efforts to conquer it - the veritable squirrel girding herself to empty the ocean!

Back in Palace Hill, I had a mountain of letters to handle - some mine but mostly those of Venerable Sumangala. A bulky letter of Little Father had been hand-carried by a student from Orange Island. I opened it first. It contained a copy of a letter of Colonel Olcott. A translation was urgently requested. I marked it as my first assignment for the afternoon and proceeded to open the other letters. Among those addressed to Venerable Sumangala was another from Olcott. Madame Blavatsky and he had come to Bombay in India and established a centre for the Theosophical Society at a place called Peak Village.

It was simply fascinating to read what he wrote of their activities. Venerable Sumangala and Venerable Gunananda of Scribe's Garden - the brain and the tongue of the historic debate of Panadura - had been elected as Councillors of their Society with representative authority in Sri Lanka. Pleasant-Gem-Tissa, who had been elected a Fellow of the Society a year ago, was requested to act in cooperation with the Councillors. Olcott had widened his network of active monks in the Island. There was evidence of frequent communication.

Olcott and Madame Blavatsky must have been an indefatigable pair driven by a dream, a passion, an obsession, I thought. I made it my private project to get in touch with monks corresponding with Olcott.

Olcott's letter of 18 July 1879 was short. I could post the translation that very evening. Little Father would bring out another brochure with that and other letters of Olcott. Pleasant-Gem-Tissa relied heavily on the printed word as the most effective means of communication with activists in the campaign to promote Buddhist education as the immediate objective and the revival of Buddhism and national independence as the eventual goals. Both of them recognized that Olcott as an American could play a major role in the achievement of their objectives. This view was shared by other monks and, among them, the foremost was none other than Venerable Sumangala.

I was privileged to be called upon to translate most of Olcott's correspondence for publication in brochures as well as to draft replies for those addressed to Venerable Sumangala. Quite unconsciously, I had become an active worker in a national campaign. I was obsessed with an urge to meet Olcott.

"Could you find out from Venerable Sumangala whether the two of us could visit Olcott in Bombay just to see how he organizes his work?" I urged Noble Son of Wisdom.

"No problem, Pure. I would love to see this man and more so the mystical lady of whom he writes cryptically," was his response.

Venerable Sumangala was accessible to the Siamese princely monk at any time. So within minutes, we had his response.

"Mark my word, Noble Son of Wisdom. Before you could go to India to see them, they are bound to be here. I don't think they have as strong a support base as the monks of Sri Lanka had provided for them," he had said.

I was disappointed. Perhaps, Venerable Sumangala, as a scholar and head of the College, was concerned that my studies had been a bit erratic as a result of the successive deaths in the family.

IX

At the end of the year, Noble Son of Wisdom and I had to sit an examination in Pali. A titled administrator from the Southern Province with the unlikely name of Louis de Zoysa, who was noted for his scholarship in Oriental languages, was invited to be the examiner. He was thorough. The written part of the examination was as difficult as the oral. At the end of the day the results were announced. Both of us had passed. Noble Son of Wisdom had done better, scoring ten marks more than I. I was happy for him.

"Next year in Sanskrit I'll allow you to do better" he said with his ever-present, contagious mirth.

Letters from Olcott continued to be sent for translation. A printed card dated 25 November 1879 invited Pleasant-Gem-Tissa to the fourth anniversary celebrations of the Theosohpical Society to be held in Peak Village. It was to be marked by the opening of a library, the founding of the Society's monthly journal, *Theosophist*, and an exhibition. Another facet of Olcott's wide-ranging interests was revealed by the reference to "machinery made by native artisans" which would be displayed at the exhibition. He was certainly not a one-track-minded, religious enthusiast.

The next letter which was sent for translation confirmed my impression. In it he calls himeself "a very ignorant student of the occult sciences which include Mesmerism or animal Magnetism".

He wrote:

"In that I have a perfect faith because I know that thousands have been cured of great illnesses by it and I have been able to do some little good myself by exercising the Magnetic Power."

In offering some suggestions for the treatment of a patient regarding whom Pleasant-Gem-Tissa and another scholar-monk had written, Olcott recommended both hypnotism and homeopathy. He added,

"I would most joyfully heal our sick brother were it possible and if I were in Ceylon I should certainly try to do something for him."

The College closed for a month for the Sinhala New Year which fell on the 14th of April.

Chief Monk wanted me back in Sangha-Gem-Field. The number of scholars consulting the palmleaf books in the library had increased substantially. Instead of asking for manuscript copies on paper, more and more scholars were sending texts for collation with texts in our books. The detection of variant readings and recording them needed skills. The two novices whom I had trained and who had taken my place needed some guidance. Chief Monk's letter had another somewhat equivocal suggestion.

"Some day - sooner or later - you will be the Abbot of this temple. I know that you did an admirable job when I was ill. But don't you think that you need to show some continuing interest and involvement?"

I was annoyed. It was not my decision to come to Colombo for formal education. Was he worried that I was getting too close to the kind of work Little Father was engaged in? Did he think that, as some sort of private secretary to Venerable Sumangala, I would eventually be more concerned with national issues than the parochial interest of a rural monastic establisment? Was he once again forcing me to make a choice and that too in the way he had already decided? Noble Son of Wisdom thought that I was over-reacting.

"Pure, Chief Monk knows your potentiality. I am sure what he is aiming at is to get you to decide early enough. Let's assume that you want to be a big player in the national scene? I know you can and you will. Then have you a contingency plan for your temple?"

He was as usual correct and very helpful. My parent's premature death and the murder in the family had affected my immediately elder brother to such an extent that he had begun speaking in terms of becoming a monk. He was an year older than I. What he lacked was formal schooling. But he was literate and was a voracious reader of the growing folk literature specially Sinhala verse. So if the elders still thought in terms of keeping the abbotship among relatives, this could be a solution. All he needed was some formal training.

I arranged my travel in such a way that I could spend a week-end in Kandy. I had several persons to meet. The most important among them, of course, was Slim-Jewel. I needed to be reassured that she was pursuing her new goals happily and successfully. I also had to meet Reverend Kenneth Saunders whom the rumours suggested was being sent by the church authorities to head its mission in Burma.

"He's being kicked upstairs," my informant told me with undisguised disdain for this liberal and enlightened scholar-padre.

"Here he makes friends for the church but no converts. In Burma, the church hasn't the chance of a snowball in hell in making any conversions. So why not send him there to make friends! A smarter padre can be sent here to make converts."

I felt obliged to say how grateful I was for his numerous kindensses and defended Reverend Saunders' approach as the most advantageous to Christianity in the country.

Some time with Uncle Victor, Aunt Flower and their son Autumn-Moon would be an added bonus. I arranged to reach Kandy on the 12th of April.

Noble Son of Wisdom declined my invitation to join me. He was planning to set up a Buddhist school in the northern part of Colombo where Roman Catholics under the persecution-free British Administration of the Island had shown a tendency to concentrate. Several spectacular Catholic churches were being constructed. He chose a block of land half way between the largest of such churches and the eighteenth century Dutch Reformed Church on a hillock, misnamed by Hollanders as Woolvendaal - the dale of wolves, imagining that Guadaluupe in Portuguese meant "dale of wolves." Despite the very rich and diverse wildlife of Sri Lanka, the wolf was conspicuous by its absence. With his own private funds, Noble Son of Wisdom had bought the land and a building was in progress.

"This is my 'Thank you' to the kind souls of Ceylon who have given me more than a second home," he told me.

He was planning to open the school on the day after the Vesak Festival which fell on the fullmoon day of the month of May. Pleasant-Gem-Tissa of Orange Island was to be the chief guest of honour not so much in recognition of his pioneering work in the field of Buddhist education but rather, as Noble Son of Wisdom said with a guffaw of laughter, "in admiration of the guts he had to pull that off the Police". He meant the manner in which he had the Police detained in the temple until we made it to safety in Kandy. I promised to be back in time.

Everything went as planned. I met Slim-Jewel and heard her own assessment of her progress in her studies, her work as a nursing aide at the General Hospital and her remarkable success in grappling with depression and dejection.

"Younger Sister, do you miss your little daughter?"

"Very much, Venerable Sir. I have gone to see her at least once every three weeks."

"Is there anything that I could do for you when I go to the village?"

203

"Yes. There is. Thank you very much for asking me. Can you please tell both your grandfathers not to malign me in their coffee cliques? They say that the lives of both you and your brother were affected adversely by the planets in my horoscope. Even if it is true, they should understand how much pain I had already gone through."

"I promise, Younger Sister. I will do all I can to prevent anyone from maligning you."

I was glad there was something I could do for Slim-Jewel.

I saw Ernest Dickinson by appointment. He received me with great affection in the same office in the old palace. I told him what I had heard of Reverend Saunders and my assessment of him as an exemplary representative of the Christian clergy in the Island. I was glad that Dickinson agreed with me.

He made me *au courant* with the developments in Oriental Studies in the West. Apparently the emerging doyen of Pali and Buddhist studies, Professor Rhys Davids, was in frequent correspondence with him. Dickinson could tell me how the English Professor had progressed with the translation of the Longer Discourses and was considering the establisment of an incorporated society to carry on the publication and translation of Pali texts.

"Bongyi, I nearly forgot to tell you that an English journalist with a flare for poetry had recently published a fantastic book on the life and teachings of the Buddha. He has called it *The Light of Asia*."

"My Siamese colleague had heard about it when he was in London. He has told me about Edwin Arnold," I said.

He took out a sheaf of paper from a drawer and started reading:

"I have a few excerpts which a friend of mine had copied. Listen, Bongyi:

"I will depart," he spake; "the hour is come!
Thy tender lips, dear Sleeper, summon me
To that which saves the earth but sunders us;
And in the silence of yon sky I read
My fated message flashing. Unto this
Came I, and unto this all nights and days
Have led me; for I will not have that crown
Which may be mine: I lay aside those realms
Which wait the gleaming of my naked sword:
My chariot shall not roll with bloody wheel
From victory to victory, till earth
Wears the red record of my name. I choose

To tread its paths with patient, stainless feet,
Making its dust my bed, its loneliest wastes
My dwelling, and its meanest things my mates;
Clad in no prouder garb than outcasts wear,
Fed with no meats save what the charitable
Give of their will, sheltered by no mean pomp
Than the dim cave lends or the jungle-bush.
This will I do because the woeful cry
Of life and all flesh living cometh up
Into my ears, and all my soul if full
Of pity for the sickness of this world;
Which I will heal, if healing may be found
By uttermost renouncing and strong strife.

Isn't that enchanting? What beautiful thouhgts and what expressive words? I have ordered a dozen copies. One is for you, Bongyi. I would like to present one to your Venerable Sumangala."

I thanked him for his thoughtfullness and inquired about the author.

"Edwin Arnold is a very powerful man in both political and literary circles. The Viceroy stops to talk to him if he walks up the corrodor of the Government House. He writes for an influential newspaper in London, The Daily Telegraph. I had heard him speak on several occasions in Calcutta. I thought he was more Indian than most Indians. He loves everything Indian. His endorsement of Buddhism should be a great asset to you people. You must use it to your advantage."

I found time to meet Reverend Saunders. It had to be very early morning. That was when he could find a little free time. Further, it was thought that I would be too conspicuous in my robes. For some reason he also thought it better to avoid the students.

It was more than a courtesy call. He was quite emotional. He was plainly unhappy about having to leave Sri Lanka.

"Why I dislike this move is that it is a part of an epidemic that is slowly but steadily breaking out. It is an epidemic of bigotry borne out of frustration. Our authorities in England are too far away to know what is happening. Their representaitves here are too submissive to tell the truth. We can't make any headway in this country in our numbers game. The age of conversion is gone, gone for ever. Full stop. They must know and they must be told."

"Why do you say so?" I inquired even though I knew that he was correct.

205

He said what the Blakes had often told me earlier. He believed that the best contribution that the missionaries could do is to bring science and technology along with English language and literature and Western culture to enrich and complement what the ancient civilization of the Island had bequeathed to the people. Reverend Saunders termed it not just a bequest from the past to the presentday people of the country but a bequest which should be enjoyed by the whole world as a common human heritage.

"We have a dual role, T. B. We have as much to take away from this country as to give it. The last thing we should be doing is to think that all we have to give these people is the Bible and our disconnected sectarian views of Christ and his mission. We have no right to make the people of this country feel ashamed of their culture, their religion, their way of life. Specially so, when we do sincerely admire all those things that we seek to replace."

"What do you expect your role to be in Burma?"

"Plainly, I don't know." he said with a gesture. "The British record in Burma is not very great. In 1824 we had the first Anglo-Bumese War and annexed a lot of its coast and hinterland. In 1852, we annexed a major chunk leaving the Burmese high and dry in the mountainous highlands. There are many who urge a third war. For all I know, it will come soon - within the next five or six years. They have begun maligning King Thibaw who was crowned only last year. Some say that he is a tyrant and the British should save the Burmese from his tyranny. Others say that he is courting the French and that the British should safeguard their political and economic interests. What do they want me to do? To help in the modernization of the system of education. At least that's what they say on paper."

"You sound dejected, Reverend Saunders?"

"I do. I am dejected here. It will be worse there. Our policy in education is all wrong. But we are the ones who advise the administration. Do you know how you got the present educational system here?"

"No. Reverend Saunders. I have no idea at all."

"What is now in place in the Island is what the Richard Morgan Commission recommended. You know how they made the decisions?" He paused for effect, then continued,

"Yes. Very democratically! They consulted forty-three persons. Among them was one Sinhala and no Tamil at all. There was one Roman Catholic. All others were Protestant Christians. Not a single Buddhist, Hindu or Muslim. It was on the advice of my own colleagues in the church that they decided to close down temple schools. They were the ones against the teaching of Sinhala literature on the ground that the content was Buddhist."

"Reverend Saunders, why are you angry about it?" I asked him.

"Because I think it's all unfair. As a nation we British take pride in upholding the highest principles of justice and fair play. But our religous interests make us the worst bigots.

"Let me tell you the story of a man I respect. He is J. S. Laurie, the first Director of Public Instruction to be appointed a decade ago. He lasted only one year. Do you know the reason? Taking to heart too seriously the educational needs of the people and trying to meet them in a planned manner. What was he expected to do? To placate my colleagues the Chrisitan missionaries!

"These are the injustices that I have been vocal about. I tell them not to denationalize the youth of this country. The up and coming generation should not be alienated from their national culture and heritage. There cannot be any worse crime than lowering the self-esteem of the young in any nation. When I point this out, they question my patriotism. What they would like me to do is to ensure that generation after generation of people of this country grow to become docile, submissive subjects of the great empire."

I felt very sad for Reverend Saunders. But I was confident that he would carry on his mission as a sympathetic student of national cultures and bring respect and recognition to his countrymen by the very testimony of his life and ideals. I wished him every success and was keen that he should visit Palace Hill where I would get him to address the students and the staff.

The week-end passed too quickly. I had equally productive and stimulating meetings with the new lay Buddhist leadership in Kandy. They were enthralled with the information I could share with them on Olcott and what he was planning for the promotion of Buddhism.

"You know what Venerable Sumangala told us when Noble Son of Wisdom and I wnated to go to Bombay to see Colonel Olcott and Madame Blavatsky" I told them. "He said that they would be in Ceylon earlier than we think. I hope he is correct."

All my meetings were not equally encouraging. To my great disappointment, the heirarchical leadership of both the major monasteries showed little interest in what was going on in the country. Their concept of the promotion of Buddhism was safeguarding the temporalities, which they felt, were being wrested from them by greedy planters and avaricious administrators. Their concerns, therefore, centred more on land acquisitions, tenure obligations of tenents and the appointment of lay custodians.

"Buddhism has lasted two thousand years without all this fuss on schools and children because kings and nobles were generous in their grants of land. It's our duty to guarantee the survival of the temple and the Sangha by ensuring their economic viablity," was the comment of one of them.

If I failed to see any validity in this point of view at that time, the reason could have been that I was so influenced by idealists like Kenneth Saunders, Venerable Sumangala, Pleasant-Gem-Tissa and, of course, Little Father.

"We need a Messiah to take us across this mess" I told myself. "I hope and wish that Olcott comes here sooner rather than later."

X

By dawn on the day of the New Year, the mail coach brought me to Sangha-Gem-Field. Villagers in their new clothes were streaming into the temple, chattering happily in gay festive mood. The kids were particularly talkative and active - just as the folk song said, "Elephants and kids do seldom rest still." The pious carried flowers, incense, candles and oil for lamps. Still untainted by foreign influences or pressurized by commercialization of the occasion, these simple folk celebrated this day exactly the way their forefathers had done for centuries.

The start of the New Year was astronomically fixed by the transition of the sun from the Zodiac of Pisces to that of Aries. Nature was at its best, bursting out in colourful floral splendour.

At an auspicious time which the astrologers of the community had prescribed, they had marked the end of the Old Year by extinguishing the fire at the hearths. From that moment until the auspicious moment for relighting the fire came, they did no cooking at home and generally avoided any kind of work. This period of "No-auspicious-times" was a sort of *dies non* and had to be devoted exclusively to religious activities. In fact, it was called the "Time for Merit-making." With a couple hours still left of this period, the people visited the temple to worship and meditate, seek blessings from the clergy and the elders and mingle with the community.

They were a happy crowd. Elders were particularly favoured, for this was the day when each person paid homage to those older to them and asked for forgiveness for anything done wittingly or otherwise to hurt them. In their homes, they would have fallen on their knees in front of each elder and offered him or her the traditional sheaf of betel leaves while saying, "If in the course of last year, I had committed any fault, do please forgive me." The elders would bless them and stroke their heads.

Both sets of grandparents were in the temple and I would have loved to do what the tradition demanded. But as a monk I was exempted. On the contrary, they worshipped me and I blessed them, saying, "May you live long in perfect health." I missed my parents. I remembered the days when they had brought me and my brothers to the temple. This was the first New Year without them. Lest tears show, I bade my grandparents a hasty farewell and hastened into the temple. I took a few minutes to calm myself before paying the customary homage to my teacher, Chief Monk.

Busy as he was receiving and blessing people, he chatted with me for a while. He had made plans for my immediate elder brother to enter the order.

"I think it's a good idea," he said. "After all, you are more useful to the Faith if you are free to be active at the national level. If these activities prevent you from performing your duties as the abbot of this temple, your brother will do the needful and look after your interests as well."

He proceeded to discuss the legal implications of what he had just stated. I was in no way interested. I was no longer content with painting on a small canvass. I had other dreams or rather plans for action at the national or even the international level. I was happy that another member of the family had decided to join the Sangha. As regards Sangha-Gem-Field, my main interest was to ensure that the invaluable literary treasures of this temple served as wide a clientele as possible. I wanted to brief my brother on the importance of maintaining the library.

It was a relief that this matter was settled without any hitch. All my relatives were happy about it. I teased my brother because he was the one who used to ridicule me for wanting to be a monk. He thought I was looking for a free and easy meal ticket. Now that he was becoming a monk he had his misgivings.

"I have no formal education to rely on," he grumbled. "I have to learn everything from scratch at this relatively old age."

"Take one step at a time, brother. You will soon be a competent monk. It's not one's learning that makes one a good or a bad monk. It's the degree of dedication and strength of character. I know that you have both."

He was very pleased.

With ten days to go for the brother's ordination, I planned to visit as many the friends and well-wishers of the family. I had to thank them for having shared our grief over three deaths in a row. I was received with great veneration in every home. It is a wonderful feeling to be respected by your fellow villagers - simple folk who had seen you growing up from infancy yet recognized that you were special because you have renounced the things that they held dear to themselves.

The Abbot of Bo-Tree Plain temple organized a special function whose centrepiece was a sermon by me. Hundreds of monks participated in an overnight chanting of the Book of Protection and in the two early morning and mid-day almsgivings. An afternoon meeting was announced through a printed notice as a reception to "*our own Venerable Pure-Wisdom, the promising scholar of the Learning-*

Awakening College at Palace Hill; a leading light in the national campaign for the revival of Buddhism and restoration of political freedom; and translator of J. M. Peeble's book on the Great Debate and the letters of Colonel Henry Steel Olcott to the Venerable Sangha of Sri Lanka."

I felt embarrassed by the exaggerated description of my modest involvement with the work of such national stalwarts as the Venerables Sumangala and Pleasant-Gem-Tissa. I thought that Little Father should have been the recipient of these honours.

To my utmost surprise, the Smiths attended the function. They were given seats just behind me so that they could talk to me and I could tell them what was happening. They had made no progress with Sinhala. If I had ever seen two unhappy people, they were the Smiths.

"We have asked for a transfer to an African colony," explained Mrs. Smith. "Reverend Smith can show real progress in a country where there is no organized protest or any strong organization to protest. Here, he is getting nowhere. We are really frustrated."

I understood what she meant and did not ask for any further information. She was bitter about the role of the Sangha. In my mind, I contrasted the Smiths with the Blakes and Reverend Saunders. The Blakes had made this village their home and its people their friends and admirers. Even in death, they are remembered and loved. Similarly, Reverend Saunders had found a mission for himself in the Island though the local church authorities did not appreciate it. Smiths wanted to get out; yet somebody, somewhere, thought that they were doing all right where they were!

Again to my surprise, Reverend Smith accepted the Abbot's invitation to say a few words. He made a few kind references to me as an old boy of his school and one of the best products of the educational system that his Mission was proud to introduce and maintain. He thanked the villagers for their courtesy and kindness.

A tinge of bitterness was discernible in a brief reference to his own work as superfluous and insignificant. If one heard his speech as I translated it, one would have thought that it was a farewell for the Smiths.

I made a very brief speech as I was due to give a sermon in the evening. Switching to English for the benefit of the Smiths I said,

"The late lamented Reverend Thomas Blake once told me that on occasions like this one had a choice of two speeches: A long one or a short one. The short speech is 'Thank you' and the long speech is 'Thank you very much.' I choose the long one and say, 'Thank you very much'".

211

The attendance at my sermon was unprecedented. The Abbot must have mounted an enormous publicity campaign. I was surprised to find R. M. and his family very close to the pulpit. The Government Agent had sent three coaches full of officers from the Provincial Office and Uncle Victor was taking care of them.

I had chosen my texts from two sermons of the Buddha:

"Do not accept anything
    On mere hearsay or tradition,
    On account of rumours,
    Because it accords with your scriptures,
    By mere supposition or inference,
    By merely considering reasons,
    Because it agrees with your preconceived notions and, therefore, seems acceptable, or
    Because the preacher is a respected person."

                                     (Sermon to the Kalamas)

"I do not preach from a desire to get disciples.
Let him who is your teacher continue to be your teacher.
Let that which is your rule continue to be your rule.
Let that which is your mode of livelihood continue to be so.
Let those points in your doctrine as are wrong and reckoned as wrong by those in your community, remain so still for you.
Let those points in your doctrine which are good, and reckoned to be good by your community, remain so still."

                       (Lion's Roar to the Udumbarikas)

With the approval of the Abbot I had wanted to share with an audience in this part of the country some thoughts which were being discussed on a day-to-day basis in the Western and Southern Provinces. I used these texts to underscore that, starting with the Buddha's own admirable initiatives, Buddhism was dogma-free and was not only tolerant as far as other religious persuasions were concerned, but also non-threatening.

I portrayed the emerging times as an age of science and technology and stressed Olcott's assessment of Buddhism as science-friendly.

With no aforethought intention, the sermon ended in a fervent appeal to set up our own schools where our culture would be promoted and our spiritual values and ideals upheld. My peroration smacked so much of a piece of political oratory that the audience was confused on how to express their acclamation.

Those in front, who represented the elite applauded in typical British manner, while the villagers intoned as tradition demanded "Sadhu, Sadhu, Sadhu".

I had been asked to remain seated so that any one in the audience could come up and speak to me. The R. M. was the first to approach me.

"Venerable Sir, you have a great friend and admirer in Mr. Ernest Dickinson, the Government Agent. He told me that you would sooner or later bring a great degree of recognition to the whole Province." He spoke in English.

"Thank you, Sir," I replied also in English. "Thank you very much for being here to listen to me. I hope you were not offended with my strictures on our current system of education."

"Not at all, Venerable sir," he responded and the tone of his voice was genuine and sincere. "If you plan to set up any Buddhist schools in this region, please don't hesitate to involve me in your campaign. I have taken your message very seriously."

How much of his offer emanated from his knowledge that the Government Agent held me in some esteem and how much from the incompetence and bigotry of Reverend Smith and his wife I could not fathom. I was too modest to think that my sermon could have made all that difference.

If I had a pledging session for a Buddhist Education Fund, I could have collected a few hundred rupees - even a thousand or so.

"You planted a healthy seed in very fertile soil, Little Name" was the compliment of the Abbot of the Bo-tree Plain temple. "If your Little Father forgets, you'll have to speak up for the ancient Kingdom of Kandy."

XI

A week after the ordination of my brother with the monastic name of Moon-Gem, I was at the library explaining to him the kind of requests it received from foreign and national scholars. The two novices who were earlier trained by me were at hand. The new monk showed more interest and understanding than I had expected. I was quite pleased that the services rendered by this exceptional collection of ancient books would continue uninterrupted.

In walked Chief Monk with a folded piece of paper of the tell-tale pink colour of a telegram. If his face showed anxiety or apprehension, it was quite normal. A telegram invariably brought bad news.

"I don't know for whom it is," he said as he gave it to me to be opened and read. "It's a relief that you are here. Otherwise, I'll have to look for somebody to read it."

I knew what he meant. There had been times when a telegram had to be rushed to Bo-tre Plain where White Padre or Mrs. Blake had to help with a translation.

The telegram was addressed to me and it was from Noble Son of Wisdom relaying a message of Venerable Sumangala.

RETURN IMMEDIATELY (STOP) OLCOTT AND BLAVATSKY ARRIVING IN CEYLON MID-MAY (STOP) VENERABLES PLEASANT-GEM-TISSA AND PURE-INTELLECT WANT YOU IN ORANGE ISLAND TO ORGANIZE RECEPTION IN GALLE AND HELP AS INTERPRETER-TRANSLATOR (STOP) - NOBLE SON OF WISDOM

In my mind's eye, I could visualize Venerable Sumangala chuckling with delight as he gave this message to Noble Son of Wisdom.

"Didn't I tell you that they would be here before you could get to Bombay?" he would have asked.

"That's your life, Little Name," Chief Monk said as I explained to him the contents of the telegram and its significance. "I can only wish you every success."

Within forty-eight hours of the receipt of the telegram, I was at Palace Hill. Noble Son of Wisdom had moved to a room in his school in northern Colombo. A student monk volunteered to fetch him. We

214

saw Venerable Sumangala together. How very perspicacious I had been. He chuckled as I had envisaged and asked,

"Didn't I tell you that they would be here before you could get to Bombay?"

I was in for a hectic time. The grand opening of the school of Noble Son of Wisdom had to be postponed. But he was determined to get the institution working on schedule.

"How about a soft opening by you, Venerable Sir?" he asked Venerable Sumangala.

"Good idea. Why don't we invite Venerable Gunananda? We should never forget that he is the man behind all that's taking place."

Resourceful organizer that the ex-Ambassador was, the soft opening was grander than most of the formal events I had seen. This was my first meeting with the hero of the Great Debate. Venerable Gunananda was a medium-sized, dark-complexioned monk with bright eyes and a prominently large mouth. Suffering from a dysfunctional kidney, he looked frail. He looked much older than he was. When he began his speech to the audience of a little over hundred, the old fire for which he had been reputed burst forth with every word he uttered. He did not say anything much or anything new. But even the most commonplace idea was conveyed with the fervour of an apostle. He had his audience in his palm to be moulded like a clod of clay to any shape he wanted. His gestures were equally mesmerizing. With a raised index finger, he jabbed into the air as if each jab etched his utterances on rock for all time to come. As everyone else, I was spellbound. Poor Noble Son of Wisdom, what a treat he missed! Yet his eyes never left the speaker even for the briefest moment.

Venerable Sumangala introduced me to Venerable Gunananda in glowing terms.

"This Little Name represents the generation which is going to take over the campaign from us. So far he's doing very well. He is our translator/interpreter *par excellence*."

He used two words for bilinguist and interpreter which had come into vogue in Sinhala with extended pejorative meanings of "a denationalized nonentity" and "a talker on other people's causes". Their good-natured laughter, in which the audience joined in, was intended to put me at ease.

Both of them agreed that I should speak a few words. I tried to be as eloquent as I could, switching into English to conclude with what was mainly a well-deserved eulogy to our Siamese benefactor.

Venerable Gunananda had precise information on the arrival of the delegation of Indian Theosophists.

"With Colonel Olcott will be two of the co-founders of the Society from America: Madame H. P. Blavatsky and Mr. Wimbridge. The rest of the delegation consists of three Hindus and two Parsis, the wife of one of the Hindu delegates and a servant. They will reach Colombo on the 16th but will land in Galle the next morning. I hope to welcome them in Colombo on board the ship and proceed to Galle to be in time for their arrival. I want to persuade Olcott to take the leadership in our campaign."

"Shouldn't we sound others before we make such a move?" queried Venerable Sumangala, who in the very wording of the question gave his consent to the proposal.

"Indeed! We should have everybody's concurrence," Venerable Gunananda replied. "What we should remember is this. The powers that be do not take us for granted any more because Dr. Peebles had drawn the attention of the world to our plight. We need a spokesman to whom the authorities here and in London and the world outside would listen. The Little Name could consult 'Orange Island' and 'Betel-Village' on our behalf."

I knew that "Orange Island" referred to Pleasant-Gem-Tissa. Little Father had told of an equally enterprising and active monk from Betel-Village. He had a very long name and I could not recall it. But I did remember two bits of information: The first was that he was born in 1795 into a Kandyan aristocratic family and he had come to the low-country while Kandy was still an independent kingdom. The other was that he established his own printing press, called "Aid to Lanka"- the first ever by any Buddhist - in 1860 and published the pioneering Sinhala newspaper "Light of Lanka" from 1862. I looked forward to meeting him.

Thus I had a special mission on my hands when I took the afternoon train to Black-Ford with the idea of taking a late evening stage coach or an overnight cart caravan to Orange Island.

I was enthusiastically received by both Venerable Pleasant-Gem-Tissa and Little Father.

Here I was fresh from the village with ample news on the family and our temple. Little Father inquired about nobody. He had no interest in small talk. He settled down to work with me on a bilingual "Praise Paper" which was to be read at the reception to Olcott and party.

It was said to be the worst tropical storm in the living memory of the people of Galle. It lasted the whole night. When the dawn broke on the 17th day of May 1880, the rain ceased and the clouds dispersed, promising a lovely sunny day.

We were at the jetty, surveying the horizon for the coastal vessel which would bring our distinguished guests to their destination. When the boat anchored about five hundred yards from the jetty, the members of the reception committee embarked on a barge decorated with banana trunks, tender coconut leaves and flowers to ferry the visitors ashore. I was invited to join them in my capacity as the interpreter.

Within minutes we were back at the jetty to a tumultuous ovation by the thronging crowd. Their joyous intonation of "Sadhu! Sadhu! Sadhu!" reverberated over the Dutch ramparts. With hardly a policeman in sight, the crowd was orderly and our visitors could be taken in procession on an 'honour carpet' of white cloth to the carriages which were to take them to their appointed residence.

All eyes were on Helena Petrovna Blavatsky, who looked every inch an aristocrat. Her compelling presence was underscored by huge eyes, straight and wiry hair, a round and kindly face and an agility which defied her obesity. She exuded energy and power. She must be a fantastic woman, I thought to myself, recalling some of her writings which I had helped in translating from her widely acclaimed book, *Isis Unveiled*.

By her, but just half a step behind, walked Colonel Olcott, tall, straight and smart. His elegantly tailored dark suit made him look an affluent businessman with immense confidence in himself. Yet, his pepper-and-salt beard and whiskers, bushy and puffing sideburns, broad and prominent forehead, long and wavy hair reaching the collar of his pure white shirt and pince-nez spectacles sitting on his large nose gave the impression of an itinerant preacher. His well-coordinated gait, however, gave away his rank and training as a military officer. He was visibly enjoying the public attention even though he appeared to be slightly unnerved by the closeness of the crowd.

Along with the other members of the reception party, I fell back so that the delegation would be better seen by the people. The wife of the Hindu delegate, Man Noble, a delicate and fragile little lady, however, insisted on allowing us to go ahead of her and the servant Babula. I had to arrange a young member to take charge of them lest they got lost in the crowd.

With our guests in carriages, the procession of dancers, drummers and musicians and of men, women and children carrying flags, poles with colourful flower arrangements and parasols and mock spears meandered through the fort and its hinterland and reached the home of Victory-Gem. An unending line of curious people passed the house, peeping inside through every door and window accessible to them to get a brief glimpse of the visitors. While the Indian delegates had no difficulty in coping with interfering crowds, the three Americans and specially Colonel Olcott were uncomfortable. He wanted the hostess' son to do something.

"This is no doubt as strong a friendliness that the people could show us and we are doing our best to put up with it." said the Colonel. "It has gone on the whole day and we can't get a breath of fresh air and it is becoming a great annoyance."

"Bear with us, Sir. Most of these people have walked for miles at great inconvenience to show how much they appreciate your vision and mission."

I thought it fit to add a word of my own.

"Sir, why don't you take turns, come out and speak to a few of these people? I will interpret. That way I could keep the people away from the doors and windows."

My little ploy worked. Olcott was the first to scramble to the top of a table in the compound and greet the people whose enthusiastic applause pleased him very much. He was a wonderful speaker, full of humour. His photographic memory baffled me. He described his first view of the Island.

"I'll tell you what I saw when the ship entered the harbour. A beautiful bay; a verdant promontory to the north, against which the surf dashed and foamy jets ran high against the rocky shore; a long, curved sandy beach bordered with tile-roofed bungalows almost hidden in an ocean of green palms; the old fort, custom house, lighthouse, jetty and coaling sheds to the south, and to the east the tossing sea with a line of rocks and reefs walling it out from the harbour. Far inland rose Adam's Peak and his sister mountains."

What a stupendous word-picture, I thought.

Mrs. Blavatsky had a great treat for the crowd. What the Colonel did with his oratory, she did with her occult powers. She raised her right hand and made motions of ringing an invisible bell. Its silver chimes filled the air and even the sceptic in me - a product of the Buddha's repeated appeal to rationalism - had to vouch that I heard clearly her "astral or fairy bells." Requests for more were politely complied with.

Mr. Wimbridge was inordinately wordy and I failed in my efforts to make his lugubrious statements intelligible to our semi-literate villagers. He talked, *ad nauseam*, about the goals and objects of their

Society and referred to controversies in his homeland, which had no relevance to the simple folk of rural Sri Lanka. I had about the same experience with the Indian delegates. Their theme was the spiritual glory of their Motherland.

None of them had either the verbal mesmerism of Colonel Olcott or the mysterious charm of Madame Blavatsky. What would have been an unending parade of speeches and miracles on the improvised podium had to be brought to an end as I had to go to the nearby temple for my mid-day meal, well ahead of noon.

Happy-minded Tissa the Ornament of Dharma of Betel-Village, who, due to the sheer length of his name, was simply called Venerable Betel-Village had played a major role in the reception at Galle on account of his seniority. A typical busy-body which the national campaign specially valued, he was a great organizer. At eighty-five, he was young in spirit and indefatigable. He kept the delegates busy with all kinds of activities, which included interviews with several teams of monks from different temples and sects. When the day was over and they longed to call it a day, he would enter into long discussions on abstruse philosophical arguments about Buddhism and Hinduism. Olcott dubbed him the sharpest of the logicians in the Buddhist Sangha and praised him as a particularly persistent disputant, very valuable, very kind.

Among the activities organized to impress the people was a demonstration of the occult powers of Madame Blavatsky. She opened the session by rapping lightly on the head of a person standing nearby with a folded newspaper and all in the audience heard an incredible din while the victim shouted that the rap inside his head was bewildering. She proceeded with what was introduced as her handkerchief phenomenon.

Mr. Victory-Gem was given a new hand-kerchief which he opened. Clearly embroidered on it was the monogram of Madame Blavatsky: HPB. He was asked to fold it, hold it aloft in front of him for a moment and open it. Lo and behold! The monogram HPB had been mysteriously replaced by his own name. A deafening applause lasted minutes.

She repeated the miracle with a person randomly picked out from the crowd. To the great consternation of the person concerned and all around him, her monogram was replaced by the word "Dies." He protested that if it was his name it was spelled with an 'a' as Dias. Betel-Village rose to the occasion and with great tact and wisdom questioned young Dias.

219

"Sir, you told us how you spell the name in English. But how do you write it in Sinhala or how do your friends call you?"

"Venerable Sir, you may be correct. We write and pronounce it in Sinhala as Di-es or rather Di-yes."

A mystery solved and her claim to miraculous power vindicated, she proceeded to astonish her crowd and wound up the performance with a long session of fairy bells which cheerfully rang in the air for minutes. She also produced a booming explosion like the striking of a large steel bar. For a finale, she caused the great table on the podium to tremble and move. The audience cheered and asked for more. But even the most enjoyable feast had to come to an end!

Seated close to Olcott in case he wanted my assistance as an interpreter, I had a chance to talk to the great man.

"Aren't you a bit amused with all our Portuguese and Dutch names?" I asked him.

"Not amused at all, Reverend Priest," he replied. "I am surprised and appalled. You have your own Sanskrit names which are infinitely prettier and more appropriate. Retaining Portuguese and Dutch names which were taken from motives of policy during their regimes, I must confess, degrades and dishonours your nation."

I made a mental note of this as one of the issues he was bound to address in greater detail in the coming weeks. By the end of the evening, my admiration to this man of spirit had redoubled.

Olcott might have given a dozen short speeches a day during the first few days at Galle. I had the privilege of interpreting more than half of them. There was a special reason why I was preferred. The yellow robe that I wore fascinated him and a bilingual Buddhist monk fascinated the people. A shaven headed Asian monk in robes standing besides a long-haired and bearded American in white, he felt, had a theatrical effect which captivated the audience.

His main public address was fixed for the 22nd of May and the subject announced was Theosophy. Olcott was keen to deliver a major speech and wanted to draft it carefully. But he hardly found a minute to himself. He told me in utter despair,

"Reverend Priest, I am quite afraid to trust myself to extemporaneous discourse. I must jot down my thoughts. But I might as well try to compose an aria in a machine shop where fifty blacksmiths were hammering on anvils, fifty turning lathes were whirling and fifty were gathered about to criticize my personal appearance, my pen and my handwriting! Our house is a Babel. Even

220

our rooms are occupied by a friendly mob from morning till night. What can we do?"

"Nothing, Sir," I replied. "Nothing at all. Expect it. Get used to it. In due course you will learn to recede into your inner consciousness and work serenely in the machine shop. You will also learn to think and work as you run."

He patted me on the back spontaneously, saying, "No wonder you fellows are free of all the tensions we Westerners grapple with!"

We laughed together.

In spite of his having to think and improvise on his feet, his first public lecture in the Island proved to be a great success. Betel-Village presided. Olcott's speech was preceded by two formal admonitions by Venerable Sumangala and Venerable Gunananda. If the first was sober in tone and erudite in content, the latter spewed fire and urged action. Olcott was a happy combination of both. An audience of over 2000 monks and laymen listened to him with rapt attention.

The hypothesis that British officials would listen to a fellow white man irrespective of his religious persuasion or opinion was proved by the presence of the entire British population of Galle on this momentous occasion. Stanley Williams, who passed all his efficiency bar examinations with tuition from Pleasant-Gem-Tissa and Little Father, was now the second in command in the Provincial Office and was responsible for this turn-out of the forty-five officials and planters and their families. Venerable Sumangala was quick to point it out. He wished that Olcott would succeed in building on this fund of goodwill and understanding.

The following morning when we met, Olcott gave me a sheet of paper.

"This is what I wrote in my diary last night. I want to give it to some of the High Priests. Isn't it better if I have it in Sinhala?"

I agreed and retired to the temple nearby to work on it. It was an impressive piece of prose:

This was the prologue to such a drama of excitement as we had not dreamt we should ever pass through. In a land of flowers and ideal tropical vegetation, under smiling skies, along roads shaded by clustering palm trees and made gay with miles upon miles of small arches of ribbon-like fringes of tender leaves, and surrounded by a glad nation, whose joy would have led them to the extravagance of actually worshipping us, if permitted, we passed from triumph to

221

triumph, daily stimulated by the magnetism of popular love. The
people could not do enough for us, nothing seemed to them good
enough for us: we were the first white champions of their religion,
speaking of its excellence and its blessed comfort from the
platform, in the face of the missionaries, its enemies and
slanderers. It was that which thrilled their nerves and filled their
affectionate hearts to bursting. I may seem to use strong language,
but in reality it falls far short of facts. If anybody seeks proof, let
him go through the lovely Island now and after fifteen years and
ask what they have to say about this tour of the two Founders and
their party.

I brought him the translation in the afternoon, with some
suggestions on how to make it self-contained and self-explanatory.
Olcott agreed and suggested further,

"I think you should begin with what I wrote in the diary on the eve
of our sighting Colombo. *'New and great responsibilities are to be
faced: momentous issues hang on the result of this visit.'* "

I returned to the temple to interpolate the new additions and fair-
copy the translation. I went back to the home of Mrs. Victory-Gem
around dusk. The delegates were seated round the dining table. They
seemed to have some kind of meeting. It did not take much time to
realize that the atmosphere was charged. It was not a friendly meeting.
They were engaged in some acrimonious exchange of hard words -
hardly what I expected from a self-proclaimed "Brotherhood of
Humanity".

I thought it polite not to barge in. I found a seat in the verandah. In
a little while, Mr. Wimbridge came out.

"Can you find us an interpreter?" he asked me bluntly. There was a
measure of urgency in his tone and I excused him for his departure from
common courtesy.

"Why? I am an interpreter". If my voice betrayed annoyance, it was
spontaneous. "I have been doing that for you for hours over the last five
days. Now what's your problem?"

"Hell has broken loose. We want to speak to the High Priests and
we like to do it through a lay interpreter."

"I am sorry I cannot do what you want. Not until the request comes
properly through your President," I insisted although I had no right or
any delegated authority to do so.

He returned to the table in a huff. For the next few minutes, the noise-level of their dispute had risen from dissent to rudeness to downright abuse. I was amazed and appalled.

The abuse came mainly from Madame Blavatsky. More than a quarter of what she said was not intelligible to me. But I had enough experience with the typical English Billingsgate from my school days that I guessed she was an adept in its Russian-American counterpart. She was assiduously searching for the juiciest of insults to whomever was disagreeing with her.

I was in a quandary. Olcott had asked me to bring the translation that very evening and I had done so. Should I wait for him and be an unwilling evesdropper to a dispute which seemed to have divided the delegation sharply into two groups: Madame Blavatsky and Colonel Olcott on one side and the rest on the other? To my great relief it was Olcott who came this time to the verandah to speak to me.

"I am sorry if that fool Wimbridge offended you, Reverend Priest," he started. He called all Buddhist monks priests. "I want you to come in and write for me and Madame Blavatsky a communique. We want to issue it to the public tonight itself in both English and Sinhala."

One of the Parsi delegates had to give his seat to me and he stood behind me. In the absence of a white cloth covering it, I spread my handkerchief before sitting down. Olcott looked very amused.

"Reverend Priest, Madame Blavatsky and I have decided to embrace Buddhism in public. For several years we have been acting up the precepts of Gautama Buddha and professing his philosophy." Olcott said calmly. I was not surprised as I had read his letter to Pleasant-Gem-Tissa two years ago. There he had said that both of them would some day make a public profession of Buddhism and enter its fold.

"Our colleagues disagree," he continued. "They say that to accept one religion as our personal faith is contrary to the spirit of Theosophy and detrimental to the interests of the Society. We don't agree

"Shall we either go to the temple and meet Venerable Betel-Village or send a carriage for him? He'll have some advice to give us," I proposed.

"We don't want any of these yellow-clad shavelings. They have had a circus in town with us and we have been manipulated like so many donkeys and clowns," shouted one of the opponents, whom I could not identify. I felt I was being deliberately degraded.

"Reverend Priest, please bear with us," said Olcott in a conciliatory spirit. "These gentlemen are under tremendous pressure. They are not as bad as this all the time."

If the last sentence was meant to elicit a little humour, it failed. Instead, in a long drawn drawl, Mr. Wimbridge raised a point of order.

"May I respectfully submit, Mr. President, that this is still a meeting of the delegation and any invitation to a non-member should have had its prior approval."

Olcott never failed to surprise me. He apologized and that too most sincerely. He led me to the verandah and returned to propose formally that my suggestion be approved and that I be invited to the meeting.

In minutes I was back at the table and Wimbridge apologized to me for his tactless reference to Buddhist monks as yellow-clad shavelings.

"Don't you worry, Sir," I replied. "After all, that's a correct description of our exterior. You wouldn't be offended if I say that you, with your unkempt bushy hair, are like a scarecrow in a rice field. Would you?"

Madame Blavatsky laughed loud and the rest joined in. It was an effective antidote to the tension which had hitherto made the meeting disorderly.

"I am relieved by your abundance of forbearance and your great sense of humour," Mr. Wimbridge continued. "To come to our not-so-internal dispute, we are shocked by what the President and the Corresponding Secretary have decided to do. In USA we will be accused of being sectarian and overly partial to one religion. In India, all our Indian fellows and members will desert us. Hindu India had abandoned Buddhism centuries ago. The average Indians don't know it and even those who know it, don't think much of it."

"That's right," joined in a Hindu delegate. "Our great God Vishnu descended to earth as Buddha to preach heresy so as to prevent too many people going to heaven. He preached against sacrifice and the caste structure. Our people will have nothing to do with the Society when they learn that its two distinguished Founders declare openly that they are Buddhists."

"That's not our reason to object," said the Parsi delegate who chose to stand behind me. "We understand Theosophy to be an admirable amalgam all that is good and true in all religions. The Founders must not jeopardize this concept which is what brings all of us in different faiths together."

"Let's take a break," said the President presumably to prevent the resumption of the dispute. "When Venerable Betel-Village comes, we'll reconvene and seek his advice."

Mrs. Victory-Gem who had been very disturbed by the noisy meeting came out with a cup of tea for me and inquired,

"Why are they quarrelling? Have we done anything wrong?"

No sooner I told her that Madame Blavatsky and Olcott had decided to be Buddhists, she brought her palms together, raised her hands to her forehead and said, " Aney! Sadhu!" - a veritable expression of genuine joy.

On arrival, I apprised Venerable Betel-Village of the dispute. The meeting was reconvened. There were enough chairs for all and those for the two monks were covered with white cloth as demanded by tradition. The senior monk asked for the floor and I translated sentence by sentence.

"Friends, we, Buddhists, are not in the numbers game. We never have been. The Buddha himself had made it very clear that he was not preaching with the intention of having converts or disciples. Did we even hint that the distinguished Founders of this important international Society should align themselves with Buddhists, leave alone adopting Buddhism as their personal religion? No. Whether they want to proclaim themselves as Buddhists or not is of no concern to us. Our esteem for them will remain the same in either situation. They gain nothing in this country by announcing themselves to be Buddhists. If by becoming Buddhists they feel that they adopt a philosophy of life more akin to their spiritual needs, that's indeed a personal gain which we must not deprive them. I can speak for the entire Sangha of this Island and say that we would welcome them into the fold of Buddhists if that is their conviction but we will in no way demand or even suggest it. One doesn't have to make a public profession to live as a Buddhist."

"Thank you, Venerable Priest," said Olcott. "We want to proclaim ourselves to be Buddhists. We do this out of our own free will. It is a personal decision and I am asking my friends and colleagues to accept it in that spirit."

Madame Blavatsky nodded her head in assent.

Acrimony had died down. There was no dissent. Immediately the meeting began to discuss the modalities of their conversion. Venerable Betel-Village had a few suggestions to make.

"Colonel Olcott, Madame Blavatsky and friends, I leave the decision to you. If you wish to have a public ceremony, give me three days and I will have one organized with a few hundred monks and a few thousand lay Buddhists besides important government officials. If you wish to do it privately, I will administer the Triple Gem and Five Precepts here and now."

One of the Parsi delegates inquired what the Triple Gem and Five Precepts meant. Venerable Betel-Village asked me to explain.

225

"Among Buddhists there had been no ceremony for admission or confirmation - nothing similar to baptism, communion or donning the holy thread. From the days of the Buddha, when someone wanted to follow the Path he preached, the practice had been for that person to take refuge in the Buddhist equivalent of a Trinity, that is, the Buddha, his teachings and the community of his disciples, the monks and nuns. In our terminology, they are Buddha, Dhamma and Sangha. Then the new convert, so to say, takes upon oneself the fivefold discipline of avoiding killing, stealing, improper sexual relations, falsehood and heedlessness caused by liquor and drugs."

Olcott consulted Madame Blavatsky briefly and opted to make their conversion a public event.

"So it shall be," intoned Venerable Betel-Village gravely.

He could have as well engraved these words on the granite faces of Wimbridge and the other delegates.

XII

Everyone active in the national movement to revive Buddhism was there. Venerable Sumangala and Venerable Gunananda had travelled all the way from Colombo. Present also were the heads of mushrooming chapters of the Amarapura or Burmese Sect created by groups of monks who had obtained their higher ordination in Burma. So was the founder the newest sect which claimed affiliation with Lower Burma and accordingly called Ramanyaka. The venue was a little known temple of the last-mentioned sect. The extensive temple grounds was a vast sea of heads.

Venerable Betel-Village's incredible foresight and indomitable energy had proved effective. He was achieving much more than mere favourable publicity for the public declaration of Buddhism as the personal religion of the two Founders of the International Theosophical Movement.

For decades it had been his mission to bring about better understanding and amicable relations among monks of different sects, sub-sects and chapters. With no doctrinal or even ritualistic specificities, these numerous divisions had come into being on social and administrative grounds. While he was unable to check the proliferation for which the British Administration of the Island was more than indirectly responsible, according to their own records, his call for unity had been well heeded.

Specially the Siamese Sect with its headquarters in Kandy deferred to Betel-Village as he hailed from Kandyan aristocracy. The most visible impact was that the monks of the Siamese sect in the low-country agreed to cover both shoulders as monks in Burma.

On the 25th day of May 1880, this doyen of the Sangha congratulated himself on his success. His life's mission of unifying the Sangha of the Island had not been in vain. Here was proof that various subdivisions would join hands whenever the need arose and they would transcend their petty differences. The enormous gathering of monks from all parts of the Island was to him a show of strength. Little Father and I represented the Sangha of Kandyan origin.

Madame Blavatsky and Olcott knelt before the huge Buddha statue. Betel-Village as the most senior monk present intoned the Pali formulae to take refuge in the Buddha, the Dhamma and the Sangha and the Five Precepts. Both of them had a good deal of trouble catching the words in a new and unfamiliar language and repeating them. Fortunately, a friend of Olcott who knelt behind them whispered the formulae word by word for them to repeat. The vast crowd held its breath while these two solemnly progressed step by step to the last Precept. The ovation that followed was later described by Olcott as "*so mighty as to make one's nerves tingle.*"

Olcott was asked to speak. Once again, I was the preferred interpreter.

"Buddhism is not a new and exotic religion to either Madame Blavatsky or me," he said. "We have read thousands of pages of published material including translations of scriptures of all main traditions of Buddhism"

I was stuck. What did he mean by the scriptures of all main traditions? So insular was my knowledge of Buddhism that I had no idea at all that his reference to plurality was justified. I translated his statement wrongly. But no one corrected me. Were the rest of us as ignorant as I was? At that time in Sri Lanka, we all could have been.

"Over the last three years, we have been consulting the Chief Priests of this country through correspondence. We had many of our knotty points explained by them. We had continued to have face-to-face discussions for hours since our arrival. Even before coming here, Madame Blavatsky has shown her deep understanding of the fundamental message of the Buddha in her two-thousand page magnum opus, *Isis Unveiled*. I am in the process of distilling my knowledge into a manual which I propose to call the *Buddhist Catechism*. We have previously declared ourselves Buddhists long before in America, both privately and in public. What we do today here is only a formal confirmation of our previous professions."

Madame Blavatsky nodded her head vigorously. Recalling the stormy meeting a few days ago, I was surprised that Wimbridge and the rest of the delegation sat stone-faced. Apparently directed to them was the rest of the speech.

"It would be dishonest and useless to mystify the fact of our embracing Buddhism because we do it in the presence of hundreds of monks and thousands of lay devotees. We are to be completely accepted as Buddhists as anyone else present here. But let us make two clarifications. First, it is one thing to be a regular Buddhist and quite another to be a debased modern Buddhist sectarian."

Here, again, I fouled up the translation. I could understand a Christian sectarian because the Reformation led by Martin Luther and the Counter-Reformation had loomed large as teacher after teacher in my two schools used the history classes to bash at what they called the Papacy of the Roman Catholics. But I was yet so ignorant that I thought that a Buddhist sectarian was an oxymoron. Once again, no one corrected me.

"Secondly," he continued. "Speaking on behalf of both Madame Blavatsky and myself, I can say that if Buddhism contained a single dogma that we were compelled to accept, we would not have taken the Five Precepts or remained Buddhists for ten minutes."

The crowd reacted with a loud and prolonged applause. Olcott proceeded to a spirited peroration which I tried to render to the best of my ability. I was never sure if I did justice to it.

"Our Buddhism is that of the Adept Gautama Buddha, which was identically the Wisdom Religion of the Aryan Upanishads and the soul of all ancient world-faiths. Our Buddhism is, in a word, a philosophy, not a creed."

With this meeting my stint in Galle ended. I was wanted at Orange Island which was to be the next stop for Olcott and party. Pleasant-Gem-Tissa and Little Father had identified jobs for me to do there.

On the 26th, I took the early morning stage coach for the six mile ride. At the stand, I bought a copy of a newsy ballad, which its author-publisher-seller was reciting aloud. Similar to what I had read on the Great Debate in my school days, this long poem was meant for the man in the street to see the week's events through the eyes of a peer. I read it avidly many times.

The monsoon blows in gales abundant
To bring the rains we sorely need
To grow the crops in our land so green.
But in its wake the storms bring in
The good and the bad alike.

The self-same winds that blew into Galle
The marauding fleet of Laurenco d'Almedo
His plundering hosts of white invaders.
Ringing the death-knell of our faith and creed,
The ruin of a nation under the trampling feet
Of the Portuguese, the Dutch and the British.

Verily this time the storm only hails
A mystic woman of captivating eyes
And a white Sadhu with a becoming beard
Goading us to action with hopes renewed.
"We come because we need you,

The gentlest race of serene Buddhists"
They say, "Yours is a creed of peace and tolerance
Which the world today in crisis seeks.
Give us your serenity, your wisdom, your culture."

What do we need to be convinced
We are no mean slavish underlings?
Proud heirs to a worthy heritage
Simply by our birth, dear friends,
In this land of a glorious past,
In this Isle of verdant splendour.

Harken, my friends to the clarion call
Of the Colonel who fought to free slaves
Of his own country and have come overseas
To free us from slavery of mind and spirit.

Amidst a myriad "Sadhu! Sadhu!! Sadhu!!!"
They kneel before the Sangha and loudly proclaim
"We have long been Buddhists of piety infinite
Formally do we now declare with your blessings
We dedicate our lives to revive in your land
Its noble heritage with values sublime."

"Sadhu! Sadhu!! Sadhu!!!" the crowd responded.

To a nation struggling to stand on its feet
You indeed are a saviour in time.
May the Triple Gem and all the gods
Protect you for ever, Colonel Olcott -
Our White Messiah, our faith, our hope.

I had memorized the poem by the time the coach reached Orange Island. As I climbed the hundred steps to the Rock-Reflection Monastery, I was saying to myself.

You indeed are a saviour in time
Our White Messiah, our faith, our hope.

Book Three

HOW DOES YOUR GARDEN GROW?

I

No sooner had I reached the top of the stairway than I was met by an acolyte who directed me to the room of Pleasant-Gem-Tissa.

"We are waiting for you, Little Name," the scholar-monk said very pleasantly. "You have another special job."

Except Betel-Village who was still in Galle with Olcott and his party, the leading lights of the Sangha were assembled in his parlour. I went on my knees and worshipped each one of them including Little Father who was there to take notes of the meeting.

It was Venerable Sumangala to whom the floor was given to instruct me.

"Pure-Wisdom, we are very concerned with what is taking place in Galle. Colonel Olcott is a serious man of science. His letters to each one of us from America and India showed that his interest in Eastern religions was genuine. None of us doubt that he was sincere in embracing Buddhism as his personal religion and that he is as devout as any one of us."

He paused to make sure if any one wanted to add anything and continued,

"To be frank, however, we are not that sure of Mrs. Blavatsky. All she wants is to entice people to her brand of Theosophy through her magic, which they call an occult phenomenon. What might have worked with her American audiences would not have the same effect here. Indian magicians at any market place perform more astounding tricks. Village girls get into a trance and talk with spirits. Credulous as our people are, they are more likely to be amused and entertained by these phenomena than enthralled and carried away. Her raps and bells are becoming a joke."

Once again, he looked around and was encouraged by nods of agreement.

"If Colonel Olcott doesn't distance himself from her weird performances, he is bound to lose credibility. And this we cannot allow. He is the best ally we have so far found and we cannot afford to risk any loss to his prestige. He should not be open to ridicule either by the missionaries and their supporters in the Government or by our own people".

"I tried my very best with what little English I could command to explain that our people are not impressed by the embroidered handerchiefs and the like," added Venerable Gunanada. "Our sorcerers can get a mango seed to grow into a plant, bear fruit before your eyes and share the ripened fruit with the onlookers," .

"We have to impress on Colonel Olcott that the occult phenomena of Mrs. Blavatsky could harm our movement," continued Venerable Sumangala. "What we want the Little Name to do is to have a confidential chat with Colonel Olcott and tell him what we feel".

I was not surprised by their disappointment with Madame Blavatsky. I, too, felt that her occult performances distracted from the seriousness of their mission of founding a Universal Brotherhood of Humanity. Now that they were professed Buddhists, I found her reliance on occultism to win people to Theosophy quite incongruous. I had been amused when she mentioned her conversations with Masters or Adepts who made aerial visits in the night from the mountains of Tibet to approve what she and the Colonel were doing in Galle. I was equally amazed when Colonel Olcott seemed to believe her reports.

Pleasant-Gem-Tissa who had been silent so far thought it fit to caution me.

"Little Name, be very tactful. We have no idea what their relationship is. Are they wife and husband or are they lovers? Or is their friendship purely platonic? Do not sound critical. You must not put him or her on the defensive. If you sense any resentment on his part, don't proceed but come back to us."

It was clear that the senior monks assigned very great importance to what I was expected to achieve. I was not given any other tasks in the elaborate preparations which were being made to receive Olcott and his party. Little Father had a long chat with me in the afternoon. Pleasant-Gem-Tissa underscored the concerns of the Sangha that the manner in which the visit of the Theosophists was being handled could be detrimental to the dual cause of the revival of Buddhism and the attainment of an immediate measure of Self-rule and eventual independence from the British.

"We appear to be working at cross purposes," he said. "He raises funds for Buddhist Publications - no doubt an important activity from his point of view in propagating Buddhism in the West. But what we want here and now are schools for our children, presently left to the tender mercies of missionaries who have only one objective. You must tell him this also."

What a responsiblity for a twenty-two year old monk whose experience in diplomacy was zero! What a price to pay for my fluency in English! I missed Noble Son of Wisdom who was busy with his new school in Colombo. I wished I could have had his guidance.

I walked down to the beach and sat on a rock. Rough waves dashed in succession on the rock sending forth a cool spray of brine which was most refreshing. The navy blue water of the sea fringed by foamy white crests of waves reflected a cloudless sky of sapphire blue. On the horizon was a deceptively immobile ship. It was heading for Colombo as I could discern from the bellowing smoke.

The more I tried to concentrate on the stupendous task of convincing a man twice my age that his partner, companion, friend and perhaps even lover be disciplined if not disowned, the more I was distracted by memories of other challenges which I had faced in my relatively brief life.

The beautiful sunset was a moment of relief. The orange hued sky merged with the silvery sea at the point where the sun, three times larger than it was when in mid sky, sank slowly and majestically. What a glorious way to say good-bye to a land lit, warmed and made rich in its verdure. It was a fitting subject for meditation - not so much on the unwholesomenesss of life as my training and vocation would prompt but on the beauty of nature and its perrenial message of hope. Involuntarily as it so often happens, my thoughts were on Slim-Jewel and the other life I would have had if our destinies had unfolded differently.

"Look at me," I told myself, "a monk commited to life-long celibacy. Over there is Slim-Jewel - a widowed mother pursuing her own career. But would I brook anyone who would express less than full confidence in whatever she did, said or thought? Is she alone in this world to fight her many battles in the arduous task of being a single parent to her beautiful daughter?"

Neither query had the remotest relevance to the problem I was grappling with. But I was still trying to answer them as I climbed the steps back to the temple.

Refreshed by a night of rest and reflection, I looked forward to the next day. The triumphant entry of the Theosophists to Orange Island was so spectacular that the receptions they had been given in Galle faded into insignificance. Of course, Galle was fully represented in the vast crowd and more prominently among special invitees. But so were the coastal towns right up to Colombo and beyond.

It was not a case of overdoing what Venerable Betel-Village had done most painstakingly. The fact was that Pleasant-Gem-Tissa was an infinitely better organizer with both vision and imagination. Garlands, bouquets, "Praise Papers" and speeches overwhelmed the visitors. Colonel Olcott gave a most inspiring speech. Conspicuously absent were the antics of Madame Blavatsky. She was the smiling recipient of floral tributes but remained in the background just as the other delegates. Even Wimbridge had receded to the background.

As I translated the various speeches from Sinhala to English and English to Sinhala, I looked for any clue which would explain this change. The closest I came was in the speech of Venerable Gunananda.

"I welcome most heartily our 'White Buddhists' who, of their own free will, embraced Buddhism as their personal faith. I also welcome the delegates of the Theosophical Society who are with them," he began making very clear that Colonel Olcott and Madame Blavatsky were now different from the rest of the delegation. In the course of his brief but brilliantly worded speech, he said further,

"It was not a miracle that these two personages born so far apart - one in the east of America and other in Russia - should meet in a joint endeavour and, in pursuance of it, take the bold step of singling out the precept and practice of the Buddha for their inspiration and guidance. The miracle is that no miracles played any part in their conversion - if the unfelicitous word 'conversion' is in any way applicable to the public declaration of their convictions.

"What seemed to have won them over are cold logic, clinical investigation and dogma-free openness which characterize the teachings of the Buddha. As you all know, the Buddha discouraged all miracles save one. The exception was the Miracle of Instruction.

"When challenged by an appeal to give back life to a dead child, what did the Buddha do? Did he display his miraculous powers, which we believe he possessed? No. It would have shameful exhibitionism if such powers as he possessed was utilized sorcerer-like to give back life to just one individual. Of what use could it have been for humanity?"

He narrated the charming story of Slim Gotami who carried her dead son to the Buddha and asked for a remedy to revive him. The Buddha's response was to send her begging for a handful of mustard.

"A handful of mustard could have been got from the poorest home. But it had to come from a home that had seen no death. She wanders through the city and finds no house which had not been visited by death. She returns to the Buddha to thank him, 'Master, you have revealed to me the truth.' She entered the Order to follow the Buddha's Path to Immortality. That is how the Miracle of Instruction works."

The beaming smile of the Colonel who nodded vigourously in agreement evinced some unknown victory he had recently gained. Positively, he had had his way, for there were no more raps or bells or embroidered handerchiefs. Olcott had made his choice.

The glum stare of Madame Blavatsky spoke volumes. Was it the beginning of parting of ways for the two stalwarts? I was curious as much as I was relieved. I was spared an agonizing mission. Particularly refreshing was Olcott's rousing address which the crowd received through my rendering with frequent applause and a long and enthusiastic ovation.

"I am here to work with you, my spiritual friends, on a Buddhist Theosophical Movement. If there is any religion which could be linked to Theosophy without the danger of creating an oxymoron, it is Buddhism. They are so compatible and mutually enriching. Help me, my brothers and sisters, in my dual strtategy of defining Buddhist Theosophy on the one hand and promoting Universal Buddhism on the other," was his peroration.

I had no idea what he meant by Universal Buddhism. I had no doubt that my literal rendering of the two words conveyed nothing to the listeners, just as they meant nothing to me.

"Let's get down to business," Pleasant-Gem-Tissa told Little Father as soon as the welcome meeting was over. "Get the children to class and let our visitors see the school in session."

The visitors quenched their thirst with the deliciously cool and refreshing water of the king coconut, served in the bright orange goblet, which nature had provided to make the divine beverage fittingly presentable. In the meantime, Little Father rounded up the teachers and the children.

Teaching was in progress by the time the visitors, in single file, entered the school hall. Colonel Olcott at the head of the line, preceded by Pleasant-Gem-Tissa and me, appeared a bit confused. He and perhaps the rest of the team had not seen an open-hall school in which several classes were conducted in one space, undivided by partitions. Long desks and chairs were arranged in two rows for each class - boys in one and the girls in the other. Each class faced the teacher whose table and chair and the blackboard on an easle were by the wall. Zigzagging boundary lines between classes which sat facing outward were narrow corridor-like spaces that facilitated circulation. The Colonel stood between two classes straining his ears to distinguish how clearly the children in the last rows heard their teacher.

As we reached each class the pupils stood and welcomed the visitors saying 'Good morning' in English.

"What do you teach?" Olcott asked each teacher. As the subject was given, he would add, "Ignore our intrusion. Please continue teaching."

Like a detective looking for clues to solve a major crime, he went from class to class slowly.

Had he been an inspector of schools? He observed everything - dust on the desks, a loose panel on the bookcase, a child wiping his runny nose with the sleeve of his torn shirt. He asked incisive questions. He examined the textbooks and pupil's exercise books. He asked me to translate the list of contents of each textbook. He was meticulous in his note-taking. He would have continued longer. But the lunch hour for monks was announced and Little Father and I had to return to the temple.

When we met after lunch, the senior scholar-monks were present. Again, it was my duty to translate a long statement of Olcott which turned out to be a scathing attack of what he has seen in the school. He was frank and his remarks were cutting. Was he really angry? Or was it simply hystrionics? Nothing that was done in the school was correct.

"You call this Buddhist education?" he asked mockingly. "All that's Buddhist about it is that you get children to chant some unintelligible Pali stanzas at the beginning and the end of the school day. See the books you use. Readers written and published by missionaries, full of Biblical stories and anectodes from the West. 'George Washington and the cherry tree' is a good story. I was happy when the whole class knew who Washington was. 'King Arthur and his Roundtable'! This isn't even history! But where are the stories from your own culture? You have a whole treasure house of stories with which to inculcate appropriate values to your children: the life of the Buddha, hundreds of Birth Stories of his previous lives, fables from India, your own recorded history of over two millennia, your folklore!"

Had he heard our comments on his efforts to raise funds for Buddhist publications? If so, he was defending himself. He was sore that a letter of Venerable Sumangala discouraged his plans to translate the Buddhist Canon in Pali into English. I felt bad because it was I who drafted it and the strong words I used reflected my inexperience and limited command of English rather than the scholar-monk's judgement. I had said that it was a matter next to impossible to translate the Buddha's discourses without losing their "energy, sweetness and propriety." I was at a loss to recall what actually I meant!

Even then, he was correct. We had been so engrossed in setting up schools that we had not thought of the curriculum contents or methods of teaching. As long as the children were freed from the possible danger of conversion to Christianity, we had been content.

Olcott's remarks were an eye-opener. The senior monks admitted their mistake and thanked him profusely. The most eloquent among them was Venerable Sumangala.

"You have opened our eyes, our dear friend," he said. "You have come to us as a messenger of the gods bearing a light with which we can see what was hitherto in the dark. Your present mission is to set up as many branches of the Theosophical Society which you and your illustrious co-worker, Madame Blavatsky, can establish. But come again as soon as you can and lead a national Buddhist educational campaign. In the meantime, do please continue to tell us what we do wrong."

What modesty, I thought as I translated his statement.

Olcott was ready to offer his own concept of Buddhist education.

"During our stay in Galle, we were honoured by visits of several dignitaries of the Roman Catholic Church. They wanted to talk to us and find out what we did and what we planned to do in the Island. I don't think they felt threatened. They were interested. We appreciate their readiness to speak to us, just as we deplore the arrogance and the aloofness with which other missionaries rejected every overture on our part to meet them. They did not want to speak to us and they made this very clear. All they have done so far is to put obstacles in our way. They are the sworn ..."

Madame Blavatsky who sat beside him whispered something to his ear and the Colonel nodded his head in agreement. On my part, the unfinished sentence was not translated.

"Yes, that's it," he said. "That's not what I wanted to say. The Catholic priests who saw us were from France, Italy, Belgium and Spain. They seemed to have no political interest and their concerns with regard to the educational needs of the country appeared genuine. For example, they stressed that the missionaries had a double standard as regards the language of instruction and its content. They conducted a handful of exorbitantly expensive English schools for the rich and the privileged. We haven't yet seen any but, from our Indian experience, I can imagine that they could be as good as the best schools of England."

I would have liked very much to interject my own observations as I knew the system from within. But I was only his voice. An interpreter has to remember that his job is purely mechanical!

"The aim was," he continued, "to produce suave young men who conversed in English, thought like the British, behaved like them and could eventually work for them. In these schools, they wouldn't allow national languages, specially Sinhala, or the history of the Island to be taught. What's the reason? Buddhism. Buddhism pervades your history and literature. Whatever history they taught began with the arrival of the Portuguese in the sixteenth century. But for the masses, they conduct vernacular schools. Just look at the word. *Vernacular*. It comes from the Latin word *verna*, meaning a homeborn slave! How pejorative!"

Once again, Madame Blavatsky whispered to his ear and he looked embarrassed.

"Our illustrious Corresponding Secretary reminds me that the word had outgrown its original meaning and is widely used to designate anything indigenous. She also tells me that the missionaries whose primary interest is the propagation of Christianity would not have bothered with English education at all if the British policy in the country did not assign so high a premium to English as the magic entry requirement to government service, professions and the social elite."

Suddenly, he raised his voice.

"You have taken only one half of this strategy. Why do you take as your model their Sinhala schools. Where will that lead you to? Nowhere! Nowhere! Nowhere!"

Resuming his normal tone of persuasion and conciliation, he outlined his concept of an educational effort which would give rise to a Sinhala Buddhist elite. He urged that priority be given to establishing English Buddhist schools which would match the best of the missionary schools.

"I will scout the whole world and find dedicated teachers and administrators who would man such schools," he said in conclusion.

I was overjoyed when he invited me to walk with him on the beach. I took him to the spot where I had spent the previous evening. We sat on the same rock and discussed the implications of the reform measures he had proposed in the course of the day.

Somewhere in the conversation, I had slipped and his reaction was swift and angry.

"Tell me, my dear young priest, are you by any chance a fifth columnist in monk's robes? You are so touchy whenever anything is said against the missionaries."

I had no idea what a fifth columnist meant until he explained the origin of the expression.

"The army usually marches in four columns," he explained. "If it has sympathizers and collaborators in the enemy camp, it is tantamount to having an additional column looking after its interests from within. You and for that matter the other priest, your uncle, give us the impression that you are far too beholden to missionaries for whatever they had done for you. If you are on our side to play any sinister role,

240

let me warn you. Get back to where you came from or I will not hesitate for a moment to expose you. I will have you hounded out of the Sangha, if that is the last thing I do in Ceylon."

If I over-reacted to his statement with peevish pique, the fault could have been my youthful arrogance. I got up abruptly and, without a further word, walked back to the temple. He called after me twice and I ignored him.

Back in the temple, I recounted the incident to Little Father. He appeared to take it lightly.

"Ultimately the truth prevails, son. You don't have to labour it," he said. "The Colonel will know who we are and why we take the positions we take. If we are spies of Christians in the Buddhist camp, whom are we spying for? Reverend Thomas Blake who is dead and gone? Reverend Kenneth Saunders who has been kicked upstairs to Burma? Give the Colonel time. He'll find out who we are."

His advice was for me to continue my work assisting the delegation, specially as he, himself, would resume his work in setting up another school in a remote village up the Gin River. But that was not to be.

Venerable Sumangala wanted me in Colombo to make preparations for the visit of the Theosophists to the capital.

We left Orange Island a little after midnight and reached Black Ford in time for a quick lunch at a temple near the railway station. We found seats in an early afternoon train to Colombo.

Right through the journey I thought hardly of anything other than the undeserved rebuke of Olcott and my peurile reaction. I wondered how he would interpret my absence. Would he inquire why both Little Father and I were not in the entourage? Or would he rush to the conclusion that we had taken cover because he threatened to expose us? Would he congratulate himself or even crow a bit that his instinctual powers saved the Buddhist activists of not one, but two, secret agents of the missionaries - or rather two dangerous fifth columnists?

Wimbridge had told me of the Colonel's many successes as a special commissioner of the War Department in America.

"You should read his article 'The War's Carnival of Fraud'. He went after very powerful people both in the administration and among military contractors. He could smoke out frauds as snakes from an anthill. His expertise was so higly recognized that he was asked to investigate allegations of a conspiracy after the assassination of President Abraham Lincoln. Nothing escapes his eye."

I laughed to myself to think how in Olcott's eyes Little Father and I would be another pair of snakes.

I would have have liked very much to tell Venerable Sumangala what transpired between me and Colonel Olcott. But it was not possible. He travelled in an upper class compartment. The train was unduly delayed on account of floods and damage to the track. We reached the College long after sunset.

It was strange to be back in my quiet cell in Palace Hill. Galle and Orange Island with the hustle and bustle of Olcott's visit seemed to be on another planet.

Here was peace. The overpowering tranquility of a monastic cell. Solitude is always a healing balm. The stillness of the night which made the plaintive cry of every tiny insect audible was in sharp contrast from the turmoil of the world outside. It was an invitation to savour, even briefly, the solace and joy of a tamed mind - a mind where thoughts of conceit and competition, avarice and aversion, malice and jealousy were superseded by those of goodwill and compassion.

Far away in another world were the angry speeches and exposed nerves, the blandly stated half-truths of innuendo and imputation, self-assumed and shamelessly proclaimed righteousness and the "Holier than Thou" attitude of the people I was with only a while ago. What dismayed me was that their words and deeds passed for proof of piety and devotion to the Word of the Buddha, the Prince, nay, the King, the Emperor, of Peace. How senseless!

I sat cross-legged on the little bed, recited excerpts from the Book of Protection, practised for a while the basic meditation on In- and Out-breathing and filled my mind with thoughts of loving kindness:

May all in misery be free from misery
May all in fear be free of fear
May all in sorrow be free of sorrow
May all beings be well and happy

Exhausted by incessant activity of over a week and a day of tiresome traveling, I fell into dreamless sleep.

As duty demanded, I joined in the group chanting at dawn. The reward for my assiduity was a chance to meet Noble Son of Wisdom. Usually he resided in a room at the new school to which he devoted all his time and energy. On this day, however, he had been asked by Venerable Sumangala to be at the College for a meeting.

"You have become a big-time impressario for Olcott and I am cooling my heels with no classes in Sanskrit," he told me by way of greeting. "When is your circus coming to town?"

If he expected me to be annoyed by his comparison of Olcott and his entourage to a circus, he would have been disappointed. I agreed with him that we had hitherto handled the visit very much as a circus. I told him of the raps and bells of Madame Blavatsky and the efforts of

243

senior monks to extricate Olcott from the so-called occult sciences. These, in the assessment of the monks and the more intelligent people, were blatantly comical. I lost no time in telling him of my last encounter with Olcott and how I reacted to his innuendo.

"You did right, Pure," he said. "I know something of this man and his Russian girl friend. He was discussed at a meeting of the Psychic Research Society in London - I am not sure but it had some such name. I was there to give a talk on the Siamese traditions of spiritualism and its connections with Buddhism. As I was a Buddhist someone wanted to know whether I knew Olcott and Blavatsky. I had to plead ignorance. You will be interested in what he had to tell me."

The arrival of the senior monks to the morning ceremony interrupted our conversation. We could resume it only after breakfast.

When Noble Son of Wisdom visited me in my cell, I asked him,
"Why were you asked whether you knew these two persons?"

"This gentleman had read a letter in an American newspaper in which they had declared themselves to be Buddhists. He expected me to know it."

"You mean long before they came to Ceylon."

"Yes. Pure, that was at least three years ago. Madame Blavatsky has been the more enthusiastic of the two. She called herself a natural Buddhist pantheist, whatever it meant."

As Noble Son of Wisdom recalled what he heard at the meeting, I took down notes.

"Yes. I remember why the members of this Society were so excited about these two people and their profession of Buddhism. Olcott came from a Puritanical Calvanistic religious background and Blavatsky was reputed to be a Russian aristocrat professing Russian Orthodox Christianity. Even as a young man, hardly twenty years of age, Olcott had taken an interest in what they called the occult sciences and begun to write on spiritualism. It was a craze in America - as a matter of fact, in Europe too - for people to dabble in all kinds of encounters with the spirits of the dead, to explore life after death and to have seances where they believed that they actually conversed with their dead relatives who, as obliging spirits, volunteered when called to talk through mediums."

Olcott had been a student of the phenomenon. He was neither overly credulous nor sceptically critical. This had endeared him to people who approached the subject with an open mind. To him it was an interesting academic pursuit. It brought him in touch with a growing circle of intellectuals through whom he was introduced to the emerging sciences of the mind, philosophy and Asian religions. He had become

244

liberal, eclectic and cosmopolitan as far as his religious persuasions were concerned. But he was hardly a man of the spirit.

He knew the importance of economic success. His passion was for scientific agriculture. He was twenty-four when he set up a Farm School. He wrote several successfull books on agriculture and campaigned for reform and modernization of agriculture. One of his main interests had been in utilizing advances in technology for the development of farm machinery. His competence in this field was so well recognized that he was able to transform his career as a journalist to that of an agricultural reformer.

As Noble Son of Wisdom recounted what he had heard of Olcott's achievements in scientific agriculture, I jotted in the margin of my notes, "How does your garden grow?" I have no explanation why this line from a nursery rhyme I had learnt from Mrs. Blake should come to my mind at this precise moment. Did I feel that Olcott should help our country in the field of modern agriculture rather than dabble with things in which he might not be altogether competent? I would not deny that I harboured a few hostile thoughts against him at this particular moment. I was still hurt that he had accused me and Little Father as of being the secret agents of missionaries. Or was it that I considered his self-assumed mission to be to convert our lovely island into a lovelier tropical garden?

Now as I write of my conversation with Noble Son of Wisdom exactly sixty-eight years ago, I cannot recollect all my thoughts. But the line seems to serve me best as the caption for the third part of my narrative which would deal with how the seeds and seedlings he planted lovingly had blossomed and borne much fruit.

"It was as the agricultural editor of a newspaper," continued the charismatic Siamese monk, who still in the robe of a mendicant, exuded the power and elegance of the prince he was, "that he went to investigate the claims made by Madame Blavatsky of spiritual powers. He was overwhelmed by what she showed him. Olcott - the man of science and technology - had been wavering in his faith in spiritualism. One might have even called him an open-minded sceptic. But after this encounter with Madame Balvatsky, he was the strongest ally of so-called occult sciences. She, in turn, saw in his mastery of language and organizational capacity what she needed to take her message to the nation and the world. Since then they have been an unrivalled pair pedalling an unlikely medley of Egyptian myth, Tibetan mysticism and Indian religious lore."

245

"Wasn't he about forty and she an year older when this took place? What were they all this while?" I asked as I found Noble Son of Wisdom to know more of them than I had imagined.

"Olcott had had a checkered career. He was a journalist before he became an agricultural educationalist and entrepreneur. When the American Civil War broke out in 1861 he was twenty-nine and he joined the Union Army. Chronic dysentry obliged him to leave the battle front and take a commission in the War Department."

"That's where he became the investigator *par excellence*?"

"That's right. Apparently these investigations convinced him of the usefulness of a knowledge of law. He studied Law and ended up as an attorney in the city of New York. He was quite influential and had a lucrative practice. Right through all these career changes, he continued with what I think was his real passion - writing, investigating and reforming. I think he fancied himself to be some kind of universal reformer."

"And Madame Blavatsky?" I asked.

"Little is known of her. Her claim of Russian aristocracy is not doubted. Nor her boast that she had travelled widely. But whether she went to Tibet or met all those fanciful Masters and Adepts and the like is another kettle of fish. What I think is that she is well-read and has an enormously active imagination. She's no charlatan; nor is she a scholar. Oh! She does have some charisma!"

The bell rang to announce the time for lunch. It was another day when the mid-day meal was being offered by some important person and we had to join the ceremony.

I was thankful to Noble Son of Wisdom for the information he could give me of the backgrounds of two people who, in a deeply meaningful way, had begun to influence my life.

I knew that my estrangement from his entourage was temporary. How I looked forward to their arrival in Colombo and to see their reaction when I rejoin them!

The patron of the almsgiving that day was a man of great wealth and influence. Benefiting from the economic opportunities in a colony of an extensive empire, the family of Hewavitharana - a name suggestive of military links and meaning 'Military Investigator' - had made good.

The patriarch of the clan was Don Carolis, a successful designer of modern furniture for which he imported from Burma the veritable king of timber - Burmese teak. His Portuguese name was indicative of the

246

impact of foreign rule in the maritime regions of the Island. Hailing from the Southern Province and from a village not too far from that of Venerable Sumangala, Don Carolis was a close friend and supporter of the scholar-monk.

The monks donning their robes in formal fashion to cover both shoulders and carrying their decorative fans assembled in front of the image house to form a single file according to seniority. Specially invited was Venerable Gunananda who had transcended lurking caste and clan prejudices of contemporary society on account of his brilliant oratory and single-minded devotion to the national revival movement. A colourful procession of flag- and flower-carrying devotees, tom-tom beaters, trumpeters and dancers led the monks out of the College premises around the block of new homes sprouting to the south and returned to a large tent which had been erected on the front lawn.

To display his esteem of the Sangha rather than to manifest his piety, Don Carolis himself was crouching at the entrance with a basin of water to wash the feet of the monks. Near him was his fifteen year old son, Don David, with a towel to dry the feet. Though still the most junior of the ordained monks, Noble Son of Wisdom and I were not too far from the senior monks. The majority who were students of the College were novices.

As my feet were dried by Don David with a gracefully deft motion of both hands, I could not take my eyes away from him. There was something magnetic and captivating in his eyes. I smiled and he smiled in return. His handsome face lit from within as he smiled. I had seen this glow in his face at Galle when he stood holding his mother's hand at the jetty to welcome Colonel Olcott.

For some inexplicable reason, right through the ceremonies of the almsgiving my eyes hardly ever left Don David. Perhaps, he had noticed it himself. When gifts were being handed to monks individually, he came with his mother to where Noble Son of Wisdom and I were seated. The slight limp which made him jerk as he moved toward us evoked a feeling of sadness in me. He was such a handsome boy with sharp eyes, gracefully curved lips and wavy hair.

Don David went on his knees and worshipped us.

"I heard you in Galle," he said in English. "You translate so well. I wish I could do that as easily as you do."

"You will, son. All you need is a little practice," added Noble Son of Wisdom.

Don David was certainly modest. He interpreted briskly and accurately what his mother said to the princely monk of Siam and the latter's replies. His command of both languages was excellent.

247

"How come you have such a wonderful command of the Sinhala language?" I had to ask.

I knew that national languages were neither taught nor encouraged in prestigious missionary colleges. He was studying at St. Thomas' College, which was one of the most exclusive schools run by Anglican missionaries.

"My parents insist that I should master Sinhala and also learn some Pali. The Chief High Priest Venerable Sumangala teaches me personally."

"Do please meet us when you are next in the College," I said.

"Most certainly, Venerable Sirs. Could I come to ask you some questions?"

The question was directed to both me and Noble Son of Wisdom.

It was clear that the almsgiving of the foremost supporter was the reason for the hurried return of Venerable Sumangala to Colombo. Immediately after the event, he along with Venerable Gunananda left for Panadura, the scene of the Great Debate, where a special meeting was being organized to welcome Olcott.

I remained in Palace Hill to attend to a series of tasks which he had assigned to me. One of them was to prepare and publish a brochure on Olcott's first week in Sri Lanka. Two purposes were to be achieved. One was to have a permanent record of the momentous incidents of a week which later historians were bound to characterize as a landmark in the national and Buddhist revival of the Island. The other, more urgent task was to get more people to listen to Olcott and to be encouraged and inspired by his identification with the efforts of the Sangha.

To Venerable Sumangala, Olcott was an indispensable ally. But his usefulness depended on the extent to which Buddhism was given primacy of place in preference to the hazy eclectic notions of Theosophy.

Enthused as I was with every challenging assignment, I spent the next couple of days in a frenzy of inspired activity. By the time Olcott and his party arrived in Colombo with an unusually violent monsoon storm, I had a few hundred copies of my brochure printed and ready for distribution.

II

The first public address by Olcott in the capital was scheduled for the next evening. The subject was to be "Buddhism and Theosophy". Venerable Sumangala had invited important Government officials and many had accepted his invitation. Among them was the Colonial Secretary, the most senior British administrator of the Island next to the Governor, and the Inspector General of Police. Leaving nothing to chance, the scholar monk had arranged a closed-door consultation with Olcott along with Gunananda and Subhuti of Curse-Sword.

On arrival at the College, the Colonel was surprised to see me. I was present at the meeting to interpret and take down notes.

"I thought you ran away, young priest," he told me.

I knew what he was driving at and had no intention to offer him any explanation. I was relieved when Venerable Sumangala, recognizing a tinge of hostility in his tone, said somewhat sharply,

"We monks don't run away. We don't turn back either."

Softening his tone considerably, he added,

"You know the last words of the Buddha. 'Don't turn back. Go forward.' " He recited the relevant Pali text melodiously.

Whether my presence at the meeting and the scholar-monk's remark in my favour convinced Olcott that I had not run away for fear of his threat to "expose" me as an enemy in hiding, I had no way to know. But as the meeting proceeded he became warmer and more cordial.

"How much we missed you in Black Ford and Panadura. We really had trouble with our interpreters. Wimbridge had the most unnerving experience of his life. About half the audience burst out in mirthful laughter at practically every sentence uttered by the interpreter. I was puzzled because Wimbridge was no humourist. He was making a dry as dust proclamation on religious tolerance. I had to ask someone what was going on."

"What was going on, Sir?" I inquired as I had no clue.

"It was funny." he replied and took out a piece of paper in which he had jotted some notes. "When Wimbridge said, 'Let us take a material case,' the translation came as '*Let us take a box full of materials.*' 'One should never attack anyone's religion' was rendered as '*Never beat a man of another religion*'. 'We must learn to get on with a world of diverse beliefs, values and aspirations' I hear was the most mangled. It came in Sinhala as '*We must practise how to climb to the top of the world of different myths, prices and breathings.*' But this was the funniest. 'Our only asylum is in faith and tolerance' became '*In belief and patience is our only mad-house.*'

"One more. It referred to me and my instant friendship with the Sangha. Wimbridge said, 'What a hit our leader made with the Venerable Priests', and the interpreter brought the house down. He had said, '*What a blow* (literally, mind you) *our leader gave the monks.*' Those who understood both languages found the whole thing hillarious. If they could not control their laughter, you can't really blame them."

"Did you have any trouble when you spoke, Sir?"

"Fortunately not. With my horrible experiences with Hindi, Marathi and Gujerati translators, I have learnt to speak plain English, if a bit high-flown at times. No idioms, no figurative speech, no imagery, no metaphors and certainly no innocent-looking strings of verbs and prepositions."

I knew what he meant by strings of verbs and prepositions. They had been my biggest bugbear. Make, get, hit, do, and speak look all so innocent until each little preposition that is added creates veritable mayhem. I had been made conscious of the importance of the place of each word in a sentence. It was Reverend Blake who once showed me that the simple sentence 'I hit him in the eye' could produce seven different sentences, each with a distinct meaning, according to where the word 'only' was inserted.

I wondered how I had fared as a translator.

"What have you heard about my efforts, Sir?"

"With your work, the speakers have a major grievance."

I was dismayed. Only the guffaw of the Colonel restored my self-confidence.

"You know their grievance? People say that your translation is always better than the original speech."

He laughed again and continued in a serious tone,

"I did ask several about your interpretations, young priest. They all agree you are superb. Accurate, faithful and eloquent. I could judge from the way you translate into English. You have the knack of conveying the emotions of a speaker as well as the sense of his words. Keep it up, young priest. Your country needs you."

He patted my arm lightly. I needed the reassurance. What was unsaid but yet eloquently expressed by his kindly face was

"Let's forget what happened in the beach the other evening. Let's be friends."

What a remarkable man!

I discussed the gist of the morning's deliberations with Noble Son of Wisdom. I wanted his comments on my minutes of the meeting. It would have been quicker if he could read them. But they were in Sinhala.

What I found enigmatic was the particular attitude of each of the three senior monks towards Olcott.

Venerable Gunananda, who was more a propagandist than a scholar, empathized with the "White Buddhist". They were both on the same wavelength as regards what moved crowds, fired up people and won support for a movement. Drama, eloquence, demogogy, half-truths, innuendos had their use, they both agreed.

"What is said is no doubt important," said Venerable Gunananda. "But how it is said is far more important."

He appealed for a free hand to be given to Olcott specially in respect of his scathing attacks on Christianity and its missionaries.

"He has a legitimate grievance. You know what happened in Black Ford and Panadura. At the instigation of the missionaries, the Government Agent forbade the use of any state building for the Colonel's speeches. So meetings had to be held in the open air."

"Was it before or after the reception which the Hindu Police Magistrate gave the Theosophists?" inquired Venerable Sumangala. "Is it true that Madame Blavatsky went into a vituperative attack on Christianity and missionaries at this reception?"

The Colonel confirmed that the buildings issue came after this reception. He also gave the impression that Madame Balvatsky went overboard on this occasion. According to him, this was her day. She found in Mr. Dawn-Mountain the sympathy that goes hand in hand with a less intellectual but more emotional religious fervour. It was so natural that it drew out her most charming traits.

The Colonel proceeded further, "She had a field day with her raps, angel bells, embroidered handerchiefs and astral letters. This visit with the Tamil Hindu dignitary has so far been the pleasantest episode of our tour. As regards her attack on missionaries, you know what I wrote in my diary. I wrote, 'As a dessert, or rather *pousse-cafe*, my colleague abused the missionaries in her best style.' "

The retired diplomat was eager to know more about the dispute over the use of public buildings. I read to him what I had copied from another entry out of Olcott's diary:

> *The same afternoon we had a taste of the other style of official; the Government Agent - a most satrapy grade of public servant - having forbidden the use of any public buidling, even the verandah or steps of the school-house, for my lecture. The poor creature acted as though he supposed*

> *the Buddhists could be overawed into deserting their religion,
> or into believing Chirstianity a more lovable one, by
> excluding them from the buildings that had been erected with
> their tax-money and that would be lent to any preacher
> against Buddhism. But the fields and the sky were left to us,
> the one for the lecture-hall and the other for the roof, and the
> meeting was held in a coconut grove.*

I thought that Noble Son of Wisdom would be interested in one more entry. This was after the meeting at Panadura.

> *The Missionaries had been doing what little they could
> since our landing to try and weaken our influence with the
> Buddhists, so I paid my compliments to them and their
> questionable policy. In truth, these Protestant Missionaries
> are a pestilent lot. With the Catholics we have never had a
> hard word.*

I continued my resume of the day's meeting with observations on the other two scholar-monks who briefed Olcott.

Subhuti's encounters with foreigners had been limited to scholars. His worldwide network of corresponding scholars included such distinguished Western scholars as Viggo Fausboll of Denmark, who translated the Dhammapada into Latin in 1858, Robert Childers, Rhys Davids and Rheinold Rost of England, Herman Oldenberg of Germany and Minayeff of Russia. What he expected from Olcott was some support to emerging research.

"These scholars in the West need our support," he argued. "You know what Fausboll calls the human and literary resources we have in this country. 'Living fountains of Buddhism'. They must have facilities to tap these rersources. Buddhism will make a bigger impact in the West through the academia than through the efforts of activists. It will take a long time, no doubt. But the results would be permanent."

Olcott appeared to be hardly impressed by arguments in favour of an academic approach. He wanted action. He wanted competition. He urged dramatic action, nay, open warfare. He saw in Buddhism a commodity which could be in high demand in the West, if only the Buddhists from traditionally Buddhist countries would cease to be lotus-eaters and adopt the ways of aggressive marketing. He had some hard words for even members of the Sangha - lazy, anaemic, complacent, leisure-loving etc. etc.

His only apology was, "Present company excluded."

Venerable Sumangala, as usual, represented the middle path. By temperament he was a bridge-builder and what concerned him in every issue was a form of *modus vivendi*. He knew officialdom the best. He could gauge the political power wielded by the missionaries. He had his own vision of a national and religious revival. More than that he had an admirable capacity for conciliation - firm, friendly and yet purposeful - compromising yet not overly yielding.

"Our dear friend and most distinguished lay supporter," he began his concluding remarks. "We thank you and accept with all our gratitude your brilliant idea that the educational movement should concentrate on setting up prestigious schools where English, modern science and Western culture would be taught besides our own national history, literature and languages, Buddhism and native values.

"We agree with you that Buddhists should have access to government service, business, the plantation industry, the medical and legal professions and the like. So let's get busy with this single goal. There are many things to do. There are also a few things we cannot, should not and, in my case at least, would not do.

"We have to survive in this country. We do not want to antognize the administration. We have many friends at every level. There are more enlightened officials than one is prepared to give credit for. We urge for Self-rule and eventual independence. These changes have to come from the politicians in London. We have to make this very clear distinction. So the first thing is to avoid is indiscriminate criticism. The same applies to missionaries. They are fighting a losing battle. Any day now the church will cease to be an official part of the Establishment."

I was reading my notes. Noble Son of Wisdom touched the paper to interrupt me.

"He never ceases to baffle me," he said of Venerable Sumangala. "He knows everything."

I smiled and continued to read.

"They'll lose money and with that a major part of their influence. When that happens, all their arrogance will go. Let's bide our time. It's not our culture to attack the falling or the fallen. Also remember. Not all of them are bigotted. We have friends among missionaries. Let's be sober. We don't have to attack Chistianity either. I think we have won that phase of the battle."

"How very enlightened!" interjected the Siamese monk.

Venerable Sumangala made his point on Theosophy with similar tact.

That night Olcott was at his very best. He was no rabble-rouser. He appealed to the intellect, to commonsense, goodwill and understanding. It was appropriate to the audience which consisted of many senior officials of the Government, editors of newspapers and men of substance and influence among Colombo's elite. Apparently benefitting from the private meeting that morning, he offended nobody. He won a great deal of admiration. The British dignitaries shook hands with him. The people mobbed him as he left the hall. They wanted to touch the man who had moved their hearts so deeply.

A sober and definitely more serious phase of work was in the offing. More time was spent in Colombo in the planning, organization and identification of strategies. Private discussions superseded public speaking. Olcott's speech at the Learning-Awakening College, which I translated, was on "Nirvana, Merit and the Education of Buddhist Children." It was a veritable blue-print for action. Repeatedly, he underscored "*the risk that the people ran in leaving their children to be prejudiced against their ancestral religion by its professed enemies, who were in the country for no other object than this.*"

His performance at the historic temple of Kelaniya near Colombo was stupendous.

Some tensions were, however, evident in the delegation as Olcott became more and more a Buddhist campaigning for an educated Buddhist elite and less and less a Theosophist building a Brotherhood of Humanity. The delegates from India, specially those representing Hinduism, were at times crochety. Did they sense that his earlier partiality to Hinduism had begun to wane?

I discussed this phenomenon with Noble Son of Wisdom. His mature observation was typical of his balanced view of life.

"Pure, you remember the story of the Buddha who went to intervene in the battle of his relatives and their neighbours the Koliyas. He sat under a tree between the warring armies but chose the shade which was on the side where his relatives were. We all have our partialities in our hearts however much we try to overcome them with our heads."

He continued,

"Pure, imagine that tomorrow morning the whole world wakes up to find that all differences in colour, race, intelligence, physical attractiveness, economic and social conditions and cultural attainments have disappeared. By twelve noon, humanity would have invented some way to claim that some are more equal than the others."

Changing moods, tensions, bickerings and plain moroseness of the delegation which trailed behind Olcott provided much grist to my mill in the study of human nature. Equally interesting was to observe the reactions of Madame Blavatsky who had been relegated to the background, at least in public.

The cosmopolitan atmosphere of Colombo seemed to have the effect of fragmenting the delegation. Each member showed a tendency to contact people of his or her own religious persuasion. How so much good could still come collectively from this rankling crowd was a wonder. But I could see that each in his or her own way did reach many people. As a result, the Theosophical Movement was making visible headway in the Island. Branches of the parent Society were being established in various towns with steadily increasing enrollment.

Olcott sensed the growing tension between those whose commitment to Theosophy was unadulterated by any partiality to Buddhism. He was a consummate diplomat and patient negotiator. He worked out a formula by which he could keep all parties happy.

The reconciliation of the two trends, however, was eventually evident in the scheme which Olcott contrived for Venerable Sumangala's wholehearted involvement in his movement. This leading light of the Sangha was elected a Vice-President of the Colombo Theosophical Society and, at the same time, the Chairman of the Monk's Division of its Buddhist Branch.

Thus, relatively free of the tensions of the first part of the visit of the Theosophists, all parties were happy. If it was a period of adjustment and acclimatization culturally and spiritually, it was well spent.

The trip to Kandy, the offical citadel of Buddhism in the Island, was eagerly awaited. Natually, I expected to be a part of the entourage. With the catastrophic experiences Olcott and his colleagues had with interpreters, I felt I was indispensable to them.

I looked forward to being once again close to this great man and to observe his admirable approach to problems and difficult situations. In spite of the incident at the beach of Orange Island, for which he did make magnanimous amends, I continued to hold him as my model of a popular leader.

A few days in Kandy had other more personal advantages. A chance to see Aunt Flower, Uncle Victor and and their son and, of course, Slim-Jewel and possibly her daughter, would be a bonus.

IV

"Little Name, I am not taking you to Kandy," said Venerable Sumangala when I saw him with the letters I had drafted for him. "Let the folks in Kandy do things their own way."

I had no idea why he thought so. But the deference due to a senior monk prevented me for asking for a clarification. It was not for me to plead for reconsideration. I had to obey.

The scholar-monk, however, ensured that I had no time to mope. I was entrusted with a number of tasks which he had thought out very carefully. They were not just to keep me occupied. Each was designed to make sure that the momentum of the national educational campaign was maintained unabated.

"Speak to your Siamese friend, Little Name. Tell him our problem regarding school text-books. Pleasant-Gem-Tissa will be here to work with you," he said in his laconic style.

Just before Venerable Sumangala took the train to Kandy with an acolyte, the pioneering campaigner for Buddhist schools of Orange Island arrived with none other than Little Father. It was a pleasure to see them. I told Little Father of my twofold disappointment and he had an explanation.

"Son, there is a great divide between the monks of Kandy and those in the low country. To the prelates of Kandy, it is a question of hierarchy and authority. Their status comes from their office and its antiquity. Monks here have to earn their prestige and public admiration through ability and hard work. That's why those like Venerable Sumangala who gravitated to the top are remarkable men of high intelligence, energy and stamina. But that's no guarantee that they are loved by those in authority."

"Is their some kind of jealousy or rivalry?" I asked him.

"Naturally, but neither party would admit it. What complicates the issue is that the Sangha has unconsciously revived an institution which has no relevance in modern times."

Little Father explained how the new administrative units which kept on mushrooming in the low country Sangha were based on caste lines.

"They call themselves sects but there are no doctrinal differences or disagreements. If at all, there are some variations in minor rituals according to where the founder of the sect obtained his higher ordination in Burma."

256

Little Father assigned blame to the British administration of the days when Kandy was still independent. It was alleged that aspiring monks of the maritime regions were encouraged to seek higher ordination in Burma. As far as the administration was concerned, it was an attempt to eliminate the religious influence of the Kandyan Kingdom against which the British had waged a number of unsuccessful wars. But that was not the whole story.

As in all such cases, there was the question of supply and demand. The unserved and the underserved communities in the South of the Island wanted their own institutions.

"The Siamese Sect should have its share of blame too," Little Father said. "It really did not accommodate the rising aspirations of the major occupational communities of the low country."

"You mean castes?"

"Precisely. But I prefer to call them occupational groups rather than castes."

I had known precious little about caste in my home in the hills. There the majority community lived by agriculture and they were called the "Cultivator Caste." Claiming superiority over them was a loose aristocracy which either claimed relationship with the old royalty or held high offices in court or district administration. They were said too be of royal blood although the etymology of the term which designated them was often disputed. Then we had a sprinkling of people who performed odd jobs which were rated low or menial. These included washing clothes, working with leather, drumming and dancing in ceremonies of exorcism, making pottery, blacksmithery, hair-dressing etc. Each knew his or her place in society just as we came to know how to treat them from our infancy.

The only untouchables were those who lived across the river in Sangha-Gem-Field. But they were the most beautiful people I had known. My mother's explanation sounded convincing though I had no way of knowing whether it was correct:

> *Once upon a time they belonged to royalty. They disobeyed the king, who reduced them in caste by getting them to eat beef, slaughter animals and bury the dead, both animal and human.*

The system which operated in the low country was one of substantial occupational groups which, Little Father said, were now in competition, not in their original occupations, but in the modern sector economy.

257

"The communities which once were exclusively engaged in fishing, cinnamon-peeling and making jewelry are no longer limiting their livelihood to their traditional occupations," said Little Father. "They have benefited from modern education, adopted lucrative economic activities and achieved positions of national prominence and leadership. But our fault is that we think that these things have never taken place."

"Very un-Buddhistic, don't you think so?" interjected Noble Son of Wisdom.

"If you are referring to our colleague Venerable Pure-Intellect, he is a rare bird who has overcome petty caste prejudices," intervened Pleasant-Gem-Tissa. "He is one man who is working for everyone's benefit whether one is a cinnamon-peeler, fisherman, cultivator or any other occupation or caste."

Translating it to my Siamese friend, I added quite mischievously,

"If you are referring to my Little Father, you are barking up the wrong tree."

I had forgotten that Noble Son of Wisdom had acquired enough knowledge of Sinhala to know that my translation was quite unfaithful to the original.

"You, rascal. How often do you do this to me.

We discussed these and other social and cultural issues arising from the fact that the hill country had remained isolated for over three hundred years. We understood why the prelates and senior monks tended to be aloof and cagey.It was now clear why only Venerable Sumangala went to Kandy and why he wanted to maintain a very low profile.

"I am sure that Olcott will note this and will go to the bottom of the issue. He has such a sharp mind," I told Little Father and he agreed.

"Wait till he notes this unneccasry and unjustifiable rift. He will become a champion of reconciliation and unification."

I wanted to share with Little Father my disappointment in not being able to see Slim-Jewel to find out how she was progressing with her studies and work. But I could not summon enough courage. I did not want him to think that my life of renunciation had any reservations.

We were a happy quartet. Pleasant-Gem-Tissa assumed leadership not only because he was the most senior but also the most experienced.

Noble Son of Wisdom was bristling with ideas emanating from his hands-on involvement in setting up and conducting a veritable replica of an English independent school.

258

Little Father knew the practical financial and administrative difficulties. His head was full of names and figures: writers and illustrators, printing presses and unit costs.

"You know how long it takes to compose with lead letters a page in Sinhala? Six hours if the man is really competent. As against the English apphabet of twenty-six capital and simple letters, we have to deal with three hundred letters, inflections and conjunct letters. To be fast the composer has to remember where each lead letter or component is, pick each item according the text and arrange it on a metal tray. Up to five proofs have to be read as there is always the possiblity that letters are put in wrong slots. When each page is dismantled after printing, the lead letters are returned to the slots. This job is usually done by an apprentice. It's time more than cost that holds up printing Sinhala."

We gained insights into matters we had taken for granted.

My experience in two schools under the guidance of two of the most enlightened padres was equally relevant as far as the quality of learning materials was concerned.

Complementary as each was to the rest of the team, we could minimize discussion and reach quick decisions. Our target was to have a blue-print of a project ready by the time Olcott returned to Colombo.

"Would you teach Buddhism as a subject?" queried Noble Son of Wisdom.

"Why not?" asked Pleasant-Gem-Tissa and Little Father in unison.

"Why do you raise it as a question?" I asked him.

"No religion can be or should be taught as a subject in a school," argued Noble Son of Wisdom. "Whenever we try, all we present is a caricature of the religion retricted to liturgy, mythology and lists to be learnt by rote."

He made a strong case for making religion the essence of the communal life of the school. Truth, honesty, tolerance, non-violence, compassion and such other values had to be learnt through emulation of sincere role-models rather than through precept and commandment, he underscored. What he opposed most was the idea that religious knowledge could be tested and graded.

"There can be no Pass or Fail in religion. Either all pass or the whole exercise is meaningless. The only criterion for passing is that the life and conduct of the pupil reflects the values which the relgion seeks to inculcate in him or her."

For a moment I thought that we had reached our first impasse. Both Pleasant-Gem-Tissa and Little Father stressed that affective objectives of learning depended heavily on the knowledge base and the skill levels that were reached directly through the interaction of the teacher and the pupil in well designed learning siutations.

"I agree," responded Noble Son of Wisdom to my great relief. "Give the knowledge base through literature and history. Your literature is rich and varied. Your history is full of appeal. Let every school have at least one monk as a teacher-cum-chaplain. Let him be the living testimony to the values that Buddhism seeks to inculcate. The temple and not the school should be the principal centre of religious knowledge and training of the community."

"Very good, Princely colleague," replied Pleasant-Gem-Tissa. "We may still need text-books. Let me write one and see how far we can agree on its contents and methods."

My task was to make the first draft of our proposals. In a single sitting we approved the final version. By way of appreciation, Pleasant-Gem-Tissa took me around the new temples springing up in and around Colombo and introduced me to a number of most inspiring and stimulating monks - men of learning and action. There was a spirit of renaissance which was unmistakable.

Venerable Sumangala returned from Kandy ahead of the visitors. He sent for me within minutes of his arrival.

"It's good that I didn't take you, Little Name," he said. "There was nothing much that we could have done. It was all ceremony and little substance - chiefs in bulky regalia, torch-lit processions and formal addresses by the prelates and dignitaries. The only thing worthwhile was the exposition of the Sacred Tooth Relic. "

"Did the Colonel's speeches go well, Venerable Sir?"

"Yes. But I wished they were better organized. For half the time he was inaudible as the crowd cramped in the temple building were restless and moved about making much noise. Even the appeals for silence went unheeded. Eventually, the location was changed to the lawn and he could be heard."

He proceeded to give the gist of Olcott's speech and intinctively I jotted down notes. It seemed that the missionaries had engaged themselves on the previous evening in preaching against Buddhism in the streets of Kandy and spreading all kinds of calumnies against Olcott and his delegation.

"You know what the undaunted White Buddhist did? He took out his watch, adopted a challenging pose and shouted,

'Last evening you went around the streets of Kandy abusing Buddhism and insulting me and my fellow-delegates. You took advantage of your self-imposed superiority as white

*men and as favourites of the administration. In your
cowardice, you knew that the harmless natives would not
confront you. Here I am. I give you five minutes. Let any
Bishop, Archdeacon, Priest or Deacon of any Church come
forward and prove their assertions that Buddhism is a false
religion.'*

"He stood for five minutes with watch in hand. But nobody dared
come forward. There were at least five missionaries in the audience. He
repeated the challenge and when nothing happened, he said,

> *'The people of this country are at perfect liberty to treat
> the missionaries and their falsehoods as they deserved.'*

For a moment, I had horrible visions of the insensed crowd turning
to violence and that mayhem would ensue."

"Why didn't that happen, Venerable Sir?"

"Because you were not there, Sangha-Gem-Field. If only you did
the translation ..... "

The senior monk laughed like a little child. I knew what he meant.

When Olcott returned to Colombo, I complimented him on his
stand in Kandy. I told him what Venerable Sumangala said about the
old soldier's call for defiant action and why it fell on deaf ears.

"That's meant to be a compliment to you, young priest. I really
wished you were there," was his kind response.

"We have a lot to do and so little time," he lamented as he outlined
his idea of unifying the Buddhists of the whole world. "It's all absurd.
Northern Buddhism versus Southern Buddhism. Sheer ignorance.
Neither knows the other. What's worse. Neither knows that they
subscribe to the same body of teachings. They share a common
platform."

I had to plead ignorance. Though a monk of well nigh five years of
monastic training, my knowledge of Buddhism was limited to the few
books I had to memorize to qualify for higher ordination and the texts
through which Noble Son of Wisdom and I studied the Pali language.
It was only very vaguely that I understood why the traditions of Burma,
Siam and Sri Lanka were referred to as Southern Buddhism or rather
the Tradition of the Elders. All I knew about Northern Buddhism as he
called the form of Buddhism in China, Japan and Tibet was that the
monks or priests in Japan married and had families. Olcott did not laugh
at my ignorance. Nor was he derisive in any way.

261

"I don't blame you, young priest. The older and the more learned monks on both sides could be worse. But, you see, prejudice can be worse than ignorance."

There was little doubt that he had given much thought to this problem. He elaborated his plans to outline the common doctrines or what he called the "common platform." He hoped to get important dignitaries of each tradition in each country to subscribe to a document.

"That's my plan for Universal Buddhism. The Buddhists of the world will unite on this common platform," he declared.

His eyes shone with hope and determination. Only after this long explanation, did I understand what he meant by this expression a week ago. I regretted my ignorance and the resulting gaffe in the translation.

Our conversation was frequently interrupted by Madame Blavatsky who kept on calling Olcott downstairs every now and then - to have a photograph taken with somebody, to talk to someone or simply listen to one of her innocuous comments. When through sheer exhaustion, the Colonel declined to come down, she came up to join us.

"It's all right to talk of the universal problem, Mr. President. What have you in mind for the problem right in front of your eyes?" she asked Olcott.

If I noticed a taint of sarcasm in her question, it could have been that I was over-sensitive. But Olcott too was irked by her question.

"How many times have I explained to you that the sects in Ceylon have no difference in dogma between them?" he asked Madame Blavatsky. "They only mean that one set of monks received their ordination from Siam and that the others from different parts of Burma."

"You do agree that a problem exists here, Mr. President. Why don't we do something."

"Let's see" was the Colonel's laconic reply. He was tired.

I was also privy to several discussions which Olcott has with the senior scholar-monks. In additon to the permanent trio, Betel-Village, Venerable Gunananda and Venerable Sumangala, senior members of the staff of the Learning-Awakening College participated in these meetings. They had many issues to settle with the Theosophists, who, at this stage of their visit, were deeply engrossed in setting up branches of the Theosophical Society and enrolling members. As I interpreted various statements to and fro, I had a tough time. Whenever feelings ran high, a comic intervention by Madame Blavatsky proved providential.

Being told that monks were barred from even the slightest physical contact with women, she would roll for Betel-Village, whom she addressed as "Her Father in God", a cigarette and pass it on to him on a

262

fan. She laughed all the time and made the old monks share in her merriment.

The exceedingly hot weather, the incessant interaction with all kinds of people and long processions which welcomed them and conducted them through towns and villages took a toll of the visitors. Even the indefatigable dynamo of the group, Colonel Olcott of excellent physique and spirit, was eventually exhausted.

He became ill and was confined to bed for a couple of days. But hardly any change was made in the volume or tempo of their activities. I was spared much of the turmoil by Venerable Sumangala who dissuaded me from undertaking too many engagements.

Olcott would plead with the senior monk to let me interpret his speeches to large crowds. He repeated his request after a trying experience with an incompetent interpreter.

"Here I was, Venerable High Priest, trying to talk to several thousand people," he told Venerable Sumangala. "The interpreter chosen for it comes up to me and tells me that I should talk very slowly as he does not understand English very well. Then he sits in front of me in a crouching position, clasping his knees with his hands. For a moment I thought he had read Homer and watched to see what words 'should escape the fence of my teeth'. It was terrible. Every now and then he would ask me to repeat what I had said. It was oratory under every imaginable difficulty."

Venerable Sumangala relented and during the last days of Olcott's travels in the South, I resumed the original role of his personal interpreter. It was pleasant to be close to him. He was a sensitive man with a great love of nature. He and for that matter Madame Blavatsky fell in love with Horror-Ford where they were accommodated in the government rest house. He showed me his diary entry:

> *We were all agreed that we had never seen so delightful a house in the Tropics. The lofty ceilings, the floors of red tiles, the walls of laterite, thick and cool, a wide verandah at the back just over the rocky shore of the sea, the rooms at least thirty feet square, the sea-breeze sweeping through them night and day, a bathing place on the beach, abundance of flowers, a good table and a sympathetic landlord - we had nothing left to desire. H.P.B. declared she should like to pass a whole year there.*

263

As we proceeded further south, I could discern a changing attiutde in the people as well as in the delegation of Theosophists. Olcott was a celebrity and hence an object of adulation and curiosity.

More and more time was spent on long and fancy processions and crowd-rallying entertainment. To the visitors these lavish demonstrations of admiration and affection had the attraction of picutresqueness and novelty. They loved the exotic dances and the fascinating puppet shows. To the organizers these were the essential means of attracting large crowds. But the whole thing usually got out of hand.

The audience was not only restless but the chaos was aggravated by early leavers jostling with late arrivals. All attempts to restore order and silence were in vain. Speeches were hardly heard. Once the people had taken a good look at the visitors and touched Olcott and Madame Blavatsky if they could come near enough, they were no longer interested in the proceedings.

I was not surprised when Olcott felt utterly frustrated for I shared his feelings. We were for the most part speaking to the air!. Our post mortems were very severe on ourselves. Were we repetitive? Had the novelty of the campaign faded? Were we doing too many things? Was it time for a little respite? But the wonder of all wonders was that the impact of the visit did not seem to diminish in any way. The overwhelming presence of Colonel Olcott and Madame Blavatsky in their midst was by itself an overpowering message.

Just as our shared frustration reached its zenith, Olcott surprised everyone with two remarkable initiatives.

The first was quite dramatic. It was a joint session of the representative monks of the Siamese and Bumese sects with an agenda of unification and joint action.

I was too junior to be among the fifteen monks representing the Siamese Sect. My presence there even as an interpreter would have upset the fine numerical balance the Colonel wanted to maintain betweeen the two groups. What I know of this meeting is from a note which Olcott had written nineteen years later.

It says,

> *The Convention met at 1.00 P.M. A necessary preliminary was the giving of a breakfast to the thirty delegates - fifteen from each sect. To avoid all friction, I placed the two parties in adjoining rooms communicating by a wide door. ... When all was ready I stood in the common doorway and read the call of the meeting, then my Address which was well interpreted as I*

264

delivered it. I also read my Executive Notice announcing the creation of the Buddhist Section. Remarks having been made by seven leading priests of the two sects, a joint committee of five each of the two bodies with Venerable Sumangala as chairman, was chosen to carry out my plan, and the meeting then adjourned sine die. This was quite a new departure, joint action having never before been taken in an administrative affair; nor would it have been now possible, but for our being foreigners who were tied to neither party, nor concerned with one of their social cliques more than with any other. We represented Buddhism and Buddhistic interests as a whole, and neither party dared hold aloof for fear of popular disfavour, even if they had been so inclined.

Olcott was indeed more than pleased with the outcome of this effort. His note continued,

I am bound to say that I have never, during the subsequent nineteen years, had reason to complain of a change of this good feeling for our work by either sect. On the other hand, they have given a thousand proofs of their willingness to help, so far as their natural inertia of temperament permits them, the great revival movement which is destined to ultimately place Ceylon Buddhism upon the most sure and stable footing, since it is that of the goodwill of an educated and willing people. It has ever been a cause of regret to me, personally, that I could not have devoted my whole time and energies to the Buddhist cause from my early manhood, for I feel sure that by the time of our first visit to the Island in 1880, I could have brought about the complete unification in sympathy of Northern and Southern - to use an absurd misnomer - and could have planted a school house at every cross-road in this lovely land of the palm and the spice grove. However, let that pass as a 'might have been', my time has not been wasted.

The other equally dramatic initiative was to summon a Convention of newly formed lay Branches of the Theosophical Society. The venue was Galle. Delegates came from practically all major cities and towns visited by Olcott and party. It was a gathering of emerging and potential leaders. I was slow to grasp the significance of the meeting until Noble Son of Wisdom decided that he should be an observer.

"Pure, something big is about to happen. All this while here as well as in Siam and Burma, the monks were the leaders of the movement to revive Buddhism and in the wake of it to bring about a national consciousness. The lay people have been their humble and obedient supporters. What Olcott is doing is to get lay involvement in an organized manner. I am sure this would not be to the liking of the monks."

"Why?" I asked him.

"Because the monks do believe in all sincerity that Buddhism is a monastic religion and the laity has no role other than as givers of requisites."

He used the Pali expression which meant "suppliers of the needs of monks in the form of food, clothing, shelter and medicine."

The emerging lay leadership, inspired by the indomitable Olcott, were ready to make decions and design plans of action on a wide variety of issues.

They urged the secularization of schools in the sense that they should cease to be centres of proselytization.

They discussed ways and means of rescuing Buddhist temporalities from spoliation.

The designed projects for the preparation and distribution of Buddhist propagandist literature.

They even broached on the touchy and sensitive subject of restoring the senior monks' disciplinary control over their juniors and pupils.

Himself a layman, the American Theosophist saw it not only fitting but even profitable that the Buddhist laity should be brought to deal with broader issues of their religion. Such issues, however, had been hitherto considered out of bounds for the laity. But it was not so much by any decree or demand of the Sangha.

Age-old traditions had resulted in unquestioned confidence in and respectful submission to the Sangha. After all, to a pious devotee, the community of monks was the third of the Noble Jewels or the Refuges of the Buddhist Trinity (Buddha, Dhamma, Sangha).

Olcott, of course, was scarcely conscious of what a far-reaching revolution he had launched through his last minute conventions of the Sangha and the laity. He had rushed where angels would have feared to tread.

"There's nothing anyone could do now, Pure," commented Noble Son of Wisdom at the close of the lay convention. "The flood-gates have been opened. Either the monks and the laity will fight to the bitter end and, in the process, destroy whatever is left of Buddhism in the Island. Or, and I don't rule that possibility out, they will join hands, pool their resources and usher in a new era of cooperation on an equal footing."

"I hope it will be the latter," I said.

"Me too."

V

With the two spectacular conventions to crown six weeks of incessant activity, Colonel Olcott and his party prepared for a tearful farewell.

Even the robust physique of the American Civil War veteran proved unequal to the tropical sun, the hot peppery curries, the long walks on all kinds of terrain, the long hours of meetings and consultations and the emotional stress of dealing with Madame Blavatsky's changes of mood.

At Sand-Village, he had once again to take to bed for a couple of days. Although his spirit compelled him to go on an outing or two to visit temples or address meetings, he was not his old self. He needed rest and I had no option but to take the matter into my own hands. At first he dismissed me as an unnecessarily fussy interference. But he did not take too long to acquiesce.

The Colonel's exhaustion and failing health had given me an opportunity to be closer to him. After the few ups and downs we have had in our two month old association, we developed a friendship based on mutual esteem and affection. As far as my position as a young monk permitted, I tended to him as a son would to a father. Much to the consternation of Madame Blavatsky, who was both possessive and protective, I took over the control of visitors and ensured that no one disturbed him. When he was up and restless, I would chant to him verses from the Book of Protection. He enjoyed the music of the chanting and was keen to know the meaning of the texts.

"Isn't it remarkable, my young priest, that in none of these benedictory verses do you really invoke anyone? No God, no angel, no saint nor any supernatural power or messenger. You make a sensible statement like how one should practise loving kindness to all beings and then say 'May the truth of this statement make me well and happy.' You really think it works! Where does the magic come from? I know it works. It must be you, my little magician. Or is it my witch-doctor?."

If his laughter was not as loud and hearty as on earlier occasions, it was because he was not in the best of health. And he was quite emotional about the impending departure. Yet, neither his curiosity to learn nor his keenness to continue the work he had begun showed any signs of abating.

"You know, my young priest, what I really regret," he told me one day. "My mistake of not taking advantage of an opportunity of the rarest nature. When we were riding on the crest of the wave of popular

268

enthusiasm, I should have begun fund-raising. We could have collected a couple of hundred thousand rupees to found schools and publish literature. It will never be possible to recreate what we lost. But try I must."

When the day of sailing arrived, he was overly moved. He invited me to see him off on the boat. In fact, I was the last to leave his cabin.

"Happy is the day that brought me to this Island," he said over and over again as he recounted what he had achieved and what he was planning to do further. "I'll be back sooner than you think." Then he beckoned me to his side and whispered to my ear,

"Next time, I come alone."

This curious statement confirmed my vague suspicion that he and Madame Blavatsky did not see eye to eye on their programme in the Island. Was she jealous that he had carved for himself a niche in which her presence was not absolutely essential? This was not the time to ask him. It was a sad leave-taking for both of us.

He hugged me as a father would. His eyes were moist. Young as I was, I could cry without shame. He hugged me again as he opened the door for me.

VI

Two of the most sensitive, thoughtful and considerate persons I had met in my life were waiting for me in the jetty when I got there in the last barge. I was embarrassed and offered my apologies.

"You didn't ask us to wait, did you?" asked Venerable Sumangala.

"You had no way of knowing we were here," added Noble Son of Wisdom, "Didn't the Colonel try to take you to India with him? He has become very fond of you lately."

"Yes, indeed, lately," joined the senior scholar monk with his usually mirthful laughter. "Some time back, the Colonel thought that the Little Name was a Fifth Columnist planted in the Sangha by the missionaries."

I had no idea that he knew of this episode or how.

A horse carriage thoughtfully placed at our disposal by a renowned philanthropist in Galle brought us to the temple in China Garden through a city that had long gone to sleep.

"Tomorrow at nine we leave for Colombo and the very next day we begin our class in Sanskrit," announced Venerable Sumangala, as Noble Son of Wisdom and I worshipped him at the door of his modest room. "Back to our normal lives."

The Siamese princely monk had requested that a bed be rolled into my room so that we could be together.

"I don't know whether you want to be alone. I thought you have to unwind yourself and perhaps a long chat with me might be the best way to do it."

"How thoughtful of you as always. Thank you, thank you, your Venerable Royal Highness."

No sooner had those words passed my tongue than I was struck by remorse. I felt that the unusual form of address could offend him. I only wanted to be light-hearted. But he might have thought I was sarcastic. He detected agony in my face before I could apologize.

"Pure, I am neither Venerable nor Royal, my fellow Seeker for Salvation. But Highness I really can be! You are my senior in the Order by a couple of hours. But I am your senior in age by a couple of decades. Never forget either."

He laughed.

As he had rightly thought I did want to speak. There was none better than him both as a patient and understanding listener and as a wise and practical adviser.

270

"How very interesting that you should ask me whether Colonel Olcott tried to take me with him! Perhaps, he wanted to. One day he gave me a piece of paper in which he had copied a comment written in the log book of the Rest House at Sand-Village by Professor Ernst Haeckel. When I read it, I had the feeling that the Colonel was trying to tell me why he was not persuading me to leave the country."

I rummaged in my bag for the slip and handed it over to Noble Son of Wisdom. He read,

> "*Ceylon is really a paradise of natural beauties for one who can appreciate them, and I do not wonder the reluctance the Sinhalese have ever shown to venturing to foreign lands, even for profit.*"

"I think you are correct, Pure. But you were disappointed, weren't you?" he added further.

"To be frank, yes. The more I was with the Colonel, the more I wanted to be close to him and get involved in the work that he was doing. The more he criticized my people as lazy and ignorant, the more I wanted to work for him and show that there could be exceptions to the rule. The more he argued that we Buddhists had very little knowledge or the understanding of the teachings of the Buddha, the more I wanted to disabuse his mind. But these are not tasks to carried out in between public lectures and interminable interviews. There's such a lot he should know of us and there are a myriad things I want to learn from him. Whence his energy? Whence his clarity of thought? Whence his wisdom?"

Noble Son of Wisdom touched my hand lightly. I stopped what was fast becoming a soliloquy.

"You're young, Pure. You have a million things to learn. First exhaust the resources you have here. The sky's the limit after that."

I agreed. I told him of my childhood dream of being a missionary taking to the world the benign teachings of the Buddha. I recalled how the Abbot of the Bo-tree Plain Temple encouraged me when I thought that I was dreaming the impossible.

Late into the night we talked of our respective ambitions at various stages of our lives and how few of them one could really achieve. The former diplomat drew many lessons from his life experiences.

"Whether you like it or not, you have a role to play in life. What it is will be fashioned by your hopes and expectations, goals and ambitions. Every disappointment takes you closer to what you are best equipped to accomplish with your innate talents and acquired skills."

"Is this another way of reiterating what our teachers and specially Western missionaries din into our ears as 'Failures are the pillars of success?' "

"No, Pure. What I mean is that every failure should show us what new and further skills we need to acquire."

Eventually, we planned our studies. While I was busy with Olcott and his party, he had mastered the Sanskrit script and grappled with the intricacies of the grammar of a language which had ten tenses or moods each with nine forms for its verbs, three numbers for its nouns and twenty-seven forms of a noun according to what function it performed in a sentence. I had a lot to catch up.

Yet I had an advantage. I read the script with ease - a spin-off benefit from my days of managing the library of the Sangha-Gem-Field. I had a head full of Sanskrit texts, specially in verse, which enabled grammar to be learnt in practical application rather than in abstract.

"Pure, the Principal hopes to have the examination just before we break up for the New year in April. That would be eight months. Eight months in which you have to catch up with me and beat me."

We wished each other 'Good Night' and closed our eyes.

Within minutes, however, the Siamese friend and colleague asked me softly whether I was asleep. Though awakened somewhat rudely, it was only polite to reply in the negative.

"Pure, I forgot to tell you something. I went to Kandy and ran into your brother the monk. We chatted about the family. There's a rumour floating in the village that the outcaste girl across the river had had a son from your late brother. He wondered whether you had any idea about how best to handle the matter. Why don't you write him a letter tomorrow.

"Thank you. I will."

Sleep did not come back to me for hours. Something upset me. Was it the pride of an upper caste villager whose nephew by blood was allowed to grow up as an outcaste? Was it pity that the unfortunate girl, his mother, already trampled by society for a mere accident of birth, had another burden to bear? Was it anger that an errant brother complicated the lives of two women and in addition had brought untold misery to an innocent child? Was it sympathy for the girl I once loved dearly who has to live with a deep feeling of guilt that a half brother of her daughter was a disadvantaged child with a destiny worse than death? What social discrimination would he encounter right through his life? What depths of poverty would he fall to as he became excluded from society as a veritable untouchable?

272

In the midst of these bleak and dismal thoughts a ray of sunshine did appear.

"He must be a very handsome boy!" I said to myself. "What a handsome father! What a bewitchingly beautiful mother!'

I hoped that his physical endowments would give him some relief in an otherwise condemned life. I was restless. A feeling of helplessness overcame me.

"What am I doing here? Planning to spread Buddhism in the world? For whose benefit? To spearhead a national and Buddhist revival movement in the country? To establish schools so that a new Buddhist elite could be prepared to take over the nation in due course? All these for others when a son of my brother's own blood, a scion of the proud clan of Valour-Lion, languished in the huts of the outcastes across the river. It is not correct. It is not right. It is not fair."

With the first crowing of cocks at dawn, I found paper and pencil in the dark and slithered out of the room to the preaching hall to write two letters: one to Chief Monk, my maternal uncle who in the strict matriarchal organization of the family was its spiritual head and the other to Slim-Jewel who in the genuine simple ways of an unspoiled village girl generated hope of understanding and compassion.

An acolyte undertook to post them. It would take several weeks before I had replies from them. Still I felt a sense of relief. I had taken the matter in hand and sought advice from two persons who could take a more objective view of things than I could from my sequestered corner in life and society.

I walked to the spot by the ramparts where I had my first dip in the sea in the company of Noble Son of Wisdom. The cold bath in the silvery water refreshed me to some extent. The red-hued dawn clouds hanging over the hill of medicinal herbs across the harbour symbolized hope - hope for an unseen baby for whose future I had a commitment.

Venerable Sumangala and my Siamese colleague noticed my red eyes, when I met them in the refectory. Perhaps, they thought that I had given vent to my grief over the departure of Olcott with tears. They were considerate and left me to myself right through the forty mile coach ride and the two hour train trip.

The philanthropist Don Carolis was himself there at the station to take us to the College in his new horse carriage. He had something to tell the senior scholar-monk:

"Venerable Sir, My son David has taken a great fancy to Madame Blavatsky and her accounts of meeting and corresponding with Adepts and Mahatmas from the Himalayas. Please talk to him without letting

273

him know that I had spoken to you. He is a dreamer and likes to read and discuss all kinds of religious and spiritual experiences. I do not want these outside interests to interfere with his studies. In every school, he had been a very good student."

"That I know," replied Venerable Sumangala. "At this age, young ones are curious and that's a very good thing. I will talk to him. But don't you worry. He's born to be a great man, a great leader."

Both of them knew that the reference was to Don David's horoscope. But what each considered to be the hallmark of leadership was certainly different. To the father, there could be no doubt that the son should shine in the emerging high society of Colombo.

A good night's sleep in my own little cell revived me for the strenuous course of studies which started promptly at eight in the morning. The class proceeded well. I was not very far behind. In fact, at times, I surprised them both with apt quotations where some abstruse grammatical structures had been applied. The first day set the tone for the days to follow.

Six hours of Sanskrit a day with three teachers - each a well-intentioned slave driver - was no fun. The indispensable memorization of rules and texts called for as much time after as during the classes. In between, Noble Son of Wisdom attended to urgent administrative matters of his school and I continued to handle the correspondence of Venerable Sumangala.The fullmoon, the new moon and the two quarter-moon Sabbath days as well as the Sundays were free. When they occurred together, the sense of relief was greater. We went for long walks, visited friends in other temples and kept in touch with the developments in the national and Buddhist revival movement.

But this routine could not last too long. To the table of Venerable Sumangala came a mountain of letters from all parts of the country. Daily I would find that the time I spent with this correspondence had to be increased. Within months, it had begun to demand every leisure hour that I could find. My resourcefulness in recruiting several volunteers did not relieve me of the growing burden.

Something was happening to the people. Unknown to us a great sleeping giant had woken. It had a thousand demands and all I was doing was the mechanical job of bringing them to the attention of Venerable Sumangala. He was working round the clock and visibly enjoyed it.

"Little Name, do you see what has happened to the country?"

274

He proceeded to narrate the story of the shorter of the Indian Epics where the mythical king of Lanka had to wake up his brother, the giant Pitcher-Ears, when the kingdom was invaded by Rama and his monkey army.

"The sleeping masses of the country, like Pitcher-Ear, have woken. Things will never be the same again - neither for me nor for you."

VII

Venerable Sumangala was correct. There was indeed a great awakening. Olcott has started a veritable engine of perpetual motion - an engine which fuelled itself from within.

Things were happening everywhere. People wanted Venerable Sumangala to lead them or inspire them or they simply wanted to report to him.

Invitations for meetings and functions came in the hundreds. People were organizing themselves in associations and societies to agitate for their rights, to create institutions to meet their religious and social needs and mobilize resources.

Schools were being planned and established. Textbooks were being written and published. Sunday classes in Buddhism were started in temples.

Rural development, temperance and social services attracted men and women of foresight and energy.

People articulated their apprehensions and aspirations. Brochures and pamphlets were widely circulated. They counselled people to awake, arise and save the heritage.

Draft memoranda meant to be addressed mainly to the British administration were being circulated. Venerable Sumangala was often the first to receive a draft for his comments and more importantly his signature .

His signature carried immense weight.

From my vantage point I could assess the magnitude of the momentum. From the silent leadership which the scholar monk gave I could also grasp the mechanics of action which steadily and truly led the nation to a national and Buddhist revival. But the leadership did not always emanate from his humble monastic cell through letters and messages. We travelled widely; held meetings of scholar-monks at the College; addressed public gatherings; and met government officials, almost all of whom were his friends or admirers.

All this, of course, was to be my leisure or own time activities. Not for a single moment was I allowed to forget that my primary responsibility was to study Sanskrit. Of course, Noble Son of Wisdom was always there to remind me what I had not done or what I needed to do to catch up. On very rare occasions, I had to miss a class. I settled down to a night of four to five hours of sleep and I felt good.

With all such responsibilities and an unrelenting schedule, my own problems receded into the background. I had letters from Chief Monk and Slim-Jewel unopened for two days before I found time to read them with the attention they deserved.

My brother, the monk, had written a letter on which Chief Monk had scribbled his signature faintly and illegibly. There was no doubt that he was not merely infirm but also ill. Could it be that he had had a second stroke? The letter said nothing. It began with a brief appraisal of what he had heard of my role in the visit of Olcott.

"I am very happy, Little Name, that you distinguished yourself as the finest interpreter that the visitors have had and that the Colonel himself has spoken very highly of you to many of my friends."

Only after a long homily on what I should do as regards my studies and the future that he dealt with the matter on which I had asked for counsel.

"It is true that Middle Banda has a son from his illegitimate relationship. The boy is two years old. I have not seen him. But those whom I sent to the village of the outcastes tell me that he is fair and handsome. But there is nothing we can do. It is his fate to be born to a mother who deprives him of a place in society........"

On and on the letter went into an abstruse discussion on the ineluctability of one's moral responsibility for what one had done in one's cycle of birth and death.

I was annoyed. I did not ask for a discourse on the theory of Karma. I knew all about it. It had been the easiest explanation for anything that went wrong in life. From the earliest days I remember of my infancy, I have heard it. Even the landslide which deprived my family of most of its landholding has been blamed on my Karma.

To say that one pays his dues for what one had done in one or more of one's previous lives may be a good point to make when urging people to avoid irresponsible and unethical conduct. But I always felt that it was grossly unfair to punish anyone without giving him or her the slightest chance to know what the crime was. The simplest code of natural justice demands that one should have the right to proffer an explanation and plead one's case.

Why should that child suffer material deprivation and social discrimination - a lifetime of oppression and isolation - for something that he would never remember or recall?

I read the letter patiently and felt sorry for the old monk. Helpless as he was as a monk - very much as I was - he was trying to dissuade me from getting involved. "*What Karma had ordained, we cannot change*" was his pitiful conclusion. But I was disappointed. I sincerely thought that he would do something to save the child from his grave fate.

Where was compassion? Where was that Loving Kindness on which we meditated every morning and night?

I hoped that Slim-Jewel's letter would be more helpful. It was long. It started on a cheery note and that was promising. She had gone to visit Aunt Flower and Uncle Victor and it was a joint letter though mostly written by her. She was chirpy as her three old daughter, Moon-Beam, was on a visit with her for the incomparable festive season of the last capital of the Sinhala Kingdom.

People in Kandy were always in happy and buoyant spirit during the season of the great pageant of elephants and dancers. It was the time the town played host to the rest of the Island. Thousands came to witness the grand spectacle. It was time to host friends and relatives in one's humblest home and to make merry.

I could discern subtle and also not very subtle hints from Slim-Jewel's first visit to Kandy. I could recognize the naughty hand of Aunt Flower who never failed to tease me.

"Do you happen to know where that bushy haired young man in flannel trousers and navy blue blazer who showed us the Temple of the Sacred Relic is? We wonder what he is doing now."

Such remarks did bring memories which I had long tried to subdue. Suppressing memories - whether pleasant or otherwise - was an uphill task. Forgetting my monastic vows, I allowed my mind to dwell in those sweet moments when life appeared in the sharpest of lovely colours.

I knew that three persons who held me in the deepest affection wanted to make me feel great. At one point Aunt Flower had inserted in her handwriting,

"Here, Slim-Jewel says that when you next come to Kandy she would cook with her own lily-white hands a whole meal for you and all your yellow-robed chaperons."

Uncle Victor had added,

"If she manages to keep your Aunt out of the kitchen, you will certainly have a decent, edible meal."

I could visualize the three of them writing the joint letter seated round the dining table after the kids had gone to sleep. How much they had enjoyed the innocent fun of teasing me and thus demonstrating their undying love.

It was only in the ninth or tenth page that they referred to my middle brother's son.

"I had no idea that elder brother had a child from his first love until I read your letter. No one tells me these things as they think that I would be upset. I was no doubt upset. The letter brought back such sad memories. I went home immediately.

"With the eldest brother and my sister, I went to the village taking some food and presents of clothing and toys. We had arranged to meet by the river and she came alone with the baby. From the moment, I saw him, I could not take my eyes away. Fairer than Moon-beam but with a skin that glistened as of gold, he looks so sweet, so lovely."

In a different handwriting, possibly that of Uncle Victor, the next sentence read.

"When he grows up he will break the hearts of all the girls on both sides of the river!"

"He has the father's face and the mother's eyes," the letter continued in Slim-Jewel's handwriting. "He came to me when I called. I hugged him with an affection that was so natural that I was amazed. I carried him all the time we were there. He loved the sweets which my mother had made. When we wanted to leave, I handed him back to the mother. You wouldn't believe, Venerable Brother. He clung on to my neck and refused to budge. I was inclined to take him with me but eldest brother dissuaded me, saying, 'She may be poor and helpless but to any mother her baby is a priceless treasure.' She went on her knees and worshipped the brother and cried. She said, 'I know you will bring him up as a prince but he is all I have.' I felt so sad that I drew her near to me and she hugged me as a sister would. Did I become less of a human being by touching her or her touching me? Why do we condemn her and her clan as untouchable? We continued to discuss various things until the little fellow fell asleep in my arms and I could give him back to the mother."

I could visualize the scene as I knew the verdant coves where boulders provided convenient arenas for lovers to meet and villagers to have their conclaves. I turned to the next page which was the last.

"My dear Venerable Brother, can you guess what she told me when she took leave of us? 'It is a joy to have the baby now. Everyone helps me to bring him up. But you never know what happens in the future. The clan may force me to marry a widower and he may have his own children. Or they might force me to go more often on begging rounds and he will be hardly cared for. If I have no way to bring up the baby, can I bring him to you? I know you are a goddess, my golden jewel. Otherwise you will not want to see my face after all I did to disgrace you and bring you untold suffering. Will you take him and bring him up as your daughter's own brother?' Without a moment's hesitation I said 'yes.' The eldest brother and my sister asked her to contact them at any time if such a need arose. You know! She went away happy, as if a very big burden had been removed from her head."

The letter ended with a brief note from Uncle Victor and a mischievous query in a postscript from Aunt Flower whether it was true that student monks of the College crept into Muslim restaurants in the night to eat egg and chicken fried rice.

"When you join them, do you wear a sarong and pretend to be a Muslim brother? Or have you brought with you your flannel trousers and blazer?"

How very irreverent can my favourite Aunt be! I laughed spontaneously. I felt so relieved, nay, so happy. With a brief note saying why I was doing it, I resealed the envelope, pasted a slip of paper and addressed it to Little Father care of Venerable Pleasant-Gem-Tissa. Let him have the news and enjoy a little innocent fun with memories of his ebullient sister, I thought.

Whatever depressive feeling I had when I read Chief Monk's letter disappeared when I read the humour-filled letter of the other three. I wrote a letter to Chief Monk and added a note to my brother, the monk, to whom the cover was addressed to let me know if the elder monk was ill. I gave them the news of Slim-Jewel's meeting with the baby.

I wrote another jointly to Uncle Victor, Aunt Flower and Slim-Jewel, with their names in that order. I told them of my recent exposure to the delegation of Theosophists and their "antics." It turned out to be a humourous letter. What I could recall of the silly attempts of Madame Blavatsky to outshine Olcott, the frequent bickering among the other members of the Delegation and Olcott's only-partially-successful effort to keep the motley crowd together was indeed quite funny. I wrote without malice. It was an edifying commentary on their human nature. I admired them without reservation for their dedication to a noble cause like founding a Universal Brotherhood of Humanity. I admired them even more for being frail humans with all human foibles, yet still setting their eyes on the stars.

I did not overlook the postscript from Aunt Flower. I added at the end:

"My Dear Aunt of impeccable memory, have you forgotten that I don't eat chicken and eggs even by day?"

I went to bed with a happier heart. Reflective of the mood was a strange dream I had. It was a family reunion. I was not sure whether I was still a monk. But I went to the family gathering with two children who clung to my hands: one was Moon-Beam and other was her half-brother from across the river.

The human being is undoubtedly· the most adaptable animal. No other living creature could create its own physical, intellectual and emotional environment and modify it at such short notice as a human being.

A middle-aged Siamese Prince who had until recently lived in the lap of luxury in a Western capital which claimed to be the centre of civilization of the modern age and myself, a rural boy of a feudalistic society from a remote village in the central mountains of a less developed island, were studying the classical language of poetry, drama, religion, philosophy and science of the great Indian subcontinent. Neither was prepared for the austere life of a monastery and for the ever-mounting demands of a relentless routine. Yet we were happy with what we were doing and looked forward to every day as a new day of intellectual adventure.

Each one was nudged by a keenness not to disappoint the self-effacing teachers who took the task of teaching us as their sacred mission and also by a subtle whim to excel the other in the final examination which was mercilessly drawing closer, day by day.

Both had obligations beside our studies: He ran with his own resources a school which was daily gaining in stature and reputation. I was handling the ever increasing load of correspondence of Venerable Sumangala and contributing in my own modest way to the intellectual underpinnings of the visible national and Buddhist renaissance of my Motherland.

We worked long hours, helped each other in every possible way and built upon a friendship which both cherished. I was of course the greater beneficiary. I learnt so much from him. His counsel was ever so valuable when I was befuddled. But he would say that he owed more to me as I made it easier for him to deal with the pangs of enforced separation from his children. Often, I felt that he equated me to his eldest son who was then completing his University studies in Oxford.

During our walks along the recently developed Galle Face Promenade, he would tell me about his family and specially his eldest son.

It was a pity that, as 1881 dawned, we were so involved with our studies and other obligations that these walks and talks became less and less frequent. We both regretted it. Yet we found a little time, specially after lunch, to chat about matters which were of personal interest to us.

Writing letters in lighter vein to Uncle Victor, Aunt Flower and Slim-Jewel and receiving theirs added a spark of joy to the otherwise humdrum monastic life. Noble Son of Wisdom had news from both England and Siam to share with me from time to time. It was not always happy news. Deaths and illnesses of dear ones gave us pain and we shared the grief as best as we could.

My grandparents died in the course of an ill-advised off-season pilgrimage to the Buddha's Footprint on Adam's Peak. While descending the sheer, cliff-like, rocky cap of the mountain, a gusty wind had blown off all those who were clinging to a rope to help themselves downhill. Their bodies were recovered hundreds of yards below the peak.

During the same week, the Abbot of Bo-tree Plain, my spiritual preceptor, had passed away peacefully in his sleep and was found dead on the following morning. In both cases, my eldest brother sent telegrams to me as well as Little Father informing of the tragic news but requesting us not to come.

In the case of the grandparents, the relatives of all victims of the accident had, quite sensibly, agreed to have the cremations at a convenient point en route to the Peak. The funeral of the Abbot was to be held within three days. It was suggested that the three month almsgiving in April would be the best time for us to come.

Noble Son of Wisdom too lost several of his close relatives. He hoped that he would be lucky enough to attend the funerals of at least some of them. This was quite an intriguing statement until he explained the national custom,

"You see they are almost all from royalty. A person of worth is never cremated in a hurry in Siam. According to how much the family is able to spend, the body will be treated and kept in a temple where monks will hold special ceremonies daily for a very long time - several years in most cases. If things change in Bangkok and I am able to return, I may be in time to pay my respects to some of them."

I felt sad for him. How much he yearned to be free! Exile, even when self-imposed, must be exceedingly painful!

A letter from Reverend Kenneth Saunders arrived with the postmark of Calcutta, India. At first I thought that he could have been there on a visit. But when I read the letter, I was very happy. He had received a letter I had sent him wishing him a merry Christmas and happy New Year. He was no longer in Burma. He had been elevated to the rank of a Bishop and had been assigned to the office of the Metropolitan, the Asian Head of the Anglican Church, whose headquarters were in the Indian Capital. He did not sound overly elated but that was Reverend Saunders.

His joys came to him from what he could do to serve humanity - "the God's most beautiful creation without discrimination of colour, caste, creed or class", as he defined humanity. He reiterated such sentiments.

I was not surprised to read his comments on what was being currently lamented in the Island as the greatest blow levelled against Christians by their own government, namely, the Disestablishment of the Church.

"Many of my colleagues and superiors are very upset. From now on they have to raise their own resources. In this way, we will be like all other denominations. This is the real test for our dedication and ingenuity, as clergy, and our usefulness and indispensability, as far as our flocks are concerned. If, as they say, our schools will close down and our numbers will dwindle simply because we are no longer a department of the government, we have no right to any credit for what we proclaim as our successes. We deserve what we have got. My task here is to inject some new thinking and to energize our padres and missionaries. To me it is a challenge to be called upon to earn my own keep!"

Towards the end of the letter, he invited me to revive my plans for study abroad. He recalled how much I craved to go to Calcutta after my studies in school.

"T. B., you lost your chance for no other reason than the petty policies and groundless bickering of my own colleagues. But I can now invite you to come here and do your higher studies. You can come as you are. A shaven-headed Buddhist monk in yellow robes could be quite a rarity in Calcutta. If what you want to study are Oriental Languages, the University and its ever-increasing fraternity of colleges could give you the best of facilities. You will be eligible for a scholarship which could look after all your needs. Think of it and let me know."

Living in the Learning-Awakening College at this time were several scholars from Calcutta. Vedic scholars of recognized erudition in Sanskrit and Indian lore, they had come to Colombo to learn Pali and Buddhism. I showed one of them the letter of the Right Reverend Bishop Saunders, the Assistant to the Metropolitan of the Anglican Church of Asia.

"Don't miss the chance, my friend," was his advice.

News travelled fast. Over the next few days every one of those Pandits urged me to go to Calcutta. I was obliged to tell Venerable Sumangala and his advice was practical and realistic.

"Ask yourself what you want to do over the next decade. If for that you need a degree from a University, this is your chance. Sit down in your cell and list your pros and cons. When one list outweighs the other, you'll know what to do."

This I did. The list of cons far exceeded the other. I saw a role in the Island in the movement which the scholar-monks had set in motion in their wisdom and Colonel Olcott accelerated with his supreme capacity to move people and mobilize resources. I had to be there when Olcott returned. How many times would he have to return, unless, of course, he settled down in the Island? Ten, twenty or thirty? I had to be there to work with him - to be his voice and ears for my people.

With such a self-assumed mission, I wrote to the Right Reverend Saunders a polite letter of thanks and told him how my destinies were now linked to an American promoter of Buddhism and a kingpin in the national awakening of the country. I gave a vivid account of how Olcott was raising the masses from their complacency and despair and galvanizing monks to action.

"As long as this White Buddhist works for the benefit of my Motherland, I have to be in readiness to assist him," I said in conclusion.

VIII

The examination in Sanskrit was conducted by one of the scholars from Calcutta. Both Noble Son of Wisdon and I fared well in different aspects of the subject. I did better in a single mark by scoring 461 out of a maximum of 500. It was nothing to crow about. But we had our good-natured fun as to who beat whom and who allowed himself to be beaten out of gracious compassion.

The greater joy came from the decision of Noble Son of Wisdom to spend the Sinhala New Year vacation with me in Sangha-Gem-Field. We arrived there by mail coach early in the morning of the tenth of April. We looked forward to a month of rest with a visit or two to Kandy. In the two monasteries there, the Siamese colleague wanted to take a look at a number of Siamese manuscripts which had to be identified.

Chief Monk had had a second stroke and he was recovering from the paralysis. But he was very weak. Sometimes, he was incoherent. How capricious his mind had turned to be.

"Birth, sickness, old age and death - you simply cannot cheat them," I said to myself, recalling the Buddha's teaching of the twelve links of Dependent Origination.

My brother, the monk, had grown in the course of just one year to be a responsible and highly respected manager of the temple. He was no scholar. He had learned to recite the Book of Protection and deliver short standard sermons appropriate to the occasion. He was popular with the villagers. His main qualification for their esteem and affection was that he was physically present among them. In contrast, I was an outsider, a visitor or, as one of the lady devotees put it, "our sun and our moon - but so far away." I was not offended. She was right.

It was my brother's idea that a three day chanting of the Book of Protection concluding with an almsgiving for a hundred monks and culminating in a public meeting was the appropriate way to honour the Abbot of Bo-tree Plain Temple three months from his death. It was proposed to the monks of the temple and they consulted the lay supporters. With some minor modifications in detail, the proposal was accepted.

The corresponding ceremonies for my grandparents were fixed in a way that inconvenience was minimized to all potential participants. The mid-day almsgiving to offer merit to them would be held on the first day on the chanting. On the eve, Little Father would be invited to deliver the customary sermon on death. That was to be on the sixteenth of April. The public meeting in honour of the late Abbot was thus to be in the afternoon of the twentieth and I was to be the main speaker in both Sinhala and English, if any of the invited officials came from Kandy.

All I had to do was to send a telegram to Little Father. The rest of the arrangements were taken in hand by my brother, the monk. How he mobilized everybody!

I was full of admiration and was glad that sooner or later I would step down in his favour so that the village could have an efficient Abbot who was in no way distracted from his duties to the flock.

The next few days the monks of both temples had to undertake the difficult and time consuming leg work. Tradition demanded that we should go personally to invite monks for the chanting as well as the two almsgivings. I volunteered to cover the two monasteries in Kandy.

"It is like visiting the cave-temples of Dambulla and hunting iguanas at the same time," said my brother quoting a popular national proverb whose parallel in English would be "Killing two birds with one stone." He was right.

Now, that Chief Monk was indisposed, I was obliged pay the New Year visits to the prelates and the senior monks of the two Chapters with suitable presents. It had to be on the very next day. Here again, my resourceful brother, whose monastic title was aptly the "Performer of what had to be done" had made timely preparations. Forty-six trays of presents had been already put together and two men named to take them with me to Kandy. The prelate, his two deputies and twenty members of the Executive Committee of each Chapter were thus taken care of. Noble Son of Wisdom joined me.

While I went from member to member of the two Executive Committees of the two Chapters, beginning with the Flower Garden Monastery, and attended to the customary etiquette, Noble Son of Wisdom ransacked the libraries of the two monasteries for Siamese manuscripts. We returned on the third day on the New Year's eve which was the thirteenth. We both had a lot to report to each other.

I had been bombarded with hundreds of questions on the bona fides of the two White Buddhists from America. Many a mind had to be disabused. All manner of misrepresentations, half-truths and innuendos had been reported. What I heard only showed how very gullible one could be when one is secluded in a traditional monastic system which had yet not begun to look beyond its portals. I defended Olcott and expressed my sincere confidence that he would be a great ally in enabling our people to regain their lost dignity.

On the part of the Siamese colleague, he had made the discovery that most of the manuscripts which the Siamese monks had brought or presented to the two monasteries were copies in Siamese script of ancient manuscripts of Pali works in Sinhala characters which had been taken from Sri Lanka to Siam a few centuries earlier.

"How much my country had benefited from the literary treasures of your Island!" he said.

"We are far more indebted to yours," I replied. "The Great Siamese Upali Sect, whose headquarters we visited during the last few days, owe their very existence to the restoration of the Sangha in which your monks played the crucial role."

Ceremonies began and proceeded as planned with neither delay not disruption. Every event was a acclaimed success. The quiet collective efficiency of the rural masses who rose to such an occasion with alacrity and resourcefulness was astonishing. I had known it all the time. But Noble Son of Wisdom said it most eloquently.

"You know what I had observed of your people - these simple village folk whose extreme humility and submissiveness conceal their many accomplishments. This is hardly a feudal society. If, at all, it is a truly cooperative society of equals who know and recognize that each person has a talent to contribute to the general well-being. They must have been at it for centuries if not millennia."

It was the assessment of a man of immaculate credentials for judging people in action.

An occasion to demonstrate the innate ingenuity of the organizers arose when the public meeting in honour of the Abbot was about to begin. A letter addressed to me from India had been redirected from Colombo. But none among them could decipher the Colonel's handwriting. One of them took the letter to Aunt Flower.

The moment she saw that it was to me, she made a sign to me with her hands and opened the letter. Being an inveterate non-conformist who did not believe in such niceties as respecting other people's privacy, she began to read it quite nonchalantly. She called the man back and whispered something to his ear.

It took over five minutes for the man to bring the letter to me. I was getting nervous as the prelate of the Flower Garden Monastery was already being conducted to preside over the meeting. With hardly a minute to spare, the man brought the letter to me saying,

"I am asked to give this letter to you now, only if you promise that you will bring the American gentleman here and set up a school for us."

"Was it my Aunt's idea of a joke?" I asked him.

"No, Venerable Sir. She told me to ask you for something before handing over the letter. We had a meeting at the back of the hall and decided that this is what we would want from you."

As the presiding prelate stepped on to the stage, I promised to make a fitting statement during my speech and grabbed the letter.

It was a happy letter. I was glad to read it even as the Five Precepts were being administered to the lay people. It was newsy as well as humorous. Olcott was at his best. Madame Blavatsky was on the war path. She had dissuaded him from carrying on his programme in the Island. Mahatmas had withdrawn their approval, she had told him. But he was coming. He had given the date and the name of the ship. I noted some parts of the letter which I thought I should read to the meeting.

I was the last of the monks to speak. Three rambling speeches by the prelate and a member each of the Executive Committee of the two Chapters had taken over an hour. It had been a gruelling time for a score of officials who had graced the occasion.

I began in English giving the letter in hand as my excuse. I had a captive audience as I switched from one language to another so that neither the visitors nor the villagers would be bored. I related with a few humorous words how I had to get my own letter by promising not only a school but also a visit by Colonel Olcott to Bo-tree Plain. His next visit to the Island would not be too far away, I said, reading at the same time his letter where the date of departure from India was stated.

"What a joy it is that he will land in Galle in exactly a week. You know what he says about our country and the people."

I read from the letter and translated each sentence into Sinhala:

"I saw the people as they are, at their very best; full of smiles and love and hospitable impulse, and have been welcomed with triumphal arches and flying flags, and wild Eastern music and processions and shouts of joy. Ah! Lovely Lanka, Gem of the summer Seas, how doth thy sweet image rise before me as I write the story of my experiences among thy dusky children, of my success in warming their hearts to revere their incomparable religion and its holiest Founder. Happy the Karma which brought me to thy shores."

288

I wove Olcott's words on the incomparable religion and its holiest Founder into the next sentence which elaborated the purpose of the function that evening. I explained why we stood in the utmost debt to the recently departed representative of both the religion and its Founder in our community.

I continued bilingually and held on as long as I thought the audience was with me. The end was less of a peroration but more of an appeal, very much in the tone of Olcott the fund-raiser.

"How shall be honour this great son of the Buddha? We need no temple. We need no preaching hall. We need no pagoda. But we need a Buddhist school - an English Buddhist School in his name so that our children will not be kept away from the fountains of modern knowledge, science and technology. This is my proposal. Please make your pledges to me or to my Venerable brother when the meeting closes."

A monk's speech was never applauded. I had absent-mindedly omitted the concluding wish that the late Abbot attains the bliss of Nibbana. Hence only a few in the audience marked the end of my speech with the usual response of Sadhu! I was truly mollified.

Giving the impression to a bewildered crowd that it was only a pause and not the end of the speech, I turned back and resumed in the tone of the traditional reciter of the text imparting merit. I referred to the Abbot and to my grand parents and wound up with the list of blessings for them and for everyone in the audience.

Finally, I raised my voice and recited as melodiously as I could, "May all of us meet again in the same preaching hall, listen to a sweet and profound sermon from the Buddha Maitreya himself and attain the supreme bliss of Nibbana."

The resounding response of Sadhu ! Sadhu! Sadhu! was indeed soothing music to my ears.

Relieved of my responsibility, I could make a more leisurely survey of the audience. I could spot many of the people I wished to see on this occasion. Chubby and prosperous-looking, Aunt Jasmine sat like a dowager queen surrounded by her five children. Slim-Jewel's parents and their children sat together with my eldest brother and his family. My other brothers were all there, scattered all over. But the one I really wanted to see was not there.

She was not there on the first day: neither for the almsgiving to confer merit on the grandparents nor the inaugural ceremony of the chanting of the Book of Protection.

I was too busy that day to talk to Aunt Flower or Uncle Victor who could have given me some information. This day, I hoped they would not leave too early. I was soon to be disappointed. Even while the meeting was on and the R. M. or the Country Gentleman was delivering a speech in English which I was translating, Uncle Victor and Aunt Flower left the preaching hall.

Within minutes, they had taken the coach back to Kandy.

The R. M., whose speech was a superlative panegyric on the late Abbot, sounded so pro-Buddhist that I had to be very careful to avoid any impression that the overtones were added by me. He seconded my proposal to have a school in the village and pledged an initial donation of a thousand rupees. That was beyond my wildest dreams.

It did not, however, take too long to find out what had happened during the year I had not visited Bo-tree Plain.

Reverend Smith had been transferred to an African colony where he hoped there would be a greater receptivity to his message of Redemption. The Mission was cutting down its budget and could not afford a missionary, let alone a couple, in a small village where hardly any progress had been made in the propagation of Christianity. A catechist from the south had been sent on a temporary basis. The Christian leadership which the Blakes exercised and a semblance of which the Smiths maintained was no more. The school had gone to rack and ruin. The church was not even half-filled on Sundays. Many recent converts were reverting to their traditional religion. Even those like the R. M. who were still affiliated to the church were no longer as anti-Buddhist as they once were.

Venerable Pleasant-Gem-Tissa's student, Stanley Williams whom I had met in Galle an year ago as a newly arrived Civil Servant from England was now the Assistant Government Agent of the Central Province. He was invited to speak a few words. What an impression he made!

Starting in Pali, the sacred language of the Buddhists, to quote a verse from the Canon wherein the Buddha says "Rare in the world are the grateful who acknowledge what is done for them", he switched on to fluent classical Sinhala. It was a short speech in which he extolled the Sangha for being custodians of learning. He concluded with a verse from a fifteenth century poet whose didactic poem was familiar to all in the audience. What an ovation he received!

The foreign and English-speaking visitors along with the R. M. remained behind for over an hour or so to talk on Colonel Olcott and the Theosophists. Noble Son of Wisdom endorsed my observations, while underscoring that the involvement of the laity in the propagation of Buddhism was an innovation which would have some remarkable repercussions. It was a lively discussion. The collective thinking of the group was eloquently expressed by the Assistant Government Agent:

"This is how I see it. Sooner or later, Olcott will be replaced by a national - in all likelihood a young man from within the movement he had set in motion. Conscious of national sensitivities and values, such a person will work out the ground rules for the Sangha and the laity to collaborate. I expect progress and not chaos. Lay leadership and involvement is nothing new to Buddhism in Ceylon.

"Wasn't it a layman who was appointed in the second century to decide whether some new teachings that came from India were heretical or not? Aren't some of the best interpreters of the doctrine in the thirteenth century lay scholars? Isn't it true that the the new wave of Buddhist scholarship in the maritime region resulted from the efforts of some lay scholars who were exposed to the renaissance of Buddhist learning which took place in Kandy in the eighteenth century?"

I wished I had known those instances from my own country's history to allay the fears of Noble Son of Wisdom when he first expressed them in Galle.

By the time we dispersed, there was hardly anyone in the temple. I had to return to Sangha-Gem-Field without finding out why Slim-Jewel was absent.

Alone, I walked up the hill and gazed for a while at the spot where, as a boy of seventeen, I dreamt I would have my dream home with Slim-Jewel as its queen ruling over a brood of kids!!

IX

With a week left before the arrival of Colonel Olcott, I had only a couple of days to meet the people I was obliged to see, arrange for more effective care for Chief Monk and perform such other monastic administrative duties for which I was still responsible as the senior pupil of the Abbot. The transfer of these duties to my brother, Venerable God-Protected, was not favoured by the monastic community. Their assessment of my brother was that he was excellent for pastoral duties, to borrow an expression from the Christian Church, but not for anything more.

They hoped that I would complete my studies in Colombo and return with greater glory to serve as Abbot and also exercise effectively the resulting leadership in the Chapter and the Sangha. One thing they did not or would not understand: I was already painting on a much wider canvas and would never be able to return to miniatures! At least, this is how I thought at that moment.

With barely enough time to reach Galle by nightfall of April 26, Noble Son of Wisdom and I left Sangha-Gem-Field. We had a couple of hours in Kandy before the evening train. My Siamese colleague visited the Horse Peak Monastery while I walked along the lake bund to Royal Spout to pay a surprise visit to Uncle Victor and Aunt Flower. Only a servant boy was at home. Being new, he did not know who I was. The more I tried to get some information from him, the more I realized that we were engaged in a dialogue of the deaf. There was no stationery to leave a note. It was all a wild goose chase - an hour to go and another to return to the railway station.

There was still an hour for the train. I sat on a bench and took out a book of Sanskrit declensions to memorize. From time to time, I looked towards the entrance of the station to see if my Siamese colleague was coming. On one such occasion, I was surprised to see a pair of outcaste women begging at the gate. As their custom went, they both had their upper bodies bare. My own innate modesty and the strict monastic discipline precluded my taking any further notice of them, even though at first sight, one of them looked vaguely familiar.

She resembled so much the girl that my brother had shown me across the river as his sweetheart many years ago. I was in a predicament. I was very keen to talk to her. Whether or when she planned to give the baby to Slim-Jewel? Does she know why Slim-Jewel was not in Sangha-Gem-Field for the New Year? As a monk I could not beckon to her. Nor could I ask someone to fetch her to me.

Within minutes my problem solved itself. The foreign-looking Siamese monk attracted their attention and they turned around to see where he was going. I stood and turned around to greet my friend and I could not help seeing what she was doing. She looked at me intently for a couple minutes, realized that she was only half-clad, pulled out a piece of cloth from her bag, covered her upper body, approached us, knelt down and worshipped each one of us thrice.

I did not know her name. In any case I could not or would not use it. Monastic language has its special usages. I had to call her "Virtuous One" or "Lay devotee". I combined both and using the appropriate feminine form, addressed her,

"Virtuous devotee, Are you not from across the river in Sangha-Gem-Field?"

"That I am, Venerable Sir. The wretched woman who applied black soot on the faces of your worthy, honourable family. The woman who brought so much shame and grief to so many."

"That's everyone's Karma," I said mechanically but regretted immediately.

I knew how much it had hurt me when people tried to brush off everything as Karma, including the catastrophic landslide on the night of my birth. But this was not the place for a homily on responsibility, moral conduct or any such theme. She was nice enough to approach me. Or she may really have a need to meet me.

"Virtuous devotee, they wrote to me after they met you. I am in favour of the plan and I told them so."

"Thank you, Venerable Sir. The golden jewel is the noblest woman I have ever set my eyes on. She is a goddess. Not only did she forgive me for all I had done to bring unspeakable disaster to her life, but embraced me as a sister and assured me that she would bring up the boy as her daughter's own brother. That was very noble of her."

"That she is. I agree. When do you think you may have to give us the baby?"

Her face clouded on hearing the word "us". But it soon cleared. On second thought, she appeared to take the collective first person plural as a reference to the whole family. If she did so, she was right.

"It looks as if I will be forced to do it much earlier than I had thought. I was expecting the golden jewel to come to the village for the New Year. But I was told that her baby first and she herself later went down with chicken-pox. I hear that she's having a really bad attack. Fever with deliria for many days and scabs all over her body."

293

How providential! It was bad news, no doubt. But I could go to Galle with some peace of mind. I had conjured up in my mind far worse calamities as I walked along the lake bund.

As the train put into the platform, we bade good-bye to the woman and went in search of suitable seats.

"Pure, you can't blame your brother. She is even now a very beautiful woman," said Noble Son of Wisdom. "She carries herself well too. One thing I agree with her wholeheartedly. Slim-Jewel must be the noblest woman to volunteer to bring up her murdered husband's illegitimate son by an outcaste woman."

Each word he chose to describe the situation highlighted what he was stressing in Slim-Jewel's character.

The railway compartment was soon filled to capacity. I gave up my window seat as no one, out of deep respect, took the vacant seats beside us. For some reason the train was unlit. As the sun set and pitch darkness engulfed us, I closed my eyes to meditate and relax.

Occasionally when I opened my eyes, the fascinating flight patterns which myriads of fireflies made as they flew around and settled on shrubs brought joyful memories of a carefree childhood. My mind was clogged with a flow of thoughts which I could hardly control. It was difficult to clear the mind and go back to meditation. I panicked as I had been conditioned to believe that my foul and inappropriate thoughts would bring dire consequences of the worst order.

Recalling my teachers' instructions on antidotes for such thoughts, I admonished myself silently:

"Pure-Wisdom, you are a monk. You have renounced your family, career and all that lay life involves. There's no turning back, now or ever. Your one and only duty is to keep your mind pure and focus your sole attention on your own salvation from the cycle of birth and death.

"The more you think of your family, your childhood, your joys and affections, the more you become attached. The more you think of things that had gone wrong and things you failed to do or get, the more you become angry. The more you think of what could or should have been done, the more you become confused.

"Hasn't the Buddha preached that Attachment, Anger and Confusion are the root causes of all evil? Wake up, Pure-Wisdom. Be a good monk. Cleanse your mind of worldly thoughts. Meditate on the qualities of the Buddha. He's your role-model.

"Think of death and its imminence. Life is but a drop of dew on a blade of grass. Meditate on the human body for what it is - a heap of decaying, foul-smelling, and putrid flesh and bones. Fill your mind with thoughts of Loving Kindness for every being in the universe."

Over and over again, I admonished myself. I recalled the monks of the time of the Buddha and how they admonished themselves and reached the end of their misery. I repeated in Pali those sections from the Canon where these same ideas were expressed in greater detail.

Little by little, these thoughts took root. I felt lighter and my mind was free of the concerns that had kept me on tenterhooks. I was reconciled to my place in life and society - a monk dedicated to a life of poverty, chastity and service. I saw what I had to do - no more doubts and no more distractions. It was such a joyous accomplishment.

By the time the train reached Colombo and stopped at the station closest to the College, my worries over my brother's child and cares and concerns of Slim-Jewel had been laid to rest. I was determined to root out of my mind the recurring pattern of thoughts which revolved around Slim-Jewel and what could or should have been in our lives.

In addition, I had formulated the confessions I was going to make when the monks met for the next fortnightly confessional ceremony. With the next recitation of the two hundred and twenty-seven rules which applied to the life of a monk, my commitment to uphold everyone of them would be unwavering and unswerving, I promised to myself.

"I didn't disturb you," said Noble Son of Wisdom as we climbed the stairs to the street. "You must have been very tired."

"Thank you very much," I replied, for it was not the place to tell him of the thousand conflicts I had grappled with.

When we reached the College premises, an observant acolyte saw us, opened the doors of our cells and offered two welcome bowls of steaming hot ginger tea.

Venerable Sumangala had left for Orange Island with Venerable Gunananda and I was expected to meet them there. Immediately after the morning chanting and breakfast, I took leave of Noble Son of Wisdom and boarded the first available train to Black Ford. I had a seat in the connecting coach and was in Orange Island a little after nightfall.

At Olcott's own request no elaborate arrangements were made to welcome him. He had wanted time to do some writing and begged that no public receptions be organized. Yet the news of his coming had travelled and a large crowd did gather outside the harbour building. Three hundred children from the school which was established during his first visit lined the Harbour Avenue up to the school. Olcott and his friend were to be accommodated in rooms on its upper floor.

295

Senior monks, led by the eighty-six year old doyen, Venerable Betel-Village, and important lay persons were at the jetty. The members of the Galle Theosophical Society were ready to take care of him. Among them was Virtue-Gem, a renowned scholar of Buddhism and Oriental Languages. He was a Sub-regional Administrator, designated by a South Indian title "Mudaliyar" meaning "the First" or "the Top Man." Both the administration and the people held him in high esteem . Pleasant-Gem-Tissa was indisposed and sent a letter to the Colonel through me.

Olcott arrived with Mr. Bruce who was introduced as a friend and a Fellow of the Theosophical Society. The monks chanted benedictory verses. A tentative time table for his work in Sri Lanka was discussed briefly.

"I need ten days all by myself to complete a manuscript and to have it translated into Sinhala," Olcott told the monks."Then I will be with you to launch the campaign for the Buddhist Educational Fund."

He worshipped each monk individually and thanked them for their presence at the jetty to receive him. He was very happy to see me and nearly embraced me before he realized that it was against our custom.

"My dear young priest, I was hoping you will be here. Can you stay behind and help with the translation of a book I have written?" he asked me.

"Yes. indeed," replied Venerable Sumangala when I looked up to him for approval.

"Meet me tomorrow in the school," Olcott told me as he joined his hosts who had already loaded their baggage into the carriage.

"You can remain here till about the tenth of May." said Venerable Sumangala reminding me that the College would reopen on the eleventh. "I have not thought what the two of you should do this year. How about some advanced Pali and Sanskrit together with some Prakrit? I don't think our Siamese friend would want to read any classics in Old Sinhala. But you had better begin."

Thus reminding me once again that my primary duty lay in pursuing my studies, he asked someone to take me to Middle Road in China Garden. Only at the temple did I realize that my bag with extra robes and under garments, towel and handkerchiefs were at Orange Island. The Abbot had a newly donated parcel of "Eight Requisites" brought to me and I had all I needed, from robes to the razor.

By the time I arrived in the school at seven in the morning, Olcott had already had breakfast, taken his friend on a walk on the ramparts and given him a detailed account of the city and its history.

The vast green esplanade in front of the imposing Dutch fortress was deserted. Seagulls in their hundreds hovered overhead as a veritable canopy. A few brave crows intruded into their territory, adding colour and relief to an otherwise all-white backdrop. Their combined cacophony muffled the sound of breaking waves - the soft hiss of the sweeping white-brimmed waves wafting the fishing boats gracefully to the shore on the left and the harsh, crashing bruit of the fathom-high waves which pounded incessantly on the crop of boulders on the right. To walk across this dew-laden green carpet early in the morning amidst the raucous music of Mother Nature was to enjoy Galle at its best. My eyes feasted on the blue sea that wrapped around the granite ramparts.

"Sit in a quiet place and read this," he told me and handed over a loosely bound manuscript. The cover identified it as "Buddhist Catechism" by Henry Steel Olcott. "I must have read ten thousand pages of the most authoritative literature on Buddhism in several languages. To begin with, can you please go through it in one go and let me know what you think?"

I chose a well-lit classroom and appropriated for myself the desk and chair of a teacher. I started reading,

1. Q. Of what religion are you?

A. The Buddhist.

2. Q. What is Buddhism?

A. It is a body of teachings given out by the great personage known as the Buddha.

The method sounded so familiar. It was so Buddhist. It, however, took a while to remember the first lesson that was given when I became a novice:

Q. What is one?

A. All beings subsist on food.

Q. What is two?

A. Name and Form (The Buddhist explanation of a being as an aggregate of psychological factors and matter)

Though the technique was old, Olcott was using it to give a comprehensive account of the life of the Buddha, the main doctrines of Buddhism and a bit on its rise and development. It was so absorbing. What an orderly presentation? How logical! How lucid and captivating! I read it in one sitting and finished it with just enough time to walk back to the temple for the mid-day meal.

297

Walking to and fro, I could formulate my comments to the writer. I had to congratulate him, nay express my sincerest gratitude. It was the kind of book we had long wanted. There was little in it that I did not know. As children we did have an exposure to the main tenets of Buddhism through a unique system of informal education which had been in vogue for centuries. Stories and narrative poems with which parents and grandparents regaled the children, temple murals which served as effective visual aids and frequent sermons which marked many an event in one's life-cycle were the main elements of this system. Knowledge seeped into one's innermost consciousness. But could they be retrieved or recalled easily? Here was the strength of Olcott's presentation. Step by step, the reader was taken over a vast body of knowledge. Olcott's method gave a structure. For the first time, I could say with confidence, "I know" and not "I think I know."

The Colonel was quite pleased to hear my comments, which I started with the caveat that I have not checked whether the information contained in the Catechism was altogether in keeping with what was taught and accepted in Sri Lanka.

"That's a detail which I want to settle with the chief priests. I need the translation for that purpose."

It was too big a task for one person. To my great relief, Virtue-Gem not only translated almost half the book but went over the entire text to ensure uniformity of technical terms and style. Within a week the translation was ready and Olcott could take the steamer to Colombo on seventh of May.

While we were busy translating the Buddhist Catechism, Olcott and Bruce were not idle. They wrote several pamphlets specially for monks and pursued the Colonel's mission of unifying the sects of the Island. He also met eminent monks of the various sects. One of them who impressed him the most was the prelate of the Ramanya sect. Though another Burmese sect, but originating in another city, this sect was emerging as an independent unit under the dynamic leadership of its founder, Venerable Mango-tree Plain. He was urging reform in the Sangha and that was exactly the same thing that Olcott was doing.

The American Buddhist whose aspiration in youth had been to be a universal reformer admired reformers. He was full of praise for Venerable Gunananda not only because he was a "silver-tongued orator" or a "wrangler and no ascetic", but because he was a champion of change. As regards the new prelate of the third sect, Olcott had a similar admiration as he was a "monk of great force of character, fine education and quenchless energy." Their target was the Sangha and

298

their rallying cry was that the Sangha had become lazy and unobservant of their duties: the religious education of the people was being neglected and there must be change.

Olcott was pleased that his ideas were being accepted and acted upon by a progressively widening circle of monks themselves.

It was a bubbling activist who took the steamer to Colombo to accomplish three tasks in the course of the second trip to an Island where he had found a mission to accomplish. He wanted to have his book approved by the leading scholar-monks and have it published within months. Once that was done he wanted to launch a fund-raising campaign with an intensity never before known in the Island. The third was to consolidate his efforts to unify the three sects - Siamese, Amarapura and Ramanya.

By the time I collected my luggage from Orange Island and returned to Colombo, the Colonel had already made arrangements to have his book read and approved by Venerable Sumangala. The senior staff of the College had been mobilized to scrutinize every word.

As guardians of orthodoxy, the Sangha had been scrupulously painstaking, right through history.

I had heard of a scholar of immense learning who came from India in the fifth century. He was planning to translate the Canonical Commentaries which were in Sinhala into Pali. Whereas Sinhala was restricted to the Island, Pali, the language of the Buddhist Canon, was the lingua franca of the then Buddhist world. The scholar-monks of the Great Monastery of Anuradhapura insisted on testing his competence. He was given two verses on which to comment. If only the commentary showed that his knowledge of the teachings of the Buddha was adequate, was he to receive their permission. The Indian scholar, of course, was equal to the task and produced the excellent compendium of Buddhism, "The Path of Purification."

It is with a similar desire that the monks set about their task to find out if Olcott really knew Buddhism as they accepted it. The White Buddhist had brought his thesis. So they did not have to emulate their predecessors of the Great Monastery and demand a written treatise. The stalwart scholars of the College sat with Olcott and Bruce. I was there on a side to assist them to collate the text and the translation and interpret to and from English.

The scholars scrutinized every word. Eight hours on the first day brought them to the middle of page 7. It was a friendly meeting. Monks argued their case and Olcott explained. Compromises were reached easily. Progress though slow was steady. The next day proved to be similar. They could do roughly a page an hour.

Half way through the discussions on the third day, they came to Olcott's definition of Nibbana or Nirvana - the Buddhist summmum bonum, the ultimate bliss of its Path of Deliverance.

"Just a minute," said the Deputy Principal of the College, Venerable Friend of Gods, a scholar of very great repute, beckoning me to interpret his statement. "What is this talk about the survival of some subjective element in the state of Nibbana?"

"We cannot accept this," joined another scholar.

Always fair and accommodating, Venerable Sumangala called upon Olcott to explain, while he himself started re-reading the original and the translation.

"What's the problem?" asked Olcott and his tone was not altogether pleasing. "I know your strong views about Nirvana and I have presented it in the way your school accepts. But I must tell the truth."

"What is the truth? Do you imply that the truth is not what we accept as Nibbana. Is that what you say?" asked the Deputy Principal.

"Why don't you understand what I say" challenged Olcott. "There is no agreement among Buddhist metaphysicians on what Nibbana actually is. The Mahayana schools of Tibet, China, Japan and Mongolia believe that some sort of subjective entity survives in Nibbana. What I mean by the truth is that this disagreement exists? Don't you know it?"

Unfortunately the last question sounded a bit too rude - in tone more than in content. Olcott had been critical about the general level of the education of monks and so far the scholar-monks had agreed with him. Generally, they had never been averse to constructive criticism, based on the Buddha's advice that one who exposed your faults was your best friend. They were themselves dissatisfied with both the level of the education of monks and the learning facilities provided to them. To them it was a problem to be solved through effective counter-measures: hence their pioneering effort to revive the ancient system of education, the publication of the national literature and the training of teachers.

Olcott went a bit too far when he cast aspersions on the erudition of the present company which consisted of the best of national scholarship. The Deputy Principal was red with anger. He stood up.

"What do you mean, Mr. Olcott? You claim to have read ten thousand pages. Did you read a single work in the original language? I doubt it. What's your ability to check if a text is faulty or the translation is incorrect or the book you read is not the relevant text for a particular school of Buddhism. I have read them in the original Sanskrit, the very ones which the Chinese and Tibetans translated into their languages. I have read them with the traditional commentaries and relevant treatises. Mr. Olcott, you asked the wrong man whether he knows what the Mahayana metaphysicians say. Isn't it one of your sayings that little knowledge is a dangerous ...."

Interrupting the scholar-monk's sentence half way, the Colonel also stood up. I positioned myself between the standing debaters so that I could hear better and to do a correct rendering.

"How dare you insult the pioneering scholars of the West who had taken so much trouble to bring the knowledge of your religion to the rest of the world?" he asked, gesticulating with his hand raised and the index finger pointing to Venerable Friend of the Gods. "You must be eternally grateful to them. I may not know whether a text is correct or whether a translation is accurate. But I go by the international reputation of these scholars. I have not read trash and I want you to know it."

Venerable Sumangala, always the calm and peaceful negotiator, felt that exposed nerves served no purpose. He wanted to terminate the argument. He requested his deputy to take a seat and beckoned to Olcott to do likewise.

"Let both parties be fair to each other. My white devotee, we may be a few but there is a growing number of monks in this Island whose knowledge of Buddhism in its fullest diversity ranks as high as that claimed by your authorities or even superior. You have no access to what we can reach through our mastery of Pali and Sanskrit. As regards Chinese and Tibetan sources, we are certainly familiar with the translations you have used. But that is not the point."

Olcott stood as if to interrupt the scholar-monk and looked at me. I motioned him to sit down and he complied. The monk after a moment's silence continued.

"You have written a good book. You want to publish it here for use in our schools and for the use of beginners. If you take out this sentence about the disagreement of Buddhist metaphysicians, you get our approval. Otherwise, you can have it published anywhere else in the world for we cannot prevent you from doing it."

As Venerable Sumangala had chosen to speak in Sinhala, I had to translate it. I did it maintaining not only the sense but also the tone of reason and finality which the scholar-monk had adopted.

"Venerable Sir, you do know that metaphysicians disagree on the subject," pleaded Olcott.

"They may or they may not. But that's not the point. This a book for students and beginners. It is not a comparative study of the evolution of Buddhism in its various cultural settings. What you have to tell is what the Buddha taught. If you see any contradictions in his statements it is perfectly in order to point those out. Here there are no such contradictions. Metaphysicians are people like you and me - mere students. My advice is that you define Nibbana as the Buddha did, unless you have proof that your metaphysicians are themselves Buddhas who have already attained Nibbana and know about it better."

It was a stubborn, obdurate Olcott who refused the face-saving way out which the wise monk had provided him.

"I know your trouble. None of you with all your scholarship had attempted to do anything like it, a concise book summarizing all that one should know about your own religion. This is a novelty, something you have never seen before. Your trouble, I must say, is your strong inherited tendency towards passive resistance to all innovation in the fixed order of things. I will fight this tendency inch by inch, as one might say. I am an Anglo-Saxon bull-dog whose Puritanical....."

To Olcott's utmost surprise, the scholar-monk, without even waiting for my interpretation, stood up gently, motioned to the other monks and left the room while he was in mid-sentence. Only Bruce and I were left with him. Olcott was quite agitated when he saw that the two manuscripts were folded and pushed towards the end of the table where he sat. This signal that the discussion was over hurt his ego.

It was my duty to be with the monks. I wished them "Good Evening" and retired to my cell.

A much-sobered Olcott sought me in my cell a few minutes later. Bruce followed him.

"Young priest, where did I go wrong? I thought we were having a frank and serious discussion."

"Yes, Sir. You did, until you started insulting them. Venerable Principal gave you a gracious way to get out of the impasse. Instead of using that opportunity, you attacked him. At first you insinuated that the monks were jealous of your book which you claimed to be a

302

novelty. Then you charged them with passive resistance. That was the worst part. Here, they were not passive. They fought vehemently against what they thought was unacceptable. And you began calling names!"

"Is that so, Bruce?'" he asked turning to his friend.

"Worse! Olcott, Much worse! This young priest is too polite. You were a darn fool."

It was a genuinely remorseful Olcott who asked me for counsel.

"I don't know what to do. If Venerable Sumangala were to cancel his promise to give his certificate of approval for this book and if he were to publish his reasons for that decision, the usefulness of my educational monograph will be destroyed beyond repair. It will be worse because any breach between him and me will make our school project ten times more difficult. I am prepared to do anything not to damage the friendship that has so far bound us. My dear young priest, please think of a way."

He was distraught and inwardly troubled. I felt sorry for him. With compassion overshadowing the anger over his intransigence, I began to think of ways to solve his problem.

I called an acolyte and asked him to find a sheaf of betel leaves. It was not a rare commodity in a temple because the monks chewed betel in large quantities. A sheaf of betel with a dried tobacco leaf was a customary gift any lay visitor might bring to a monk as a mark of respect.

"Take this, Sir. Go to the room of Venerable Sumangala. Offer it as any local devotee would and apologize to him," I told him.

He found the scholar-monk in his tiny cell in front of the two blossoming cannon-ball trees. Within a very short time I was sent for and I was happy that they were back on talking terms.

"My virtuous white devotee," Venerable Sumangala began in Sinhala. "It is not that we do not feel the greatest friendship to you or that we do not appreciate the great good that will accrue to us as well as others elsewhere from the book you have written. But your rigid and intolerable attitude in a matter of no major significance made me wonder whether you are qualified to interpret Buddhism to others. It is not a body of knowledge. It is a spirit, a way of thinking and acting. It's a way of life. Tolerance, patience and flexibility are its essential characteristics."

303

Venerable Sumangala stopped so that I could translate it for the Colonel. Mortified by the rebuke, he was speechless. The monk continued:

"Whether metaphysicians of any country agree or not is not the point. But to us what was important is that you blatantly disregard the Buddha's own definition of Nibbana. He says clearly that it was a state unconditioned, beyond classification as either annihilation or eternalism and more importantly unreachable through logical inference or argument. What your metaphysicians would have tried is to apply their tools of logic and as I told you none of them had become a Buddha. Do you understand the point I am making?"

"Yes, Venerable Sir."

"So, all we say is that your sentence about later metaphysicians has no place in a definition of Nibbana for students and beginners. Is that clear?"

"Yes, Venerable Sir."

"You will delete it?"

"Yes, Venerable Sir."

"We meet tomorrow at the usual hour. But we will go over the whole manuscript from the very beginning. There may be things we had glossed over."

I could read discomfiture written large on the mild and composed face of the old veteran. If that was what he meant by passive resistance, I would rank it the most effective strategy against obduracy and arrogance. I was sent away to inform the rest about the resumption of the discussion. They chatted for a very long time. As friends they did not need an interpreter!

The subdued author submitted to the revision of the text right from the beginning. Long discussions ensued but the monks had their way. Finally the revised text was duly approved and ten weeks later on 24 July 1881 both the English and the Sinhala versions appeared simultaneously with a certificate signed by Venerable Sumangala. He said that he had carefully examined the Sinhala version, it was in agreement with the Canon of the Southern Buddhist Church and he recommended it "to teachers in Buddhist schools, and to all others who may wish to impart information to beginners about the essential features of our religion."

As I recalled this momentous encounter between the monks and Olcott, I checked what the Colonel had to say years later when he recorded his impressions of the event. He had written in his diary:

"It was not that the priests did not feel the greatest friendliness for me and the high appreciation of the possible good that might accrue to the nation from our school project, but the conservative instinct was too strong to be pacified at once, and points that had been passed upon had to be reconsidered, and long discussions entered into as to the spirit of the Buddhist sacred books, before I could be allowed to go to the Press with my work. I am perfectly convinced that if I had been an Asiatic of any race or caste, the book would never have appeared, the author would have been tired out and have abandoned his effort. But knowing something of the bull-dog pertinacity of the Anglo-Saxon character, holding me in real personal affection, they finally succumbed to my importunity."

I cannot help but smile as I read his account. Truth, after all, is what one is most comfortable in believing!!!

X

One thing true of the bull-dog pertinacity of the Anglo-Saxon was the Colonel's capacity to have several irons in the fire at the same time. I had observed it at first hand in my close relations with Reverend Blake and his wife and Reverend (now Right Reverend Metropolitan) Saunders. Even while the monks were getting ready to scrutinize his manuscript, he sat with Venerable Sumangala and Venerable Gunananda and prepared a plan to raise popular subscriptions for the "revival of religious interest among the people" through the establishment of Buddhist schools.

He also had a document of support ready to be sent for signature of eleven of the most renowned scholar-monks who were at the same time the most influential members of the Sangha. They were also the leading pioneers of the Buddhist Revival Movement. With their support, the whole Sangha and the lay population would be behind the Colonel.

On the eighteenth of May, before the crisis over the definition of Nibbana occurred, these documents had been sent out with the request:

> *"As my time in the Island is limited, you will oblige me by signing and returning this paper by the first returning post in case you are as willing as last year to aid me with your valuable name, learning and advice."*

Armed with letters from the leading lights of the Sangha, Olcott started his field visits with Venerable Gunananda even as the book was being printed. His first plan was reviewed in two months and rejected as a bad one. He argued that delivering one lecture a week on Sundays would "require more than one man's life-time to get together the sum large enough to do much for Buddhism in Ceylon." He wanted three or four lectures per week to be arranged in different places. This he did and his own accounts of these trips are indeed most picturesque:

> *Journeying by clear days and days of pouring tropical rains; nights of moonlight, of starlight, and heavy showers; nights sometimes, when sleep is broken by the ear-splitting sounds of the jungle insect world, the horrid yelp of the jackal pack, the distant noise of the wild elephants pushing through the cane groves, the ceaseless shouts of the driver to his lagging bullocks, and his country songs, mostly in falsetto and usually discordant to keep himself awake. Then the*

mosquitoes swarming about you in the cart, with their exasperating drone, menacing slow torture and white lumps swelling on the skin.

Then the arrivals at the villages; in the dawn; the people all clustered along the road to meet you; the curiosity that must be gratified; the bath under difficulties; the early breakfast of coffee and appas - a thickish sort of rice cakes - with fruit; the visit to the monastery; the discussion of plans and prospects with the Buddhist monks; the lecture in the open air; or if there is one, the preaching pavilion, with great crowds of interested brown-skinned people, watching you and hanging on your interpreter's lips.

Then come the spreading of the printed subscription-sheets on a table, the registering of names, the sale of Buddhist tracts and catechisms; the afternoon meal cooked by your servant between some stones, under a palm tree; perhaps a second lecture for the newly arrived visitors from neighbouring villages; the good-byes, the god-speeds of rattling tom-toms and squeaky pipes, waving of flags and palm fronds, the cries of Sadhu! Sadhu! and the resumption of the journey in the creaking cart.

So on and so on, day after day I went all over the Western Province on this business, rousing popular interest in the education of the children under the auspices of their own religion, circulating literature and raising funds for the prosecution of the work.

Superb master of the theatrical effect that he was, Olcott interrupted his trips long enough in the first week of July to proceed to Galle and to convene a second Convention of the Sangha. It marked the anniversary of the first convention where fifteen monks from each of the two sects were fed in separate rooms. In all there were now sixty-seven monks representing the two sects that met on the previous occasion and the new one that was emerging. This time they met in one hall and were fed together.

Whereas I was excluded on the last occasion, lest the fine numerical balance between the two sects be disturbed by my presence, I was present on this occasion and was called upon to interpret several speeches.

As usual Venerable Gunananda made the most heart-warming statement. Olcott was overjoyed. He called it another feather in his hat in that the monks of the three sects had joined together to pledge their support to his work. It was a treat to see him chuckling with joy at the end of the Convention. He attributed his success on such occasions to his Yankee ingenuity.

The most convincing display of his Yankee ingenuity was when after a few months of riding double-bullock carts, he began to design and construct the equivalent of a pioneer's covered wagon for his trips.

It was a two wheeled travelling cart on springs. It had ample sleeping accommodation for four. By a simple change of longitudinal seat planks inside, he could have a writing room, a dining room for eight, sleeping room or an omnibus-like arrangement to seat eight passengers on two rows of cushioned seats.

Lockers projecting from the sides held table-furniture, tinned provisions, a small library and his bathing kit. There were two large lockers under the floor for baggage and sacks of vegetables and currystuffs. A chest in front held the tools, spare ropes and hooks for water-bucket and cattle-trough etc. A secure shelf over the axle was for the driver's cooking pots. A tight canvas roof on hoop-iron ribs gave ample protection from the tropical sun and the monsoonal torrents.

I was amazed when I saw it and its many uses. I was thrilled whenever I could ride in it. To every village we went, this travelling cart proved the most effective magnet in drawing large crowds. They came to see its wonders and stayed to listen to the Colonel and the scholar-monks who accompanied him.

Venerable Gunananda was his regular companion. He could be with him all the time as he had no ecclesiastical obligations.

He was, no doubt, a very senior monk, respected for his erudition, oratorical skill and courage. But for a minor misdemeanour, the Sangha had reduced him in rank and he was equivalent to a novice.

Every ordained monk had to observe the Rainy Season Lent from the fullmoon day of July to that of October. They had to be at the same residence in which they had agreed to remain and an absence of only six nights under exceptional circumstances was permitted. Monks completing the Lent also participate in a ceremony of presenting a special robe to the Sangha.

Venerable Gunananda was exempted from this obligation as a result of his loss of rank. That was a special advantage in that he could devote his entire time to travel and to the promotion of the National Buddhist Educational Fund.

308

Venerable Sumangala joined Olcott on special occasions, particularly when meetings or functions were arranged in important towns and townships. The scholar-monk was otherwise too busy with his mounting duties as academic head of the College. Besides his own programme of lectures, meetings and consultations, he had to deal with a daily mountain of correspondence. In this, I was more than a part-time private secretary. He continued to teach Pali and Sanskrit to an expanded class which included six Indian students from Calcutta. Their presence made the class more challenging to me and to Noble Son of Wisdom.

Whenever Olcott visited Colombo or went to Galle, Venerable Sumangala would find time to be with him. On all such occasions, I too had the privilege of being with them. Their friendship, if at all, was only strengthened by the crisis of the Buddhist Catechism.

Whenever present with them at a meeting, I was accorded the distinctive honour of being the main interpreter. Olcott would say kind words in public on my language ability as well as of the calm and collected head that I carried on my shoulders. Sometimes, I was quite embarrassed. But I knew why he went out of his way.

He was grateful that my simple strategy of sending him to the senior scholar-monk to tender his apologies in the traditional fashion saved a crucial friendship. I must have been with him when he delivered about a third of the "begging lectures" he made during this trip which ended on the thirteenth of December 1881.

Every day I spent with Olcott, I learned something new. He gave me news of what was happening in the field of Buddhist studies in the West. He was quite excited when he heard about the founding of the Pali Text Society by Rhys Davids.

"This is a step in the right direction, Young Priest. Scholars in Europe and America are in need of critically edited texts and good translations. I am happy that our friend, Mudaliyar Virtue-Gem has persuaded many of the scholar-monks of the Island to join it. As a result, Rhys Davids has decided to concentrate on the Buddhist Canon and its Commentaries. Isn't that wonderful?"

He was equally excited about a brief visit to the southern tip of India in October to found a branch of the Theosophical Society at Tinnevely. He was accompanied by three Sinhala Buddhists to represent the Theosophical Societies of Sri Lanka. For them it had been an extraordinary experience. Olcott had taken a coconut plant as a token of goodwill from the Island and was planning what he called an "ever-to-be-remembered incident" of planting it within the Tinnevely Hindu temple compound "by our Buddhist delegation as an act of religious amity and tolerance."

From the vivid account, the Colonel wrote in his diary, it had been a memorable event, replete with processions, bands and a crowd of five thousand. He says,

> *"I tried to speak in the hope that, when they saw my lips moving and my body swaying, the crowd would give me a chance, but my bad throat compelled me to stop very soon. Then, when the case looked hopeless, a light-skinned, intellectual-faced Brahmin, naked to the waist, arose in his place, towering above the squatting multitude, and, raising both arms full length above his head, pronounced the sacred salutation: 'Hari, Hari, Mahadeva-a-a!' The clear resonant sound rolled far and wide and silence fell upon the chattering multitude: I could even hear the sparrows twitter and the crows cawing outside. Instantly, I began my discourse and got through it more or less successfully.*
>
> *It was an appeal for religious tolerance and brotherly love, for theirs, their fraternal reciprocation of the good feeling which had brought over these Sinhalese, whose ancestors were Indian like theirs, and whose religious teacher was recognized by them as one of the Avatars of Vishnu. It seemed to be I touched their hearts, for there were all the outward signs of friendliness.*

Reading this account nearly two decades later, I wondered why it had not occurred to anyone that Olcott could have led a similar delegation to the Jaffna Peninsula in the north of the Island and encountered a similar experience.

For my part, I have to admit at that point in time, I did not have the foggiest idea that a strong outpost of the South Indian Tamil and Hindu Culture did exist within our own geographical and political boundaries.

Such ignorance was in spite of a fairly decent English education received at the hands of some of the finest missionary teachers in Kandy at a reputed school which was a meeting place for several ethnic, religious and linguistic groups.

How much more ignorant would have been my contemporaries from the southern maritime region of the Island!

Even as a child in Sangha-Gem-Field, I had seen South Indian estate labourers whom the British planters were importing in ever-increasing numbers. It was believed that they were exceptionally good for the back-breaking work in the coffee estates which were rapidly being replanted with tea. All the average villager claimed to know about them, however, was that these indentured labourers were mostly untouchables, extremely poor and ignorant, who believed that dried fish grew under tea bushes!

At least one Muslim family had settled in each village that I knew. I was familiar with the language they spoke which was a mixture of Tamil and Sinhala. Externally they were easily recognizable as men shaved their heads just as Buddhist monks did and the women covered their heads and faces when they stepped outside their homes. But I had never met up to this time a single Tamil Hindu from the North of the Island. Even if I had met one accidentally, I would have thought that he or she was another immigrant from South India.

As I had gone to Colombo with Venerable Sumangala on the day after my altercation with Olcott on the beach of Orange Island, I missed the opportunity to meet the Police Magistrate of Black Ford. Dawn-Mountain was reputed to be of a very distinguished Tamil Hindu family from Colombo. I had overheard the senior scholar-monks discussing this family, as one of its scions was an eminent scholar. Their observations as well as the tone had always being one of appreciation and admiration. Again, I had no idea that this family originated in the North.

Uncle Victor had told me of the increasing recruitment of Tamil officers to government service and spoken about their unwavering allegiance to the crown as well as to their land and kinsmen. He, too, spoke about these officers with unreserved admiration as honest, hard-working, and diligent to a fault.

"Our white superiors simply love them," he would say in support of his assessment.

That being the scope of my total knowledge of this important segment of population with whom we had shared our Island for millennia, I was in no position as a young monk of twenty-three to suggest to Olcott that he should seek out sympathizers for his movement in Jaffna. Knowing him, as I do, he would have undertaken such a mission with alacrity. As the wise American would do under

311

similar circumstances, I too have no other option than to record this missed opportunity as another "would have been."

By the time Olcott returned to India, the Buddhist Educational Fund stood at five thousand rupees in deposit and nearly fourteen thousand in pledges. So, in pecuniary terms, the seven months on the road had not been very profitable. Olcott himself asked for nothing and he did not receive a rupee for himself.

"I should have done all this last year when the whole country was boiling with excitement and enthusiasm over HPB's and my visit." he told me before his departure. "We could have collected ten or twenty times this amount."

"You couldn't think of every thing, Sir," I told him. "Besides, this educational movement was a natural evolution out of experience. You could not have anticipated it?"

"You are right, Young Priest. I am not totally unmindful of our gains."

He was a very happy man as he recounted his successes.

"Many times, Young Priest, I thought of chucking up everything and letting the ungrateful power-seeking nonentities to make their own funds and found their schools by themselves. I was so disgusted with their petty jealousies, contemptible intriguings and red-tape checks and regulations. You know why I did not do so?"

"Yes, I know, Sir," I replied. "You knew that none among them could do what only you could do."

"Well said, Young Priest. That was the reason. I had undertaken a duty which only I could fulfil. They have no experience. They are so divided with their caste prejudices and antipathies. And what of their local jealousies!!! When you see how they treat themselves, a little ingratitude or jealousy or pettiness to me appeared so trivial." He laughed.

"See, young priest, what a rich harvest I have reaped. At last, I have put together a board of trustees and a board of managers. I have brought together some dedicated men of vision and ability. Schools are springing all over. Twenty thousand children have been so far rescued from hostile religious teachers. Buddhism is reviving and the prospects are brightening. Not a bad record! Not a bad record at all!"

I congratulated him sincerely.

"Thank you, young priest. I could have done more if only I knew a few things."

"Such as ...?"

He thought for a while as if to collect his thoughts and said,

"It was a foolish policy to leave a village with subscriptions unpaid. When the excitement of the moment was over the makers of promises thought to themselves, 'rupees are rupees.' School houses existed only in the minds. But rupees are something real and tangible. So they clung to them."

"Don't we all learn from experience, Sir?" I asked.

Our farewell was as moving as on the previous occasion. We both regretted that we had not spent enough time together. But he was enthralled by my account of the progress I had made in my studies.

While he pushed forth his programme of Buddhist schools, I had read the great Indian classic, the *Cloud-Messenger*, by its celebrated Sanskrit poet Kalidasa, the original biography of the Buddha in Buddhist Sanskrit which formed the base for Sir Edwin Arnold's "Light of Asia", fifty of the Middle-length Sermons of the Buddha from the Pali Canon along with relevant Commentaries and Sub-commentaries and a third of a Prakrit poem called the "*Building of the Bridge*" which dealt with an episode of the Indian Epic Ramayana.

His second embrace had the impact of an eloquent message of encouragement.

The first part of 1882 passed quite rapidly. Eight of us in the class were preparing for our examination in April. It was more exciting than when only Noble Son of Wisdom and I were competing for higher marks in a friendly manner; the ex-diplomat described it as a home-and-home match. Each of us had our strong and weak points. To me the grammar of the various Prakrit languages and dialects was a bugbear. I had to seek extra assistance and a young teacher obliged me.

In February, I was forced to take a week off. Chief Monk passed away in the General Hospital in Kandy after a week in a coma which followed a massive stroke. The R. M. had him admitted to the Planters' Ward - a special modern health care facility reserved for the growing affluent class of tea estate owners and their senior managers. Chief Monk was given the best possible attention.

It was a solace to me that I reached his bedside while he was still alive. I was holding his hand when Chief Monk opened his eyes, looked vacantly at me, turned his head to a side, and became motionless. The nurse who responded to my call for help declared him dead. I was devastated. I felt I was an orphan.

My sense of helplessness was further magnified when I realized that I had succeeded to all his spiritual and ecclesiastical responsibilities. I sat on a chair in the verandah, buried my head in my folded arms and cried. I had taken with courage and philosophical detachment the death of my parents, my grandparents, my preceptor the Abbot of Bo-tree Plain temple and my brother who was plucked out in the spring of his life by a ruthless murderer. Was it grief or self-pity or was it an inexplicable mixture of both?

My brother, the monk, touched me on the shoulder lightly,

"Younger brother, I know how sad you must be. He was a God to us. But should we not control ourselves and attend to what needs to be done?"

He was so calm and composed that I felt embarrassed. I let him take the lead. We made the decisions regarding the funeral and rallied the people to whom we had to entrust various responsibilities. At the request of the Most Venerable Prelate who came to the hospital within an hour, the funeral was to be held in the River Temple of Blood-Sand where, as tradition held, eminent members of the Sangha were cremated.

A massive gathering was present for the final rites. Present were representatives of both the Catholic and Anglican Churches. The Government Agent himself had come to represent the Administration. I arranged all three of them to speak. Little did I realize until they had spoken that they were there to honour him as my teacher. It was particularly embarrassing when I had to translate the Government Agent's kind words of appreciation of what I had added to the fame and the reputation of the temple of my village and its Abbot.

The day after the funeral, I paid the customary courtesy calls on the prelates and their deputies and the members of the Executive Committees of the two Chapters and consulted them on my predicament as the new Abbot who was prevented from performing his titular functions.

"The Little Name, God-Protected can certainly look after the temple and serve the community," said the prelate. "But he is still a novice. See that he comes for Higher Ordination this year itself. We know you have studies to complete and perhaps other duties to perform - more important ones for the entire nation. For us you are the Abbot. But who looks after the day to day functioning of the temple is your business."

The monks of the region and the lay devotees who were summoned to the temple at Sangha-Gem-Field were informed of the counsel of the

314

prelate. It was a mere formality. My recommendation that my brother Venerable God-Protected be appointed the Acting Abbot was agreed to.

The R. M., whose association with the temple and the Sangha had become even closer than in the previous year, spoke on behalf of the congregation, moved a vote of condolence on the death of Chief Monk, praised me for my devotion to the national cause and expressed the fullest cooperation to the Acting Abbot. This formality was appropriately concluded before the sermon on the eve of the seventh day from Chief Monk's death could be delivered by me.

I chose as my topic a saying of the Buddha: "The form of a mortal perishes but not his name and clan," meaning that good name and fame survive one's death.

The next morning I had a visitor. The Catechist who was now in charge of the church and the school came to pay his respects to the new Abbot of the temple with some of the senior members of the staff.

"We offer you our congratulations as an old boy of our school" he said and Sam Silva the head master offered me a tray of jasmine flowers. I was touched by this gesture and my thoughts went to the days of Reverend Thomas Blake and his wife and told them of the wonderful spirit of tolerance and cooperation which once existed.

I invited them to participate in the almsgiving which was to take place shortly. I was pleased when they accepted the invitation.

Returning to Colombo the next day, I told Noble Son of Wisdom of the visit I had from the new representative of the Christian community.

"That is wonderful, Pure. On second thought, I must say that you had witnessed a minor miracle."

It was a mysterious statement, the kind that my Siamese friend had a knack for using to capture attention.

"Don't you know who this Catechist is? Haven't you read Peeble's report on the Great Debate of Panadura of 1873?"

"I read it. But I do not see the connection," I replied.

"This is the same Catechist F. S. Fortune-Pride who came out with the silliest arguments against Buddhism in that Debate."

"You mean the one who argued that the Buddha did not practise the loving kindness that he preached, because as a baby of seven days he caused the death of his mother."

"Precisely! And much more," said Noble Son of Wisdom.

315

I felt sad for the faithful Christians of the region who certainly deserved better leadership. I thought of dropping a note to the Bishop of Kandy along with the letter of thanks I was writing for his gracious presence at the funeral of Chief Monk.

Back to books and the burning of midnight oil. Extra lessons on Prakrit; Revision with Noble Son of Wisdom; Volumes committed to memory.

The examinations were to be conducted by a renowned lay scholar and a public servant of the rank of Mudaliyar from the City of Gems, Louis Corneille Victory-Lion. His imposing personality cowed us. But he was kind and flexible. Gruelling oral tests were preceded by a three-hour examination paper in which incisive questions were asked, not merely to elicit what we had committed to memory but more importantly to assess our abilities in critical analysis. At the end of the long day, he took our answer scripts home, promising to send the results next day.

Were not Noble Son of Wisdom and I happy when the results came? We were at the top tying for the first place with an average of ninety-three marks. The rest of the class trailed behind us, five passing the examination and one failing quite badly.

My Siamese colleague and I celebrated our success with a long walk to the Colombo jetty and a harbour cruise to take a good look at the newer and bigger ships which had made Colombo a regular port of call.

Walking back through the gas-lit major streets of the city, we made plans to visit Sangha-Gem-Field during the Sinhala New Year holidays this year too.

I resolved not to be distracted by whatever feelings of affection and concern I harboured in the innermost recesses of my mind for Slim-Jewel. Never again the excruciating mental torture and the humiliating confession of last year, I told myself.

XI

New Year celebrations were no longer the same at Sangha-Gem-Field. It was not that the customs had changed or people had adopted new ways.

I was no longer a carefree young monk who could enjoy the company of friends and do what he liked to do. I was the Abbot. To have an efficient brother to look after the details was a great asset. But he could also be a nuisance.

He had worked out what formal visits had to be undertaken, when and with what kinds of gifts. He had laid out the full programme for the two important days when the temple would be full of devotees. In this programme, I had to be doing something every two or three hours - conducting the congregational worship associated with symbolic offerings of food and beverages at the image-house at noon and at sunset; two sermons and a frequent sessions of just being seated for people to pay their respects with sheafs of betel and to receive my benediction. Being used to more intellectual activity and less adapted to ceremonial formality, I must have shown my exasperation at least to my closest friend, critic and counsel.

"Pure, you are like an Ambassador who has an efficient and conscientious private secretary," he teased me. " One who pops his head into your office every now and then says, 'Your Excellency may be pleased to meet so and so, pleased to lunch with so and so, pleased to sign the book of condolence at such and such embassy, pleased to meet Minister so and so, or pleased to go home now that the office is closed!!!' "

"You had one like that?"

"That comes with the territory, Pure. So take it easy. What you cannot resist, you must learn to relax with and enjoy."

"Isn't that the advice you said the London Police gives potential victims of street rape?"

"Your brain must be a filing cabinet! Pure, you remember it?"

We laughed heartily. I felt better. After all, playing Abbot was not altogether a bad experience. After some time, I was really enjoying it.

Not only relatives and friends but unseen admirers from neighbouring villages and newly arrived government officers of all grades utilized the New Year holidays to call on me. The R. M. came with his family. Quite by accident, the Catechist came at about the same time. I received him with the respect due to a man of religion. To

317

chat in greater comfort, all of us repaired to the preaching hall where we could be seated round a table.

"We would like to talk about the new school," the R. M. said. "Not only have I brought my contribution, I have collected a few thousand rupees from my family and friends."

I felt very uneasy. It was an year ago that I promised that I would invite Olcott to visit the village. He had been in the Island for seven months and I had done nothing. In fact, I had hardly given any thought to the proposal I made. But to my great relief, the senior official continued,

"With the death of Chief Monk and all other problems you must have had, we did not think we could have begun the school this year. The delay has made us reconsider some of the earlier ideas."

The enthusiasm with which the Catechist shook his head indicated that some consultations had been in progress. I listened carefully.

"After all, Bo-tree Plain is a small village. Whether we like it or not, a school does exist there. How about our building the school in memory of the late Abbot in Sangha-Gem-Field which is fast becoming a small town?"

I who had slept over my own proposal for a whole year had no right to object.

"Sir, you are the best judge of the needs of the area and I would abide by your decision without any reservation."

"We have a site in mind. It's government land. Mr. Stanley Williams has promised me that it could be given on a ninety-nine year lease if you make the application."

"That's very good, Sir. I have known Mr. Williams from the time he was a cadet in Galle."

"Yes, he knows also your uncle, Venerable Pure-Intellect."

"How shall I make the application?" I asked.

"I have it all ready, Venerable Abbot. You have only to sign it."

An acolyte found a dried up ink-well and an old feather pen in the room of Chief Monk. A few drops of water produced enough ink for me to sign my name in the appropriate cage of the application form.

"One more thing, Venerable Abbot, Please don't invite Colonel Olcott here until we have got the school functioning. We must show that we do things on our own. We are not waiting for anyone to come and raise funds for our school. I want the people to do it themselves. Do you agree?"

Had he heard of the whinings of the Colonel when he was in a bad mood? I thought to myself.

318

Not only did I agree but thanked the R. M. profusely for his leadership in the project. He stood up along with the family and made a request that baffled me.

"Venerable Abbot, my family and my Jewel's family have for generations been Buddhist. She is still Buddhist. I was converted in school and Reverend Blake baptized all my children. On this auspicious day of New Year, we want to return to the religion of our forefathers. Would you please administer the Three Refuges and the Five Precepts to us.".

I was moved and tears welled in my eyes. I looked at the Catechist. He did not look surprised. But I seemed to have expected him to say something.

"I am not surprised, Venerable Sir," he said. "Over the last few years, we hardly make any new conversions while most of the people are returning to Buddhism or Hinduism or, worse still, to Roman Catholicism. That's the trend now."

He looked sad even though he tried to be disinterested. I sent for my brother and asked him to make arrangements for the R. M. and his family to take their precepts in the Image-house. I took leave of the Catechist.

He bowed to me bringing his hands together as any devotee would do. Two milennia of Buddhist culture still lurked in his background, I thought to myself.

"Thank you, Venerable Abbot, for the letter you wrote to His Lordship the Bishop," he said. "It was a big sacrifice for me to come all the way from the coast to run the school and the church. His Lordship agrees that a missionary couple has to be assigned to Bo-tree Plain. A new couple coming from England is expected to take over in a couple of months."

"I am happy that I could be of service to you and the community at one and the same time."

Instead of leaving, he followed me to be present at the ceremony where the leading member of the Christian community of the region was formally resuming his traditional religion. Mindful of the adage that one should never apply salt on an open wound, I limited the ceremony to the administration of the Three Refuges and the Five Precepts and joined the other monks in chanting benedictory verses.

Even the shortest speech would have sounded too loud a cry of victory. But victory for whom?

Noble Son of Wisdom travelled to Kandy every now and then to continue his work on the Siamese manuscripts that he had discovered in the two monasteries.

I found time to check how the resources of our library were being utilized. I was happy that its fame had travelled all over the world. Scholars asked for copies of manuscripts and the two monks to whom I had entrusted this work were doing a good job.

They were motivated by the fact that they had many corresponding friends all over the .world. They were airing and polishing the manuscripts systematically. There was nothing on which I could give them any direction.

To the members of my extended family, my assumption of office as the Abbot was a cause for joy and pride. The elders thanked me for helping to keep the position within the family or rather the clan, if that was what they meant. They visited me frequently and made sure that the temple missed nothing. It was a treat to meet the little ones. The only one I had known, besides the kids of my eldest brother, was Moon-Beam. While Slim-Jewel continued to work and study in Kandy, she lived with her grandparents and aunts. She was nearly five years old. My Aunt Jasmine's children were bigger. They had been baptized Christians but came to the temple with the rest of the family.

When I saw all the kids who were at the temple on the New Year day, I thought of the advice which Olcott used to give the villagers. He advocated that every temple should have a Sunday School where the rudiments of the religion were taught to the children from their infancy.

I discussed the question with the two young monks who were handling library inquiries. They jumped at the idea. I engaged a drummer to go all over the village announcing that a Sunday Religious School would commence on the following Sunday.

It was a case of putting the cart before the horse. When the children streamed in by their hundreds accompanied by parents and adults, I had not enough mats, nor teachers to take classes nor people with any idea as how to bring order in the vast crowd. I thought of Olcott's Yankee ingenuity!!!

Standing on a table at a corner of the temple compound, I asked them to sit on the ground. After they were made to utter "Sadhu! Sadhu! Sadhu!" several times, there was pin drop silence. I administered the Three Refuges and the Five Precepts. Order thus resumed, I asked for volunteer teachers from among the adults. To my great satisfaction, two ladies and ten men volunteered.

It was not the time to find out whether they were competent to work as teachers. I was glad that there were enough warm bodies to take over the crowd. With four monks ready to assume the responsibility of running the school, a staff of sixteen teachers was in place. Before grouping the children according to age and gender, I spoke of the importance of learning the religion in a formal setting. I repeated a lot of the arguments of Olcott. The children as well as their parents showed much enthusiasm.

I asked myself why I did not do this earlier. I had no reply. Perhaps my thoughts must have been elsewhere whenever I visited the village.

"You were overly pre-occupied with Slim-Jewel whenever you came home," an inner voice told me loud and clear.

Teachers found convenient shady spots where their pupils could sit in a circle in front of them. As if the institution had gone on for ever, the school was now functioning.

Teachers improvised the contents of lessons even though they had no idea that morning that their services would be so required. I walked around. Little ones memorizing the Pali stanzas; bigger children being told stories with moral values; the oldest children in a question-and-answer session with one of the monks.

I wished there was one person to see this miracle - yes, Colonel Olcott. He would have admired this spontaneous demonstration of Sinhala ingenuity!

Noble Son of Wisdom arriving from Kandy by the morning mail coach was surprised by the unprecedented activity in the temple premises. He would not believe a word of my account of surprises and improvisations.

"Don't tell me all this happened in one morning?" he said repeatedly.

"You have been here many Sundays before this?" was all I could tell him.

The month passed quickly and we were making arrangements to return to our books. We were to be in different classes. I would do classical and ancient Sinhala while Noble Son of Wisdom would proceed with his Sanskrit and Pali.

On the eve of our departure around midnight, I had a visit from my eldest brother, who was married to Slim-Jewel's eldest sister. He had brought some country palm molasses to be taken to Venerable Sumangala. But that was not the only purpose of his visit. He had something to tell me and suggested that we go to his place.

"Venerable Brother, the outcaste girl has brought that boy and they are at my place," he said. "And I don't know what to do."

I left with him to his place. We walked through the village each carrying a torch of dried twigs soaked in wild nut oil. Our shadows stalked like mighty giants behind us. On the way I asked him what the actual problem was.

"No one in the village should know what we are doing. If anyone were to know that the boy adopted by Slim-Jewel is a son of an outcaste woman, that child's future will be as bleak or even worse. What we are trying to do by giving him a new start could be totally nullified," my brother explained.

"This is a simple question of logistics. I have an idea. I don't have to go all the way to your place. Can you drive Chief Monk's buggy cart?"

"No, our second brother can. He used to take Chief Monk around."

"All right. Find him. Ask him to get the cart ready. Go first to your place in the cart and send it here with the child."

Back in the temple, I woke Noble Son of Wisdom and asked him to be ready for departure by two in the morning. My estimate of time was perfect. We left the temple with the two year old snuggling at our feet and fast asleep on the floor of the buggy cart.

Trotting down hill all the way at a steady speed, we were in Kandy by dawn. When Slim-Jewel came to congratulate me on the assumption of office as the Abbot and also pay her respects on the New Year Day, I had told her of the wild goose chase exactly an year ago. So she had given me not only the address but also the directions to her place. She had rented a house not too far from the Horse Peak Monastery and closer still to the new Catholic convent with a girls' school.

I had hoped to reach her place either before she left for work or after she returned from her night shift. When the second brother went in to call her, she was up and dressed, although it was her day off.

"We have brought you a priceless treasure," I told her. This is exactly how I felt about my middle brother's son.

She rushed to the cart, worshipped both me and the Siamese monk, gathered the sleeping baby in her arms and pressed him to her bosom. What love! What affection!

Only after the baby was laid on her bed and tucked in snugly did she invite us in, spread white sheets on two chairs and went on her knees to worship us again.

"Thank you, Venerable Brother. I am so very happy," she said.

She and my second brother went about getting breakfast for us while we chatted about the meaning of our fly-by-night adventure.

"Away from the prejudice-ridden rural society, we want to give this boy as fair a chance as possible to start a life without oppression," I explained.

Having nothing in Siam comparable to the untouchable outcaste of the Island's hill country, Noble Son of Wisdom was at a loss to grasp the full import of what I was saying. But he was conscious of the great concern of the family and he appreciated it.

Slim-Jewel presented a sumptuous breakfast of rice hoppers and spicy fried onion. We made a brief ceremony of it to share merit with my dead brother and to offer blessings to the young addition to the family. We chanted the Discourse on Loving Kindness and other appropriate verses in Pali.

I was curious as to how Slim-Jewel was planning to combine her career as a nurse in training and a student of English with the care of the new baby. Despite my total ignorance of how a single parent household would operate, I wondered if Slim-Jewel was a bit unrealistic or even over optimistic.

"How are you going to manage, Slim-Jewel? A child of two cannot be left at home alone while you go out to work and study," I asked her.

As usual, she surprised me with her resourcefulness. I recalled how I had once compared her to the mother squirrel in the Buddhist legend who tried to empty the ocean with her tail so as to save her young ones from drowning.

"I have had a whole year to think about it," she replied. "And I was very lucky."

She called out a woman in her early thirties. She came from the kitchen and worshipped us.

"This is Golden Jewel. She will look after not only this baby but also Moon-Beam whom I plan to admit to the convent school in January."

She related the story of Golden Jewel. She was married to a sharecropper and had a fairly comfortable life. Her husband died of malaria last year and she was hard put to look after her three old son. Yet she managed to find enough work until the child fell ill. He was simply withering away , losing weight steadily and showing not only symptoms of malnutrition but deep-seated infection. The child was brought to hospital and admitted to the ward where Slim-Jewel was a Student Nurse.

One night, Golden Jewel was found sleeping on the verandah of the ward and Slim-Jewel brought her home. Thus for four or five months, she had a place to stay and could go to hospital to see her child daily. In spite of all that Slim-Jewel was able to do by pleading with doctors, the boy died and Golden Jewel was devastated. She had no place to go. There was none in the village who could help her.

"Without this Buddha-like jewel I would have been long dead as my husband and my son," said Golden Jewel sobbing.

This was the second woman I had heard who compared Slim-Jewel to the compassionate Buddha.

"So everything seems to be well thought out. How do you propose to legalize the adoption of the child?" I asked Slim-Jewel.

"Uncle Victor has found a way to do it without involving his mother. I have thought of a name. But I am not sure if you will approve it."

"Why?"

"I want to give him his father's name: Middle Banda Valour-Lion. You know that I go as Valour-Lion?"

I did not know. She did not have to. In our culture, women retained their names after marriage. Only in Westernized families in big towns was the new fashion coming into vogue. But her magnanimity baffled me. She did not appear to have the slightest bitterness toward her wayward husband. She had no hesitation about keeping his memory alive through this living souvenir of his indiscretion.

Was she a masochist to inflict pain of mind upon herself? Or was she an angel whose benevolence knew no bounds?

"I have no reason to disapprove either."

"Thank you, Venerable Brother. What I plan to tell the more inquisitive inquirers is that I adopted this child to be a brother to my daughter as I do no want her to grow up as a mean, selfish, self-centred only child."

We wished her good luck and left her to attend to the baby who had woken and was crying.

Noble Son of Wisdom was truly baffled. With Slim-Jewel's newly acquired proficiency in English, the conversation had been bilingual and he himself knew enough Sinhala. He summed up our joint impression of this brave young woman,

"If she represents the typical womanhood of your country, yours is a very fortunate nation."

XII

Back in the classes. Noble Son of Wisdom was with the five Indian students who had passed the examination. They were reading another fifty of the Middle-length Discourses of the Pali Canon with the relevant Commentary and Sub-Commentaries and Kalidasa's much celebrated poem "*The Chronicle of the Solar Race*" in Sanskrit.

I was in another class with a score of younger monks who had already done several years of preliminary studies in the traditional system. We read a ninth century text summarizing the rules of discipline for monks. It was in such archaic Sinhala - almost in its Prakrit or Middle Indian form - that every word had to be traced etymologically to its original Pali or Sanskrit before one could understand it. We also read an equally difficult, but far more interesting ornate poem called the "*Diadem of Poetry*" or "*Diadem of Poems*".

Attributed to a scholar king of the twelfth century, it dealt with the story of a previous life of the Buddha when he was born as a very ugly prince. His younger brother, by contrast, was very handsome. Though the heir apparent to the throne, the elder brother would not agree to take a wife. He feared that no woman would want to live such an ugly man. But when his parents insisted, he made a statue in gold of an exceedingly beautiful woman and told them he would only marry a girl resembling it. Although it was meant to delay the search of a bride or even make it impossible, a girl was found and the marriage arranged. The couple met only in the dark and the marriage continued, for the bride thought her husband was the handsome younger brother.

This Oriental equivalent of the story of Beauty and the Beast has a similar happy ending. The ugly prince has to show himself when he had to defend his country and on this moment he had shed his ugliness and was a charming prince.

The poem was full of picturesque descriptions replete with similes, metaphors and a wide range of figurative speech and clever play on words. But it was not an easy book which one could read for pleasure in one sitting. One really had to study and study hard.

"Why don't we begin with the simpler poems and easier texts and go to these archic works when we know enough of the language?" one of my class-mates asked the teacher.

"How do you eat the kernel of a coconut?. You have first to break the hard shell. Then you eat the sweet kernel" was his bland reply.

To me it summarized the underlying pedagogical principle of the system of monastic education.

We studied grammar from a thirteenth century book which was hardly twenty pages in print. How condensed it was could be understood from the fact that the commentary that we used ran to two hundred pages.

I found it easier to study it with an annotated translation into English which James d'Alwis, a highly reputed national scholar-lawyer-legislator, had published thirty years ago. With an introduction to the history of Sinhala literature of over two hundred pages, it was a sizeable volume. It was meant for new recruits to the Civil Service who came from England. I could vouch for its relevance and usefulness as I learnt more of my language, its history and the creative genius of the nation from this one book.

After two years of concentration on Pali and Sanskrit, it was fun to study classical Sinhala. But I missed my Siamese colleague. We met quite often. We discussed problems of Sanskrit grammar and sometimes read Kalidasa together. I discovered the degree to which the author of the "*Diadem of Poetry*" was indebted to Sanskrit literature for his imagery.

With Olcott away in India, there was a lull in the fund-raising and publicity activities. But if the correspondence of Venerable Sumangala was an accurate barometre, the national and Buddhist revival movement had not relaxed its momentum.

On the eighteenth of July, 1882, Olcott arrived in Sri Lanka for the third time. I was among the first to see him. He was exhausted. The four day trip had been the worst he had ever experienced. The monsoons were bad enough but every unoccupied cabin had been laden to the ceiling with sandalwood, licorice and onion. Their combined odours together with the foul smell of damp cotton mattresses and the burnt engine oil had made him sick. We listened to his complaints with genuine sympathy.

A few days later the target of his complaints had become the Buddhist Theosophical Society and its members.

"All my efforts of the Western Province trip have been frittered away. I am sick of listening to all these paltry excuses," he told Venerable Sumangala. "Only one hundred rupees has been collected out of the pledges amounting to thirteen thousand rupees. Added to this, the Trust Fund has been used up in running expenses. They have also spent fifty rupees belonging to the Buddhist Catechism Fund."

"What do you plan to do?" the scholar-monk asked with concern.

"There's nothing left for me but to just go to work again, re-infuse life into everything, wipe out the story of the half-year's idleness and set the machinery in motion."

327

"That' the correct spirit, my virtuous devotee. But you must speak to the members and tell them what you feel."

A series of meetings followed. I was in one in which he proposed that the Buddhists must adopt a system of voluntary self-taxation similar to that levied in the Christian Churches.

"I remember my father. He set apart ten percent of his earnings for religious and charitable work. Do you know what you, vociferous promoters of Buddhism - you, who like to call yourself Colombo martyrs - had given to the Buddhist revival movement?"

He paused for the question to sink in.

"Three fourths of one per cent of your incomes! Imagine! Not even one per cent. See how much we can do if you had given ten per cent of your incomes to the cause."

If the Colonel managed to make the audience feel bad, their blank faces did not reveal it.

A week later when the Colombo Theosophical Society celebrated its anniversary, a banner in large letters carried the message, "The Past you cannot recall. The Present is yours. The Future will be what you make of it." Was it the members' response to their benevolent critic? I wondered.

After the anniversary dinner, Olcott went to Galle where to my surprise he celebrated his fiftieth birthday in August! My notes had his date of birth as 2nd of February 1832.

Two things happened which prevented me from meeting Olcott during the rest of his stay in the Island. He decided to cover the Southern Province with the intensity and thoroughness that he devoted to the Western Province in the previous year.

A couple of days before the beginning of the Rainy Season Lent, a request came from none other than the R. M. that I should accept the invitation of the people of the region to spend my Lent at the Sangha-Gem-Field. Venerable Sumangala, through whom the request was channeled, thought it a good idea and gave me leave from the College.

Travelling on Saturday to Kandy, I was able to take the morning mail coach to Sangha-Gem-Field. The Sunday School was in progress. Once Venerable Gunananda had told me that the most effective decoration in any place was the human being, especially the child. I had never seen our temple premises   so beautiful as as on this morning. Under every shady tree a cluster of children was reciting verses, listening to stories and learning from their teachers. I felt drawn to my own temple in a manner that I had never felt before. It was a good beginning.

An unprecedented crowd attended what so far had been a purely ecclesiastical ceremony. The lay supporters of the temple had been assembled to request the monks formally to observe the Rainy Season Lent in the temple. The R. M. was there with a sheaf of betel to make this invitation in a solemn manner, promising on behalf of the entire congregation that the creature comforts of the Sangha would be taken care of by them. This was something that had been learnt from the new sects in the South - possibly a Burmese tradition.

I saw immediate implications. This period when monks were to be staying indoors was going to be one in which they could interact with the people directly and intensely. I was alive to many possibilities arising from such interactions.

An age-old tradition of giving each family a ticket (called in Pali, *salaka*) to entitle it to supply the monks with a morning or a mid-day meal or at least the evening beverage on an allotted day was revived. On every Sabbath, determined according to the phase of the moon, a sermon would be delivered by a monk. Preceding the sermon two ceremonies involving congregational worship would take place - one at the sacred tree of enlightenment, called Bo-tree, which included watering the tree; and the other at the image house when beverages, called medical requisites in a broad sense, would be symbolically offered to the Buddha.

The village and temple got closer as a result of these intense activities in a manner I had not known in earlier years. The community approved these initiatives. Families chose days of special significance to bring alms to the temple such as birthdays and death anniversaries. Mention was made of such events in the course of the thanksgiving sermons. The enthusiasm of the people urged me to think of further initiatives. I revived the practice of teaching children individually to master literacy and to read the "Century Books' in Sanskrit.

Within a month the temple was a hive of activity. There was no time when a score of people - specially the young - were not in the temple. It was my brother's idea that the end of the Rainy Season Lent should be marked with an offering of 84,000 lamps. Collecting and making oil, cutting zinc sheets into 4 inch by 4 inch squares and beating them on a mould to make lamps, finding rags and rolling wicks out of them and erecting arches and platforms out of slit bamboo and arecanut trunks to hold lamps made the temple premises a veritable factory. What skills the young ones learnt in the process!

329

I was so involved in a new life - a life of activity with the community - that the idea that I could go out for a few days without breaking my vow never occured to me.

I could not help but be very grateful to the White American Buddhist from whose speeches I had derived such inspiration and to the temples in the South where I saw the closeness of the temple and the community resulting from participatory activities.

It was one thing to able an interpreter of another's ideas or to learn things by observation: it was an entirely different and stimulating experience to do things yourself.

As usual, after the days work, I sat for a few minutes of worship, meditation and reflection. On every such occasion, I expressed my grateful thanks to all who have directed me to a life of useful dedication.

The Lent of three months was over. Thousands came from all over the Province to see the fairy land of lights which the offering of 84,000 lamps created. I invited Noble Son of Wisdom to deliver the sermon that evening. It was a pleasant surprise when he spoke in elegant and lucid Sinhala.

That night we sat until early hours of the next day chatting about our respective experiences. These three months had been the longest period during which we had not been together. He told me of his school and its success. I told him of the new school in Sangha-Gem-Field which the people were determined to run in their own way. He was not surprised that the school had already come into being with about a hundred students, that I functioned as a regular teacher if not its temporary headmaster, that we needed more material and human resources and that I felt a commitment to my native village that I had never felt before.

"You know, Pure, what Venerable Sumangala told me?" he asked, but continued without waiting for a reply from me. "He said he would not be surprised if you wanted to continue in the village after Lent."

"What made him say so?"

"He said that you have matured to your responsibilities and come to that point in life when you experience an inner urge to do what you have yourself preached or heard other people preaching. He is also happy that you are not tagging along with Olcott."

"Why? Why did he say so?"

330

I was baffled when he described how the Colonel had found a new interest and begun to enjoy popular adulation as a faith healer. It seemed that the Catholic church was claiming to have discovered a healing pond not too far from Colombo quite close to a very important Buddhist shrine and Olcott had urged monks to put up a counter show. When he found that monks had no interest in such matters or that kind of competition, he had started the healing business by himself.

Even while on the travels in the Southern Province to raise funds, his healing mission had overshadowed his earlier role.

"Can he really cure?" I asked Noble Son of Wisdom.

"So everyone claims. He is said to have learnt all these newfangled things about hypnotism, mesmerism and animal magnetism. Hundreds vouch that they had been cured of the most serious disabilities like paralysis, lameness, excruciating pain."

It was now December and I was hoping that we could find a good headmaster for the school so that I could return to my studies. What the prelate advised me to do, I had accomplished to his satisfaction. My brother received his Higher Ordination even though the festivities connected with it was kept to a minimum as a mark of respect for the late Abbots.

As and when I found time, I had read the "Diadem of Poetry" and the Vinaya text in archaic Sinhala. As far as the grammar was concerned, I had no problem whatsoever as I read the English commentary replete with interesting examples from literature. Even if I were to go back in January 1883, I would be able to sit the examination in April.

While my work in the village occupied my fullest attention, a corner of my heart urged me to continue my formal education. In two or three years, I would be able to sit the Final Examination of the College and get a certificate for it. Occasionally, as my day-to-day responsibilities mounted, I thought of accepting Right Reverend Saunder's offer and going to Calcutta to earn a Bachelor of Arts degree from the University.

When Olcott left Sri Lanka in November, I was not there to bid him farewell. In a note hurriedly written from Bombay, he alluded to my absence and said he sincerely hoped that I was prevented from coming down due to my obligations in the village. He seemed to wonder whether I had abandoned him as the senior monks had done when this White Buddhist lay devotee of theirs became an itinerant faith-healer.

Some degree of disaffection about Sri Lanka was also discernible in another statement in the letter. He was hoping to continue his healing mission during the next year in India.

At the same time there was trouble brewing for him in the Theosophical Society itself. Rows were frequent among the members in Bombay. Olcott was disturbed to find that even the messages Madame Blavatsky claimed to receive from her Mahatmas and Adepts were becoming tainted by contradiction, uncertainty and such other mortal failings!

In a cryptic sentence, he said that he would next come to Sri Lanka when, and only, when he was specifically invited by the people and after they had realized that he was the only effective ally that they and their ancient religion had in the world.

Corresponding as I did now with a growing galaxy of Pali and Buddhist scholars in the world, led by Rhys Davids, I was not prepared to agree fully with his description of himself as the only ally of Buddhism. But from the point of view of political and social activism, his assumption was correct to a significant extent.

The school grew in enrollment. I was lucky to recruit a few more teachers on account of my contacts with scholar-monks in Galle and Colombo. Two townships in the Island were getting recognized as reservoirs for teachers with above-average competence in English: Baddegama on the bank of Gin River, about twelve miles from Galle, and Kotte, about six miles from Colombo. Two of the oldest and best organized English schools of the Church Missionary Society happened to be in these two places.

Increasing internal trade and resulting economic opportunities had set in motion a pattern of immigration from the coastal region to the interior. Young men who were not only more adventurous but also endowed with entrepreneurial ability, were looking for fresh pastures.

To remote rural areas like Sangha-Gem-Field, the infusion of sophisticated low country people was an advantage at the early phase of development, specially when they chose to serve as teachers. They brought in such invaluable life experiences to the hill country which as a whole had been late in entering the modern world - perhaps by at least three centuries.

On my twenty-fifth birthday, on the fourth of February in 1883, I was unusually fortunate. Little Father came from Orange Island with a teacher from a school in Galle, who wished to settle in the hills. By the time they got out of the coach, he had fallen in love with the verdant mountains, valleys laden with fruit and vegetables and the winding road which opened new vistas every few miles. Little Father's skill in mobilizing human resources for a network of schools had convinced him that Mr. Edward Perera would provide the leadership which the region lacked.

It took less than an hour for me to make up my mind that we had the right person. We called on the R. M. that evening and, with his concurrence, Mr. Perera was appointed the headmaster of the school. I was now free to resume my studies in Colombo.

Back at Palace Hill, I worked mostly with the Deputy Principal, Venerable Friend of Gods. He graded as excellent the progress I had made with self-study. With a view to giving me more time to study, Venerable Sumangala asked me to deal only with foreign and English language correspondence. In the room in which I worked earlier, the volunteers I had gathered together had set up a veritable office for the scholar-monk.

Bureaucracy was at work in a fairly advanced state. Division of labour, specialization according to skills and competence, work distribution according to subjects or geographical regions and routing of papers through supervisory levels were the order of the day in an office where ten or fifteen monks worked during their spare time. The output in both quantity and quality was certainly more satisfactory than when I worked either by myself or through a few selected volunteers.

I expressed my admiration of the new system to the young monk who appeared to be in charge.

"We couldn't do without it," he explained. "To match the work you did to satisfy our Venerable Principal, we had to replace you by ten of us."

I was pleased. Even to a monk who had renounced everything, a bit of recognition and appreciation is a soothing balm! But my joy knew no bounds when it was confirmed by Venerable Sumangala who asked me to resume my functions as his private secretary immediately after the examination.

XIII

The twenty-fifth of March 1883 was a special day for the Buddhists of Colombo - specially for those who were admirers of the courageous role which Venerable Gunananda played in the national scene. It was the day on which an image of the Buddha was to be ceremonially installed in the image house of the newly constructed temple in a northern ward of the capital. The temple was aptly named the "Foremost in the Island," for that is how the nation felt about its Abbot Venerable Gunananda.

As usual, the ceremony was marked by an almsgiving to which practically every important monk in the country was invited. I was there along with Noble Son of Wisdom and, as our seniority demanded, we sat together. After the mid-day meal, we stayed in the same place, as the procession bringing the image was due shortly afterwards.

Nothing guarantees punctuality in our society more than a belief in the astrologically determined, auspicious time. We had no doubt that the image would be brought in time for its installation at the prescribed hour and minute. But that was not to be.

From a group of utterly frightened men running for their dear lives, one had enough courage to rush into the temple and tell Venerable Gunananda what was happening. With his characteristic presence of mind, the orator-monk clambered onto a table and addressed the thousands of devotees who were attending the ceremony.

"A little mishap on the way has delayed the procession," he said, as he appealed all to sit wherever they were. "Whatever you hear, please do not panic. Remain where you are. Please do not leave the premises until I ask you to do so."

While the senior monks retired for a consultation of their own, the rest of us were kept wondering and speculating. Noble Son of Wisdom was sent for by Venerable Gunananda and that added to the mystery.

"Catholics must have attacked the procession," ventured one of the junior monks. "There has been a lot of tension lately in this part of Colombo."

"Why in this part of the city?" I asked him.

"It is an exclusively Catholic area and they don't like what they call the Buddhist and Hindu infiltration. One of my Catholic friends from school called this part of Colombo 'Little Vatican'."

I knew that some of the most impressive Catholic churches were in this area. But I had no idea that the Catholics were anti-Buddhist. In the recent struggle with the government on the reform of educational laws, the Catholics had supported very strongly the right of the Buddhists to establish schools. They urged the abrogation of laws which favoured Protestant Christian churches with stipulations about the distance between schools for purposes of approval for grants-in-aid.

My praise of such support was dealt with derision by the younger monks. One of them said,

"Don't you see that they are doing? It's just what we do when we want a little extra rice or curry at an almsgiving."

The analogy was clear and telling. When monks sit to eat, they never ask for anything for themselves. If one were to need something by way of extra rice or curry or water, he would call upon a lay devotee to serve the monk seated next to him.

"You mean that the Catholics are doing this to help themselves?"

"Precisely," replied the younger colleague.

I felt quite foolish as I had taken them at face value.

There was no sign of a returning procession and the tension grew. I was beginning to be nervous. The reality of an attack by Catholics was inescapable. A Buddhist procession with tom-toms and pipes passing in front of Saint Lucia Cathedral on Palm Sunday morning did not appear to me to be purely coincidental.

Three hours later, a few people straggleed in with the statue which fortunately had not been damaged. The Police Officer who accompanied them was a Britisher or a Dutch Burgher, as far as his complexion showed. He was astounded to see the thousands of able-bodied men of all ages seated in the temple compound.

I could discern that expression easily as I had seen it often on the faces of officers who had no idea of the degree of tolerance, patience and discipline that our people could show even when provoked.

"How was this done?" he asked and my bilingual skills made me the instant spokesman for the crowd.

"What do you mean? What happened?"

The Police Officer gave an account of a three hour melee which a force of eighty constables could not quell with their batons. It had left one man dead and forty seriously injured.

"If someone had incited this crowd to join the fray, there could have been hundreds of casualties and even the Cathedral could have been pulled down brick by brick."

"We not only preach but also practise tolerance, non-violence and peace," I told him, as I could now understand the importance of the steps which Venerable Gunananda took with foresight when obviously he was informed of the riots.

"I am glad you did so at least today," he said.

I did not mind the tinge of sarcasm because I had learnt to associate it with lower grades of the Administration.

For the next seven or eight months, the commotion on what was now called the Kotahena Riots remained unabated. Newspapers carried all kinds of interpretations and allegations depending on with whom they sided.

Some claimed that the Buddhists provoked the Catholics by conducting a procession which mimicked theirs in which the statue of Virgin Mary was carried. Some took offence that the procession was held on Palm Sunday which had a special religious significance to the Catholics. Some argued that tom-toms and pipes should have been silenced as the procession passed the Cathedral. There was also an unfounded allegation that the procession carried an effigy of a monkey on a cross.

On the other hand, it was established that Catholics could be accused of pre-meditated preparedness for a riot. As the procession came close to the Church, the church bells were rung and about a thousand men carrying clubs, sticks and swords descended on the unarmed processionists. The fact that the one dead and almost all the injured were Buddhists went to prove that the processionists had had no intention of creating any disturbance.

The Police and the government blamed the Catholics and even admitted that the attackers had been under the influence of liquor. Catholics and Buddhists accused certain individuals and took them to courts. The Governor appointed a Riots Commission. But the problem, as in all such cases, was to associate a particular act of violence with a particular person and prove it in a court of law. For this, there could be no reliable evidence.

To the Buddhists, however, the government's position constituted a failure of justice. Monks and the lay leadership did all they could to get the government to act.

As the time for the Rainy Season Lent drew closer, I was wondering whether I should remain in Colombo to assist Venerable Sumangala to deal with the enormous volume of correspondence pertaining to the aftermath of the riots. But he thought otherwise. He felt that the whole issue was under control and government should be allowed time to act on the petitions addressed to it.

"I know that the present governor Longdon is not as much a lover of our culture and civilization as Sir William Gregory was and not a tenth as sympathetic, but the British do have a reputation for justice. We have to give them time," he said, in stressing that nothing extraordinary would happen in my absence.

As the aftermath of the Kotahena Riots had prevented me from going to Sangha-Gem-Field for the Sinhala New Year, I was eagerly awaited not only by my brother but also the leading members of the laity whose involvement with the temple had grown conspicuously. All my initiatives were flourishing. The Sunday School had twenty teachers and over five hundred students. Inspectors of the Department of Public Instruction had given Edward Perera and his staff glowing reports after the first annual inspection of the school. Another batch of classrooms were being built to cope with the increasing demand for admission. The temple itself had been recently renovated and colour-washed.

"Things happen here not because of me but in spite of me. I almost feel I am superfluous," I told Slim-Jewel who made it a point to come from Kandy, as she was working when I visited Uncle Victor and Aunt Flower.

"You should add one more to your list of successes," she said as she gave me an account of how her extended family was shaping.

"Moon-Beam loves her brother so much and it is lovely to see how he responds. It must be in their blood. Often, I feel I am the odd person out."

She had entered the girl in the first grade and the boy in the nursery class of the Convent. Golden Jewel accompanied the children to school and generally looked after their needs. Slim-Jewel continued her studies and had adequate confidence in English to proceed to formal training to be a qualified nurse.

I could not help but reflect how Little Father, Aunt Flower, Slim-Jewel and I myself, hailing from a remote village in the mountains of the Island, could emerge into a new society with unlimited opportunities and benefits, simply through education. I wished I could encourage more of the deserving and eligible young people from the region to follow our example. I thought of delivering the next sermon on an unusual subject: "Education as the ladder for social and personal improvement." I was sure that I could find a suitable text from one of the discourses of the Buddha.

337

When I received a telegram from Venerable Sumangala asking me to come as soon as the Lent was over without completing the robe-offering ceremony, I guessed that the efforts to get justice had failed. I returned forthwith.

I stepped right into a series of high level meetings and consultations. Each ended with the conclusion that any hope of getting any justice was not in Colombo but in London. But each session appeared to drive Venerable Sumangala into a visible state of nervous depression. It worried me. I inquired from his nearest colleagues and students but no one had a clue. Only the Deputy Principal said that the senior scholar-monk was constantly asking his visitors about the conditions of prison life.

I sent a message to Noble Son of Wisdom and he came over to spend a night at Palace Hill. Having listened to what I had observed and what the Deputy Principal had told me, he decided that we should talk to Venerable Sumangala directly.

We saw him in his room. He was alone. We announced ourselves and he called both of us in. He was reclining on an ebony couch which was exquisitely carved.

"I sent for you Little Name because there is something which worries me," he said as we worshipped him and sat on two small chairs which were usually meant for lay visitors. "It's all my fault. I should have waited till you came."

It was Noble Son of Wisdom who chose to speak first.

"Venerable sir, you did well to ask Pure-Wisdom to come. Perhaps he has already made a diagnosis. He has observed that you become pale and disoriented every time somebody suggests that action has to be taken in London to get any justice in the matter of the Kotahena Riots. He has also found out that you have some or preoccupation with regard to prisons. Please tell us what your problem is so that we can look for a solution."

A faint smile brightened his face.

"I should have remembered that Little Name is a wonderful detective," he said. "I recall how you found your lost uncle. You are right, Princely monk."

He sat upright on the couch, placed his feet on the floor and arranged the robe to cover his feet.

"In the absence of Little Name," he continued, "I signed a letter to a very important political leader in London condemning the Governor and asking for his removal from office. Now I feel that I have committed sedition and am liable to be arrested, tried and sent to jail. Will they get me to break stones for the road or beat coconut husks? At my age, how can I endure such hard labour?"

338

He looked as helpless as a child lost in a crowd. As the ex-diplomat explained step by step that governments acted differently and none of the consequences he feared could arise from his having made representations to imperial authorities in London, the senior monk punctuated each sentence,

"I know that you must know it. You were there."

Yet, at the end, he looked as unconvinced as he was at the beginning.

We proceeded to marshall all the resources at our disposal. We found a copy of the letter. We had it examined for any improper or illegal expressions. We consulted legal opinion. It was after a promise given by a leading lawyer that the scholar-monk relaxed.

"Venerable Sir, I guarantee that you will never be arrested, tried in court and never sentenced to prison because I will defend you and every Sinhala Buddhist in the country will finance your case," the lawyer told him.

Possibly, he slept soundly that night. When I saw him at the group chanting early in the morning, he called me to his side.

"Little Name, I agree with all others that we should seek justice in London. But we cannot do it. We are constrained by having to be loyal subjects of the British crown. Ask Venerable Gunananda whether we should send for Colonel Olcott."

Within days, a cable signed by both the senior monks and leading Theosophists and Buddhist leaders was despatched to Olcott. He arrived in Colombo on the twenty-seventh of January 1884.

How prophetic he had been in his last letter to me. He said that he would return to the Island if only he was invited.

There could not have been a more earnest invitation.

XIV

Olcott lost no time. Immediately he founded the Buddhist Defence Committee. It elected him an honorary member and empowered him to travel to London as its representative. As an essential preliminary step to his meetings in London, he travelled to Kandy and met the new Governor Sir Arthur Gordon who had succeeded Longdon. The Colonel thus ensured that he could not be accused of not making an effort to get justice locally.

Assiduous lawyer that he was, he ensured that he had the proper proxy to negotiate on behalf of the Buddhists. This he wanted from the notable scholar-monks. To prove its authenticity they wrote it in Pali and, of course, appended an English translation. The letter vouched for his knowledge of and devotion to Buddhism. As further proof of his identification with the Buddhists, it authorized the Colonel to administer the Three Refuges and the Five Precepts to anyone interested in becoming a Buddhist and stated that such conversions would be recognized by the Sangha of Sri Lanka as valid.

Armed with with this certificate of his Buddhist identity, he landed in London in April and sought the intervention of the Colonial Office on behalf of the Buddhists of Sri Lanka. He went fully prepared for his mission with memoranda from various sources and detailed information and data on the conflict. The British Administrations of both India and Sri Lanka had their own versions of the influence which Olcott wielded.

As I later learnt from the Colonel himself, Lord Derby, the Colonial Secretary, did not meet him lest such recognition at the highest level in the British Government would enhance White Buddhist's stature and influence in the two countries. The British had been for some time wary of a rumour current in South Asia that Colonel Olcott was being regarded in some religious circles as a messiah come to re-establish a virtuous rule and usher in prosperity.

Such a rumour did exist among Sinhala Buddhists whose folklore spoke of an Emperor of Righteousness named Diyasena. He was to appear two thousand five hundred years after the death of the Buddha. I was, however, not aware of anyone in the Island who even vaguely thought of Olcott as a possible Diyasena!

Though disinclined to add a further feather to Olcott's cap and make the prophesy of Diyasena a self-fulfilling one, the British could not treat him lightly. So they had him met by the Assistant Under-Secretary, R. H. Meade.

While anyone else would have treated this as an affront and refused to proceed any further, the goal-oriented perseverance of Olcott goaded him to pursue negotiations as energetically as he had planned. He was specially encouraged by a message from Lord Derby that the British Government regretted the lamentable failure of justice in a matter in which the Buddhists had real grounds for complaint.

Only bits and pieces of news on the negotiations came from messages which Olcott sent the National Defence Committee through ships that called at Colombo. All were encouraging.

When, ultimately, we heard of his return with good news, we organized the most lavish reception to our old friend and ally who was now a new hero.

Venerable Sumangala was very pleased. He had consistently considered the American Buddhist to be the most valuable ally in dealing with the British Administration. He had said so to leading members of the Sangha and the laity on many occasions. He had a personal reason to be grateful to Olcott.

Lord Derby's apology to the Buddhists, though worded somewhat obliquely, seemed to convince the scholar-monk that, after all, he had not committed an unforgivable crime by complaining against the Governor to his superiors in London.

Olcott returned just a couple of days before I was to leave for Sangha-Gem-Field. Once again, I had planned - this time entirely on my own initiative - to spend the Rainy Season Lent in my temple. I felt that I had many tasks to oversee. Not only Sumangala but also my other teachers agreed that I was doing the correct thing.

"Young as you are, you are more than the Abbot of that temple, Little Name. You have become the funnel through which all good things seem to pour into to your still undeveloped mountainous rural area," said the Vice-Principal, Friend of the Gods.

They assigned me work which included the study of the first ten discourses from the Collection of Long Discourses of the Pali Canon and the first ten cantos of "*The Birth of the Prince or War God*", another epic in Sanskrit by the famous poet Kalidasa. In classical Sinhala I was to read the two works of Gurulugomi, the "*Flood of Nectar*" and the "*Illuminator of the Doctrine.*" I also had assignments in Pali and Sanskrit Grammar.

I was at the mammoth meeting to welcome Olcott and had to interpret from and to English. I was fortunate to be assigned the

341

statement which the Colonel made as well as the eloquent addresses of appreciation and gratitude of the leading monks.

Olcott was loaded with garlands and bouquets flowers. As a bearer of good news, he sounded buoyantly optimistic and even imperious. It was certainly his day.

"The miscreants who attacked the procession will be arrested and duly punished," he said to the tumultuous ovation of the crowd who hardly heard his caveat about finding fresh reliable evidence.

To the Buddhists who were not demanding a pound of flesh from their attackers, the mere acceptance by the British Government in London that they had real grounds to complain was more than satisfactory.

The monks were relieved that the new laws about the management of Buddhist temporalities would not be pursued. They needed to put their own houses in order before the Administration could take over any of their rights or assumed a role of supervision.

"There will be no more interference with your processions and you will have the right to use tom-toms and pipes with no restrictions," he announced as one more concession that he had obtained for the Buddhists. Again a deafening ovation marked the announcement. But the wildest and the most joyous was reserved for the last announcement.

"The Colonial Secretary's Office assured me that as from the next year the thrice blessed Fullmoon Day of the month of Vesak, marking the anniversaries of the Birth, the Enlightenment and the Demise of the Buddha, will be a public and bank holiday."

That was more than the Buddhists had expected. They were conscious that none of these concessions could have been obtained without the intervention of Olcott. So pitiable they were in their servility to a foreign imperial power that they believed that no national would have been given the hearing that Olcott as a White American with impressive credentials from that rapidly growing nation could receive. Despite my admiration for two British clergymen who had influenced my life for the better, I shared that belief.

Olcott, however, was quite modest. After the meetings when I met him to say that I would be back in my village for the next three or four months, he approved my new vision and goal. We had a friendly chat as usual.

"There wasn't much I could extract from the Colonial Office," he told me. "The gesture about the holiday comes from the new Governor who seems to be more amenable and recognizes the importance of

Buddhism in the culture and politics of the Island. I heard while in London that the Venerable Sumangala had befriended Sir Arthur Gordon."

He also gave me a bit of gossip about the sudden removal of the previous Governor. It had something to do with the transfer of his son-in-law to the office of the Colonial Secretary. When its propriety was questioned, he seemed to have asked whether it was too much for a father to ask that his daughter be close to him. The powers that be had not taken kindly to such a response.

I invited Olcott to visit my school and requested that he should come in his travelling cart. I could imagine how enthralled the people would be. It certainly was a far cry from Chief Monk's buggy cart which was once the most wondrous thing they had ever seen.

He could not accede to my request. The glory he had enjoyed over his successful intervention in London on behalf of the Buddhists and the limelight of admiration he earned from them were marred by a series of unpleasant incidents among the Theosophists in India. In a brief note of apology on disappointing me, he wrote,

> "*All that I have believed in are being questioned and my own conscience raises many a question I cannot answer. All I have built over the last decade are being demolished and I am fast revising the unreserved and unwavering trust and affection I have had for my closest friend and partner.*"

To my surprise and curiosity, the letter ended with a request for information on how one became a Buddhist monk.

The three months in Sangha-Gem-Field was sheer joy and tranquility. What were once difficult projects to start were now simple routine. My weekly sermons drew crowds and I became not merely a repeater of the Buddha's teachings but a channel for public information and education. The school was doing well and the Board was active. More students, teachers, buildings and learning aids and materials were the visible signs of success. It was at this crucial point that the registration of the school had to be elevated from grade C to grade B. Only this elevation in registration would enable it to develop either as an English only or a bilingual school. My personal preference was for it to become an English only school.

A week after the end of the Lent, I was about to leave for Colombo when the R.M. accompanied by the other members of the School Board saw me to discuss an urgent issue. It related to the question of the imminent upgrading of the school.

"Venerable Sir, Mr. Edward Perera has brought us some information which we want to check with you," started the R.M. who was the chairman of the Board. "He says that the Buddhist agitation in the Western and Southern Provinces is against the conversion of the Buddhist schools into English only or Bilingual schools. It seems that the prevailing public opinion is to discourage the conversion of Buddhist schools to English schools."

I was amazed. Apparently, I had become out of touch with the original educational movement which the monks in the Southern and Western Provinces had set in motion on their own initiative before the arrival of Olcott. I had been so closely involved with the National Educational Movement which he was spearheading and which was strongly supported by Venerable Gunananda and Venerable Sumangala. I had also been so engrossed in my own studies that the issues of a national nature hardly came to my attention. My only means of knowing them was the correspondence I handled for the scholar-monk. Even when I was in Palace Hill, I handled only a fraction of his correspondence, that too when someone wrote in English.

All I could do was to promise that I would consult Venerable Sumangala and other scholar-monks and let the Board have my advice as soon as possible. But before I left Sangha-Gem-Field, I wrote a long letter to Little Father and asked him to advise me on what I should do.

I had arranged to spend a Saturday in Kandy before taking the train to Colombo. I was so keen to see the little boy whom I aided in smuggling to Slim-Jewel's home before anyone in the village could know. We were to meet at Royal Spout where a luncheon was arranged less formally than on other occasions. I was to be there alone.

It was a delight to see the young boy - a two and a half foot replica of my late brother. Moon-Beam was overly solicitous and protective of the brother. Theirs was a mutual love which every gesture and grimace expressed eloquently. It was an affectionate threesome and I had never seen Slim-Jewel happier.

"The little fellow completes our lives," she said. "It's such a joy to have him."

I called him. He came up to me, rolled on the ground in his own version of the traditional salutation due to a monk and touched the end of my robe. Stroking his head, I asked him,

"What's your name, Son?"

"Eat what's given and run away," he replied tilting his chin up with a slight shake to the left.

"Is that your real name?"

"I don't know. I have many names. Mother calls me 'Treasure.' Sister calls me 'Booby.' Teachers call me 'Middle Banda.' It's my little uncle who told me that my correct name is 'Eat what's given and run away.' "

I was glad to hear how Autumn-Moon had begun to tease his new-found nephew.

"Do you like the name that your little uncle has given you?"

He thought for a while and replied,

"No. But it's better than Saiya. I didn't like when the people in the village called me Saiya."

"You proud little rascal," I said, as I gave him an affectionate hug. Tears welled in my eyes as I thought of my late brother whose son this boy was, not only in looks but also in his proud and confident disposition.

Slim-Jewel and Moon-Beam took turns in narrating amusing incidents in which the little Middle Banda was the hero. If there was any visible strain in Slim-Jewel on account of her new life of responsibility, she looked a little tired.

"To have the greatest time with the kids I have opted for the midnight shift six days a week," she said. "I go to night school for my English after they go to bed."

Quite out of context, she complained that life was about to produce another problem for her. Uncle Victor was under orders to go on transfer to the District Office in the capital. It would be a great blow to Slim-Jewel who would lose the moral and material support of the most intimate and helpful members of the family. Her complaint broached a subject which they had decided to place before me.

Uncle Victor did not like it either. He was concerned that Aunt Flower would be lost in a big city without her friends and family. Colombo in her mind was a dirty, dusty dump. She had heard so many negative things about the rapidly expanding capital which had fast become an alien environment.

"There's only one person who can help us," Uncle Victor told me. "Ernest Dickinson has just returned from furlough in England and has been appointed as Government Agent of Colombo."

"What do you mean? Can he say that he doesn't want you in his office?" I asked.

345

"No. Not exactly. He can tell the Colonial Secretary's office that I could be more effective here in the Native Department in view of my direct links with many important persons in the region including the most influential clergy of all denominations."

The Native Department of a District Office was a quasi-political unit which dealt with law and order issues and therefore had its ear to the ground. Uncle Victor was correct in assuming that his connections would help the Administration. He was also correct in his assumption that Dickinson would appreciate why a person like Uncle Victor had a special role to play in the Province.

"I didn't know he was back. I certainly can tell him. But is there a position you can be placed in?"

Uncle Victor had done his home-work. He had everything so clearly worked out. His solution was quite plausible.

I looked forward to meeting Ernest Dickinson whom I recalled as the best friend I had in the Administration. I was also happy that I would be able to get something done for Uncle Victor.

This time I was better prepared for my classes. I had done my assignments and knew exactly where I needed the assistance of the teachers. Noble Son of Wisdom met me within hours of my arrival. He had a lot to tell me about the aftermath of the Kotahena Riots and the impact of the negotiations of Olcott in London.

"One thing is definite. Olcott is a national hero. None will outshine him. And why? The holiday. You simply cannot imagine what a moral booster it has become to the entire Buddhist population," he told me.

He also had a story to tell about a Buddhist Flag. A local committee had decided to base the flag on the six colours said to have emanated as a halo from the body of the Buddha: blue, yellow, red, white, orange and a mingling of all five. But what they designed was a pennant with the five main colours horizontally and their mingling marked by five vertical strips. It was nice to be taken in processions and hung on walls. But it was not a flag.

Once again, Olcott had shown his Yankee ingenuity. He trimmed the vertical strips to be the same breadth as each of the horizontal strips. Out came a flag which was of the correct proportions and could be flown from a pole. According to the information Noble Son of Wisdom had, this modified flag was to have been introduced at the function which was disturbed by the Riots. Now the plan was to have it ready for the first Buddhist holiday on the twenty-eightieth April, 1885.

The other piece of news related to young Don David. He had been taken out of Saint Thomas' College as a mark of protest after the

346

Kotahena riots. He had now become an avid reader of Theosophical and occult literature. He spent all his time either in the Pettah Public Library or in the house of the Agent for Theosophical Society publications. His parents worried that he was fast becoming an idealistic visionary.

"I was waiting for you to return to have a long chat with the boy," he concluded.

During the next few days I found time to visit Ernest Dickinson in his office and also to have a long chat with Don David.

The Government Agent was as cordial as he was when I first met him in Kandy. We recalled with amusement how I became a fugitive charged with my brother's murder. With the Buddhist holiday very much a reality, we recollected how his ploy to attend my higher ordination was perhaps the first occasion when the whole idea was first mooted. He was interested in what I was doing with Olcott and how I evaluated his work. Only after an hour of such small talk did I broach the subject of Uncle Victor's transfer.

"He's the man I would love to have here," he said and I was much discouraged. But he continued, "I see the point he makes. If he's of the correct seniority for the post in the Native Department, I'll move to have him appointed to it. If he isn't, we can appoint him to act ad interim. I'll see that he gets a challenging list of duties."

Promising to see him as often as it was convenient for both us, I hastened to the College where Don David would be waiting for me with the Siamese monk.

Slim and handsome, Don David had celebrated his twentieth birthday only two months ago. He was smartly dressed in flannel longs and a long-sleeved white shirt. His jet black hair cut and fashioned in the Oxford style then in vogue was held down with a shiny cream. He sat on a bench to our right. Against the setting sun whose soft rays played on his wavy hair, his profile with the prominent aquiline nose resembled a oversized copper coin with the familiar figure of the reigning monarch. He spoke softly but with enormous confidence.

"I had to leave school without passing the Matriculation Examination. Removing me from a Christian school was my father's way of objecting to the injustice surrounding the investigation into the Kotahena Riots. But to me it is a boon."

He gave us a brief account of the books he was reading.

347

"I read Sinnet's *Occult World* with a thrill of joy. I read an article of Madame Blavatsky about "*Chelas and Lay Chelas*" and I wrote a letter to the 'Unknown Brother' and the Himalayan Adept and forwarded through Madame Blavatsky. When Colonel Olcott came in January this year I went to see him and became a member of the Theosophical Society. The more I read these writings on occult sciences, the more I am disturbed by the fact that our monks are sceptical about our being able to attain the highest levels of the Path of Deliverance of Buddhism. What do you think? Can one of us attain Arahatship if we follow all the instructions given in our sacred books?"

I knew that he had asked this question from many a senior monk and received the standard answer that no Arahat, that is, a saintly achiever of liberation from suffering, had been produced over the last thousand years. I hesitated to reply. Noble Son of Wisdom discussed the tradition in his part of the world.

"Don David, I do not know what the belief is here in the Island. But I can speak about Burma and Siam. In our forests are monks steeped in meditation and some sincerely believe that they had attained various levels of the Path. Some have the reputation of being Arhats. But the achievers themselves do not go about advertizing themselves. Our meditators certainly believe that the teaching of the Buddha continues to be efficacious. If someone works hard at it, the final goal is within reach."

"That's very encouraging, Venerable Sir. I wish our monks would think positively and strive to achieve that goal without saying that we have to wait until the next Buddha, Maitreya, comes into being."

"I see in that statement a tinge of Mahayana teaching," added the Siamese colleague. "Are you familiar with the theory of Bodhisatvas in Mahayana Buddhism?"

"Not very much. I am afraid I do not know enough of Buddhism. I am so much more familiar with Himalayan Adepts and Mahatmas that they are real to me. Morya and Koot Hoomi are as real to me as you two are. My father is very concerned. He thinks I am wasting my time. But I do not really know how to combine this interest of mine with the practical needs of life."

Mature, wise and tactful, Noble Son of Wisdom encouraged the young seeker to pursue his spiritual quest while paying heed to parental advice on a practical course of life. He stressed the Middle Path and showed how its basic principle of moderation applied to every issue. It was a delightful conversation with a promising intellectual.

"What I think, Venerable Sir, is that I should go to Adyar, spend some time with those who profess to know occult sciences, see how they relate to my own inner quest and what I wish to have in the Island for the good of the masses. Then I can make a final decision on my mission in life."

"Wonderful," we both responded in unison. He was tickled by our choosing the same exclamation.

Never did I think that in a couple of weeks I should be running several errands for this young man. In December 1884, Madame Blavatsky arrived with Mr. and Mrs. Cooper Oakley. C. W. Leadbeater came from London. Olcott arrived with Dr. Franz Hartmann from Madras to accompany the party to Adyar. Don David had obtained his father's permission to go with them to India.

It so happened that on the morning of their departure his father withdrew his permission as he had had an unlucky dream.

Young David was adamant. Venerable Sumangala agreed with the father. But on repeated appeals form the young man, he asked me to accompany a scholar-monk of the college to seek Olcott's advice. He was short and to the point. If the father objected, no one could go against him. But Don David showed his mettle in refusing to surrender.

Our final court of appeal was Madame Blavatsky. Hers was the simplest solution.

"If we don't take the boy, he is sure to die," she said in a tone that was endowed with some mysterious superhuman authority.

Don David thanked me profusely as Madame Blavatsky led him by his hand up the gangplank.

Returning from Adyar, Don David came to my cell one afternoon to thank me again for the errands I ran to get him permission to accompany Madame Blavatsky and party. He was very excited.

"Venerable Sir," he said, choosing to speak to me in English. "You remember what I told you and the Siamese princely monk. I was right. I did find my mission - but in an entirely unexpected manner."

"Did you really see any of the Mahatmas or Adepts?" I asked.

" No. But Madame Blavatsky may have consulted them."

"What did she tell you?"

"She called me to her room one day and asked me to sit by her. She showed some articles and pictures which represented Himalayan Masters and Adepts paying their devotion to Lord Buddha. Then she told me, 'Young man, it is not for you to study occultism. Study Pali and read its vast literature. All you should know is in it. You should work for the good of Humanity.' She laid both her hands on my head and

349

blessed me. I felt as if a great darkness was lifted from my vision. I now know where I should go."

"Did Madame Blavatsky put this young man on a collision course with Olcott?" I asked myself.

I had felt on several occasions that the Russian Co-Founder of the Theosophical Society was not happy that Olcott was giving greater priority to Buddhism, the national revival and educational development of the Island. Rumours were rampant that she had disrupted the Colonels' Buddhist work in Burma by feigning illness. On day I asked Noble Son of Wisdom whether my prognosis was exaggerated.

"Pure, don't you see what will happen. Sooner or later this young man is going to be the leader that the people will be inclined to accept. They will be grateful to the Colonel but follow the other. We have arena seats to watch this inevitable contest."

XV

The examinations in April were to our satisfaction. I had become used to working on my own for three months without adverse results in my performance. Noble Son of Wisdom had become exceedingly proficient in both Pali and Sanskrit. He was keen to do more advanced work.

"Tell me, my friend, what motivates you to study Sanskrit and Pali so diligently?" I asked him when I congratulated him on being the first in his class.

"Sooner or later, Pure, I will return to Siam. There, we haven't anything comparable to the great tradition of learning that you have in Sri Lanka. I want to be a pioneer in this field. Maybe I'll have time for research and may even publish a few books and articles."

He paused for a while, gulped down an invisible lump in his throat and continued,

"Isn't this a pleasant way to while away one's exile?"

1885 was not a great year for the Theosophists. The investigation into alleged fraudulent practices continued amidst charges and counter-charges from within their own circle.

The London-based Society of Psychical Research sent its representative to go into the allegations. Madame Blavatsky was reportedly wild and violent and Olcott had even considered suicide.

Madame Blavatsky whom the Psychical Society was to declare at the end of that year to be "one of the most accomplished, ingenious, and interesting imposters in history" left India for good on the 2nd of April. During her brief stopover in Colombo, Don David made it a point to visit her.

The full moon day of April, which fell on the 28th, was a day to remember. The newly designed six coloured Buddhist flag dominated the sky. People thronged to temples to observe the Eight Precepts. Colourful archways depicting life-size scenes from the life of the Buddha and stories of his previous lives adorned every vantage point in bigger cities. Free food and beverages were provided in gaily decorated refectories for pilgrims and spectators. Processions carrying sacred objects criss-crossed every city, town and township. The rhythmic tom-toms and plaintive pipes created a festive ambience. Public meetings, sermons and wayside gatherings hailed Olcott as the hero of the day.

The nation had taken a holiday for the first time in well nigh four hundred years to pay homage to the Buddha on the anniversary of his Birth, Enlightenment and Demise. The procession which left the premises of the College was dominated by three large pictures of Venerable Sumangala, Venerable Gunananda and Henry Steel Olcott. What a Trio - Erudition, Oratory and Diplomacy!

It was mid-May and I was rudely reminded of an inexcusable lapse of memory. I had been so overwhelmed by diverse demands on my time since my return from Sangha-Gem-Field: the studies and the examination; Don David's trip to India and its repercussions on his goals and objectives of life; the investigation into Madame Blavatsky's occult phenomenon and its impact on Olcott; and, above all, the excitement of the first Buddhist holiday which had to be observed fittingly. But none of these excuses could be offered with a good conscience to the School Board to which a response was due from me.

Two things happened almost simultaneously. I received a letter from my brother the monk mentioning quite casually that the next annual inspection of the school was fixed for the end of June. My presence as the manager would be useful, he said by way of repeating a suggestion made by the headmaster Edward Perera. I guessed what consternation gripped the School Board. The main question of the medium of instruction of the school remained unsettled.

The same evening a monk from Orange Island hand-carried a bulky parcel from Little Father. It contained several publications of Venerable Pleasant-Gem-Tissa and a twelve page letter, neatly written in Little Father's pearl-like round letters. It was in reply to my letter which I wrote to him on my arrival in Palace Hill. It started with an apology for the delay which he explained was mainly due to the fact that he wanted to deal with the question exhaustively. That he had certainly done.

He analyzed the question of English education in Buddhist schools from every possible angle. It was clinical in its objectivity.

What is the most forceful argument against English education? He raised this as the first issue and answered it lucidly:

"Real or imaginary danger of alienation, denationalization and exodus of talent from local communities."

He elaborated with examples what the objectors meant by alienation and denationalization:

> *"The adoption of Western dress, language, customs and etiquette resulting in or accompanied by an outright condemnation or loss of interest in national language, history, religion, culture, customs etc. etc."*

Just as a smart lawyer would have done, Little Father proceeded to examine the evidence on which the objectors to English education had reached this conclusion:

> *"A Buddhist boy or a girl educated in English in a Buddhist environment is still a rare, if not non-existent animal. So all we can observe are the behavioural changes of children from Buddhist homes who have received their education in Christian or Roman Catholic Schools. The Colombo Academy and other government schools are in spirit, content and atmosphere Christian.*
>
> *"What do the majority of their Buddhist alumni reveal? Exactly what the objectors to English education highlight. Whatever be the home background and influence, this majority shows that they become totally Anglicized in their way of thinking and overall life style. They consider themselves to be superior class, run down everything in the national culture, take to ostentatious living and conspicuous extravagance, neglect religious obligations, take to the drinking of alcohol and laugh at the masses who strive to preserve the tenets of their national religion.It is lamentable that they degrade everything national and demonstrate a despicable lack of respect to their elders.*
>
> *"The most disgusting characteristic of this new class is they are shy of their peasant parents and refer to them in their circles as 'Old Man' or 'Old Lady.' The people call this class derisively, 'Black Whites'. One wonders whether the educational opportunities made available to them are for the good and for the benefit of either the community or the country."*

At this point, I thought that Little Father was one of the objectors and had put forth a strong argument against English education. But the next question he had underlined cautioned me not to jump to conclusions.

Now, as a scientist would, he raised the question:

> *"Do we have a control group to determine whether the undesirable behavioural patterns came from English education or from the alien spiritual and cultural environment provided in missionary schools?"*

"No. Not at all," he answered the question. "Objectors have no patience to make an objective assessment. They have their own axes to grind."

He categorized objectors and subjected each group to ruthless scrutiny.

"Let me take the monks first. They are honest and sincere but, on the whole, constrained by their limited experience to take a broad look at life or society.

"Among them the most vocal are the pioneering monks who revived temple schools or established new schools to counter-balance the missionary effort. I know practically everyone of them. I am led to wonder whether their antipathy to English has something to do with Olcott.

"As you will recall, it was the White Buddhist who proposed that a Buddhist Elite must be produced through a system of Buddhist English Schools. Here, to my mind, is a classic case of condemning an idea because someone else proposed it.

"An element of jealousy and hostility could also be suspected as the Colonel involved the laity as leaders of reform and implementers of change and this robbed some monks of their self-proclaimed superiority."

I paused to think. Little Father could be right. Olcott was not all that popular among monks in general. It was not entirely due to any pettiness on the part of the monks. He annoyed them with his blanket criticism of the Sangha as a whole. In his enthusiasm, he felt that monks were not active enough. He expected them to keep pace with him. His letters to monks were not always polite. To a very senior monk, he had written: "Please be ready for my visit - by not running away!"

For whatever animosity the monks might feel towards the Colonel, English education should not be the scape-goat, I thought. It would be like throwing the baby with the bath water.

How well our thoughts synchronized! That was exactly the simile with which the next page began. He examined with equal attention the self-interest of the teachers who were in temple schools and the earlier set of Buddhist schools. They felt self-sufficient in conducting the schools as they were.

As long as a teacher could reduplicate himself or herself through the education imparted in a given school, he or she had no reason to think of superior goals which would change the *status quo*. Such change would have the immediate effect of eliminating these same pioneering teachers.

No species is known not to resist self-destruction!

"Here, in the eyes of these teachers," argued Little Father, *"the better is the enemy of the good. I mean their personal good*!!!"

He had reserved his wrath for the last category of objectors to English education. He identified several persons basking in political and social limelight who objected to the conversion of Buddhist schools into English schools. They gave valid reasons and reiterated much of what the monks and teachers had advanced. But the difference was that their children continued to receive the best of English education in the Colombo Academy as well as important missionary schools. But their hearts bled for the children from Buddhist homes of modest incomes and rural areas. They urged that 'these innocent children' should not be exposed to the demoralizing horrors of an English education.

"These hypocrites are convinced that they are engaged in a great national service," continued Little Father. *"But what is their motive? Plain and simple. They want to keep English education their exclusive monopoly. In the guise of defending national culture, these self-centred good-for-nothings defend their own privileges."*

In conclusion, Little Father repeated what Colonel Olcott had been stressing in his fund-raising campaign for National Buddhist Education. This was his last paragraph:

"We want our doctors, lawyers, engineers, accountants, administrators, investors, entrepreneurs, teachers, technicians, journalists, clerks and the like. ***Our schools must produce them with a love for the land and the people and an appreciation of our spiritual, literary and cultural heritage.*** *The longer we neglect to do this, the longer shall we be under foreign rule.*

Son, resist. Do not surrender the rights of the Buddhist child to please anyone."

I read the letter twice over. It said more than I needed to make up my mind. I weighed his arguments against the reality of an isolated rural community. It could hardly afford to lose too much of its talent to the modern sector. That night, I wrote a letter to the R. M., the Chairman of

355

the School Board. I urged that our school should be an English-Sinhala Bilingual School.

Noble Son of Wisdom extolled my decision, not on any social or educational ground, but on the basis it conformed to the all-prevailing Buddhist principle of the Middle Path.

I planned to leave for Sangha-Gem-Field in time for the annual inspection of the school. That gave me enough time to discuss what I should study in preparation for the final examination of the College in April 1886. Stock was taken of the progress I had made in the three languages: Pali, Sinhala and Sanskrit. A notable lacuna was in formal study of prosody and rhetorics in any of the languages. My first assignment was to do a thorough comparative study of the metres, sound patterns and figures of speech in the poetry in all three languages. It was fascinating to find how the Sanskrit model had been modified to suit each literature. The most difficult was the work on Sinhala rhetorics which was ascribed to King Sena of the tenth century.

In Sinhala, I was required to read three major prose works of the thirteenth century and two poetical works of the greatest poet-monks of the fifteenth century. Fortunately, there were palmleaf manuscripts of all these books in the library.

In addition, I had to revise all the work I had done over the eight year course at the College. The final examination covered this entire subject-matter and instant recall was the order of the day.

A remarkable work on polity presented through fables was prescribed to improve Sanskrit composition. As its translation happened to be one of the books of Pleasant-Gem-Tissa which Little Father sent me, I had read it already. For Pali, what was prescribed was an abstruse analysis of Buddhist psychology. It was too difficult for self-study. I needed much guidance more on the content than on the language. It was taken out of my holiday allocation of work.Reverend Blake's story of the suitcase and conservation of time had been my saviour at all times. The extended stay in Sangha-Gem-Field, necessitated by the school inspection, promised to be an exceedingly difficult period. In reality, an Abbot was at the beck and call of everybody even though the reverse appeared to be true. If my own goals were to be accomplished, crevice time would have to be pressed to maximum use.

All were happy with my decision to ask for the status of a Bilingual School. Particularly so was Patrick Patrick, the new Inspector of Schools. A product of Westminter School in London and Chaltenham

Teacher's College in Gloucestershire, he was an idealist in many respects. He had volunteered to serve in a colony and was delighted when sent to Sri Lanka. Though he had hardly spent a year in the Island, he had already got a little tired and utterly impatient with missionaries who tried to dictate terms to him.

One of them had reminded him of the fate of Mr.J. S. Laurie the first Director of Public Instruction in 1869 whose job on paper was to provide a general education to all children in the country.He had taken his job description seriously and started to work in earnest.

"Laurie thought he was in England," this missionary had told Patrick Patrick. "Colonies are not run the way the masters run their own country. When he failed to understand this we had him ignominiously removed even before he could enjoy the sun and the sands or the glory of his exalted office for a year. I am warning you in case you do not know."

This had happened when I was yet in the primary school. The Inspector gave me the details of Laurie's career.

Such were the stumbling blocks which were buearucratically hurled in Laurie's way that he had in utter frustration complained to the Colonial Secrtetary that the office of the Director of Public Instruction was "a misnomer and a farce." Of course, such frankness was not tolerated. The Governor had him removed from office on the ground that his retention in office "was fatal to the interests of education in Ceylon."

The Inspector stayed behind for an informal, heart-to-heart chat with me. He was intrigued to find an English-speaking monk. As we conversed, he was astonished to find that I had had the privilege of having as complete an education as anyone of my age could have received in England. I spoke gratefully of the Blakes and of Right Reverend Saunders. His eyes shone when I told him that the latter was not only my teacher and school principal but also my sincerest friend.

I think the fate of the school was determined on this conversation as on its performance. He took leave of me after assuring me that he had no difficulty in recommending the upgrading of the school, as I had taken a wise decision.

The Rainy Season Lent passed with the usual spate of activities. My week-end sermon had become a regular feature and I was flattered to find that people travelled from Kandy and Matale to listen to me. Among them were Uncle Victor, Aunt Flower, Slim-Jewel and the three kids Autumn-Moon, Moon-Beam and Middle Banda. I was more than thrilled to see the avuncular and sisterly attention Middle Banda had from the other two.

I made every sermon topical. Edward Perera, who was the most pleased about the status of the school, had made arrangements to have them taken down to be published in the form of a book.

For the closing ceremony of the Lent, I invited Noble Son of Wisdom who delivered another excellent sermon in flawless Sinhala, to the delight of the entire audience.

After two days we left Sangha-Gem-Field. Once again, I had to miss the Robe Ceremony as the Final Examination I faced was no piece of cake.

Back in Palace Hill, studies commanded my undivided attention. Every teacher expressed readiness to help me. Among the twenty students preparing for the Final Examination, I have missed the largest number of classes on account of my obligations to the community whose Abbot I was. Five of us formed a study group. It proved to be the best way to ensure that each had memorized his texts correctly.

One morning, in November, I was sent for by Venerable Sumangala who had very thoughtfully relieved me of handling his correspondence. Don Carolis was with him.

"I know, Little Name, you are devoting every minute for your studies for the Final Examination," commenced the scholar-monk. "But our dear friend and supporter has a problem about which you and your Siamese friend might be able to do something."

Don Carolis worshipped me and handed over a neatly written letter which began with the usual benediction and endearing references to father and mother. It was a letter which Don David had addressed to his parents.

"Please read it," said Venerable Sumangala.

Young Don David was asking his parents for permission to leave home to reside in the headquarters of the Buddhist Theosophical Society so that he could devote his entire life as a celibate devotee to the promotion of the Buddhist Faith. He had asked them for a paltry monthly allowance of five rupees (then equal to US $ 3.66).

"Did you speak to him on receipt of the letter, Sir?" I asked.

"Yes, my wife and I both did. I appealed to him, reminding him of his obligations as the eldest in the family. One day he might have to take care of his younger siblings. But his mind is set. Mother has given her blessings. But I would still urge him to take a job and be independent."

358

I looked at Venerable Sumangala and awaited his instructions.

"Your Siamese friend and you should talk to him. Maybe, you could persuade him to accede to the father's advice about doing a job."

It was, as usual, a pleasure to see Don David. He had already moved into what was meant to be a store-room in the headquarters of the Society. Not only was it windowless but the ceiling was barely a few inches above our heads.He had moved in a camp bed of the variety called a "donkey bed" - an exceedingly primitive contraption made by fixing a stretched-out burlap rice bag to a frame of rubber wood. A neatly arranged table contained a few books and a pile of paper, leaving hardly a square foot or two for writing. He was using a stool until he could find a chair. Under the table was a metal food-carrier in which lunch had been sent from home. The unmistakable glow of happiness on his face contrasted with the sparse living conditions. He had found his place in life and he was overjoyed.

I let Noble son of Wisdom to do the most of the talking. He congratulated Don David.

"We have similar traits, Don David," he said. "My small room in the school is a little bit more comfortable than yours. But that's because I designed it for me to live in. But both of us do this by choice. I am a king's son, whatever that means. You can live like a king. There's no doubt that we have been inspired by the example of our teacher the Buddha, the Sage of the Sakyas. I can only give you my blessings and wish that you achieve whatever goal you set for yourself."

"I am happy to hear that, Venerable Sir. I am not as lucky as you both are and this makes me sad."

"Why do you say so?' I asked him.

"I would gladly be a monk. My parents would understand such an urge better and give their unreserved blessings. But you know my problem."

It was not necessary for him to elaborate. No one with any physical deformity could be ordained. His was not in any way a major deformity. He limped visibly when he walked.

We discussed matters of common interest allowing him as much time as he wished to elaborate his ideas on his chosen mission.

"My trip to the Headquarters of the Theosophical Society in Adyar opened my eyes. I think that Madame Blavatsky knew what was coming when she advised me to give up occult sciences and concentrate on Buddhism. To my mind she was a true friend of Buddhism. Her trouble was that she wanted to be the subject of everyone's adulations. So she went too far with her occult phenomena. In Adyar, she has no place.

Her excesses in the practice of occultism have brought her disgrace. An Indian Subba Row has taken her place and people like Cooper Oakley think that his occult powers are superior to hers. Olcott is doing all he can to distance himself from her as far as he can. He has even thought of coming here or going to Burma to be ordained as a Buddhist monk. Hinduism is taking over the Theosophical Society. Gradually the Buddha is losing his place to Shankara and his monistic Vedanta."

Were we listening to a young man of barely twenty-one? His analysis of the situation was sound and his judgement accurate. I had no idea who Shankara was or what his Monistic Vedanta taught. But this was not the time to ask him. It was clear that Buddhism was losing ground to Hinduism in the heasquarters of the Theosophical Society.

Noble son of wisdom and I had to agree with his conclusion:

"The future of Buddhism is our responsibility. I want to dedicate my life to its service."

Once the seriousness of his dedication was acknowledged, he had no objection to following his father's advice. Both Noble Son of Wisdom and I were pleased with our role. Venerable Sumangala and Don Carolis were grateful.

Don David applied for a job in the Department of Education. The Director of Education was so impressed with his penmanship that he was immediately appointed as an Assistant Clerk. Shortly afterwards he sat the competitive Clerical Service Examination.

My routine of study was once again disturbed when Olcott arrived in Colombo with C. W. Leadbeater in February 1886 to continue the campaign for the Buddhist Educational Fund. I called on the Colonel and found him in a bad mood.

Recent events in Adyar had taken a toll of him. He looked tired, distraught and unhappy. More indicative of his state of mind was his unusual reticence. At fifty-four he looked a decade or two older.

He was, nevertheless, courteous and made inquiries about my studies and my experience as an Abbot. I told him of my school and the decision that I had taken to make it a Bilingual School. His body shook up in a tremour as something snapped within him.

"I am a big fool, Young Priest," he said. I have been at it for the last six years. But not a single school has come up. This time it is going to be different."

A few days later, I was not surprised to read in a newspaper that the Colonel was threatening to call off his campaign and return to India. The diatribe was levelled against the Buddhists in general.

"No one has come forward to accompany me," it said. "It is useless my wasting my precious time if no Buddhist cares even to join me on the tour."

I was in a predicament. I should have offered to join him on his tour and serve as his interpreter. But I was preoccupied with the examination which was to be in two months. To make amends, I went to see him. I sincerely thought that my personal success in the academic field was not as important as the national service in which he was engaged.

But someone had beaten me to it. Don David had seen him earlier and agreed to take a few months' leave from his job so as to assist the Colonel in the campaign. Olcott was elated.

The Colonel took another important decision and that was to establish the Buddhist English School in Colombo. He wanted to name it after his hero of the Great Debate, Venerable Gunananda. An agreement on the name proved elusive and thus was born what in due course became Ananda College. Leadbeater who continued the campaign trail, even after Olcott returned to Adyar, became its first Principal. Olcott's idea enunciated at Orange Island on his first visit reached fruition six years later.

One more memorable event took place shortly afterwards. While on tour with Leadbeater, Don David was appointed to a post on the the results of the General Clerical Service examination. He did not think twice before he sent in a letter of resignation.

Don Carolis was disappointed. He took Don David, on his return, to the Colonial Secretary to have the resignation withdrawn. But Don David declined. Later, he narrated the event to some of us saying, "With delight I left."

The Final Examination lasted two full weeks. Twelve three-hour question papers covered the whole gamut of grammar and literature of Pali, Sinhala, Sanskrit and Prakrit, subject-matter of the textbooks studied in depth, prosody and rhetorics as well as exercises in prose and verse compositions in the first three languages. I did well and expected to have the ordeal of formal studies behind me.

To celebrate the newly gained relief from the pressures of study, I took a trip to the south. Little Father took me to a number of flourishing schools mostly in temple premises. He was however disappointed that English Buddhist Schools were still a far cry away.

"Opponents of English education on high moral grounds are still on the increase," he gave as the explanation. "The way we are going we will be a nation of transport, toddy and arrack contractors, farmers, teachers and monks. The Buddhist will ever be doomed to the lower middle class without leaders, without intellectuals and without professionals."

On the day of my return to Colombo, Little Father had a special piece of advice:

"Go to the Buddhist English School which is near the Learning-Awakening College, befriend Leadbeater, offer to be a teacher, chaplain or whatever, and study how an English school is run."

This I did.

The results of the examination was issued in May. Not only had I passed in all subjects with distinction but I was awarded the Golden Medal for the best student. A position as a teacher in the College was mine for the asking.

To work with younger students who promised to be future leaders of the nation was positively more attractive. I went daily to Leadbeater's school and was virtually its Chaplain and teacher of Buddhism.

In July, I went to Sangha-Gem-Field with a week to spare for the commencement of the Rainy Season Lent.

XVI

After a very long time I was at my own temple without the pressure and anxiety of a forthcoming examination. For the first time in my life I was experiencing the delicious pleasures of sheer relaxation. The incredible joy of having nothing to do!

I had more time for the village folk who came to see me. I read what I had long laid aside. I could visit the school and actually teach a class or two in place of absent teachers. I made myself available to students who needed counselling. I visited the sick, the old and decrepit in their homes. Chief Monk's buggy cart was in constant use. Some days I went as far as Palm-branch Stream where a small community of Christians still remembered Little Father who accompanied Reverend Thomas Blake.

I paid courtesy calls on Abbots of famous temples in the region. I chose a Saturday morning to pay a visit to my old school. I met the new missionary couple, the Wilkins. Reverend Paul and Mrs. Rebecca Wilkins reminded me of the Blakes. They looked alike and their attitudes to life appeared to be similar.

"We had long wanted to see you," said Reverend Paul trying to figure out how I should be received. I let him shake my hands. But I had to explain to Mrs. Wilkins why I was treating her differently.

The Wilkins had been inspired by the writings of Bishop Bigandet of Burma and Bishop Copleston of Sri Lanka. They had also read reports of the missionaries, specially of the Church Missionary Society. Rebecca Wilkins, in particular, had been intrigued by the agonizing accounts of the setbacks to which the Church had been subjected.

"The incredible story of the rapid recovery of the Buddhists and threats posed to Christianity through emulation by Hindus and Muslims, fascinated me to no end. At one time, I wondered if they were mere sob stories of missionaries in order to ferret out more funds. Finally, I persuaded Paul to ask for an assignment here so that I could write a book about it."

"Now that the cat is out of the bag, Reverend," asked Reverend Paul. "What do you think about her idea?"

"All depends on the purpose of the book," I replied.

"I am a student of Anthropology. I have a Master's degree in it. I wonder whether I could study what is happening in the Island in the domain of religion from an anthropological standpoint and write a thesis for my doctorate."

I needed a lot of explanation before I understood the full implications of what she was engaged in. Neither my English education nor the mastery of the traditional knowledge in four languages had prepared me to comprehend the new developments in modern higher education in the West: Who would give the highest academic credit to the study of a passing phenomenon in the life and history of a tiny Island?

"It's not a passing phenomenon in a tiny Island, Reverend Pure-Wisdom," she said. "What happened to Christianity here may provide answers to what is happening to it elsewhere. It could even suggest answers to the whole question of cyclic changes in religion, spirituality and the like.

"Where did Christianity fail? Is it its total reliance on political patronage? Is the Disestablishment of the Church the cause for the onset of decay? Is the Christian world so divided and prone to infighting that it dissipates its energy in self-destruction? Or is it its inability to face the challenge of modern science?

"Where does Buddhism find its source of regeneration? Is the tolerance which it has demonsrated in history, sometimes to its own detriment, the hidden secret of its survival over centuries with marked periods of revival? Is Christianity too rigid, whereas Buddhism has grown into a remarkable diversity serving the needs of people of different cultures and different temperaments?

"Answers I could find to any of these questions will have universal relevance."

While Rebecca Wilkins and I were engaged in this academic discussion, the padre, himself, went to the kitchen, prepared tea and served me and his wife - her first, of course - two cups of tea.

I thanked him and added in a lighter vain,

"I wish I can teach my compatriots to be as polite to their wives and serve them first."

"Don't you tell me, Reverend. That's how I find out when I pay my visits to big shots in the region how far they deviate from their traditional norms and customs. When the gentleman of the house does things, I feel grateful to my compatriots. They have at least left one visible mark."

As if it to assuage any criticism that was levelled against the local custom, he laughed aloud. I was amused because the self-deprecation was on my part.

"My wife is the brain of the family, Reverend." he said further in good humour. "That, of course, makes me the man about the house. You know what I mean?"

I formed a good impression of the missionary couple. They were easy-going and were not taking themselves seriously. I promised to be available to her for whatever information or guidance she would need in her research. It was a good visit and I wished to see them again.

The Rainy Season Lent had become a period of intense activity in the temple ever since I became its Abbot. This year my relaxed presence seemed to have contributed to a visible increase in activity. My brother was still the Organization Man. The three fullmoon days were to be marked by three events.

One was the revival of an ancient mode of preaching called the "Two Seat Sermon." Two monks were on the pulpit and one initiated a subject on which the other made his comments drawing on the commentaries and the narrative literature. It was not a debate but could be a test of erudition, especially for the second monk. The monk initiating the subject would choose a text from the Canon or raise a question and the other monk had to know the subject-matter thoroughly to provide an explanation. It could last three to four hours and the audience even took sides as to which monk performed better. On the whole, it was an effective way of teaching the doctrine to the people. To make the encounter of the two monks topically more interesting to the people, Little Father was invited to be the monk initiating a subject. I was persuaded to be the commentator. We were indeed well matched and the Two Seat Sermon proved to be a great hit.

The next was the re-enactment of the encounter between the Greek King Menander of Bactria, a kingdom to the west of the Indian Subcontinent, with a Buddhist monk named Nagasena, meaning Serpent-Army. This king of the second century before Christ was said to have had several in-depth dialogues on many issues relating to Buddhism and eventually embraced it as his personal religion on account of the monk's convincing answers.

I was glad that the re-enactment of the dialogues between the king and the monk would be an opportunity to educate the people on this period of Buddhist history. I had a further reason to be pleased. One of the sons of the R. M. had agreed to be dressed as a king and to play the role of Menander, on condition I represented Nagasena. That event too was a great success. The proud father of "King Menander" had the preaching hall filled with his relatives and friends and specially the class-mates of his son from Kandy.

365

Buddhists were perhaps the earliest in the world to use visual art for educational purposes and made sculpture and paintings on every wall and rock space in temple premises an accessory to teaching the religion. Yet, they seemed to have frowned on performing arts in general. I was therefore quite curious to find out how this particular episode which was so dramatic in quality could be a technique for teaching the more philosophical aspects of the doctrine. I was further intrigued when I found that the Pali work "*The Questions of Menander*" was translated into Sinhala for the first time barely a hundred years ago. I figured out the re-enactment of the dialogue could be something of recent origin. But its effectiveness was beyond question.

The most elaborate event was a seven day chanting of the Book of Protection, to be followed by the recitation of a special text in highly Sanskritized Sinhala of benediction by a teen-ager in the guise of a god. Clad in raiments of silk and adorned in gold jewelry, the boy would be taken in a long procession with tom-toms and pipes and hundreds of dancers and led to the temple in time for the recitation.

It was a feat of memory and we decided to let the best student of the Sunday School to be assigned this task as an honour and a reward. I was personally happy when the boy chosen was son of a very poor share-cropper, who despite the economic constraints of the family, assigned high priority to the education of his children.

The boy's performance was fantastic. An appreciative R. M. offered to pay his school fees and living expenses in an English Boarding School in Kandy.

Edward Perera kept to his word. The texts of my weekly discourses including the Two Seat Sermon and the Menander Dialogue were presented to me for revision. A modest booklet containing them was printed in time for the Robe Ceremony. I was thrilled as it was the first publication to bear my name.

This year, too, I invited Noble Son of Wisdom to the Robe Ceremony and planned a little surprise.

The day began well before dawn when the web of white cloth was brought to the temple from the weaver's house in a grand procession. The monks measured and cut into nearly thirty shapes which represented the square and rectangular paddies and the long, narrow ridges of a rice-field.

At a time when robes were nothing but a patchwork of rags picked from the dust heap and the cemetery, such a pattern for joining the pieces of rags served an aesthetic purpose. From generation to generation this pattern, which the Buddha pointed out in a beautifully laid tract of rice-fields in the Gangetic Basin, had been faithfully preserved.

By the time of the mid-day meal, the pieces were sewn together and the robe dyed into a soothing shade of yellow. The dye came from chips of wood from the jak tree. It was spread in the sun to dry as the monk to whom the robe was assigned had to wear it that very day.

To the great delight of Noble Son of Wisdom, the Sangha in an elaborately conducted ritual of assigning the Austerity Robe - as it was called - named him as the recipient and consequently the preacher of the evening's sermon. He chose his text "*To live in an agreeable land and to have merits acquired in the past*" from a discourse of the Buddha on great blessings.

Noble Son of Wisdom stayed with me for a week. I had to catch up on many matters and he had always been the most reliable purveyor of news.

He told me of the growing interest in the Buddhist shrines of India, generated by the visit of Sir Edwin Arnold in January 1886. I recalled the fervour with which he appealed to the Buddhists of Sri Lanka to save these sacred monuments. He was quite blunt when he said that they were being desecrated by people who either knew nothing of their sanctity or by fanatics who thought that the Buddha was an enemy of their faith. I wondered who in Sri Lanka would take the lead.

Venerable Sand-Village was indeed a very fine scholar and his mastery of Sanskrit was of the highest order. But he seemed to lack the charisma of a leader who could rally people around him and rouse them to action. He was, however, a fervent and reliable supporter and, according to my Siamese friend, had become a source of encouragement to Don David.

"Their collaboration has become the talk of the town," said Noble Son of Wisdom. "Venerable Sand-Village is sixty-one and a scholar of the highest reputation. Don David of twenty-two more or else tells him what to do and what to write. Not only does the scholar-monk comply with all such requests of the young man, but encourages him to make them. He must see something in Don David. Otherwise, I cannot think of an explanation for such docile compliance."

"Docile is the last epithet that would ever apply to Venerable Sand-village, " I told him. "He is a fighter in his own right. You know how he treats Colonel Olcott. He shows quite openly that he does not think much of the White Buddhist. He hardly replies to his letters or joins him in the fund-raising campaigns. Of course, Venerable Sand-Village's foreign hero is Sir Edwin Arnold. They had known each other for some time. I am more inclined to agree with your observation that the scholar-monk sees Don David as a promising leader. If he does things that young man asks for, it must be the scholar-monk's way of encouraging him."

Noble Son of Wisdom had more to say of Don David. Since taking up his residence in the tiny room in the headquarters of the Buddhist Theosophical Society, he had become the General Secretary of the Buddhist Section, Manager of the Buddhist Press, Manager and *de facto* Editor of the Sinhala Newspaper, Moon-Ray (*Sandaresa*), Manager of Buddhist Schools and Assistant Secretary of the Buddhist Defence Committee.

His tour of the Island with Olcott and Leadbeater in the Colonel's travelling cart had made a great impact on the aspiring reformer.

My Siamese friend brought a cutting of a newspaper in which Don David had written,

> *My tour of Ceylon is an eye-opener. I saw for the first time the grim realities of life, which the villagers, uncared for and ill-provided, lived in remote areas without roads and houses, schools or hospitals. I am convinced that the greatness of a nation depended not on the prosperity and comfort of a few urban families but on the happiness and contentment of the masses who formed the nation's backbone. I realize the need for freedom so that the people could guide their destinies without being down-trodden and subdued by Colonial masters who are neither equipped nor inclined to appreciate the national heritage and the latent potentiality for greater and mightier achievements.*
>
> *There is something about an alien rule, no matter how beneficent, that stupefies.*
>
> *I dream of the day when Ceylon would be independent, the religion of the people restored to its pristine glory. the simple un-affected ways of Sinhala culture recognized and upheld and the people made more enlightened participants in the scientific and technological achievements of modern times.*
>
> *To this end I have to be active and activity means agitation according to constitutional means."*

"Hurrah!" I exclaimed. "Or should I shout Sadhu! Sadhu! Sadhu!? This is a fantastic statement from a young man of twenty-two. It's my dream too. If only this could be realized without rancour, acrimony and blood-shed."

"Yours is a truly blessed nation to have young men who think so far," responded the Prince of Siam in yellow robes.

When Noble Son of Wisdom returned to Colombo, I settled down to send out New year greetings to my growing number of friends. Every steamer sailing into Colombo or Galle brought me their greetings and newsy letters, besides requests for information on various subjects they were interested in.

With the kind of multifarious activities in which I had engaged myself, I too had a lot to write to my friends and correspondents all over the world.

My letter to Right Reverend Kenneth J. Saunders had crossed with his. His letters were always welcome. It seemed that he had a very efficient secretary who ensured that all those who had sent him greetings last year were to receive the first batch of cards. He added a lengthy letter in his own handwriting to congratulate me on my Abbotship and the success at the examination. He was full of admiration for what I had tried out in the temple. He concluded his newsy letter with the usual invitation:

"I do hope you will some day comply with my repeated advice to come to Calcutta for your studies. Do it soon, while I am still here. There are a few rumblings that someone may want to come here and I might end up in Canterbury."

I wrote him a reply. I told him of my experience in the school set up by Leadbeater in Colombo and underscored that I was beginning to see the value of a University education. I thanked him profusely for making so generous an offer to me even though I was a Buddhist monk, actively engaged with the forces which were undermining the efforts of his colleagues in the Island. I went into detail so that he could safeguard his interests if I were ever to become a bone of contention.

I also had a letter from Professor Rhys Davids outlining the success of the Pali Text Society and thanking me for copies of manuscripts I had found for editors of various Pali works. He also mentioned the encouraging results of a visit to America where he promoted the study of Pali and Buddhism. He was in the process of writing a book on 'Buddhist India.' He had annexed a list of requests for copies of manuscripts. It gave me the impression that the entire Pali Canon might be available in Roman script to scholars of the world long before the

369

same became accessible in full to Sinhala Buddhists in their script. I sent him a reply congratulating him on his many achievements.

I had no letter from the Colonel and that distressed me. Our contacts had been few and far between. But that was not all due to my pre-occupation with my studies. The Colonel has made only a few short visits to the Island. His entire energy was being diverted to his work with the Hindus in India.

Madame Blavatsky's departure from India apparently was not the end of the troubles she was instrumental in creating. Again as Noble Son of Wisdom had found out from his friends in London, she was earnestly seeking a new power base to challenge Olcott. Between his efforts in reforming Hinduism and guarding the Theosophical Society from splintering, he had little time for Sri Lanka.

Fortunately, some of the men whom he had introduced were engaged in good work and the grateful Sri Lankans did not rush to criticize him. At least not at this moment.

Venerable Sumangala had sent me several encouraging notes on what I was doing. I had not told him anything. But news in the Sangha travels fast. He congratulated me on reviving the now-lost innovations in teaching the religion to the masses.

He was interested in the boy who recited the benedictory text at the end of the seven-day recitation of the Book of Protection. If he wants to study in the Learning-Awakening College, the scholar-monk would offer him all facilities, board and lodging and other expenses included. He could remain a lay man, he had clarified. But the boy, renamed from the pejorative Setuva to Buddhadasa, the Servant of the Buddha, was now in a school in Kandy as a ward of the R. M.

With regard to Olcott, he made a very brief comment:

"We are expecting too much from this one man. I am doing my best to get Venerable Gunananda and others to realize that we must rely on ourselves rather than blame him if progress is slow."

Tactful as he was, he did not tell me that Olcott was now a spent force. He knew me as not only an ardent admirer of the Colonel but also his most earnest defender!

I made up my mind to go to Palace Hill at the earliest possible opportunity and informed him accordingly.

My letter to Olcott, which accompanied a New Year card, was meant to cheer him. I wished him a happier and more productive year in which I hoped to see him more often and for longer spells in Sri Lanka. I showed that I not only understood but also admired what he was doing in India for Hinduism.

"We in our tiny Island so close to an overwhelming land mass and a sea of population would never have peace and tranquility, unless the cradle of our civilization emerges from servility and grows in political stability and economic prosperity," I wrote. "A poverty-ridden India can swamp us with a stifling exodus of its ignorant masses, as we in the mountains have already begun to experience. What you do in India may some day save us."

I also congratulated him on a recent speech in which he had restated the objectives of the Theosophical Society. I was glad, I said, that he had dropped involvement with the occult phenomena from the Society's functions.

I offered to be a full time chaplain or teacher if an English school was established in Kandy.

XVII

Once again, I was there in January 1887 to welcome Olcott on his arrival in Colombo. He was slightly emaciated and his drooping eyes revealed the weight of the troubles he faced stoically by himself.

Madame Blavatsky was not making things easy and he was never sure what she would do next. A statement he had made in one of his articles to the effect that "*One should accept nothing, whether written, spoken or taught by sage, revelator, priest or book, unless it reconciled itself with one's reason and common-sense*" had been construed by some to be an attack on her.

Olcott's more urgent concern to was deal with the displeasure that his co-workers in the Island had begun to express quite openly. He tried his best to win back the confidence of his long-standing friend and hero, Venerable Gunananda. In this he failed and was quite apprehensive of the public meeting scheduled for the eighteenth of February at the orator-monk's temple at Kotahena.

"If I am criticized, I have no other option but to apologize," he told me. "The rapid increase of my work in India has compelled me to neglect what was so successfully begun in Ceylon. I know the effects have been really bad. Will you be my interpreter? I want them to understand not only what I say but more importantly what I feel."

I agreed and I was there. Venerable Gunananda had rounded up all the leading monks and the lay leadership. He was an accomplished impresario who could summon meetings with the highest and most powerful representation at very short notice.

He attacked the White Buddhist mercilessly. He could wield the rapier as effectively as the bludgeon. He had his own interpreter who, if at all, made the criticism sound harsher and more ruthless in somewhat bookish English than in the monk's original. What was lost on the Colonel and his handful of foreign Theosophists was the humour with which the consummate orator tempered the bitter truth.

The gist of the attack was that the Theosophical Society had become a Hindu organ and that the Colonel was a puppet who had no strength of conviction to live by his avowed commitment to the religion he proclaimed as his own. The Buddhist Theosophical Society was not spared either.

Two men suffered visibly: Olcott because he had to admit his negligence of the Sri Lankan front: and young Don David who felt that he was responsible for whatever was wrong with the Buddhist Theosophical Society.

Colonel Olcott, however, won the day with his humility. His was a sincere declaration of "*mia culpa*" and a fervent promise to redress.

People had not forgotten that he made the Buddhists of the Island proud the day a public and bank holiday was declared in honour of the Buddha. Besides, other speakers specially Venerable Sumangala and Subhuti of Curse-Sword, took the sting off the criticism by sounding more reasonable and charitable.

Both Olcott and Don David made amends quickly.

Olcott reinvigorated the campaign for Buddhist education and set as his immediate target an English School in Kandy.

With the help of Venerable Sumangala of Sand-Village, Don David campaigned on two fronts: one against the practice in vogue to give children Christian first names and the other against meat-eating. Don David, himself, changed his name to Dharmapala, meaning Protector of Virtue.

These initiatives were to be followed shortly with a similar campaign against Western dress which was gaining currency in the economically and socially better off Sinhala families. He advocated the Indian Sari for women and a modification of the South Indian banian and cloth for men.

The fervent young Dharmapala was a full time partner of Olcott and the Theosophists who were brought from time to time to accompany him. I was, therefore, no longer essential to the campaign for a National Buddhist Educational Fund. As I was no longer the secretarial assistant to Venerable Sumangala, I was not there to accompany him to important functions. But I was not totally out of the picture. Whenever tricky memoranda had to be drafted or scrutinized, the scholar-monk would seek my assistance.

I found myself treated more as an adviser than the Private Secretary I was as a student. I could certainly discern that a certain amount of recognition and respect came to me even from senior monks since I became the Abbot of the Royal Monastery of Sangha-Gem-Field. But I was uneasy. It was as if I had lost a ring-side seat at the precise moment when the game was becoming more engaging and interesting. I took solace by recalling several occasions when I had to leave the Rugby field when the match was at its most tantalizing point.

I discussed my frustrations with my closest friend and colleague who had never failed to be by my side whenever a major crisis came my way. With years of experience in real life as an administrator and diplomat, the Siamese princely monk set me thinking with a simple statement:

"Pure, what you have still to learn is that you and you alone and nobody else are your best friend."

He was correct. I have been at the beck and call of people. Whatever prominence I had in activities at the national level, I had not achieved through my own initiative. Now at the age of twenty-nine, I was being reminded that I had to do things myself. He was right. The few things I had done on my own at the temple had brought me personal satisfaction as well as praise and recognition from others. Why not something more spectacular?

In the train from Colombo to Kandy I mulled over several projects and struck upon one as the most feasible, provided, of course, the prelate was in agreement. I met the prelate late in the evening as he was reading the latest issue of Moon-Ray in the verandah of his unpretentious dwelling house. I knelt before him and worshipped him thrice.

"Ah! The Abbot of the Royal Monastery of Sangha-Gem-Field. How are you and what brings you here?"

He was pleased to see me.

I told him of my visit to Colombo and meetings with Colonel Olcott.

"You don't hear much of him these days," the prelate said. "All I read in the paper is on the son of Don Carolis who talks some good sense. Do you know him?"

I told him of our meetings and my impression that he would soon be a recognized Buddhist leader in the country.

I had to wait until I was asked whether I had anything specific to discuss with the prelate. In our culture, to ask anyone the reason for a visit or a meeting would be rude and unacceptable. I remembered how my father taught me this rule of etiquette. This was his story:

"One season, things were so bad at home that we had to consume the stock of seed rice which ordinarily would not be touched. I had to borrow a few bushels of seed rice. But I did not know from whom. So I went first of all to an uncle who appeared to be the most prosperous. He didn't ask me why I came. If he asked me I would have been obliged to tell the truth. Then if he was in some dire difficulty and could not lend me the seed rice I wanted, he would have been very embarrassed. So we chatted about everything else: health of family members, a pending lawsuit over the partition of a property, the outcome of his recent land deals, prices of vegetables and transport costs and so forth. As we

374

talked, it dawned on me that my uncle has had even a worse year than I had both due to illness in the family and costly business failures. I made my visit appear a purely social affair and left his place without asking him to help me. It was on my third visit to a cousin that I found that the question could be posed. He was very pleased to oblige me. It takes time, son. But no one is embarrassed."

The situation as regards the proposal I wanted to place before the prelate was in some ways identical. It was important for me to know how he reacted to what was happening in the country and how he viewed the new institutions which the national and religious revival had brought into existence in the maritime regions. Apparently he was pleased with whatever he had read in the newspaper, which under the management of young Dharmapala, hitherto known as Don David, was better focussed on national issues.

"Now, our Abbot, there must be something that must have brought you at this hour to see me?"

"Yes, Venerable Prelate, I have an idea which I want to place before you to seek your advice. I am wondering whether we should have in Kandy a College for the formal education of our novices and younger monks ......"

"You mean an institution like Learning-Awakening or Learning-Adornment?"

"Yes, Venerable Prelate."

"You really think that these new-fangled things have any relevance to us? Aren't our novices and younger monks given a good enough training in their temples?"

My heart sank. Did I pose the question at a wrong time? Is he against the revival of the ancient system of formal education for monks which Venerable Sumangala pioneered. Or, was he unaware of the history of monastic education? How should I answer his questions? Should I tell him that the Learning-Awakening and Learning-Adornment Colleges were based on ancient models which were well documented in our literature?

I could tell him of the Cremation Ground College of Polonnaruva of the twelfth century or of the two Colleges of the fifteenth century headed by the great scholar-monks, Rahula of Ferry-Village and Forest-Gem of Kera-tree-stone. I had memorized the verses in the two Messenger-poems which described these two institutions and gave valuable information on the student-body, teachers, curricula and methods of study. Did the prelate want to be convinced? Or, had he made up his mind?

The awkward silence was broken by the prelate.

"I am not against your idea, Little Name," he said in an affable and friendly tone. The choice of the informal form of addressing a young monk was even more encouraging. "All I want to know is what you think. You see. You are the best qualified person to answer my questions. You know what we do. You are a graduate of the College at Palace Hill. Didn't you win the gold medal? You also know what has happened since the most notable revival of learning which the King of the Sangha, Refuge-maker, brought about one hundred and thirty five years ago. Tell me, Little Name. How did the Two Chapters in Kandy lose the leadership in learning that they enjoyed at that time?

It was not always that a young monk of twenty-nine is asked by the highest administrative and spiritual head of his sect to speak his mind, even if he was prematurely appointed the Abbot of an important temple. I was mindful of the importance of tempering truth with tact. But such an abundance of caution was not demanded.

As I proceeded with a historical analysis of the factors which isolated the temples in the erstwhile Kandyan Kingdom from the laity, the prelate proved to be more critical of his predecessors and colleagues than I could ever have dreamt.

"It's a bitter truth, Little Name. Our temples do not belong to the people. We do not depend on the charity and the goodwill of the people. We thrive on past royal patronage. Our major concern is with the management and protection of the temporalities. I ask myself often the difference between me and the scholar-monks of the low-country. I am the elected head of the Chapter. But they have charisma and natural leadership.

"In fact, I asked Colonel Olcott when we had a special exposition of the Tooth Relic for him. What he told me had made a big impact. He said, 'Venerable Prelate, they had to earn their prestige. In your case, as I see it, your are either born into it or have it thrust on you'

"I have also observed what you do. Your school is a thriving institution. The R. M. in his fifties comes to you for advice as if he is only a humble acolyte. You are a legend in the region. Everyone speaks of your Sunday school and your new ways of teaching the doctrine to the people.

"Little Name, I have long waited to see when you will come up to me to tell me what we should do."

I could have never have had a more encouraging response. But I wanted one thing clarified.

"Venerable Prelate, with your blessing I will begin action immediately. I wish to have your approval on one matter. To build an institution, we need public support. It is no secret that the economically better off people in the town are those who have emigrated from the low-country. We will have to bring them in."

"Yes, Little Name. That's another bitter truth."

The College was aptly named in honour of the last King of the Sangha in the Island's history. Without the restoration of the monastic order in 1753 with the direct assistance of the reigning monarch and the cooperation of the Dutch Regime of the low-country, Buddhism and Buddhist scholarship would have long been dead.

It required much coaxing for the prelate to assume the Principalship. Despite his sound background in Buddhism acquired informally through self-learning, for the most part, he was either too modest or lacked confidence. I promised to take care of the administrative and organizational details and also to handle the bulk of teaching responsibilities until a qualified staff could be recruited.

My first obstacle was in finding enough students. Personal messages sent to all temples affiliated to the Chapter brought discouraging responses.

They led to the painful discovery that young monks were an extremely rare commodity. I could imagine what was going wrong. My own uncle, Chief Monk, delayed taking a pupil until I grew up. The temptation to keep the Abbotship within one's family was too great to be eradicated from the feudalistic mind-set of most senior monks and their families.

With the approval of the prelate, I embarked on a tour of temples with increased recruitment to the Sangha as the target. The ageing buggy cart proved to be an asset.To my greatest delight, I discovered that every temple had bands of acolytes, who were aspiring to be ordained. There was no dearth of candidates.

It would not be correct to say that my mission was a hundred per cent success. I met some of the most die-hard conservatives who had a hundred arguments why an expanded Sangha was not desirable - so obsessed were they by their dwindling resources resulting from shrinking landholdings!

From their point of view, there was reason to be anxious. The best of temple land had gone into coffee and tea plantations as a result of the Waste Land policy. Encouraged by the neglect of state responsibility to protect Buddhist temporalities, tenants flouted tenure terms and temples were indeed impoverished.

The low-country model of temples supported by the laity that the monks served was rejected as either too risky or too cumbersome.

In spite of this opposition, enough novices were recruited for the College to start by the end of 1887 with an enrolment of thirty-seven, of whom twenty-eight were novices recruited as a result of my campaign. A temporary hall, roofed with woven coconut fronds, on the slope to the north of the walled bathing well by the lake, housed the College.

The headquarters of the Flower Garden Chapter was not an homogeneous monastic institution. It was a conglomeration of many temples, each of which was connected with an important temple in the Region.

When a senior monk came from one of these temples to serve in the Executive Committee or as a prelate or one of his two deputies, the practice was to set up a self-sufficient dwelling house. Each such dwelling house not only carried the name of the original temple but was maintained by it.

As the College flourished, I was allotted a piece of land so that a dwelling house for me could be constructed. My five lay brothers, under the expert supervision of the one in robes, constructed a spacious house in no time. I could accommodate the two new teachers who had been my batch-mates at the College in Palace Hill.

The R. M. bought a bigger carriage for him and his family and refurbished the old carriage. He donated it to me with a horse. It was certainly more comfortable and faster than Chief Monk's buggy cart.

The prelate spared no effort to make a success of the College. He worked as a regular teacher and taught Buddhism to the first grade every afternoon. He used Olcott's Catechism to provide the framework for his course and utilized the original discourses of the Buddha to amplify what the Colonel had discussed briefly. The spirit of dedication to learning, which the prelate demonstrated, galvanized the Sangha.

The other two teachers and I knew enough of the strengths and weaknesses of the curriculum of the Learning-Awakening College to concentrate on a new curriculum, better graduated according to age, aptitude and achievement of individual students. My exposure to senior secondary education in a modern Christian school came handy in this exercise. We tried to draw on the best of both systems and our students were delighted with some of the elements we introduced.

Enrollments had doubled in the first year and two more teachers had joined us. The anniversary was marked with a prize-giving. Stanley Williams was invited as the guest of honour and he surprised everyone with a fluent speech in Pali on the value of learning. Two students responded in Pali and Sanskrit. But theirs were prepared speeches which came nowhere close to the eloquent presentation of the Assistant Government Agent.

It was fulfilling work. The College was my first priority. I went to Sangha-Gem-Field as often as I could. I made it a point to see Aunt Flower, Uncle Victor and Slim-Jewel and their children at least once a month.

It was a pleasure to see them prospering in their own chosen ways. Uncle Victor was the acting head of the Native Department. One of his duties was to find background information for the Government Agent's Diary. With the Government Agents's interest in the social organization, laws and customs, beliefs and cults and folk-tales of the Kandyan villagers, Uncle Victor spent days in the field collecting data which were as edifying to him as they were useful to his superior officer. As a result, Uncle Victor had become a treasure house of interesting stories to the great delight of the children and, of course, myself.

I admired Slim-Jewel's single-handed efforts to bring up her young family. By sheer dint of hard work, she passed the necessary examinations and was confirmed as a nurse. She worked in a ward where nuns of a Catholic Order volunteered as nurses and nurse-aides and did some of the most menial work. She was full of praise for their efforts and urged me to get Buddhists to be similarly conscious of the importance of social service.

I wished I had the resources. It was a pity that the Order of Buddhist Nuns had disappeared and the Sangha did not have a female counterpart. The prevailing opinion among the senior monks was that it was beyond their powers to restore an Order of Nuns.

The Rules of Discipline as laid down by the Buddha required a minimum quorum of nuns with higher ordination to recruit new nuns. This quorum was not available in Sri Lanka, Burma, Siam or Cambodia.

The more I explained to Slim-Jewel the obstacles against the resuscitation of the Order of Nuns, the more she expressed her disapproval of the die-hard conservatism of the Sangha.

"Why can't they find the quorum of nuns from other Buddhist countries," she argued.

She always concluded by saying that I could do something if I really wanted!

My brother's son grew up in stature and confidence. That he was handsome was beyond question. Slim-Jewel loved him as though he was of her own flesh and blood. Moon-Beam took special care of the brother and took pride in the sisterly authority she exercised over him.

Every time we met, I would tease him about his name.

"Don't call me by that name," he once told me. "I am not "Eat when given and run away.' I am Middle Banda Valour-Lion."

"Don't you remember that you told me that you liked to be called 'Eat when given and run away'?"

"Maybe, when I was small. Little Uncle gave that name to tease me. I am a big boy now. I don't remember anything and I don't want to remember anything. This is my sister. That's my mother. I am Middle Banda and you are my father's brother."

A long and firm speech for a lad of seven!

When he was out of the house playing, we adults analyzed his mature replies and decided among ourselves never to raise any questions about his very young days. He was consciously trying to forget whatever memories he had of his childhood. Slim-Jewel had done her best to enable him to be integrated into the new family. She had a few jolts in the process.

Twice, his biological mother had come to see him, but thoughtfully as a topless outcaste beggar. When on the second occasion, the little boy insisted of giving her more money and wanted to hand it over himself, Slim-Jewel had a cold sweat.

At her requast, I had to go to the settlement of outcastes across the river to advise the woman not to visit the boy under any pretext. I was tactful and stressed the need to enable the child to take full advantage of his new environment.

"But, Venerable Sir, I am his mother. He is my own flesh and blood," she pleaded with me on that occasion. "I turned my own blood into milk and fed him. I want to see his face from time to time. Otherwise my grief of separation from him will kill me. But I'll never let him know who I am. I promise."

I could understand the pangs of a mother and promised to make suitable arrangements.

Though the College kept me busier than I had expected, I managed to keep in touch with my growing circle of friends, admirers and well-wishers.

Ernest Dickinson, who was still the Government Agent of the Western Province, was one of the earliest to congratulate me on deciding to set up a monastic College in Kandy. He did not fail to remind me of a promise I had made nearly a decade ago:

"Bongyi, you have an unfulfilled promise to keep. I hope you remember it."

For over three months, I went to the Octagon of the Temple of the Sacred Tooth Relic after the evening service and prepared a comprehensive catalogue of the palmleaf manuscripts and also arranged them in logical order to make them more accessible to readers. I reported the conclusion of the mission to Dickinson through Stanley Williams who wrote a glowing account of what I had achieved.

I sent a copy of the catalogue to Rheinhold Rost of India House in London, saying that researchers would like to know the holdings in another important library in the Island. Over several decades he had proved to be the best focal point of contact with the expanding galaxy of Oriental scholars in the West.

Noble Son of Wisdom who was in constant communication with me did surprise me with a dawn visit to celebrate the tenth anniversary of our joint higher ordination.

Without the fanfare of elephants, drummers and dancers and the comic relief of our fancy royal raiments, we offered flowers and lamps at the Temple of the Sacred Tooth Relic and retraced on foot the route of the procession that took us to the historic Chapter House where higher ordination was conducted.

To my surprise, though not to his, the prelate and other senior monks were assembled in the Chapter House to chant benedictory verses and to bless us. The Siamese monk certainly outshone me with a brilliant speech in impeccable Sinhala.

XVIII

I wrote to Colonel Olcott regularly even though he was no longer as prompt in replying. Occasionally I would get a letter from someone in Adyar and invariably the news was disturbing.

Madame Blavatsky was active in England. She had set up her own Esoteric Section of the Theosophical Society, written a new book called "*The Secret Doctrine*", found a coterie of supporters who subscribed to her views and begun to publish her own journal called "Lucifer."

It was abundantly clear that an impassable chasm had developed between the founders of the Theosophical Society. Colonel Olcott had told somebody that he was in such a state of nervous unrest such as that of a person in a bombarded town.

A letter I received from the Colonel around the end of 1888, however, showed that he had reason to believe that better times were ahead. He was an incurable optimist and at the nick of time things turned up to sustain his optimism.

This time the oxygen of rejuvenation had come to Olcott in the form of a Buddhist delegation from Japan. He was flattered by the fact that no less a person than the renowned Buddhist reformer of the Land of the Rising Sun, Zenshiro Nogouchi, had come to Adyar, called him 'a Bodhisatva (Buddha-to-be) of the nineteenth century and invited him to Japan to lead a Buddhist revival.

"I hope to travel via Colombo and hope to see you, because I have something very important to entrust to you," his letter continued. "You will recall the many discussions we had on a rapprochement of the various traditions of Buddhism into a United Buddhist World. I have been working on a common platform to which the Buddhists of all traditions could subscribe. I wish to discuss that with you before I take it up with our high priests. I have never forgotten how your presence of mind saved me from impending disaster."

He never forgot to express his gratitude for my little role in getting his Catechism approved by the scholar-monks of Palace Hill.

Around the same time, I received a card and a longish letter form Right Reverend Kenneth J. Saunders. It dealt mainly with conclusions he had derived from a study of contemporary religious reforms in India.

"Whatever the Christian missionaries had done in Ceylon, Burma or India, the single most important outcome is the revival of the national religions," he wrote. "None of my colleagues like to hear this and half would not believe it. But I am more than ever before convinced that Christianity played an essential catalytic role in bringing about the revival of Buddhism in Ceylon and Burma and the reform and modernization of Hinduism in India."

He discussed various movements that had been launched to reconcile into a logical whole the different cults and practices which constituted Hinduism. He made fine distinctions with regard to the different approaches to divinity, individual soul, authority of ancient scriptures and forms of worship. He analyzed the plurality of religious or spiritual experience within Hinduism and argued that a form of devotionalism similar to that of Christianity was gaining currency.

I read the letter several times. I understood what he said as he wrote so very lucidly. But I had no idea of the issues discussed. I was totally ignorant of the basics which he had taken for granted. It was a revelation - a rude eye-opener. Here I was with twice as much education that an average monk could have had in Sri Lanka. But I knew nothing of either Hinduism or the very background to the religion which I had inherited as mine.

A chill went down my spine as I thought of the request embodied in the letter of Colonel Olcott. What if I find myself in an equally vulnerable position as an ignoramus of the highest degree as regards the different traditions of Buddhism. What do I know of Buddhism in China or Japan or Tibet?

I recalled Chief Monk's story of the frog in the well whose entire universe was circumscribed to the tiny circle of the sky it saw from the bottom of the pit. I was a frog in a well, so insular and so ignorant. I had to do something to remedy this deficiency.

I called on Colonel Olcott just before he embarked on a ship to Japan. He gave me a copy of fourteen paragraphs into which he had tried to summarize the beliefs and doctrines which were common to the three main traditions of Buddhism: the Tradition of the Elders of Sri Lanka, Burma, Siam and Cambodia; the Great Vehicle of China and Japan, and the Vehicle of the Thunderbolt of Tibet and Mongolia. I was requested to have it translated into Sinhala so that it could be discussed with the senior scholar-monks on his return.

One look at the document convinced me that my premonitions were right. How could I know that these fourteen points were common to all three traditions when I knew nothing more than the tradition into which I was born?

I also had an opportunity to discuss Japanese Buddhism with Zenshiro Nogouchi. He was exceedingly polite and gentle. He answered my questions most patiently. But how long could I expect him to explain rudimentary aspects of a vast tradition?

If nothing else, I had to learn more of Buddhism and Hinduism.

With Noble Son of Wisdom, I paid a visit to Don David who had now renounced that name along with his Western clothes. We were received with due respect by Dharmapala, and conducted to the elegant office from which he carried on his multiple functions on behalf of the Buddhist Theosophical Society. He was excited about the forthcoming visit to Japan. He was grumbling that he had not enough time to prepare for the trip. At our request, he explained:

"I went to Adyar without knowing what to expect, what to see or what to study. That's not the way to visit a new place. I came back without the foggiest idea of what was happening in Madras. Pettah library has at least ten books on Japan. But I could hardly read two. Something very great is happening in that country over the last two or three decades. They call it the Meiji Restoration and what I understand is that some major efforts are being made to modernize education, urban life and industry. I wish we do not go from temple to temple and lose the opportunity to observe how an Asian country could enter the twentieth century on par with the Western powers."

"Didn't you talk to Sensei Nogouchi?" asked Noble Son of Wisdom.

"I did and he had left me more confused. He says that there were some fifty or sixty sects or Buddhist traditions in Japan and a compilation called the Lotus Sutra and its numerous commentaries are the main source for Japanese Buddhism. They revere this book with a formula similar to that we use to pay homage to the Buddha. He also tells me of Buddhist priests who are married, have children, do business and retain temple properties as family heirlooms for generations. These he contrasts with an austere meditating sect called Zen whose discipline and devotion are held to be the most exemplary. It seems there is also a sect similar to Tibetan and Mongolian Buddhism where worship is accompanied by magical incantations, symbols, and mystic gestures or signs. I am sure there is much to learn."

I told him of the fourteen-point common platform for which Olcott planned to obtain the consensus of diverse Buddhist traditions. Not only did he know about it but had his own interpretation of the Colonel's objective.

"I think the Colonel wanted to do something spectacular in India to mark the tenth anniversary of his arrival in Bombay in 1878. That was one reason for him to have concentrated on India during the last two years. But the unfortunate scandal on Madame Blavatsky's occult phenomena upset his plans. My guess is that he wants to do something next year to mark the tenth anniversary of his activities in the Island. I would suggest an English school in Kandy and another, possibly in Galle, similar to Leadbeater's school. But his horizons are wider now. He may be wanting to emerge as some sort of Asian Apostle of Buddhism. That's how I see his efforts for what he calls a United Buddhist World. It's a good thing."

It was the sympathetic assessment of an admiring friend. The Colonel would have been happy if he heard himself being described as a potential Asian Apostle of Buddhism. My own parochial interest was in a school in Kandy. I said so and requested Dharmapala to let the Colonel know of my interest.

"All we want is a devoted young man who would run the school until it gets registered and recognized," he replied with authority. Obviously, he was donning the invisible hat of the Manager of Buddhist Schools of the Buddhist Theosophical Society.

We chanted three discourses of the Book of Protection along with the usual benedictory stanzas, tied a holy thread which the Siamese monk had thoughtfully brought with him and wished Dharmapala a safe journey to Japan. He went on his knees to worship us.

"Pure," said Noble Son of Wisdom as we left the premises of the Buddhist Theosophical Society. "You were talking of a young man to set up a school in Kandy. I met recently a likely candidate - a young man who has a tremendous background. Very much yours but the other way around. He comes from Kelaniya, very close to the temple, and belongs to a very influential family. From his childhood he has been closely associated with the 'Other Place.'"

"You mean the Learning-Adornment College of Venerable Light of the Doctrine of the Red-Flower-Grove?" I asked.

Venerable Sumangala and Light of the Doctrine were pupils of the same teacher. Two years after the former established the Learning-Awakening College in Palace Hill within the city of Colombo, the latter established in Kelaniya a similar institution by the name of Learning-Adornment College in 1875.

Though totally unintended by the founders, the two institutions had developed a healthy rivalry between them and each one's specificity was marked by their policies and traditions. Over the last decade or so, they had developed into a kind of relationship which the Sri Lankan historians associated with the Great Monastery and Sanctuary-Peak Monastery of ancient Anuradhapura or Flower Garden Chapter and Horse-Peak Chapter of present Kandy and which British and American scholars associated with Oxford and Cambridge in England and Harvard and Yale in USA.

While Venerable Sumangala sought government assistance and obtained a grant-in-aid, the other wished to maintain their independence through self-reliance. If the Learning-Awakening was overly traditional, the other place was more innovative in content and methods of instruction. The most easily distinguishable specificity was in the use of the two n-sounds and l-sounds in spelling in Sinhala. Another was that they tended to wear the robes as they did in Kandy with the right shoulder bare while at Palace Hill we covered both shoulders.

If Noble Son of Wisdom intended to tease me because my loyalties, perhaps his as well, were to the College at Palace Hill, I did not react. So he continued,

"His name is Don Baron and he carries the family name Jayatilaka. He had a first class grounding in classical Sinhala and in both Pali and Sanskrit until he was thirteen. Then he was admitted to Wesley College where he received a perfect English education. He knows his Buddhism and its history. He's a born scholar with an insatiable thirst for knowledge. How much he knows and what questions he raises in search of further knowledge!"

I was sure that Don Baron was an unusually promising young man because the Siamese colleague was not in the habit of dispensing his praise too liberally.

"What's he planning to do?" I asked.

"To cooperate with Colonel Olcott in setting up another English school - possibly in Kandy. He's such a great admirer of the Colonel."

"That will be wonderful for two reasons. Now that Leadbeater's school is showing signs of rapid progress, one in Kandy would be timely. The other is to start a school with a national as the head, if that's possible. Such a move would give a correct signal to our people. It'll be a tragedy if people begin to think that a Buddhist English school should have a foreign head to give it any stature."

"I'll tell Don Baron what you said when we next meet. He comes to discuss with me how schools are run in England and how my son is progressing in Oxford. He has hitched his wagon to a high and distant star."

"I would like very much to meet him."

"You should. You have so much in common."

"Study abroad" advanced from a desire, to an urge, to an obsession. I was fortunate that I had a patron saint in Calcutta ever ready to help me. I wrote him a detailed letter explaining why I made up my mind to take advantage of his kind offer.

I waited impatiently for a reply. Three weeks later came a letter which bore the welcome post mark of Calcutta. But it was not what I had expected.

A personal assistant of the Right Reverend Metropolitan had written to say that he was out on a mission in Burma and would not be back for a month. But so certain I was of Right Reverend Saunders' favourable intervention that I began making arrangements to find people to take over my various responsibilities.

My brother was already the *de facto* Abbot of the temple and he could carry on more effectively once I had completed the necessary paper work to transfer the management of the temporalities. The R. M. was prepared to be the Manager of the school in addition to being the Chairman of the School Board. Edward Perera undertook the supervision of the Sunday School.

All these arrangements I could make myself. But to find someone to undertake my managerial, supervisory and teaching duties at the King of the Sangha College required the concurrence of the prelate. I could not go to him until I had a positive reply from Calcutta.

The telegram had been delivered in my absence and received by none other than the prelate himself. By the time I returned from a visit to Uncle Victor and Aunt Flower, it had been opened, read and translated to the prelate by one of my colleagues in the College.

"Are you planning to go to India for any studies, Little Name?" asked the prelate whose tone did suggest a tinge of concealed annoyance.

"I am hoping to, if one of my school teachers can still help me," I said trying my best to indicate that nothing more than some tentative inquiries were in progress.

If I had not told him when I wrote to the Metropolitan, it was simply because I was not required to do so. As the prelate and the head of the Chapter, he had no control over me as our organization differed in this respect from the Christian Church. I was free to do what I considered fit as long as I made satisfactory arrangements for my duties to be covered.

"I am glad that you have a good friend in Padre Saunders," he said handing over to me the opened telegram. "I remember him. He was a very nice man."

I read it and could not believe my eyes.

"ALL ARRANGEMENTS MADE. MUST BE HERE BY SECOND WEEK OF JULY. REPLY ACCEPTANCE IMMEDIATELY."

Maybe, my face shone or there was a twinkle in my eye.

"You are happy and you want to go? Have you enough time? Hardly two months."

I told him of the steps I had taken in anticipation of Saunders' reply.

"Venerable Prelate, as regards my responsibilities in the College, I postponed any discussion with you until I was sure that I could go this year."

"I am sure you have something in mind."

I told him what I had thought out. He was pleased that I had identified two staff members: one to take over managerial and logistic functions and the other to handle academic supervision.

"I will miss you, Little Name. What eluded you at sixteen is coming to you at thirty-two. You are destined to have a University education and I can only congratulate you."

In appreciation of the prelate's encouragement, I worked in the College to the last possible day and travelled to Colombo with just a day to spare to catch the boat to Calcutta. I saw him just before my departure.

He wished me well and asked me to remember "Son, you have a land of your birth to serve". He recited the line from a popular Sinhala verse.

It was a busy day in Colombo. I paid my respects to my teachers at Palace Hill, obtained letters of introduction from several Indian students and called on Venerable Sumangala. He received me with affection and wished me every success. As a parting gift, he gave me a copy of the *Great Chronicle* which he and another scholar had translated into Sinhala.

"Read this on board the ship. Little Name," he advised. "You will land not too far from Tamluk, the ancient Tambalitti, from where the boat bringing the sacred Bo-tree from Asoka the Righteous left. The

Rose-Apple Continent is the sacred land of our religion. Do take some time off to see the places hallowed by the presence of the Buddha."

It was ironical that he was advising me to see the Buddhist monuments in India, the Rose-Apple Continent of our classics. Apart from the temple at Kelaniya and those in Kandy, the only site of historical significance in the Island I had seen was the Temple of Light near Matale.

Exactly two thousand years ago, the Buddhist Canon and its Commentaries were reduced to writing for the first time at this historic monastery where an impressive array of massive rocks carry ancient inscriptions.

Every morning in the course of worship, I had recited the list of sixteen sacred spots associated with the tradition of the Buddha's three visits to the Island. I had been to Kelaniya. My grandparents died while climbing down the peak of the Buddha's Footprint. Possibly, I would have a glimpse of this sacred mountain from the ship and visit the site of the Bo-tree in Buddha-Gaya before I see its surviving sapling at Anuradhapura!

The afternoon was entirely left free for a leisurely meeting with Noble Son of Wisdom. I had a vague premonition that this would be the last time we meet. I shuddered at the thought of its possible implications. I wished him long life in the best of health. I added a silent wish for mine as well. He, too, apparently had a similar prognosis and was giving it a more logical explanation:

"We may not meet again for a long time, Pure. Maybe, never in our present states."

He had purchased my ticket and refused re-imbursement. I had to be on board at ten in the night for the boat was to leave early in the morning the next day.

We had our mid-day meal together in his modest room at the school. We recalled our first meeting in our fancy royal raiments on the day of higher ordination eleven years ago. I expressed my gratitude for his many acts of kindness. He, in turn, said how much he valued my friendship and the sense of belonging that I had developed in him toward everything Sri Lankan. Both of us gave vent to sloppy nostalgia and tried to capture a few moments of togetherness in a relationship which had been rich in its diversity and intense in its commitment. I saw in him a father, a brother, a friend and a colleague. I said how privileged I was to have come to know him. In his sincere modesty, he paid the same compliment to me.

A tap on the door announced a visitor. It was Don Baron who had been asked to come so that we could meet. Neither of us needed an introduction as Noble Son of Wisdom had told each about the other.

I was impressed with the tall, slim, handsome young man, smartly dressed in a Western suit - grey flannel trousers, white silk shirt, navy blue muffler with white polka dots, black blazer, patent leather shoes and felt hat. His roundish face with sparkling eyes glowed as he gave us a benign smile and bent forward to remove his shoes.

Once inside the room, he went on his knees and worshipped us. He refused to take a chair that was offered to him and remained seated on the floor. We talked of our studies. He had registered for the degree examination of the University of Calcutta and was planning to take the examination the following year.

"What you are doing is certainly better, Venerable Sir. What I plan to do is to go to England some day and get a higher degree from Oxbridge and also take the Barristers from one of the Inns."

It would be a palpable lie to say that I understood every word of what he said. It required some lengthy explanation before I realized that the ambitious young man knew where he wanted to go in life and how. I told him of the recent revelation of the depth of my ignorance and the resulting urge to spend a few years in formal study.

"To know how little you know! Isn't that the highest of all knowledge?"

"Yes, Sir," I replied. "But the discovery is truly devastating."

"Venerable Sir, my visit today is not just to say 'Hallo and Good-bye' to you. I wish to have some advice from you. I am told you know Colonel Olcott from the day of his first arrival in the Island nine years ago. I hope to work with him closely and, if possible, set up a school like the one that Mr. Leadbeater is developing here in Colombo. I hear you did some work there also."

"Let me see. You have three questions. First about Olcott. I came to know him and Madame Blavatsky around the time that I lost my parents in quick succession. They had been a sort of substitute parents at a time I was feeling my way in life. So personally, I have the highest esteem and affection for them both. At one stage, I was close enough to them to see them as real human beings rather than the idols who were the subjects of the adulation of the masses. With all their human weaknesses, they have made a unique contribution to the national awakening and the Buddhist revival of the country......"

"Venerable Sir, you seem to have some reservations when you emphasize their human character."

"Not at all. Not at all," I pleaded. "My affection for them has remained unwavering because I recognize them to be human. Specially the Colonel. I see him as ambitious, self-righteous, short-fused, rigid and over-bearing. That makes him a steam-roller. No obstacle is too great for him. He brooks no nonsense. Nothing that he has so far accomplished would have been possible if he was goody goody all the time. What you should be happy about is that he is on our side. He is sincere when he upholds the religious heritage of India and Sri Lanka. He has no patience for the kind of sectarianism that prompts us to see differences between Buddhism and Hinduism. Will you be bothered if his critics say that he is changing sides: a Buddhist in Sri Lanka and a Hindu in India?"

"I don't think that would bother me very much."

"You must also remember his Yankee characteristic of being sure of everything and frank to the point of calling you the most abominable names. Will that bother you?"

"Can you please give me an example."

"You must have heard him attack the monks as lazy, ignorant and unmotivated. He once called me a Fifth Columnist of Christian Missionaries in the Sangha and threatened to expose me and my uncle if that was the last thing he did in the Island. How would you react to such an insult?"

"I would go by his motives and will not be overly concerned if he genuinely wants to get something speeded up."

"Would it bother you if he starts a project and half-way goes to India and forgets about it until he next comes here?"

"That depends on whether he delegates authority."

"No. He's more a visionary and less a practical manager to think of such details as delegation. But this is a good point to take up the case of Leadbeater. He knew this aspect of the Colonel. So he never bothered to seek delegation of authority or ask for any other instruction. They set up the school together but Leadbeater took charge of the nuts and bolts. The school has prospered and the people of this city are the winners. Olcott has since moved into other fields. Now his mind is on unifying the three traditions of Buddhism and building a Unified Buddhist World."

"Thank you, Venerable Sir, you answered my third question, too. You are convinced that Leadbeater is a good role-model and his school is the prototype for a school, say in Kandy."

"Provided, you, Sir, can be like Leadbeater and do it alone."

"I understand, Venerable Sir. You have been most helpful"

392

We continued our discussion on Kandy of which he knew little, other than of a few prosperous families who had recently migrated from the low-country and taken control of the town's growing commercial sector. I gave him names of people to contact and wrote out a few letters of introduction. I liked his enthusiasm and moreso his methodical preparation for an activity which was yet to be put on the drawing board.

This remarkable quality of foresight was bound to make him a great national leader in the future, I noted this in my diary that day.

After Don Baron left us, we had some tea and returned to a review of a friendship which had left an indelible mark in both of us. Our plan was to leave around dusk to the Buddhist Theosophical Society to spend a couple of hours with Don David or rather Dharmapala. But Noble Son of Wisdom thought it better if we went there earlier.

If there was any reason for this change of plan, he did not tell me. We sent my trunk to the jetty through a teacher with the ticket and walked to the headquarters of the BTS.

We were taken to the office of the young recluse and we found him busy drawing a cartoon.

"I didn't know that you are also a cartoonist?" remarked the Siamese colleague.

"It's one more way of giving a message. Yes. Venerable Sir, I like to draw."

He showed the cartoon which depicted a rustic-looking Sinhala man being blinded, robbed and harassed by a group of men, each in a distinctive dress to depict their ethnic origin.

"You see, Venerable Sirs. England the mighty metropolitan of an empire over which the sun never sets has an Alien Prevention Act. But our little Island is not so protected. On the other hand, the Administration encourages aliens from all over the world to come here and exploit the natives."

He held out the cartoon.

"This is an Afghan from faraway Afghanistan. He comes here and establishes himself as an itinerant loanshark who exploits the small fry. This is a Chettiar from Cochin and he is the big-time money lender and import-export agent. The trade is in the hands of these recently arrived Moors in Fez cap. This is the labour supervisor of a tea estate who gives work only to immigrant South Indian labour. On horseback with a whip in hand is the planter and even his whip falls on this innocent man. I want to publish it with a poem in which I will identify each type of Alien and urge for an Alien Prevention Law for the Island."

393

"Makes sense," remarked Noble son of Wisdom.

"We have to fight on many fronts, Venerable Sirs. But education to my mind is the first and the most important. I am happy that both of you are active in this field."

The young agitator did not hide his disappointment over my decision:

"You are wanted, here, at this crucial juncture. The least I can say is that this is not the time to be selfish and self-centred. What we do or do not now will decide whether we can be once again a great nation. Any way, you have made up your mind and I wish you every success. But do come back soon and give us a helping hand."

I wanted to explain but was prevented by Noble Son of Wisdom.

"We need scholars as well as agitators," he told Dharmapala. "You will give him your blessings if you have read his first book."

I had no idea what he meant until he took out a copy of "*Sermons of a Rainy Season*" which Edward Perera had published.

The young recluse leafed through the book for a while.

"Remarkable! Very well-said. I agree, Venerable Sir. We certainly need scholars or rather thinkers like you."

In a more relaxed ambience, we discussed tasks in hand and those yet to be conceived. I sounded him on my childhood dream of being a Buddhist missionary in a foreign land.

"We have our hands full here, Venerable Sir. Before we think of propagating Buddhism abroad, we must set the house in order here."

In a tone no less vituperative than that of Colonel Olcott discussing the same subject, he found fault with everybody, the Sangha, the laity, the Administration for their failure to safeguard Buddhism. Of monks he was the most critical.

"All day long they chew betel until the spittoons overflow."

"I think, Sir, you are over-reaching yourself," I had to say even if he got angry. "This kind of blanket criticism of all and sundry does us no good. Do you know what hundreds of monks are doing at this particular hour? They are writing books, teaching students both lay and clergy, raising funds to maintain schools, building temples in remote unserved areas, attending to the sick,....."

"I am sorry, Venerable Sir. I am really very sorry. I should be more careful."

I returned to the subject of propagating Buddhism in foreign countries. Again, his mind was set. I asked him whether he remembered the plea made by Sir Edwin Arnold about the restitution of Buddhist Monuments of India to Buddhists. He thought for a while.

"If you are thinking how you can still be useful to the Buddhist cause from India, this is something worth pursuing. You have a point here, Venerable Sir."

Agreeing to be in touch by mail, I wished him a successful career as a Buddhist leader and set out to the Jetty. We walked along Norris Street in front of the Fort Railway Station.

Turning to face the Railway Station, Noble Son of Wisdom pointed to the centre of the open esplanade:

"Pure, do you know when yours would once again be a great nation? When you have your own rulers who will instal a statue in honour of Olcott here and name this the Olcott Boulevard."

"Where will they have a statue and a road for Don David - Dharmapala?" I asked in jest.

"Right in the heart of the elitist quarter of Colombo," he replied in a jiffy.

"They will both have statues and roads?"

"No doubt, Pure. So will Don Baron."

"How are you so sure?" I asked him.

"Pure, yours is a grateful nation. Your history shows it."

XIX

What a thoughtful friend I had in Noble Son of Wisdom! He orchestrated the formalities at the jetty to ensure that I got on board without delay. He sent me by an earlier launch and tarried behind to ensure that my baggage was properly taken care of. But what I did not know at the moment was that he had synchronized my embarkment with a surprise welcome committee on board.

I had hardly put my head out of the launch when I heard a familiar voice of a child saying in a loud whisper, "Coming. He's coming."

At the top of the gangplank were Autumn-Moon, Moon-Beam and Middle Banda in gleaming white dresses with flowers in their hands. Behind them were Uncle Victor, Aunt Flower and Slim-Jewel. What a surprise! What a pleasant surprise! Tears of joy ran down my cheeks.

"This is an idea of Stanley Williams," explained Uncle Victor. "He gave a letter to the shipping agent for us to be on board to give you this surprise send-off."

"That's wonderful. I am so happy," I said as I wiped away the tears with my handkerchief. "Did the Venerable Siamese monk know you were coming?"

"Why? He sent a teacher with a carriage to meet us at the Station - the same carriage in which your trunk was brought to the harbour."

I could not help but laugh. Apparently the dramatic gesture of locating the site for a future statue of Olcott had a more mundane objective of verifying whether the train had come in time. Noble Son of Wisdom never failed to surprise me. So endearing he was in everything he did.

The kids enjoyed their first ever visit to a luxury passenger liner. They had a rollicking time. A crew member not only ensured their safety as they ran all over the decks but saw to it that they had a plenty of cakes and sweets to eat. Aunt Flower and Slim-Jewel were struck by the sheer luxury of the furniture and fittings, chandeliers, carpets and candlebras and shining silverware.

Stanley Williams' letter had some magic effect on the shipping company. My ticket entitled me to a second class cabin which I was to have shared with an Indian businessman. Now I was given a first class cabin all to myself with the compliments of the Captain. Any visitors coming to see me off were to be given dinner and allowed to stay on board until the last launch left the ship.

These were real privileges. But more than anything else, these extra specials guaranteed for me the best attention of the crew right through the voyage.

My Siamese colleague came on board an hour later with a young and handsome compatriot.

"I have brought you a Lay Provider," he said, using the correct term in Sinhala to signify a layman who accompanied a monk on a journey and looked after his creature comforts. "Mr. Prasong is in the Siamese Legation in Calcutta and he is going back after his holidays in Bangkok. You can call him Mam Luang, which means that his father was a Prince."

"Like you?"

"Yes, my brother."

It had been a chance meeting for neither had any idea that the other was in Colombo. The nephew had gone to Kandy and made inquiries at the Temple of the Sacred Tooth Relic. Apparently there was no monk that day who knew Noble Son of Wisdom or, more likely, understood what the foreign gentleman was inquiring about.

"Pure, just imagine. I am here for eleven years. The first Siamese I meet after all this while is my nephew, my elder brother's son. Doesn't it augur something?"

The charm, the elegance and the class confidence of the young scion of royalty were patent. Equally evident was the deepest veneration he had for the Buddhist Sangha. We chatted for some time and, then, I was left to be with my family.

The Captain invited us to his table for dinner. A lot of explanation was needed before he understood why the two monks would not eat after mid-day.

To my surprise and relief, the two ladies from Sangha-Gem-Field had no problem either with the Captain's humour nor the array of silverware. There was no doubt that Uncle Victor had done a fine job in their orientation.

Uncle Victor narrated amusing stories from Sinhala folklore and the young diplomat found parallels from Siam. The Captain was a consummate conversationalist and could contribute to any subject intelligently.

If travel broadens one's mind, the evidence has to come from the captains of luxury liners!

397

"Separation from the beloved is suffering" is a quote from the very first discourse of the Buddha. But the last few hours on board with the family as I had known and my closest friend had been passed in pleasant company.

That within an hour I would say good-bye to them and start alone to a far-off land did not occur to me until coffee was served and the Captain announced that the last launch would leave ten minutes to ten - that was, within twenty minutes.

Noble Son of Wisdom blessed me by placing his fan on my head and chanting the stanzas of benediction. He took out from his inner shirt pocket an envelope and gave me;

"Pure, promise me that you will open this only when you are in dire distress."

"Some magic?" I asked less seriously.

"Yes, Pure. Very effective."

He took an earlier launch and told Uncle Victor that the teacher would be at the jetty with the carriage. I could not thank my Siamese friend enough. I wished that he be well and that we meet again very soon.

The kids were exhausted. The smallest had curled himself on a sofa in the lounge and was fast asleep. Autumn-Moon worshipped me perfunctorily. Moon-Beam did likewise but asked whether I would return in a similar boat and they could on come on board to receive me. Uncle Victor and Aunt Flower asked me to take care of myself and not to worry about home folk.

"We'll go often to Sangha-Gem-Field and do the needful," they assured me.

The last to worship me was Slim-Jewel. It took an inordinately long time for her to suppress her sobbing and wipe out the tears before she could rise.

"Venerable Brother," she said. "You have been a great strength to me in my widowed life. Please look after yourself. You are the only light in our miserable life."

She pointed to herself and the two children.

"Sister, write to me if there is anything I should know or do. There's no sacrifice that I will not make for you and the two children."

"Thank you, Venerable brother. It's comforting to have that assurance from you."

It was neither the time nor the place to show one's emotions. The deck was teeming with passengers and their visitors. Parting is to die a little, they say. That applied to all who were then on the deck.

Uncle Victor carried the sleeping Middle Banda and each of the other ladies led her own child.

Slim-Jewel pressed into my hand a soft ball of tissue. I tightened my fist lest I drop it.

Suppressing an overwhelming lump on my throat, I slunk back to the lounge. A monk for fourteen years! But still human to feel the pangs of separation from the beloved and shameless to shed tears, though in the privacy of the cabin!

I opened my hand and spread the tiny lady's handkerchief on my palm. Two strands of hair of the children with an unspoken plea: "Never forget them." Conspicuously absent was anything to represent her own selfless self!

I lay on the berth, dazed and emotionally exhausted. My moist eyes looked vacantly at the porthole for hours.

The clanging of bells woke me. The boat was about to leave. I washed my face quickly and went to the upper deck. A steward led me to a deck chair and brought me a steaming cup of tea.

"Sit here, Sir. You'll have an unforgettable view of the Adam's Peak as the boat pulls out of the harbour."

"Wonderful!" I said and thanked him profusely.

It was indeed a wondrous spectacle. As the boat moved westward into the ocean, the city of Colombo faded into a hazy shoreline. Dominating the eastern sky and framed majestically by the reddish backdrop of the rising sun stood the monarch of the mountains - Peak of the Buddha's Footprint.

Mesmerized by the sheer scenic beauty, I watched it recede further and further, before I thought of my grand-parents who died at its feet. I recited stanzas in their memory and wished that they attain the ultimate bliss beyond death and rebirth.

The boat turned left and cruised southward. The hazy shoreline at the horizon was hardly discernible. A school of porpoises frolicked along the boat and a flying fish would lose its bearings and land on the deck. Passengers came out to watch the teeming sea life. The sight of a giant turtle drew crowds to the prow and experts distinguished between the sharks and the bluefins, bonitos and the mullets and explained how a porpoise differed from a dolphin.

It was another world. I closed my eyes and let my innermost thoughts gel into rhymed quatrains of mellifluous Sinhala in a metre so aptly called "The Music of the Sea":

My Motherland, the verdant isle of nature's
bounty!
Thy gleaming shore line fades in a no-man's
land
Where a cloudless morning sky dives into an
inky sea.
When will I see thy smiling face again?

I see in my mind's eye so clear
The striding hill by the bubbling river.
The home of my fathers - rustic, simple but
brave,
The salt of the earth, the sweetness of virtue.

What did my catastrophic birth portend?
By a quirk of nature - a massive landslide,
A family condemned to work and want
Raising its head in dignity with goals sublime.

What a childhood! But what a score?
In blue grass fields of Soccer and Rugby,
In halls of oratory - a debater applauded,
Flaunting with pride the rise in fortune
In speech, in gait, in a blazer emblazened.
The joys of innocence which soon did vanish!

The girl of my teenage dreams
A widow with cares of an errant mate's progeny,
Unloved and anxious, frightened and insecure,
Reaching to the skies undauntingly courageous.

Me, a monk in a saffron robe
Treading a Path with milestones so becalming
Of love, compassion and service to all,
Free from greed, malice and delusion
To reach the bliss of neither birth nor death.
Struggling yet in the worldly scene

400

For good of the many, welfare of the many.

Who rides so tall in the bobbing barge?
Bespectacled, bearded and sombre,
Erect as a soldier but without his sword,
Meek as a preacher but without his cross?

A gardener with a passion to grow more lushly
A bed of roses where pebbles vanquish
                    mimosas.
Staring through me and the throngs on the
                    shore
At a land he sees as a befitting site
For a garden of everlasting peace,
Of tolerance and virtue - a paradise of
                    righteousness.

It's my home, Sir. My isle of bliss and beauty,
Of balmy plains and meandering rivers,
Of brawny men and comely girls
Cowed down but briefly by alien force.
We strive to be free as the wafting breeze,
As the birds of the air and beasts in the forest.

Henry Steel Olcott of Orange, New Jersey
Of the mighty land on liberty's crest!
You brought us hope and a vision so fresh
Uplifted by you the nation looks ahead.

You are our guide, my mentor supreme.
How does your garden grow?

401

Book Four

**OFT A LITTLE MORNING RAIN
FORTELLS A PLEASANT DAY**

I

On board the ship time passed quickly. I read and studied for the most part of the day. I had my breakfast served early in the morning in the cabin and went to the dining room only for lunch and well before noon. Mr. Prasong would be there to see that I was properly served. In this he was most solicitous.

We would chat for some time but generally on the weather or something similarly innocuous. He was a tight-lipped diplomat and no amount of coaxing could persuade him to give me any information as to a possible future for Noble Son of Wisdom in his Motherland. I would leave by the time the other passengers came in for lunch and Prasong would join the very important people at the Captain's table.

I read the Great Chronicle and was baffled by the objectivity of its author who praised even invaders and usurpers for the good they had done. I knew most of its contents. But to read it as an epic and to appreciate it as history was a different experience. I brushed up my Sanskrit grammar and read all the works of Kalidasa. It was not easy to get back to formal studies. I worked hard to recapture the lost discipline.

I joined the Captain regularly at tea-time. It was the typical English tea ceremony. Invariably, he would propose a subject and I would be looked upon to provide the information. Oriental culture in general and Buddhism and Sri Lankan history, in particular, loomed large and the circle of participants grew daily - much to the Captain's satisfaction. He loved to preside over what was to all intents and purposes a University Seminar on Asian Culture. He was intrigued by my account of the re-enactment of the dialogue between the Greek king Menander and the Buddhist monk Nagasena.

"At tea on the last day, let's try it out here and I will be the Greek king," he proposed. Without the book, I had to write out the questions by memory. It proved to be as hilarious as it was educative. The Captain ad-libbed and dragged me into an in-depth discussion of the fundamental teachings of Buddhism. It was a debate set in modern times and my interlocutor was not a Greek king thirsting for philosophical speculation but an idealistic scientist losing confidence in religion.

Thanks to the Blakes and Saunders of my early life and Olcott of the last decade, I was a matching partner. At the end of the performance, I was showered with gifts including thoughtful donations of money. The Captain's gift was a set of pens and a letter to the shipping company requesting that my reservations at all times be upgraded to the first class.

403

"I never had so much fun since I left the naval school," he said in genuine appreciation. He invited me to the bridge to experience the thrill of sailing out of the Bay of Bengal into and up the Hooghly River. He showed with his left hand, the expansive Gangetic delta with multiple estuaries and said,

"In the third century B.C., ships came down from Patna the capital of the mighty Maurya Empire and sailed all the way to the north of Ceylon. Tamluk, there, was a thriving port."

"Yes, Captain. I am reading about it in the country's history. The third Mauryan Emperor, Asoka the Righteous, sent his daughter Venerable Nun Sanghamitta in a boat this way to found the Order of Nuns in the Island. She carried a sapling of the tree under which the Buddha was enlightened," I said.

From the gusty Bay of Bengal to the gentle murky brown waters of the river was a noticeable change. The alluvial plain as far as the eye could see was dotted with clumps of trees and palms like oases in a desert. Wherever the land rose a few feet were clusters of adobe houses with gleaming white walls. Before the monsoon rains began and the river turned muddy, what was now a desolate mud hole had been a bee-hive of activity,

"You should have been a month ago," said the Captain. "For miles, it looked like ants gathering food for the rainy season."

How glorious it would have been two or three months earlier, I thought to myself. A sea of green rice-fields! A giant tapestry of nature where clumps of trees and the mounds of human settlements stood out as a pattern of leaves and flowers on a green background!

A pilot guided the ship around treacherous sand banks and tongue-shaped islands. The Captain was chatty. He prepared us to expect the onslaught of crowds when the ship docked at the quay.

"I have a message for you, Sir," he told me. "Be in your cabin until you are called for by a man called Ram. I have heard of Camels and Foxes and even Bulls and Bears. But this, Sir, is Ram."

He thanked me for making the trip most memorable. Our improvised debate had whetted his taste for more Buddhism. I promised to keep in touch and to have a copy of Olcott's Catechism delivered to him through the Shipping Company in Colombo.

Ram turned out to be the Metropolitan's personal assistant, a stout gentleman in a white drill suit, white shirt, black tie and bowler hat. A well-groomed moustache compensated for his lack of height. The smile which exposed most of his betel-stained teeth endeared him to me

404

instantly. Was he as efficient as he looked? In minutes, I was on the quay where a stack of trunks were said to be mine. No amount of protestation that I came with just one trunk was of any avail. Again, it had been arranged by Uncle Victor in collusion with Noble Son of Wisdom! Five extra trunks which I insisted the Customs should open.

"Sorry, sir. They would never do it," persisted Ram. "Never as long as I tell them you are a dear friend of Right Reverend Saunders."

With my curiosity yet unsatiated, I mounted the carriage. It edged its way through what was literally a sea of people and crossed the tantalizing pontoon bridge at Howrah. The impressive river front revealed the grandeur of the capital of British India. The incessant commentary, as Ram pointed in different directions, hummed in my ears. It did not matter that none of the names he dropped had any meaning to me. One thing was certain - he was proud of the city. He loved it and hoped I would do likewise. The carriage jolted to a halt and he craned his neck out to see what had happened.

"You are very lucky, Sir. You couldn't have had a better omen. Success,success and success all the way."

All I saw was a human cadaver with only its pale grey face visible in a bed of marigold garlands. We let the procession of mourners pass us.

"You mean to meet a funeral procession?' I asked him.

"Yes, Sir. Not only that. For it to go in front of you. You are very lucky."

On the twenty-fifth of July 1889, I landed in the city where I had hoped as a boy to come in 1875 and was greeted by the lucky omen of a funeral procession! This is what I formulated in my mind as the diary entry for the day.

With my future successes in the new land mystically guaranteed, we rode through busy streets to the Office of the Metropolitan. He received me in his sumptuously furnished parlour. We looked each other over and shook hands for a full two minutes before either of us found words to greet the other after twelve years.

"You look the same, T.B. If at all, you have blossomed with age into a figure of visible authority," and patted me on the back exactly the way he did when I was a student. To parents and teachers, one really never grows up.

I faltered for a second, wondering how to address him and he noticed it.

"You have a choice, T. B. Either you can be my friend and call me Kenneth or Ram could give you all my titles for a more formal address," he laughed so loud that I had no choice.

"Reverend Kenneth, may I say?"

"As you please, young fellow."

The Right Reverend Kenneth Saunders with greying temples looked shorter than I remembered. He always loved good things in life, saying often that God did not create them for the pleasure of the sinners only. He had put on a little weight but was not fat. He looked every inch to have the glamour, the authority and the sanctity of the exalted office he held.

"You are an incurable flatterer," was his response to my grateful reminiscences of what a wonderful teacher, an exemplary mentor through my teen-ages and an unchanging friend he had been to me.

I was to sleep the first night at his place. It had never occurred to me to ask him if he had married since we last met in Kandy. In the carriage, I asked him.

"Yes, T. B. How is it that you never guessed it? I am married to the Church."

It was a typical British under-statement. If at all, he was married to the whole of humanity. That, of course, I knew from the very first day I carried him a bowl of soup at the request of Mrs. Blake.

"What have you smuggled in?" he joked, when he saw six trunks lined in the verandah.

"It bothers me too. I hoped the Customs would open them and I would then have known the contents."

"Why not now? I will get your tea served here and someone will help you to open them. What's your proverb: 'Why probe a bag when you can open it?' "

It was an hour and a half later, after he had taken his dinner alone that he saw me in the verandah. The contents of the trunks were out.

Heaped on a side were packets of tea with distinctive red labels of the Gartmoor Estate which never tired of boasting that its high quality tea fetched over twenty pounds sterling a pound in the London Tea Auctions. Similarly heaped were balls of palm molasses wrapped in dry banana leaves. So were dozen bundles of cinnamon. The rest consisted of bed-sheets, towels, extra robes, slippers, tins of tooth powder and soap.

Eh! what's all this? Its is like a trousseau that a young bride brings on her marriage day," teased Right Reverend Saunders. A moment later, he spoke admiringly of the affection which motivated the family and my Siamese colleague to make me feel so wanted and also so self-sufficient in my new environment. "TO MAKE NEW FRIENDS" was painted in the inner lids of the trunks which contained, tea, molasses and cinnamon.

As I repacked what I needed for my immediate use into two trunks, the Metropolitan kept me company. We talked late into the night on friends and acquaintances, recent events in the country, the impact of Olcott's efforts, the emergence of a national leadership and of possible consequences in the political scene. I told him of the Wilkins and of the research which Mrs. Wilkins was doing on the decline of Christianity in Sri Lanka.

"I am glad you told me this. I must write to her and send her some material I have put together. I have a tentative theory that what the Anglican Church loses in the Island will be more than compensated by the expanding presence and influence of the Catholic Church. I want her to test it in the field."

"Do you have a feeling that Buddhism will fall back into a secondary position?"

"Never again, T. B. Not after all that energy your monks have put in, all that organizational efficiency which Olcott had infused in lay Buddhists and all that you tell me about these young men like Don David and Don Baron. But I am inclined to believe that there will be a constant eight to ten per cent Christians - mainly Catholics - in your population?"

"Any basis to your belief, Reverend Kenneth?"

His was quite a complex theory. But the major part of his argument was based on the tolerance and goodwill which he thought would always be forthcoming from the Buddhists and Hindus of the Island. I was ashamed when he spoke to me of the success of Christian missions in the North of Sri Lanka, specially the Jaffna Peninsula.

Scotland or Ireland was more familiar to me than the northern part of my own homeland. He had to tell me of the apprehensions with which the British administration in the first decade of the nineteenth century received missionaries from the newly independent United States of America.

"To my countrymen the events of 1770s were still too fresh in their mind. They wouldn't trust the American missionaries anywhere close to the capital. So, they were sent to the furthest corners of the Island. They served the people well."

I recalled what Uncle Victor had told me about the influx of young men from Jaffna Peninsula to the clerical and other services in the Administration. But beyond that I knew so little of a substantial population which shared the same Island home. Did they know about us? I asked myself. What would the future hold if we grew up without knowing the history, culture, achievements and aspirations of each other?

407

When I posed this concern of mine to the Metropolitan, his answer was simple:

"Disaster, T. B. Disaster. Unmitigated disaster. But people like you can do something. I hope you address this question when you return to the Island. In the meantime, it may help you to study a bit of the Hindu culture and the history of this subcontinent."

Next morning, Ram loaded two of the repacked trunks in the carriage and accompanied me to a University hostel in College Square. My new life began with little ceremony. Two coolies or labourers trundled my trunks into a room on the ground floor. Ram had the keys. It was a slightly damp room with a musty smell after a spell of monsoon rain. It was sparsely furnished. The sagging bed of ropes woven on a clumsy frame on unstable legs was bare. The table and chair could best be described as rickety. The only new thing was a kerosene oil lamp with a chimney made in Belgium. In view of my age rather than my monastic status, I had the room to myself and it was also the closest to toilet facilities.

"I'll survive," I said to myself. But Ram was not taking the situation lightly.

"Mark my word, Sir. You will have brand new furniture before the day is out."

I told him that as a monk I was used to living in modest accommodation.

"You may be, but not when you are friend of the Right Reverend Saunders."

It was the second time in two days that I was reminded of my specially privileged circumstances as a friend of the Metropolitan.

Ram knew exactly what to do next. He took me the Registrar, a mild-mannered man of fifty, seated at a wooden table laden with brown and grey files of different sizes. Shelves along the walls were bulging with bundles of files and documents wrapped in red cloth. They looked like over-sized pillows.

"Come in, Guruji. Take a seat," he told me with the utmost deference. He stood up and saluted with his hands clasped in traditional worship. "I am told that you are a very important and learned Buddhist Guruji of Lanka."

This was the first time I was so addressed by anyone. In Sri Lanka, 'guru' simply meant a teacher. But in India, as I found out in due course, the term applied to one's spiritual teacher and the suffix -ji was an honorific signifying veneration and esteem.

408

I sat in the only chair in front of the Registrar and Ram stood at the side with both his hands on the table.

"Right Reverend Saunders wrote to the Vice-Chancellor personally and everything is ready for you, Guruji." the Registrar said after consulting a slim file he had in the drawer. "Here's the card for the warden of the hostel. He bills me for your board and lodging. Here are cards for your three professors in English, Sanskrit and Philosophy. Give them the cards and they will have your name entered in class-lists. One more thing. You are a special student and hence exempted from the first year. In recognition of your mastery of the Pali language, you are invited by the University to teach a first year class in Pali."

He took out of the same file, a timetable, a class-list and an envelope.

"You'll meet your Pali class on three days a week for one hour from five to six. And you begin today in the front corner room of this building."

I looked quizzically at the envelope.

"That's your monthly cash allowance of fifteen rupees for your sundry expenses."

What a deal the Metropolitan seems to have negotiated with the University.

"Guruji, the Vice-Chancellor-sahib will want to see you one of these days and I will let you know when."

Ram took me to the three Professors and we met them in quick succession. All of them looked British. But R. R. Wilson, the Professor of Philosophy, introduced himself an Anglo-Indian, meaning that he was of mixed parentage. S. N. Griffith, the Professor of Sanskrit and D. L. Marrs, the Professor of English were from England and looked forward to serving in India for a couple of years.

They asked me more or less the same questions on my educational background, the books I had read, level of competence in the subject and my career goals. My reading in English literature was rated more than adequate but in Sanskrit I was required to take a test. The subject with which I had very little familiarity was Philosophy.

Professor Wilson laughed derisively when I said that I had read Madame Blavatsky's "*Isis Unveiled*".

"You have wasted a lot of your time with those charlatans. They call Buddhism a philosophy? You will have a lot to unlearn. Any way I will see how you fare in the first term."

If they expected me to be discouraged, it did not happen. I was determined to do well.

409

We came to the hostel in time for lunch. I was happy to find that I was not the only monk in the dining hall. To the east of Calcutta, close to the border of Burma, was an ethnic group called the Chakmas of Chittagong and they were traditionally Buddhist. There were several Chakma and Burmese monks who were being served at a special table an hour before noon. I joined them and they were pleased to meet their new instructor in Pali under such informal circumstances.

If I had any misgivings whether I would feel embarrassed due to my conspicuous yellow robe, they disappeared in the morning even before I met my fellow Buddhist monks. There were quite a number of turbanned yellow-clad monastics of the Ramakrishna Movement. Their leader called Lord Discriminatory-Wisdom-Joy (Swami Vivekananda) encouraged them to acquire modern knowledge and serve humanity. The students, too, wore clothing more informally than in a comparative setting in Sri Lanka. The white cloth wrapped around the waist and tucked in between the legs - called Dhoti, meaning white garment - and the matching white chemise which reached down to the knees was more prevalent than the Western dress. If one was in full Western suit, he was bound to be a member of the staff, a freshman or a visitor. Into this medley of sartorial fashions mine merged quite easily.

The monks took me over from Ram and gave me the vital information that would facilitate my life in the campus. We ended in the room where the first class in Pali was to be given. There were fifteen students - twelve monks, two men and a solitary woman.

It had to be a beginner's class. While the monks knew the texts they chanted, they could hardly write or translate them correctly. The male students - one of them a Chakma - did not have even that slender acquaintance with the language. The girl who was from Mandalay, the royal city of Upper Burma, had some rudimentary knowledge of the language. She told me that, at one time, a knowledge of Pali - specially its grammar - was an essential pre-requisite for marriage for a Burmese girl.

I devoted the major part of this inaugural class to telling them how the Buddha's democratic and egalitarian sensitivities prompted him to present his teachings to the people in their own idiom in preference to Sanskrit which was the language of the elite and the erudite.

"The Buddha preached to the man in the street. So he preferred for this purpose the language of the street." I said as I compared Sanskrit and Pali words to show their convergence and divergence. The students laboriously took down copious notes. I failed in drawing them into any discussion. I was somewhat disappointed.

410

My disappointment was premature. Outside the class they had many questions. They were keen to tell me that their language, Bengali, was similar to Pali in that it derived from Sanskrit and that the morphological and sonal simplification I illustrated with regard to Pali would apply to their mother-tongue as well. Before I reached the hostel, one of the lay students Hemendu (Winter-Moon) by name had appointed himself my private tutor in Bengali.

Ram was in my room to greet me. He had wrought a miracle. A four post bed with a thick mattress covered in white sheets had replaced the primitive rope bed of the morning. A larger writing table, two book cases and two lounge chairs with a low centre table between them gave the room an air of luxury.

"All these must have cost someone an arm and a leg'" I said recalling a typical American idiom I had picked up from Olcott or more likely from Madame Blavatsky.

"Not at all, Guruji, our bachelor Metropolitan has enough furniture to spare for a dozen students!"

"Does he know?"

"No. He will. His orders to me are very clear and simple: 'My brightest student from early days in Ceylon should have nothing but the best.' He is so proud of you."

I was eager to know whether Ram was privy to any more information. But it was not the right time to ask. What prompted Right Reverend Saunders in his kindness was nothing but the sheer goodness of a man who had transcended race and religion.

From the next day, I settled down to a routine of fifteen hours of classes and three hours of tutorial discussions a week as a student, three hours as a teacher of Pali, four to five hours a day at the library and every spare minute in the room to reorganize the notes and to write tutorials on assigned subjects. Long hours had never bothered me. The joy of learning was a great stimulator.

Not all lecturers were equally inspiring; nor were all subjects. But the system demanded hard work. Somebody who had never seen you and whom you might never see would grade your papers and determine whether you deserved to pass or not. It was meant to guarantee fairness in the sense that every student had the same obstacles to overcome.

The University of Calcutta was a complex academic organization which operated through a network of affiliated colleges. The University *per se* was an examining body. The College to which I was assigned had a special relationship with the University where only post-graduate work was done. As such, I had quite some difficulty in being able to understand where one ended and the other began.

411

The Professor of Sanskrit was pleased with my performance at the test. But more helpful was a junior assistant lecturer who guided me through texts that I had not studied at Palace Hill.

I never saw the Professor of Philosophy after the first day. Again, a young lecturer took interest in me and filled the gaps in my knowledge. He encouraged me to take several papers in Indian Philosophy which included the study of Buddhism in all its traditions. I read most avidly every book or article which showed how Buddhism spread from its original base in India to the rest of Asia and what contribution each branch or tradition of Buddhism made to philosophy.

The annual examinations were purely internal. With my natural need for high achievement, I felt I could have done better. The result was that I decided to use the long vacation for an extra spurt of effort.

Temperamentally, I could never be a lop-sided bookworm. I participated in as many College activities as I found compatible with my life as a monk. For one thing, sports were out and so were musical and dramatic performances.

I did not miss a single excursion whether organized for students or the staff. Not only did I get an opportunity to observe the rural life of Bengal but also to visit many Hindu temples including the famous Temple of Goddess Kali after which the city was named.

The most memorable tours outside Bengal were to the incredible Sun-temple of Konarak and the fabulous Jagannath Temple at Puri. The explicitly erotic art of these temples enabled me to understand the significance of a trend in religious experience which manifested itself almost simultaneously in Hinduism and Buddhism. Indian philosophical and religious thought was no doubt full of enigmas. The most difficult to comprehend was the way in which sexuality and spirituality merged into a seamless web in the traditions which produced the astounding erotic art of Konarak and Puri.

I was particularly interested in guest lectures specially those which dealt with science, anthropology and technology. I had no idea that India had so many aborigines. These anthropologists had fascinating information on the life, beliefs, customs and taboos of Santhalis, Gonds, Mundas and Todas. I wished similar information should be gathered by somebody about the Veddahs of my country. Indian archaeologists were making breath-taking discoveries and every now and then one of them would address us on his findings.

On one occasion, I was swept off my feet when a scholar stated that the attribution of the hitherto discovered Edicts to Asoka the third Mauryan Emperor was based entirely on the authority of the historical records maintained in Sri Lanka.

412

"If not for the *Great Chronicle* and the *Island Chronicle* of Ceylon, we would never have known that *Devanapiya* of the Edicts and Asoka were one and the same; nor would we have known anything on the life and career of this great emperor without these same records. India is silent on an emperor who could easily be her greatest," he said.

The Bengali Poetry Circle was my favourite. Sanskrit and Sinhala both came to my aid when I began studying Bengali, a mellifluous language with a vast vocabulary and one specially suited for poetic expression. I was thrilled when a maiden attempt on my part to write some verses in Bengali was appreciated even by the Professor of Modern Indian Languages. Winter-Moon Sengupta, my self-appointed Bengali tutor, was the hero of the day!

Bengalis in general had a soft corner for the Sinhalas. Their legends spoke of a Victory-Lion (Vijay-Singha) who went from their part of India to conquer Lanka and establish the Kingdom of Sinhalas. Our own tradition as recorded in the Chronicles was that the grandmother of Victory (Vijaya) the founder-king of the Island nation was a princess from Bengal. I took great delight in learning their language, literature, culture and customs. I was invited to some homes and I liked their curries which resembled Sri Lankan cuisine.

I reserved Sunday mornings to keep up my correspondence with the family, the temple and a carefully selected number of mentors, friends and Buddhist leaders. At least once a month, I met Right Reverend Saunders and spent a couple of pleasant and profitable hours with him. He was engaged in a comparative study of Buddhism and Hinduism. We would analyze some of his observations and conclusions.

Once in three to four weeks, Uncle Victor, Aunt Flower and Slim-Jewel wrote a single letter together, each chipping in to comment on something another had written. Gossipy, humorous and on the whole entertaining, these letters could quite paradoxically either create or dispel bouts of homesickness. Usually, the three kids did a drawing or wrote a few affectionate words.

My brother the acting Abbot wrote a monthly report on happenings in the temple and occasionally included a note from the R. M. on the school.

Venerable Sumangala replied to every letter regularly. Somebody efficient had taken my place there. His letters invariably dealt with what was happening in the country. He was the born optimist who saw promise of good in every challenge.

413

Noble Son of Wisdom understood exactly what I wished to know and his letters were as descriptive as they were analytical. Every time he met Dharmapala or Don Baron Jayatilaka he sent me a detailed account of what they discussed and what impressions he formed of the conversation.

"Don David's visit to Japan with Olcott has brought about a significant change in the young man's attitude to education," he once wrote to me. "As you may remember he has always been very enthusiastic about science. It is rumoured that he had once told the Principal of his school that missionaries should be teaching the people English, science and Western culture rather than Christianity. Now Don David wants technical education to be the primary objective of the schools under his management. As the reception to this idea from teachers and parents alike appears to be quite cold, he is talking of establishing his own demonstration school. He is such a bundle of energy. Don't be surprised if I write to you next time that such a school has already come into being."

Similarly, he wrote to me of Don Baron:

"If Don David is visionary and exuberant, Don Baron is cool, calculating and practical in a good sense. He sees decades ahead and prepares himself for future challenges. He is basically a scholar but he sees no contradiction in objective study and active involvement in pressing social problems. I think he will be Olcott's choice for the school in Kandy, which is no longer a dream or a proposal. I do all I can to promote the idea that young Don Baron could run a school as well as any person we import from elsewhere."

Although Olcott had been for the most of the year in the same country that I was in, he replied to none of my letters. All I got from the Headquarters of the Theosophical Society in Adyar was a cryptic unsigned note criticizing Olcott. I could imagine the old Colonel being pulled in all directions. At one time, he wanted to resign from the Presidency of the Theosophical Society and free himself to pursue exclusive Buddhist interests. In fact he had written,

> *"I could very soon build up an international Buddhist League that might send the Dharma like a tidal wave around the world."*

At another time, he gave precedence to the Theosophical Movement which he, as a founder, felt obliged to protect from what he called the machinations of Madame Blavatsky.

In a letter I wrote the day after my annual examination, I asked him not to be discouraged by any "badmouthing" by vested interests and to

414

proceed as he had hitherto done with a balance in both spheres of activity. I quoted a verse from the Canonical text, The Path of Virtue, as the Buddha's stand when maligned:

I bear up words of insult,
Like an elephant in war
The piercing arrows;
For the most of the world are without virtue.

II

I started my final year of studies with renewed enthusiasm. I was also better prepared as I used the long vacation revising what I had already learnt and reading books prescribed for the Final Examination. The memory-training which I had gone through as an integral part of monastic education was an invaluable asset.

The workload was to be heavier as I had an additional class in Pali to teach, as well as more tutorial discussions to attend. On the material plane, I had never been in a more stimulating ambience or had such abundant facilities.

I looked forward to a very successful year. I was not disappointed. Everything was exactly as I had anticipated.

News from Sangha-Gem-Field and Kandy were consistently good. Venerable Sumangala was as active as ever and his letters summarized the gains of the national and Buddhist revival. In one letter , he said,

"Now the entire hundred chapters of the *Great Chronicle* are accessible because of an excellent translation by Louis Corneille Victory-Lion. You may remember this scholar. He was once your examiner. I have sent you two copies of this great book. One is for you and the other for the University Library. It is a blessing that the Government continues to assist Oriental learning."

Don David who was better known now as Dharmapala sent me an interesting letter which could more appropriately called a list of questions:

"Are you still studying? Have you found time to preach Buddhism to the people of the Buddha's own Motherland? Have you met any monk or Lama who had developed tranquility and insight through meditation? If you have, find out what they know about reaching the higher attainments of the Path in this very life? Have you taken an interest in the question of restituting Buddhist shrines to Buddhists which Sir Edwin Arnold had raised? What do you know about the introduction of technical education to school curricula? Do you know what the Burmese and the Chakma Buddhists think of Colonel Olcott's Fourteen-point Buddhist Platform and his proposal to set up an International Buddhist League? Is it true that there is a widening rift in the Theosophical Society and Madame Blavatsky is having her own way in Europe?"

I replied to each of the questions to the best of my knowledge. I commended him on his interest in technical education and suggested that our school in Sangha-Gem-Field could be a venue for an experimental programme:

"I have always been worried about the current tendency to limit the education given to rural children to the so-called three R's - Reading, Writing and Arithmetic" I wrote. "Missionary vernacular and Anglo-vernacular Schools have Christianization of the people as the main goal and they have no interest in their future vocational orientation. Already educated youths are moving in large numbers to towns in search of better pastures. But as they have no saleable skills, they end up doing odd jobs and live precariously. I would like to see if schools can really help in developing skills in agriculture, cottage industries and crafts which are income-generating."

My faithful purveyor and analyst of news, Noble Son of Wisdom, was in constant communication. He had continued his studies in Palace Hill and passed the Final Examination of 1890, winning the year's gold medal.

"This is not a mean achievement for a middle-aged man, whose son too is graduating from Oxford University about the same time," he wrote. "Now I have irrefutable credentials to establish my competence in Pali, Sanskrit and Buddhism. This is in preparation for a new career in Siam, as I am optimistic that my self-imposed exile would come to an end sooner than I had ever thought possible."

I congratulated him immediately on both counts - his brilliant success at the examination and the likelihood of his returning to his Motherland. I had a hunch that the chance meeting of his nephew on the day he came to see me off could be the beginning of some negotiations with Bangkok. I knew that he would tell me more about it when he was in a position to do so.

Towards the end of the year, he sent me a more detailed letter. It sounded like an annual report on the conditions in Sri Lanka. Olcott had come with C. F. Powell and Dr. J Bowles Daly. Along with Dharmapala they had continued the campaign for the National Buddhist Education Fund. The school in Kandy was a reality. It was started with young Don Baron Jayatilaka as the Principal. Olcott had spoken of a young Englishman by the name of F. L. Woodward who was expected to head a school in Galle. It seems that Woodward claimed to have cooperated with Olcott in similar work in his previous lives as well. It ended with a piece of advice.

417

"In January 1891, there will be a Theosophical Convention in Adyar. It is Olcott's wish to have his Fourteen-point Common Buddhist Platform approved at this convention. Don David would certainly be there. If you can find the time, I would advise you to attend this meeting. You have not met Olcott or Don David for quite some time. You have to meet them from time to time lest they forget you."

The ninth to the twelfth of January were not the most convenient days. But the College authorities excused me from attending my classes but insisted that my six hours of Pali to the two classes had to be made up.

It was a lovely journey by train.

One of my classmates told me that in India the taste of well-water and the language changed every twenty-five miles. I felt that the list had to be completed by adding garments, ethnic or racial affiliations, food and religion. So diverse was this great land that the mere observation of these differences as people came and left the railway compartment was a study of the unfathomable divergence and yet the underlying harmonious oneness of humanity. Whatever be their differences, they reacted alike to heat, cold, thirst and hunger. A welcoming smile was received with a smile. A kind word was gratefully acknowledged. Roughness and unkindness brought fear or anger. The ultimate wish of every human being was to be left alone or dealt with kindly.

Perched on a luggage rack, where a railway attendant spread my hold-all and arranged sleeping accommodation for the whole trip, I watched the passing human scene with the greatest interest.

Adyar helped me to understand Theosophy. Sacred symbols of all known religions which were prominently displayed signified its ideal of a Universal Brotherhood of Humanity. The shrines and the library further highlighted its acceptance of religion without boundaries. I congratulated Colonel Olcott on how apposite the concept was.

"I am happy to see you here and I am very pleased with what you see as our message and our motivation. But, Young Priest, never forget that all great movements and revolutions come under the inviolable law of unintended consequences. You may see things and you may hear things. You will like some and some will disturb you. Then remember this law."

Was it the comment of a disappointed man? What made him feel so insecure? What was he warning me about?

The Convention was a stately meeting. Speeches were formal. Discipline was exemplary. Disagreements, when expressed, were duly prefaced with apology. Sarcasm was absent and bigotry eschewed. What decorum! What courtesy! What commitment to the good of the humanity! I was deeply impressed.

The motion on approving the Colonel's Fourteen-point Common Buddhist Platform elicited praise and gratitude for his deep commitment and erudite summary of the quintessence of Buddhism valid for every tradition. The participants signed the document and it certainly was another feather in Olcott's hat. He deserved the unsolicited encomia that were showered on him on this occasion.

I had several occasions to discuss matters with Don David or Dharmapala . He preferred not to be called by his Christian name any more. He signed the Common Platform in the name of the Buddhists of the Island. He spoke of a major change of mind he had experienced since we last met. He attributed this change to the impact of a meeting he had with Sir Edwin Arnold when he was in Sri Lanka in February 1890. My talks with him confirmed what Noble Son of Wisdom had written to me in one of his letters:

"Our young friend, Dharmapala , spoke to me in great earnest about the protection of Buddhist Shrines in India. He hopes to visit shortly the shrines which mark the spots where the Buddha attained enlightenment, delivered the first sermon and passed away. Sir Edwin Arnold who was in the Island recently seems to have convinced him that there was a role Dharmapala could play. Perhaps, Sir Edwin's friend, Venerable Sumangala of Sand-Village, also might have had a hand in this. The more interesting change is his growing interest in spreading Buddhism in foreign lands. He is quite serious when he says that Ceylon should pay back the debt of having received Buddhism from Asoka by re-introducing Buddhism in the land of its birth. I am sure, Pure, you will find him more in agreement with you than on the day you last met him."

How right the Siamese ex-diplomat was! Dharmapala did ask me to cooperate with him. He urged me to develop close links with Burmese and Chakma monks who were in the University and to preach Buddhism whenever and wherever possible to educated Indians. He felt that the only way to get Buddhism accepted in India was to convince the emerging intelligentsia of the prestige which their country had earned on account of the Buddha. There was no doubt that the budding leader had done a lot of thinking.

He and his Japanese friend, a monk by the name of Reverend Kozen Gunaratana (Virtue-Gem), invited me to accompany them to the Buddhist shrines which they were due to visit immediately after the

419

Convention. I would have agreed but for a minor diplomatic situation. Colonel Olcott asked me to accompany him to Burma where he expected the Burmese Sangha to approve the Fourteen-point Common Buddhist Platform.

Accepting either one's invitation would have been misunderstood by the other. I also had misgivings about Olcott's choice of Burma as the first country to visit. It was a wrong move, I felt, although I could not explain why. To avoid any controversy, I pleaded that my teaching commitments precluded me from being absent from Calcutta.

Immediately the Convention was over, I returned to the College. In deference to the request of Dharmapala , I convened a meeting of the staff and students interested in Buddhism and spoke to them on three themes: Olcott's Common Platform for Buddhists, the spiritual and cultural impact of the Buddha on the Asian continent and the protection of Buddhist shrines in India. It was a well attended meeting. Many asked for more information.

The questions revealed that theirs was not a passing interest. Another meeting was fixed for the following week and after three sessions was born what was called a Buddhist Study Circle.

We met regularly once a month. We found speakers mostly from among ourselves. Dharmapala was so right in predicting that young intellectuals would first accept the Buddha as the greatest son of India and their interest in Buddhism would be built on the national pride they enjoyed on account of him. The challenge which I had to face was to find out ways and means of popularizing the Buddha and his teachings without being overtly evangelical. I knew enough of the pitfalls which the missionaries had failed to avoid both in Sri Lanka and India.

Perhaps, my most successful move was to get Right Reverend Saunders to speak on his research in Buddhism and Hinduism. The largest hall in the University was packed to capacity. He made me proud. I was delighted when he spoke of me as his most distinguished pupil. To the massive audience in rapt attention, he presented a historical analysis of the role of the Buddha in the evolution of Indian philosophical and religious thought. At one point he said,

"As a result of my travels in Asia I have come to the conclusion that no other human being has had as many shrines, statues and memorials built for him so consistently for so long a period as the Buddha has. That in itself has been the prime motivation for the growth

420

of serene and sophisticated artistic traditions in every country where Buddhism had been or is now prevalent. This alone should make every Indian very proud that one of the greatest sons of their Motherland had shaped the culture of a whole continent for around twenty-five centuries."

His unprejudiced, unbiased objectivity won him the highest encomium of the Vice-Chancellor who presided over the meeting.

After this meeting, the Buddhist Study Circle had ample volunteers and I was able to let it grow as a student activity. It did really well.

My Pali students in both classes acquired competence in the language quite satisfactorily and before long were reading extracts from the Canon and Commentaries. I was therefore able to guide them into a methodical study of Buddhism in the Buddha's own words. My selections and notes were growing into a book which I hoped to publish in due course.

In the meantime, I made steady progress in my own studies for the first degree. I had an advantage that my class-mates did not have. In English, in particular, my asset was that I had learned the language from teachers who spoke it as their mother tongue. I had also used it longer in diverse ways in real word situations as debater, interpreter, public speaker, drafter of documents and so forth. In Philosophy, my chronological maturity was certainly helpful. That was the only way I could explain my facility in grappling with abstract ideas which baffled most of my classmates. As regards Sanskrit, even the Professor observed that the foundation given at Palace Hill was the best imaginable. I hoped to do well in the Final Examination. But by nature I would not relax. I continued the grind.

News from home - both Kandy and Sangha-Gem-Field - continued to be good. I had a letter from Don Baron asking whether I could be counted upon to keep my word in helping him with the new school in Kandy. He was encouraged by the reception given both to him and the school by the people of Kandy. For this he claimed no credit. He praised the charismatic leadership of Colonel Olcott.

"But it will take a little more time and much coaxing and convincing before the elite of Kandy decide to send their children to our school."

I replied that Don Baron could count on my joining him in his effort.

Noble Son of Wisdom also had a lot to say about Olcott. It seemed that he had made a tactical blunder in going to Burma first to get the approval of the Burmese Sangha on the Common Platform. He had obtained twenty-three signatures in Rangoon on the third of February and came to Colombo post-haste to make amends.

The monks had their own way of handling such situations. Having encouraged Olcott to proceed with the idea of unifying the Buddhists of the world on the basis of the doctrinal unity underlying external diversity, they would not withdraw their support to him. But nor were they overly enthusiastic.

It was left to the Colonel's long-standing friend and admirer, Venerable Sumangala, to rally round the hierarchy of his own sect in Kandy and a few confidantes so that the document received only five signatures in Sri Lanka. The list of signatories convinced me that Venerable Sumangala had put in an enormous effort to get even these signatures. Conspicuous by their absence were many of the leading lights of the national and Buddhist revival in the maritime regions.

As though this was not enough, the monks refused to subscribe to the second proposal of the Colonel. Neither the proposed International Buddhist League nor its affiliate a Sinhala Buddhist League was endorsed by them. Nor did they agree to the major fund-raising campaign that he proposed.

I wondered whether I could have campaigned for a little more support. I thought that I could have obtained Little Father's assistance in getting more signatures from the senior scholar-monks of the South.

The next few months were a virtual nightmare. It was too close to the examination that I was apprised of it scope. It was to cover what had been prescribed for all three years of which the first I had missed altogether.

It meant reading at the last moment several prescribed textbooks in Sanskrit and English and getting a good grounding in Deductive and Inductive Logic. My classmates helped me with notes and copies of their tutorials. I felt as if a trick had been played on me. It was so annoying and time-consuming.

Ultimately, the examinations came. I found the question papers to my satisfaction. Yet, it was a relief when all nine sessions were over and the long vacation began. After the lapse of several months, I returned to my old routine. I reread the letters which I had only glanced through. What a wealth of news awaited me.

I began with letters from my brother. It had become necessary to dismiss a teacher and the School Board seemed to have done it with proper recourse to justice. My views had been asked about replanting a piece of temple land with cocoa which was said to be a successful cash crop. I asked my brother to consult the R. M. and to do whatever he advised.

The first letter of Noble Son of Wisdom generated mixed feelings. I was delighted that the Siamese Palace had begun to communicate with him and his assistance had been requested by King Chulalongkorn (Little-Ornament) himself to modernize the system of administration of the country. I was sad that his return to Siam and possibly resumption of lay life would be a personal blow. For over twelve years he had been my closest friend and counsel. Already I began to feel abandoned. But I wished him well and hoped that his twelve to thirteen years as a monk would be of benefit to his country specially in resuscitating a tradition of scholarship.

His other letters and a letter of Venerable Sumangala spoke of Dharmapala and his new self-assumed mission. It seemed that his pilgrimage to shrines associated with the principal events of the life of the Buddha had a profound impact on him.

On the twenty-second of January 1891 he had been at the shrine marking the spot where after six years of study and striving the Buddha attained enlightenment. It was in the hands of a Hindu sect and the imposing shrine was being used as a chapel for the Hindu God of Destruction, Shiva. What shocked Dharmapala was an animal sacrifice which was in progress.

"How could such cold-blooded slaughter be committed in the shrine most sacred to the name of the Buddha, the Prince of Non-violence!" he had asked himself.

I could understand his reaction. Once, a classmate took me to a temple dedicated to Kali, the consort of the same God Shiva in her terrible form. At first, the image itself shocked me - Kali with a garland of human skulls, trampling a vanquished enemy and drinking blood out of a skull. There was a series of animal sacrifices - several bleating goats and a frightened buffalo slaughtered in front of the shrine. The priest slit the throat of each animal with a sharp knife and threw the head and torso of the goats to his left and right. The protesting buffalo was held by several assistants and that was all I had the gall to watch. I felt dizzy and had to depart from the scene hastily. The very thought that a shrine dedicated to the Buddha at least a millennium ago was the scene of similar ritual was indeed revulsive.

Dharmapala had vowed to safeguard the serenity of the shrine and was rallying the support of Buddhists with the slogan "Save Buddha-Gaya".

Both Venerable Sumangala and Noble Son of Wisdom hailed the campaign as timely and relevant. Reportedly, it was also supported by Colonel Olcott.

Right Reverend Saunders encouraged me to register for post-graduate studies leading to a Master's Degree. My preference was for Philosophy. I decided to remain in the hostel during the long vacation and once again Ram displayed his ingenuity by making arrangements for my meals.

Some time during the long vacation, I received a circular letter from Dharmapala in his new capacity as the General Secretary of the Maha Bodhi Society. Maha Bodhi, meaning 'Great Enlightenment' was an appropriate name for the organization whose main objective was to safeguard the sanctity and serenity of the ancient Buddhist shrine.

The Society had been established on 31 May 1891 with the Grand Lama of Tibet as the Patron and Venerable Sumangala as the President. One each from Burma, Japan and China and two from Sri Lanka were appointed Vice-Presidents. I was happy to find that Subhuti of Curse-Sword and Venerable Sumangala of Sand-Village were the two Vice-Presidents from Ceylon.

It was a truly international body. Representatives, most of whom had already taken action to establish branch societies in their cities or regions, were from Bangkok, Tokyo, Kyoto, Colombo, Rangoon, Thayetmyo, Akyab. Chitttagong, Darjeeling, Calcutta, California and New York.

Colonel Olcott was its Director and Honorary General Adviser. Unmentioned in the list of office-bearers but vicariously present through Venerable Sumangala of Sand-Village was Sir Edwin Arnold, the originator of the idea of restituting Buddha Gaya to the Buddhists.

The Secretariat was to be in Calcutta and I looked forward to being involved in its activities. I congratulated Dharmapala and offered him my cooperation.

Another circular letter from Adyar announced the death of Madame Blavatsky and the departure of Colonel Olcott to London. She had died of influenza on eighth May 1891 and Olcott had arrived in London on the fourth of July. Nothing more was known as Noble Son of Wisdom, too, had received only the same communication. He, however, surmised that Olcott could be meeting in London with his friend and long-time

424

worker in Theosophy and Vice-President of the Society, William Quan Judge, to discuss the future leadership of the movement.

The indefatigable purveyor of news and rumours, the Siamese ex-diplomat, however, had information of an aspiring leader - a woman of inexhaustible energy and remarkable political acumen. He said that her name was Annie Besant and her leanings were more to Hinduism. It had been rumoured that she was really a Socialist and her choice of Hinduism was based on her ambition of being a popular leader in India. She was expected to make it her permanent home.

Having seen the tense relationship that Olcott had with Madame Blavatsky, I hoped that the new comer to the movement would not make the late years of the White Buddhist in any way miserable. I wrote him a long and consoling letter and addressed it to Adyar with a note on the cover to hold it until he returned.

With a "First Class First," meaning in University parlance that I had not only obtained a first class honours Bachelor of Arts degree but was also the best student of the class, I was admitted to a Master of Arts degree in Philosophy.

Remembering what prompted me to resume my studies, I opted to write a dissertation in lieu of several examination papers. The subject I proposed was "The Rise and Spread of the Mahayana Tradition of Buddhism." It was accepted and I commenced my research immediately.

The degree gave me a new status in academic circles. Even Professor Wilson changed his attitude and became more respectful if not entirely friendly. I was more a member of the staff than a student. I taught three classes of Pali and the total enrollment was over seventy. On the material plane, my allowance was raised to fifty rupees and I was transferred to another hall of residence. In a larger room, the Metropolitan's furniture added glamour and luxury.

My routine changed little. Of course, I had fewer classes to attend. I spent more time in the library and in informal discussions with my teachers and fellow students.

The Buddhist Study Circle had grown in popularity and membership. I persuaded the new office-bearers to invite Dharmapala for a lecture. I forwarded the letter with my own invitation to the Secretariat of the Maha Bodhi Society in Calcutta. He accepted the invitation and suggested that his subject would be "The World's Debt to the Buddha."

It was another impressive session. He was undoubtedly the most eloquent speaker on Buddhism I had met so far. His command of English was astounding and his mastery of the subject-matter was remarkable. He made the Buddha and his teachings come alive to an audience that was already enthused by the credit that India gained by simply being the home of the Buddha. He fielded his questions expertly. He concluded by inviting everybody to an international Buddhist conference which he was in the process of organizing at Buddha Gaya for October 1891.

During the next few weeks I spent whatever time I could spare at the Secretariat of the Maha Bodhi Society as a volunteer. There was so much to do to organize the international conference. We had no precedents to go by. As far as we all knew, this was going to be the very first of its kind. Of course, we did tap our own experience of the Adyar Conventions of the Theosophical Society.

If Colonel Olcott was available, it would have been a great asset. But he was in Japan enlisting support for his Common Buddhist Platform. As we heard via the grapevine much later, he was not having an easy time. Most of the Japanese felt that the fourteen points were inadequate to cover the essentials of Buddhism as they knew it. Ultimately, a compromise was reached. They agreed to say that they were "included within the body of Northern Buddhism."

Exactly at this time, while Olcott was pleading for support from the Japanese Buddhist clergy for his Common Buddhist Platform, Dharmapala had two more feathers added to his cap.

On the twenty-fourth of October, he delivered a speech at the prestigious Albert Hall in Calcutta. The subject was *"Buddhism in its relationship with Hinduism."* Not only did a fairly large audience appreciate his rich and well argued presentation but the Indian press was impressed with the message of "love and peace from his Buddhist brethren." The Editor of the *Indian Mirror*, I felt, epitomized in an editorial on the third of November 1891 the sentiments of the people who heard or read the speech:

> *It is strange and remarkable that the Buddhists should have turned wistful eyes to India at the present time. India dates her misfortunes since the date of the disappearance of Buddhism. Why should not this unlooked for return of Buddhism in the form of a Buddhist colony at Buddha Gaya bring back with it the hope that Hindus will recover their place among the great nations of the world? This is not a mere vague undefined hope; it is one which we expect to realize before long. The Buddhists form a very large portion of the world's population. The Hindus have kept themselves aloof from millions upon millions of Buddhists of*

China, Japan, Burmah, Siam, Tibet and Ceylon. ...... Why should we then hesitate to take the hand which the Buddhists now proffer us in right, pure friendship? It was India that gave them their saving faith. Should we not take them to her arms? And in that case her sons will not only be found between the limited area, between the Himalayas and Cape Comorin, but millions upon millions of sons outside and beyond will work for her with all the zeal and ardency of sons that had been disowned, but are now restored to their long lost mother's affections.

The other achievement of Dharmapala was the most successful international conference under the sacred Bodhi-tree at the site where the Buddha attained enlightenment two thousand four hundred and seventy-nine years ago. Thus went his own record of the event:

The first memorable event in the Maha Bodhi Society's progressive career is the holding of the Inter-national Conference at Buddha Gaya on October 31, 1891, almost simultaneously with the preliminary conference of the World's Parliament of Religions in Chicago. On a spot facing the sacred Bo-tree under whose shade the ascetic Prince Siddhartha attained supreme wisdom, delegates from different countries sat in solemn conclave and discussed the future programme of Buddhist activity.

I was keen to attend the Adyar convention at the end of 1891. I had several reasons. I had not met Olcott for a whole year. Our correspondence had been perfunctory and formal. People spread all kinds of stories about his mental stability. It was rumoured that he was back again talking of Adepts and Mahatmas. He was claiming to receive messages from them. Every night, he was said to be expecting Madame Blavatsky to appear in a dream and give her ideas on what he was doing. I would be sad if the era of his perfect rationalism had come to an end.

I also wanted to test my hypothesis that Dharmapala had challenged Olcott's leadership in Sri Lanka and the latter was piqued about it. If either of them had difficulties as regards his relationship with the other, I would be among the handful of persons in a position to help. I would have been the happiest to see them cooperating fruitfully and I looked for every glimmer of hope that this would happen.

Adyar would have been the best place for any mediation between them. I made it my self-assumed mission. My loyalty to both of them demanded it. I was further convinced that it was my bounden duty to keep them together for the sake of the yet-to-be-accomplished objectives of national and religious revival of Sri Lanka

427

III

The University approved my leave and I was about to purchase the tickets. That very morning, a messenger from the Siamese Legation brought me an important-looking letter in a large red envelope. Inside the cover was a letter addressed to me. I knew immediately from whom it was. I guessed its contents from the manner in which it was sent. It was from Noble Son of Wisdom. Even as the messenger reverently waited for me to sign the receipt, I opened the envelope and began reading the letter.

My dear Pure,

I hope this letter reaches you before my ship gets into Calcutta.

As you will recall, we met for the first time as aspirants for the noble status of a Buddhist monk in the sacred presence of the Tooth Relic. We went through the ceremonies together. The friendship that started on that wonderful night has been a joy at all times, a solace when nostalgia struck me hard and an encouragement in the pursuit of knowledge. It has been a relationship that has to this moment been one of the most rewarding to me.

Now as you will guess, I am called to shoulder other responsibilities. It had been an inexorable exile. But everything has been cleared and I am due to resume my royal duties to my King and the Nation.

I will be a Special Adviser to His Majesty on the modernization of the administration of the country. To add greater joy to me in my late years, His Majesty has also given my son an important position in the Siamese Embassy in London.

I could have left for Bangkok directly from Colombo. But I am making a detour for two very important emotional reasons.

I have not seen you for two years. I want to spend a few days with you before I change my life. So that we could be together and move about exactly as we had done from the first time we met, I will come to Calcutta as a monk.

Now, Pure, this is my other emotional reason. I want none but you to return me to my lay status. Will you please come on board the ship on the last day of our visit and administer the Three Refuges and Five Precepts and be the first to bless me in my lay clothing?

For ever,
Your cordial friend,

Noble Son of Wisdom.

Enclosed was the information on the time of arrival of the ship. It gave me barely three days.

I had to choose between loyalty and duty. Without hesitation I chose the former.

In the absence of the Metropolitan, Ram rose to the occasion and organized all that was needed for the creature comforts of the visiting monk. The Buddhist Study Circle planned a fitting reception. Mr. Prasong suggested a pilgrimage to at least the shrines marking the sites of the Buddha's enlightenment and first sermon. The Maha Bodhi Society would be our host at Buddha Gaya.

Noble Son of Wisdom had not been to Calcutta. So Ram became an instant tour guide from the jetty itself. The bobbing pontoon bridge at Howrah fascinated my Siamese colleague.

"This must be the largest in Asia," he mused. "This is the kind of modernization my country needs - bridges, roads and railways, besides, of course, schools and hospitals. My first priority, however, will be the judiciary. Having been a fugitive from an uncertain fate, I owe it to myself to give the nation a more equitable administration of justice."

I told him of my encounter with a dead body and how Ram explained that it was a really good omen.

"How is it, Ram, that you omitted this item from my programme?" teased Noble Son of Wisdom.

"Don't worry, Guruji. In due course. In due course."

It was quite funny. In ten minutes, he led us through some by-lanes to a street where we met not one but three funeral processions.

"Your luck, Guruji, is thrice guaranteed," Ram chuckled.

A room had been lavishly furnished in the same hall of residence as mine. It was indeed in keeping with his royal eminence. We had been so regular in correspondence, we had little to share among us by way of news. He was thrilled that the young king, who had taken full control of the kingdom from the regent, was determined to lead the Siamese nation into the twentieth century. He had drawn much inspiration from the Meiji Restoration in Japan. Noble Son of Wisdom's nephew whom he met in Colombo had persuaded his father to speak things out with the King. What had been most convincing to the powers that be in the court was that he had not merely been a monk but virtually exiled himself in Sri Lanka and pursued his religious vocation with exemplary dedication. The fact that he had done a full, twelve year course in monastic studies in Pali, Sanskrit and Buddhism made him a rare asset to his country.

"In a couple of weeks, I return to the service of my nation with much greater awareness of the unique culture to which my countrymen are born," he said in the course of his address to the Buddhist Study Circle. "It is His Majesty's wish that Siam enters the twentieth century as a vigorous modern nation enjoying the fruits of science and technology but, at the same time, preserving and promoting our magnificent Buddhist Culture for which we are indebted to India, the home of the Buddha."

Once again, the audience overflowed the hall. With the Siamese Legation handling the publicity, high level officials of the Administration were present along with the elite of Calcutta. His expose of the Buddhist Culture of Sri Lanka and Siam and of the historical relations between the two countries was as eloquent as it was informative. The Indians in the audience were delighted. Several asked questions. But each preceded it with an expression of satisfaction that the name of the Buddha was now being more often heard and that their national pride had thus been enhanced.

How very perspicacious was Dharmapala when he asked me to pursue this line of approach to make the Indian elite proud of their nation's historical contribution to the culture of Asia!

On the third day, we took a train to Benares - Varanasi or Kasi of literature, the holiest of all cities in India. It was the spiritual centre of Hinduism. So it had been for millennia. To the Buddhists, its significance lay in that the Buddha chose a deer park outside the city to deliver his first sermon. It was here that the Buddha addressed five of his erstwhile colleagues in study and meditation and commenced his mission of turning the wheel of teachings. Here it was that he declared:

"There are, O Monastics, two extremes to be avoided as vulgar and fruitless: the extreme of self-indulgence and the extreme of self-mortification."

430

It was here that he expounded the four Noble Truths of Suffering, the Cause of Suffering, the Cessation of Suffering and the Path leading tho the Cessation of Suffering.

Herein, again did he elaborate to the same disciples on the next day the principal teachings of the three characteristics of existence: Impermanence, Suffering and Selflessness:

> *"Everything in life is impermanent; what is impermanent is unsatisfactory and causes only suffering; when everything is impermanent and causes suffering and one simply cannot have any say on it, how can one have the selfish, self-centred concept that there was some one to say 'I am', 'my' or 'mine'?"*

This was the crux of his teaching.

Noble Son of Wisdom and I were moved to tears as we knelt and offered trays full of flowers to the circular foundation of the Tope which marked the venue of the first sermon and the ruined but still very impressive monumental Tope at the spot the second sermon was preached. We sat between the two spots and read aloud in original Pali the two discourses.

The site was being excavated by the Indian Archaeological Survey and a helpful archaeologist showed us the treasures unearthed. They included magnificent statues of the Buddha, components of the polished sandstone columns of Asoka with his Edicts and the foundations of an extensive monastic complex. Parched grains of rice and untouched food bespoke a sudden and catastrophic end of this sacred monastery.

The next day we were at Kushinagar or Kasia (Kusinara of Pali literature) where the Buddha passed away lying down under twin Sala trees. Archaeological work was in progress and the remains of another extensive monastic complex were being unearthed. The heroic granite statue of the recumbent Buddha on his death-bed evoked grief and pathos. It was not easy to keep our eyes dry.

"I haven't seen any Buddhist, who came here and did not cry," observed a young English archaeologist, who accompanied us to the spot where the Buddha was cremated. "I hope you fellows take charge of these site. They mean so much to you and absolutely nothing to the people here."

It was with great reluctance that we refused the offers made by several kind people in Kushinagar to take us to Lumbini, the royal park of Sala trees, in which the Buddha was born. His mother was on the way to her parent's home for her first confinement, as was the custom. But the child was born under a tree in this park between the cities of his father and mother. The terrain was little known and the political boundary between India and Nepal - the Himalayan Kingdom - ran between Lumbini and Kushinagar. We were reluctant to take any risks. But the disappointment was painful.

What awaited us in Buddha Gaya was beyond description. The newly created Maha Bodhi Society had organized a grand reception in our honour. It was an occasion to highlight the spiritual significance which the sacred Bodhi-tree and the monuments around it had to the Buddhists of Asia. When invited to speak, I spoke of the sapling of the original tree which Emperor Asoka sent to Sri Lanka and described what the spot where the Buddha attained enlightenment meant to us. Noble Son of Wisdom spoke more eloquently and supported the mission of the Society and expressed his support on behalf of his country. We both praised Dharmapala who, unfortunately, was not present. Colonel Olcott and he were on a fund-raising effort to buy a property close to the holy site to carry on the campaign to have the site restituted to the Buddhists.

We paid our respects to the sacred tree and visited, in order, the places around it where the Buddha spent the first seven weeks after enlightenment. We could not enter the main shrine. It had been converted to a Hindu shrine and the Mahante, as the custodian of the temple was called, would not permit us to enter. What we saw of the monastic complex in ruin convinced us how very dear the place had been to the Buddhists for many centuries, It was strewn with artistic treasures of the highest order - statues, sculptures and architectural components of exquisite beauty.

We spent a night near the sanctuary and met many Burmese and Tibetan pilgrims who had travelled under great discomfort to visit what they described as the holiest of holy places of pilgrimages. A Burmese explained that a replica of the main shrine had been constructed in his village by a Burmese king of the past. He shed tears that the main shrine was in disrepair and scant respect was being paid to Buddhist religious symbols.

Early next morning, the two of us walked to the river and were met by a group of village urchins. They offered to take us to various places connected with the life of the Buddha: where he received a bowl of milk-rice from a noble woman of the village; where he converted the three brothers who were hermits in a monastic system in the neighbourhood; and where a giant serpent is said to have sheltered the Buddha from a storm.

What baffled us was that the collective memory of the community had preserved this information and none of these urchins or their parents held any allegiance to Buddhism. We were astonished by what they knew of the Buddhist lore which we had learned from our books.

Five days later, we were back in Calcutta. We both felt that the emotionally charged denouement towards which we both moved called for fortitude. We looked upon the impending event from all angles. It was the end of a common style of living and thinking we had shared for well nigh thirteen years. It was the end of a friendship as we both had known it.

We were conscious that Noble Son of Wisdom was bound to be burdened by his royal and family duties and the bondage between us would vanish progressively and result in nothing more than occasional perfunctory communication. He had enjoyed the freedom of monkhood.

He had apprehensions about returning to the lay life of competition, intrigue and treachery. We talked things over in very great detail.

Ram joined us in some of the conversations. He was surprised to discover the depth of affection and trust that we shared. When we were once describing in his presence how much we would miss our regular communications and involvement in activities of common interest, Ram teased us:

"You two are so emotional that you sound like a reluctant couple compelled by someone to go in for a divorce."

The time came for him to board the ship. This time, the Siamese Legation arranged our transport to the harbour. Mr. Prasong attended to departure formalities personally. I was invited on board and the Captain, who had heard about my voyage in a sister boat two and a half years ago, had lunch served for the two us an hour in advance. He attended on us along with Mr. Prasong and we were deeply touched by his solicitude. In a typical ceremony, with the chanting of stanzas in Pali, we offered merit and benediction to them.

While the boarding passengers had their lunch, Noble Son of Wisdom and I retired into his luxury cabin. Although I was hardly an hour senior to him as a monk, he went on his knees and went through the ancient monastic ritual of the reverse of confession:

433

"Have you, Venerable Sir, seen, heard or suspected that I have violated any aspect of discipline that I had vowed to maintain."

Thrice he asked me and thrice I replied in the negative.

"I am so very happy that I have lived my life as a monk without a blemish. Now may I have your permission to don white clothes and return to lay life?"

I remained silent lest I break down and cry. Silence was also the appropriate response, according to tradition.

He worshipped me thrice, rose slowly and moved into an anteroom. When he returned he was in a white suit. Only his neatly shaven head showed that he had been a monk until a few minutes ago.

He knelt and worshipped me thrice. In the appropriate Pali formula, he asked me to administer the Triple Refuge and the Five Precepts. He repeated each line after me.

I was led down the gangplank to the carriage of the Royal Siamese Legation by His Royal Highness Prince Diamond-Lustre, Special Adviser on Modernization to His Majesty the King of Siam.

IV

I opened my eyes slowly. The light was too bright. I blinked a few times before the eyes focussed on a white screen which enclosed my bed. I was not in my room. I was not dreaming. That much was clear. I raised my right arm and found myself wearing some sort of long sleeved unbleached cotton shirt. A bonneted figure appeared instantly against the door. The shadowy profile resembled Aunt Flower in her uniform.

"Good Morning, Guruji," she said in a voice that chimed like a silver bell. "You had a long sleep. Do you feel all right?"

She was positively relieved, if not happy, that I had woken up. So was the doctor who was summoned by her. It seemed that the driver of the carriage followed me to the room in the hostel carrying the parcel of robes of Noble Son of Wisdom. He found me fumbling with the key. As he approached me to help, I had fainted. With the help of some of the servants of the hostel, he had carried me back to the carriage and taken me direct to the hospital. For twenty hours I had been unconscious.

"You can eat something and go home, Guruji," said the doctor after a thorough examination of my chest. "It's sheer exhaustion, Guruji. Both physical and emotional. Promise you will have a lot of rest. Best thing to do is to walk round the pond near your residence and feed the fish and the birds."

How easy it should have been if all one had to do to relieve the stress and pain of being separated from such a dear and loyal friend was to feed the fish and the birds!

I was reliving the grief and insecurity that I had suffered as a child when Little Father disappeared and, later, fate obliterated my teenage dreams. It was the same pain that I felt every time Colonel Olcott left the Island. The growing distance between the White Buddhist and myself had gnawed at my sinews as I had no explanation for such a strong spiritual and human relationship to break down. Why am I destined to lose every person who becomes important to my life? For a moment I shuddered. Is it my love that brings about catastrophe?

In my self-pity, I overlooked the joy with which the Prince was returning to his Motherland to serve the King and the Nation. I should rejoice with him. With ample time spent in the open feeding birds and the fish, to the amusement of a dozen urchins who surrounded me, I regained enough strength and serenity to return to my books.

Two things set me writing the first draft of the dissertation on the evolution of the Mahayana or the Northern Buddhist tradition. One was a cheerful letter from Prince Diamond-Lustre. He spoke lovingly of his principal wife and two minor wives and their children. Their happy reunion was a tribute to their patience, faith and hope, he said. He concluded the letter encouraging me to pursue my studies.

"I will always be your friend, Venerable Sir," he wrote. He was formal as a lay man addressing a monk. "Please be my guide in my lay life as you had been my friend and solace in my monastic life."

The other was a visit by the Right Reverend Kenneth Saunders. On his arrival in Calcutta, he had been informed of my brief illness and he made it a point to see me immediately to find out if everything was all right with me. He had passed through Madras and met some of the delegates to the Theosophical Convention . - the one I missed on account of the visit of Noble Son of Wisdom. He had news on Olcott.

"T. B., do send for a copy of Olcott's Presidential Address. It seems that he apologized to the Christians for his long-standing anticlerical position. He called himself a chief offender, of course, meaning that there was another chief offender. He is supposed to have said that if the founders of the Movement had not been so very intolerant to Christianity that the Christians in the Movement would have been a thousandfold. I was reminded of the time he accused you of being a Christian spy or Fifth Columnist."

"He must be getting wiser at sixty," I mused. "Or else, he must be wanting to dissociate himself from Madame Blavatsky or Dharmapala or both."

"You don't think that he could be sincere in his regrets?" queried the Metropolitan.

"Oh! No. I would be the last to accuse him of insincerity. He is a man of integrity. But some times he makes me worry."

"You mean when he goes back to his Himalayan Masters and Tibetan Adepts."

"Precisely, Reverend Kenneth," I replied. "And also when he appears to be in open competition with his own protege, Don David or rather Dharmapala ."

I was not surprised that the Metropolitan had made a thorough study of the growing tensions between sixty-year old White Buddhist and the twenty-eight year old Dharmapala . Nor was I surprised that the main contributor to the study was Mrs. Wilkins who had examined the effect of the disestablishment of the Anglican and Presbyterian Churches on the rise of national religions. Their conclusion was that the

436

Christian missionaries in Sri Lanka and India would be long remembered for two major developments: First, the education of the new generation of national leaders who would use their new knowledge and language ability to agitate against foreign domination in every respect; Second, a growing middle class nurtured on values of liberty, equality and democracy which would demand nothing less than that enjoyed by its counterpart in England.

It seemed that Mrs. Wilkins contended that the alumni of Christian schools like Don David and Don Baron would attract more of their kind into a vibrant campaign for national independence.

She had further predicted that the more effective leaders of such a campaign would be Christians themselves or rather Christians who in the wake of a democratic process would resume their traditional religion.

"You see, T. B., what her research has shown is that a progressive path to democracy and political freedom, and not Buddhist or Hindu renaissance, would toll the knell of Christianity. What do you think?"

"It is no doubt an ingenious theory. But I see no evidence."

I wrote a long letter to Colonel Olcott in which I explained why I did not attend the Adyar Convention, congratulated him on the spirit of tolerance of his Presidential Address and outlined the theory of Mrs. Wilkins on the role of democracy and national liberation in the revival of traditional religion. In passing, I suggested that he should continue to inspire and guide Dharmapala .

When the brief New Year break ended and I returned to my routine, I was overwhelmed by an urge to redouble my academic efforts. It was an unprecedented sensation of urgency, as if some immediate task was being neglected. I worked late into the night and completed the dissertation. Professor Wilson returned the first draft with comments on language, style and word-order. On the last page was his appraisal:

"Looks good. But as I know very little of the subject, I must take your word for the contents!"

I was not discouraged as I had expected him to say so. I was fortunate that I had several fellow students who could lead me to a few scholars outside the University.

One was a Lama who had founded a Tibetan Monastery in the foothills of the Himalayas at Kalimpong and was engaged in research on the origin of Tibetan Buddhism - the major representative of the third school or tradition called the Path of the Thunderbolt or the Path

437

of Magical Incantations. He read my draft and offered substantial comments.

Another resource was the esteemed Brahman scholar, Sarat Chandra Das, who was reputed to have made the first recorded visit by an outsider to the heart of Tibet. He had been a personal friend of B. H. Hodgson who, as British Representative in Nepal, brought the wealth of Mahayana Buddhist literature in Sanskrit to the attention of the world scholars. Das was in the process of setting up an Indian counterpart of Rhys Davids' Pali Text Society. His comments were incisive. He made me revise whole sections and the result was a well-documented, coherent and readable text.

I submitted the dissertation to the University and began in earnest my studies for the six examination papers which I had to take an year later.

Neither my studies nor the teaching assignments precluded me from being in touch with my little circle of mentors, teachers, friends and family. Despite advancing age, Venerable Sumangala was still engaged in his manifold activities. He replied to my letters regularly. His optimism for greater days for the country and the people remained unabated. He encouraged me to complete my studies as soon as possible and return to the Island.

"We need you here very urgently," he said in one letter. "Our College is attracting so many foreign students that we need you on the staff."

Equally enthusiastic was Don Baron whose English High School in Kandy was progressing steadily:

"I am looking forward to your return, Venerable Sir. We have a lot to do together. The King of the Sangha College at the Flower Garden Monastery is doing quite well but not so splendidly as when you were there. My latest project is to establish a monastic residence for visiting monks near the Railway Station. Our ancient monasteries are still too conservative. They do not accommodate the monks from the low-country who belong to sects other than the Siamese. I have set up the Residence-Donor Society and its membership comprises mainly the low-country business men who are prospering in trade and professions in and around Kandy. I am inviting that illustrious scholar of Palace Hill College, Venerable Pleasant-Tissa of Crystal-market, to be the abbot of the new temple in the Field of the Gods."

I met Dharmapala whenever he was in Calcutta. The Maha Bodhi Society consumed all his time and energy, even though he did not neglect his many functions in the Buddhist Theosophical Society of Colombo. He found his work rewarding. Branch Societies were being established in many cities and countries. "Save Buddha Gaya" had become a household slogan. He was riding the crest of his popularity.

Though lukewarm in their personal relations, he and Olcott continued to cooperate with each other. For the dual purpose of exchanging information on the growing network of collaborators and of disseminating knowledge on Buddhism, he started the Maha Bodhi Journal. So impressive was his work that Sir William Hunter added a chapter on Buddhism to his "*History of the Indian Empire*". It commented on the work of Dharmapala and made a special reference to his Journal:

> "The first number of its Journal opens with the following words: The Maha Bodhi Society has commenced its mission for the resuscitation of Buddhism in the land of its birth."

Prince Diamond-Lustre wrote from time to time. He enjoyed his work but complained about the drudgery of lay life.

"Venerable Sir, How correct the Buddha was when he said that the life of a householder was full of obstacles and how free like the space the life of a monk was! But I do enjoy the opportunities I am having to do what I learnt as a monk in your beautiful country."

He gave few details of what he was doing. Apparently he was very busy.

Letters from Sangha-Gem-Field were invariably short and infrequent. I had become superfluous and my brother had grown to be an esteemed leader. I was happy for him as well as for myself. I could now concentrate on the wider national or even international role which I always thought was the intention of my mentors.

My three morale-boosters from Kandy never wavered. Their letters had been my source of joy, solace and encouragement. The three kids too joined them with their own little messages and drawings. The failing health of Little Father was disconcerting. He had been in hospital twice and Aunt Flower had arranged for him to be in Kandy. He was uneasy and was anxious to return to his work in Orange island. Slim-Jewel spoke of her long hours of work - a full eight-hour day at the hospital and the many hours of sewing she was doing to supplement her income.

"I am a regular dress-maker to my colleagues in the hospital and their friends. Lucrative though it is, I do not much like the pressure of deadlines which force me to work very late into the night."

I had only a very short letter from Olcott. He was busy, he said, with work which he should have done in India long ago. He did not specify what it was. He was keen to cooperate with Dharmapala in promoting the wide-ranging agenda of the Maha Bodhi Society.

"We are planning for September or October a joint visit to Burma to raise funds and to establish in Akyab a Branch Society," he wrote.

To me it was happy evidence that two men who were indispensable for the promotion of Buddhism were still friends. Theirs was the relationship of a relentlessly protective father and a spoiled child. At least, that was how Olcott preferred to describe the ups and downs in their interaction.

Proof of better relations came on the twenty-fourth of October 1892.

The establishment of the Headquarters of the Maha Bodhi Society in Calcutta and the announcement of its objective of regaining for the Buddhist World the custody of its most famous and holiest shrines had stirred up ignorant prejudices and bigoted protests among a small section of the Hindu Community. Dharmapala with his enlightened Hindu supporters in Bengal thought that it would be imprudent to suffer the anti-Buddhist discussion to go unchecked . So they requested Colonel Olcott to make a plain public statement of the actual relationship and mutual sympathies between the Hindu and Buddhist religious systems.

That balmy Monday evening Colonel Olcott spoke most enthusiastically to a large audience at the Town Hall. By him on the stage sat Dharmapala to whom the speaker made several complimentary references. Olcott explained and supported the goals and objectives of the Maha Bodhi Society which he said was established with his concurrence. He urged that no time be lost in coming to a mutual understanding. Hindus trusted Olcott and he had generously lent his goodwill to his brilliant if somewhat stubborn protege. It augured well for the future. I was overjoyed.

Next month when Olcott and Dharmapala left together for Burma to raise funds for the Society's programme in Buddha Gaya, I was thrilled. When Olcott's speech on Kinship between Hinduism and Buddhism appeared in print with a glowing introduction by Dharmapala

I felt relieved that one of my worst nightmares was over. Thus for me the year ended well.

I had no idea that 1893 was to be a year of turmoil. It began with four months of intense study. The examination was difficult as it had to be for a degree of Master of Arts in Philosophy. I felt that I had acquitted myself creditably. My students in Pali fared well in their examination. Among them was a brilliant young monk from Chittagong whom I would gladly recommend to take my place on the staff of the College. I was planning to return to Ceylon immediately after the examination.

Right Reverend Kenneth Saunders arranged a farewell function in which I was asked to speak on Buddhist Scholars of the West with special reference to Bishop R. S. Coppleston's recent book "Buddhism: Primitive and Present in Magadha and Ceylon." I spent most of my day in the library as I wanted to deal with the subject exhaustively. I returned to my room only after the library closed for the night.

That night I was unusually tired such that even the single letter which had been slipped into my room under the door led me to a debate whether it could wait till the next morning. But the handwriting on the cover prompted me to open it immediately. This was perhaps the only letter which had been addressed by Slim-Jewel in her own handwriting. Usually, Uncle Victor addressed the cover in his large legible civil service scroll. It was unusual in another aspect. It was not a morale-boosting epistle written jointly by my beloved Gang of Three. Slim-Jewel had written alone. Besides, it was in verse.

I raised the wick of the oil lamp which a servant had thoughtfully lit for me before my arrival. I sat on the bed and began reading.

"Venerable Brother,

May the blessings of the Triple Gem and the
Protection of the gods be with you.

To gods have I appealed with devotion   unswerving
But an answer I have yet to receive.
To a living god whose heart I know and trust
I turn for help in dire distress

A sentence worse than death have I received:
My eyes dim fast and ere too long

441

Into abysmal depths of darkness
Am I doomed to be cast.
Between blindness and death
The latter I would gladly choose.

Often have the curly thin petals
Of the dazzling red blossom of Gloria Superba
Invited me to taste its seducing root
To lead me softly to blissful sleep everlasting.

Shamefully would I now admit
I told them "No" the day you donned a beggar's
        robes.
I couldn't say "Yes" when they called me next
When my child's dear father
In faithless squalor died and left us doomed.
They beckon again from the fence next door.
What should I tell them now?

"No again, Oh, sweet ender of sorrows,
Grief I must bear for it's my sad lot?
No yearning do I have for a life of my own,
For mine ended the day I said 'No' to your kin
By the river whose gurgling waters
Chided my weak, fumbling heart."

Oh brother, my saviour, my harbinger of hope,
A girl of fifteen looks rosily for a future
Beauty and brains in unison had decreed.
An orphaned lad whose mother I replace
Walks jauntily in pride as all around
Have nothing but praise for his charming ways,
His bewitching looks, his thirst for learning.
Who'll care for them if I seek my Peace
In selfish neglect of maternal duty?

But a burden I should never be
A frail woman to be led by her hand and fed
        with theirs!
Why truly need I live without my daily joy
Of seeing their smile-lit faces brighten
To cheer a toiling Mum?

Tell me, my brother, Give me your word.
You'll see them through life
As a father would do -
A father they never had.

Your beleaguered sister,

Slim-Jewel.

I read it several times. The words were clear and compelling. But the meter she had deliberately chosen came from a poem of boundless pathos. There, a mother searched in vain for her children she presumed to be lost in the forest. She did not know that their infinitely pious father, qualifying to become a saviour of humanity as the Buddha, had given them away to serve in an indigent household. Verses put into the mouth of this wailing mother never failed to draw tears and sobs even if the poem had been heard many times before. It happened quite often as this poem with its evocative sentiments was read at every wake, where in honour of a departed one, friends and relatives stayed awake the whole night.

Tears ran down my cheeks and the mist in my eyes had to be repeatedly wiped out to proceed with the reading.

What should I do? What should I write to her? How does one comfort a woman of thirty-four when her oncoming disability is complicated with her responsibilities to bring up two young children? How can I be a father to them? Vowed to a life of renunciation and poverty, I lived on what others gave me. In my present state of a monk there was nothing I could promise. Once again, I felt powerless and useless.

To say that sleep eluded me that night would be a gross understatement. I thought in circles. I chastised myself for my credulity at a time I could have asserted myself. But I was only a boy of seventeen then? And worse still, a docile product of the culture in which I was nurtured. I was shocked to hear of her repeated plans to kill herself. I was grateful that she was wise. I made several attempts to write a comforting letter. All that resulted from this futile venture was a floor strewn with discarded paper crushed nervously into unseemly balls!

By dawn I trudged to Ram's house. He was being shaved by his barber. Conscious of a deftly swung razor, the ebullient Man Friday of the Metropolitan was disposed to giving me a patient hearing. I told him

443

of the sad chapter of my life and of recurring occasions when I had accused myself for all the woes of Slim-Jewel.

"Guruji, you are a young man and your future is still ahead of you. Grief is not the answer. Let's talk to the Metropolitan and he is bound to find you a solution."

"When?"

"Why not today? Say by nine."

I returned to the hostel to tidy myself and to put on a newer robe. That proved to be providential. A letter from Uncle Victor greeted me as I opened the door. I tore it open and read quickly. It was a hastily written note, brief, precise and to the point. He had heard that Slim-Jewel had written to me and wanted to put me at ease.

"It is serious but not altogether hopeless" he wrote. "Surgery is the only solution. But it can be done by a Harley Street specialist only in London. I will let you know what we are planning to do."

Instinctively I opened the trunk in which I had kept the envelope which Noble Son of Wisdom gave me on the day I left Sri Lanka. It was there with my important documents. The brown envelope bore his clearly written notation: TALISMAN SANS PAREIL. NEVER KNOWN TO FAIL, SPECIALLY WHEN THE WORLD AROUND LOOKS DARK AND BLEAK AND HOPE HAS FLED. I opened the packet carefully. I could not but smile at his unfailing sense of humour. Was I not surprised? It was indeed a talisman which could solve all problems, specially the one I was now grappling with. A thousand pounds sterling in crisp five pound notes!

I put the packet in the trunk and joined Ram, who had come in a carriage to take me to the Metropolitan.

"You look far more relaxed, Guruji. What happened?"

I told him about Uncle Victor's letter and the universally effective talisman of Noble Son of Wisdom.

"It's good, Guruji. You can take her to London."

"Should I?" I asked tentatively. "I thought that my Aunt would be more useful."

Alerted by Ram through a messenger, Right Reverend Kenneth Saunders awaited us in the verandah. It did not take too long for him to grasp the problem and to offer solutions.

"Now, T. B. as money the root of all difficulties is not a problem, let me do a little scouting for you: someone to meet the party on arrival in London, a place to stay, the best doctor we can find to do the operation and ....."

444

"Thank you, Reverend Kenneth. That's a lot already," I said without allowing him to complete his sentence. But he continued.

"...... a way to see how a nervous young monk of my acquaintance could be there to chant a little benediction and prepare the patient spiritually for the operation."

I took a while to realize that he was referring to me. He was not laughing. He was quite serious.

V

Thus was I amidst the milling crowds at Southampton Jetty when a luxury ship from Australia berthed on a warm sunny morning of the Mid-summer day. A young Anglican padre who had been my friendly guide since my arrival a week ago, told me,

"You know. Today is the day that we British hail as the longest day of the year and the French across the channel bemoan as the shortest night."

It was the twenty-second of June, 1893. Aunt Flower in a long flowing dress and a matching hat walked down the gangplank. Slim-Jewel in a less pretentious dress and a tiny hairdo held on to her left arm. Only the tan on their faces set them apart from the rest of passengers who disembarked displaying the sheer joy of being back home.

They spotted me and whatever nervousness I saw in their faces when they emerged from the ship vanished. How very thoughtful Reverend Kenneth had been!

"I am here on a study tour funded and arranged by the India Office but, of course, imaginatively inspired and orchestrated by my ever-mindful God Father," I told them as we took a train to London. "Rheinhold Rost, the Librarian, handles my programme and he has invited you to use his spare room on two conditions. You keep it clean and you make for him one of your fabulous curry dinners."

"That's simple," said Aunt Flower. "We have brought all the condiments, some rice and palm molasses, too."

"Don't forget to invite me," added Reverend Stephen Reeves, who briefed the ladies on their appointments with the doctor and the hospital. Everything had been meticulously organized.

"Thank you, Reverend Reeves, I am grateful to you for all the trouble you have taken," said Slim-Jewel pronouncing every word clearly though diffidently.

"Wonderful. So both of you speak English."

Within a week, Slim-Jewel was back from hospital and all she needed was a long period of rest. As her sight improved, she became more cheerful. She could read with ease the letters sent by Moon-Beam and Middle Banda. Autumn-Moon had sent a drawing of the Temple of the Tooth. Uncle Victor gave the news. He had his hands full with three kids. Golden Jewel was a resourceful helper.

I spent a couple of hours in the evenings with them. After an interval of five years, there was so much of news to exchange. During the rest of the day, I helped Rost to identify and catalogue a number of Sinhala palmleaf manuscripts which the India Office had acquired. He had many visitors and most of them I knew by name and their contribution to Indological and Sri Lankan studies. Needless to say, these were the happiest days in my life.

Members of a Ladies' Club took over the two ladies when Slim-Jewel was declared fit enough to tour London and the environs. They took turns in taking them to places of interest and I looked forward to meeting them in the evening to have their reactions to what they had seen and done. The day they were taken for a ride in a horseless carriage, their excitement knew no bounds.

Another thoughtful suggestion from Reverend Kenneth had been that the two Sri Lankan nurses should have some "hands on" experience in a London Hospital. They spent several weeks on what proved to be the best professional education they had ever had in their careers.

I was sad to see them go. I accompanied them by train from Waterloo Station to Southampton and stayed with them on board until the visitors were requested to disembark. Slim-Jewel fell at my feet and cried as she thanked me for making the treatment possible.

" I would have died without you. I couldn't have lived a day if I went blind."

My stay in England continued for two more months. Summer was not the best time to visit centres of Oriental learning. But most of the scholars went out of their way to receive me and in some instances their students too. Rhys Davids were an impressive couple and I marvelled at the energy and stamina of Caroline Rhys Davids who took a very keen interest in Buddhist Philosophy. To some I was a curiosity - a living representative of the exotic culture they studied. But to the most I was a resource person who could fill in information they lacked or give the traditional interpretation of things which were not clear to them.

One of the most striking personalities I met was the stately aristocratic bureaucrat, Sir Robert Chalmers, who had chosen Pali and Buddhist literature as his special fields of study as a student of Professor T. W. Rhys Davids. This young man was in correspondence with Venerable Subhuti of Curse-Sword and gave me a fascinating account of his discovery of the story of Baarlam and Joasaph and its possible link with the story of the Buddha-to-be Prince Siddhartha. He surmised that Joasaph was a corruption of Bodhisatva, the appellation by which the Buddha in his lay life was referred to in literature. I did not dream at that moment that I would next meet him as the Governor of Sri Lanka.

To me all these encounters meant that I was privileged to be born an heir to a great spiritual, literary and artistic heritage. By the time I left England, I had a fair idea of the width and magnitude of the emerging intellectual discipline of Oriental studies, the key players in the scene and the progress they had made. I had also made some lasting friendships. I could never be more grateful to the two men who made this possible - Right Reverend Saunders and Dr. Rost.

On the way back I enjoyed the voyage better. During my trip to England, a combination of anxiety and sea-sickness made me miserable. I spent most of the time in the cabin. I hardly ate a square meal for fear of being sick. This time, the Mediterranean Sea was quieter and I had become more immune to motion sickness. I spent most of the time writing my impressions and observations to go into a report which was required by my sponsors.

At Port Said we berthed for a day before entering the Suez Canal - that incredible man-made waterway connecting the Mediterranean Sea with the Red Sea. This ingenious feat of technology had shortened a trip between Calcutta and Southampton by almost a month.

There I had a pleasant surprise again due to Reverend Kenneth's ingenuity. He had sent the results of my examination and a message of congratulations through the Captain of a ship which was scheduled to be in Port Said a few days ahead of us. Another "First Class First" with a Master of Arts degree with distinction was an accomplishment to celebrate, said the Captain of our ship. But he knew enough of the constraints of the life of a Buddhist monk to not insist. Yet he made an announcement during lunch and it changed the rest of my voyage dramatically.

It was not in any way like my first voyage to Calcutta. More people recognized me and some stopped to have a chat. A few invited me to tea so that they could discuss Asia in general and Buddhism in particular. A civil servant and a few planters going to Colombo had many questions to ask. They were glad that I had confirmed what they had heard from returning officers and planters.

"They all say that yours is a lovely country and you people are really very nice." I was proud that my country and people were so appraised.

There were many British nationals going to India to pursue a wide variety of careers. Among them was a young archaeologist who was on his way to join the Archaeological Survey of India and was interested in the study Buddhist monuments. I had many hours of stimulating conversations with this young man of learning and culture. A thorough desk research he had conducted in preparation to his field assignment had yielded him a wealth of information. He had an hypothesis that the Buddhists in India were pioneers in founding long-lasting institutions and building them in more permanent material like stone because of direct Greek influence.

"I have reason to believe," he said, "that Asoka's grandmother was a Greek."

He was referring to the third emperor of the Maurya Dynasty of the Third Century before Christ. He embraced Buddhism as his personal religion and eschewed war in favour of peace, reconciliation and moral upliftment of humanity. This emperor played a major role in spreading the Buddhist Faith in and outside his empire which covered more than present India but did not include the southern Dravidian regions or Sri Lanka. Asoka the Righteous, as we called him out of veneration, has been the greatest hero of our history. Buddhism was introduced to the Island by his own son Mahinda and daughter Sanghamitta.

The Bay of Bengal as the South East Monsoon was tapering was a veritable terror. Every evening the sky became dark suddenly and storms with thunder and lightning and pouring rain tossed us mercilessly. As a monk foregoing the evening meal, I was spared the messy experience of balancing a soup-laden spoon in mid air with tricky gyrations of an acrobat! One clung to one's bed for fear of being thrown violently on the floor. But the agony lasted just a couple of days and we were sailing up the Hooghly, swollen and muddy brown with the rich alluvial soil which was being wastefully washed to the sea. As far as the eye could see the erstwhile rice fields were pools of muddy water whose sediments would enrich the soil for a bumper crop in the next season.

I was received by Ram who informed me that the Metropolitan had plans for me. The postponed farewell function was now rescheduled and it was not merely a farewell but a celebration of my recent success. It was to be a day after the Convocation or Graduation Ceremony and the guest list had grown to include academic and social celebrities. I looked forward to it as an opportunity to thank publicly my many sponsors, mentors and friends. Their generosity and kindness had seen me through a life of achievements hardly conceivable by a man of my circumstances. At the top of the list were the Metropolitan himself and His Royal Highness Diamond-Lustre, once known as Noble Son of Wisdom.

449

The function was a great success. I was pleased to hear what the speakers had to say about me. They had no reason to flatter me. My speech was well received. Right Reverend Kenneth Saunders had the last word. He picked on my summary of my life's experience. I had said,

"I do think that my achievements are nothing more than or different from what any person would have made if he or she had the same opportunities that I have had."

The Metropolitan's response was that anyone could have the same opportunities but only those with self-confidence, perseverance, wisdom and dedication could made use of them. I felt that he was correct. I am not the only student to whom he stretched out a friendly hand. How many grasped it?

I was disappointed when Dharmapala was unable attend the function in my honour. He was busy getting ready to proceed to Chicago in the United States of America where the leaders of world religions had been invited to attend an international parley. Its ambitious convenors had called it the Parliament of World's Religions. In a friendly letter, he had explained how its principal organizer, Dr. John Henry Burrows, had been impressed with the very first issue of the Maha Bodhi Journal and invited the young editor to be a member of the Organizing Committee of the Parliament. In that capacity, he had done all he could to find a suitable representative for Southern Buddhism. Several whom he approached had declined on various grounds. He wrote,

"Some of my best friends and trusted advisers, not anticipating the good results which were likely to come out of this great historic Parliament, pooh-poohed the idea, and thought that the Parliament was simply the means for the glorification of Christianity."

Despite such discouragements, he had planned to attend the Parliament and speak on behalf of the Southern Buddhists. He was fortunate, he said, that two Buddhists from California and New York were financing the trip and had requested him to give a series of talks. His own motivation for the trip came from the fact that he might visit Japan and China on the way back and enlist support for the restitution of Buddha Gaya and other shrines to Buddhists.

In my reply, I wished him a very successful visit to the United States of America. I also told him of the choice which the Hindus had made to be their spokesman. I had occasion to hear him at a lecture he

450

delivered at the University. Vivekananda or Bliss of Discriminatory Knowledge was brilliant as an orator - erudite, forceful and exceptionally convincing. He was the disciple of a saintly man of admirable qualities of piety and dedication, whom the people in veneration called Ramakrishna the Supreme Swan.

"If oratory, substance and an inspiring message are to be the ingredients of success at the forthcoming Parliament, I have no doubt that the two of you will bring great distinction to yourselves and much credit to our region in Asia," I added.

Leaving Calcutta was a painful wrench. Five fruitful years in Calcutta had made me a man. In quarters that mattered, I was known and respected. A widening circle of friends and admirers loved me. Whatever diffidence that plagued me at times on account of my humble background and limited life experiences disappeared steadily. I was ready to face life with renewed vigour.

I could make a rewarding academic career in Calcutta. The College would love to have me continue as a lecturer in Pali. There was a steady flow of students from the Chakmas and border regions of eastern Bengal. Even the University was ready, on a strong recommendation by the Professor, to consider me for an academic position in the Department of Philosophy. The Archaeological Survey of India had discussed how I could be brought in to be a regular consultant on the Buddhist heritage which constituted the major part of its work.

In the spiritual domain, I could be directly involved in the growing activities of Dharmapala and his Maha Bodhi Society. I could have accomplished my boyish ambition of being a celebrated Buddhist Missionary in foreign lands. The young intellectuals of India were ripe for Buddhism. There was so much interest and I had already proved to be a favourite speaker.

But something inexplicable was drawing me home. It was not mere nostalgia but a deep and stirring sense of patriotism. I felt that I had been too long away from the important work of national development. I had a promise to keep with Don Baron. Now that the failing health of Little Father took an active worker away from the campaign for educating the underprivileged Buddhist children of backward villages, I was convinced that I had an obligation to take his place.

On a more domestic note, there was also a vague impression that I had a role in the nurture of my dead brother's two children. Though in robust health otherwise, Slim-Jewel's eyesight remained a cause of concern. The operation only guaranteed the status quo without further deterioration. Besides, both children were of an age when some

451

guidance from a male adult was needed. All these created the feeling that my return to the Island was for a multiplicity of purposes and

.

every one of them was important and urgent.

It was with mixed feelings I boarded the ship. My tourist class ticket had secured for me a first class cabin on the strength of a Captain's letter given five years ago! I was a celebrity. The Captain and the crew spared no efforts to take the best care of my needs. The voyage gave me ample time in a tranquil atmosphere to embark on a serious in-depth investigation into my own self.

I was in time for the funeral of Little Father. It was a grand occasion. A thousand monks found their way to Kandy where he died after a prolonged illness. Seven-days of lying-in-state had been arranged at the residence of the Abbot of Sangha-Gem-Field at the Flower Garden Monastery. My brother, who by now had become a senior monk of great prestige and much influence, had set the sky as his limit in according to Little Father the highest ecclesiastical honour. He had asked Uncle Victor to meet me on landing and rush me to Kandy. *De jure*, I was still the Abbot of the Monastery and I had to play my role.

My appearance on the scene on the fourth day after his death redoubled the flow of mourners and on-lookers. Most had decided to come a second time so that they could offer their condolences to me. That he was my mentor and role model was highlighted in every obituary that appeared in the newspapers, both Sinhala and English. So was the story of his disappearance and the successful exploits of Noble Son of Wisdom and me as detectives.

By the time the day of the funeral arrived, Little Father had risen in the eyes of the media-manipulated public to be a hero without a parallel! I had one more occasion to witness the indomitable prowess of "mouth-to-mouth" communication. I was convinced that Little Father deserved it all. But what was being said of him should have been more poignantly stated while he was still alive. It would given him the solace that every sacrifice he made in the service of his religion, his nation and his country was worth the while. That unfortunately was not to be. I regretted it very much and blamed myself as the most unconscionable defaulter.

The most coveted tribute to Little Father came from the monks. He was no ecclesiastical luminary. He was neither a scholar nor a famous preacher. He had no books to his credit. Nor was he the preceptor or tutor of distinguished disciples. He was only a campaigner - an activist and that, too, in the field of lay education. But every important monk was there to pay their last respects to a humble brother who dedicated every minute of his time and every ounce of his energy to serve the disadvantaged children of rural Sri Lanka.

I had the most challenging task of ensuring that as many as twenty-four messages of condolences in verse and thirty orations were packed into the five-hour period from one to six in the afternoon. That was after dissuading as many others who wanted to say a few words in his honour. Of course, I had to request a few special visitors to join in. Among them was Ernest Dickinson, now a senior officer in the Attorney General's Office in Colombo, who felt obliged to attend the funeral personally.

"I would not be surprised if Venerable Pure Intellect would rise from the bier and chide us all for wasting our time attending his funeral," began Dickinson. "He would ask us why we were not devoting this effort to raise funds to set up one more school in a remote village."

That I thought was the most comprehensive epitome of my Little Father's life and career.

Dickinson was spending a few days in Kandy. I invited him to Sangha-Gem-Field and he accepted my invitation gladly.

I had every reason to be proud of what my brother had done. The temple was spotlessly clean and in the best of repair. The school had grown and had been repeatedly rated the best school in the region. That was remarkable specially because the Christian School at Bo-tree Plain had gone down rapidly. The Sunday School, too, was flourishing. We arranged hurriedly a colourful event where Dickinson would be the guest of honour. It was a joint Prize Giving of the School and the Sunday School.

After the function, he met me in my room in the monks' residence. We spoke of the changes that had taken place in the country since we last met over five years ago. He knew what I had done during this period not only as I wrote to him somewhat frequently but also because our common friend Reverend Kenneth Saunders had apprised of my progress. We spoke frankly and had no hidden or open agenda. We were two friends who valued our mutual esteem and affection. From the sublime we came down to the ridiculous. From national revival and agitation for independence we digressed to gossip and personal lives. At one stage, he was asking me about my plans for the future.

"Bongyi, my friends wrote to me from London to say how very concerned you were over Slim-Jewel's operation. The nurse had told the surgeon something that reminded me of a couplet in the life of the Buddha. You remember, Bongyi? 'Happy indeed is that woman whose husband is a man like this.'"

"I didn't know I was being watched," I replied with unconcealed embarrassment. "It's true I was very concerned. She had appealed to me for help and her letter in verse was heart-rending."

"Can I tell you something? Life has its own designs and they do not even enter our dreams. Ever since I heard about the disrobement of your bosom pal, the Siamese Prince, I had expected to hear similar news about you."

"Really?"

"But the Metropolitan assures me that your commitment to monastic life and moreso to the tasks in hand in the country is solid and unwavering. He thinks that nothing short of an insurmountable catastrophe in the lives of your brother's widow and children would swerve you away."

"He's very right."

"Yet," continued the elder administrator. "I want to give you an assurance. If at any time, you are compelled to return to lay life for whatever reason, do let me know first. I would happily take care of what needs to be done then."

It was not clear what he was offering or whether it was something I could ever accept. But I was grateful that he had thought of me and had alternative plans for my life, if a need arose at any time. I assured him that the need to make use of his kind offer was not likely to occur - at least, at the moment.

"In our tradition in Sri Lanka," I explained, "one becomes a monk for life. Temporary or short-term ordination is unknown to us. In Burma, Siam and Cambodia, people do become monks for short periods. You know. They compare the Sri Lankan form of ordination to marriage."

I was so confident that I would be a monk to the last day of my life.

Fortunately, the August vacation which coincided with the annual pageant of the Temple of the Sacred Tooth in Kandy enabled me to rest a bit. I accepted no invitations to go out of the temple. Of course, I had to deal with a stream of visitors, who came to see me more out of courtesy if not curiosity. There was little doubt that my five-year absence had made me a rank outsider in my own village. The temple and its many activities went on without any intervention on my part. I was no longer wanted. At times, the stabbing pangs of grief caused by what appeared to me a conspiracy of rejection burnt deep into my

454

heart. In time, I learnt to rationalize and accept the situation. A change of residence to Kandy appeared to be the best solution.

On the day the Kandy Buddhist High School reopened, I visited Don Baron. As Principal, he had done a wonderful job. It was a flourishing school. I told him that I had come to fulfill my promise. He was so pleased that he gave me the time-table of an absent teacher and led me to his class. That very afternoon, I resumed my position as a teacher in the Buddhist College of the Flower Garden Monastery. It was quite convenient that I had residential facilities close to both institutions.

I settled down to a routine which was as reassuring as it was rewarding. It did not take too long to be back again in the national scene. The ageing leaders, notably, Venerables Sumangala of both the Learning-Awakening College and Sand-Village, Gunananda of Scribe's Garden, Pleasant-Gem-Tissa of Orange Island and Subhuti of Curse-Sword, welcomed me back with a visible sense of relief. With renewed energy, I was back in the loop.

How very warmly I was received by the old and the young campaigners for religious revival, educational development and national liberation! Olcott made his infrequent visits but his impact on the growing English medium Buddhist schools was incredible. He found some remarkable men of learning and devotion to run these schools as well as to teach in them. But the towering stalwart in the national scene was young Dharmapala . He was unrivalled. Any hostility or indifference shown by an increasingly cantankerous Olcott did not seem to affect him.

Chicago added immensely to the burgeoning prestige of Dharmapala . His world tour was exceedingly successful.

In Hawaii, he met Mary Elizabeth Foster who was to be the patron of his numerous activities in the fields of Buddhist education with a technical and vocational bias, social services for the benefit of the poor and the disadvantaged, and revival of Buddhism in Sri Lanka and India.

I joined him in his tours to mount public awareness and raise funds. It is through these tours that I had a glimpse of the glory and the majesty of the ancient civilization of the nation as reflected in the ancient monuments which lay in ruin.

I began to take an interest in rock inscriptions which were being discovered in various parts of the Island. Once deciphered and interpreted by palaeologists and linguists, they proved to be a fantastic

455

source of information on the evolution of the Sinhala language as well as on the history of the nation. The *Island Chronicle* and the *Great Chronicle* which date from the fourth century and the sixth century of the Common Era trace our history from the fifth century before Christ. These inscriptions corroborate and amplify much of the information recorded in them. Whatever little time I could find from my teaching and national services I devoted to study the historical content and significance of these inscriptions.

As often as I could I spent several hours a week with Moon-Beam and Middle Banda. A replica of her mother in beauty and charming ways, the sixteen-year girl was doing well in school and was preparing for the Matriculation Examination of the University of London. Her ambition was to be a doctor. She had found what she needed to do to enter the Colombo Medical College, which was fast gaining prestige as a seat of higher learning. It was particularly popular with students from Burma and Bengal. She was equally keen on being conversant with Sinhala which was not taught even as a subject in the Convent School.

"Venerable Little Father, I want to be a doctor to save children like the son of Golden Jewel," she told me once. "But how can I do it if I do not know their language well enough to talk to them?"

"I thought you three spoke in Sinhala at home and you are quite good."

"Not any more. When mother was studying English we made it our home language to help her. Then we continued to do, so that my brother would benefit. Now we have become quite unconsciously an English-speaking home. Any Sinhala we use at home is to give orders to Golden Jewel."

"That is interesting," I said. "I am glad you speak English so well and so does your brother."

Classes in Sinhala were the remedy. Both kids were eager learners. To my great surprise, the fourteen-year Middle Banda took his work even more seriously than the sister did.

"I want to be like Mr. Stanley Williams," he told me. His aim was to be an administrator of a District.

With such high goals as tender teen-agers, the pair studied diligently. They had a million questions to ask. I was flattered by the confidence they had in me. They discussed their fears and apprehensions as much as they planned their future lives with me. I had loved them dearly. But meeting them weekly transformed itself to a close similitude of parental love and care.

One day, it was Moon-Beam who had to tell me something in confidence:

"Venerable Little Father, I have a feeling that mother is going through some problem in the hospital. Last week she had had trouble in giving an injection to a patient. This week she failed to draw blood from a patient's arm. At the third attempt she broke the needle and had to seek help from another nurse. The doctor had not been very kind to mother when the patient developed a large haematoma on his arm. She has been transferred to the office where she has to keep records and place orders for supplies. She is very unhappy."

I was perturbed. I knew what her unhappiness could lead her to. I went to see her immediately. She was fomenting her eyes with pomegranate leaves on the advice of a practioner of indigenous medicine. She had not expected me. She ran inside, put on a house-coat. and came out saying,

"I hope the children didn't tell you anything. I asked them not to. You have far too many things to do than worry over the miserable fate of a wretched woman. Besides, Venerable Brother, you have done more than you have to."

She was upset. She tried to check the tears but in vain. She clung to the door jamb and cried while Golden Jewel found a white sheet and spread it on a chair so that I could sit.

"Never mind what the children said. Tell me what the problem is," I told her.

It turned out to be far more serious than I had visualized. The operation had been only partially successful. Her ordinary vision was quite good. But she was hypermetropic to a point that anything within two feet was only a blur. Even as a clerical worker in the office she had to keep the papers on the table and stand up to be able to read.

What she had not told the children and was very reluctant to tell me was that she was soon to be retired on grounds of physical disability. A medical board to review her case had already been constituted and it had tried every possible remedy that medical science knew. Spectacles were of little help. If the board decides to terminate her services, its recommendation would be final. She cried bitterly as she gave me all the details speaking in a mixture of English and Sinhala.

"Death is preferable to what I am going through. On less than a third of my salary, how can I bring up the children? Until eyes went bad, I was supplementing my income as a seamstress. Moon-Beam looks forward to joining the Medical School in Colombo. She wants to be a doctor. Just to get a Licentiate in Medicine and Surgery, which is the least qualification necessary to practise, it would take five to six

457

years. Middle Banda already talks of being an administrator. He is only fourteen. He has to study for ten more years. His chances become better if he could do his higher studies abroad. I want to live for them and I want them to achieve their ambitions."

Her sobbing moved me to tears. I had no idea how I could comfort her. I felt weak and helpless. I wanted to say something encouraging. But I had no opportunity.

Moon-Beam and Middle Banda were returning home. Their carefree laughter was so loud that they were heard long before they were seen. That gave Slim-Jewel and me a couple of minutes to wipe our eyes and change the topic of conversation.

The children rushed in and were surprised to see me. They fell on their knees and worshipped me. They stood by me until I spoke to them.

"You seem to be having some fun. What's it all about, Son?" I asked the little fellow who seemed to be tickled by something that had transpired between him and his sister.

"We were arguing as to who is superior: a doctor or a Government Agent."

"Who won?"

"Who else?" asked Middle Banda whose eyes twinkled with mischief.

"What a happy family! What a catastrophe lurked around the corner!" I thought. But I had no solution to offer. I missed my Siamese colleague.

The next day I discussed my dilemma with Don Baron.

"I know what bothers you, Venerable Sir. If the family could be ensured a steady income, the children could continue in their schools and Slim-Jewel would be less anxious. I know that you will want to see your brother's children achieving their ambitions. But you are a monk. I wish I could pay you a salary for your work. You are the most qualified teacher on the staff and the experience you have brought is unique. But however much I try, our conservative board members in Colombo will never agree to employ you on a salary as long as you are a monk. To be very frank, they may even be more reluctant to employ you if you give up robes."

That night I knew what options were open to me. I could remain a monk and let Slim-Jewel and the two kids fend for themselves. I did have access to substantial sums of money as Abbot of the Royal Monastery of Sangha-Gem-Field. But to use such funds for family

458

purposes would be not merely unethical but an unpardonable act of moral turpitude. From our infancy it had been ingrained in our minds that to take anything which belonged to the Sangha (the Order of Monks) would result in rebirth as a crow, a dog or a denizen of hell. Even a blade of grass in a temple belonged to the Sangha.

I could, of course, return to lay life. But I would need a job as the school will have no place for me. The stigma attached to disrobing was so strong that even the proverbial loving kindness of a pious Buddhist would not permit him or her to show the slightest favour to an ex-monk. It was tragic.

Should I take the offer so kindly made by Ernest Dickinson? All that he could do was to appoint me to a post in the British Administration. Could I become a servant of the government without recanting all that I had hitherto advocated in favour of national identity and liberation? Was it not an act of betrayal to those with whom I had worked all these years? Will I go down as a traitor?

Right through that week, I evaluated every idea that occurred to me. The more I examined various options, the more I saw that there was only one course of action open to me. My moral conflict was narrowed down to a last question:

"In this life-time, what is of greater relevance: expediting my liberation from the cycle of birth and death or the future happiness of the children of my brother whose indiscretions had jeopardized them?"

By Friday, the answer was clear and final. I took the night train to Colombo.

VI

Venerable Sumangala was pleased to meet me. I told him of my decision. He was so understanding.

"I have only one regret, Little Name," he said. "Will you have the courage and serenity to face calumny, backbiting, vilification and disparagement which will be your lot from the moment you lay this robe aside? No explanation by you or anyone else will be heeded by your unreasonable critics and slanderers. But let that not desist you from doing what you consider important."

The identical sentiments were voiced by Venerable Gunananda, the Monk with the silver Tongue. But he added a comment that was very encouraging.

"Pure-Wisdom, Don't listen to anyone who asks you not to join government service. We need men like you to have experience in running the country. The fanatics who say we should have nothing to do with the British haven't the foggiest idea of how a country can be governed if and when the colonial masters leave. We really should have more men like you inside."

To have the blessings of the two of the most important men in my life was sanguine. I wished I could have also consulted Colonel Olcott and Dharmapala . But they were in India making arrangements to buy a property in Buddha Gaya for the Maha Bodhi Society. I had the vague impression that Venerable Gunananda reflected very much the pragmatic thinking of Dharmapala .

Monday morning I went to the Office of Mr. Ernest Dickinson in the Law Courts Complex of Colombo, which not only retained a Dutch atmosphere but also the Dutch name Hulftsdorp. I sent the usual slip requesting an interview and waited outside his office. He was at a conference with the Attorney General, I was told by a passing clerk. The longer I waited the more I reviewed my plans from various points of view. At one point I thought of calling it off and returning to Kandy. It was at that precise moment that the peon with a red sash led me to Dickinson's office.

"Bongyi, Or should I begin calling you T.B.? You don't have to tell me anything. Yesterday I took a walk and visited Venerable Gunananda. The poor fellow had not been too well recently. He told me everything. In fact, it is your case that I was discussing with the Attorney General."

I was simply flabbergasted. While I was on a slow train, my destiny seemed to ride a super express.

'Thank you, Sir. I hope he told you the whole story."

"Yes. Perhaps a little more. You are indeed a very courageous man."

Slim-Jewel's retirement on medical grounds and my appointment as the Interpreter-Mudaliyar to the Judicial District of Kandy took effect in the same week. I had to go through a ceremony to take my oaths before a judge of the Supreme Court who had his sessions in the Royal Audience Hall of the Kings of Kandy. Located at the foot of the Upper Garden Forest, barely a hundred feet to the northeast of the sanctum sanctorum of the Temple of the Sacred Tooth Relic, this architectural gem was an open hall ventilated by a fragrant breeze from the forest. Rows of elegantly carved timber pillars supported a majestic rafter-and-reefer-meshed Kandyan roof with its characteristic double slopes forming an obtuse angle of roughly 135 degrees. Nineteen years ago, I had taken Aunt Flower and Slim-Jewel to show the intricate carvings of the pillars.

Today both them were there, seated in the third row. In fact there were six others with them. One of them was my brother the monk who had been appointed the Abbot of the Monastery. In two days the Flower Garden Chapter would promote him to the rank of a Chief Monk and the Government Agent would hand him the Act of Appointment. The R. M., who had continued to be the Board Chairman of the school and the chief lay supporter of the temple, was there in his resplendent attire of a Kandyan chief - glittering blouse, forty yards of cloth draped bulgingly around the waist and thighs, golden shoes and a square hat with tassels. The rest were Uncle Victor and the children. Moon-Beam, in a white saree worn in Kandyan style, was the cynosure of all eyes. I could not help but reminisce that Slim-Slim looked exactly like her when we first visited this revered monument.

I was in the official attire of a Mudaliyar - a title transplanted from South India meaning the First Person. It was held *ex officio* by the Regional Administrators of the maritime provinces and conferred as an honorific to men of eminence in service to the Government and the public. I had a choice. I could have come in a Kandyan outfit similar to what the R. M. wore. It was Uncle Victor's idea that the more appropriate would be the uniform which went with the title.

Among my papers was a description of this uniform by Colonel Olcott. It was an entry he had made in his diary in May 1880 when he met a Regional Administrator:

[He] wore the country dhoti and a single-breasted last-century coat of blue cloth, with long skirts, turn-over cuffs, twenty large gold buttons down one side of the front and as many loops and lacings of gold lace opposite them, and the same ornamentation on the collar and the cuffs. A gold-laced scarlet baldric, passed over one shoulder and under the opposite arm, supported a short sword with a gold scabbard. A huge golden medallion-plaque, as large as a desert plate, was suspended diagonally in the contrary direction by a gold chain. A heavy and richly embossed gold girdle was buckled about him. His feet were bare and wore leather sandals.

The only item missing was the circular tortoise-shell comb which was an integral part of this costume. It was omitted not only because it needed long hair which could be tied in a knot at the back of the head and mine had hardly grown an inch and a half. It was also because Dharmapala , in his campaign for a simple national dress for males, had made the horn-shaped ends of the circular comb a subject of ridicule.

"Colonial powers have taken you to be fools and given you a pair of horns to prove it," he would say to crowds that cheered his bitterly sarcastic attacks on the upper classes who tended to ape their colonial masters. The circular comb was a Portuguese intrusion!

The day began for us with a visit to the Temple of the Sacred Tooth. The monks on duty were as friendly as when I was a monk. I felt a bit awkward to be in an alien formal attire. But the senior monk put me at ease saying that the kings of Kandy came in full regalia to make their offerings to the Tooth Relic.

It was the opening day of the Kandy Assizes of the Supreme Court and the presiding judge was John Spencer. For all intents and purposes he looked and behaved like an Englishman. But his slight tan set him out as a Burgher, that is, a descendant of the Dutch who once ruled the maritime region of the Island. The imposing wig of horse hair and the black cloak made him a figure of authority. The Government Agent as the Fiscal of the Central Province had some formal documents to present to the court. All this had to be done in strict compliance with age-old protocol imported from England.

While these ceremonies were in progress I sat on my assigned seat and gazed on the judge. I had seen the craning necks and moving lips of the audience. I was not merely an object of curiosity but also malicious gossip. Most of them knew me as a monk and even heard me criticizing the policies of the Administration. To them I was a renegade, a turn-coat. Fortunately I was prepared by no less a person than Venerable Sumangala to expect this reaction.

As regards my own moral dilemma, a sympathetic letter written by the scholar-monk Subhuti had a quotation from the Buddha:

The lay and the home

less alike,
Each supporting the other,
Accomplish the true doctrine -
The peerless refuge from Bondage
(Itivuttaka 107)

My mind went back to Sangha-Gem-Field where I disrobed. It was a very sad moment when I came in lay clothes and my brother administered the Three Refuges and Five Precepts. I thought of the day I did the same to Noble Son of Wisdom. It was a very private affair between two friends on board a British ship. But I had asked my family and many important members of the community to be present. I delivered to them a sermon on the text quoted by Venerable Subhuti. It was my last act as a monk. On that occasion, I told the assembly what I was about to do and why.

Seated in the front row of the court, I was careful not to day-dream. So when my name was announced and I was called upon to affirm loyalty to the Queen and her government, I was ready. I was not required to swear on a Bible as a concession had been recently made exempting non-Christians from that formality. I faced the judge, raised my right hand and repeated the words of a court official. I signed some papers presented to me, using my lay name Tiny Banda Valour-Lion. In a couple of minutes, the ceremony was over and the judge retired to his chamber for an half-hour recess.

I was delighted when the Government Agent asked me to join him and the judge in the chambers for a cup of tea along with Uncle Victor, Aunt Flower and Slim-Jewel. To say that I was clumsy and uncomfortable would be to put it very mildly. But Justice Spencer was a very kind man. He had heard about my background from Dickinson and treated me more as a friend than a court official.

"I welcome you to join an illustrious band of scholars the Government has been able to attract to the services," he said. "It is the most enlightened thing they have done." He listed those whom I already knew such as Louis de Zoysa, L. C. Victory-Lion and Edmund Virtue-Gem.

When the court resumed, I was on my feet interpreting the opening statement of the Crown Counsel in the first case to be tried by this Assize: a murder that had taken place in a tea plantation. I still sounded like a monk in the pulpit but consciously modified my idiom and diction to suit the sordidity of the real world.

I had no doubt that I had returned to lay life and the change had been recognized, when Middle Banda teasingly imitated my gestures and mocked the way I interpreted.

We all had a lot of fun as we sat around the same table and enjoyed a sumptuous lunch well after noon. It was thoughtfully hosted by Uncle Victor in a restaurant close to the court.

Thus ended another chapter of my life and a new one was opened.

Two decades as a monk could not be erased overnight. Everything, to begin with, was a problem: the hair, the clothes, eating three meals a day, social graces, uninhibited speech and, above all, managing money. Uncle Victor and Aunt flower had invited me to be their house-guest. It was propitious as the two of them and Autumn-Moon helped me in the transition.

My young cousin, at eighteen, had little respect for anybody. I teased him by calling him Uncle Autumn in the tone in which Moon-Beam and Middle Banda addressed him. His devastating criticisms or more often his derisive sarcasm proved to be really effective, as most of what I had learnt from Mrs. Blake as social graces and table manners had long been forgotten. About to enter the Law School, Autumn-Moon was interested in what went on in the courts. He accompanied me there whenever he could and I would introduce him to legal luminaries from Colombo who were retained by wealthy clients. Two of us became close friends.

I continued teaching Sinhala to all three children. Middle Banda was a remarkably fast learner. Of course, he was the youngest and hence the most obedient as regards doing home work and assigned readings. Moon-Beam had an agile mind. I told her that she had a well-arranged file cabinet inside her head. She was so methodical and, to my delight more than surprise, very assertive. She had learnt to survive with the two boys!

The biggest problem for Slim-Jewel was the unaccustomed leisure. She did not know what to do with time hanging on her hands. In spite of the best possible spectacles we could get dispensed in London, her near sight was too blurry to read or sew.

"How long can I talk to Golden Jewel and on what?" she would ask in desperation. "Not only is she illiterate but she has her hands full with running the house."

Slim-Jewel and her two children spent the week-ends at Aunt Flower's home in Royal Spout. Uncle Victor had bought a horse carriage. We went in it to visit friends and see places. We dubbed the week-end dinners the feeding time at the stable because the adults and the children - seven in all - made so much noise teasing one another. The good-natured humour which was the hall-mark of Uncle Victor's personality pervaded the house. The joy of a happy home was a long-forgotten experience. I thought of my parents and the happy environment they provided for me and my brothers.

When I received the first month's salary, I handed it over to Slim-Jewel. I did it as though it was a routine which had been in vogue for ever.

"Be my banker, Jewel." I told her. "I have some money for my expenses. So you can use the whole amount."

I felt miserable when with a surge of emotion she fell at my feet and holding them with her soft hands cried. She was so very grateful. I held her by the shoulders and made her stand up:

"I am not a monk any more, Jewel."

Once I had picked up the intricacies of the work in the court, I too found time hanging on my hands. The monotony of the repetitive and unimaginative legal processes bored me. I needed to do something creative to stimulate the mind. I returned to my books.

Stanley Williams on a holiday in Kandy asked me to collaborate with him in a study of the Kandyan laws. It was a far cry from Philosophy and Buddhism to indigenous law of an obscure kingdom which was no more. But in my new incarnation as a court official, it had a greater relevance. I began with a critical edition of a standard work of unknown authorship but possibly a few centuries old. It was aptly called "*The Compendium of Law.*"

I made some thrilling discoveries in several palmleaf manuscripts. Among them were the informative responses given by the Sangha to a questionnaire of the early British administrators of Kandy on how the kingdom was administered. Gradually I regained the position I held as a link in the galaxy of international and national scholars. Once again,

Rheinhold Rost of India House was the pivotal point of contact. It was indeed very satisfying. Yet a part of me cried for greater involvement with the public.

I yearned for the kind of hands-on participation I had in national and Buddhist revival movement when Colonel Olcott and Madame Blavatsky first arrived in the Island or when I handled the correspondence of Venerable Sumangala. It was not a case of mere nostalgia. I had the impression as though I had been sidetracked from something which was as indispensable as the very air I breathed. I was being choked out of existence. That was the way I felt.

Venerable Gunananda had assured me that I would be able to play a more exciting and productive role in the national awakening as a lay man than I had as a monk. Many lay organizations were active in the development of education, promotion of Buddhism or constitutional agitation for a measure of Self-rule. Yet, none had responded to my offer of cooperation in their activities.

Had they forgotten me or begun to distrust me? Was an ex-monk unacceptable to them? How deep was the stigma attached to leaving the Sangha?

I was being referred to by the designation "Discarder of the Robe" which though correct as a description of what I had done was palpably pejorative. In circles which mattered to me I was a pariah - an abominable outcaste. Out of sheer frustration, I met Don Baron to seek his advice.

"Mudaliyar," said Don Baron, addressing me formally. " I am not surprised. We are a nation riven by all kinds of prejudices and the discrimination of ex-monks is only one of them. I will do something about it."

He kept his word. I was invited to give the inaugural address of a new organization he set up to foster literary and cultural interests. Wide publicity ensured a large audience. Again, curiosity played its part. Many were curious to see the ex-monk who had the audacity to face the public!

Speaking on the literary heritage of the country, I surveyed the Sri Lankan literature in Pali, Sinhala and Sanskrit spanning at least twenty centuries. To many of the listeners, it was an eye-opener. I urged that the study, the preservation and the propagation of this vast literature was an urgent task to which the youth of Kandy should address themselves. As requested by Don Baron, I proposed formally the establishment of what would translate into English as "The Pavilion of Muse." The motion was carried by acclamation.

Don Baron from the chair called for nominations for office-bearers. I could not believe my ears when I was nominated as the President and a loud and long applause indicated the unanimous acceptance of the motion even before it was seconded.

Was this the spontaneous response of the audience to my talk? Or did the genius Don Baron stage-manage it in his own masterful manner? I was never to know.

He vacated the chair after congratulating me generously. The rest of the elections resulted in an executive committee comprising the creme of the creme of Kandy.

But Don Baron did not stop there. At the annual general meeting of the Temperance Movement of the Central Province, he proposed my name for the post of President and that too was accepted with acclamation.

He invited me to be the Treasurer of the Residence-Donor Association which had already set up a monastic residence in Field of Gods for monks visiting from the low-country and abroad. Already a visiting lama had reordained himself as monk of the Southern School of Buddhism and decided to live there. He was a source of information on Tibetan Buddhism which was hardly known at this time. The Abbot of this monastic establishment, Venerable Pleasant-Tissa of Crystal-Market, was a remarkable monk whose reputation as a scholar was on the ascendancy. Meeting him periodically was a perquisite of this office.

From time to time, I received communications from the Theosophical Society in Adyar. I was planning to attend the annual sessions at the end of 1894. I was still concerned about the rapidly evaporating cordiality between Olcott and Dharmapala . But the uneasy truce that had prevailed over the last few months had been encouraging. Yet an anonymous note in an envelope post-marked Madras did not look too friendly to Dharmapala .

It asked simply whether the recipient had read the "*Diary Leaves of the Buddhist Representative to the Parliament of World's Religions in Chicago*". The question more precisely was whether the reader took notice of the writer's proclivities. What was annexed was a laboriously copied extract on women of Burma and Japan. About a year ago, I had read the article in *The Buddhist* which was edited by Charles Leadbeater. I had no recollection of anything objectionable. But taken

467

out of context, the quoted part of the article was meant to damage the image of young Dharmapala as a budding Buddhist leader:

> *Burma is the land of free women. She is the lord of the soil. ... The graceful figure of the Burmese woman clothed in rustling silks, her beautiful hair decked in beautiful roses and jasmine, her neck and fingers adorned with valuable rubies and diamonds, who will not be fascinated by her charms? The Burmese girls are seen in their best attire only on festive days or in the temples. The Promenade of the Grand Golden Pagoda in Rangoon on festival days is an impressive spectacle. Hundreds of gay young girls, some laughing and chatting, some distributing food to the pilgrims, some offering flowers before the stainless shrines of the gentle Tathagata, one almost imagines that he is in the midst of a company of fairies! The Burmese girl is graceful: but the sweetest flower of womanhood is to be found in Japan, the land of the chrysanthemums and cherry blossoms.*

I was very angry. I wrote a letter of protest to Colonel Olcott saying that I would hold him responsible if this kind of garbage emanated from the Adyar Headquarters of the Theosophical Society. I did not have the nerve to accuse him directly nor any evidence.

At the earliest opportunity I asked Don Baron whether I had over-reacted.

"Perhaps so, Mudaliyar," he replied."You should have laughed it off. After all, Dharmapala is not a monk. He has taken no vow of celibacy. He is a healthy young man of thirty with a good eye for beautiful girls whose charm and grace he knows how to appreciate. There's nothing wrong. Our literature is full of pious monks who composed some of the finest poetic descriptions of beautiful women."

He quoted from memory some of the most evocative verses from classical Sinhala poems.

That night I wrote another letter to Olcott telling him of the common-sense and reasonable reaction of Don Baron. I apologized to him if I had hurt his feelings by being undiplomatic in my earlier letter.

"It looks, Sir, that I am wanting in many wonderful attitudes, approaches and graces of the lay society. But believe me I am learning fast." I added by way explanation.

Dharmapala was quite tickled when I narrated this episode to him a few months later.

"The old rascal can be up to anything," he said. "But he is the kind of gentleman who would have signed the note."

I had no doubt been very comfortable as a house-guest of Uncle Victor and Aunt Flower. As they would be insulted if I offered money in payment for board and lodging, all I could do to compensate them was to help their son in studies and do some marketing every week. Week-ends brought Slim-Jewel and the two children to Royal Spout. Golden Jewel, their faithful servant-companion-counsellor, accompanied them. That was a relief for Aunt Flower who had steadily learnt to hate household chores - specially cooking.

We had a lot of fun. But all good things had to come to an end. Uncle Victor could not remain in Kandy any more. With another promotion he was transferred to Colombo. With a month of grace he had obtained through an appeal, he had to be in Colombo by 1 April 1895. I had to find another place to live in. Due to my continuing diffidence as a lay man, it was a major headache. But not for Aunt Flower.

VII

Quite often Slim-Jewel and I had tried to figure out how it all happened. Before we knew exactly what we were doing, Uncle Victor had obtained for me a commodious government residence. With him and another colleague as witnesses, Slim-Jewel and I had our marriage solemnized by the District Registrar of Marriages in his office. Moon-Beam had taken a day off from Medical School to stand beside her mother as a Bride's Maid. The strapper of a cousin in formal dress was my Best Man

Everything from the wedding dresses to the reception had been masterminded by Aunt Flower whose undiscovered talents as an excellent impressario were vividly evident.Our relatives from Sangha-Gem-Field came in their best outfits. My eldest brother and his wife, who was Slim-Jewel's sister, took the place of our departed parents.

It was on the second of March 1895, marking the eightieth anniversary of the fall of the Kandyan Kingdom.

"What a coincidence, Mudaliyar!" joked Don Baron in a toast he proposed. "You choose this particular day to surrender your independence! What should I offer you: my commiserations to you and my congratulations to the victor? Felicitations, Mrs. Valour-Lion!"

The day passed quickly like a happy dream. Just before sun-set, an improvised procession with dancers and drummers deposited us in our new home. Left to ourselves Slim-Jewel and I were enthralled by the turn of events. For the second time in my life I felt that my dreams had the habit of coming true not at my pace but theirs. The first experience was with my belated resumption of higher studies in Calcutta. This time it was different.

Dreams of two persons were now being realized with a long delay of twenty years. Helping to take out the dozen dazzling gold necklaces which adorned her as a bride, I looked at her with affection and saw only the unblemished beauty and the ravishing charm of the girl for whom I dreamt of having a house built on a cliff commanding the most beautiful scene. That part of the dream too had come true. I put my hand on her shoulder and slowly turned her to show the view from the bedroom window.

Below us lay the Kandy Lake with its cute little island, to our right the imposing building complex of the Temple of the Sacred Tooth Relic, the Audience Hall and the old King's Palace framed by the Upper Garden Forest, and to our left the well-laid out city of Kandy with the long and straight Trincomalee Street vanishing in the horizon. It indeed was the happiest moment of my life. I am sure it was hers too.

It did not take long for the new family unit to get adjusted to a quiet, happy and productive life. I was pleased that Slim-Jewel understood the rigid set ways that my long years as a monk had ingrained in me. Her tolerance of my eccentricities baffled me. Often I was so ego-centric that I forgot her presence in company. She would patiently remain in the bleaches until I took the initiative to bring her to the centre of the arena. In time, of course, I learnt to do it promptly and naturally. She was equally considerate about my intellectual and social life.

She, in her turn, realized that I needed a few undisturbed hours when I could pursue my research and writing or attend to the growing mail from the organizations in which I was active. Some respectability had been restored to me since I married Slim-Jewel. While I could not explain how it happened, I was more acceptable in associations which once rejected me as "a discarder of the robe"!

Slim-Jewel's life centred on the two children. Both of them were equally dear to her. I marvelled at her exemplary impartiality or, more precisely, her readiness to side with Middle Banda when her own daughter was in conflict with him.. Nothing brought out her innate magnanimity of the noblest kind more poignantly. I had loved both of them. Now with the authority of a father figure I could get involved in their lives and their loving response gladdened me immensely.

Moon-Beam was a diligent student and her teachers were impressed by her sense of social responsibility. She wanted to specialize in preventive medicine rather than choose a more lucrative career in curative specializations.

"Little Father, I don't want to be a doctor to make money," she told me when she came home on a short break. "The poor health of our people is all due to causes that can be prevented through education and simple measures of good sanitation."

She talked of malaria and cholera which she explained could be greatly controlled with environmental sanitation and personal hygiene.

"I would rather save thousands through precept and example than cure the few that come to a hospital or a dispensary."

"That's very noble of you, Moon-Beam," I said. "But remember always that no general in history had won medals for preventing a war."

"They do, Little Father," she said with her characteristic laughter. "You don't see them. They wear them on their hearts inside."

I knew I had a daughter who was exactly after my own heart.

471

Middle Banda passed the London Matriculation Examination with distinctions in English, Mathematics and Geography. As far as opportunities for further education in Kandy, there were hardly any. We could send him to Colombo for another year or so to do the Intermediate Examination in Arts. Slim-Jewel and I debated long hours as to the advisability of sending the boy to Calcutta or England. While we both thought that he was too young to be sent out to the wide cruel world, Uncle Victor came up with the most feasible solution.

"SEND SON IMMEDIATELY (STOP) COLOMBO ACADEMY WILL ADMIT HIM TO INTER-ARTS CLASS IF HE PASSES ADMISSION TEST (STOP) TEST SCHEDULED FOR NEXT SATURDAY FOR CONVENIENCE OF OUT-STATION CANDIDATES"

was his telegram.

Obtaining leave from the courts, I took Slim-Jewel and Middle Banda to Colombo with two days to spare before the test. It was a wonderful family reunion. Moon-Beam joined us whenever her classes and clinical assignments made it possible. We arranged to go on board a ship in order to relive an experience we shared a long time ago - when all of them surprised me on the night I sailed to Calcutta. We had breakfast in a typical South Indian cafe and savoured the lentil sourdough pancakes with hot curry and coconut chutney. The dinner was in a Chinese restaurant which Uncle Victor had discovered not too far from home. As culinary experiences, both were new to us and we admired how Aunt Flower was becoming quite an adventurer.

Middle Banda sat for his test in English, Mathematics and General Knowledge. In the meantime, Slim-Jewel and I paid a visit to Palace Hill. Venerable Sumangala was very pleased to see us. When we began talking shop mainly about Olcott and Dharmapala , Slim-Jewel excused herself and visited the shrine room.

While her errant husband's progeny sweated in an examination hall, she did what only a mother does. To assist him in securing success, she invoked the blessings of the Triple Gem and the favourable intervention of the Hindu gods from whom the Buddhists sought help in times of anxiety.

Though very feeble, Venerable Sumangala walked with me to the shrine-room and chanted the Three Discourses from the Book of Protection and wished for success in Middle Banda's examination. I was touched by Slim-Jewel's initiative as well as the kindly gesture of the senior scholar-monk.

With such spiritual reinforcement, we did expect the young fellow do well. He saw the carriage and sprinted to it. The youthful exuberance with which he greeted us was enough proof that he had no doubt about his performance. I had planned to leave for Kandy on Tuesday night. It was providential. The results were posted on Monday afternoon and we could meet the Principal on Tuesday.

I was a bit embarrassed when he said that he had met me as a monk and he had heard from the Metropolitan himself about my achievements.

"We are glad to have your son with us," he said and I was pleased that he was not too specific as some others were to describe him as my step-son. "Next time you come to see him, I want you to address the morning assembly."

"Thank you very much. Do you have any subject in mind."

"How about "*Disce ut discede*" - Learn or Depart? I hear that Oriental literature is full of didactic statements on the value of learning."

"If that is the intention, why don't I speak on the Sanskrit saying 'Learning gives discipline.'

His eyes shone as if he recognized something.

"I know the verse. Doesn't it give a causal series? Please refresh my mind."

I recited the verse in Sanskrit and gave him a rough and ready rendering:

Learning gives discipline
Through discipline one earns approbation
From approbation one attains wealth
From wealth comes virtue
Thence happiness.

"That's right. Think of more of these. My students do not get enough exposure to the literary wealth of their own culture."

Middle Banda laughed all the way home:

"Little Father, the way the Principal interviewed you, I thought he was going to admit you to the Academy on the results of my test"

I was happy for the young fellow and thought of his father whose life was snatched away in its prime. How much he resembled him in appearance as well as in behaviour?

473

One stray thought, however, bothered me. Neither Slim-Jewel nor I had told his mother of the plans we had made for him. Slim-Jewel, to begin with, and both of us since had made it a point to allow her to see her son and have the satisfaction of watching him grow up to be a fine gentleman. I made a mental note on how to remedy this thoughtless omission.

As Uncle Victor undertook to look after his book list and transportation, we left for Kandy as planned. Slim-Jewel held her tears bravely until Moon-Beam and Middle Banda bade us good-bye. She wept from the moment the train started. Even I felt a large black vacuum in my heart as though a part of it had been wrenched. There could be no solace from words. We travelled in silence.

Buddhism has been criticized by many Western scholars as a pessimistic religion. Of the Four Noble Truths which form the foundation of the teachings of the Buddha, suffering or misery, as the word Dukkha is usually translated, is the ineluctable nature of existence. The Buddha in his very first sermon defined suffering as birth, sickness, old age or decay, death, association with the unpleasant, separation from the beloved, the failure to acquire what one desires and all forms of grasping or cleaving.

With both children in Colombo, the veracity of separation from the beloved as suffering was patent to both of us. Slim-Jewel turned to religion as a source of solace and I was happy that I could guide her in theory as well as practice. She developed a great interest in meditation.

Yet, we bowed down to the tenets of popular Buddhism for the significance it had to Slim-Jewel's unusual circumstances. As often as we could, we went to the Temple of the Sacred Tooth, expressed our adoration to the Buddha with flowers and lamps, and invited gods and deities to partake of the merits we had acquired. The Temple Square was a must on each occasion. There we worshipped a deity who belonged to the Northern School of Buddhism. Called simply, "Lord", he in that tradition was the foremost Buddha-to-be who surveys the world. He was also the personification of compassion.

Right across, at the foot of the Upper Garden Forest, was the temple dedicated to the Hindu god Vishnu whom we adored as the protector of Buddhism in the Island. We never neglected to pay our homage to the demon-king of the New City, whose tiny chapel was in the same compound.

At each place, Slim-Jewel would engage a lay priest who would, in a sonorous chant, invoke the deity concerned to bless the children, improve her eye-sight and bring prosperity to the household. Our round

474

of temple visits ended with the chapel dedicated to the twelve-armed, six-headed Hindu God of War who rode a peacock. There a Brahman priest from South India made the invocation in a mixture of Sanskrit and Tamil.

We enjoyed the walk as much as the ritual. The glowing sensation of religiosity was equally gratifying. But at the courts, my friends in good humour dubbed our frequent temple rounds "the Valour-Lions' insurance renewal." With all my rationalism and idealist interpretation of the Buddha's teachings, I would not grudge the comforting feeling that Slim-Jewel derived from it.

Gradually I involved her in the work of the Temperance Movement. Though shy at the beginning, she summoned enough courage in due course to enlist the support of the women in preventing the establishment of new taverns as well as in having some taverns shifted or closed.

Temperance Movement had its subtle political agenda. Liquor had been always known in the country. The literature portrays drunken scenes and also offers fervent admonitions against drunkenness. The classic, the Diadem of Poetry, which I studied at Palace Hill, had one of the most explicit descriptions of a Bacchanalian saturnalia. But the Fifth Precept of lay Buddhist discipline discouraged the consumption of liquor. Any drinking of liqour, specially in rural areas, was done in privacy by men only, usually with excuses for succumbing to the temptation of a bad habit. So it was easy to blame the Western colonial powers as having introduced social drinking and made liquor more freely available. In marginal urban society, the consumption of alcoholic beverages was proving to be a problem.

Apparently as the problem was real and getting out of hand, the Administration did not bar government servants from holding office in the Temperance Movement. Yet due to my innate sensitivities, I desisted from uttering anything which could even be remotely considered as critical of the Administration.

Steadily we settled down to a quiet and easy-going but infinitely fulfilling life. I had adjusted myself completely to lay life. I enjoyed my work and revelled in being appreciated by my colleagues. We both enjoyed the many opportunities we had to interact with people. Slim-Jewel proved to be a generous hostess. We looked forward to the vacations when children returned home. They joined us in our temple rounds. As time permitted, we included the historic temples in the vicinity of Kandy. Very soon, they became connoisseurs of art and architecture and mediaeval paintings of which an enormous heritage was within walking distance.

The highlight of the year 1896 was the trip I made with Middle Banda to Madras for the Annual Conference of the Theosophists at Adyar. It was a special session as it marked the tenth anniversary of the opening of the Library on the twenty-ninth of December in 1886. Moon-Beam was not free as she had clinical assignments even during the Christmas week. Slim-Jewel chose to be at home in case the daughter managed to sneak away for a day or two.

Middle Banda had completed a successful year of studies at the Colombo Academy and sat the Intermediate in Arts examination of the University of London. He was awaiting results. The family had a major decision to make as regards his future: Calcutta or England? Madras was going to be his first exposure to a foreign environment.

I had another very important reason to go back to Adyar. I wanted to meet Olcott and explore the possibilities of patching up the relations between him and Dharmapala . The last quarrel between them was caused by a disagreement on buying a property for the Maha Bodhi Society in Buddha Gaya. Ultimately, the nature of the property which each insisted on was not the issue. It turned out to be an ugly struggle for power. Dharmapala asserted his right to supersede the Adviser and Director of the Society. Olcott saw no other option but to resign from office and membership of the Maha Bodhi Society.

As a friend and ally of both persons I had been receiving all kinds of memoranda with explanations and mutual criticisms. The older and more mature party in the conflict still looked upon the younger and the less experienced as a spoilt child. Dharmapala had nothing but the highest respect for his mentor but was disturbed by the fact that Olcott's increasing attention to India and Hinduism irked him as an act of breaking faith. Yet, they agreed that there was much to be gained by cooperating on matters in which both had a shared interest. In this perception of the problem on their part, I saw some hope.

It was a much changed man I met at Adyar. The death of his soulmate Madame Blavatsky, his own indecisions swinging from rationalism of his Buddhist inclinations and the credulity in Adepts and Mahatmas of his Theosophical background, accusations of partiality to Buddhism or Hinduism by opposing camps and growing bickerings among Theosophists themselves had taken a big toll. Even his youthful fire and enthusiasm had dwindled and with it his noble ideals. The Olcott Free School and the other schools he had set up for the untouchable outcastes of Hindu society and hence nicknamed 'Pariah

Schools' were shanties and lacked the quality and efficiency he demanded of Buddhist schools of Sri Lanka.

Middle Banda, who unbeknown to him had been saved from a fate as bad or even worse than that of a South Indian Pariah by Slim-Jewel, was appalled when he visited the Olcott Free School.

"Little Father, how can you motivate these children by offering to do nothing more than preparing them to be servants to Europeans and Eurasians?"

At sixty-four Olcott looked twenty years older.I would not find him free for more than a couple of minutes. Several conversations which I tried to steer toward a possible improvement of his relations with Dharmapala ended abruptly and inconclusively. He was constantly preoccupied and his span of attention was pitiful.

"I can't believe he is the same man who swept you off your feet, Little Father," commented Middle Banda after one of the conversations in which Olcott revealed beneath his polite exterior some of the worst traits of an intolerant and cantankerous egoist. "Did he always have a chip on his shoulder?"

That was a good question. But I had no answer. It is always sad to see one's heroes of youth fade into insignificance as they grow old. But to have nature's course complicated by the transformation of personal qualities which one admired in them is to witness the greatest of all tragedies.

We returned to Sri Lanka utterly disappointed.

The only gain from the trip was that Middle Banda made several friends in India and England, toured the city of Madras, gained insights into the life of Saint Thomas, the Apostle of Jesus Christ, and visited the astounding rock-cut temples and sculptures at Mamallapuram and the ancient centre of Buddhist and Hindu culture of Kanchipuram. Besides, it was the first opportunity that we had to be together and discuss on an one-to-one basis values and ideals, concerns and apprehensions, and long term goals of the young man whom I had learnt to love as my own son. The bonding between us which was strengthened by this visit compensated in more than one way for my failure to soften Olcott.

It was Olcott who in the course of a conversation referred to my angry letter about the extract from the report of Dharmapala about the women of Burma and Japan.

"Let me make one thing clear, my friend," he said. "If I sent that scurrilous note out I would have signed it."

I recalled what the offended party had told me. How very well Dharmapala knew and appreciated the lofty character of his erstwhile mentor!

VIII

Once again, Right Reverend Kenneth Saunders stepped in with immeasurable kindness and limitless generosity. Back in England, he was an important church dignitary at Canterbury. In his laconic self-deprecating humour, he described himself as a glorified messenger boy for the Archbishop. Whatever he did, he had not ceased to be the ingeniously resourceful friend-in-need. On this occasion, Middle Banda was the beneficiary.

For months Slim-Jewel and I agonized over his impending departure to pursue higher studies in London. We met his biological mother in Sangha-Gem-Field and explained what was happening. The tall and handsome young man in a bluish shirt and grey flannel trousers and a Scottish muffler loosely wrapped around his neck knew nothing of the significance of this meeting. Or, at least we thought so at the moment.

He and Moon-Beam were fascinated by the white waters of the noisy cataract which made this part of the Great Sand River particularly beautiful. The tears shed by the outcaste woman were more of joy than of grief. She had come with her other two children who were in their early 'teens. Their father had left her a few months ago for a younger woman and she lived by begging as did most of her tribe.

In contrast to Middle Banda these two boys, though equally handsome in face and features, were malnourished and ill-clad. They lacked the brightness and confidence which came from learning or schooling. As naturally as kids often do, they joined Moon-Beam and Middle Banda and showed them what they knew of the secrets of the river - little pools which abounded in fish and eddying waters which sucked in whatever came near them. What camaraderie they enjoyed despite the gulf between them!

The sight of the half-brothers of Middle Banda in dire poverty, compounded by social discrimination, moved Slim-Jewel to tears.

"If only I had the energy I had before, I would bring up both these children for you," she told their mother.

"I know, my mother of a Buddha," the other responded, expressing her depth of gratitude with the emotionally pregnant words she chose to address Slim-Jewel.

Hardly had Middle Banda reached London and commenced his studies at Imperial College than we set about getting his half-brothers a new lease of life. It was not unusual for children from rural areas to be inducted to affluent homes in cities as a cross between a servant and a retainer. Naide the elder found a new home with Uncle Victor and Aunt Flower in Colombo and was renamed Virtue-Servant . Setuwa with the new name Victory-Servant joined us in a home which missed the spontaneous laughter of his more fortunate half-brother. It was a solace to both of us.

Slim-Jewel found a new energy with her self-imposed mission of providing the thirteen year old a remedial education. Together we worked hard with the goal of getting him to a school within two to three years. That was hard work - but exceedingly rewarding. Victory-Servant proved in every way a worthy recipient of our love and attention. We compared notes on the progress of the two brothers and were pleased that Virtue-Servant did as well.

Letters from London were always cheery. The one I cherished most came with greetings for the dawn of 1898. I read it avidly.

> *My Dearest Little Father,*
>
> *I have never had any doubt in my mind that you are a very great man, worthy of my deepest affection. What I had never realized is that many others in the world rate you even higher. Every letter of introduction, you gave me, had brought me friends who go out of their way to make me well cared for.*
>
> *They hold themselves in debt to you for many services you had rendered to them. How could you have done so much for these people, most of whom you had never met? These are highly placed scholars, administrators and public figures in British Society. Those you had met briefly when you accompanied mother for her eye surgery have a thousand questions to ask about you and your scholarly work. I wish I had known enough of you to satisfy their curiosity! Why not do a comprehensive curriculum vitae with a list of your publications and if possible a list of the persons in England you had helped from the time you became a junior monk at the Sangha-Gem-Field Monastery?*
>
> *Could you please do me another favour? I have met several family members of Reverend Thomas Blake and his wife. They want to know all about them. If you could please write an appreciation of them as you knew them, I will copy it to them and even get it into one of the periodicals which are interested in what missionaries do abroad.*
>
> *Do please have something ready on Right Reverend Kenneth Saunders. The rumours are that he is in for a very eminent position*

in the church administration. If you could write an article on his work in Ceylon and India, I may find a newspaper or magazine interested in publishing it. You could not have found for me anyone better "in loco parentis". For more personal matters, please refer to the other letter which is addressed to both mother and you.

I remain,
Your beloved son,
M.B.W.

The other letter was in the family's accustomed informal or irreverent style. It was full of funny stories on embarrassing *faux pas* of foreign students in College. He seemed to have had a fair share himself. He had a lot to say of the Diamond Jubilee of Queen Victoria. He was just in time to participate in some of the celebrations. He analyzed the impact of the jubilee celebrations on the weakening of the republican movement in England. What touched both Slim-Jewel and me was his compassionate note on what we had done for the two sons of the "*Lady of the River.*" But the annex to the letter kept us wondering. Neatly written on expensive-looking stationery was what he called a doggerel:

O Lady of the River!
Your kindly face which befits a queen
Has charm and grace that belie your beggarly rags.
Do your sons in their impish curiosity
Ask you what palace you left and when?
What crime did you commit to be banished in disgrace?
Or did the fires of youth in your soulful heart
Urge you to leave your royal garb in favour
Of a young man's warm and tender embrace?

I wonder every time I had seen you in the bleaches
Chatting with my parents in grateful tones,
Showering me with eyes so serene your boundless affection,
Yet so keen that it be discreet.
Have you been a mother, an aunt, a sister or granny
In a life long hidden by a faded memory?

481

In a dreamland from time to time I do
encounter
Your face with a tear, a smile, a fondling kiss
As my mood of the moment has need.
Your sons to me are dear as though
We shared something which made us what we
are.

You are a riddle and in vain I seek
An answer to a question I cannot ask aloud
Why do you haunt my solitary thoughts?
How do you travel so far over the seas?
O Lady of the River!

The poem needed a bit of paraphrasing before Slim-Jewel grasped its significance.

"Is it time that we told him the truth?" she asked me.

"Shouldn't we first talk to Moon-Beam?" I suggested. "Besides, we cannot do it by letter. We will do so when he is next here with us."

"Can you do something in the meantime? Can you build on the natural love he seems to have for his half-brothers?"

How thoughtful and generous on the part of Slim-Jewel!

I had an unusual opportunity to redouble my attention to young Victory-Servant .

Justice Spencer asked me to accompany him to Jaffna where he was due to hold the Assize of the Supreme Court. Several cases where the services of a Sinhala Interpreter-Mudaliyar were needed had been lumped together. It was envisaged that a stay of four to six weeks was entailed.

En route to Jaffna, we planned to spend a week-end in Anuradhapura, the first capital of the nation from the fourth century before Christ to about the tenth century of the Common Era. I was allowed to take someone to attend to my creature comforts. I took Victory-Servant with me. He had progressively passed the level of a servant and become as close and beloved as a son. The Judge actually took him to be a child of Slim-Jewel!

To say that the splendour and marvels of Anuradhapura held me enraptured would be an under-statement. But to have the opportunity to brief a senior Judge of the Supreme Court of the wonders of my own ancient culture was an enviable privilege.

My in-depth study of the *Great Chronicle* of the Island had prepared me for what to expect. I, too, was visiting the sacred city for the first time. But I had enough information to identify and date most of the monuments and to refer to some interesting episodes of their history. I drew immense pleasure in my dual mission of impressing the Judge of the Island's past and interesting the curious Victory-Servant in the loftiest exemplars of his heritage.

What an infinitely more rewarding experience it would have been if I had brought Middle Banda before he went to London, I thought. Just as I did, he would visit these places one day with a prior knowledge and appreciation of Stonehenge, Saint Paul's Cathedral, Westminster Abbey, the Tower of London and the city's many bridges! I had at least one advantage. My brief pilgrimage with Noble Son of Wisdom to holy shrines of Northern India associated with the living Buddha had given me a balanced view of the cultural achievements of the East of the past and the West of the present. If Middle Banda was inordinately mesmerized by the splendour of the West and thoughtless of his own culture, the fault would be entirely mine. So did I blame myself even as I attempted to visualize the glory this vast buried city manifested in its heyday.

As I led my eager learners through what little had come hitherto under the archaeologists spade, I waxed eloquent on the three tree-clad ruins of once-majestic Topes; meandering foundations of building complexes and columns of rock which took the place of concrete elements in ambitious superstructures; gracefully tapering columns with carved capitals which carried copper roofs; elaborate entrance points with lacey moonstones for door mats, balustrades in the shape of an elephant's trunk and exquisitely carved guardstones of flower-bearing deities of serene beauty; and rock-lined ponds which rivalled the best swimming pools of Colombo. At every point Justice Spencer expressed his gratitude for enlightening him in an area which he missed in his general education.

"Mudaliyar, next time I come to Kandy, I want you to address the bar on the glory of Anuradhapura as they could be as ignorant as I had been so far," he said at the Rest House by the Tissa Lake where we had a delicious dinner of fresh-water fish.

The highlight of the day was when Victory-Servant brought me a cup of tea at bed-time.

"Can I ask you some questions please," he began in perfect English but continued to pose them in his mother-tongue. Slim-Jewel and I had put him through an accelerated course in English over the last half-year.

483

How successful we had been we could now gauge as the young lad had picked up correctly the sense of much of the details I had given Judge Spencer.

I was glad that I had introduced him to the Judge as one of my nephews whom I had decided to adopt as a son. That was what I decided to do. I was so convinced of the largeness of Slim-Jewel's heart that I went to bed with the most gratifying thought:

"How wonderful to have a son at home again!"

Jaffna was an entirely new world. It was as dissimilar from the rest of the Island as one could imagine.

From the moment we passed the little causeway which connected the Peninsula to the mainland, our eyes met nothing but majestically swaying palmyra palms on vast flat stretches of pure white sand. The intense dry heat was tempered by a steady sea breeze. Villages of crowded huts were on both sides. Their roofs were thatched with slate-grey coconut fronds and around each hut was a high fence of thickly woven cadajan. The residents seem to demand privacy to an extent I had never seen elsewhere. Winding alleys led in all directions.

Hardly any land around a settlement remained unutilized. Rice fields framed by rows of lush-green Suriya trees were being tilled by swarthy men in variegated loin-cloths and white turbans. They advanced in a line in unison. The coordinated raising and lowering of long-handled hoes bespoke long years of shared experience.

In vegetable gardens, men on their knees tended beds of eggplant, chilie and onion. The fence posts had grown into trees and were laden with the long drumstick-like beans, after which the tree was named. Creepers of bitter gourd clung to the side. The scene reminded me of my childhood days at Bo-tree Plain where vegetable-growers tended their plots in the undulating hilly slopes with abundant water. Here in the hot and dry loamy plain, the water came to the vegetable beds along shallow drains. The water was drawn manually from deep wells which dotted the entire scene. It was a curious contraption - the well sweep.

A colleague of mine who hailed from the Peninsula had described to me how the well sweep worked. But to see it in action was flabbergasting. On a sturdy frame by the well was supported like a see-saw a horizontal log of twelve to fifteen feet. From one side was suspended a bucket on a pliable stick which reached the water in the deep well vertically when that end of the log was lowered. Lowering the bucket into the well and drawing it with water out to the surface was deftly accomplished by a young a man who walked on the log to and fro. Scores of young men were engaged in this bizarre form of

484

acrobatics and one wondered how they balanced on the narrow logs so long.

Victory-Servant was all eyes. He had so many questions to ask. I wished I had known the answers to most of his incisive questions.

Even before we reached the town of Jaffna, I was convinced that I for one had lived half a century in the Island with absolutely no knowledge of the life and customs, language and religion, hopes and aspirations of the people who had shared this Island home with us for so many centuries. With my exposure to India, I knew a little more of religious and linguistic diversity than the average Sri Lankan. On the contrary, my childhood in the hill country had created in my mind an indelible prejudice that Tamils were Indians of depressed economic and social status and had been brought by the British planters as indentured cheap labour to develop their tea and rubber plantations to the detriment of the Kandyan peasantry.

Other than in recent years as a lay man and government employee, I had hardly met anyone from the North and had no idea that a distinctly separate culture flourished unknown to and unappreciated by the rest of the country. It was this realization which made the month in Jaffna an unforgettable cultural experience.

With an observant understudy in Victory-Servant , I explored the vicinity of Jaffna with the same avidity that I did my research in a library.

We had lodgings in the sprawling King's House inside the Dutch fortifications of the eighteenth century. It was a quaint place even without the legends of its ghosts! Rooms were spacious and the high ceilings and large windows made them cool and comfortable. On one side was the impressive Dutch Groote Kerk or Great Church. Victory-Servant was pleased that I had a bed for him brought into my room.

My Tamil-speaking counterpart, Mudaliyar Shiva-worshiper, was a scholar or more precisely a historian. He had laboriously gathered data on the hypothesis that the Sinhalas were the earlier settlers of the Jaffna Peninsula. His evidence for the theory came from the *Great Chronicle*, the local legends, place names and archaeological monuments.

He organized a trip for the visiting Judge and other court officers to the northernmost beach of the Peninsula which local tradition connected with the arrival of Emperor Asoka's daughter in the third century before Christ. It was a lovely sunny day and the white sandy beach glistened

485

for miles. He took us under the shade of a ficus tree which I could immediately identify as the holy Bodhi-tree of Buddhist worship.

"This, Your Honour, is where the ancient Rose-apple-leaf Port was," began Mudaliyar Shiva-worshipper. "From here to the mouth of Hooghly near Calcutta was a seven-day voyage. The ship carrying Emperor Asoka's daughter and her companion nuns landed here. She brought for the King of the Island an invaluable momento - a branch of the tree of knowledge under which Lord Buddha attained enlightenment."

Justice Spencer had read the *Great Chronicle* in the revised translation of Victory-Lion and he recollected some of the episodes narrated in it.

"So, it was somewhere here that King Tissa, the Beloved of the Gods, walked into the sea until the water reached up to his neck to receive the sapling?" he asked.

"Yes, Your Honour, and that plot of land is still called the Compound of Tissa. The King camped there waiting for the ship to arrive. The tree under which we are standing was planted by the king himself. It has gone down in history as a tree produced from one of the eight berries of the sapling."

Some of the details given in Shiva-worshipper's heavy accent were beyond Victory-Servant . I filled him in. His eyes shone with disbelief. Only a few days ago had I told him the story of the Sacred Bodhi-tree at Anuradhapura. He would not believe that the tree was over two thousand two hundred years old and that its history could be traced from literature. To see the place it was received by the King himself was particularly exciting.

"Young man, how do you like to be where a King once stood?" asked Justice Spencer.

"Very good," he replied after some hesitation as he could not find better words to say what he felt.

My colleague took us on other trips as well. We visited villages which had names which were definitely Sinhala in origin - at least, the meaning fitted the settlement only when the Sinhala original was applied to it. The village still known as the place to find a good carpenter carried the name "Settlement of Carpenters." "Slimy Pond, "Upper Pond", "Upper Plain" "Gem-set Pavilion", "Copper Palace," "Lime Village" and so forth were expressive Sinhala names even in their Tamilized form. We spent a whole day in the near-by island which still carried the name by which it was referred to in Pali and Sinhala literatures. "Areca nut Island" was famous as the site of a Buddhist monastery. Though there were no ruins in this island, the main Peninsula had a cluster of Buddhist ruins at "Kaduru-tree-Grove" of the Lime-Village. This again was a monastery known in literature.

All these easily recognizable Sinhala place names occurred in an area where hardly any Sinhala families lived fifty years ago. A sprinkling of Sinhala migrants mainly from the Southern Province had just made a bid to explore economic opportunities here, very much in the same spirit they came to the hill country.

We knew a bit of this rapidly growing community of Sinhala traders - mainly bakers of bread and cakes, who had migrated into a geographically, linguistically and culturally different part of the country.

The two cases of homicide that were being tried by the Assize had taken place in this community. In one a well-to-do businessman had been clubbed to death and the suspects were from a neighbouring village. In the other, a baker from Galle had been stabbed by his nephew with a poker in a fit of anger. I spoke to some witnesses.

My overall impression was that they were quite happy in their new surroundings. Almost all had nice things to say about their neighbours and customers.

Shiva-worshipper won the admiration of Justice Spencer for his objectivity and thoroughness. The more he showed his erudition, the more I felt ashamed for having known precious little about his culture and history, his language and religion. What a self-destructive sense of self-sufficiency! I did not know whom to blame. I was sure that I had to own up to my own guilt for an unpardonable act of omission.

We planned a sailing trip to the Naga Island which the Sri Lankan Buddhist tradition associated with one of the three visits of the Buddha. An enterprising Buddhist monk was building a shrine in this tiny island.

"There's no problem, Your Honour," said Shiva-worshipper. "I could take you there. But I do not think that the reference in history is to this little coral island. The whole of the Jaffna Peninsula and perhaps the major part of the Northern Province to north of the Great Sand River and Flower Garden River was the Naga Island."

He brought an impressive book in support of what he said. It had a map of Tabrobane by a Greek cartographer of the early centuries of the Christian era.

487

"This is the map of Ptolemy of this part of the world, Your Honour," he told the Judge. "Greeks apparently thought that the Island was much bigger than it really was. But some of the details are really astounding."

The Judge was impressed by the evidence which came from ancient Greece - so high was his admiration for the Western Classics in which he was well versed.

The Government Agent lent us his boat and sent a young officer of the Provincial Office to accompany us on our outing to the island. Tom Bradley was a Civil Service Cadet and Jaffna was his first duty station. He had completed the first year of training and was under transfer orders to the General Treasury in Colombo.

"I love this place, Sir. There's so much to do and so much to learn" he told Justice Spencer as we sailed out of the port of Kayts which in Tamil was called "Guardian Port of the Land."

It was a sunny day. The boat skimmed over a calm sea and the palmyra-fringed shoreline receded into the horizon as we meandered through a series of islands. Picturesquely located was a small Dutch fortress on a tiny island.

"You know what the Dutch called this place, Sir. They called it the heel of the ham. If you picture Ceylon as a huge ham, hung by its heel, this is it."

Tom Bradley had something to say of every island. He was a purveyor of folklore. We could not have had a more entertaining guide. He persuaded the Judge that the visit to Naga Island was incomplete without extending it to the largest of the outlying islands which the Tamils called the "Straight Island' and the Dutch had renamed Delft.

"You have to see the wild horses and the Portuguese Castle and possibly some of our blue-eyed descendants via Lieutenant Nolan," Tom laughed.

"Not mine, of course," said the Judge in mock anger. He was mindful of his Dutch ancestry and had possibly heard about the story of the Irish lieutenant and his escapades in Delft.

It turned out to be an incredibly memorable day. To be shown a grand Hindu temple by a budding British administrator was a novel experience. Victory-Servant , who trailed behind us, befriended Tom. Over a hot fish curry served with rice, my son of choice stammered his way through confidently in his rudimentary English.

Tom followed the tradition of the Civil Service. Not only had he learned enough Tamil to communicate with the people but studied their history and culture. As the boat sailed back into a darkening evening, he narrated episodes from the history of the Tamil Kingdoms in Jaffna which he felt could be traced to about the thirteenth century.

"But the Tamils might have been here before from at least the annexation of the northern region of India into the Cola Empire in the eleventh century. When King Valour-Arm the Great of the twelfth century had to issue orders to the authorities who ran the port at Kayts, he did it in Tamil."

The more I learned about the antiquity and history of the people in this part of my country, the more I blamed myself for my ignorance. I shuddered at the very thought of the consequences which could ensue if the people in two parts of the same small island grew in isolation without mutual knowledge and appreciation of their heritage, aspirations and apprehensions. Over the next weeks, I discussed this question with many of the new Tamil friends I had made in the Peninsula.

"You are quite right, Mudaliyar," said Justice Spencer. "The only people who come from the south to the Peninsula are petty traders. They are viewed as economic exploiters and can hardly be welcome as goodwill ambassadors even if they want to be friendly and cooperative. On the other hand, the Peninsula sends out lawyers, doctors, engineers, accountants and teachers to the south. They mingle with their peers among the Sinhalas, Burghers and Muslims. I am impressed with the high degree of camaraderie that had grown among them. But the vast masses on both sides will remain ignorant of each other for all times."

Shiva-worshipper felt that the isolation was not altogether accidental. He thought the Administration wanted it that way.

"Mark my word, friend. 'Divide and rule' is the law of imperialism. Some day we on both sides will pay the price."

"I have lived in the south and so have many of my friends" said the Office Assistant to the Government Agent in his heavy accent with y's before every initial vowel and distinctly rolling r's. "We like the country and the people. But we like to return here because it is only here that we feel really comfortable and at home. I cannot have my weekly sesame-oil bath and stay in the sun in Colombo. Do you know what an unmatched joy it is to sit on the well-wall under palmyra palms and savour fermented toddy from a cup made of the leaf of the same palm? You can miss the annual festival of the Temple of the Good Village one year but the next year your spirit wants you to come back."

After six weeks in Jaffna Peninsula, it was time to bid farewell. Not only had I acquired many good friends but had made up my mind to study Tamil and delve into its literature. I had begun the study of the

489

typical Hindu faith of the Sri Lankan Tamils. Their preferred deity was Shiva the Destroyer while his sons the elephant-headed Ganesha and six-headed and twelve-armed God of War, Skandha, were the most popular. I was intrigued with the philosophical base of their faith, which they called the "*Dogma of Shiva*".

Victory-Servant had actually begun to speak Tamil and even Shiva-worshipper commended him for being a fast learner.

"I had very good teachers among the servants in the kitchen of the King's House," he said in Tamil to the utter delight of the historian-linguist.

"Very good, my lad," Shiva-worshipper replied in his own brand of Sinhala.

IX

I returned to Kandy with new insights and renewed fears. We are indeed a divided nation or more precisely many nations within the confines of a small island.

Could we or should we turn it into a melting pot in which all elements will lose their identity and emerge together as a stronger and durable alloy?

Or should we be satisfied that all we could produce is a colourful quilt where each component will preserve its colour, form and design and yet create a thing of beauty by harmonious coalition?

I had decided to make my own little contribution by devoting the next few years to a thorough study of Tamil language, literature and culture as well as Sri Lankan Hinduism. If only I could complement the work of Shiva-worshipper and trace the Tamil contribution to the evolution of Sri Lanka's rich culture!

I had, of course, a couple of urgent things to attend to. The first was to give effect to the decision I had made about Victory-Servant. My letter to Slim-Jewel and Moon-Beam had apparently been adequately convincing. The proposal met with their instant approval. My letters to Uncle Victor and Aunt Flower were equally productive. They wanted to adopt Virtue-Servant. We commenced action simultaneously and with the cooperation I could enlist from the court and the District Registrar, the process was discreetly concluded without disclosing whatever adverse information which could affect their future.

It was a moment of great jubilation for both families. We managed to give them a new life. Unless they chose to divulge their childhood memories to anyone on their own accord, none but a heartless and indefatigable inquisitor would unravel their humble beginnings and the consequent social stigma.

One a Perera and the other a Valour-Lion, they were destined to share the fortunes of a decent life which birth had denied them.

The next challenge was to cope with a crisis which many of us in Kandy had long dreaded. Don Baron, ten years my junior in age, was fast proving to be a man of such abilities and ambitions that the hill capital was too small for his self-fulfillment. Sooner or later, he had to step into the national scene. His friends in Colombo recognized it. They found an opportunity. A converted Buddhist of Dutch Burgher descent, A. E. Buultjens, had replaced Charles Leadbeater as Principal of the first of the English Schools which Olcott had established in Colombo, This remarkable man of vision and wisdom was ailing and an understudy was needed to ensure the smooth transition of headship in the event of his early retirement. Don Baron, who was the obvious choice to succeed Buultjens, was now needed for grooming. Mindful of the opportunities which the capital would provide him for his many-sided interests, he agreed to the proposal.

On my return from Jaffna, I found Kandy in turmoil. What a vacuum in the intellectual and social life of a growing city this young man was going to leave!

Farewells with processions, "praise-papers", adulatory speeches, garlands and presents were easy to organize. Slim-Jewel had become a veritable adept. But to find replacements for the various offices Don Baron held in religious, literary and social service organizations taxed the resources of the small community of intellectuals.If I ended by having to bear a heavy share of the burden, it was entirely due to the confidence the departing leader expressed in no uncertain terms.

At the last farewell party which Kandy gave Don Baron, I was bold enough to make a series of prophetic statements.

"Our loss is Colombo's gain, nay, the whole country's gain," I said. "This rising star in the national leadership will not only succeed Mr. Buultjens as the Principal of the premier seat of Buddhist education. He is bound to carry on and expand the many activities which the illustrious Buddhist of Dutch Burgher origin had undertaken in social and political planes. As we move towards the ultimate goal of Self-rule under the benign protection of the British Empire, I see clearly in my mind's eye the role which Mr. Don Baron Jayatilaka will progressively play. He will be the nearest we hope to have as a scholar-statesman on the Greek model of a Philosopher King."

My speech was received with a standing ovation. Even the new Government Agent congratulated me in person, adding in passing,

"You sly fox, I liked your reference to 'the ultimate goal of Self-rule under the benign protection of the British Empire'."

"I couldn't say anything else," I replied in mock seriousness. "So soon after we gave Her Majesty the Queen such a rousing Diamond Jubilee celebration!"

I was not too visionary when I spoke of Don Baron. The first thing he did on his arrival in Colombo was to set up the Colombo Young Men's Buddhist Association on the model of the Christian international YMCA movement and to assume the editorship of the newspaper "The Buddhist".

492

I also had news waiting for me about Olcott and Dharmapala . Their cooperation in a joint effort to bring Buddhism to the untouchables of South India took them over many a rough stretch of road both literally and metaphorically. Yet they were together. It was rumoured that Dharmapala was keen to get Olcott out of the movement and, with that objective in mind, had repeatedly urged him to return to Sri Lanka to revive his Buddhist activities there. Not only did Olcott refuse to do so but imputed that the younger man's motive was to get his chestnuts pulled out of the fire by someone else.

Tensions were inevitable. But the formation of the Dravidian Buddhist Society or South India Sakya Buddhist Society in the middle of 1898 gave some hope of possible rapprochement for the umpteenth time. If truce it was, it did not last long. Exactly a month later, Dharmapala wanted to dissociate himself and Sri Lanka from the Theosophical Movement and proposed that the Colombo Buddhist Theosophical Society should change its name to the Colombo Buddhist Society. To Olcott, it was nothing less than the secession which he had dealt with in a different plane during his involvement in the American Civil War.

I wrote to both parties pleading that each had promises to keep; the goal of national and Buddhist revival yet remained to be achieved; and they should haul the burden together and mobilize the still untapped intellectual and spiritual resources of a generation they had helped to bring forth. I had no reply from either. Their time and energy were being frittered away in mutual recrimination. Every piece of news of their bickerings gnawed at my heart. How unfortunate we were as a nation, I said to myself.

Even this dark cloud was not without its own silver lining. The efforts of Olcott to further English education within a Buddhist setting had begun to bear fruit. The schools in Colombo, Galle and Kandy had prospered. They were serving as models for others. Olcott had kept to his promise of finding dedicated men to manage them and teach in them. Whatever be the outcome of the current contests of will and bitter conflicts, I was sure that the credit which Olcott deserved for this service could never be detracted.

I had reason to be pleased with what the Temperance Society under my leadership could achieve in the Province. I had kept it strictly confined to the discouragement of social drinking and the prevention of the proliferation of taverns. "Local option," as the process of eliciting public opinion on the location of taverns was called, was an effective instrument. It enabled socially conscious people to undertake widespread educational activities on the evils of alcohol abuse. The frightfully burgeoning instances of homicides caused by sudden provocation had an obvious correlation with drunkenness. Hence, the Administration treated alcohol abuse as an urgent concern of Law and Order. Yet, the excise revenue from locally brewed liquor and the custom dues on imported spirits and wines were far too attractive to be given up by the adoption of total prohibition. On very rare occasions, I had to discuss this ambivalence of the Government when over-zealous members urged stronger agitation. Otherwise, I steered clear of all political issues and treated Temperance as a purely ethical issue in which each person had to make his own decision voluntarily.

I had occasionally to caution Slim-Jewel to temper the more belligerent attitude of the parallel women's organization. She had herself become a vocal campaigner in more than one front and an active band of the growing, leisurely, middle class women had joined her. In order to reflect their wider interests, they renamed their association as merely the Women's Organization. They had soon made contacts with similar bodies in the rest of the country, including, to my sheer delight, a newly created association in Jaffna. Their concern centred on all vices: liquor and drugs, gambling, prostitution and abuse of women and children, social and caste discrimination, indebtedness and many more. What an active president Slim-Jewel was! Her professional training as a nurse and the inspiration she received from her daughter's campaign for preventive medicine led her to hands-on projects in various parts of the Province.

Both of us had the leisure and the inclination for public service because our children demanded so little from us. Moon-Beam was perpetually having written or oral examinations. Slim-Jewel had the schedule with her so that she could do the regular round of temples to invoke the blessings of the supernatural for her daughter. No engagement however important would ever take her away from this self-imposed maternal duty. With or without this external aid, Moon-Beam was faring well. She was among the top ten of her class and her teachers as well as the superintendent of the teaching hospital had nothing but the highest compliments for her.

The news from London was consistently heartening. Middle Banda enjoyed his honours course in Western Classics and continued to write doggerels which were becoming progressively obscure due to frequent allusions to Greek and Roman mythology. His letters invariably sent me to the Planters' Library which was located in the ancient bathhouse of the royal harem. He had chosen Lincoln's Inn out of the four Inns of Court to do his dinners in preparation for admission to the British Bar as a barrister. We had hardly any worry on his count because of the immeasurable compassion of the Right Reverend Kenneth Saunders.

Victory-Servant continued to make good progress in English and Arithmetic. The private teacher who coached him in regular school subjects was confident that his ward could pass the entrance examination to my old school. So, no one was surprised when he was admitted on a partial scholarship - partial simply because his parents were in an upper income bracket.

With nothing in the home front to distract me, I pursued my studies in Tamil with the help of a colleague who was generous with his time and patient with my innumerable *faux pas*. He introduced me to the Tamil code of law called "The Custom of the Land" and I began a comparative study of the systems of law in the two parts of the Island. It was indeed most rewarding.

One more step taken by Dharmapala also made 1898 memorable. It testified to his ever-mounting dedication to the cause of Buddhism and national revival. Hitherto he had been a lay man. His white outfit over which he wrapped a white sheet was described "the dress of a Buddhist student." To convey his ultimate commitment, he took the Vow of Homelessness and dressed himself in the colour of the Buddhist monks' robe. In this semi-monastic state, he began to call himself Anagarika Dharmapala, Homeless Dharmapala . It is by this appellation that he has since been known both nationally and internationally.

Years passed and life had nothing but the best. Ours was a happy and contented home. We welcomed the dawn of the twentieth century as the era of our children. We looked to their future with hope and enthusiasm. It never occurred to either me or Slim-Jewel that ours was a family where biological parenthood was not a matter of any significance. Only Moon-Beam was a progeny of Slim-Jewel. But in love and mutual devotion our bondage with the three children - Moon-Beam and Middle Banda having the same father and the latter and Victory-Servant having the same mother - was matchless.

Sometimes, I regretted that I had no children of my own. But Slim-Jewel would catch me in such moods, sidle up to me and say "You have a ready-made family that loves you so dearly." All three children called me "Little Father" but In their undivided affection I was their beloved father. It was indeed an experience of the rarest joy to me.

495

Moon-Beam obtained her Licentiate in Medicine and Surgery with honours and joined the Department of Public Health. Her option to specialize in preventive medicine was heartily endorsed by her superiors. We had a party to celebrate her dual success. To our utmost delight she added a third aspect to the celebrations.

"Little Father, would you please ask Mother if she would invite Timothy to the party?" she asked me shyly.

"Who is Timothy, Moon? And why have I to ask Mother?"

"Because -" she replied and mischief was written across her face.

"Tell me two things about him and I will do your bidding"

She told me more than two things. But the gist of her bubbling asseveration was that Dr. Timothy de Lanerolle and she had been friends from the day they joined the Medical School and the friendship had grown over the years to a romance.

"With the blessings of both Mother and you, we would like to get married this year." she concluded.

Never was an easier task assigned to me by anyone. Perhaps, Slim-Jewel thought of her own youth. Her tangled life had prepared her to empathize with her daughter to a degree I could not have imagined. I had expected a protest and an assertion of the inalienable parental right to find a partner. Instead, tears of joy ran down her smooth cheeks and a smile confirmed that the daughter's request was heartily granted.

With a little bit of home work, we conspired to enhance the status of the party. It was Moon-Beam's turn to be surprised.

Timothy came with his parents - a genial couple from Galle in immaculate Western dress. They were both teachers in two leading schools of the town. Almost behind them came a dozen relatives of the family who had travelled all the way from Galle and Colombo. Their dress, manners and speech set them off as representatives of the new middle class which was in the ascendancy.

Slim-Jewel and I had our families represented by our closest relatives. The contrast was striking. Ours were stalwarts from the village in their pure white long shirt and cloth which under the influence of the berating speeches of Dharmapala was fast becoming a popular national dress. Our Jewels - as we called the womenfolk in general - came in colourful saris draped in the typical Kandyan style. Our friends from the city and its environs fitted one or the other group. Between them, as a class by itself, stood the few Britishers and Burghers whom I had invited from the Provincial Office and the Courts. Mudaliyar Shiva-Worshipper, who made a special trip from Jaffna, and a Muslim colleague from my office made the gathering fully representative of the racial and religious diversity of the Island. It was an engagement party for Timothy and Moon-Beam.

"I should have guessed it," said Timothy, every inch a statuesque French nobleman, tall and fair with a prominent nose and a strong chin. "I should have guessed it when Mummy asked where the 'Arthur's Seat' was in Kandy."

As if by accident, the Chief-monk of Sangha-Gem-Field showed up at the termination of the party to chant benedictory verses from the Book of Protection to bless his niece! It was a happy day.

"Thank you for all you did for Moon-Beam", said Slim-Jewel when our visitors had departed and we retired to our room in the early hours of the next morning. "I cannot wait for the day they get married."

"I too, Jewel. I love being the Bride's Father."

Every event in the family had a strange way of being brought back vividly to our memory three or four months later. That was when we received Middle Banda's reactions usually in a funny doggerel. To his new brother-in-law he had the following to say,

Parlez vous francais, mon cher beau-frere
Monsieur le docteur Timothy de la Narolle?
Connaissez vous un arrier-grandpere
Ambassadeur au pres du roi de Kandy?
A cause son arrogance, happily we have
A family so noted for charm and brains.
Brains from the French? I dare say 'No'
Charm of diplomacy? I do concede.
Riches of your mind you trace indeed
To a noble lady, the daughter much cherished
Of the revered Guru of His Majesty the King.

When after some effort the French lines of the doggerel were deciphered, we were amused by the allusion to the French Ambassador Laisne de Nanclair de la Narolle whose arrogance cost him his liberty. King Royal-Lion the Second condemned him to his human menagerie which already had a few scores of Europeans.

Robert Knox had left a detailed account of the ambassador and his men and their frequent quarrels. Middle Banda had traced the family history and found out that the imprisoned ambassador ended up by marrying the daughter of the royal teacher and founded a renowned dynasty, noted for physical beauty and intellectual gifts.

497

Were we not doubly amused and pleased, of course, when Timothy asked his parents about his family's history and found out that its surname, which they hardly used now, was really "House of the French Ambassador."

We could, however, never find out how Victory-Servant came to address Timothy at all times as 'His Excellency'. The only clue was his school report. The remark of his English teacher read: "Young Valour-Lion reads widely and has shown a keen interest in accounts of diplomatic missions and military expeditions to the Kandyan Kingdom. He has opted for French lessons."

We teased him saying that he was apparently preparing for his one and only role at the sister's wedding.

"Yes, indeed," was his good-natured response.

The next mail from England brought us happy news of the culmination of Middle Banda's multi-chanelled preparation for his ambition of being an organizational leader. He had passed his examination in Western Classics with First Class Honours; done his dinners at the Lincoln Inn; devilled for no less a person than Gerard Foot, an eminent criminal lawyer in a renowned family of legal luminaries; was called to the Bar as a Barrister; sat for the Indian Civil Service Examination; and received his posting to Mandalay, the erstwhile Royal capital of Upper Burma. All this said in a lilting doggerel brought tears of joy to the eyes of Slim-Jewel and Moon-Beam.

If I sniffled a bit myself, I was not ashamed. With single-minded perseverance, the boy had done well. I relived the unforgettable experience of smuggling him from the village of outcastes to Slim-Jewel, much against my stringent monastic vows. My feet tingled with the very memory of the two-year old toddler who snuggled himself to sleep on the floor of the buggy cart, clinging on to my feet for security and warmth.

"Father, you are crying too," said Victory-Servant , himself sobbing for a different reason. "We'll not see him for a long time again?"

"Little Father, how could he manage by himself in Mandalay?" inquired Moon-Beam who always thought that Sri Lankan men were lousy house-keepers.

"We haven't still come to the end of his letter. Let's see if he has any ideas about it. He plans things meticulously."

Occasionally we had read of his admiration of a Scottish lass among his poems published in the Sunday Observer.

"You mean that his Scottish lass is real, Little Father?" asked Moon-Beam.

It was real. He had met her while working for Gerard Foot.

"It was love at first sight and I confessed it to the senior counsel," continued his lengthy letter. "His advice was, 'Young man, there's a cure for love at first sight and that's a second sight.' I have had more than one sight and our love for each other had only increased with each sight! So, my dearest Mother and Little Father, I seek your blessings for our marriage, which will take place with enough time for a restful honeymoon on board the ship to Calcutta. Right Reverend Kenneth Saunders is putting his remarkable ingenuity to concoct a half-Buddhist-half-Chistian ceremony!"

Fay MacAndrew, nicknamed Rose, was undoubtedly a very pretty girl. The little Indian ink portrait which he had done himself depicted a cheery girl with bright eyes, a shapely nose and lovely lips.

"Why can't they come here on their way. They can marry in Colombo and we could all be there," suggested Moon-Beam.

"Sorry, Moon. He cannot be reached in time to make that suggestion."

"How wise and practical!" sighed Slim-Jewel as she unburdened her mind to me in the privacy of the bed-room. "I dreaded his coming back to the Island either to work or to seek a bride. You never know. There could be some wicked person who knows about his background and would seek to destroy his happiness. Now he and Rose can have a life of their own. Nobody can hurt him now. Thank you for being his saviour in more than one way."

I shared her apprehension and was relieved by the course of destiny. The next Sunday Observer, however, had this to say about him:

Our regular correspondent from London, M. B. W. of Sangha-Gem-field, whose humour-filled doggerels are eagerly awaited by our readers, has been appointed a Gentleman Cadet of the Indian Civil Service and is currently sailing to Calcutta with his bride Fay Rose MacAndrew en route to his duty station in Upper Burma. Being a Barrister of the Lincoln's Inn, he is tipped to be the Police Magistrate of Mandalay, the erstwhile Royal Capital.

Farewell, Sweet England

Alone to thy shores I came,
A seeker of knowledge and skills,

Welcomed by the cultured,
Shunned by the bigoted,
Received with love by friends and theirs,
Tested in patience, forbearance and courage
By the few whose warped minds
Craved damnation in their folly
For tanned skin and jet-black hair!

"I'll paint you on the wall with charcoal," one   told me.
"I'll honour you with a portrait in pale chalk," I said
"If only the wall is black and your weak little chin
And the ugly nose are less repulsive."
Challenged to a fight, we boxed each other
Until blinded by blood-clotted eyes
We flung our arms in a comic dance
To the cheers of a growing ring of amused colleagues.
Urged by them, we shook our hands and hugged but briefly.

A friend he has been ever ready to help
Raising his voice and sometimes his hand
In defence of his buddy from the East.
Never again did I feel estranged
In this decent land of courteous dignity.

That was my England ere the sweetest Rose
To bloom in the highlands of Scotland
Led me with charm to heights of sheer delight.
Her scenic homeland of the free and the brave,
Where hills and dales and expansive lakes
Filled my eyes with tears nostalgic,
Vied with mine in nature's bounty,
Despite the absence of elephants!

Never yet could any surpass
The beauty of her eyes,
Her honey-sweet voice,
Her divinely inviting gait -
A goddess of the rarest gifts!

Immersed in serenity, perfumed with love,
Waving thy flag of an empire's pride
Together we seek a mission sublime
In the land of the gentle Burmans,

500

Amidst shrines that revere the Buddha's virtues.

We take with us thy foremost creed:
"The world is what we make of it
With law and order, science and industry;
Open is Freedom for all and sundry
To earn with effort and to cherish with joy."

Farewell, Sweet England,
Wish us well.
In the mountains of Mandalay
Thy name we shall serve
With honour and humility
For the good of the many
For the benefit of the many. (M.B.W.)

X

The wedding of Moon-Beam and Timothy was a grand occasion. Victory-Servant kept to his word. As the intended brother-in-law, it was his duty to welcome the bridegroom by symbolically washing his feet. By way of a reward, the bride-groom threw into the basin of water a gold ring, The budding actor-linguist bent down, retrieved the ring, bowed low to Timothy and said in all seriousness,

"Merci beaucoup, Excellence, mon cher beau-frere."

His exaggerated gestures and the eloquently articulated foreign words were so funny that the outburst of laughter was a fitting start to the ceremonies.

Anybody who was somebody in the Administration, professions and business were there by invitation. It was a splurge. The best of wine and the finest of food. We had spared no effort or expense. Moon-Beam's flowing white wedding gown came from Paris and Timothy had his suit stitched in Saville Row in London. For Slim-Jewel, a sari was bought by Ram in Calcutta and sent through a visiting Padre. The dining room of the hotel was decorated gorgeously. An all-white band played 'Here comes the bride' as I proudly led Moon-Beam to the hall. I wore my official dress of a Mudaliyar for the special occasion.

It was a proud moment when the Government Agent himself solemnized the wedding in his capacity as the Provincial Registrar of Marriages and followed with a homily on the hopes and obligations of the emerging new generation of the twentieth century. The dazzling couple walked up to a three-tier wedding cake set in the centre of the hall and I stood by to offer them my silver sword to cut the cake.

The band played Western music and the couple stepped into the dance floor. Many couples joined them. It was magnificent. Slim-Jewel and I regretted that our preparation for the new century had not included a course in ball-room dancing.

Guests all seemed to enjoy the occasion. In our excitement we had failed to realize that our relatives from Sangha-Gem-Field were in a quandary. They felt like fish out of water. They had grouped themselves in a corner and sought security in their togetherness. The food was strange and so were the implements with which they were supposed to eat. The only relief they had was from watching the dancing couples. That, too, in shock and amusement than any appreciation of the music or the graceful moments. Joining them thoughtfully and helping them to enjoy what they could of the day was Don Baron, who as Principal of the ever-growing Buddhist School in Colombo, was already a nationally recognized personality.

The day ended with a thousand handshakes and salutations with clasped hands - each form being adopted according to the cultural background of the guest. Last to leave was Don Baron. He did both and we reciprocated.

"Did you invite Dharmapala ?" he asked me.

"Yes. But he responded in the negative."

"Did he say why?"

"I don't remember. Why?"

"Find out, Mudaliyar."

During the hectic weeks of preparing for Moon-Beam's wedding, neither Slim-Jewel nor I had any time to go through our mail with the meticulous care that we usually accorded to it. We had simply grouped all letters into three categories: acceptances, regrets and gifts. We counted the acceptances and filed the regrets which accompanied gifts of cash or vouchers from shops. Among the regrets in the third group was the letter of Dharmapala .

It began with the straight forward response "I will not be there for your daughter's wedding." Apparently that was all that either Slim-Jewel or I read. Now we read the whole letter:

Dear Mr. and Mrs. Valour-Lion,

I will not be there for your daughter's wedding. My reasons are many and would like to explain in person because of the esteem in which I once held you and would like to hold you in the future.

You two hailing from the hallowed village of Sangha-Gem-Field, which once sheltered the Sacred Tooth Relic, were the last people I would have expected to ape the West blindly and make fools of yourselves. I am ashamed of you. There's still time to rethink. If you drastically modify your plans, do please let me know. I may still be there to bless the young couple.

If you do not or would not, you will have to count me out.

I remain,

Yours sincerely,

Homeless Dharmapala .

Only one thing remained to be done and that was to meet him. In the following week we would be in Galle for the Home-Coming of the couple. A stop-over in Colombo was ineluctable.

On a sunny morning in mid-April 1904, Slim-Jewel and I went in two rickshaws to Aloe Avenue on our fence-mending mission to Homeless Dharmapala. He was seated in the verandah reading a book. He got up to receive us. I lagged behind to pay the two rickshawmen.

"Mrs. Valour-Lion, I will excuse Valour-Lion this time because of you. How can a healthy man of his stature be so inconsiderate as to get this half-starved man, less than half his size, to pull him uphill from the station?"

Here we were: two adults six years senior to him in age. With hardly an education to compare with mine nor the long experience I had in the world of monks and in the world of men, he towered over me in his moral high ground. His tongue-lashing left us feeling ashamed and morally inadequate. His caustic comments on my rickshaw ride extended to the wedding which we had given Moon-Beam.

"How soon you betrayed all that you had stood for, Valour-Lion! What happened to your moral sense? What happened to your patriotism? You have become one of *them* and in your poor imitation you are worse. Aren't the two of you simple village folk? Are you ashamed of the ways of your ancestors?"

"We came to tell you how sorry we are and give you the assurance that we would make amends for our excesses," I managed to say at the very first opportunity that I could get a word in.

"I appreciate it. Let's sit down and talk."

We entered the living room and sat on a sofa and he drew his rocking chair close to us.

"I am glad you admit what fools you have been. What a bad example you set to a young couple who are starting their life! This is how our youth get alienated from our culture, our customs, our religion, our values. Their happiest day was a mockery. All of you became slaves of British commercialism. Suits from Saville Row! Benares Silk Saris from Calcutta! Scotch whiskey and French wine! I was appalled when Don Baron told me how the whole thing passed."

Suddenly he rose and in a fit of anger came up to me shaking both his fists.

"Do you know how much you humiliated your relatives from the village? You made them feel small. You demeaned them. You degraded

504

them. You made them lose face. They did not know how to eat what you served them. They had never used fork and knife. You served them liquor in the presence of their wives and children. Do you know what they felt?"

"Homeless Dharmapala , you are right. We had done many things thoughtlessly. In our anxiety to give as good a wedding for Moon-Beam and Timothy, we made many mistakes.You know what we regret most. Both us compromised our positions of leadership in the Temperance Movement. But believe me. We did not order any liquor. Our fault was that we had not checked what the package deal included. About our relatives from the village, we are again very sorry. We will be eternally grateful to Don Baron who made it a point to be with them and to make them feel at ease."

Once the tensions settled and we had enjoyed a drink of fresh king coconut, our conversation turned friendlier. He filled me on what had happened in his numerous religious, social and educational activities since I became less and less involved directly. He spoke most enthusiastically of what he had observed in America and Japan as achievements of technical and vocational education and was keen to establish industrial schools here and in India. He was planning a long world tour to study the systems of Industrial Schools in USA, Britain, Holland, Denmark and Italy.

He took leave of us and went inside. He returned with a very slim hard-cover booklet called "*History of an Ancient Civilization*". Its smart appearance showed that it was not printed in India or Sri Lanka.

"This is for both of you," he said, handing over the booklet to Slim-Jewel. "You'll see that I have decided to be on the warpath. There's no looking back."

If he was a visionary, his dreams were not altogether unrealistic. Independence, to him, was a measure of self-government similar to that New Zealand had already had for half a century. This he expected to achieve in forty to fifty years. But he was keen that the colonial masters began immediately to prepare the people for democracy through education and economic development.

"My model is Japan and I am confident that we can do what they have done in education, in science and industry and in employment-related vocational and technical training."

While he spoke, I looked surreptitiously at the date of publication of the neatly bound booklet. "Los Angeles, 1902" - two years ago and I saw it only that day. That was how much I had veered away from a cause which I had thought was my life's mission. I felt so ashamed.

"Time up to be born again," I said to myself. "Better late than never."

"The sweet, tender, gentle Aryan children of an ancient, historic race are sacrificed at the altar of the whiskey-drinking, beef-eating belly-god of heathenism. How long, oh! how long will unrighteousness last in Ceylon! Humanitarians of England, France, Germany, Austria, Russia and the emancipated people of the United States of America, we solicit your sympathy."

It was a wet, chilly Sunday morning in November. The unseasonable rain with loud peals of thunder and frequent lightening had kept me awake most of the night. I was still in bed half awake. Loud and clear in an emotionally charged voice was delivered what even in my groggy state I recognized as the closing paragraph of Dharmapala 's *"History of an Ancient Civilization."*

Has he made an unannounced visit to Kandy? Was he at my door step?

The voice and diction were unmistakable.

"The bureaucratic administrators, ignorant of the first principles of the natural laws of evolution, have cut down primeval forests to plant tea; have introduced opium, ganja, whisky, arrack and other alcoholic poisons; have opened saloons and drinking taverns in every village; have killed all industries and made the people indolent," the speech continued.

"In the name of Humanity and Progress, we ask the British people to save the Sinhalese race from the jaws of the demon of alcohol and opium let loose for the sake of filthy lucre."

A loud peal of thunder following a flash of lightening sounded like a prolonged applause. I got up from bed, washed my face and dressed up quickly. The speech continued.

"The revenue of the Island for the year 1900 from taxes and excise duties was over eighty-one million rupees or twenty-seven million dollars at three rupees per dollar. Fourteen million rupees go to pay the salaries and pensions of British officers and two million go to England for the military establishment. Tea planters remitted fifty million to London. Thirty-nine million rupees worth of goods are imported from England and British colonies. We do not grudge the enormous profits which the imperial power makes of its colonies. After all, you do not run the empire for nothing or as the Sinhala villager says,'One doesn't break a honeycomb merely to lick the fingers."

506

The voice faded in the clap of thunder but came back again louder and clearer.

"But what appalls us is that only a pittance, if at all, is ploughed back to develop the industrial base of this country, to modernize its food production or for the education of the future generation. Out of a population of three million, only one hundred and eighty-eight thousand children went to school. Compare this with another small country - also a colony of another imperial power: Finland. Out of a population of two and a half million, half a million children were in school, nearly eight thousand in universities. What did we spend on higher education in this Island? Less than the Governor's salary? Yes, less than ten thousand rupees a month!"

The speaker paused for the point to sink in. Changing to an audible whisper, he continued in a tone of mock seriousness,

"I will tell you why we have to send all this money to England. She expects it. Yes, she is always expecting. That's why we call her Mother England."

That was in substance what Dharmapala had said in his booklet. But something was missing or different. It was too prosaic to be his language and lacked the ire and the pungency of the original. In its place was satire and humour. That had to be so.

Standing by the open door and talking out loud into the mist-laden lake and the Upper Garden Forest across the valley was Victory-Servant in a ludicrous version of the signature pose of Homeless Dharmapala, with a yellow bath towel wrapped around his neck to boot. I could not help but laugh. He made exaggerated belligerent gestures to his invisible audience.

I approached him quietly and put my right arm around his neck. He shuddered and stopped his recitation.

"What's up, son?" I asked him.

I am practising for the year-end gala. I will dress up like Homeless Dharmapala and imitate his pyrotechnics. At the rehearsal, everyone laughed including the teachers.

"Why do they think it so funny?"

"One thing, Little Father, I make the whole thing funny with my ad-libbing and gestures. But the truth is that my audience lives in another world and thinks nothing of the issues with which we are concerned."

"That means you are not making a fool of Dharmapala ?"

"Not at all, Little Father. To do that would be to laugh at you and Mother. I adore him for what he says and writes. What I want the people in my school environment to know is that our secluded Western-oriented upper class society cannot last too long in its sheltered silk-cocoon of privilege and advantage. Through humour at least, I want to

507

make them aware of the legitimate grievances of our people. Whom else should I imitate and mimic but the man I sincerely hope to emulate?"

I was not merely relieved. I was happy. Right along the line, Slim-Jewel and I had done something right.

I wrote to Dharmapala how Victory-Servant was using his booklet for a skit in the year-end gala of his school and explained the young man's intention. A reply came promptly. He approved of the strategy and mentioned what he was in the process of doing.

"I will myself be soon resorting to humourous verse and cartoons to convey my message. Satire is a powerful weapon. I never thought of the stage. My congratulations and best wishes to your ingenious son." the letter said.

The news that followed was disturbing. On his way back from Benares where he had established his first Industrial School, Homeless Dharmapala had gone to Adyar to pay his respects to his seventy-two year old mentor, Colonel Olcott. What could have been an opportunity for the revival of their old friendship was lost on account of Olcott's derogatory remarks on the authenticity and the sanctity of the Sacred Tooth Relic.

"Olcott showed bad temper and broke off friendship after a period of twenty years. I am sad. He initiated me to the Theosophical society in January 1884."

He said nothing more. I felt sad for both of them. They needed each other and we needed both of them. It was true that Olcott was rapidly becoming senile, erratic and cantankerous. But we were all engaged in our dedicated mission for national and Buddhist revival because of his precept and example. We were all his products, if not disciples. I wrote a long letter to Homeless Dharmapala and persuaded him to be more understanding of the foibles of an ageing man whose services to the Island and Buddhism should not be forgotten.

Many other common friends had advised him similarly. So he did extend a hand of reconciliation. Maybe, the young rebel was not clear enough in his offer to renew the friendship. Olcott's response was to go into print with his theory that the Sacred Tooth relic was a fake. It hurt the Buddhist susceptibilities to an extent that Olcott lost much esteem. Homeless Dharmapala was indeed the beneficiary. He rose to the rank of the foremost Social Legislator for the Sinhala community. It was on his palm, so malleable that he could fashion its thought and action the way he wanted.

Quite unconsciously, Slim-Jewel and I in our various positons of influence in the Temperance, religious and social activities of the Central Province had become the "Voice in the Hills", as Don Baron described when we attended his wedding on the twelfth of August in Colombo. His beautiful bride Jasmine was the daughter of a renowned scholar who collaborated with Venerable Sumangala in the editing and the translation of the *Great Chronicle*.

"The Voice" for the Island as a whole was Don Baron, now the Principal of the most prestigious Buddhist School in Colombo, the President of the Young Men's Buddhist Association of Colombo, the Editor of "The Buddhist" and a live wire in the Buddhist Theosophical Society.

Victory-Servant passed the Matriculation Examination of the University of London with distinction. But his late start had made him over-age for the scholarship which would have come with his level of excellence. Slim-Jewel and I had to take a decision as to where he should be sent for his higher education. Unlike his older siblings, who had clear professional goals, he had none. He liked to study history.

While we debated whether to send him to England or to Calcutta, I had once again to accompany the Judge of the Supreme Court for his Assizes in Jaffna. The new judge was a Muslim and an ardent admirer of Siddhi Lebbe who was a pioneering campaigner for the education of Muslim children. He knew of Middle Banda and read his poems in the Sunday Observer. On his own initiative, he wished to know what we were planning for Victory-Servant .

On the first Sunday in Jaffna, we had an invitation for dinner at Jaffna College, preceded, if we liked, by a swim in the sea and a tour of the village whose name in Tamil was derived from a Sinhala original meaning the settlement of carpenters.

The beautiful modern campus with brand new class rooms and auditorium spread through a grove of palmyra palms. Playing fields and tennis courts were well kept. Smartly dressed students in white shirts and long or short trousers were all over. It did not resemble any of the seats of higher learning I had visited in Britain. Could this be a replica of an American College?

I was not left too long to wonder. Reverend Kennedy, the Principal, received us in friendly informality.

509

"I am Reverend Kennedy of Boston and I am trying to create in this sandy plain a little corner of my alma mater, Harvard."

"You are succeeding, Reverend Bill", replied Justice Jabbar.

The dinner was simply splendid. The College Glee Club sang American songs like the "Red River Valley," "Home on the Range" and "Gone are the days". A sample of what was called "Southern Spirituals" was particularly moving. Food was delicious. The typical Jaffna delicacy, *Cool*, the mixed seafood curry which Reverend Kennedy called "our version of Spanish Zarzuela," was *la piece de resistance*. The bean soup and a home-baked apple-pie were appreciated by the Judge as reminders of Thanksgiving in Boston. Nothing else was needed to convince me that we were in a different cultural milieu. But the Glee Club resumed its programme as coffee was served. A medley of Tamil songs ranging from sonorous psalms and Hindu devotional songs to hilarious folk ditties was a treat.

Quite amusingly, I had to be the translator of the Tamil lyrics to both the Principal and the Judge. As I surveyed the happy faces of the singing lads representing a wide spectrum of race and religion, the conviction dawned in me,

"What a wonderful cultural milieu to which to send Victory-Servant for an year or two!" I thought.

Both the postprandial speeches were brilliant. They were witty and full of substance. Reverend Kennedy - who kept on insisting that he be addressed simply as Bill - spoke of his mission as unsettling the young mind so that it shook away prejudice, dogmatism and bigotry and opened itself to science and technology and, more than that, to unbiased critical thinking. The Judge's response was a tribute to the American spirit of liberty and democracy. He regretted that the flowering new culture of the United States of America was confined to the Jaffna Peninsula.

'It is a pity that we do not meet the pragmatic down-to-earth padre of Reverend Kennedy's vintage down in the South," he lamented. "It was all because the American Missionaries were prevented from contributing to the education of the majority race of the Island for fear of political contamination. You see 1810 was not too far from 1776 and the leaders of the day still had nightmares of the American War of Independence. But what a narrow-minded policy it has proved to be?"

He analyzed the history of education from the Dutch times with such clarity and concern that he sounded more a well informed educationalist than a jurist. He praised Reverend Kennedy for the attention paid to Tamil language, literature and culture.

"Let me make a prediction. It will take the rest of the Island three more decades to create anything which comes close to Jaffna College in quality and coverage, in ideals and achievements."

Even before the prolonged applause subsided, I had made up my mind,

"This is where I would send Victory-Servant ."

I recalled my first visit to Jaffna when the young boy accompanied me as my servant and returned home to be our adopted son. Jaffna had everything to do with his destiny. Mudaliyar Shiva-worshipper approved my decision and volunteered to act *in loco parentis*.

With a fortnight to get Victory-Servant to Jaffna College, we received sad news from Colombo. His brother, Virtue-Servant , who was adopted by Uncle Victor and Aunt Flower at the same time Slim-Jewel and I adopted Victory-Servant was tragically killed in an accident. As we found out later, it was not exactly an accident. It was a stunt gone bad.

To impress his school mates, he had occasionally performed a daring prank of jumping from a moving tram-car to another going in the opposite direction. With remarkable agility and split-second precision, he had done it several times to the bewilderment of passengers in both tram-cars. He had been warned by the conductors who did not consider his stunt funny. On this day, the window that he aimed to enter by was half-closed.

Before the drivers of the two tram-cars could stop, his torso had been stretched as on a torture rack of a mediaeval dungeon. He died instantly.

On receipt of the telegram, Slim-Jewel and I made immediate plans to go to Colombo to help in the judicial proceedings and funeral arrangements. Victory-Servant was to accompany us. But it occurred to Slim-Jewel that it was our duty to inform the biological mother.

"What shall we do? Change our plans and go there tomorrow?" I asked.

"Why don't the two of you go as planned. I'll go to the village and bring her along," volunteered Victory-Servant .

511

Thanks to a quicker and more efficient telecommunication system in the region, it was not necessary for anyone to go all the way. A telegram to my brother, the Chief Monk of Sangha-Gem-Field, brought back a reply in two hours that the biological mother of the two boys and, of course, of Middle Banda would be at the Kandy Railway Station by nightfall.

One nagging problem remained to be solved and Slim-Jewel as usual had thought of it before I could. Out of her wardrobe she took out several outfits which would fit the woman and had one laid on the bed for her to wear on the trip.

Leaving Victory-Servant with a long list of do's and don'ts, we departed for Colombo as we had planned. Providentially, I was there in time for the hearings of the Inquirer into Sudden Deaths and Coroner. My mind went back to the murder of my elder brother over two decades ago. Only the village headman was there to write a report. Concepts of law and order and the processes of enforcement had developed so rapidly that no efforts were spared to fix responsibility. The Colombo Municipality urged that the guardians of the dead boy be brought to book. With my long experience in the courts system and the sharp mind of Autumn-Moon - our second barrister in the family - just out of the Law College, we adopted a defence strategy which worked.Uncle Victor and Aunt Flower were spared with a stringent reprimand.

Victory-Servant came in time for the funeral with the woman across the river whose real name we never knew. In Slim-Jewel's clothing, she looked dignified and presentable. She could easily pass for a Kandyan woman from a good family. Her natural beauty despite the age was a significant asset.

Uncle Victor with his Christian training and outlook had little difficulty in treating her as an equal member of the family. Aunt Flower and I demurred a bit but we joined Uncle Victor in insisting that she joined us at the table and used the guest room bed. She needed an enormous amount of coaxing. We felt sorry for her. It had been dinned into her ears that she was an outcaste, an untouchable and she had accepted it. The dignity we accorded to her as the mother of our children actually embarrassed her. She spoke to us with immense deference. We had to caution her not to address us, at least in company, in a manner that would reveal her social standing.

She was grief-stricken. Her life had been one of many tragedies. The death of Naide alias Virtue-Servant exacerbated the pain she already experienced in not having the three sons with her. The conviction that they were for ever liberated from the shackles of their

512

birth in a socially and economically depressed outcaste community had been her only solace.

Eight to ten hours alone with Victory-Servant enabled her to savour a bit of the joy she felt the day we met her by the river to show Middle Banda on the eve of his departure to England. Once more, she saw another of her sons grow into the kind of gentleman from whom she begged in the streets. It had deepened her sorrow in that another son who could have had a similar destiny had died of his own folly. She showered all her love on Victory-Servant but had carefully avoided mentioning that Middle Banda too was her son. Whatever they discussed had had made a deep impression on Victory-Servant.

"Little Father, can you ask Small Grandmother Flower to keep my mother with them? She has no one to return to in the village" he asked me the day after the funeral of his brother.

For a moment I was not sure whether I heard him referring to her as 'my mother.' It was the very first time that he did so since we adopted him. He told us what she had gone through. The man who had fathered the two boys were no longer with her. She was too old to attract another husband or lover. She eked out a difficult existence. Kindness and compassion were not common commodities in her community.

About to retire from government service and planning to settle down in a suburb of Colombo from where they could watch the rising fortunes of their only son, Autumn-Moon, Uncle Victor jumped at the idea. Aunt Flower approved it heartily.

"You all will be Buddhas," said the woman whom we renamed Lucy. "I did not think that the Little Gentleman will remember what I told him in the train. For the fourth time, you are my saviours."

She cried profusely and both Aunt Flower and Slim-Jewel put their arms around her and took her to the kitchen.

"Thank you, Mother. Thank you, Father." Victory-Servant told us in the train. He recounted to us what Lucy recalled of his thirteen years in the village and what she had suffered in the hands of ruthless people.

"One more good deed, Boy Scout. Be prepared for more." was my response as I drew him and planted a loving kiss on his head. Slim-Jewel wept all the way. Perhaps her mind was on the many ways in which her own destiny was entwined with Lucy's.

"When you write to Middle Banda about the death of Virtue-Servant , don't say anything about his relationship to Lucy," she said when the train approached the Kandy station.

513

"No, Jewel. But I have to tell him that his Lady of the River was now the Lady of a Stream at Kotte!"

I was referring to the Water-Colour Stream by which Uncle Victor was building his retirement home in the now ruined fifteenth century capital of the Island.

"What's all this about a Lady of the River?" asked Victory-Servant in English. I promised to show him the doggerel which Middle Banda sent us from London.

XI

While in Colombo, I managed to find just enough time to call on the ailing Venerable Sumangala. The seventy-eight year old scholar-monk was visibly weak but his indomitable spirit had not left him. He looked every inch the unchallenged leader he had always been.

"You look well, Sangha-Gem-Field," he said when I knelt by his couch and worshipped him thrice as I had always done.

Perhaps he could not recall my lay name immediately. But to be called by the name of my village which was prefixed to my name as a monk showed how alert he was. We talked about his poor health and my work and family. He had read some of the poems of Middle Banda in the Sunday Observer.

"He does have some keen insights and a fine sense of humour to go with them," he commented. "I am glad that he married an English girl and decided to work in Burma."

I knew what he meant and I was very grateful. I recalled how his decision to support my becoming a layman and a government employee was a source of solace to me and Slim-Jewel.

We drifted to a discussion of the two personalities who meant a lot to both of us.

"If I did not have this great respect for what he had done, I would have said that the White Buddhist was crazy," said the scholar-monk with the utmost compassion. "Our man, also, is far too impetuous."

By 'our man' he referred to Homeless Dharmapala , whose attempts to revive the old friendship with Olcott had failed miserably. I felt a sense of guilt as I had urged the younger man to extend a hand of reconciliation. The rebuff was too harsh.

"Now no one can bridge the gap," continued the scholar-monk. "What was a private altercation between them had become a public debate. Olcott has taken the quarrel to print and calls 'our man' a 'spoilt brat', 'vainglorious boy' and 'pertinacious popinjay'. What hurt most Buddhists is that he questions the authenticity of the Sacred Tooth Relic. He has published an article to say that the actual Relic was destroyed by the Portuguese and what he have in Kandy is only a replica carved out of deer horn."

"Is there anything we could do, Venerable Sir?" I asked him.

"Very little or nothing, Sangha-Gem-Field. We are simply helpless. What I am trying to do is to ensure that his hostile attacks on Sri Lankan Buddhist leaders, institutions and beliefs do not detract from the gratitude we owe him for his unparalleled services to our cause. I hope he does not make things too difficult for the very few friends he has left in the Island. The last thing we want to do is to plead senility or insanity in defence of his irrational utterances."

Homeless Dharmapala was not in town. Venerable Sumangala had a high opinion of what the young man was doing.

"He is fighting in too many fronts. But he is doing well all round. So there is no way to hold him back in any way and to ask him to concentrate on the essentials."

Recently, I had to keep myself informed of his doings from the pages of the Journal of the Maha Bodhi Society. It had blossomed into a veritable Buddhist forum with a growing international readership. I was pleased to have more uptodate information from Venerable Sumangala.

"We continue our main struggle to urge for the restitution of Sacred Buddhist shrines of India to Buddhists," he said.

The emphasis on the first person plural was most possibly to remind me that he continued to be the President of the Society and shared the responsibility for the legal proceedings set in motion in Buddha Gaya.

"Since becoming a Homeless, 'our man' has gained an immense following here. No one - not even myself - can command such crowds as he could. You know what I call him: 'our social legislator.' I like what he does with the crowds. He has become the most effective adult educator and what he does is to raise the consciousness of the people about what oppresses them."

Venerable Sumangala appreciated the multi-pronged message of Homeless Dharmapala .

What was particularly highlighted was his dual approach. He criticized the government for neglecting education, specially vocational and technical education. But without waiting for the government, he had begun setting up schools in imitation of those he had seen in operation in other parts of the world.

He was urging the government to pass an Alien Prevention Act, similar to that of England, to control the fast growing immigrant population of Indian import-export merchants, traders and petty businessmen, Malabar jewellers, Marawadi textile dealers and Afghan and Chettiar money-lenders. At the same time, he was urging the Sinhala villagers to come to the city and become entrepreneurs in the

516

commercial district of Colombo called Pettah, where foreign interests were taking root.

Homeless Dharmapala spoke, wrote and encouraged others to do likewise on pressing issues. His solution for most ills was self-reliance. He generated confidence by drawing heavily on the nation's long history and rich culture. Adherence to Buddhist principles and upholding plain and simple living were his antidotes against the burgeoning tendency to ape the West.

"I wish I was as young and resilient," murmured the scholar-monk who was visibly exhausted after his long and lively recital of the contribution of "Our Man". He needed a drink of warm water before he continued.

"Something really admirable in Homeless Dharmapala," continued Venerable Sumangala, "is how he is inspiring so many young people to do something for the country. A young man with a flair for writing is being encouraged to write stories in imitation of the English novel and to use these stories to propagate the ideas he holds important: national names, customs and dress, study of national history and literature and, of course, promotion of Buddhism. This young Piyadasa Sirisena writes beautiful prose as well as verse and his novel will be a great breakthrough. He comes here to talk with me from time to time."

He also spoke of another young man who had taken to the study of history and archaeology.

"We are urging that the Buddhist monuments in India should be restituted to Buddhists. Our own monuments in the ancient cities are in ruin and neglected. This young man is groomed to take the battle to authorities here."

At the next meeting of the Temperance Movement in Kandy, I gave an account of the multiple approaches of Homeless Dharmapala towards national and Buddhist revival. It was unanimously agreed that he be invited as the guest of honour for the forthcoming annual general meeting.

Victory-Servant travelled to Jaffna alone. His first letter was not as cheery as we expected. The emotional stress of the death of his own brother and meeting and caring for his birth mother had been greater than we thought. From the salubrious hill climate of Kandy to the dry heat of the Jaffna Peninsula was too big a change. He began with a bout of fever. We passed an anxious week until we had a letter from

517

Reverend Bill saying that Victory-Servant was well and had his first dip in the ocean.

With the children dispersed in three places - Moon-Beam with Timothy in Galle, Middle Banda and Rose in Mandalay and Victory-Servant in Jaffna College - Slim-Jewel and I were once again left high and dry. Our only regret was that distance prevented us from enjoying the pleasures of being grandparents. We had had a few days with Moon-Beam's bouncy baby son. As regards Middle Banda's daughter, all we had was a promise that they would touch Colombo on their way to London on furlough.

Our most faithful Golden Jewel ran the house and looked after our non-stop stream of visitors. Perhaps, unconsciously, to compensate for the woes of a fractured family, we redoubled our efforts in the organizations through which we served the people. Since we bungled with our daughter's wedding, we had promises to keep. Jointly we planned a rousing welcome to the uncrowned king of the masses - Homeless Dharmapala .

It took months before he could find two days to spare. We grabbed the opportunity. The widest possible publicity was given to his visit and the people of Kandy arranged a glamourous procession to conduct him from the station to our place and later from there to the meeting in the Esplanade in front of the Temple of the Sacred Tooth Relic.

It was a sea of heads. He held the audience spell-bound. His eloquence matched the message which he presented logically. None was spared. He attacked the Sangha for being lethargic and inactive. He blamed the government for everything from neglect of education to erosion of the top soil of the Kandyan hills. He urged people to return to righteousness and simple life.

For two hours he held forth and there was not even the slightest murmur from the crowd that took in his admonitions with eager attention.

His histrionics added spice to his pungent utterances. Right in front was an unkempt young man in shabby clothes.

"Come here, young man," he beckoned to him. "How much is a ball of soap?"

"Maybe half a cent."

"Good, take this cent. Buy your self a ball of soap. Wash your clothes. Dry them. Bathe yourself. You understand. Apply soap liberally. Comb your hair. Come back before the meeting is over."

Presiding over the meeting, I was amused to find quite a score of similarly unkempt and shabby young men leaving the grounds!

Homeless Dharmapala resumed his speech as if the digression with the young man was a part of the strategy to emphasize his point that we as a nation failed to do little things that would reinforce dignity and pride. His eyes roamed constantly in search of such details. For a moment I shuddered when his eyes fell on the three merchants attired in tweed coat and cloth.

Immigrants from the low-country, they were among the most successful and affluent. Their gold watch chains and cuff links matched the expensive suits. For a while which looked an eternity, the speaker focused his gaze on them. Slowly he left the podium and walked up to them. In respect, they stood up and greeted him with clasped hands.

"Would you mind giving me your combs?" he asked politely. All three reached for their heads simultaneously and gave him the tortoise shell circular combs.

He returned to the podium and held aloft the combs.

"How very dignified you look without these silly horns you had on your heads! Please do not put them on any more. These only serve to remind us that the Portuguese were once the rulers of our Island of righteousness," he said as he broke the combs into pieces. The merchants were mortified. The audience was shocked to silence.

On the theme of aping the foreign powers that continued to rule in the Island, he waxed eloquent. Once again, he surveyed the audience as if in search of another digression. At that precise moment walked in the young man whom he sent out for a bath.

"Come here, young man," he called him to the podium. "See what half a cent of soap can do."

I could hardly believe my eyes. His white banian and striped sarong were spotless. He was himself clean and looked handsome.

Homeless Dharmapala put his arm around the young man's shoulders.

"Now, I am proud to call you my brother. What do you do for a living?"

"Nothing. I have failed to find any work."

"Can you learn to make lentil-balls?"

"Yes, Sir. I think I can."

Homeless Dharmapala reached for his purse and gave him five rupees.

"This is your capital. In six months you must return it to the Maha Bodhi Society. Buy the utensils and the lentil you want for the first two days. The balance must be deposited in the Post Office Savings Bank. Whatever profits you make also must be deposited every week. You understand."

The yellow-clad social reformer was all compassion. An enthusiastic audience applauded as he wound up with another of his typical admonitions.

"Look at the South Indian who comes here with hardly a cent in his pocket. If he is lucky, he gets a job in an estate as a labourer. But if he does not get work, does he sit on a culvert wall and blame everyone around for their misfortune? He goes round collecting bottles and old newspapers. He does this until he has enough money to set himself as a seller of roasted gram and lentils. Within months, he runs a grocery store and our foolish people will be going to him for credit. Why should this happen in this country where its own young men loiter around in the streets? I you love your nation, give up your lazy habits. Take the South Indian bottle man as your role model. Learn to raise your head in dignity."

As soon as the meeting was over, I rushed down to meet the three merchants whom I felt had been publicly humiliated.

"I am very sorry, if you are hurt by what he did to your combs and what he said," I told them.

"Thank you, Mudaliyar," replied the seniormost among them. "We are glad that he opened our eyes."

"Only this morning I scolded my daughter who said that the circular comb looks exactly like a pair of horns - the very words that the honourable Homeless used. I think both of them had a point," said the next in seniority.

The youngest and the most prosperous among them went further: "This man is really speaking a lot of sense. I want to ask him how I can help him."

After taking leave of the monks on the stage, Homeless Dharmapala joined us. He apologized to them saying that his was a spontaneous, if rash, reaction. The merchants offered him their support.

"Carry on with what you do. You are the real patriots. What you do will make our nation truly great and independent. If you really want to help me, get more and more of our people to take to economically productive activities. Encourage specially the young men."

I was very glad that the meeting was a great success. Two European planters who were in the audience joined us to congratulate Homeless Dharmapala . I was taken aback by the spirit of camaraderie they showed Dharmapala .

"We are saying the same things in Ireland," one of them said in perfect Sinhala.

In strict adherence to the eight precepts which he had vowed to observe, he refused to eat any solids after noon. Over a glass of coriander and ginger, we talked late into the night on his plans and aspirations, concerns and conflicts.

"Poor Olcott," he repeated every time the ageing warrior was mentioned. "I love him as much as I loved my father. But what can I do? He rejects me and spares no opportunity to insult me. His closest friends ascribe his change of behaviour to senility. But others even think that he had gone crazy after the death of Madame Blavatsky."

"What do you think?" I asked bluntly.

"I don't judge him. He had long been my mentor, my friend, guide and counsellor. I wish him well. But when my human feelings get the better of me, I meditate on the ineluctable law of impermanence. There go I, I say to myself, but for the grace of my relative youth."

XII

When a few months later, an altercation between Colonel Olcott and Venerable Sumangala was reported in the newspapers, I knew that Homeless Dharmapala , if at all, had played only a minor role. It was Olcott who had created the problem. After years of involvement with Hinduism in India, he had revised his views on some aspects of Buddhism. He brought out the fortieth edition of his *Buddhist Catechism* to reflect his new interpretations.

On seventeen questions, his answers were found to be at variance from those which Venerable Sumangala had approved in earlier editions. To protest against Olcott's unilateral revision of a book which still carried the certificate of authenticity which the scholar monk had issued, he resigned from the Theosophical Society. Referring to Olcott's views on the Sacred Tooth Relic and other issues, Venerable Sumangala minced no words:

"Such an uncalled for attack we could expect only from an enemy of our religion."

I felt that I should intercede immediately. I wrote to both the senior monk and Olcott urging them to negotiate a solution. Recalling my intervention while I was still a student twenty years ago, I agreed to meet them in Colombo and sit with them to iron out the differences. The White American did take me seriously this time. I had a reply accepting my offer as a mediator. His concern was realistic.

"If Venerable Sumangala turns against me, I become instantly vulnerable to any campaign that Dharmapala mounts against me. He can stir angry feelings of the masses against me and I will be obliged to sever my connection with the Island," he lamented.

The repentant author revised the objectionable answers and the compassionate protagonist of peace and tolerance lived up to the tenets of his faith. A friendship cherished out of gratitude was restored.

There could, however, be no reconciliation with the youthful firebrand, who insisted that Olcott should recant the pan-religious stand of Theosophy and express his undivided partiality to Buddhism. Nothing I said or wrote had any effect on Dharmapala .

"Theosophy is irreconcilable with Buddhism," he replied. "Buddhism is opposed to all existing religions."

I wondered about both the accuracy and relevance of this statement.

"If there is anything irreconcilable with Buddhism, it is bigotry and intolerance," I said to myself, but had no guts to write to the man whose mounting rage had robbed him of good sense and brought him to the brink of fanaticism.

This act of omission I regretted an year later when the hero of my youth - my mentor in more than one sense - died, shattering whatever hopes I harboured on bringing these two men together again.

Travelling from a visit to New York to see his family, the seventy-four year old Colonel had a fall on board the ship. A month in an Italian hospital in Genoa barely enabled him to continue his trip to Colombo. Despite all his admirers and friends could do for him during the two weeks he spent in a nursing home, he regained just enough health to proceed to Adyar on the eleventh of December 1906. Slim-Jewel and I were sad to see him go. What a caricature of the man whom I met in my youth on the day he landed in Galle!

"Impermanent are all aggregates; they rise and they fall", I said to myself and wished him a speedy recovery.

There was still so much he could do for the good of humanity. But my mind kept on reminding me not to expect miracles. We would never be destined to meet again in this life.

He passed away on the seventeenth of February 1907. The news, though not unexpected, made us very sad. We held a fitting memorial service. We had it on the second of March - the ninety-second anniversary of the loss of independence of my Motherland. I persuaded Justice Spencer, now in retirement, to preside. He made a moving speech.

"Judge not this man from what you have heard of him. You are too close to him to make a detached, value-free assessment. Yet, look around for his real achievement: an ancient nation raising its head in dignity and seeking a place in a brave new world. He was there when this nation most wanted him. His farsighted actions continue to produce the kind of committed men and women to whom the reins of this nation will soon be given rightfully with confidence," he said in conclusion.

That night, I sat until the early hours of the morning and unburdened myself in three emotion-filled letters to my fractured and scattered family. Moon-Beam and Timothy were in Colombo, Timothy gaining a reputation as a successful surgeon and his wife and mother of two an active itinerant campaigner for public health. Middle Banda and Rose were in Rangoon. He was the District Judge and his wife - the White Buddhist of the Valour-Lion family - the founder-principal of the first ever modern Buddhist girls' school in the Burmese capital. Victory-Servant had graduated from Jaffna College and was reading for a Master's degree in history in a mid-western Methodist College in Illinois, USA. Reverend Kennedy had obtained for him an assignment as a Teaching Assistant.

I wanted them to know how much the White Buddhist had influenced my life and thereby theirs. That, I felt, was the least I could do to ensure that in their grateful hearts his memory would dwell with unstinted affection.

"What I am and whatever values of liberty and service I may have inculcated in you all came from this great and noble man who inspired me to reach out for the unreachable and dream the impossible. Whenever you think of your Little Father, who had tried to be more than a father to you, add a thought of gratitude to Colonel Olcott and wish, 'May his journey in the cycle of birth and death be short and may he attain the ultimate bliss of Nibbana.'"

I also wrote a similar letter to His Serene Royal Highness Diamond-Lustre. I recalled our common experiences with the White Buddhist when we were both monks.

Slim-Jewel came to my study with two cups of tea and till dawn we talked of Olcott's greatness. What death could do to a person! Only a few months ago were we complaining of his intransigence and obduracy for which the more charitable explanation we gave was senility.

Hardly a fortnight from his death, we missed him dearly. His selfless dedication to the cause of a human brotherhood and his unmatched contribution to the promotion of Buddhism rose in our minds as the cream of the cream of his life's activities. We cried without shame.

Our home had been a bee-hive of activity. My religious, literary and temperance activities occupied all my leisure. I was the President of this, Secretary of that or Treasurer of yet another of national or regional organization which mushroomed in the wake of the leadership of men like Homeless Dharmapala and Don Baron.

Slim-Jewel had her own share of responsibilities. Her mission was to shape that superior half of the national energy which found

524

expression in diverse ways. If my organizations did more with words than deeds hers were the opposite. Hers were in the midst of real problems - helping wives to combat drinking and gambling; finding homes for orphans; feeding the homeless and raising funds through all kinds of innovative strategies; and above all, enabling the women to raise their heads in dignity to assume their rightful place in society..

Golden Jewel - now a plump middle-aged woman - rose to every occasion with inner reserves of stamina which characterized the Kandyan peasant. There was hardly an evening or a week-end when our home was not the venue of a meeting, a reception or a workplace for some project or another.

Our involvement in so many activities was not without challenge. If I made it a point, with studious assiduity, to steer my societies and associations clear of anything which would even be slightly political in nature, hers could be more vociferous in their comments on, if not criticisms of, the policy and action of the Administration. But our leadership certainly helped to keep any agitation within constitutional and legal bounds. There were times when the high officials in the Government and specially the judges with whom I was closely associated appreciated our restraining influence on public sentiments. I was hard put to withstand a popular cry that one of my associations should invite a rising star in the emerging national political scene.

F. R., as he was affectionately called by both his colleagues and the populace, hailed from a distinguished family with the surname Senanayaka . He was the acknowledged leader of an active band of young men of solid English education who had acquitted themselves creditably in legal and medical professions or were wealthy entrepreneurs. Associated with him were close relatives of Homeless Dharmapala . Don Baron, who still concentrated most of his efforts on educational development and the promotion of Buddhism, was a sympathizer of their philosophy of politically inspired agitation.

"Invite him for all I care," was the advice which I received from the Government Agent himself. "But don't you get caught in the chair when he attacks the Government and asks the British to quit the Island!"

The sneering laughter was more expressive of the disdain he had for both me and the emerging new leaders of the nation.

It was the laughter which incited me to action. I went to Colombo and met the executive committee of the Temperance Union. We deliberated a course of action for a long time.

There was Dr. W. A. de Silva whose munificence kept many a national and Buddhist organization in action. He had a remarkable way of ensuring that he capped only successful ventures. To many who came to him with appeals for financial aid, he would blandly say,

"You want to build a school in your village. Very good. The roof is mine" or

"You are building an image house in your temple. Count on me for the pinnacle."

All three Senanayaka brothers, D.C., F. R., and D. S. were the most vocal, the youngest demanding nothing short of confrontation. F. R. appealed for patience and long term results.

"We certainly can have a temporary victory by staging a demonstration in Kandy," he told mostly his own brothers. "But what if the sentiments we arouse lead to violence? What if the jobless criminal elements take control of the situation and begin to riot and loot for their own benefit? Any victory we win must be in keeping with the solid principles of non-violence and tolerance we hold as dear as our own lives."

No one would disagree with F. R.. His was the voice of reason.

Don Baron had a practical and, of course, absolutely legal solution to the problem I posed to the Committee. He persuaded the Temperance Union to have its next Annual General Meeting in Kandy.

We can all be there. F. R. can be the main speaker. Mudaliyar can act as host. We achieve all we want. Won't we Mudaliyar?"

I agreed. I counted on F. R. to keep the emerging young leaders in line. Four hours in the train to Kandy. I drew up my plans for a memorable event.

Four letters awaited me - two from England, one from the United States of America and one with the prominent royal seal of Siam.

Edged in ominous black was the envelope which caught my attention first. The news it brought was devastating. The Right Reverend Kenneth Saunders had passed away in Canterbury after a brief illness. I buried my face in my hands on the table and wept with unbearable grief. Golden Jewel, bringing me a cup of tea, was shocked and summoned Slim-Jewel. I told her the news and she was inconsolable. We recalled the innumerable kindnesses we had received from him from the first day I carried him a bowl of soup to his sick bed at the behest of Mrs. Blake.

"He was a saint walking on the earth for our sake," lamented Slim-Jewel. "It is only one's father or brother who would have done what he did when I went to London for my eye surgery."

526

We concluded our long session of grieving for the departed mentor and friend-in-need with plans for action.

"Slim-Jewel, we have two things to do and in this order," I told her. " First we have to arrange a fitting memorial for Reverend Kenneth. After that we invite the Temperance Union to hold its Annual General Meeting in Kandy. That's when F. R. would give the speech that our people demand."

While Slim-Jewel went back to the kitchen to instruct Golden Jewel on what to cook for lunch, I read the letter from Siam. It was a pleasant letter. The Prince was cheerful even though his health was not as perfect as he wished. He complained of chronic back pains, which confined him to days of bed-rest, much against his wishes. He was dictating his memoirs in which he threatened to expose all my "shady deals"! For no reason, tears welled in my eyes.

"Am I about to lose another of my soulful friends?" I asked myself.

Letters from the two sons we read together. The news they brought cheered us up.

Victory-Servant had made up his mind on two matters in which he had earlier asked for our advice. On both matters Slim-Jewel and I, after much deliberation, decided to leave them to his good sense. He had given up the idea of becoming a Methodist Minister. But he was sticking to his plans to marry a Minister's daughter. He had secured a teaching post in his intended Father-in-law's College. As we could guess he was going to teach history. Apparently to facilitate his assimilation to his new environment and certainly out of his own convictions, he had agreed to be baptized a Christian.

Once again, both of us were relieved or rather overjoyed. It was a relief that both our boys found careers and wives abroad because their unfortunate past as children of an outcaste woman from across the river would never haunt them. At least, that was what we thought then.

The joint letter from M. B. W. and Rose was full of thanks for the visit we had paid to them on board the ship which took them to England on furlough. Rose spoke lovingly of the impression we had made on the two kids. Middle Banda was hoping to get some leave for further studies. They invited us to visit them in London and join them on a grand tour of the Continent.

The Vicar of Kandy did not believe his ears when I told him that I had come with plans to hold a fitting memorial for the Late Right Reverend Kenneth J. Saunders.

527

"I don't know much of him," he confessed. "Of course, I have heard all kinds of stories - not all them very complimentary to a church superior."

"You mean, bigotry had no place in his life,' I retorted.

"So, you seem to know these stories?"

Despite the chilly start, we sat down to work out the details of a service in Saint Paul's Church and a public meeting at the adjoining Buddhist School. The Bishop of Colombo whom I invited to preside over the meeting was equally surprised how and why a person whom he had taken to be a "firebrand" in the national re-awakening movement should take the initiative to commemorate the services of a church luminary.

The fourth of February, 1908 began with a visit to the inner shrine of the Temple of the Sacred Tooth Relic. It was my fiftieth birthday and Slim-Jewel had arranged to have the morning offering assigned to us. The two prelates of the Flower Garden and the Horse Peak Monasteries were present to bless me. So was my brother the Chief Monk of the Royal Monastery of Sangha-Gem-Field. The monks chanted verses of benediction and the prelates told the milling crowd of worshippers how much they held me and Slim-Jewel in esteem and affection. It was a good start of a birthday which was to include the memorial service and public homage to my most outstanding benefactor.

We rushed home to change into formal dress to join several hundreds of people who had gathered to express their gratitude to a man whose humanism knew no boundaries of race or religion or region. The Bishop of Colombo read a eulogy on Right Reverend Saunders and the Vicar departed from the order of the ceremony to afford me a few moments to share with the congregation my memories of my teacher, mentor and life-long friend.

The public meeting in the afternoon was worthy of the saintly churchman it was designed to honour. Both prelates attended it and spoke lovingly of his devotion to Buddhist scholarship. The Government Agent was there to welcome the Bishop who presided over the meeting. They had much to say of his contributions to the Church and the Empire. The Principal of his old school recounted what his illustrious predecessor in office had done for education. I chose to be the last speaker.

I spoke in both Sinhala and English and I could not help being emotional. Not only Slim-Jewel but several others in the audience wept as I recalled incidents from the life of a holy man whom they had not seen for a long time but whose goodness was vivid in their memories. I

528

wound up abruptly lest I choked and receded to the back of the dais to get hold of myself. It was a relief that the vote of thanks was brief.

The Bishop thanked me profusely for organizing the function. The Government Agent joined him, saying,

"Jolly old Mudaliyar doing for us what we should be doing! Healthier this way, Old Chap!"

They both wished me a very happy fiftieth birthday.

The Annual General Meeting of the National Temperance Union in May was a spectacular event. A procession which, to all intents and purposes and glamour, was a mini replica of the August Pageant of Kandy conducted the delegates from the railway station to the venue of the meeting. The whole city was decorated with the Lion Flag and the six-coloured Buddhist Flag of Olcott's design.

Thousands lined the streets to take in a glimpse of the men and women in the vanguard in a determined effort to regain national independence. F. R. was their hero though Don Baron as the returning prodigal son was hailed with more enthusiastic ovations. At the door of the meeting hall, I received the stalwarts with the traditional sheaf of betel while each organization in the host committee garlanded them.

The meeting commenced with W. A. de Silva in the chair and the routine affairs were rushed through in a thoroughly business-like manner. Don Baron introduced F. R. and he made a brilliant speech in which temperance was the peg on which many a theme of national interest was cleverly hung.

F. R.'s brinkmanship was tantalizing. Just when a peroration bordered on sedition and the plainclothes men from the Central Investigation Department craned their necks to catch every single nuance of his statement, he would pay a tribute to the British Administration in general or to a particular political leader in England. It was an amusing game of words and he sent his pungent points home with a superb sense of humour.

Right through the session, the spirit of two men stalked the hall: Olcott who inculcated in us a genuine appreciation and pride in our heritage and Homeless Dharmapala who had made us ashamed of our complacent inertia.

Speaking here were men of action, lawyers and physicians, planters and entrepreneurs, well-versed in the theory and practice of politics. If they were masters of the art of the possible, they showed no readiness to be cowed by either argument or show of power. As a mere member of the audience, though given a seat in the front row, I was no more than an observer. But what I saw pleased me.

Before me unfolded the promise of a glorious future when men and women of the island would decide for themselves what is best for them and their children.

If Olcott was a dreamer redesigning the world to conform with his own fond model and Homeless Dharmapala was lighting bonfires to bring light where darkness reigned, these speakers were careful planners of action. They expressed themselves clearly and their logic was flawless.

"Sooner or later, we shall rule our destinies. We ourselves or our children will sit in the Councils of State and solve our problems. No more will there be a need to import officers to attend to our affairs. But such a future shall never dawn unless we eradicate the horrible scourge of drunkenness. We are here to redouble our efforts to achieve the goal of a liquor-free society and that indeed has to be our first lap in the inexorable march to freedom," concluded F. R. to the applause which lasted a full five minutes.

Repercussions to the week-end's demonstration and meeting were quick to follow. On arrival in the courts in the Audience Hall, I received word that the Government Agent would like to see me. I had gone in the ceremonial dress with scabbard and all as it was the first day of the Kandy Assizes of the Supreme Court. Somewhat self-consciously I walked to the old Royal Palace. It was a place I had known from my 'teens and the Government Agent's office had been the location of several minor victories - specially the day I came as a fugitive from Orange Island and returned a free man. Memories of those days crowded in my mind as I sat on a wooden chair in the corridor until my arrival was announced.

Much had changed indeed. The intellectually motivated young civil servants of those days had been replaced by veterans of the Boer War of 1899 - 1902. The erstwhile friendly, fruitful collaboration with native scholars in exploring the language, religion and culture of the Island had given way to rankling suspicion and distrust. There were still exceptions - but very few indeed and none to my knowledge in Kandy.

I sat out the time the self-assumed ruler of the Province took to impress on me his superior authority. I was not surprised by it at all even though this same man had been extremely cordial when we last met at the Memorial Service to the Late Reverend Kenneth.

530

At last, after what seemed a whole hour, the peon with the red sash took me to his office. The growl on his face was incongruent with his "Good Morning" and "Nice to see you again". I greeted him with traditional politeness and awaited an invitation to take a seat. He was absentmindedly messing around with some papers on his table - no doubt, another way of re-emphasizing who the top dog was! He looked up suddenly,

"Oh! Mudaliyar. Sit down. Sit down." he said.

As I sat, he stood up, a towering figure - every inch an imposing soldier. Second Lieutenant John Smith, elevated to the Ceylon Civil Service   in re-cognition of active war service in South Africa, was struggling to gain some inner composure. He too was dressed in his ceremonial best because as the Fiscal of the Province he had a role to play in the noon ceremony of the inauguration of the Assizes. Seeing me in my black attire with sash, sword and gold chains, he laughed mockingly,

"We aren't dressed for a fight? Are we?" he said disarmingly.

" I am, Sir," I said patting the hilt of the silver sword.

This time it was genuine laughter and the tension which up to this moment could have been cut with a knife almost vanished.

"You are a clever fox, Mudaliyar," he said in a more friendly tone. "You found a way to eat the cake and have it. But I wish you had not been there at the door with betel leaf to receive the seditionists."

Though he laughed, he meant what he said. I could not let him get away with such a statement.

"Sir, these are the emerging leaders of this country and I hope to live here long after all of you leave on retirement or earlier. They are not seditionists by any stretch of imagination. If they were, you could take them to courts..."

"And have the further humiliation of seeing them being acquitted by our namby-pamby judges and becoming heroes. Say, on the contrary, they are found guilty. They become instant martyrs. We have no options, Mudaliyar."

"But you know that they cannot be tried because their loyalty to His Majesty Edward VII has never been in question. They say nothing more than the Honourable Members of the Opposition in the House of Commons say on our plight."

"I know. I know. But things are different when our loyal public servants curry favour with them and sit alongside them in a public meeting."

'Sir," I said sternly. "You can ask for my explanation and proceed with disciplinary action, if you so desire,"

531

That he was disappointed with whatever he had planned to do this morning was clear from a brief sigh which escaped his lips.

"You know our mistake. We educated you fellows and now you can talk back to us in our language with our logic."

"Yes and no, sir. We had to agitate for our education and pay dearly for it. Of course, great men of vision like Reverend Kenneth were there on our side."

"That's the problem. Soldiers, not scholars and saints, should run the empire."

"I see your point, Sir. So the natives could be overrun and subdued like the Zulus, the Bantus and the Hotentots," I said softly to disguise the mounting anger within me.

The watchdog over imperial interests was impatient. It was clear that he did not like the turn in the conversation. I had touched a raw nerve in John Smith who until his commanding officer died in action was a Platoon Sergeant of the British Army in Cape Town.

"Mudaliyar, we'll be both late for the Supreme Court."

He stood up abruptly and offered his hand which I took in mine out of sheer politeness and shook weakly.

"Well done, Sir," said the peon with the red sash in Sinhala. By the end of the day the encounter with the Government Agent would be the talk of the town. It could even figure as a news story in the popular newspaper of Homeless Dharmapala , "*The Sinhala-Buddhist*," of which the editor was the up and coming novelist, Piyadasa Sirisena.

The customary tea in the chambers followed the ceremonial opening of the Assize of the Supreme Court. John Smith introduced the guests to the Acting Justice Eugene Jayewardene . In the pecking order I was about the last in the line.

"Our illustrious scholar Mudaliyar is an old friend. We have had very good times together in Jaffna. Haven't we, T. B.?" said the judge before the Government Agent could tell him who I was. "How far have you gone with your theory that Sinhala was an Indo-European Aryan language, profoundly influenced by the phonology, morphology and grammar of Dravidian languages?"

"I had two papers published, Your Honour," I replied. "One in London and the other in Berlin. In fact, Sir, I have been invited to speak on it to the Royal Asiatic Society in London in August and the

Oriental Congress in Berlin in September. I hope Colombo approves my leave."

"They have, T. B. As an exceptional case and on grounds of sympathy. That's how I know that you will not go to Jaffna this year with me."

Discomfiture, written largely so far on John Smith's face, turned into an ugly frown. It became more and more vicious and noticeable as the Judge proceeded to discuss the main findings of my research with regard to the Dravidian influence on Sinhala language, as observed by the loss of the aspirate, alternation of sa and ha sounds, formation of the plural, non-declension of the adjective with the noun qualified and so forth. The Judge was deeply interested in the details.

"How the hell do you get exceptional leave on sympathetic grounds?" Smith asked when we were alone.

"My wife needs another eye operation. Hers is a very bad case of optical muscular debility. Her peripheral vision is all right. But she can hardly read or write or sew. She had held on with the operation done in London nearly twenty years ago."

"You were in England twenty years ago!" He exclaimed. "A lucky bloke, you really are!"

In the guise of someone deeply concerned with Slim-Jewel's eye condition, the Government Agent ferreted out information on how my trip was being financed and what kind of connections I had in Germany. It was time to exaggerate. In my experience, that was the most satisfying way to handle the green-eyed monster.

"My travel is jointly paid by the organizations I address in Europe. But my wife's passage and all our expenses come from our three children. We are having a family reunion and a grand tour of the Continent. Some sort of belated fiftieth birthday celebration for me."

"What the heck! You have three children abroad and they are giving you a holiday! What are they any way?"

Undaunted by his condescending tone, I told him all.

Timothy had just completed advanced training in surgery and had been awarded with honours a Fellowship of the Royal College of Surgeons. He had taken Moon-Beam to Paris to savour the land of his ancestors and of Loius Pasteur, the indefatigable campaigner for preventive medicine. They spent a week studying the latest techniques of immunology and infection-prevention at the Pasteur Institute in Rue de Docteur Roux, Paris XVeme. On return to London, she had gone to

533

see Sir Joseph Lister, the First Baron, who had given her a temporary posting in his outfit. Her experience with hygienic problems of the Tropics had brought her close to Sir Joseph.

Middle Banda and Rose were on furlough in London with their children and he had extended his leave to brush up his knowledge of British and South African Case Law.

Victory-Servant , now an Associate Professor of History in an American College and married to the daughter of its President, had decided to start his first sabbatical leave with the family reunion in Europe.

"What's more," I said with bloated glee. "They have already placed an order for my birthday gift - a first edition 1908 Model T Ford car with right hand drive."

Possibly John Smith had had enough of bad news for one day. He left a half-drunk cup of tea on the table, wished a brief good-bye to the Judge and walked briskly out of the chamber.

The Judge invited me to join him for lunch at his official residence.

"You should be a bit more discreet, T. B." the Judge admonished. "You are dealing with a class of new Civil Servants who have reason to be jealous of the natives like us. We are visibly better placed and more successful than they could ever imagine or hope to be. They hate to see us doing well and are frightened that they will soon be replaced. Don't throw live embers on dry grass."

I thanked Justice Jayewardene profusely and wished that I would never have to regret my boastful encounter with the Government Agent.

XIII

London in July was sheer delight. The presence of all the Valour-Lions in one place enhanced it.

Slim-Jewel's operation was remarkably successful. In recognition of his acclaimed eminence, Timothy was invited to join the surgeon and his team in the Operating Theatre. In two weeks she was out of the hospital with a perfect bill of health. Within the same two weeks, with Beckie and Rose as my mercilessly severe and uncompromising instructors, I obtained my licence to drive a motor vehicle.

We set out on a relaxed tour of the Lake District or the Wordsworth country, as Middle Banda preferred to call it. Refreshed by a week's rest by Lake Windermere, where we commandeered the whole of a modest hotel, we visited the hills and dales and massive lakes of Scotland. Castles had to be done sparingly as they were not exactly the kids' favourite.

It was a lot of fun. The extended family of eight adults and four children from four corners of the world had bonded itself into a harmonious unity. Grand-children were an inestimable joy. So were our British and American daughters-in-law. Moon-Beam arrogated to herself the role of the bell-ringer, as she called herself. All acknowledged her mature leadership. With Timothy as a careful planner, nothing was overlooked - even the tiniest details as regards the diaper change for the baby were meticulously planned.

"Our surgeon in action," we hailed him when with a pencil jabbing a piece of paper he would explain the day's schedule. We made "surgeon" sound "seargent"!

With experience gained in Scotland we boarded a boat to Oostend to begin our month long tour of Western Europe. We had ready-made guides in the family.

Victory-Servant , for easier integration into the environment of a conservative Christian College, had modified his first and last names to an Anglicized form as Vickie Wickie. His petite wife Elizabeth preferred to be called Beckie. Vickie and Beckie were as jovial a couple as their names sounded. Vickie knew history and Beckie's interest was geography. Timothy's speciality was European nobility and heraldry. We were a learning community.

"Back to our university on wheels," became Timothy's standard announcement whenever we began a stretch of travel by train.

535

The kids found a doting grand-mother in Slim-Jewel. She narrated folk tales and Buddhist stories. That she was systematically introducing them to the cultural heritage of their Motherland was patent when the elder kids would approach me to ask questions on history and literature.

Rose and Beckie, too, were ardent students. They never failed to flatter me by hanging on every word I spoke. Middle Banda and Rose had a wealth of information to share on the life and culture of the Burmese. Through the eyes of Vickie and Beckie, we saw America as the haven of private enterprise and cornerstone of democracy.

When the month was over, what dominated our memories were not so much the exciting places we saw and the stimulating persons we met but the close intimacy which made the Valour-Lions a loving, harmonious family. No family could be more heterogeneous than we were. That came out most vividly in a festive dinner which the children organized for us in Southampton on the eve of our departure.

It was a raucous party even though none consumed any liqour. We were all teetotallers by conviction. It was the genuine joy of a family which enjoyed the mutual company of its members. As coffee was being served, Vickie in mock seriousness called the meeting to order.

"Valour-Lions have important business to conclude," he said. "I call upon our spokeswoman to present it."

Moon-Beam rose with a rolled parchment in hand. It was tied in a rainbow-coloured ribbon. The large double bow looked a veritable flower. Timothy, every inch an aristocrat, rushed to her side, took the parchment, removed the ribbon delicately and held up the parchment to his wife to read. She began in an imperious voice befitting a royal declaration:

We the three Valour-Lions, respectively by *birth*, *acceptance* and *adoption*, with our spouses and progeny, do hereby declare solemnly with unbounded love, gratitude and admiration that henceforth Mudaliyar Tiny Banda Valour-Lion shall be referred to by us as FATHER and not LITTLE FATHER and shall be entitled to all Rights, Honours and Privileges that go with the new designation.

May it be known that the said illustrious Valour-Lion earned this honour with devotion, kindness, generosity and affection beyond the call of duty.

Signed in recognition thereof,

536

Moon-Beam Valour-Lion de Lanerolle
Timothy de Lanerolle
Middle Banda Valour-Lion
Fay Rose Shefield Valour-Lion
Vickie Wickie (aka Victory-Servant Valor-Lion)
Beckie Wickie (aka Valour-Lion)

Moon-Beam handed the parchment to Middle Banda who choked slightly as he began to speak.

"Father, we owe you an apology. We do not know whether we had thanked you for what you have done for each one of us. If we did we may have only said 'Thank you' perfunctorily. But we want you to know one thing. We have thanked you in every moment of our lives. We accepted you not merely as a father figure at an age we needed one badly but as a role model in every way. Our love for our Motherland and our culture we learned from you. It is in respect of your ideals that we pursued our studies with diligence and worked toward goals that you would approve. It is out of respect for you we remain teetotallers and uphold temperance. Every day in our lives we ask ourselves how best we could serve the fellow human beings so that our Father and, of course, Mother would be proud of us. Father, we want you to know, even so late, that we say, 'Thank you, Father," with our action and that is at every moment of our lives. We pay you the highest compliment of emulation."

Tears streamed down my face. Slim-Jewel was crying with joy. Middle Banda gave the parchment to Victory-Servant or Vickie who endorsed every word of the previous speaker.

"Father, I called you Father ever since you adopted me as your son. You are the only father I have known in all my life. I regret that my unfortunate brother could not benefit from what you offered both us as a boon of the highest value - a new start in a decent life. I think often of what my life would have been if my birth mother was less wise and more selfish. I also think of my fate if I was made to remain a mere retainer in your home. But you both elevated me to the status of a son and gave me opportunities to prove myself. I may have disappointed you lately. But your magnanimity humbles both me and Beckie. Have faith, Father. We too uphold your ideals so you will be proud of us. "

He approached me and Slim-Jewel as if to hand us the parchment. Instead he kissed us on both cheeks and handed the parchment to Timothy.

537

Timothy spoke with his mind rather than his heart. He was not altogether devoid of deep sentiments of affection and gratitude. But he chose to recount my life of scholarly and professional achievements. It was informative and I was pleased. This young man really knew what I had done and where I had made a mark. He was truly the scribe of the family, as Vickie the historian was soon to remark. I knew who in the family could write my biography if I ever deserved one.

The parchment was like a baton in a relay race. It went to Rose who said nice things of her husband and thanked us for the thoughtful, considerate and self-sufficient man we had made of Middle Banda. When her chance came, Beckie brandished the parchment in high spirits and spoke of Vickie the clown who kept everyone happy and laughing.

"Thank you, Father and Mother, for giving the world this wonderful man, Vickie. Thank you, Father, for taking him to Jaffna where you made him your son."

The parchment returned to Moon-Beam who slipped back the ribbon with the lovely bow and gave it to her daughter. She snuggled behind me, slipped her arms over my shoulders and held out the parchment.

"Open it, Grandpa," she insisted. "I'll show what we had done."

Thoughtfully adorning the space around the signatures were tiny pictures of a cow, a car and a train and a tiny little thumbprint in red.

"These, Grandpa, are from the tiny weeny Valour-Lions."

"The three of you could have signed your names, couldn't you?"

" We thought about it, Grandpa. As the baby cannot sign his name, we thought we all must do the same. Don't you like our pictures?"

What love and thought had gone to the planning of this event. Now that the baton was in my hand, I rose to speak. Tears welled in my eyes. I choked. With a string of "Thank you! Thank you! Thank you!" smothered by sobs, I sat down speechless. Slim-Jewel touched my face. Before I knew what was happening, I was on the shoulders of the three men who lifted me aloft as they danced shouting in unison with the rest in the room "For he's a jolly good fellow."

"We really have done something right,"I told Slim-Jewel when we were alone in our bed-room.

"No, my dear husband, it's not me. It's you who did everything right."

538

On the way back by ship where we spent most of the time together by ourselves, Slim-Jewel and I spoke incessantly of our lovely family. The eve of our departure left with us the loveliest of memories.

The night before the ship arrived in Colombo, I told Slim-Jewel,

"Thank you, Jewel, my beloved wife. Thanks to you alone do I have this sense of utmost fulfillment. Think of it. I am a Father by acclamation! By choice! And.. and.. and... not by accident!"

She took my face in the palms of her hands and laughed at the stammered closure of my peroration.

On our return to Colombo, we had to stay a few days in the city until the car was released by the Customs and arrangements could be made for it to be transported by train to Kandy. The last thing I wanted to do was to drive to Kandy and make a triumphal entry.

It was a blessing in disguise. It gave us a chance to be with Uncle Victor and Aunt Flower. An added pleasure was to see Lucy, the mother of two of the children who with their wives declared that they would call me Father. She was an asset to my relatives. A full-fledged member of the family, she took care of the household. Slim-Jewel and I told her of our holiday with the three children and their families and the surprise party on the eve of our departure from England. Lucy hung on our lips and sighed. No doubt, she was thinking of the son who had the same chance but did not make it. She could have also thought how much she was herself deprived of the joy which was legitimately hers.

"May you both be blessed with Buddhahood," she said. "I can close my eyes in peace. My children have been liberated from the horrible destiny which was theirs by birth."

We also made the best use of the time by visiting old friends. The most inspiring among them was Venerable Sumangala. At eighty-two years of age, his unfailing memory and alert mind baffled us.

"I heard that you were in London and I wanted to ask something from you, Sangha-Gem-Field," he said, calling me as he always did when I was a monk. "The Royal Asiatic Society of Britain has conferred on me a Fellowship and Professor Rhys Davids is asking me to accept it. I should accept it, don't you think?"

"You know personally half its membership, Venerable Sir. And half of them are your students, I am sure."

539

"That's it, Sangha-Gem-Field. That's my dilemma. My friends and students cannot be impartial judges of my suitability to receive this honour."

Physically weak and easily tired, he nevertheless kept up the argument until I gave all the possible reasons why he should accept the recognition.

"You may be right, Sangha-Gem-Field. Before you go, please draft me a letter."

I wrote it, had it signed by the scholar-monk and mailed it myself.

Homeless Dharmapala was not in Colombo. His litigations with the Hindu contestants for the temple at Buddha Gaya were not proceeding the way he wished. While the battle was on, he lost several skirmishes. These would have discouraged any ordinary person. But Homeless was no ordinary person. I thought of visiting the editor of the *"Sinhala-Buddhist."*

Stocky and round-faced, Piyadasa Sirisena looked more a successful business man - a neo-nationalist entrepreneur - in tweed cloth and coat with starched shirt and tie and Oxford shoes than a frontline fighter in any ultranationalist movement advocating simplicity and the elimination of conspicuous consumption. Nevertheless, he impressed me as a man without frills.

"Come in, Mudaliyar. Take a seat. It's nice to see you again," was his spontaneous reception.

Within minutes we were talking on the extraordinary man we both admired.

"This indeed is a fine job," said Piyadasa Sirisena, "Yes, if only you can keep pace with the whirlwind. He is here today and there tomorrow. From wherever he is he writes his weekly column 'What one should know.'"

"Isn't that a fantastic column?" I asked him, as I had read it avidly and had not missed a single contribution. "I look forward to reading what I missed recently."

"He writes on every imaginable subject. His ultimate aim is to educate the people. He loves to be on the brink of sedition and I know the Administration is having every word translated and checked. They want to take him to courts but they worry about the outcome. To Homeless that is a fine position to be in. A typical cat and mouse game!"

Piyadasa Sirisena was full of admiration for the human dynamo that kept a whole nation ticking. If he had any complaint, it was that Homeless Dharmapala was too involved in the international mission of the Maha Bodhi Society.

"He should be here, leading the people to Self-rule. He can achieve in ten years what in his mind he had scheduled for half a century."

"What do you mean?" I asked him.

He explained to me the political target of Homeless. I realized that the people had begun to refer to him simply as Honourable Homeless. It was a fifty-year plan for Sri Lanka to reach the level of Self-rule that New Zealand was already enjoying. He argued that this time was needed to educate the people to govern themselves and to develop a sound economy with national investment and involvement. Hence the emphasis placed on vocational education alongside a good general education combining science, technology, history and culture of the West with national history and literature.

What he urged the government and the people through his writings and speeches was to develop the national human resources, preserve the environment and remove obstacles to the flowering of the national culture.

"What are you doing with your own talents, Mr. Piyadasa Sirisena?"

"All I do in my humble way is to let my readers understand the message of Homeless. I write my editorials in the *Sinhala-Buddhist*. I love to write Sinhala verse and I want to use the romantic novel as a medium for social reform."

"That's a lot," I told him. "I am one of your fans."

It prompted him to pull out of the drawer of his messy paper-ridden table a sheet of paper. He read or rather recited in a melodious voice:

Right through history in our lovely Isle,
Sri Lanka, the home of the Lion-Race,
Our fathers reached the sunny summit
Of glorious feats of science and spirit.

For centuries had they known and mastered
The art of building massive mounds of bricks
Which only the Great Pyramid of the Pharaohs surpassed.
They tamed the torrential monsoon floods
With mighty dams across rivers
Until every drop of rain which fell

Served man before it flowed to the ocean.
Their ten-storeyed mansions for the comfort of monks
And seven-floor palaces for kings and princes
Bespoke of luxury with art endowed
Right down to the privy seats,
Carved of granite with beauteous motifs.

Heights of fame did they also reach
In pursuits of the mind:
Philosophy, Religion, Poetry and the like.
Heirs to the Buddha's timeless teachings
Monks and nuns by piety induced
Preserved in texts and elucidated with comment
His Words of Wisdom, Love and Liberation.
Braving the storms of endless seas,
They spread outward to lands unknown
From Burma and Siam and further to Java
Beyond thenceforth to the ports of China,
Not as the merchants of worldly goods
As the lay men did with courageous enterprise,
But as Knowers of Peace
And Teachers of the Path of Peace
Of the Lion-Race destined for ever
To guard and declare the Buddha's Way.

Thus, my friends, were your ancestors engaged
In piety and beauty and noble deeds.
Where were then the men who rule us now -
These imperial rulers with ways imperious
Parvenus to life's nobler callings?

Vandals they were on destruction bent
Against whose fury the civilized prayed
To God or gods to tame their wild ways.
Did their prayers work?
Steadily the Norsemen rode non-chalant
Shrouding in gloom, as they trod,
Whatever was left from time immemorial
Of the Glory of Greece and the Splendour of Rome,
Sweeping to corners the gentle Celts
With their flowering culture and the knowledge of stars
Of the lording Druids reshaping into Culdees.
These vandals by many a name known

Plunged before them a smiling continent
Into a Dark Age of Ignorance.

Out of this chaos through war and violence
Arose petty nations to carry their mission
 To a world where people with serene ways
 Led lives of relative calm and dignity.
With might as right they call themselves
The bearers of the "Whiteman's Burden"
Of civilizing the civilized!

I tell you, my friends, in truth sincere
We are no slaves under the whip of a master.
A nation with a history so illustrious
Has need to raise its head in pride.
So should we show the world without fear
Our burning urge to be free as the wind.

   Show it with the names you choose
   With the dress you wear
   The language you speak
   The religion you profess
   The values you uphold
   The customs you cherish.

And, above all, through unity and comradeship
With all alike who share with you
This charming Island:
Our paradise on earth.

"Bravo! Excellent!" exclaimed Slim-Jewel. "What a wonderful idea to get our people to be proud of their country!"

"That's exactly my idea, dear lady," said Piyadasa Sirisena. "But I do not know whether I am overdoing it."

I thought I should be frank with this man of talent who spelled through novels and poems the message of Homeless Dharmapala .

"You certainly are overdoing it if by that you mean that you have resorted to inexcusable exaggeration. Nothing is black or white. But that's how you have chosen to compare the British against the nationals."

"I know, Mudaliyar. I know it," he said in a tone of reconciliation. "But we are at war. Don't they say something like anything is fair in love and war?"

543

"Can I ask you two questions?"

"Yes, Mudaliyar."

"Why do you address this message solely to the Sinhalas or the Lion-Race as you prefer to call them?"

"I am the editor of the *Sinhala-Buddhist*. That's our audience. As Homeless would say, the Sinhala Buddhist is our patient. It is to cure him that we prescribe our medicine. We do expect leaders of other communities to address their clienteles similarly."

"You mean people like Six-face Navalar and Siddi Lebbe who reach out to Hindus and Muslims."

"Precisely. You know that we support them"

"That's fair enough. Now my second question. You are berating Western culture as if it has nothing to give us. And that's not true. Aren't you creating unnecessary prejudices which would be detrimental to our own well-being?"

"Yes we do, Mudaliyar. I personally hope that better sense will prevail when we regain independence. Now we use every available weapon. But when we are on our own, we will have to undo much of the damage. That's a task for men like your sons. I read last Sunday an article in the Observer signed as usual M.B.W."

"Can't you make their task easier by being less contentious and more moderate?"

"I'll try, Mudaliyar."

We left chummier friends than we had been. Slim-Jewel could not conceal her unreserved adulation.

The man we most wanted to meet was the hardest to contact. Don Baron was a veritable whirlwind. Leadbeater's School, now renamed after the closest disciple of the Buddha, namely Ananda, was indeed his first love. The school was prospering under his leadership and guidance. Its reputation matched the older and better financed missionary schools. A loyal and proud clientele supported Don Baron. He had made the school a fountain of talent moulded by his precept and example to serve the people.

"One thing I must say about Don Baron Jayatilaka 's brand of Buddhist education is that its product has a greater awareness and deeper consciousness of national issues and are ready to contribute their mite in solving them," was the evaluation of my erstwhile mentor Ernest Dickinson. He had retired from service and chosen to live in a suburb of Colombo. "If there is any Ceylonese who could one day take over the political leadership of this country, my bet is on Don Baron."

544

The reason for Don Baron's unavailability was that he was active in so many different fields. Not only was he the Principal of the most successful school to be founded by Colonel Olcott, but he was virtually in control of the Buddhist Theosophical Society which managed the entire system of Buddhist education. He had been the General Manager of its schools ever since he returned to Colombo from Kandy.

At his time, he was being urged by influential members to become the Secretary of the Society. It was a tottering organization which needed new blood and additional resources. Don Baron, the born reformer and resuscitator, faced his new tasks with vigour and single-minded determination. That, of course, was not going to make him very popular with those elements which had other reasons to be associated with this most important Buddhist organization. Already, Don Baron was caught in the midst of a tumultuous power struggle.

What drew most animosity was the success he achieved in getting the Society's newspaper, *Moon-ray of the Muse)Sarasavi-sandaresa)*, back into a paying proposition. It regained its position of influence among Sinhala readers. The quarrel which had a profound impact on him arose from the decision which he as its editor took in changing how the issues were dated. Hitherto, only the Buddhist Era was used. Don Baron was a practical man and he was conscious that the country had adopted the Christian calendar to all intents and purposes. He began using both calenders to date the issues of the newspaper. What a rumpus it created at the annual general meeting! He had ultimately to bow to the majority of the members and revert to the exclusive use of the Buddhist Era. He was hurt and dispirited.

As if all problems should come to him all at once, he was drawn into a legal battle in which his much-admired friend, Homeless Dharmapala was indirectly an adversary. The pioneering industrial school that Homeless had founded in a suburb of Colombo had been under Don Baron's management. Now Homeless' organization, the Maha Bodhi Society, was entering the field of education in the Island and his family wanted the industrial school to be under its management.

All this would have made an ordinary man run away from the public scene. But Don Baron was not an ordinary man. His numerous interests sustained him. He was active in the Royal Asiatic Society and the Oriental Studies Society which gave him ample opportunities to pursue his literary and historical research. Equally active was he in the Colombo District Schools Committee to which he was appointed by the government.

545

It was the eve of our departure to Kandy. Slim-Jewel and I were both disappointed that we would leave without seeing him. But that was not to be. We were about to retire for the night when a toot of a car horn took Uncle Victor to the verandah.

"I am sorry, Mr. Perera," boomed the familiar voice of Don Baron. "I have to say good-bye to our Mudaliyar and his charming wife."

He was returning from a meeting of the Board of the Royal Asiatic Society. What a thoughtful gesture!

We would never have guessed that he was under so much pressure. He was bouyantly cheerful. There was no rancour or malice in anything he said. He laughed at the concerns we expressed.

"All this is a part of the game, Jewel. We thrive on it," he told Slim-Jewel who asked about the criticisms levelled against him in some quarters.

We shared information on our common friends. He spoke of his plans for the immediate future. It was clear that he was beginning to think that he needed wider experience and a learning retreat away from the Island was the answer. I encouraged him referring to my own experience in Calcutta and my study tour in England.

As I walked with him to his car, he put his arm around me.

"Be ready for some surprises when you return to work," he warned me. "The mood of the colonial officialdom is rapidly turning hostile. It doesn't take kindly to the constitutional reforms which are imminent simply because they would set the trend for an elected leadership from the people. People like us are the most vulnerable to victimization - more you than me. Yet, I would rather let the dust settle down and return to the melee with enhanced credentials."

"You mean, you will enter politics?" I asked him.

"Eventually, Mudaliyar. I am sure you too may have to do so."

XIV

The car arrived in the same train we took to Kandy. It was delivered within an hour. A porter was loading the baggage under the direction of Slim-Jewel while I was examining the car before signing the papers. The new car with foreign plates was as conspicuous as a Kandyan chieftain in his traditional garb.

"What a beauty!" commented a Scottish planter whom I had met several times in the courts. "It's not British, is it?"

"It's American," I said casually so as not to convey even the slightest hint of being boastful.

"Lucky bloke! Look at me. A double dyed white master. Waiting for a rickshaw to take me to the hotel."

His guffaw was meant to dull the sardonic barb of sarcasm.

"We are in for a lot of trouble," said Slim-Jewel in Sinhala.

"Weren't we warned?" I told her. "To be pre-warned is to be pre-armed."

"Home sweet home," we said together as we entered home and were received by Golden Jewel who seemed to have gained a few more pounds in our absence. She was happy to see us. But the two men servants paid more attention to the car than to us.

"Better leave this at home and walk to office as you always did, sir." was the gardener's advice.

"Why?"

"Evil eye, sir."

After a restful week-end, I walked to the office not so much in deference to the gardener's advice. I really needed the exercise. It did not take too long for me realize that there was something wrong. It was in the way the colleagues received me. We had been a friendly crowd sharing our joys and sorrows. We never missed a chance to be cheerful. The air of foreboding was thick as the morning mist over the Kandy Lake. The way in which the chief clerk followed me to my office was ominous. I had to ask him what was wrong.

"You have orders, Mudaliyar," he said calmly.

Three ugly brown covers of unpolished paper with OHMS (On His Majesty's Service) in red contained the orders. Though they were sealed and addressed to me personally, the office knew their contents ahead of me. The office copies had already reached the chief clerk.

The first was from the the Director of the Combined Services of the General Treasury in Colombo. It simply stated that, with effect from my return from overseas leave, I was transferred on promotion to the Provincial Office to be the Mudaliyar of the Native Branch. The hand of John Smith was clear in this move. He wanted to have me directly under his supervision. As long as I was not asked to uproot myself from Kandy, I had no reason to protest. As regards working for the Government Agent, I felt no threat either.

The second was from John Smith himself. He regretted that the quarters I used belonged to the Courts and as such I would have to vacate them within two months. I had to find a house myself because the Provincial Office did not have any quarters suitable for me. That too would cause no problem. A monthly house rent allowance would be added to my salary. A place closer to office and accessible to medical facilities would be certainly more desirable.

"We aren't getting any younger," I told the chief clerk.

The last of the envelopes and in fact the bulkiest was meant to be the last straw that would break the camel's back. I read the letter and the enclosures twice before I understood what John Smith's real problem was.

Dear Mudaliyar Valour-Lion,

Congratulations on your promotion to the post of Mudaliyar of the Native Department of the Provincial Office. I look forward to working with you for the advancement of the Province. Your deep knowledge of the history, literature and culture of the Island and close contacts with major public figures, institutions and organizations would prove to be an advantage in the solution of complex and sensitive issues assigned to this Department.

As I am anxious to maintain the best possible working relations between us, I wish to make myself very clear on the question of your public social activities which might conflict with your duties in the new post. It may not have been brought to your attention that your long tenure as the President of the Temperance Movement in the Province has been in contravention of long-standing official instructions, a copy of which I annex for your easy reference. Apparently, your superiors hitherto had not drawn your attention to this contravention because your duties have been purely of a routine nature as an interpreter in the courts. It will be in your interest to have yourself released of this position with immediate effect.

As regards your literary and religious activities and your spouse's leadership in the Women's Organization, I reserve the right to review the extent to which they are in conflict with your new duties and revert to them in due course.

548

Please feel free to discuss with me any matter in which you may need further clarification.

Yours sincerely,

John Smith
Government Agent,
Central Province.

Enclosed with the letter were copies of circulars and minutes on the touchy questions of the civil liberties of Government Servants.

The chief clerk, a gentle god-fearing Hindu in his early fifties, was a man for whom I had enormous respect. We had been friends from the day we first met at the Good-Village Temple in one of my early visits to the Jaffna Peninsula. He read my emotions in my face.

"Mudaliyar, it's a promotion. You are within your rights to decline it," he told me in Tamil. Officers from the North had a special bondage with me as I could speak their language.

"What will you do if you were in my situation?"

"Mudaliyar, don't call me an opportunist. I would accept the promotion, move from the quarters, resign from the Temperance Movement and get into the Native Department. You'll be more useful to the causes you espouse than you could be anywhere else."

"You really think so?"

"Ask your leaders, Mudaliyar. I am sure they will agree with me."

Slim-Jewel was surprised to see me at home for lunch. I showed her the letters and told her of the chief clerk's view.

"I seem to agree with him. But you have a whole heap of options," she said. She was as lucid as she was persuasive: decline the promotion; or accept it and bamboozle John Smith until it is time for retirement; or apply for early retirement and join the embryonic caucus of active politicians.

"Whatever you choose, you'll not be a loser. I will be with you. And so will the children and their spouses."

I returned to office, applied for leave for three days and took the late night train to Colombo.

I started with Ernest Dickinson who felt that the chief clerk had a point. Don Baron held the identical view. Venerable Sumangala was ill and I had no intention to bother him with the question. Uncle Victor who had worked in the Native Department encouraged me.

"If you have any political ambitions, that's where you can cut your teeth," he stressed.

The man whose advice I was most anxious to obtain, namely Homeless Dharmapala , was not available. The only one to urge me to retire and join their campaign immediately was Piyadasa Sirisena, the editor of the *Sinhala-Buddhist*.

I also spent a day at the office of the Colonial Secretary, chatting with colleagues and amassing relevant information on current affairs.

On the third day I returned to Kandy not only confident but adequately prepared for a head on clash with the Government Agent, if that was what he wanted.

I think I surprised or even disappointed John Smith. He expected a fight, a veritable row. Here I was conceding like a lamb. He could not believe that I had agreed to all the conditions he had laid down. To my acknowledgement of the orders, I annexed a translation of the letter of resignation from the Temperance Movement:

Respectfully written to the Honorary Secretary of the Temperance Movement of the Central Province,

Honoured Sir,
    The enclosed correspondence from the Government Agent of the Central Province makes it clear that I have to resign from both the membership and the presidency of the Temperance Movement. Accordingly I do resign hereby from both with effect from today.
    May the Movement continue its invaluable service to society.

Yours Honestly,

T. B. Valour-Lion

John Smith, seated at the same desk where I had met many an exalted and friendlier predecessor, read my letter and frowned:

"My correspondence was not meant for public diffusion," he said angrily.

"They were not marked confidential. Or even if they were, I had to give a reason for my sudden resignation."

550

He bit his lip and crossed his arms on the chest.

"I demand an explanation in writing."

With this brief encounter began what I dreaded to be a long, tedious, tendentious and futile phase in my career. But my fears were unfounded. All I went through was an uneasy week-end. Poor Slim-Jewel had to listen to my grievances, apprehensions and regrets. My repeated efforts in drafting a satisfactory explanation as demanded by John Smith resulted in only a heap of paper balls in the waste basket and shattered nerves!

I went early to office on Monday to consult a couple of friends. The whole office was agog.

"Sir, do you know what has happened to the Government Agent?" asked the first I met at the door.

He did not have to reply it as a friendly voice boomed from behind me.

"Hello, T. B. I have news for you."

It was Stanley Williams with whom I had had years of exciting cooperation in unravelling the legal foundations of Kandyan customs. He led me to the room he once occupied as the Assistant Government Agent.

"I came last Friday minutes after you had met Smith. I had to bring orders from the Colonial Secretary."

Believe it or not, I never thought that as pompous and self-confident a man like John Smith would ever stake his career for ten rupees and fifty cents, equivalent at the time to one British Guinea or a little over three US dollars! An astute young officer in the audit service had discovered that the Government Agent had travelled on three consecutive days to the same village and one of them was the public holiday to mark the birth, enlightenment and death of the Buddha.

"Could the Government Agent really hold an inquiry into illicit felling of trees in a crown forest on the Vesak day?" the audit clerk had asked himself.

His meticulous investigation revealed that John Smith had really been in the village, spent three days as a guest of a superintendent of a tea plantation, done all the work he claimed he had done exactly as was suspected - in one day. The rest had been spent partly in hunting wild boar and partly in exploring some settlements of the aboriginal tribe, the Veddahs.

551

John Smith had done his best to blame an inexperienced accounts clerk. But the final outcome of the long-drawn inquiry which had taken place while I was in Europe was too harsh a punishment: immediate dismissal and repatriation to South Africa from where he was recruited.

"Isn't it too harsh a punishment for defrauding a paltry sum of ten rupees and fifty cents?" I asked Stanley Williams.

"That's only the tip of the ice-berg."

I did not press for more information. I was not interested. I could guess that John Smith, who advocated that the empire should be run by the military, was not a hot favourite of the gentlemen of the Civil Service. I was delighted that my new boss was not only a friend but a man of integrity - a sincere admirer of the culture of the people he was sent to rule.

Whatever the grievances with John Smith, one thing was true. My work in the Native Department would have been extremely difficult if I continued to be the President of the Temperance Movement. Stanley Williams insisted that there could be no objection to Slim-Jewel continuing her useful work in the Women's Organization. We were not required to change houses. I was allowed to continue my affiliation with literary and religious activities. In fact, he became the patron of and an occasional speaker and visitor at the Pavilion of the Muse.

We resumed our long-suspended, comparative study of the Kandyan "Compendium of Laws" of which we were co-editors and its Tamil equivalent, "The Customs of the Land." Once again, life was on an even keel. If, at all, I was busier than ever and so was Slim-Jewel.

Timothy and Moon-beam came on transfer to the Kandy General Hospital. It was Moon-beam's idea that we should enjoy the grandchildren. She was a great asset to Slim-Jewel. Each needed the other. Their joint campaign to eradicate smallpox, cholera, tetanus and typhoid fever through vaccination and periodic inoculation stretched the resources of the Women's Organization to the maximum. I began to teach Sinhala and Buddhism to the kids. It brought memories of the days when Autumn-Moon, Middle Banda and Moon-beam were my eager students.

Timothy the surgeon had his own literary interests. Our Sunday lunch, alternately at theirs and ours, was a resumption of the University on Wheels of our European tour. Middle Banda and Rose visited us with their children on their way to and from England. Middle Banda had already published three collections of his poems. Rose was struggling with the treatise she had been planning to write for several years.

"It's all in here, Father. I don't know how to get it out!" she would say pointing to her head.

"Let's do it together," I volunteered. Half a day we struggled and the result was a list of chapter headings.

Rose was on her third chapter when they returned from England. Vickie and Beckie wrote to us frequently. They were always bubbling with accounts of things they did together or said to each other. They looked forward to the next sabbatical which they hoped to spend in Sri Lanka.

Slim-Jewel and I went several times to Colombo. Uncle Victor passed away. Aunt Flower decided to remain in their house near Colombo. Lucy, the birth mother of Middle Banda and Victory-Servant alias Vickie, was her friend and companion.

The health of Venerable Sumangala was deteriorating rapidly. Don Baron was at the height of his popularity and, consequently, a subject of controversy in his immediate circles. He resigned from the Buddhist Theosophical society and set his mind on further studies in England.

Homeless Dharmapala was embroiled in a protracted legal battle with the Hindu custodian of the Buddha Gaya Temple in a case that the latter had filed in 1906. Determined to strengthen the foothold of the Maha Bodhi Society in India, Homeless bought a building in Calcutta for its headquarters. He needed support and Slim-Jewel spearheaded the campaign in Kandy. It was always a cheerfully optimistic philosopher in flowing yellow robe and shawl who received the donation with gratitude.

"Jewel, my unwavering supporter. We'll have the shrine restituted to the Buddhists very soon."

He was not so hopeful when we met him in July 1910. He had to contend with two forces who joined hands with the Hindu custodian. He had a severe blow in that the court case was settled in favour of the plaintiff.

"I can understand the attitude of the British. It is politic to side with the man of the place, specially when he represented the majority of the population," he said bitterly. "But why do the Japanese go against me? We are of the same religion. Yet for some obscure political reason, they formed a coalition with the Hindus."

"Did you say that their motive was political?" I asked.

553

"That's what I hear. The Japanese want to create some political centre at Buddha Gaya. Very strange! But that could be true!"

He had little more to say. That he was utterly hurt and disheartened by the expulsion of Sri Lankan Buddhists from Buddha Gaya was obvious.

"They even ordered us to remove the Buddha Statue," he lamented. "Mind you! From the spot where he attained enlightenment!"

"But you are not giving up, are you?" joined Slim-Jewel.

"Not as long as I have the support of people like you," he replied with a courteous bow to Slim-Jewel.

What a swift recovery! The gloom on his face disappeared. He was back again the undaunted fighter. He planned for greater things. Once again his thoughts were on the situation in the Island.

"Let the dust settle down in India. Meanwhile, I must resume the campaign for a national revival in the Island. The momentum of the Olcott days has to be restored. But who's there to lead? Whatever be our differences, I have faith in Don Baron. But he's leaving the Island tomorrow for higher studies in Oxford. Did you know?"

"Yes. We do. In fact, this time we came to see him off."

We met Homeless for a second time after the departure of Don Baron Jayatilaka. I had a message from the departing scholar-activist to the nationally acclaimed social legislator. To me it was a great relief that two men who were indispensable for the future of the Island respected each other.

For over an hour we discussed Homeless' plans for a national revival.

"Two things are before us," he told me and Slim-Jewel with a tone and histrionics meant for an audience of thousands, "Either to be slaves and allow ourselves to be effaced from national existence or make a constitutional struggle for the preservation of our nation from moral decay. We have a duty to perform to our Religion, to our children, and our children's children and not to allow this most holy land of ours to be exploited."

He was bristling with ideas. He berated the Government and the people for the increasing consumption of liquor and the lack of access to good education. He had a new concern: the influx of foreigners - the Indian Tamils as plantation labourers, Borahs and Marwadis as merchants, Afghans and Chettiars as money-lenders and so forth. With the insights gained in the Native Department, I could understand his apprehensions about the Government's open door policy. He gave high

554

priority to a campaign to convince the Government that Sri Lanka needed an Aliens Preventive Act as much as England.

We were about to leave when Homeless took my hands in his in a rare demonstration of affection.

"T. B., when are you due to retire?" he asked me.

XV

The dog barked and the gardener tapped on the bedroom window. Late in the night of the twenty-ninth of April 1911, I raised the wick of the kerosine oil lamp and opened the front door to receive a telegram. A telegram was always a foreboding of disaster. Slim-Jewel followed me to the door and took it from my shaking hand while I struggled to sign the acknowledgement. The gardener had the presence of mind to get the ten cent tip to the messenger.

The news of the death of the Most Venerable Sumangala, though sadly expected, came as a red-hot knife that ruthlessly pierced my heart. The excruciating pain was unbearable. Involuntarily, I knelt on the ground, crouched with my forehead on the floor and cried relentlessly. The grief was worse than when I lost the elder brother who was mercilessly stabbed and left to die in the river and than when my parents who followed him swiftly heart-broken by sorrow. It was first the Blakes, my childhood mentors, then Olcott, the hero of my youth, then Reverend Kenneth, my ever-present friend-in-need and now Venerable Sumangala, my spiritual father.

Why was I destined to suffer this grief? I asked myself out of self-pity.

Of little use at this moment were the years of inculcation of the sublime truth of the Buddha that everything was impermanent, suffering and misery ensued from impermanence and there was no self to claim anything for itself. Sorrow and self-pity overwhelmed me as they would any illiterate peasant.

Slim-Jewel rose to the occasion. She got in touch with the organizers of the funeral and made arrangements for us to be there in time. She had even accepted an invitation that I would speak at the ceremony on behalf of the alumni of the Learning-Awakening College.

Stanley Williams paid us a visit in our home to express his sympathies.

"I know what you feel, T. B.," he said. "If I remember what you have told me, Venerable Sumangala had been everything to you: a teacher, a father, a mentor. He even encouraged you to revert to lay life and serve the Government, didn't he?"

A monk's funeral usually tended to be a garish show of bad taste with devotees vying with one another to show how much they cared for the departed. Unseemly decorations and outlandish processions turned the event to a carnival. The crowd gathered mostly out of curiosity. The long drawn eulogies and sermons did not improve the situation either. I was happy when I found that an enlightened committee had concentrated on a dignified ceremony in keeping with the high ideals which Venerable Sumangala held in his life. Speeches were short and relevant. No eulogies were needed when the mere statement of what he had done and achieved was most poignant.

Homeless Dharmapala turned to me to congratulate me on my oration.

"When are you due to retire?" he asked me again.

"On the fourth of February 1913," I replied. "I will be fifty-five then and qualified for early retirement."

"Excellent. I launch my national revival movement next year. You will retire in time to join me."

I nodded my head in assent.

"It's a promise,T.B.," he said."Not to me but to the nation, I mean, the poor and the down-trodden."

On the very first day back in office, I met Stanley Williams and told him all about the discussions I have had with Homeless. I felt it my duty to keep him informed lest I compromise the trust the Government Agent had placed in me.

"I cannot and will not ask you to drop your friends whatever be the colour of their politics. I appreciate your keeping me informed. I know that you know what it is right to do."

That was a much needed vote of confidence in the following years when circumstances drew me impulsively to a deepening awareness of what I needed most to do in life: from a mercenary Government Servant, I wanted to be a genuine public servant. I was serving the wrong clientele. But the transition had to be decent and without damage to my personal sense of duty and responsibility.

If I needed my hunch to be fortified, it came most unexpectedly from the visit of Justice Jayewardene's brother.The recent constitutional reform had changed the composition of the Legislative Council. It was to consist of eleven officials besides the Governor and ten unofficials. Six unofficials were to be appointed by the Governor as before: two from Low-Country Sinhalas, one from Kandyan Sinhalas, two from Tamils and One from Muslims. The other four unofficials were to be elected on an ethnic basis: two by Europeans, one by Burghers or the

557

descendants of the Dutch and one by the Sri Lankans with a certain standard of education. The principle of election introduced for the first time had a significant impact on the political life of the Island.

Even though just one "Educated Ceylonese" was to be elected, the contest became lively and the resulting campaign tested the people's ability to rise above petty rivalries and prejudices. I was therefore not surprised that Eugene Jayewardene was actively campaigning for the Tamil Hindu candidate.

"The educated Ceylonese have one chance to show that we can rise above communal differences and choose the right man to represent us," he said and I admired the noble sentiments.

When the results of the election were publicized, I had reason to feel happy.

"We *are* ready for Self-rule," I told a friend.

"I wonder!" he interjected and proceeded to spell out the sordid aspects of the election. He thought that what pervaded were despicable caste prejudices which even the so-called educated Ceylonese were determined to perpetuate.

"Communal unity my foot! The caste, my friend - it's the caste that mattered. It cuts through race and language."

He could have been right. He supported the Sinhala candidate who lost. A nation riven by caste could be riven by anything - language, religion, class or even education. To me the need for a national revival was obvious. And that was to forge unity, wipe out bigotry and put the public good ahead of old bickerings.

I wrote on those lines to Homeless. His response which came nearly a month later made me really sad. He spoke of caste as though it was an incurable malady. The instances of discrimination he listed spanned the entire national life, including, most surprisingly the monastic system and even the newly founded Buddhist schools. Do we have any hope? I asked myself.

No one could be more aware of the dangers of caste discrimination. I had two wonderful sons who, if their birth caste was known, would have been condemned to life-long misery. They by their excellent service to humanity had reconfirmed the Buddha's assertion that nurture and not birth made one noble or otherwise.

The more I thought of the divisive factors in operation in the country, the more I was convinced that there were greater issues than liqour and drugs, denationalization and proselytization, conservation of national resources and Self-rule. I began to draw my own program for forging unity and eradication of discrimination.

Each day, I began with an hour of reflection on what to do and my notes were growing into a sizeable book. I shared my insights with Don Baron who was pursuing his studies for a degree in Law in Jesus College at Oxford University while at the same time as fulfilling requirements at the Lincoln's Inn for admission as a Barrister-at-law.

With wider social involvement, he saw eye to eye with me more than any other national leader with whom I tried to discuss the issue. One of his most thought-provoking statements struck me as most significant:

"To achieve all that you want, there is one sure-fire method: get the women to be active in politics. Get them into our councils of government. They are more sensitive to public issues than we men can ever be. I admire the women, called Suffragettes, who fight for the vote in elections."

I needed little proof. I had seen how Slim-Jewel and her Women's Organization attacked problems. There rarely took 'No" for an answer.

XVI

1912 dawned uneventfully. Even as the new constitution came into operation, the agitation for further reforms arose. As promised, Homeless started his national revival campaign.

It was to all intents and purposes a resumption of the same kinds of agitation which had intermittently carried on over the last two decades: national dress and names; return to righteousness with no liquor, drugs or meat; back to Buddhism, national history and literature, values and customs; Self-rule under the protection of the British Empire; and as the underlying remedy for all ills, more and better education.

The *Sinhala-Buddhist*, ably edited by Piyadasa Sirisena, spearheaded the campaign with informative articles on the national budget, decisions of the legislative council and actions of the Governor and bureaucracy. The hand of Homeless was all too evident when with strongly worded criticisms of the Administration he came by the skin of his teeth close to sedition and libel. The Attorney General engaged an army of translators to apprise him of the contents of these articles and occasionally I had a request to review some of them.

"You are in the news in London, T. B."

That was how Stanley Williams greeted me when I entered his office in the Old King's Palace. I knew there was something special for him to have sent for me.

"Must be my articles to the Journal of the Royal Asiatic Society,"

"No. But I will come to it later. I have an urgent request from the Attorney General."

He took out of the drawer a bulky package and placed it in front of me.

"T. B., the editor of an important Sinhala newspaper has written to the Governor every now and then cautioning the Administration that Homeless Dharmapala was fomenting a revolution. These have been rejected as accusations of a rival newspaper. But recently he had begun saying, 'I will not be surprised to hear one morning that Mr. Dharmapala is in the vicinity of Colombo with an army of Sinhala Buddhists.'"

It was not clear to me how I came into the picture. The Government Agent apparently read my quizzical gaze.

"The Governor has been advised by the Attorney General to take Homeless to court on a charge of sedition. Mudaliyar Simon de Silva,

560

your Nemesis, had translated his writings and made a case that the language and contents could sustain a charge of sedition. But the Governor wants to be extremely careful. We have created far too many martyrs in India and we do not want to repeat that mistake here."

"It's no doubt wise, Sir. But where do I come in?"

"The Governor wants you to review Simon de Silva's translations. As to why you are given this task there are several reasons. He thinks of you as some sort of Devil's Advocate. Your friendship with the nationalist agitators is common knowledge. The Governor thinks that you will do all you can to show that the original articles are not as bad as the translations sound. If you do so, he'll know what he has to contend with in the courts."

"Sir, I would never try to hide anything if it has to be exposed. I hope they have enough confidence in me."

"That, too, T. B. He pulled out a letter from the Private Secretary of the Governor. See it for yourself."

Once again, I thought of my British mentors, the Blakes and Reverend Saunders. How fair these British could be? In the same letter, which said that my association with the nationalist agitators was more than would ordinarily be tolerated in the case of a senior Government Servant, was the following statement:

"We are, nevertheless, mindful of his integrity and commitment to accuracy. On his reputation as an objective scholar, we can rely on Valour-Lion to give us the most accurate translation even if it damages his friends. If that becomes the case, our hands will be doubly strengthened in taking this rabble-rouser to courts."

Annexed to this letter was a press-cutting from a London newspaper. Williams urged me to read the news para. At a conference on Temperance in London, Don Baron had recounted my unceremonious removal from the Presidency of the Temperance Movement. What details he provided were not mentioned. But several members of the House of Commons who had heard about it had expressed their shock and disbelief about the Draconian measures adopted in the Colonies. One of them had gone to the extent of seeking an explanation from the Secretary of State for the Colonies.

"If at all it must have been a misunderstanding," the news para ended, quoting a senior adviser of the Secretary of State.

"T. B., There will be new instructions. Then you can resume your Temperance work," said the Government Agent.

561

A peon followed me to the office carrying the bulky package. That day I skipped lunch and worked late into the night. I read each page several times. I had covered almost half the articles when I decided to drive back home. Not a single error or overstatement had I discovered. My colleagues in Colombo whose work I was asked to review had been professionals proud of their performance. Next day, I worked likewise. My report was short and simple.

"As ordered, I had reviewed with meticulous care each article and the corresponding translation. The translations are accurate and objective. I might have at times preferred different words to bring out tone and significance of each statement. I am, however, unable to agree or disagree with the conclusion that the original articles are seditious, as such an appraisal is more a matter for lawyers than translators."

Perhaps my assessment did not satisfy some people. The Administration continued to exercise a close vigil. An year later, Reginald Fernando, the Editor of Lanka-Gem, was still writing to the Governor urging action against Homeless. He was being named as the Public Enemy No, 1. My own colleagues in Colombo were hoping that Homeless would soon trip and they would be declared correct.

All this while, the campaign gathered momentum. Impressions which it left in the minds of the people were expressed as slogans at public gatherings as well as in private homes:

> "Eighty percent of the revenue of the Island ends up in England to fatten its economy - ten million rupees in 1909 from tea and rubber alone."
> "The annual expenditure on higher education is less than the salary of the Governor."
> 'It takes one rupee and fifty cents a day to feed a prisoner whereas the grant-in-aid for educating a child is three rupees a year."
> "What we need is more of technical and scientific education than of Christian Theology and Western Classics."
> "Our cows are ill-fed and neglected, so that a market is created for condensed milk from Holland and Switzerland."
> "What we need is a body of men who, with enthusiasm, will go forward to awaken the sleeping people who are now leading a moribund life."

"We must restore our lost place in the history of he world. Once we were great, we were never conquered, and today we would have been an independent nation."

"Education is the only remedy that will save our people - not the education that makes us what we are but the higher scientific education that will make us engineers, architects, manufacturers, scientific agriculturists etc."

Homeless Dharmapala was in high demand. It took Slim-Jewel three months before her Women's Organization could have him in Kandy to be the guest of honour at its Annual General Meeting.

By this time, Stanley Williams had been transferred to the Colonial Secretary's Office in Colombo.

"Should I invite Homeless to be my house guest? Should I attend the meeting? Should I meet him at all?"

There was hardly a friend who could help me to solve the dilemma. Even though Homeless repeatedly stressed that his goal for the Island was the political status which New Zealand was enjoying as a Self-ruling entity under the protection of the British Crown, far too many in the Administration had been antagonized by his vituperative attacks. He was their "*bete noire*" just as they were his.

Six months to go for an honourable retirement! Should I jeopardize it?! Indeed, there was one who would answer my question wisely.

Homeless Dharmapala had included the event in Kandy in an extended lecture tour of the Central Province. He had come in the familiar wagon for whose initial creation Colonel Olcott credited "Yankee ingenuity". There was, of course, a major development. What was drawn by oxen was now mounted on the chassis of a motor truck. Painted on its sides was the plea to save Buddha Gaya - the hallowed site of the Buddha's Enlightenment.

I was not in Kandy when he came; nor when he addressed the Women's Organization. Slim-Jewel was left alone to look after him.

To "let sleeping dogs sleep," as Homeless had advised me in his letter, I utilized that particular week-end to visit Aunt Flower in Colombo and to tell Lucy how well her two sons were progressing in life. The third addition to the family of Middle Banda and Rose was a son and I had some photographs which I could show her. She was naturally more excited about the news I had of Vickie and Beckie. Their month-old twins were cherubs and their proud parents had inscribed "*le choix du Roi*" on the back of the glossy photograph. With Timothy's help I had deciphered what the choice of the king meant. The twins were a boy and a girl. I explained it to Aunt Flower and Lucy.

Lucy kissed the photograph. Moved by some strong emotion, she fell at my feet and touched them. Was she grateful that we had given a new life to her two boys and redeemed them from the pathetic life of poverty and discrimination to which they were born? Or, was she beholden to us that we continued to allow her even vicariously to enjoy the pleasures of a biological grandmother? It could be both, I said to myself as I raised her gently by her arms.

Age had hardly taken its toll of her. She was as beautiful as she was the day I saw her at the railway station in Kandy. A little weight she had gained. But that enhanced her figure and rendered her face glossier. For a moment I was distracted by the thought that she looked a perfect model for the fifth century frescoes of the Lion-rock.

I told them of my plans to take early retirement and to become active in the campaigns of Homeless and Don Baron.

"I am not sure whether Mr. Jayatilaka would ever return to the Island," said Aunt Flower. "All I read about him in the papers these days is that he is deeply involved with various associations and delegations in London and accepting invitations to speak in France, Sweden and places like that."

My aunt was correct. Don Baron was frequently in the news. He was active. The Toddy Bill which the Legislative Council in Colombo had passed on the twelfth of April 1912 had catapulted Don Baron to limelight. On the twentieth of June he had addressed the All-India United Temperance Association and within the week the delegation from the Island was met by a group of influential Members of Parliament. By July, the Secretary of State for Colonies, none other than Right Honourable L. V. Harcourt, had agreed to meet the delegation.

The kudos for all this went to Don Baron who was officially the Secretary of the delegation. Also reported in the local press was his address in August to the Association of Colonial Peoples. He was a regular speaker at the meetings of Temperance Societies in London. Whatever the theme, he always added a note on his concern for the situation in Sri Lanka.

Looking at it from afar, he had reflected profoundly on the causes of poverty, disruption of national values and norms, inadequate education and the increasing drunkenness and its direct result in crimes

564

of sudden provocation. His association with the burgeoning ranks of leaders struggling for freedom for India had convinced him of the only solution. We too should struggle for freedom.

My audience of two was impressed with my account of Don Baron and his message for the nation. They were fairly well informed about him and his wife as they had written extensively to the daily Sinhala newspaper 'Day-Gem." Even Lucy to whom these travelogues had been read could recall details. She recalled in particular a long diatribe that Mrs. Jayatilaka wrote on Ballroom dancing which she had seen aboard the ship. Both of them were interested in what Don Baron had written to me in his personal letters.

"Does he really say that, Tiny?" asked Aunt Flower. "Does he really say that the people he met in London are appalled about the way the Administration runs the country?"

"That's what he says, Aunt Flower. And that, too, after meeting some of the highest in the Government and the Opposition."

"Does he also say that the longer he stays in London, the more he is encouraged to struggle for our freedom?"

"Precisely. He is meeting some remarkable men from India and China who inspire him."

We chatted late into the night. It was a rare opportunity for all three of us to recall our different lives stemming from the same region. Lucy told us more about her incredible experiences as a girl among the outcastes across the river. She spoke frankly about her infatuation with Middle Banda, my third brother who paid for his clandestine love with his life.

"I didn't think of the consequences," she confessed. "That Buddha of a gentleman appeared to me as my only lifeline. He was my only salvation from a life which was daily becoming intolerable."

Aunt Flower and I listened sympathetically. I wished that Slim-Jewel was there to hear her. I knew that she bore no ill will toward the wretched woman who stole her husband and led him to an early grave, nay a tragic death. Yet, with emotions long abated, Lucy's account of herself evoked compassion.

To make her feel better, we started speaking of other things- our innocent games, the foibles of the people we knew as children, and accidents of life which brought us where we were. Inevitably, we were reminiscing on Little Father to whom I owed everything I had gained in life.

565

"Hardly a day passes without my having to recall that Little Father was the one who wanted me to go to the Missionary School in Bo-tree Plains, That was the beginning of every phase in my life."

"That includes your adventures with Colonel Olcott?"

"Yes, indeed, Aunt Flower. But as important was my meeting with the greatest of my benefactors, The Right Reverend Kenneth Saunders."

We slept late that Saturday and were up very early. Lucy went out briefly to buy hoppers and stringhoppers for a sumptuous breakfast which actually turned out to be a brunch. I had no plans for the day other than taking the night express train to Kandy.

"Uncle Victor has left behind a whole heap of files and papers," said Aunt Flower when she found that we had almost exhausted all subjects of common interest. "I don't know what to do with them. They meant something to him and that's why he had kept them so safe. I vaguely remember that he was keen that you should see them."

Two metal trunks were pulled out of the store-room. One was full of files which were carefully labelled. The other contained all kinds of news clippings, notices, pamphlets and letters, awaiting scrutiny and classification. "TO BE FILED," said a piece of cardboard pasted on the inside of the lid.

First, I went through the files. Each had its subject clearly written on the cover. The documents were filed in chronological order. Paper cuttings were mounted on plain white paper and the binding edge fortified with strips of paper. Files ranged from "Acts of blatant discrimination," "Religious persecution," "Denationalization," "Divide and Rule," "Fomenting communal disharmony" to "Justice and fairness of the British," "Sport and fair play," and "Norms and values of a democratic society."

There were bulky files on each of the Governors since Sir William H. Gregory and those of varying thickness on many of the public figures both national and expatriate. The earliest documents dated from about 1875 or the time he joined the Government service as a clerk. It must have been his hobby.

It did not take too long to realize that Uncle Victor had not only a keen historical sense but also the vision that his life and times needed to be documented. He had been a self-assumed archivist. Since his retirement, he had spent long hours in putting the documents in order. I looked in vain for evidence of attempting any analysis or critical examination of the material in hand. The beginnings of a book? For whom was he preparing this invaluable compilation?

566

"Didn't Uncle Victor tell you anything specific about these files and papers?" I asked Aunt Flower.

"I did ask him why he was doing all this sorting and filing and what the compulsion was for him to work even when his health was failing. All I remember very vaguely is that you or Timothy might find a use for them."

It is then that I ransacked his personal papers for any clue. What a delightful surprise! Pinned inside the front cover of the file with his last will was a sealed envelope. It was clearly addressed to me or Timothy. Inside was a note where we were requested to see his collection of documents bearing on the history and social conditions of our times. He hoped that we would find them useful.

I was glad that I had a task in hand when the time came for me to retire.

Before I left for the railway station that evening, I had another long chat with Aunt Flower. She was keen to know how much I was prepared for retirement.

"No wife, however, loving wants a husband hanging around in the house the whole day," she said.

"Our case might be different, Aunt Flower"

"How come?"

"I have a philosophy which enables me to face all problems as preludes to better times. This has been so in office and now it shall be at home. I simply tell myself, 'OFT A LITTLE MORNING RAIN FORTELLS A PLEASANT DAY.' "

567

Book Five

PATH AND FRUIT OF FREEDOM

I

It was not easy to make big changes in life when one was fifty-five. Retirement indeed called for changes in every aspect of one's life. In the hurry and scurry of bringing up the children and serving the people, we had failed to think of the future and to build a retirement home. With weeks to leave the Government quarters, we began to panic. But in vain.

"Why don't you take your leave preparatory to retirement and take Mother to places that you have been to like the buried cities and Jaffna?" asked Moon-Beam sweetly.

Protests about moving house and winding up office work were met with reassuring promises. Moon-Beam and Timothy would have our effects moved to a place that was available immediately for rent. No further arguments were necessary when the place available was the house in Royal Spout that Uncle Victor and Aunt Flower had once occupied. Their son, Autumn-Moon, had it as a holiday home which he hardly ever used due to his ever-expanding career as a successful crime lawyer in Colombo.

Thirtieth of November 1912 was my last day in office. The only letter in my In-tray that day was a newsy epistle from Don Baron telling me, among others, of his lecture tour to Sweden.

"If all goes well, we will be back in home sweet home by the middle of next year," he said, before proceeding to wish me a happy retirement. "Look forward to a very busy one, my friend."

I went round and spoke to my colleagues and left office as on any other day. Any feeling of sadness was off-set by the excitement of the imminent trip to the North.

I looked forward to it as a kid did the New Year gifts. I had decided and Slim-Jewel had reluctantly agreed to do it by car. It really could be an unforgettable adventure!

Travelling by car through long stretches of less known territory where nothing more than cart-tracks were said to exist was not for a middle-aged couple in mid-fifties, said both friends and the family.Their main concerns were about fuel and mechanical breakdown in out of the way places.

Serviced and polished, our four-year old Ford T was declared to be in top condition. Timothy had a contraption fitted at the back to strap two five-gallon cans of gasoline and an additional spare tyre. Moon-Beam insisted that Jamis, the gardener, should accompany us. Timothy and my Hindu Chief Clerk of the Native Department had alerted their friends and acquaintances in places we would pass. But all these precautions were superfluous.

That evening the three merchants whose combs were publicly broken by Homeless Dharmapala paid us a visit.

"Sir, we came to tell you not to worry about the trip." said the eldest among them. "Your Tamil officer talked to us about your safety on the way. We came to tell you that we had taken care of everything. Our carters travel in caravans of fifty to hundred carts. They will look out for you. You will meet at least two caravans a day. They will cook for you if it is meal-time. And the most important, we are sending gasoline with every caravan so that you will have no problem even when you cross the jungle."

I was amazed at what had been planned. I felt as if I was starting on an expedition to an altogether uncharted territory.

"One more thing," added another merchant. "Keep to the cart roads. They are quite motorable if you learn how to avoid the deep ruts made by cart wheels."

I knew what he meant as I had seen this extraordinary feat being achieved by the driver of the Government Agent's car in Jaffna.

Although I was in the best of health and Slim-Jewel had nothing but her failing sight to complain about, we took our motor tour easy. On the first day, we did hardly twenty miles. Our extensive tour of religious and cultural sites began with a day among the massive boulders of the Monastery of Light where, two thousand years ago, the Buddhist monks of Sri Lanka rehearsed the teachings of the Buddha and wrote on palm leaves the Canon and its commentaries.

Averaging twenty miles a day, we drove northwards spending as many days at each of the monuments as we felt necessary to see all that was important. The caves of Dambulla and the rock fortress of Sigiriya (Lion-Rock) merited five days while the buried city of Anuradhapura took a whole week. We travelled in luxury. We met the carters regularly and their rustic cooking was delicious even if the menu was limited.

Even in the remotest village was a Buddhist temple with at least one or two monks. It was a treat to meet them. Not all of them were educated or groomed for their work. But what each achieved in keeping the faith of the people alive was remarkable. Most had heard of Olcott and Homeless Dharmapala . Some had travelled miles to listen to them.

It was a morale-booster to both Slim-Jewel and me when a couple of monks actually knew us by name and the work we did in some of the associations.

"If for nothing else,we should thank the British for these lovely Rest Houses," quipped Slim-Jewel as we walked in the extensive garden of the Tissa-Lake Rest House where teeming monkeys held their long palavers unmindful of human presence. It was idyllic.

Seated on the bank of the man-made lake, while Slim-Jewel fed the monkeys, I gave vent to my feelings in a poem which I wrote for the Sunday Diadem:

This hallowed land of my nation's pride
Where saffron-clad saints laid their robes to dry
After a dip in the cold blue waters
That kings of yore with man-made dams
Stored for the good of man and beast.

Here in ruin lie mansions and shrines
Where milling crowds paid homage to the Buddha,
Where artists turned plain blocks of rock
To works of art of sheer delight,
Where poets sang their patriotic songs
For a land held free with courageous might.

O Monkeys! in your day-long chatter
What do you say with hardly a break?
Is it your grief you vent, my friends,
That the glorious light of our culture sublime,
Like a lamp without oil with its wicks burnt out,
Has dimmed for ever with scarcely a hope?

If so, my friends, the nearest kin of humans,
Rejoice in the signs of dawn though yet so far.
The sun of freedom will shine once again.
To our cry in unison for a land reborn
Flowing with curd and treacle and fragrant blossoms
The world shall harken and we will win.

The crumbs that fall from the master's table,
The slice that's offered in pitiful disdain,
The loaf we have gained with dint of effort

571

Shall suffice us no more and never again.
We claim the bakery to make as we want
The bread for you and me and the rest.

Add your voice to our lion's roar:
This noble land of sylvan splendour
Should rise from shambles to guide us to the day
When, in harmony and faith, we will happily proclaim
"FREE AT LAST - free as the breeze and you, my friends.

I thought for a while and wrote the caption, "*Grieve not, my monkey friends!*" Slim-Jewel walked up the lake bund followed by a stubborn monkey who asked for more. I showed her my poem. She sang the verses. Rendered in her melodious voice, they sounded great. She rubbed my cheek with the back of her fingers.

From the ancient capital to the Elephant Pass was wild country. Yet, within reach each day was a Rest House. The melodious jingling of bells and the sonorous singing of the carter's songs - heard long before we met a caravan of carts - was always welcome. The carters were kind and solicitous. The fuel they transported was quite handy. We drove ahead of each caravan until we reached another.

Occasionally, we ran into young civil servants in khaki shorts and short-sleeved white shirts on official circuits on horseback. We stopped to talk to them about our common friends and acquaintances. Invariably, every conversation ended with the cliche: "What a small world!"

It was only through one particular stretch that the carters insisted that we should travel with them.

"Any bandits?" asked Slim-Jewel.

"Only the four-legged big kind," said the lad who was washing our car.

One thing we had not thought about were the elephants in whose habitat we were unwelcome intruders. We camped overnight with the caravan near the vestiges of a man-made lake to observe wild life in the moon light. Slim-Jewel counted thirty elephants majestically approaching the water-front. How very lovingly they tended their young! What a glorious experience to see the jungle alive!

Jaffna lived up to its promise and reputation. We were welcomed by my old and loyal friend, Shiva-Worshipper, who had found for us a most charming villa by the sea not too far from Jaffna College. In

January Jaffna was as cool and inviting as Kandy or some of the other hill stations. What a contrast from the heat and humidity of April!

"You'll be in good company here," he told us. "Your son is a legend in the College and in the community too."

He could not have said anything truer. The former teachers and friends of Victory-Servant , now in Illinois as Vickie Wickie, offered us their services, invited us to their houses and made us feel at home in every possible way.

"He is still in touch with most of us," said Reverend Bill Kennedy who gave in our honour a fabulous party, replete with Jaffna delicacies and the finest songs of the Glee Club.

The surprise of all surprises was to see young Bradley of my very first visit in the College. Having found life as an academic more pleasing, he had left the Civil Service and joined the School of Oriental Languages of the London University. He was spending his sabbatical on an in-depth study of some aspects of the Tamil language and literature in which he was already an acknowledged specialist. We spent many evenings with him as our common friends invited us together. He also joined us in a trip to the large island of Delft with its wild horses and Portuguese ruins, On the way we also visited the Naga Island which tradition associated with a visit of the Buddha. Needless to say that we had much to share.

If the return trip took a whole a week, it was due to the circuitous route we took. Three carts with ample supplies accompanied us. A herd of elephants foraged just fifty yards of the cart track unmindful of our intrusion. Hundreds of deer and peacocks dotted the grassland. Every now and then, disturbed perhaps by preying crocodiles, flocks of shrieking cranes rose to the sky displaying their snow-white plumage.

We saw the fabulous ruins of Polonnaruwa, the capital in the eleventh and twelfth centuries. The incredibly vast reservoirs around it awaited repair and regeneration. Yet in their dilapidated state, they evinced the superior technical skills of our ancestors. We went in succession to every capital to which kings moved in a crucial period of political uncertainty and national insecurity. This rapid fall of capitals lasted through the thirteenth and the fourteenth centuries.

Ours was a journey through history. The hundred chapters of the *Great Chronicle*, the non-stop epic of the Island, was our guide. Our last night was at the Rest House at Elephant Rock. The booming town, noted for neighbouring graphite mines and fecund coconut plantations, owed its name to the gigantic granite rocks which resembled a herd of sleeping elephants.

"Can you imagine, Jewel, we are where King Prowess-Arm the Fourth had a team of scholars led by a Tamil monk of South Indian origin to translate the Book of Birth Stories of the Buddha into Sinhala."

"You mean the venerable book on the Buddha's five hundred and fifty past lives?" she asked me referring to the book with deference. She used the honorific with which a devout Buddhist honoured a living sage.

"Yes, Jewel. That's the book."

It came as a surprise to Slim-Jewel that for many centuries Buddhism flourished in South India and that several generations of Tamil-speaking scholars had maintained close contact with counterparts in the Island.

She was no different from most of my generation who thought of South India as the land from which the British planters brought unwanted intruders into our ancestral lands in the form of cheap labour.

In a session on the verandah of the Rest House, we talked on history and literature - a session which reminded us of our unforgettable "University on Wheels" in Europe. The only difference was that the rest of the family was not there.

"Now that you are retiring, I hope we can have more of these sessions. I know so little," enthused Slim-Jewel as we adjourned to the dining hall, where a sumptuous meal of fresh water fish was served.

I was elaborating on the role of the great South Indian scholar-monk, Bodhidharma (Enlightenment-Virtue), who went to China from South India and founded the popular tradition of meditation-based Buddhism called *Ch'an* in China. It was better known by its Japanese appellation, *Zen*.

Slim-Jewel took in every word with rapt attention.

A polite cough from the darkness beyond the door disturbed us. In came a gentleman in a white drill suit.

"Mudaliyar Valour-Lion, I presume?" he said.

We invited him in and he sat with us at the table. He apologized for the hour he had chosen to meet us and explained that his work as a doctor in the hospital prevented him from coming earlier.

"Dr. de Lanerolle insisted that I should meet you tonight itself."

If for a moment Slim-Jewel and I were nervous and apprehensive, he put us at ease.

574

"No. No. There's no problem. I was specifically asked to tell you that all are doing well, including those in Burma and America. Dr. de Lanerolle wants me to give you a message. They want you to come to their place first before you drive home. For what meal should they expect you?"

We deliberated for a while and chose dinner.

The young doctor, a native of Point Pedro, the northernmost town in the Jaffna Peninsula, joined us at dinner. A resourceful Rest House Keeper fixed for him a vegetarian meal.

"My father is the chief high priest of the Hindu Temple," he said, giving the reason why he remained a vegetarian. "I also had my training as a priest and I assist him when we have our big festivals."

He was a delightful conversationalist. He gave us some insights we had never had of the life of our northern neighbours.

"When I go home to Jaffna, in the train itself, I fold my Western suit and put it at the bottom of the suitcase. Then I wear the shirt and cloth as we all do in Jaffna. It would be preposterous and unpardonable to go home in Western clothes or to speak in anything but Tamil."

I had often wondered why my many friends in Jaffna had never been seen in Western suits outside the court or the office.

"We are overly fond of our language and our customs and traditions. When I came here I was appalled to see how easily the doctors and nurses and most of the people of the south had adopted a foreign life style. They love to dress like the English, speak English and eat and behave like the English."

He was not critical. He was only explaining how tradition-bound he and his fellow Tamil Hindus were. If he made it sound a virtue, it was quite unintentional.

"Some of my colleagues here tease me for taking my sesame oil bath every week-end. Nurses poke fun at me saying that I smell of sesame oil," he said with a good-natured laugh. "They are amused when I observe regular fasting days."

"I used to say that to one of my bosses," quipped Slim-Jewel. "I was a nurse then. But the doctor was quite thick about it."

"We all are, Madame. Or rather we have to be. Play the square peg in a round hole and be unmindful of what others say. Or else, lose your identity and lose everything with it."

He elaborated his theme. We talked until it was time for the staff of the Rest House to retire. We invited Dr. Young-Moon to visit us in Kandy.

"I would love to do it," he told us. "Your son-in-law is the model for every young doctor. It is our dream to be like him. It will be an honour to meet him."

To say that we were not elated with his admiration for Timothy would be palpably untrue.

We made a detour to see a few more sites in an area where H. C. P. Bell, the pioneering British archaeologist, had begun some extensive excavations. Our last day on the road was as exciting as every other day. We could hardly believe that the history of this part of the country extended back to centuries before the Common Era.

We reached Kandy by nightfall and drove to the house of Timothy and Moon-Beam. Jamis got down from the car to open the gate. Slim-Jewel stroked my cheek.

"This has been a wonderful experience for me, to see the country in your company," she said with a lump in her throat. "Let us hope we can do it again."

We were delighted to find that my cousin Autumn-Moon had come all the way from Colombo to meet us.

"You are such a busy man, Autumn. We are delighted to see you here."

"You are certainly right about my being busy. I have not been able to see Mother for a month."

I knew about it. It was a source of recurring pain and complaint for Aunt Flower.

"I have some important business to settle with you tomorrow," he continued, but showed no inclination to discuss it any further.

We freshened up for dinner and told Moon-Beam that we would like to eat early and go to our rented home.

"No, Father. You sleep here tonight."

Meanwhile the two young men had unpacked the car and taken our bags to the master bed-room. It would have been futile to argue. We settled down for a good meal of rice and curry - undoubtedly superior to what we had eaten on the road all these days. We retired early and rose before the rest of the house. It was a Saturday morning and that accounted for the lull.

576

The house on the slope overlooking the Great-Sand River was shrouded in the thick white mist of February. The river expressed its mighty presence with that roar to which I was accustomed from my infancy. It was exactly into a similar position that Mother Nature cataclysmically moved my home on the fateful night of my birth. I stepped into the compound and relived my childhood. My reverie into this early chapter of life brought back memories of a troubled childhood.

"Did I really cause that disastrous landslide?" I asked myself as I had done a myriad times before.

On the eve of my retirement at the ripe old age of fifty-five, I seemed to have no clear answer. But the memories of my life were not all that bad. I took stock of what I had achieved personally and what I had helped others achieve - especially Slim-Jewel and her daughter and Lucy and her two sons. I had reason to be happy.

"Above all," I said to myself. "I made a difference in the life of a lovely woman whose faith in humanity was at its lowest ebb."

I was woken from my reverie by that same lovely woman who had made with her own lily-white hands a steaming cup of tea for me.

The breakfast of milk rice with the hottest concoction of chillies, onions and dried fish from the Maldive Islands, followed by hoppers and stringhoppers with fish curry and coconut cream gravy, was a long-drawn affair. The family was still enjoying the reunion when Timothy announced that the three men had business downtown. We scrambled into his car and drove down to the vicinity of the courts. I still had no idea what the business was. My curiosity increased as we stepped into the office of a Notary Public who was my friend.

"I have them all ready, Mudaliyar. You have only to sign them," he said as he pulled out from his drawer a sheaf of papers. I recognized them to be a deed conveying a property. He handed them to me for perusal.

"What? Autumn selling his house to me?" I protested. "But I haven't that money and the last thing I would do is to leave any encumbrance to Slim-Jewel or any of the children."

"Don't you worry, Brother. All that has been taken care of," said Autumn-Moon. "I am glad that the house will still be in the family, especially that part of the family that both my father and mother adore."

To save time for the Notary Public, we signed the papers even though I still had no idea what had happened. It was in the car that Timothy explained how Moon-Beam thought out the plan and how all the others concurred.

While Slim-Jewel and I were having a whale of a time enjoying our visits to new places and expanding intellectual horizons, Moon-Beam had contacted Autumn-Moon and made an offer for the house which we had already agreed to rent at Royal Spout. Buzzing wires took care of the rest of the deal. Each of our children paid her or his share and Timothy masterminded the rest.

Slim-Jewel, when told of our morning mission, hugged Moon-Beam, Timothy and Autumn-Moon in turn and cried with joy. But that was not the end of the story.

With these kids we had been always ready for surprises. But what followed was beyond our expectations. We went in two cars to Royal Spout to a newly painted house. The garden had been relandscaped and was teeming with flowers. Even the path leading to the front porch had been redone. A lean-to garage had been constructed for the car. Moon-Beam took us around the house and showed us in a leisurely fashion all the work that had been done to make it the ideal home for us to retire in.

"Why don't they take us in?" I wondered. But not for long.

"Time up," shouted Timothy from the front of the house.

He handed the key to Slim-Jewel.

"A minute to go, Mother," he said. "Father knows the stanzas."

He was watching the second hand of his pocket watch for the exact auspicious moment. It was indicative of the extent to which they had thought of details. They had got my brother the Chief Monk of Sangha-Gem-Field Royal Monastery to work out the astrologically appropriate time to enter the new home.

Slim-Jewel turned the key and opened the door, joining me in the Pali stanzas I recited invoking the blessings of the Buddha, his Teachings and the Community of his Monks and Nuns. It was a solemn moment for both Slim-Jewel and me and we withheld our tears.

When the door opened we had further evidence of what arrangements Moon-Beam and Timothy had made for a traditionally perfect house-warming. In the centre of the hall was a metal sheet on which were placed three bricks and kindlings to form a fireplace. A new clay pot was set on it. Autumn-Moon came behind us carrying a bottle of milk, which I was asked to pour into the clay pot. Timothy handed a box of matches to Slim-Jewel.

We stood around the boiling pot until the milk overflowed and extinguished the fire. I could not help but recall that we had just performed an age-old rite - one of sympathetic magic - which might

578

date back to the early Aryans who entered India at least three thousand years ago. In their pastoral society the overflowing milk must have been a powerful symbol signifying prosperity.

Occupying more than half the living room was a structure of bamboos decorated with paper cut-outs of beautiful motives. It formed an enclosure specially prepared for the next important element of a traditional house-warming. It had a canopy of white cloth from which hung betel leaves and flowers of the areca nut palm. On a table in the centre was a pot of water decorated with the yellow tender leaves of the coconut palm. Twelve chairs covered with pure white cloth were placed around the table.

"So there is nothing you have overlooked!" I said in sheer amazement.

"Why not take a look in your rooms?" suggested Moon-Beam while the young men set about removing the fireplace from the hall.

They had done a superb job of *demanagement*. Every room had been arranged as they were in the previous house. Furniture was in place. Cupboards were neatly arranged. The wardrobes had been moved without dismantling. Even the kitchen and pantry were perfect.

"You must have put in many days of hard work. Thank you very much," I told Timothy and Moon-Beam.

We have had too many surprises for one day. We really needed a rest. Sensitive always to our needs, Moon-Beam noted it.

"Let us leave Father and Mother for a while and return when the people come."

"You mean, you have invited people?"

"Yes, Father. They will come after eight when the monks are brought to chant the Book of Protection for the whole night."

For a moment I had forgotten the significance of the elaborately decorated structure in the living room.

Moon-Beam had chosen the room I had earlier occupied in this house and made it the master bedroom. Grateful for their thoughtfulness, we snatched a couple of hours of the sleep we sorely needed.

The all-night chanting of the Book of Protection and the almsgiving for a dozen monks on Sunday morning were happy denouements to the unending display of thoughtfulness and affection on

579

the part of Moon-Beam and Timothy. The presence of Autumn-Moon throughout all ceremonies enhanced our joy. So did the close friends and colleagues who had been invited to make the events truly social. Our life in the new home could not have begun better.

II

The fifth of February 1913 was a chilly rainy day. I awoke at five as usual. The morning mist, a fluffy white blanket enveloping the house, added to the cozy feeling of a life without the burden of responsibility. Ever thoughtful Golden Jewel had left a steaming pot of tea on the dining table. Nothing else brings about that exhilarating feeling of well-being which only a hot cup of tea with milk and sugar does in the tranquility of dawn.

It was my first morning as a retiree. Untrammeled by either the routine-riden time-table or the cares and anxieties of office, I enjoyed a second and a third cup of the reinvigorating elixir in a leisurely mood that I had never experienced since I gave up the robes of a monk. I was savouring every moment of a wonderful sensation: I was free to do what I wanted and the choice was entirely mine.

"A dog has no work to do. But never walks slowly," said Slim-Jewel with a smile when she found me in the study. Her allusion was to a popular Sinhala saying which meant that the circumstances did not merit the hustle and the bustle.

"How can I, Jewel? Even when old a monkey does not walk on the ground," I retorted with a parallel saying. One does not outlive one's habits, it was meant to say. "Besides, Jewel, now my office is right here. You remember what I told them at the Farewell Party: 'It is the government that I cease to work for. But my service to the people of this hallowed Island of ours will only see an increase.' I want to keep to that promise."

Slim-Jewel who had been the public servant *par excellence* in the family needed no more explanation.

"I know," she said with a nod."Join the club."

We both laughed. It augured well for a new life together, when she had to contend with a husband who hung around the house all day.

What an inviting environment for work. Moon-Beam and Timothy had fitted the airiest and best lit room in the house as my study and a similar but smaller room at the back as a office for Slim-Jewel. Both rooms had been organized with such meticulous care that one felt urged to commence using them. All my book cases had been neatly arranged.

The files of sociopolitical information of Uncle Victor had been taken out of the trunk and carefully placed on a rack. Timothy had worked on the loose documents in the other trunk and sorted them in several categories each with a label to identify the subject. Pending my approval, he had not filed them.

That was where I began. Many of the documents could go into the files already opened by Uncle Victor. For others, new files had to be opened. An extremely thoughtful Timothy had purchased a whole stock of files, writing paper and such other paraphernalia as one would need in an office. On a side of the desk was a stack of note pads with the new address!

I divided the files into three groups - Sociopolitical Issues; Biographical Notes; and General Interest. I commenced with those which could be of immediate use in the campaign in which I would join Homeless. I made copious notes. By the time breakfast was announced I had half a notebook full of data that the campaign could use effectively.

A shivering but refreshed gardener stood at the door.

"Sir, there is nothing to beat a shower at the royal spout. It's so chilly. But afterwards you feel as if you can climb the Hantane Peak twice."

He was extolling the virtues of taking an alfresco shower at a spout which was once reserved for royalty. Hence the name of the village. The icy cold water from the mountain stream descended on you with a force which assured a vigourous massage.

With this advice was established a routine for the early part of the day: tea in a misty porch; an hour or two of paper work, and then the royal shower.

The visit to the spout had another advantage. A dozen men from the vicinity assembled there, not only for ablutions, but for socialization. It was the equivalent of the village well where the womenfolk exchanged gossip and maintained their tiny window to the world.

The men at the spout were a motley crowd, drawn from all walks of life. Weekends brought the English educated white-collar city workers and teachers. The very fact that they braved the chilly water of a pounding spout early in the morning in the rising mist of the Kandyan hills set them apart as hardy men - a local brand of Stoics. Semi-nudity indeed was a great social leveller!

"Wonderful to see you join our club, Mudaliyar" said the short dark man in his early twenties who introduced himself as the headmaster of the Roman Catholic School in the neighbouring village.

582

"We would like to have you at the school one day to meet the founder of the school."

I accepted the invitation without hesitation and a few days later drove up the hill to discover a new world. I never believed that it could exist in my very backyard.

Nestled within a flourishing plantation of coconut in the valleys and tea on the hill tops was a veritable mediaeval monastery with red walls and white windows. A winding road had a triangular playground on its left and a two-storeyed impressive school building on its right. To the left at the highest point was a grey stone church perched precariously on a hill top. Across the church on a plateau stood the Papal Seminary of the Society of Jesus, a University for priests.

If it was anachronistic in its very concept and design, it was out of place in a British Colony: the Seminary was not only Roman Catholic but typically Continental European in character.

I had been asked to come at the time the classes were dispersing. Hundreds of young priests came out of the large wooden door of the impressive building. Their white cassocks, highlighted by the scarlet waist bands from which broad strips of the same colour reached the ankle, set them apart as students or "brothers."

It was an international crowd. Their facial features revealed the many races they represented. They were noisy and vivacious - the universal hallmark of students of any clime or time.

I strained my ears to detect what was so amusing. To my utter disbelief, they were conversing in a language I could not recognize. I parked the car and opened the door to step out. "Cave canum" warned a Brother who possibly hailed from upper Burma. Reaching for my leg was a dog baring its teeth in anger. The warning was in dear old Latin.

Walter J. Peiris, my shower club member, had arived ahead of me. He came out with a youngish priest in an immaculate white cassock with the waist band and strip in jet black. The dog had been chased away. I got out of the car and walked up to the door to meet them.

"Reverend Father Augustine Berrewaerts, Professor of Astronomy in the Seminary and Principal of our school," said Walter by way of introducing the tall and slim European priest. His brownish goatee accentuated his sharp chin and his elongated pentagonal face. He offered me his right hand. I took it in mine and the gentle handshake was infused with sincerity.

583

"I have heard of you and read some of your writings, Mudaliyar. Headmaster tells me that you have retired and that you all meet at the spout to prove your mettle," he said in a thick European accent and laughed.

"What would you like to see first: the Seminary or the School?" asked Walter.

"Now that we are here, why not the Seminary first?" suggested the Father.

He led us to the parlour where visitors were received. Over a cup of tea with neither milk nor sugar, Father Berrewaerts explained what the institution did and how he came to establish his school. He spoke English fluently but very slowly. He had developed an effective technique to minimize the impact of his Dutch-sounding accent, which, I realized later, came from his own mother tongue, Flemish.

"It's wonderful to have this calm and quiet sanctuary to train our priests for Asia" he continued. "We could never find a site so beautiful, so convenient and so peaceful in a place so close to a growing modern city and amidst people who are so tolerant and friendly. At first we took everything for granted - mostly the patience and gentleness of our neighbours. If they did not spread a red carpet and welcome us into this village, they did the next best thing. They have let us grow. Everyone of us has been treated with respect and even deference."

Father Berrewaerts had been the first to raise his voice against the policy of the Seminary to ignore the community and remain a foreign implantation.

"I shouted the most against the attitude of aloofness. Then the others turned round to me and said, 'Go ahead and do what you say we should do.' It was then that I read in a paper how costly education was in this Island. One of the campaigners for national liberation had said that it cost several times more to send a child to school here than in India."

"You must have read something written by Homeless Dharmapala." I intervened.

"Maybe. I honestly don't remember who said it. The proposer did not matter. What he said was true. And that alone was relevant. So my aim was to set up a school where I would levy a fee less than one fourth charged by a school in Kandy."

"Was it possible?" I asked.

"Yes, indeed. But with the generous assistance of the Seminary at the initial stages. It put up the buildings and its teachers doubled up to teach some classes and help in various activities. But now we enter the

584

tenth year of existence and we are completely self-sufficient. In fact the new classroom block that is coming up is from school funds."

Our tour of the Seminary included the class rooms, the refectory and the library. What a fantastic library it was!

"We have your books, Sir. You are most welcome to come here and do your research at any time," said the priest in charge of the library. His accent was unmistakably Italian.

After the brief visit to the Seminary, we went to the school in my car. What was there to see in an empty school, I thought. But I was wrong. Father Berrewaerts led us to his office through a sickroom with four beds. Each was occupied. These were children who were too ill to go home after school.

"I get children from a radius of three to four miles," he explained. "They come from families of modest income. My first concern is their health. I run a clinic for them in the morning."

"Do you get a doctor or a nurse?" I asked.

"I am both, Mudaliyar," he said with a benign smile.

Walter took over and described how the morning began with dressing sores, distributing quinine against Malaria and treating kids for all kinds of diseases ranging from acute malnutrition to diarrhoea. Sometimes, a poor villager would come to get a festered wound cleaned and bandaged by the saintly priest.

While Walter spoke, the priest made tea for the sick children and made notes on what to bring each of them for dinner.

His office was more a library.

"Yes, I am the librarian, too," he said with his usual laugh. "The children come to me to get their books. Unless they can answer a few questions on what they have already read, they do not get a new book."

"That is very interesting. But how do you find the time?"

"Very simple." he said with a smile, but did not elaborate.

We went through the empty classrooms. Each desk shone in the evening light with a thick coating of wax. Not a speck of dust was visible anywhere.

Walter explained the system. Each child was responsible for the cleanliness of the school and took turns to sweep the premises. They scrubbed the desks once a month with the abrasive leaves of a tree that grew in plenty in the neighbourhood and polished them with tallow from the used candles of the church.They did all the manual work in the school, hauling things about; bringing drinking water and even keeping the latrines clean.

"Don't the children or their parents complain?" I asked, mindful of my own disappointment with the receding sense of dignity of labour in the country.

"How can they?" countered Walter, "When they see that the Principal begins the day by emptying and cleaning the chamber pots of the sick children?"

Needless to say that this was not my last visit to the school or the Seminary. I found inspiration from the selfless devotion of this Belgian scholar-priest who served his God in the most admirable way by serving the poor and needy of this impoverished and depressed part of the Island.

I frequented the library, for its intellectual wealth was inexhaustible. I met many of its professors and students. I came to know more of the school where a band of self-effacing teachers served under the able guidance of Walter. The heart-stirring stimulation of Father Berrewaerts wrought miracles with the rural youth.

All this had a profound impact on how I saw the future of my country. It reminded me of the Blakes and the Right Reverend Saunders. These were all noble examples of Christian compassion in action. I was glad that I had learnt to accept kindness without always imputing motives or being suspicious of hidden agendas.

Disinterested action without ulterior motive was not a monopoly of any particular culture or individual.

On a sunny June morning, I was invited to the King's Birthday Parade of the school. The entire student body and the staff were at school on a day which all other institutions observed as a holiday.

The children, who on other days were barefooted and dressed in short-sleeved shirts and pants of whatever colour or style the parents could afford, were in a uniform. They wore immaculately white shirts and blue drill short trousers. White stockings reaching the knees and newly pipelaid canvas shoes and bowler hats completed the attire. It was a smart turnout. The drill master, a teacher of Dutch descent, was in the khaki uniform of a sergeant major of the Army Reserve. A hundred strong brass band with a profusion of bugles attended the parade.

Assembling at a smaller ground by the school, the children stood at attention in rows of sixty according to height. The Principal conducted a formal inspection of each row in the company of the drill master while the band played a miscellany of military melodies.

586

Preceeded by a mace-wielding leader, the band conducted the platoons down the winding road to the larger field. There on a platform stood the invitees, mainly officers of the Government. In front of them under the Union Jack stood the Government Agent in all-white official uniform including the feathered solar topee hat. The Band played "God save the king" and row by row the students marched past the dais and saluted the flag and the chief guest. In less than an hour it was all over. The hours of preparation that had gone into producing this spectacle of poised discipline and elegance were justified.

"This is truly remarkable," I told Walter as we joined the invitees for a cup of tea. "What beats me is that your school puts all this effort into celebrating the King's birthday when I do not know of any other school that does so, not even the Anglican Church school I attended."

"Don't be surprised, Mudaliyar, if I tell you that I was as much puzzled when the whole thing started as a brain child of Father Berrewaerts. But he had a wonderful explanation."

I waited until all the guests departed to congratulate Father Principal on the excellent spectacle.

"That's our Annual Cricket Match, Sir," he said in his heavy Flemish accent. "The only difference is that the whole school plays instead of just a team of eleven. Besides, nine out of ten of our school-leavers end up in Government Service. It is good for them to know whom they serve and learn to respect them."

Walter added later:

"It is not a show of patriotism so to say, but rather the pragmatism of a man who thinks of only his wards."

I was eager to share my insights and feelings on what I had seen and heard in the Seminary and the school with Homeless Dharmapala as well as Don Baron. I was convinced that a change in our outlook was called for. A call for national Self-rule had to be more pragmatic and comprehensive than insular, lop-sided and piecemeal. But both my heroes were out of the country.

Homeless spent the major part of 1912 going to various parts of the country and gathering support for a national revival movement. For this purpose he used the old Olcott Wagon which had been modified to be motorable. He was also on an extended visit to Japan and Honolulu to promote his campaign for the restitution of Buddhist shrines of India to Buddhists. In fact, the day I attended the King's Birthday Parade at Walter's school, Homeless was in Honolulu meeting his benefactress

587

Mary Elizabeth Foster. As he had written to me from Japan, he was meeting her to raise funds for a Free Hospital in Colombo.

Don Baron had just completed his studies in England and was planning to set sail for Colombo. Prominent national leaders like F. R. Senanayaka and W. A. de Silva were making plans to give him a public welcome on his return in a couple of months. Newspapers had already begun adding to his name his full academic and professional titles: B. A. (Calcutta), Ll. B. (Oxford), Barrister-at-Law (Lincoln's Inn).

Until these two men were back in the Island, I had time to think and plan and to work on the precious legacy of documents left behind by Uncle Victor. I had begun sorting out the files to separate those documents which could bolster up a claim for a greater measure of Self-rule. I labelled the new files in a way that the issues dealt with in the documents would be clearer.

If their list sounded like a formidable array of serious acts of omission or commission by the Administration, I could not help it. But Timothy who came from time to time to help me had reservations on labels like "Governor - Abuse of Power," "Blatant Injustices," "Willful Damage to Environment," "Discrimination Against the Majority," "Arrogance of Petty Officials," "Exodus of National Resources," "Mockery of Education." He picked up the series which I had called "Weapons of National   Destruction" where each file was subtitled "Liquor," "Opium," "Conspicuous consumption," "Denationalization," "Influx of Foreign Exploiters," and so forth.

"Father, I would be less provocative. You are a man of peace and reconciliation. This is not your style," suggested Timothy, who looked every inch an erudite Professor. He jabbed the air with his unlit pipe of polished buffalo horn to stress his point of view.

We renamed each file. As both sides of the brownish file covers were blank we could simply refold them and write the new titles. We had no reason to believe that my titles which were now inside the back cover page were of any significance.

At the dinner table that night, we talked of Uncle Victor and the wealth of information he had collected over at least three decades. Timothy explained to Slim-Jewel and Moon-Beam what he had done with the files.

"Father, Timothy has a point. We read a Journal called *Indian Sociologist* which is published in Paris. There is a strong movement which calls itself Anarchism and it does not rule out violence as a way to gain independence."

Very lucidly, our public-spirited daughter explained to her mother and me the implications of the on-going Balkan War, the deteriorating relations between Germany and Great Britain and the British suspicions that the young Indian revolutionaries could be in tow with the Germans.

"Troubles in India could overflow to our country and don't you discount ruthless crackdowns if the Government gets suspicious."

Homeless Dharmapala returned to the Island and renewed his tours in the motorized Wagon. I was invited to join him. Thanks to Uncle Victor's archives, I was better prepared to observe and comment on matters where reform was needed.

Until I retired, I saw many things from the eyes of a complaisant officer of the Administration. I had glossed over them quite lackadaisically. Now they appeared different. I shared my feelings of shock and disbelief with Homeless.

He took me to shrinking villages which were hemmed into flooding valleys by burgeoning tea and rubber plantations. We were horrified by the disgusting sight of men of all ages haunting village taverns to drink arrack and toddy. We rounded up malnourished and sickly children who had never seen the inside of a school and took them to the nearest temple to plead with monks to open at least a Sunday school for them. We lectured to the villagers on how to be self-reliant. We met people with problems individually. In the evening the whole village would gather round our mobile home to listen to Homeless who showed slides of the Buddhist Holy shrines of India and Sri Lanka with his "Magic Lantern."

On a starry night in a village near Kandy, the crowd had just dispersed after a slide show. Homeless and I sat on a rock and chatted while the dinner was heated. We had an unexpected visitor. She was a middle-aged woman. With her were five children who ranged from about ten years of age to four.

"Revered sir," she addressed Homeless. "You both spoke about drinking. So I brought you these children because they are victims of a father's drinking."

She narrated the sad story about her sister whose children she had brought with her.

"They were a family," she continued. "My brother-in-law was the most righteous man in the village. You know what his main entertainment was. When children were small, he gathered them around

589

him at the doorstep of his modest cottage and read to them stories of the past lives of the Buddha. He did it at the door step so that the people in the village could sit in the compound in front of the cottage and listen to him. When he began the story of the Buddha as a wise vizier who saved his king by building a tunnel, the whole village gathered in front of the house to listen to it. It went on for two or three weeks."

"He must be a remarkable man," said Homeless. "We will like very much to see him."

"That's the tragedy, Revered sir. That was all before they opened the village tavern."

It was no doubt a tragic story. He was in prison for life. In a fit of temper under the influence of liquor he had stabbed his wife mercilessly.

"All my sister did was to advise him repeatedly to stop associating with the kind of people with whom he spent every evening at the village tavern. When she could hardly get a square meal for the children, she left home with the children to come to my place. She had no alternative because he hardly brought any money home."

It was all too familiar a story. Returning from the tavern, drunk to his eyes, the man chased the woman and the children until she fell. She was killed before the eyes of the children even while the four-year old clung to her.

Liquor and short temper mixed badly. The readily available kris, which villagers carried, not as a weapon for self-defence but as a useful implement, came too handy. The pointed and double-edged kris was a deadly dagger which had found its way to the Island from Java or Malaya in the days of the Dutch. In my career as a court interpreter, I had heard many a similar story and was, in fact, once angered by a senior police officer's explanation that the offenders were the knife and the short temper. He refused to see the role that liquor played.

Homeless was moved to tears. He agreed to take the two elder children to Colombo to be admitted into an orphanage. He gave the woman the amount raised that day in the village for the promotion of national revival. It was not much. But the woman could feed the two kids for a couple of weeks until Homeless would arrange some regular assistance.

While eating a dinner heated for a second time, he asked me, "Mudaliyar, are you back in the Temperance Movement?"

Was I not ashamed? It had been five months since I had retired. The Government orders no longer applied to me. But my preoccupation with Uncle Victor's files and the daily routine of the icy shower at the Royal Spout, walks to the Seminary and the exploration of its Library had postponed my return to active involvement in the Temperance Movement.

"Don't give me excuses, Mudaliyar," Homeless said sharply. "I will tell you what your real trouble is. Tell me if I am wrong. You are not sure whether the new office-bearers want you and you do not want to get there other than as President."

I was amazed. How right he was! That was my problem even though I did not think of being the President. I was waiting for an invitation from the new Committee.

The dressing down I received on this occasion was not second to what I was given after the wedding of Timothy and Moon-Beam. I listened to him silently. If I was idly mixing my rice with the curries and not taking a morsel to my mouth, it was because I had lost my appetite. Homeless could be a virulent critic and a merciless lampoonist. I heard him through until he returned to his normal self.

"I will see that you get back to the Movement. We have to campaign not only against liquor but also the proliferation of the kris. We should do something about our people's short temper."

"What have you mind?' I asked him.

"How about meditation? A calm mind has no room for sudden anger. We have to get our people back to the temples."

From the next morning, his speeches contained two more themes: the kris and sudden provocation. By the time we concluded the tour of Kandyan hills, our haul of surrendered kris was substantial. I set my mind on designing an all purpose knife which would be less lethal.

III

Returning home in time for the Annual Pageant of the Temple of Sacred Tooth Relic, I found in the mail awaiting me an invitation from Colombo. Ananda College was welcoming Don Baron who was due to arrive on the ninth of August. A letter from USA had a pleasant surprise. Virtue-Servant or rather Vickie Wickie, as he liked to call himself, was arriving in the same ship with Don Baron. With him would be Beckie and their twin babies.

Aunt Flower and Lucy had already come in advance for the Pageant. Leaving them to make arrangements for Virtue-Servant and his family, Slim-Jewel and I drove in our car to Colombo.

"Nice to kill two birds with one stone," I said as I explained our plans to my attentive audience of the five women and Timothy.

"Wonderful, Father, though your metaphor does not reflect your commitment to nonviolence" intervened Moon-Beam and all laughed.

Timothy added, "We will bring our car also so that we can all drive back in comfort."

It was very thoughtful of them and our stay in Colombo was greatly enriched by the partial reunion of the family. While I was busy with the receptions for Don Baron, Timothy assumed the role of a tour guide. Moon-Beam baby-sat to give Beckie the respite she sorely needed as a mother of active toddler twins.

Don Baron was a new man. Invigorated by his exposure to the West, he was bristling with ideas. His speeches reflected his sincerity and his unwavering love for the country. He rode the crest of a wave of popularity. Organizations vied with one another to accord him and his equally popular wife a fitting welcome after their sojourn in England. Over the four days I spent in Colombo, I attended four of them. Apart from a few moments of small talk at each reception, neither Slim-Jewel nor I could have a conversation with Don Baron or his wife. His replies to many speeches of adulation were indicative of a new line of action which he had apparently thought out for himself during his absence from the Island.

"We must work diligently until success takes us to victory," he said. "Unfrustrated by discouragement and lack of satisfaction, we must work and work unceasingly, for there is a power above all those who claim to be in power. That is the overwhelming power of democracy and moral persuasion."

He certainly merited the most enthusiastic standing ovation which the audience gave him spontaneously. Had he chosen a political career for which his training as a lawyer would be a tremendous asset? I asked myself.

We returned to Kandy with ample time to participate in the arrangements to accord them a hearty reception at the Dharmaraja College - the school Don Baron founded under the inspiration and guidance of Colonel Olcott. They had already accepted the invitation of a flourishing businessman to be his house guests. I was given the opportunity to invite them for a meal.

I had several options. It could have been a family occasion specially as I wanted Timothy and Moon-Beam and Vickie and Beckie to meet these inspiring personalities. Both these young couples were getting drawn to public service in a manner that a future dedicated to the good of the people, particularly the down-trodden and disadvantaged, was their primary goal. I could also invite the Government Agent and the judges and show off to my erstwhile superiors that I was hobnobbing with the emerging national leadership. Instead the option I chose was to invite the humble participants in religious, temperance and social service activities. Both Slim-Jewel and I were happy that we had rounded up a goodly fifty fellow volunteers.

"You always think the right thing," complimented Don Baron when he realized that he was meeting many of the people who had extended to him a helping hand. He knew so much about them or their fathers or uncles whom they now represented. By way of a postprandial speech, he addressed the crowd on the importance of national independence. Even Don Baron, at this moment, could not think of a complete breakaway from the British Empire. "Self-government under the benign protection of His Majesty's Government" was how he spelled out his goal. But his explanation of the benefits of self-determination was so comprehensive that Self-rule appeared to be the one and only goal before the nation. Once again, with his choice of words and the utmost sincerity in presentation he won the hearts of these common folk. The ovation was as enthusiastic as ever.

My wish that Don Baron and his wife should come to know our children was fulfilled when the six of them sat at a table in the garden to have their tea. It was an animated conversation in which every one of them was actively involved. That they discussed some things closest to their hearts was evident to any passer-by. I was busy with the other guests and I had no chance to participate in their discussion. It was Beckie who gave me a gist of it later.

"Father, you have an Abraham Lincoln in the making," she said, as she outlined what Don Baron was presenting as his grand design for a new nation. "If ever he achieves one half of what he plans in education, health, transport and communications and political reform, this Island could be a model for many modern nations."

"We can speak for health," joined in Moon-Beam and Timothy, who had become so integrated as a couple dedicated to the common good that they often said the same things in unison. Moon-Beam deferred to her husband and allowed him to continue.

"Father, he is speaking of a system of universal health care, free dispensaries at the village level, rural hospitals in centrally located, bigger villages and a general hospital in every district capital. I asked him about the costs and his answer was exactly what Homeless gives: a greater portion of this country's revenue must be spent right here for its development."

"Father, you know what baffled me?" asked Moon-Beam. "He is a champion of preventive medicine. He speaks of vaccination and immunization of every child by making the failure to do so a punishable offence. He would send parents to jail if that is what is required to save the infants from unnecessary death. He also wants a service of sanitary inspectors to see that the environment is kept clean. You know what he told me, 'Doctor, malaria cannot be eradicated by giving people quinine every morning. That is only a palliative. He have to attack it at the source - the anopheles mosquito breeds in every coconut shell that is thrown by the wayside.' "

"What's more, Father," said my American daughter-in-law." He makes politics look the sanest and the most relevant vocation for any right thinking person and he has won two candidates."

"Yes, Father," said Timothy. "I am almost convinced that I have a role to play."

"I endorse the idea wholeheartedly," added Vickie alias Virtue-Servant .

Late that night after listening to two more speeches of Don Baron, I told Slim-Jewel of the impact that the emerging national leader had made on our children.

"Timothy seems to be fascinated by politics," I told her.

"He is painting on too small a canvas," she said, reminding me that the metaphor had already been applied to me. "He is capable of greater things."

It was not clear as to who had taken the initiative: Homeless or Don Baron? But at the next annual general meeting of the Temperance

Movement of the Central Province, I was elected President by acclamation.

A week later, a newly created organization with an open political agenda elected me as its General Secretary. Its main objective was to agitate for an unwavering adherence to the provisions of the Kandyan Convention by the British Administration. As the centenary of this treaty was only eighteen months away, my task was to set in motion a series of publicity and public relations activities. I began with a public rally which would be addressed by Homeless Dharmapala . If I preferred him to Don Baron it was because I owed Homeless an apology in action for having run away from Kandy when he was invited by Slim-Jewel. I was now a free man with no white officer of the Government telling me what or what not to do.

I also planned something really spectacular for the centenary of the Kandyan Convention or rather the sad and gloomy day when the country as a whole lost its independence for the first time in two thousand four hundred and fifty years of history.

The highlight of 1913 was the appointment of Sir Robert Chalmers as the Governor of the Island. When the news appeared in the papers, I wrote him a letter of congratulations, mentioning in passing that I had pleasant memories of our meeting when he was a student of Professor Rhys Davids. I said that it augured well for the Colony that an eminent Pali scholar of his calibre was entrusted with its government. I concluded the letter with three Pali verses which I composed in praise of his scholarship. I sent the original, care of White Hall in London, and a copy to the King's House in Colombo.

He arrived in Colombo in October and I had the usual printed card acknowledging my message of congratulations. But enclosed in the same envelope was a personal note from the Governor in his own handwriting and an official invitation for a Levee at the King's Pavilion in Kandy in the month of November. In the note he had expressed the desire to renew his Pali studies and to work on a translation of the Middle-length discourses of the Pali Canon. He remembered our first meeting and the information I had sent on his queries on the Story of Josephat and Balaam.

The dress code for the Levee proved to be a problem. Black tail coat or uniform was the rigour. I had the right to wear the black uniform of a Mudaliyar with scabbard and gold linings. I was also entitled to go in the glamorous dress of a Kandyan chieftain. Homeless insisted that I wear the form of national dress that he was advocating - a South Indian cotton cloth draped round the waist and reaching the ankles, a collarless long white shirt reaching to mid-thigh level, an embroidered folded

595

shawl round the neck and open sandals. It had its own elegance despite its simplicity. But its main attraction was its suitability for the humid hot climate. I needed a lot of persuasion to be non-conformist.

"Don't make a fool of yourself, Father," advised Moon-Beam. Timothy, however, was anxious to see what the reaction of the officialdom was.

"All that they can do is to ask you to go home and come back properly dressed," was his argument. "We will have your Mudaliyar monkey kit in the car. You can change into it at our place."

So I modelled Homeless' version of a national dress and had Timothy to drop me and Slim-Jewel at the King's Pavilion. A military officer perfunctorily checked the invitation and intoned in a typical Yorkshire accent "Mudaliyar and Mrs. Tiny Banda Valour-Lion." Being the first one of that title at the party that evening, my sartorial oddity passed off as a uniform. Or so it appeared until I stood before the Governor.

"So this is your new national dress?" he said after receiving Slim-Jewel and me most courteously. "Very apt for the climate."

He had me to turn around to get a better idea of the dress and chatted a while on some of the scholars we knew. He thanked me for the sentiments expressed in my verses and looked forward to being in contact. I was very pleased. Slim-Jewel preened with the attention she received from the ladies in the reception line.

"The new Governor seems to know you well?" queried the Government Agent as I led Slim-Jewel to the middle of the reception hall.

"I met him when he was still a student in England and we used to correspond regularly while he was doing his research."

"Hm..Hm.." drawled the senior official. "You lucky bloke!"

I was rescued from further questioning by an Aide-de-Camp of the Governor. In a snow-white uniform, he towered over the crowd. While Slim-Jewel chatted with some ladies who were interested in her sari and the jewelry, I was taken to a chair at the back of the hall.

"The Governor is very happy that you came," he started. "He is aware of your early retirement to take an active role in politics."

"That would not be exactly correct," I explained defensively. "I would say I have taken up public service. The last thing I want to be is a politician."

"It does not matter what words we use, Mudaliyar. Whether you want to be called a politician or not, the work you are doing whether in temperance or agitation for Self-rule is ultimately politics. You are a great supporter of Homeless Dharmapala and he is no friend of the British Administration."

"But, Captain, he is a loyal subject of the British Crown and admits it in all his writings and speeches."

"So are you, Mudaliyar. But you would any day like every single Britisher in the Island to leave so that the country is run by you people."

"That would be a blatant exaggeration," I countered.

Suddenly it dawned on me that I was being led into a situation where I would have to either defend the campaign for national Self-rule or acquiesce to the indispensability of continued British rule in the country. I tried my best to wriggle out and it came to a point where I had ask him forthright:

"Tell me, Captain, what does the Governor want you to find out about me? Am I invited here as guest or is this your new way of cornering unsuspecting people for a convenient third degree?"

"Oh No, Mudaliyar, not at all," he said waving his hands to emphasize the negation of the charge I levelled against both him and the Governor. "All these questions are merely to satisfy my own curiosity. The Governor only asked me to see that you are well taken care of."

"I hope the Governor's words have no hidden meaning!" I said punning on the expression.

I laughed spontaneously and the Captain joined me and appeared to be relieved. But the conversation left me thinking of the changing perceptions of the Administration on the activities I carried out under the guidance and with the inspiration of Homeless and Don Baron. To them I was a politician to be watched!

"Valour-Lion, beware!" I said to myself as I rescued Slim-Jewel, bade goodbye to the Governor and beat a hasty retreat.

IV

When 1914 began, both Slim-Jewel and I had our hands full. Our house was once again a bee-hive of activity. We had to purchase another car towards which Vickie and Beckie made a generous contribution. It was a joke among the servants that I left in my car when Slim-Jewel came in hers and our only day time communication was what each shouted to the other in that brief moment of meeting.

An outbreak of a cholera epidemic in a nearby estate which had been mishandled at the outset kept Slim-Jewel busy for weeks. Moon-Beam took special leave of absence to volunteer at a burgeoning camp. Once an irate planter had shouted at both of them.

"You have no business to look after the idle people from the village. It's my men and women that bring you the revenue. The next time I see that you get my labourers to stand in line while you look after your --- natives, I will send in my men to tear this place down."

It was then that Moon-Beam rose to her full five feet and looked up into the eyes of the berating planter on horse back and metaphorically fired both barrels. She had to set the record straight. They were not government servants paid from the revenue that the white planter was supposed to be raising for the Government with his imported South Indian labour.

"I am here as a volunteer on unpaid leave of absence, Mister," she told him. "My mother and every one of us here are volunteers devoting our time and energy and running the risk of contracting the dreaded disease ourselves. Besides, Mister, you have no right to trespass in our camp which is in the land of the temple."

"How can you say that I am trespassing when I am rightfully in a territory which belongs to my Majesty the King?"

"For less than a century, Mister. This is our land, the land of our forefathers. Even your estate is in *our* land. I hope you do not want an argument as to who has the greater claim to this place."

"You talk too much, woman. Unless you do what I tell you to do, I will have you removed in a jiffy."

"Look here, Mister," Moon-Beam had shouted back in anger. "Before you do that I will have a bucketful of cholera-infested night soil dumped on your face to see that you crawl here to get some relief."

The enraged Assistant Superintendent raised his whip to punish the puny native woman who had the audacity to threaten him.

598

He was aiming at the face with the intention of disfiguring her. Slim-Jewel, standing by her daughter, was not allowing this to happen. She pushed Moon-Beam aside and took her place. But no whip landed on her. Instead, the planter landed on his back as a frightened horse reared, turned around and galloped away to the estate.

A smiling lad who had instantly become the hero of the camp was still holding on to the fence pole with which he had given a hard blow to the horse's back.

It all turned out well at the end. Moon-Beam rushed to the fallen planter, introduced herself as a medical doctor, applied improvised splinters to set his broken shin bone, put him into her mother's car and drove to the Kandy hospital. Timothy did the surgery and, in spite of the grievous nature of the compound fracture, managed to save his leg.

Two weeks later, a repentant and greatly wisened planter called on Timothy and Moon-Beam with a box of biscuits and a bouquet of flowers.

"It is not me that would have been disfigured if you succeeded, Mr. Harcourt," said Moon-Beam. "You owe an apology to my mother."

Thus did we have a visit which turned out to be very pleasant. He donated five hundred rupees to the Women's Organization and offered to send a box of tea every month to raise funds for her charities.

"You know, Mudaliyar, why I am beholden to your family for ever?" he asked me as he left our home. "Whether I have this leg or not was a decision in the hands of your daughter and son-in-law. They chose the difficult course to save it."

There was, quite visibly, a growing tension between the rulers and the ruled. I was asked by Stanley Williams to see him in Colombo.

"I want to discuss some very confidential matters," his letter said.

It was a pleasure to see him. Since we completed our comparative study of the laws and customs of the Sinhala and Tamil communities, our meetings had been few and far between.

He invited me home to his official quarters in Stanmore Crescent. All the houses on this semicircular road faced a well-kept lawn where the green park benches carried an engraved notice: NATIVES AND DOGS NOT ALLOWED.

I laughed it off as the product of a sick mind. Whenever something like this made my blood boil, I recalled the numerous kindnesses I had received from numerous Britishers commencing with the Blakes and Right Reverend Kenneth Saunders. The list also included Ernest Dickinson and the man I was going to see, Stanley Williams.

"All this will change some day when we regain independence," I said to myself as I rang the bell of a stately two-storeyed building in the middle of a neatly trimmed, large garden.

A servant led me upstairs and Stanley Williams saw me in his well-lit office room. Its windows commanded a view of the park I had crossed gingerly on account of the forbidding notice. I thought of mentioning it to my friend, but rejected the idea as trivial and irrelevant. Apparently, he wanted to discuss more important matters with me. He neither dilly-dallied nor minced words.

"You have been under investigation, T. B. and so is Jayatilaka . Who are your contacts in Germany?"

A war was imminent between Germany and Great Britain, he explained. Some thought that the Germans had prepared for a war for quite some time and one of its strategies had been to undermine the loyalty of British subjects in the Colonies. Don Baron and I had both been invited to address the Oriental Congress in Berlin. I had gone there earlier and the suspicion was that I had made some arrangements with some influential people there.

"Your other brother-in-arms is similarly suspected for being in tow with the Japanese as well as the Germans and the Bolsheviks of Russia. The Police think that Homeless Dharmapala is sending young men to Japan to pursue technical education in the belief that they would return with anti-British ideas. They also think that his association with the Indian Bolshevik M. H. Roy and the German-Indian Party makes him a key figure in Anti-British activities on an international scale."

"You must have some special reason why I should have this information. What I am supposed to do?"

"Let me be frank with you, .T, B," said Williams. "This meeting is not my idea at all. I have been asked to speak to you by someone who admires your contribution to scholarship."

"You mean His Excellency the Governor?"

"Precisely."

I had to explain that all my contacts in Germany were scholars and that no pressure had been exerted by them to do anything disloyal to the British regime. I told him of a young man whom Rheinhold Rost had introduced to me and to whom I have been sending material on early history. He was Wilhelm Geiger, a Pali and Sinhala scholar, who had completed the critical edition of the whole of the *Great Chronicle* and was in the process of translating it into German and English. The first part had been already published in 1912. All he wanted was to develop Sri Lankan Studies as an independent discipline.

Stanley Williams had met him and he agreed with me that scholars of the calibre of Herman Oldenberg, the editor-translator of the fourth century historical epic, the *Island Chronicle*, and Wilhelm Geiger had no political agenda.

"We have yet to clear Don Baron's name as his visit to Germany was more recent," continued Williams. "His contacts are more varied. But all his public statements have hitherto been politically correct."

"I am quite disturbed by what I hear, Sir," I told him. "Why does the great empire feel so threatened by just one country."

"An open war we can win, even if Germany finds allies in the least likely places; but a war of propaganda is another kettle of fish. We are quite vulnerable. Take my own case, Mudaliyar. It did not take too long for me to realize that the people of this Island had an advanced civilization. We had things to learn from you and we did. When men like Homeless parades his statistics, I know that he is right. When Don Baron speaks of education and Temperance, I have to agree with him. Believe me. Every night I ask myself what right I have to govern this country when its nationals can do a superb job if only we leave them the institutions we have built."

He elaborated the situation unfolding in India. He spoke of the success of Annie Besant, the successor of Colonel Olcott as the President of the Theosophical Society. From Theosophy she had moved to politics and was the strongest voice in the Indian National Congress' struggle for freedom.

"All this is a natural sequel to our policy of educating the native population and involving it in the development of new nations. I endorse this policy and so does every right-thinking administrator I know. But we have a problem with a certain war. All that the Governor wishes to know is whether you could talk to the emerging leadership of the country and urge moderation in their campaigns and possibly obtain an expression of their loyalty to the Crown. Could you do the same with the influential monks of the two major seats of learning and the chief prelates in Kandy?"

"That is a lot, Sir. All I can promise is to do my best."

That very night I was able to meet Homeless. He was back in the Island to take charge of his ancestral home and to convert it to a centre of social service. He was even thinking of shifting the Maha Bodhi School to this central location in Darley Road, not too far from the Colombo Railway Junction. He was also engaged in setting up a Free Hospital for which Mary Elizabeth Foster of Honolulu had made a substantial donation.

601

Homeless listened to me carefully. He laughed at some of the innuendos, specially with regard to sending youth to Japan. At the end, he said,

"Do please tell your friend to inform the Governor that I have been and will continue to be a loyal subject of the Crown. But I will continue to agitate to gain the rights of the under-privileged people of this country. But it will be done constitutionally. Tell him further that I will not do anything to embarrass the Administration in the event of a war even if Japan joins hands with Germany. I believe that our country's destiny is best served by gaining Self-rule under the protection of the British monarch."

I had heard him say this in public on many occasions and I knew that he was sincere.

The Principals of Learning-Awakening and Learning-Adornment Colleges expressed similar views as Homeless. They would support anything to make things easy for the new Governor whom they knew from his scholarly work and whose interest in Buddhism they admired.

The meeting with Don Baron was much less smooth. Conscious of his new position as a member of the Bar since he took his oaths as a Barrister on the twenty-third of September 1913, he wished to deal with the matter directly.

"Leave my case to be handled by me, Mudaliyar. I will deal directly with the Attorney General himself. If the Government questions my loyalty, it is *his* responsibility to see that I know the grounds. At least *he* must know that one is innocent until proved guilty."

He recognized, nevertheless, that any war between Germany and Great Britain would necessitate some reconsideration of strategies in both political and social campaigns.

I met Stanley Williams two days later in his office. He was pleased with what I had done. I promised to meet the prelates of the Flower Garden and Horse Peak Monasteries and convey to them the request of the Governor. He agreed with the attitude of Don Baron.

"T. B., that is exactly what I would have said if I was in a similar situation. It is quite possible that we as a nation has become overly scared of this impending war. If the Empire is drawn into a war, it would not be a war just between two countries. It is bound to be the first world war in human history. I dread to visualize the extent of destruction and loss of human life such a war would entail."

I felt sad for men like Stanley Williams who were decent, devoted and dutiful. The very last thing they wanted to do was to join the handful of paranoids in the Administration who would interpret the native people's love for their own country, language, religion or culture as blatantly anti-British. They were few no doubt. But in times of upheaval, theirs would be the only voice heard. I also felt sad for Sir Robert Chalmers, the man of letters with a deep sympathy for things oriental, who had to be the chief executive of this Island on the eve of catastrophe.

My lonely drive to Kandy that afternoon had remained unforgettable because everyone of the worst case scenarios I built in my mind had proved to be correct to the letter. The worst, of course, was the manner in which a war in a distant land might cost me everything I held dear in my life.

I visited the two Monasteries as requested. I met the prelates along with their Executive Committees. They listened to my message, discussed its implications and told me that they would address the Governor direct. I was relieved that my mission was a success.

For the following Sunday I summoned a meeting of all the executive committees in which Slim-Jewel and I were involved. It was a goodly gathering of six dozen men and women whose common bondage was their love for the country and the dedication to serve the people. Taking care not to scare them or to dabble in rumour-mongering, I told them what I did and heard in Colombo.

"By our decision to serve in these various associations and organizations, we have identified ourselves as leaders of action and we have therefore a shared responsibility," I told them at the very start. "The Government had taken the extreme step of violating its own constitution and principles of justice in subjecting to investigation two of the most important men of devoted action like Homeless Dharmapala and Don Baron Jayatilaka , not to speak of myself, because the imminent war with Germany has scared it. Fortunately for us we are clean. We love our country and we want change; we want improvement; we want reform. We are not advocates of anarchy. Our goal is decent and nonviolent, if forceful, dissent and agitation. It will continue until injustices are removed and the common man in the country regains his rights as a free and well cared for human being."

The repeated applause must have had some effect on me. My statement proved to be longer than I expected. But the message I conveyed was simple. We had to lie low in the event of a war. We had to hold back our political agitation until peace was restored.

"This is a promise I conveyed to the Governor. I am convinced such a degree of cooperation with the Administration is to our benefit in the long run. It is even possible - though I do not count on it - that a grateful Administration would recommend political and social reform beneficial to our country."

The discussion which followed was free, frank and fruitful. One of the senior members even asked me whether I was still a Government servant! I had a brief statement on our common position drafted and approved. It was signed by the President and Secretary of each participating organization.

With a letter explaining the action I had taken, I forwarded this statement to Stanley Williams with copies to Homeless care of the Maha Bodhi Society Headquarters in College Square, Calcutta and to Don Baron in Colombo. In a short covering letter to Williams I told him that the Governor might wish to be apprised of what the public organizations of the Central Province had decided.

The Freezer Club, as we now called the early morning regulars at the spout, had missed me during my four day absence in Colombo.The reason was that every morning Walter had come in asking whether I had returned. Even as I was being told how anxiously he was inquiring for me he came.

"We missed you, T. B. Specially I. I need your advice."

We arranged to meet on the following Monday - the day after the dinner meeting with the executive committees.

"Jewel, I am sure you have kept some left-overs for me from yesterday's dinner," Walter teased Slim-Jewel as he came in. He was clad in blue drill shorts and a short-sleeved white drill shirt. He wore white canvas shoes and the ubiquitous solar topee hat.

"That I have, Head Master. But for a moment I thought you had sent one of your teen-age students to tell us that you were not coming. I wouldn't have known what to do with all the sour young jak fruit and fish in sour sauce which I hid away for you."

The good-natured banter lasted the meal which we enjoyed together with Moon-Beam and Timothy. Imperceptibly the conversation drifted to matters serious. I told the rest at table of the action I had taken since the meeting and Walter raised the matter with which he was concerned.

"You know, T. B. that I and my family are all Catholics. My relatives back in the low-country are either Buddhist or Catholic. My own forefathers adopted the religion when the Portuguese were here, suffered immensely under Dutch persecutions, lost all our property under the Dutch law which prevented Catholics from inheritance and survived because the Buddhist king of Kandy not only gave them refuge but even helped them to build churches. So my feelings for our Motherland is as strong and genuine as that of any other Sri Lankan."

"That we know, Head Master, from the care you take of the poor children with neither prejudice nor discrimination," commented Slim-Jewel.

"I have a simple question to ask you both. Why don't you take us into your organizations which are secular in objectives and national in character. We cannot barge in unless we feel welcome."

He reminded us how, in the long struggle for the right to educate children according to the parent's choice of religion, the Roman Catholic Church took sides with Buddhists, Hindus and Muslims against the established Anglican Church.

"Now even that problem does not exist. Your Homeless was correct when he wrote some years ago that the established church would lose much of its interest in evangelic and educational services once the padres are no longer paid by the State. Theirs is a dwindling force. So many of their converts are returning to their ancestral religions. By the middle of this century all Protestant Christian denominations in the Island may amount to only about one per cent. But Catholics, who have gone through baptism by fire under the Dutch, show an increase. We are the most active in education and social services. My idea is that where we can cooperate with you, we should do so. But the call must come from your leaders who must now realize that Buddhism as well as Hinduism and Islam are no longer under Christian threat."

I thanked Walter for the sentiments he expressed so ardently. I invited him to join the Temperance and Literary Movements in which I was active and agreed to send out letters to any potential members he could name.

That night I sat and wrote a long letter to Homeless. If at all, he was the one who would be a bit difficult to convince. As regards Don Baron, it would be a piece of cake. He had always been moderate in his views and since his sojourn in England had become even more tolerant.

While Homeless Dharmapala was away in India, the Administration prosecuted the Printer and Publisher of *Sinhala-Buddhist* for publishing seditious statements and sentenced him to prison for three months. Homeless' response was to court arrest and prosecution. He sent a cablegram to the Inspector General of Police on the fourteenth June 1914:

I HAVE RECEIVED INFORMATION THAT THE POLICE AUTHORITIES ARE GOING TO ARREST ME WHEN I LAND IN COLOMBO. ALL MY WORK SHALL HAVE TO BE POSTPONED IF THE REPORT IS TRUE THAT I AM TO BE

605

ARRESTED WHEN I ARRIVE IN COLOMBO. IF YOU WANT ME PLEASE WIRE AT MY EXPENSE.

The letter of Homeless Dharmapala , enclosing a copy of this cable, contained his response to the matter I had raised in response to the plea of Walter J. Peiris:

"As I approach my fiftieth birthday on the seventeenth of September this year, I have done a lot of rethinking. I shall never compromise my position with regard to the major issues that I fight for: Propagation of Buddhism, National Independence, Educational Reform, Restitution of Buddhist Shrines to Buddhists, Service to the Poor and the Disadvantaged, and Vigilant Protest against Injustice. But I would gladly review my strategies. I am drafting a long statement which I would like to issue some day as my message to the youth of Sri Lanka. With regard to the matter you have raised, this is what my draft document contains:

> *Christians and Buddhists should unite and work for the elevation of the Sinhalese people. Religion should in no way hinder our patriotic activities and it had not prevented Sun Yat Sen, the son of a Chinese Christian, from working for the elevation of the Chinese People."*

The next morning at the Freezer Club, the bathers were amazed by my account of the spirit of tolerance which pervaded the whole letter of Homeless. They wanted to see it and I invited them home. Walter made the rare decision to be late at school.

Over steaming hot cups of tea which Golden Jewel produced in no time, we read and discussed the new spirit of inter-religious dialogue and cooperation to which all of them were committed.

"What a long way we have come," concluded Walter. "The happiest day in our lives will be when we can forget what divides us and look for what unites us. We share a beautiful country. We share a commitment to religion and moral life which each of our religions preaches. When we see the might of irreligion raising its ugly head in the great Russian Tsardom, we have to unite to fight for religion."

The spontaneous applause of fellow bathers was sweet music to my ears.

Walter rushed to his school. The rest stayed behind because Mr. Stream-Spout, the village historian and raconteur of lore, began an analysis of the news trickling into our newspapers from Europe.

"It is ominous, my friends," he said. "A month ago to the date the heir apparent to the Austrian throne was assassinated in Sarajevo and three days ago on the twenty-eighth of July, Austria declared war on Serbia. According to a political analyst that Observer quotes, Russia and Germany are both preparing for war and whenever Germany declares war Britain is bound to join the fray."

I thought of Stanley Williams' own analysis: **This is bound to be the first world war in human history.**

On the fourth of August 1914, Britain declared war against Germany. The opposing camps came to be known repectively as the Triple Entente (Britain and British Empire, France and Russia) and the Central European Powers (Germany, Austria-Hungary and their Allies). By the sixteenth of September all German colonies in Africa were in the hands of the Allies. On the first of November Turkey joined the war, allying with the Central European Powers.

As citizens of a British Colony, we were in the Triple Entente and an active partner in a war which had no meaning or purpose to us. The Administration took quick action. All political activities were suspended. A contingent was sent to the war front. Raising funds through war bonds became a major activity. It became obligatory that support be given materially and it was insisted upon as a demonstration of one's loyalty to the Crown.

Slim-Jewel and I drove to the Provincial Office and bought our war bonds from the Government Agent himself at a public rally that he had organized for the purpose. We were held as exemplary citizens even though our contribution was modest!

V

1915 began with bleak news of a war which was expanding in all directions. Offensives on both sides resulted in insignificant gains and indicated the likelihood of a prolonged war of attrition. Though still far removed from us, the vivid accounts which filled our newspapers in both Sinhala and English portrayed the enormity of the machine of destruction that had been let loose. War had already reached the Middle East. German war ships and underwater U-Boats were expected off the shores of the Island at any moment.

It was depressing to begin each day by reading the lists of the dead and missing. The war was coming nearer home. Among war victims were young men who had once been in the Island or had joined the recent contingents sent out to support the Empire's war effort. Some had been my immediate supervisors in service or friends.

Responding to a Government appeal that the Empire's war effort be helped by a substantial reduction of food imports, our voluntary organizations launched a "Grow More Food" campaign. Walter brought with him a dozen young men from the vicinity of the school to join our activities. Every willing pair of hands was welcome and theirs were unusually competent. The members of the Temperance Movement and the Pavilion of the Muse were invited to participate in a jumble sale organized by the Church in aid of orphans.

The spirit of cooperation spread to other denominations as well. Out of it evolved plans to set up a non-sectarian and non-denominational Social Service League. In appreciation of the new outlook, the Government Agent consented to be its *ex-officio* Patron.

The latter part of January was a worrisome period. Aunt Flower was ill. Twice she had blacked out. But her condition was otherwise stable and did not warrant admission to hospital. Autumn-Moon was ever the dutiful son. He took her to doctors, bought her medicine and visited her every evening to see how she was. Lucy cared for her in every possible way.

The prognosis was that the dizziness and the nausea would soon pass. But it was not to be. She lost weight rapidly and that was not surprising: She had no appetite at all. Some days she took nothing more than a cup of soup with a slice of bread - and that for the whole day. She also had problems with her memory. One morning she had forgotten how to comb her hair. Lucy was frightened when Aunt Flower could not recollect her name.

She must have had a mild stroke, said the doctor. But Lucy was convinced that Aunt was insane or under the influence of a malevolent spirit. She kept on insisting that a witch-doctor of her village could do an exorcism in no time. Aunt Flower also seemed to share this view. A concerned Autumn-Moon wrote to me and Slim-Jewel to take stock of the situation and do the needful.

"Do you believe in Devil Dance as a form of exorcism?" I asked Slim-Jewel.

"Yes," she replied, "when nothing else seems to work."

Lucy's information was correct. Not far from the settlement of the outcastes was the village of drummers - another depressed caste who traditionally cultivated the land donated to the Temple of the Sacred Tooth and provided drummers for the annual pageant in August. I met the village headman who undertook to find the best men of the cult to go to Colombo.

Ten men with their drums boarded the night train in Kandy. Timothy and I set out at dawn in our cars with the two families. It was to be Golden Jewel's first trip to Colombo. She preferred to ride with Moon-Beam to ask questions on the way. For the same reason our two grandchildren opted to ride with their grandparents. It was the pleasantest trip we had made for some time.

When we reached Colombo, almost the whole day was before us. The drummers set out to erect their flimsy altars out of areca nut palms. The "flower stands," as they called these altars, were gaily decked with all kinds of motifs made out of the creamish tender coconut leaf. The pure white areca nut flowers contrasted in size, shape and colour with the rich creamy coconut flowers. The drummers had all the help they needed. Autumn-Moon had brought more than the supplies they had ordered.

Timothy and I thought of visiting Don Baron and Stanley Williams. We intended them to be spectators of the Margosa Rite. It had the reputation of being the most sophisticated ritual based on Kandyan dancing and drumming.

We met the budding national leader as he was leaving his office to go to the courts. We walked with him to the crowded Magistrate's Court.

"I have only to let the Proctor know that I am around here," he said and we proceeded to the tiny tea kiosk for what was for me the sixth cup of tea for the morning. Tea must be quite addictive or we had taken the slogan "Any time is tea time" too literally!

We spoke of many things. The Temperance Movement, the need for a national political movement, the place of religion and the importance of developing a system of informal religious education for Buddhist children who had no access to it in schools, and his own plans for his future.It took quite some time before the conversation veered to the purpose of our unannounced visit to the capital.

"Mind if I come to see it. It is a long time since I last saw the Margosa Rite in Kandy. It is so different in concept and style from the devil-dancing of the south. The drumming leaves its resonance in your ears for months"

"I was about to ask you if you are interested. You and your wife will indeed be most welcome," I said.

We had to circle the Secretariat twice to find a spot to park Timothy's car. The time so spent was opportune. We met Stanley Williams as he was leaving the building.

"In a hurry, I presume?" I asked.

"I will be back in a couple minutes. Taking my daily constitutional in relays - ten times a day between the Secretariat and the King's House. H. E. wants to talk to me about a file."

"Don't worry, Stanley. You do not have to rush back for us. We came to ask you to come to Aunt Flower's home if you are interested in a performance of the Margosa Rite."

"Margosa Rite! Here in Colombo. I would love to and so is someone whom we both know. Can I bring a guest?"

"Yes, indeed. I mean in addition to your wife."

"Even a very important one?"

With time to spare, Timothy and I walked along the beach to the Galle Face Hotel. In surroundings so akin to what we had both experienced in England, we had a quiet lunch of four courses - soup, fish, chicken and rice pudding besides cheese and biscuits and tea. It was rarely that the two of us met by ourselves. We spoke of things that interested men.

"Father, Can I ask you a question? You may remember my telling you about my fascination with politics. Now I have a concrete proposal. Would you give your blessing if I resign my post in the Government, set up my own clinic in Kandy and take an active interest in politics?"

"What exactly do you mean by politics, Timothy?"

"The kind of politics that Uncle Don Baron is talking about. Preparing to take over the nation's Government any day the British find that we are ready for transfer of power."

"Will you serve the people better than you do now? You are a wonderful healer. You are a born doctor. Your steady gentle fingers make you a remarkable surgeon. Have you talked over this idea with Moon-Beam and what does she think?"

"She is your *alter ego*, Father. If I am a born doctor, she is a born patriot. As a relentless propagandist for preventive medicine, she considers her role to be political."

"You mean that she encourages you to be more in the public eye. She is right, son. Our nation needs professionals like you to be active politically."

"Thank you, Father. I will give a month's notice and have myself released at the end of February. I want to start my new career on the second of March, the centenary of the Kandyan Convention symbolizing our loss of independence."

He was referring to the day the last king was deposed and the Hill Kingdom of Kandy was taken over by the British. It was on the second of March 1815. I was deeply moved by what he said. I got up from my seat, walked round the table to his open arms and gave him a warm embrace. He wrapped his arms round me. Both of us had our eyes brimming with tears.

"Son, You have had all this already figured out. May the Triple Gem and the gods protect you. You have my blessings and, of course, my fullest cooperation."

"Father, can I talk to Uncle Don Baron tonight if I get a chance? How would you let Uncle Homeless know about my new mission? I should value his advice and of course his blessings"

"Do certainly talk to Uncle Don Baron. He would love to have you working alongside him. As regards Homeless, he is somewhere between London and Calcutta. We can write to him in Calcutta."

We walked back to the car. Our next stop was Elephant House where we bought enough snacks and soft drinks for the guests we expected in the evening to witness the rare spectacle of the Margosa Rite in Colombo. We returned to Aunt Flower's home.

It had been transformed into a fairy land.

Guests began to arrive a little after eight. A few of Uncle Victor's old colleagues had been invited by Aunt Flower. Don Baron came with his wife and a nephew. Aunt Flower in a white saree was in her best. She was pleased to meet old friends. She fluttered around from group to group. Few would have believed that she was the sick person for whose benefit a major rite of exorcism was about to be performed.

611

The drummers were dressing up in their flowing white costumes with red waistbands. They covered their hairy chests with a mesh of bead ornaments and wore on their arms gold-plated bracelets, shoulder plates and arm bands. Strings of tinkling bells were tied round each ankle. Some covered their heads with simple turbans while several wore elaborate headdresses, called in Sinhala *Ves*, meaning "disguise." This headdress distinguished the consummate masters of the dance.

As the ceremony was due to start after nine, Timothy had ample time to have a long chat with Don Baron. Oblivious to the cacophony of the environment, they discussed what each would like to see happening in the country and how jointly and severally they could make things happen. I watched them from far as I served drinks and snacks to our guests, I could judge the growing convergence of their thinking as each nodded vigorously in the affirmative when the other was speaking. Moon-Beam was amused too.

"Tim and Uncle seem to be taking the world apart and putting it back together again. You know Tim's dream? To make Ceylon the Switzerland of the East."

I wanted to ask her what he meant by it. But the appearance of two constables at the gate obliged me to hand the tray full of soft drinks to Moon-Beam and go to meet them. They had brought me a letter. What a pleasant surprise it was for me and the rest of the family. Aunt Flower was thrilled when I whispered it to her. So was Moon-Beam.

"How did you wangle that?" asked Don Baron and Timothy when I disturbed their tete-a-tete to tell them that we would soon have a special guest.

Timothy and Autumn-Moon busied themselves to get a special seat arranged at the most vantageous point from which the Rite could be observed. A seat on the right was set apart for Don Baron and another for me on the left of the special guest.

Sharp at nine thirty, a car with a crown in place of the number plate stopped by the door. Stanley Williams stepped out as an aid-de-camp, a navy officer in spotless white uniform, opened the door for the Governor.

I received him with the national salutation of clasped hands and shook hands.

"Thank you, Mudaliyar, for your kind invitation. Williams told me that this was a very rare rite and hardly to be seen in a city. He convinced me that I would never have a chance to see it if I did not avail myself of this opportunity."

"Your Excellency, we are privileged to have you here with us tonight," I said by way of response.

I introduced Aunt Flower and the rest of the family. Don Baron needed no introduction; nor did Autumn-Moon who had been instrumental in organizing the Bar Association reception for the Governor on his assumption of office.

We took our seats and, until the conch-blower announced the beginning of the ceremony, we spoke of our earlier meetings and the state of oriental learning.

"One thing I would like to achieve in my tenure of office is to lay the foundation for a full fledged university in the Island with special focus on oriental learning. I have already sent my despatch on the subject."

I thanked him for his initiative and told him of my experience with Jaffna College.

Aunt Flower sat with the ladies between two flower stands. She was covered from head to foot with a white cloth. The drumming and chanting commenced. The sound seemed to waft towards us from far away. Gradually the noise level rose and we were engulfed with the powerful rhythm of the different drums which, singly and collectively, produced a tremendous effect. Unobtrusively the dancers stepped between the drummers and the patient. What virtuosity!

What graceful blending of figure and movement! Drummers and dancers weaved together and what a feast it was for eyes and ears! Drummers dialogued with one another with such tantalizing variations in rhythm and resonance: The dancers kept pace: The louder the drums the more vigorous the dance. What perfect concentration on the part of the drummers and the dancers! To them as well as to the spectators there was nothing else in the world. Everyone's mind was drained of all it contained and only the strikingly plentiful sensory messages seemed to dominate. We were totally immersed in a Rite, as old as history, and nothing else mattered.

The stamina of the performers was astounding. The performance continued until midnight before the drumming relaxed and dancers withdrew behind the flower stands. It was no relief. The eye and the ear demanded more. They longed for the resumption.

"Mudaliyar, this is simply fantastic," said the Governor. "It is one thing to read about the Margosa Rite and yet another to see it. These men must be the best connoisseurs of the art."

Don Baron, whose speciality had been the explanation of national culture to anyone who wanted to learn, took over from me and gave Sir

613

Robert Chalmers a detailed account of the origin of the Rite, its history and its magical or psychological significance.

While the drummers and dancers relaxed, the medicine-man sat in front of Aunt Flower and performed a series of ceremonies in which incantations were repeated and acts of contagious or sympathetic magic performed. The Governor and Stanley Williams took copious notes and asked Don Baron to translate the incantations. To both of them, the Margosa Rite was a subject worthy of detailed study.

Drumming and dancing resumed.It was not a mere repetition of the first session. Variations were subtle but noticeable. A mellowness in drumming and a graceful lassitude in the dancing were striking. Yet they controlled the spectators and the effect on the patient was fabulous. The performers seemed to enjoy what they did. They beat their drums and danced in utter abandon.That session lasted nearly three hours.

A relaxed Governor mingled with the people asking questions and sharing his impressions. It was almost dawn when he with the Williams bid us farewell and departed. The posse of constables who had guarded the house during his presence left with him.

The ceremonies continued until sunrise. The medicine-man conducted the closing ceremonies. He read signs like the freshness of lime leaves and reddish tint on the lime fruit which were cut. Without a trace of doubt, he declared that the evil spirit which had taken control of Aunt Flower was banished to the further end of the universe.

A smiling Aunt acknowledged her perfect recovery. All were satisfied. That included those who had come to see some really authentic Kandyan drumming and dancing. No one was disappointed. It was an exceptional treat as the Governor, the erudite scholar of Buddhist literature and oriental culture, said several times before his departure. Don Baron and his wife stayed behind to have breakfast.

"It is wonderful that we have a man of learning to represent his Majesty the King in our country. What a gesture of friendship and what keenness to learn our culture! I hope he stays with us long enough to set up the University he proposes and to help us to advance faster towards Self-rule," he told me, Timothy and Autumn-Moon.

"I hope he will," said the young but hard-boiled lawyer of the family rather sardonically.

"Why do you sound so pessimistic?" asked Timothy.

"We have first to see how reacts to a crisis"

VI

The first thing Timothy did on his return to Kandy was to resign from his post. It was accepted by the Government with an officious letter which spelled out conditions. He would not be entitled to a pension and if he decided to rejoin he would be treated as a new recruit. If he expected a word of thanks for the services he had rendered outside the call of duty, he would have been disappointed. He was given his accumulated leave but that was his right and not a favour. He looked forward to getting his clinic working as soon as possible. But it was not to be.

On the fourth of February, the whole family including Golden Jewel left at dawn to the Temple of the Sacred Tooth. Slim-Jewel had undertaken the morning offering to celebrate my fifty-seventh birthday. It was very thoughtful of her to do it. The two prelates were there in the sanctum sanctorum to bless me. The prelate of the Flower Garden Monastery spoke a few words in praise of my services. He had a special word for Timothy.

"I have asked a rare man of vision and dedication to come here to meet you, Doctor. We want to bless both of you together because we expect you to work together."

Thus was Albert Land-Frontier introduced to Timothy. As they stepped forward to receive the prelates' benediction, they looked twins. Not only did they look alike, tall, slim and fair-complexioned, but they had dressed alike in snow-white satin drill suits. Young and energetic, Albert was a consummate orator in both English and Sinhala. He had recently founded a political movement which was named "The Three Sinhalas". The name was meant to signify that Kandy from where he inaugurated his movement was the meeting place of the three ancient parts of the Island, namely, Northern, Southwestern and Southeastern Divisions, called respectively the Region of the King, the Region of the Heir Apparent and Ruhuna. I had met him on many occasions as he supported the Temperance Movement and the work of the Women's Organization. He was a charmingly brilliant conversationalist, full of humour.

The prelate of the Flower Garden Monastery spoke enthusiastically of Timothy's plans to become active in politics and urged that he joined hands with the local leaders like Albert. The prelate of Horse-Peak Monastery sounded a little more cautious. He explained that the Sangha by tradition was either impartial or tilted, when needed, toward the reigning monarch. He welcomed Timothy's decision, adding as a proviso,

615

"Whenever the British in their wisdom decided to confer Self-rule to the people of the Island, there should be experienced statesmen to take over the administration."

There was no reason why we had to hurry back home. We invited Albert Land-Frontier to join us at a downtown restaurant for breakfast. The kids welcomed the treat with a unanimous ovation.

"I am glad that you chose stringhoppers and coconut gravy rather than bacon and eggs at the Queen's Hotel," he said accepting our invitation readily.

It was an opportunity for Timothy to plan his debut into active politics.

"What a coincidence, Doctor," said Albert. "You have a ready-made forum in our celebration or rather the sad commemoration of the hundredth anniversary of the loss of freedom. We want to take an oath to continue to agitate until this fair island of ours is back in our hands."

The occasion had already been planned in great detail. The new leadership of the nation were to be fully represented. W. A. de Silva, Don Baron and the Senanayaka Brothers were all invited as guest speakers. Albert was only too ready to assign to Dr. Timothy de Lanerolle, the newest member of the "Three Sinhalas," the enviable task of moving the draft resolution embodying the Organization's objectives, strategies and plan of action.

"Are you not lucky, Timothy?" I asked him.

"Yes, indeed. I am so happy, Father."

It was almost noon when we returned to Royal Spout. My Freezer Club members had surprised me with an inscribed cake. The gardener stood plaintively at the door and in his hand was a telegram. I slit open the telegram and read it twice before the message sank in.

"Jewel, Aunt Flower is dead," I was hardly able to say before a growing lump in my throat choked me. I sat on a chair burying my face in my hands to cry. Aunt Flower had been my closest relative. There was no part in my life as far as I could remember when she had not played the most decisive role in my growing up. She had been a mother, a sister, a friend and confidante, my counsellor *par excellence* and above all our guardian angel. Her optimism and humour had seen me through many a crisis in life. What would my life have been without her? What would it now be without her?

The sad news shocked all of us. Barely ten days ago Aunt Flower was in her usual buoyant spirit after what we took for a successful exorcism. That she was happy during the last days of her life was a solace.

On the night of my fifty-seventh birthday, we were back in Colombo to pay our last respects to a person who meant everything to both me and Slim-Jewel.

As the pyre was lit and the flames engulfed the coffin, a stabbing pain pierced my heart. Advanced in age myself, I felt orphaned and alone in a cruel world. She was my last link with the generation that fashioned my life.

The excitement over Timothy's debut as a politician served to some extent as a distraction. Slim-Jewel and Moon-Beam suggested that the visiting dignitaries and some of the local leaders be invited to our home for dinner after the rally. Albert Land-Frontier approved the suggestion and despatched invitations. Timothy and I were entrusted with getting a temporary hall constructed and appropriately decorated. I remembered how a similar structure was constructed for my higher ordination. The Kandyan decorative motif, the variegated "wave-bridge" in cloth, had no competition. We had the best men in the District to decorate the hall.

From early morning on the second of March, trains and buses disgorged thousands of people, young and old, who came from all over the Province to observe the hundredth anniversary of the loss of independence. Albert's inscrutable propaganda mostly through word of mouth had been exceedingly effective. The crowds were orderly. There were no untoward incidents. The heavy Police presence added to the gravity of the occasion. Sellers of ballads printed on large sheets had a field day. Their theme centred on the alleged lament of an old woman who witnessed the last king of Kandy being led away as a prisoner of the British:

> *Luckier are you, O tiny ants*
> *For you have a king*
> *While we have none;*
> *Hence do we weep.*

The balladeers sang of heroes of recent years. The scholar-monks and debaters, Madame Blavatsky and Colonel Olcott, Homeless Dharmapala and the rising generation of leaders were all mentioned with glowing tributes to their courage and sagacity. The dignitaries due to arrive in Kandy for the occasion were duly praised. I had reason to be self-conscious. I figured in their eulogies as the "Hero of Kandy, the embodiment of its conscience."

"That's overstating it," I told Slim-Jewel.

"Who are you to decide that?" she asked in mock seriousness.

617

The rally was an immense success. Speakers were brilliant. They held their motley audience spell-bound. But every speech was politically correct - Self rule under the benign guidance of His Majesty the King of England and Emperor of India to whom was expressed unwavering loyalty. Such subtle nuances, of course, were lost on the semi-literate villagers who were there out of sheer curiosity. If numbers could impress the rulers that the masses wanted Self-rule as much as the leaders, they had ample evidence.

Timothy had been agonizing for days on his having to speak in English to his own people. But he was not alone. Many of the leaders were more at home in the foreign idiom than in their own. Intimidated by scholars who spoke on these occasions a highly Sanskritized formal Sinhala, most of the Western educated people demurred when it came to speaking in the mother tongue, in which they were quite fluent. One had only to overhear them speaking to their servants at home or better still to their labourers in the workplace. Invariably their command of the juiciest invectives was enviable.

I had told Timothy not to speak to the dignitaries on the stage but to see straight into the eyes of a single man or woman in the middle of the crowd and address his thoughts just to that one person. I was taught this little trick of effective public speaking by Reverend Kenneth Saunders and what an effective speaker of Sinhala or Bengali he was!

Timothy was asked to present the resolution of the "Three Sinhalas" just after the two prelates had delivered their addresses. To everyone's surprise but to the delight of the monks on the stage and the milling crowds, he began in Sinhala and read the resolution in a simple rendering I had drafted. Of course, no one knew that the text he read was written not in the script of which he was still not very sure but in Roman characters with appropriate diacritical marks.

In the audience, he spotted the eager eyes of Golden Jewel and made her his one-woman target for a brilliant, if rather halting, analysis of the importance of moving to the world-acclaimed principle of a "Government of the people, by the people, for the people." He switched into English and with incredible fluency repeated his eulogy of democracy and independence.

He referred to his younger brother-in-law, Professor Vickie Wickie, who had convinced him that the United States of America was justified in its revolution against the British Empire on the ground of "No taxation without representation." It was a pity that much of his arguments were lost in an inept translation. Perhaps his body language convinced the crowd that he was a fighter and what he said was

618

weighty. There was a resounding ovation and those on the stage reached out to shake his hand as he resumed his seat.

I was proud. But a lurking thought nagged me,

"Goodness me, the neophyte forgot the safety net!"

The spirit of the rally was duplicated in the richly decorated dining hall in the compound of our home at Royal Spout. To everyone present, and that was almost the entire leadership of the growing political movement of the nation, Timothy was the hero. They congratulated him on his brilliance and sincerity.

"You know, Doctor, what I liked most in your speech," said the Editor of *Sinhala-Buddhist*, the ebullient novelist Piyadasa Sirisena. "It wasn't namby-pamby. Let it be an example to the others. One need not be so cowed down by the Administration as to repeat *ad nauseam* their hypocritical pledges of loyalty to the Crown."

That, to me, was the safety net he forgot. We had talked about it and Timothy had no objection. I regretted that I had declined Albert Land-Frontier's invitation to propose the vote of thanks. I told him that I wanted Timothy to have his day. But if I was the last speaker, I could have made amends on behalf of both of us.

I consulted Don Baron on how serious the omission was.

"Mudaliyar, there will be thousands in Britain who will fight to guarantee the freedom of Timothy to say what he had to say in whatever manner he chose to say it. You know they have a Speaker's Corner in Hyde Park. Anyone can go there and speak on any subject. They attack the monarchy. They criticize the Government - some of them most virulently. The Police are there, not to stop them speaking but to ensure that crowds are not unruly and that all have a chance to listen."

"If so, why do all of you make a fetish of avowing loyalty to the crown?" asked Timothy.

"For the benefit of the small men sent here to run the country," said Don Baron with a shrug of both shoulders.

"What do you mean, Sir?"

"Timothy," continued the budding statesman, "from the Governor right down to the pettiest officer in the Government, they are convinced that they are here to safeguard the interests of their monarch who rules over an empire over which the sun never sets. They are dismayed that the people they rule do not appreciate the sacrifices they have personally made to come all the way to the backwaters, leaving behind their loved ones and a life style of greater ease and comfort."

"I thought they came because they get the thrill of lording it over people - a thing they cannot do in England."

"You are perfectly right, Timothy. But they do not know that we know it. They may whine about the heat and humidity, the flies and mosquitoes and stupid natives. But what bothers them when we ask for Self-rule? It is not that they have so much trust in the House of Commons as the only capable legislature. Their fear is that this Island will no longer have a place for them. They look at the jobs they lose, the opportunities of success that may never come their way. This Island is a far better place than most of the duty stations available to them. They are seated on a well-padded branch and they do not want us to cut it. What we do is to assuage them and they are lulled into confidence. Their despatches to London praise us as a nation with the right attitude and support progressive increase of the share of responsibility assigned to us in the Government. So, as your Father says, play the game, Timothy. Play the game."

A few others joined our group and we discussed the changing profile of the British officials.

"In 1817," quipped the local historian Stream-Spout whose authority on the Kandyan Period of the Island's history was widely recognized, "every Englishman right down to the footmen of the Army had precedence over the most respected Provincial Governor. So the riots took place. Now the tables are turned. Education and wealth had made many a native equal or superior to most of the expatriate British. Young civil servants are the most affected. Native officers and clerks working under them dress better and live in luxurious homes. And some like you, Mudaliyar, have cars they can hardly afford. They see you driving in style when they are being hauled by a sweating rickshaw-puller. It must be hurting them."

"Does that mean that there will be riots again?" someone asked.

"No. Not for them to reassert themselves. But if ever there are riots, you can rest assured that the Administration will exploit every opportunity to harass the majority community."

Before Stream-Spout could go deeper into his theory, Slim-Jewel announced that hoppers were being made and the guests could help themselves directly from the hopper-makers' pans.

The dinner was sumptuous. The conviviality of the guests made the family very happy. Timothy was in high spirits. It was as it had to be.
It was his day.

After all the guests left and Don Baron and his wife retired to the guest room, I wrote two letters to Middle Banda and Rose in Burma and

Vickie and Beckie in Illinois, USA. They contained lengthy accounts of the day's happenings.

"It's very late, Father. Why don't you sleep?" asked Moon-Beam, who brought me a freshly brewed cup of tea.

"Not until I tell your two brothers the big news about Timothy."

"You are so thoughtful, Father." she said, "I don't know who would keep us together if you were not there."

The third month almsgiving in memory of Aunt Flower was on the fourth of May. We went to Colombo a few days in advance and set about making preparations. As usual the men had less to do than the women on these occasions. Timothy and I found much time on our hands. I coached Timothy in Sinhala and taught him some secrets of indigenous oratory. He was keen to become an effective speaker in the national language - already a *sine qua non* for success in politics.

We also planned to see people - scholar-monks, authors, journalists, political activists and friends. Even though it was not intended, each of these meetings gave Timothy the kind of insights which would serve him in his new career as a politician. National problems were discussed from various angles. But all proffered the same solution. As each proposed and praised Self-rule, I could discern the indelible mark which the persistent campaign of Homeless Dharmapala had made on the intelligentsia. No wonder that he was feared so much by the Administration!

Stanley Williams got us a brief interview with the Governor. He thanked me profusely for enabling him to witness the Margosa Rite at Aunt Flower's home and once again expressed his condolences on her death. He congratulated Timothy on his decision to play a direct role in the development of the country. We spent the rest of the time talking about the Governor's plans to have a University established in the Island. He was very cordial and even introduced us to a Member of Parliament with whom he was due to have a luncheon meeting.

"Mudaliyar Valour-Lion is a remarkable scholar and I envy the reputation he has gained internationally," Sir Robert Chalmers, the Governor, said. " His son is in the Indian Civil Service and is a judge in Burma. This young man is a surgeon, an Honours Fellow of the Royal College of Surgeons. He has just resigned from Government Service and announced his intention to take an active part in politics."

"Excellent!" interjected the Parliamentarian after each sentence. He shook hands with us.

"It's men like you who have convinced me already. This country should eventually be entrusted to its own leaders, subject, of course, to guidance and protection by the Empire," he said.

VII

The almsgiving was a sad occasion. Most of the monks who attended it were my class mates or contemporaries at Palace Hill. Now they were senior monks with their own temples and pupils. Autumn-Moon whose familiarity with rites and customs of the ceremony was minimal, was guided by Slim-Jewel. I had to translate for him the speeches of the monks and he was deeply moved by what they had to say about his mother. He requested us to prolong our stay and help him to dispose of Aunt Flower's belongings so that the house could be put up for sale.

Almost the whole month of May was spent in Colombo. Moon-Beam returned to Kandy for short spells to keep abreast of her work but returned to be with us. Slim-Jewel worked methodically making lists, identifying things to be given away as charity and those to be sold, and setting aside the valuables on which Autumn-Moon's decision was needed.

Timothy and I helped when things had to be arranged or shifted about. But for the most part we were out meeting an increasing circle of people whose insights and experience could be of benefit to Timothy. In this manner we had met practically every important figure in the national and religious revival and Temperance Movement. That included the Senanayaka Brothers, F.R., D.C. and D. S., Dr. W. A. de Silva, E. W. Perera, the brothers of Homeless and the Editor of *Sinhala-Buddhist*.

We also met several times a lawyer with a flair for the drama. We had no way to see any of his dramatizations. It was a pity. But our mission in Colombo was in connection with the death of Aunt Flower. It would have been a gross breach of propriety if we sought to entertain ourselves.

John de Silva, the playwright dramatist, belied his foreign name. He was a genuine patriot. He produced his plays with a purpose. It was his contribution to the rising sentiments of patriotism in the country. His songs were on Buddhism and the glory of Sri Lanka. The lilting song with the refrain

Knowers of the mass of the Buddha's serene teachings
For ever with dedication guard noble virtues

was a popular hit. It indeed was a haunting lyric bringing to life the splendour of the ancient capital of Anuradhapura with its lovely ponds brimming with lotus and water-lily and a wealth of aquatic birds. The theme of the play was the story of the pious king who sent his own head to his usurper so that the wanton killing of look-alikes would stop.

"It's a pity that drama and music were discouraged by the monks." lamented John de Silva. "I find them the most effective media to teach the masses."

He briefed Timothy on what needed to be done to promote the cultural advancement of the nation. He made a good impression on the budding politician.

"I never realized that our cultural specificities are what set us apart from the rest of world and give us an identity, foster cohesion and promote creativity. All this time I thought that all we needed were science and technology, modern agriculture, engineering and foreign languages."

"We live to learn, Timothy. don't we?" was the lawyer-dramatist's laconic response.

Moon-Beam returned from Kandy on the twenty-sixth of May. She brought the two children. Our plan was to spend the next day to see how the thrice holy day of the Buddhists which marked the anniversary of the birth, the enlightenment and the death of the Buddha was celebrated in and around the capital. Then we would drive leisurely in our two cars to Kandy and give the children a chance to see how the holy day was celebrated in rural and semi-urban areas.

In my youth Vesak, as the fullmoon day of May was called after the Sinhala name of the month, was strictly observed as a day of religious observances. But it was fast becoming a colourful festival, modelled in many ways on Christmas.

The burgeoning commercial culture had introduced new elements which enhanced the gaiety and the festivity of the occasion. Whereas a string or two of pennants and a row of clay lamps with tiny swaying flames fed by coconut oil were the traditional decorations, the candle-lit Chinese lanterns and bright-coloured paper "buckets" had become ubiquitous. Vesak greetings were exchanged and brightly illustrated cards with inspiring messages came to the stores several months in advance. Vesak carols were sung either by groups on foot or by singers who rode beautifully decorated and illuminated floats. The "Vesak Chariots" as these floats were called were either motor-driven or drawn by oxen. On the Vesak eve thousands of people flocked to cities and towns and sauntered the streets seeing decorations and carols. It was what we had arranged to do that night with the two children.

Garishly painted and illuminated "pandals" were an innovation. These were actually called archways and ordinarily were set up across roads as a symbol of welcome. The more traditional ones were made of the trunks of coconut and areca nut palm and decorated with motifs made of the the butter-coloured tender leaves and flowers of the coconut and the snow-white flowers of the areca nut. Bunches of green and red coconuts were tastefully hung to lend colour and fullness.

The new fangled structures were not necessarily archways straddling a road.They did not even look like archways. They resembled huge architectural follies on which were hung large panels depicting scenes from the life of the Buddha or one or more of his previous lives. Over the last few decades, the pandal had become a hallmark of religious identification for the growing class of successful Buddhist merchants. Jointly and singly they vied with one another to create the best-rated pandal.

The criteria ranged from the religious and educational significance of the theme, the quality of the paintings and the beauty of the whole structure to visual tricks one generated with thousands of blinking coloured bulbs. One tried to get the most commanding location for one's pandal. Around each pandal were organized such activities as sermons, recitations, musical performances and the offering of refreshments. To attract and retain the crowd for the longest possible time in front of one's pandal was everyone's objective. If one thing distracted the visitors, it was the ear-splitting din of the dynamos which generated electricity!

Alms halls were set up at regular intervals. Meals and refreshments were served in them, not necessarily to the poor and the needy. Any one in need of a meal or a drink was welcome. Invariably each alms hall had its little pandal, however modest.

Equally popular with sight-seers was another form traditional Vesak decorations which bore the prosaic appellation "Vesak cages." Made of bamboo strips and Chinese tissue paper, these could be as small as one or two cubic feet or as big as a three storied house. In fact, Timothy's research on worthwhile decorations for our tour had enabled him to locate two sites where fabulously huge and magnificent "Vesak cages' had been constructed. Each was said to be forty to fifty feet high. One had a square base while the other was octagonal. Four and eight full grown bamboos carried progressively reducing replicas of the base in the most ingenious manner. The people who made them and decorated them with paper cut-outs and tassels had worked over them for many months.

We started the day with visits to several temples. The first among them was where my colleague in robes, Venerable Noble Son of Wisdom, once resided. The school he set up there was flourishing. So

624

was the temple which housed a fair number of monks. We were there to see hundreds of devotees in white, milling into the shrine to observe the Eight Precepts. Colombo was shifting south-wards. Once deserted Cinnamon Gardens and Ant Settlement were becoming a prestigious quarter and there the affluent classes were building fabulous houses.

Galle Road was fast becoming the artery of a growing commercial district. Two Hindu temples vied with Christian churches which lined it. New Buddhist temples - though relatively modest - were being established in cross roads to which people were moving from the south. Our visits to several of these new temples showed how the social characteristics of the southwestern coast of the Island were being replicated in the capital.

Small temples proliferated and eked out a difficult existence. Each occupationally determined caste in the traditional social organization of the Sinhalas wished to have its own temple. It was a pity that parochial considerations vitiated every effort to pool resources and develop viable institutions. I remembered the valiant effort which Colonel Olcott made decades ago to bring monks of different sects together. I recalled how I had once thought of dedicating myself to the task of unifying the Buddhists. It was before I became a layman and lost myself in the day-to-day tasks of raising a family, earning a living and playing leader.

We drove into the Mount Lavinia Hotel for snacks and chose a table overlooking the sea. The kids were thrilled to slide down to the beach below and clamber up the cliff. Lucy and Golden Jewel watched them nervously. A blue sea under a bright sun spanned up to the city of Colombo in the north.

I felt a tinge of sadness and a stabbing sensation in my heart. Is this the last time I would see this splendour? I asked myself. It was so ominous. But I had no explanation for this uneasy feeling.

We spent the rest of the afternoon looking at the two gigantic Vesak "cages' in a southern suburb of Colombo and drove into to the city by dusk. We visited practically everyone of the more important pandals. We took them at a leisurely pace. Lucy and Golden Jewel were enthralled by the riot of colour, light and music. Kids showed a keen interest in the themes. Slim-Jewel played the proverbial grandmother explaining to them the finer points in each story. Timothy made notes to write an article to the papers. I had the double pleasure of seeing how the Buddhist renaissance manifested itself outwardly with so much fervour and devotion and watching the more intimate part of my family enjoying a day out with me. We wound up the day by dropping into an

625

alms hall conducted by some friends and experiencing the sheer fun and delight of emulating the hundreds who came there for a free meal.

We laughed all the way home calling one another some familiar nicknames given to people who over-eat simply because the food was free.

Although we returned home well past midnight, we planned to leave for Kandy early morning. We were invited to the Royal Monastery of Kelaniya, six miles to the east of Colombo, where, at the instance of Don Baron, Timothy was expected to speak to the devotees. We reached the shrine punctually and were received by the Chief Monk whom I knew from our days as students in the rival institutions the Leaning-Awakening and Learning-Adornment Colleges. But we had remained friends because we had a common interest in education as the engine of national revival.

Thousands of devotees who had observed the eight precepts overnight were seated around the Tree of Enlightenment. The Chief Monk led Timothy to a little platform from which he was to address the crowd. Before his speech, the monk administered to the devotees the regular Five Precepts by which the rigour of the more stringent set of precepts was relaxed. Now the devotees could return to their household lives without abstaining from sexual conduct, adornments, entertainment, eating after noon or using high and large seats and beds.

Timothy had agonized about the speech over the last couple of days .

"These people would have fasted for over eighteen hours and had no sleep", he told me. "What statement of mine in my poor halting Sinhala would justify the harassment?"

"Ask yourself frankly," I admonished him. "What's it that really bothers you? Standing between them and their well-deserved breakfast and rest? Or your diffidence at speaking in Sinhala?"

"You are very right, Father. It is the latter which looms larger."

"Well then, Son. Speak of freedom: The indispensability of freedom, if you will."

Standing besides the Chief Monk admonishing the devotees to observe the five precepts diligently, Timothy looked anxious to make his speech. He commenced well. I think he spoke to me. His eyes were fixed on mine.

"The Buddha taught us a Path of Freedom," he began. "What actually is Freedom? What did you do as soon as the Chief Monk lifted the burden of Eight Precepts from your shoulders? You changed posture, straightened your bent legs, loosened the wrap-around from your shoulders and audibly heaved sighs of relief."

Elaborating the imagery of devotees enjoying the freedom from a life of rigour, he outlined the goals and process of spiritual liberation. I was impressed not only by his depth of understanding of Buddhism but also the manner in which he was able to argue his points in clear colloquial Sinhala. He wound up his excellent expose with an allusion to other freedoms and hoped that the day would not be too far away when the destiny of the people of the fair Island would be determined not by foreigners, however competent and sympathetic, but by nationals dedicated to the welfare of the people.

Released from the semi-monastic discipline of the eight precepts, the devotees gave Timothy a resounding ovation. Don Baron who was seated among them quite unobtrusively stepped forward to congratulate him.

"Well done, Timothy." he said. "Well done. Freedom from slavery. Freedom from suffering.

That was a good start for the twenty-eighth of May. We drove through villages and small towns stopping briefly where a Pandal or a Vesak "cage" merited attention. Even the most modest hut had a row of pennants to mark the holy day and rows of clay lamps ready on oil-stained stands of split areca nut palms to be lit at dusk. White clad devotees moved between temples and their homes in measured steps. The serenity and peace which pervaded were beyond words.

We crossed the little bridge over the Great Stream at the Great Forest Falls without making our usual stop-over to see the thousands of bats hanging upside down on the branches of trees like oversized fruits. It was too holy a day to disturb them for the mere fun of seeing startled and screeching creatures flutter around aimlessly with sun-blinded eyes. We also had another reason.

A monk was beckoning to us. He appeared to be in a flurry and needed our help badly. This was a village in which the Buddhists were actually a minority. A Buddhist monk in a crowd of shaven headed, sarong-clad Muslims was indeed a rarity. I signalled to Timothy in the second car and pulled over to the shoulder of the road.

"What great fortune that you should be driving up to Kandy at this particular time," the monk said even before I could step out of the car and greet him according to tradition. "Something terrible is going to happen. Can I ride with you to Kandy."

Slim-Jewel did not hesitate. She got out of the car and joined Golden Jewel in the rear seat. The monk sat on my left and we resumed

627

our journey. He elaborated his apprehensions. His accent was a bit too strong and some words were wrongly pronounced. I attributed the strangeness of his speech to his excitement and fear and did not think of it any more.

"From early morning, hundreds of young men from Great Forest Falls went to Kandy. That is nothing unusual.They do it every time there is something in Kandy, specially when the August Pageant takes place. It is the only time these young people living in the highly segregated Muslim society get to mingle in a mixed crowd and have some innocent excitement poking fun at girls. We have all done it in our young days. Haven't we?"

"Yes, we have, Venerable Sir. But what is the terrible thing that you portend this time?"

"They are not going to mingle in the crowds. They have been summoned to the main mosque in Kandy to protect it."

"How do you know that?" I asked him.

"There is a young man who is keen on becoming a native physician. He is studying the Unani system of medicine of Arabic origin. But he also wants to study our traditional system - the Science of Longevity. So he comes to the temple to study Sinhala and Sanskrit. He had been in the mosque last Friday. The lay priest, the Maulana, had made the announcement."

"What exactly had the Maulana said?"

"I do not know. My student was very frightened of reprisals in case he was caught giving me information.. He only said that they were going to stop the desecration of the mosque by Vesak carol singers."

I understood the implications of what the young student was said to have told the monk. It had been a recurrent issue between the Muslims and the Buddhists. I had intervened on several occasions when I served as the head of the Native Department in the Provincial Office. The Muslims wanted Buddhist processions to pass their mosques in perfect silence on the ground that tom-toms and music disturbed their prayers. As they prayed five times a day, there was no window for an exception to be made. The Buddhists asserted that their institutions had predated mosques and the traditional ritual could not be changed to suit a new comer's demand. Whenever the Administration tried to intervene, the Buddhists asked for a compromise. Would the mosques in turn agree not to announce the prayer times from the minaret? The early morning call for prayer and the traditional rites of the Temple of the Sacred Tooth coincided to the minute. I could never see the end of this squabble.

I recalled the Government Agent Stanley Williams ending a frustrating effort at reconciliation with the sharp statement,

"Yes, I agree that the majority should be tolerant. But the minority should not provoke. You cannot have it both ways."

The monk's account of the mobilization of the Muslim youth was amply borne out when we reached the Railway Station of the Sword-taking. Shaven headed young men, with the unmistakable handkerchiefs tied around their foreheads, outnumbered the villagers taking their children to show them the Vesak decorations in Kandy.

"Why are you going to Kandy, Venerable Sir? What do you plan to do?"

"To undo a foolish move on my part, if nothing else."

My effort to get any more information was in vain. The monk became uncommunicative. His hissing self-deprecations uttered *sote voce* revealed a disturbed mind. I had to do some thinking myself.

Despite the monk's protests, I turned into the Police Station at the south-eastern edge of the town. I wanted Timothy to continue with sight-seeing in Kandy. But Slim-Jewel insisted on remaining with me.

The officer in charge of the Police Station was a Burgher Inspector. All the staff he had was a posse of Malay constables under a Malay sergeant. The Inspector had seen me in the courts and he was polite.

"What can I do for you, Mudaliyar?"

I told him what I thought needed to be done. The rank gave him little autonomy. He had to ask his superiors in correct ascending order. The process had to start with a *proces verbal* on my part. He arranged the sergeant to take down my statement. An hour later with no visible sign of action on the part of the Police, we were allowed to leave.

The monk was very agitated. At the gate of the Police Station itself, he wanted to be let out of the car.

"I can go this way to the Horse Peak Monastery. May you have much merit for obliging me with the ride." Once again, he sounded odd.

"I should like to drive towards the mosque if I can and see what really is happening," I told Slim-Jewel who had remained in the car while we were inside the Police Station.

"What did you ask the Police to do?" she asked me.

"I told them of a possible breach of the peace and asked them to prevent the floats with carol singers from coming towards the mosque. I told them it was quite simple. They simply had to close the road and divert the crowds to another street."

"Did they agree to do it?"

629

"They did not tell me anything?"

"That's unusual. Did the monk tell the Police why he feared a breach of the peace?"

"No, Slim. I did all the talking and I signed the statement."

"You did what?" she uttered in disbelief. Her voice was ominous. I took her burst of temper to mean that we should take the shortest cut home.

VIII

With a steaming cup of tea in hand, I sat on a chair in the verandah. It was like any other morning with the difference that Slim-Jewel had not joined me yet with her cup of tea. I thought to myself that she must be regretting her outburst of temper but waiting to see whether I had relented. I called out to her by a pet name which was her favourite. I heard her footsteps and turned to receive her. She turned pale and nearly dropped her cup of tea. I stepped forward to steady her.

"What, man? what happened to you?" Slim-Jewel shouted.

I turned around to see what had frightened her so much. Leaning on a fence-pole, was the pitiable figure of the gardener. A blood-stained bandage covered the most of his forehead and head. His cheeks were bruised and covered in iodine tincture. The left arm was in a sling. He supported himself on his right leg and the fence-pole. Apparently his other leg was badly hurt.

I gave him my chair to sit on. It needed much persuasion and insistence. Slim-Jewel helped him to drink her cup of tea.

"How did you get hurt, Jamis?" we asked him in unison.

We could not believe our ears. Slim-Jewel's intuition as regards the man from Great Forest Falls, whom we took to be a Buddhist monk, was right. The commotion which he spoke of had taken place and several people were seriously hurt. It was providential that there were no fatalities.

"The carol chariot was passing in front of the mosque and many people had gathered in the streets to see it", Jamis continued. "I joined the people who held hands and kept the crowds from coming too close to the chariot. I did that right from the beginning and the couple of policemen who were between us and the chariot thanked us for helping them in controlling the crowds. Suddenly bricks and stones were hurled at the chariot and the Petromex gas lamp blew up. The paper decorations caught fire. The children dressed as divine damsels shrieked for help. Several of us ran to the chariot and rescued the children and the musicians. In the process I was hit on my head by a brick or two and bruised on the face by the falling debris of the chariot. I was helping a burly musician to get down from the chariot and we both fell. My ankle was twisted under his weight."

"Who took you to the hospital?" Slim-Jewel asked.

"The police. But it took a long time."

Jamis had been lucky at the hospital. The Police had rounded up as many of the doctors in town as could be found to assist the skeleton staff that was on duty. Among them was Timothy. He recognized the gardener, examined his head injuries and found them to be superficial.

While Jamis was recounting the gruesome scene in the street and the hospital, two vehicles entered our premises. Timothy drove in his car first. Following him on a motor cycle with a side-car came the Police inspector and sergeant whom I had met on the previous day.

"This is a lucky bloke, Father," said Timothy. "None of the bricks were direct hits. That was so in practically every case. Otherwise we would have had dozens dead."

"Do you mean that the hurlers of bricks knew what they were doing?" I queried.

"I am sure. What it means is that the attack was not spontaneous. It had been planned and executed with care. The hurlers of the missiles must have been trained to scare people and create chaos without killing anyone."

"You are in it in a big way, Sir," said the Inspector by way of explaining his early morning visit. "Last afternoon, you come to the Police Station and make a request that we should divert the Vesak chariot from the street with the mosque. Of course, you were relying on the word of a Buddhist monk whose name or address you did not give us. What happened before the mosque was just like what you asked us to prevent. So you had prior knowledge of it. That is the first point. Among the people who were injured at the scene, the first we could identify was your gardener. Is it a coincidence? Or was he there at your bidding? That is the second point. We want to take down your statement. My superiors think that you have a background of direct involvement in political and religious movements and these could be related to the riot in front of the mosque. You can refuse, if you wish or opt to come to the Station with your lawyer."

Timothy and Slim-Jewel looked askance at me.

"I have nothing to hide and I can answer any question you wish to pose and make any statement on what I know," I said without showing the annoyance which rose within me.

"Can I first make a statement on the man in robes to whom we gave a ride from Great Forest Fall?"

"Suit yourself, Madam," the inspector responded. "Women and children first is always my policy. But I have always thought that women like to have the last word." He laughed.

632

His jugglery with cliches did little to relieve the tension which the rest of us felt.

"We took him to be a real Buddhist monk. We were very deferential to him. We saluted him the way we always pay our homage to monks." Slim-Jewel dictated.

She chose to do it in Sinhala and Timothy did the translation.

"I offered him my place in the front seat and I sat with the servant behind him. Right from the very first word he spoke to us I felt something unusual in his accent. There was an unmistakable lisp. But I thought he was too excited with whatever was bothering him. At first I believed that he was a Buddhist monk and sympathized with him. He was repenting what he had done and was anxious to set it right."

"What did he say that he had done and wanted to be corrected?" asked the inspector.

"He told us that Muslim youths were being mobilized by the local mosque to come to Kandy in large numbers to protect the sanctity of their places of worship. It had to do with something about not stopping the music when processions and carol parties passed their mosques. He claimed that he as a Buddhist monk had to take counter measures. The impression he gave us was that he had mobilized the Buddhist youths in the area to assert the rights of the Buddhists. He convinced us that he regretted his action and wanted an ugly situation prevented. He said that innocent people would get hurt if the two sides clashed. I was in agreement with my husband's decision to go to the Police Station to request that the chariot of carol singers be diverted from the street with the mosque. But I was aghast when I found out that he was not a monk at all."

"How did you find out?" asked the inspector.

"When he opened the car door and put his leg out, his robe slid at the neck. Clearly visible was a thick gold chain of the type that the affluent Muslim traders wore. No Buddhist monks wear jewelry. So when my husband and he returned to the car I was more observant. My doubts were confirmed when he said that he was going to his monastery. He pronounced the name incorrectly. Muslims have difficulty in pronouncing a vowel at the beginning of a word. He called it "Yasgiryaa" instead of Asgiriya. But that was not all. He wore the robe covering both shoulders. For that he should be a monk of the Siamese Sect from the low-country. So I looked at the only proof that would show him to be a monk belonging to the Horse-Peak Monastery. His eye brows should have been shaven. Instead he had bushy eye brows. No one covering both shoulders and having bushy eye brows could have any affiliation to this monastery. But that was not all, I watched him as he stepped up the slope to get to the street. Instead of

633

the yellow under-garment which Buddhist monks wore, he was dressed in an unmistakable black and white checked sarong. I could see an inch and two of the sarong."

"Why do you think that this man took all this trouble to disguise himself as a monk and persuade you to bring him to Kandy?"

"I do not know. But I would like to think that he was a good man who knew all about a conspiracy and genuinely made an effort to prevent violence."

The inspector looked at me.

"I think so too," I added. My esteem for Slim-Jewel's powers of observance and analysis of evidence rose sky high. I had also reason to be grateful.

"This voluntarily given statement changes the whole situation," said the inspector. "It throws a lot of light on matters we are concerned with. I will talk to my superiors and return if a statement is needed from you."

We were relieved as we would have some time to assess the situation.

Timothy had come to take a second look at the injuries of the gardener. We had from him a more detailed account of the outbreak of violence. All the injured persons with the exclusion of a musician were innocent bystanders. Not a single one among them was a Muslim or a Police officer. His patients agreed that all bricks, brickbats and stones came from the direction of the mosque and the people on the street were taken unawares. Any retaliation on their part had been limited to fisticuffs. I was relieved that what I had told the Police on the basis of the disguised monk's fabrication was false. At the same time, I was angry that the Police did not accede to my repeated plea that the carol chariot be diverted to another street.

"Doesn't look good at all to me," I said. "I am reminded of my grandfather's stories of the riots of 1848. Rumours will spread. Reprisals will be taken against Muslims all over the Island. By the time the Administration intervenes, the Muslims would have become the victims and the Buddhists the merciless aggressors. Exactly the situation most of the administrators have been looking for."

Though we had lost much of our appetite, we sat down to partake of a breakfast of hoppers and fish-curry which Golden Jewel had laid out for us.

I had a month's correspondence, journals and newspapers to go over. I sorted the mail and laid them on the table in three heaps: personal, social and religious. Then I proceeded to arrange the journals and newspapers in the reverse chronological order.The very first English newspaper, I took in my hands, had the head line: GOVERNOR LOSES TWO SONS IN WAR. What a tragedy to lose two of your grown-up sons in a worthless war, I said to myself. It had apparently happened after Timothy and I had seen him in the King's House.

I wrote two telegrams of condolences; one in Slim-Jewel's and my name and the other from Timothy and Moon-Beam. The former was long, personal and dealt philosophically with the theme of Death, quoting Buddhist aphorisms that the Governor already knew. I drove to the Post Office, despatched the telegrams and dropped in at the Police Station to see if I could meet the Superintendent himself.The Malay sergeant met me at the door.

"Hell of trouble, sir." he said even before any greetings could be exchanged. "Boutiques broken, houses burnt. We do not know what to do? Trouble everywhere, Colombo and Galle worst."

"Can I see the Superintendent?"

"No, sir. All senior officers conferencing with Government Agent."

Although I tried to get more information from the sergeant, I had no success. His limited English was one problem. The other was that he viewed me with suspicion. I could not blame him. After all, he was a Muslim and I an adversary.

Timothy had gone to the hospital in the morning volunteering to assist in surgery. He was welcomed as a boon from heaven. Whenever people took to streets to solve their problems with violence, the hospital became the score-keeper. After several hours of surgery, Timothy dropped in to see us or rather the gardener whose facial lacerations were beginning to fester.

"The tide has changed, Father. We have some very serious cases that the rural hospitals could not deal with. Spades and crowbars, long-armed farm knives, axes and the like are being used widely by both sides. Sinhalese and Muslims are brought in in comparable numbers. Women and even children on both sides are being ruthlessly raped. It is mayhem. I cannot dream how one could be so brutal and inhuman to fellow humans. The Police are not in control. Many patients whom the Police had shot appear to be innocent bystanders rather than looters and criminals."

"How do you know that, Timothy?"

"None who could wield a crowbar has yet come with shotgun injuries," he replied. "And only the Police have guns."

That evening around dusk, the inspector of Police came in with the sergeant. He brought a message from the Superintendent.

Dear Sir,

My pressing duties had kept me away from office and as a result I was deprived of the pleasure of seeing you on both occasions you came to the Police Station. I have read the statement you gave at the Station and that which your wife gave at your home this morning.These have clarified your position as someone who went out of his way to prevent violence.

It is a pity that my officers could not contact me in time. Your recommendation on the diversion of the Vesak chariot to another street, if implemented, would have prevented the tragic event. May I express my sincere thanks for your public-spirited cooperation with my officers.

I remain, Sir,
Your Obedient Servant,
I. V. Sanders
Superintendent of Police,
Central Province.

Was I not pleased? It was a vindication I did not expect, even though in a corner of my head was the old memory that the British knew the right thing to do when fair play demanded it. I added the Superintendent's name to my list of exemplary British: The Blakes, The Right Reverend Kenneth Saunders, Ernest Dickinson, Stanley Williams.

I read the letter to Slim-Jewel and thanked her again for being a fine detective.

Over the next four days, newspapers, the grapevine and Timothy purveyed grim bits and pieces of information which showed how widespread and serious the riots were. Fear psychosis had affected the masses to such an extent that whole villages were deserted within hours. People sought refuge in numbers and security among relatives and friends. Mounting casualties at the hospital bespoke the unceasing intensity of violence. The most pitiable were women and girls who in the event of any uprising had to pay the ultimate price with blood, tears and shame. I was appalled. Never in my life had I felt so helpless.

I summoned the members of the Executive Committees of various associations and societies in which Slim-Jewel and I were office-bearers. Our intention was to explore how we could collectively assist the Administration in bringing about the stoppage of riots and the

636

eventual reconciliation of the two communities. It was to take place at 6.00 PM on the second of June.

A little before the time of the meeting, Timothy rushed in from the hospital to tell us that Martial Law had been declared by the Government.

"Is it advisable to hold the meeting?" he asked me.

"Timothy, I would certainly like to cancel it but how can I do it? The people might be already on the way here."

"All right, Father. I am going to be with Moon-Beam and the children. Give the people dinner and send them home early. It is not a day for speeches."

That was exactly what we did. But that was not enough.

The next morning began as usual. Slim-Jewel and I were sipping tea in the verandah. The familiar motor cycle with the side-car pulled over under the front porch. The inspector walked in followed by the Malay sergeant.

"It's a delicate matter, Sir," he began. "We have orders from the Army Commander to have you arrested for violation of the rule about unlawful meetings. Under Martial Law any meeting of more than five is unlawful. Last night you had over forty."

"That is right. But when was Martial Law declared?"

"Yesterday. By noon it was known to all. The Headmen had it announced through tom-tom beaters in all their duty areas."

"When do you think I invited the people? Do you think that I could have contacted each one of them and asked them not to come?"

"That's a good point, Sir. But I am only a subordinate officer. The Superintendent would like to see you at the Station by nine."

I was at the Police Station earlier than nine. The Superintendent summoned me to his room immediately. He was definitely in a bad mood. But he tried to be as pleasant and courteous to me as he could.

"Mudaliyar, I do not know what to do or even where I stand," he said by way of explaining his state of indecision. "Martial Law was declared yesterday and already a '*podian*' of a lieutenant who knows nothing of this town is telling me what to do."

He must have been very angry. He chose to refer to the military officer assuming control over law and order by the pejorative expression '*podian*,' meaning in Tamil a child or more precisely an unworthy nincompoop. I could sense the beginning of turf battles and serious personality clashes. Of course, I was less worried about these than how they were about to affect me.

After bad-mouthing the lieutenant for several minutes, the law-enforcer came to the subject in hand.

"This arrogant beer-gulping jingo orders me to arrest you and keep you locked up without trial. I have refused to do it. I want to follow procedure."

"What do you mean? On what am I to be arrested? Is it because the people I had invited days ago came to my house and had dinner? It is true that nearly fifty people were there. But there was no meeting. No speeches were made. We knew of Martial Law and decided to make it a purely social gathering."

"I know it. My officers have met many of your guests and found that it was so. I want a law officer of the state, a magistrate or a judge to hear our version and yours and give us a legitimate order and that is exactly what I am going to do."

I thanked him profusely. He called an officer and dictated an indictment.

Mudaliyar Tiny Banda Valour-lion of Royal Spout, on being informed of the alleged violation of the provisions of Martial Law in that he summoned or caused to be summoned an assembly of about fifty persons to his residence during the evening of the second day of June 1915, surrendered himself willingly and without duress to the Police this morning at nine. He admits that an assembly of persons, who had been invited before Martial Law was declared, took place as alleged. He also avers that the meeting for which they were invited was abandoned and those present were treated to a dinner and no discussions or speeches on any subject took place. As a prominent social worker in the Province, a distinguished scholar and a retired Government Servant with an immaculate reputation, Mudaliyar Valour-Lion had intended to mobilize leaders of voluntary organizations to bring about a reconciliation between the two parties in the riots. A decision of the court is solicited in view of the pressure that is being exercised by the military command that he be arrested and detained without trial.

Wheels of justice moved fast. By noon I was arraigned before the Town Magistrate. Police presented the case. I made a statement. The military command, though summoned, was not represented. The judge asked a few questions on what transpired at my place in the evening. Within minutes, I was discharged. I drove home to the relief of my family.

"The rule of law still persists," commented Timothy.

638

"But for how long?" asked Slim-Jewel.

The riots subsided in days. Timothy's services were no longer required at the hospital. Rumours, however, were rampant. The gardener recovered fully. He became a purveyor of news or rather gossip. The Police and the military had been empowered to shoot at sight anyone whom they suspected to be rioters or looters. Gruesome stories of military and Police excesses were recounted.

For all intents and purposes, a reign of terror was said to be prevalent. Reinforcements of Punjabi and Marathi soldiers were allegedly brought in and their ruthlessness was beyond imagination. I had no way to verify the accuracy of the rumours.

A monk travelling from Colombo brought me an unsigned note from Don Baron. It said that the Administration was about to arrest and detain in remand all leaders of the majority community and the activists in the Temperance Movement would be specially targeted. The charge would be sedition and conspiracy. I was asked to be in readiness for a spell in jail. Don Baron, the optimist, saw that much good would come out of this measure.

"Our emerging leaders have had no time or opportunity to think and talk among themselves. Now we could do that as guests of His Majesty."

Again, through the grapevine, I got the news of the arrest of the the Senanayaka Brothers, F.R., D. C., and D. S., Dr. W. A. de Silva, playwright John de Silva, Don Baron and the brother of Homeless Dharmapala . A case was being built, my informant said, to prove that the emerging Sinhala leaders were in tow with the Germans. If that was true, I should be in the list of dangerous men or suspects. I had been to Germany on invitation just as Don Baron had a couple of years after me. I told my family and Slim-Jewel, the effervescent optimist, scoffed my apprehensions away with a laugh,

"All you did was to say that Sinhala was a distant cousin of German. Not a big deal!"

Two days later, a posse of foreign soldiers was at my door. At least, the platoon commander was polite and considerate. I recognized him instantly. He was none other than Charles Harcourt whose leg was saved by the timely intervention of Moon-Beam and Timothy. As a reserve in the Ceylon Rifles, this planter had been called to service and he seemed to enjoy it. While I was getting a few of my basic necessities together, he was recounting to his soldiers his encounter with Moon-

Beam at the cholera camp and how the wife and husband team of doctors attended on him without malice.

"I want to be nice to their father," I heard him say as I came out, "even though he would love to have us out of the Island as fast as possible."

He kept to his word.

The spacious and elegant residence of an erstwhile Kandyan chieftain in King's Street was the remand prison. Its large rooms had been transformed into cells with steel barriers. A cell could hold eight prisoners. There were already fifteen when I was locked in. Harcourt, apparently, had some influence and had me housed in a tiny windowless store-room. It was a luxury to be in a cell all by myself.

As more and more people were brought in every day, the prison became a living hell. Lavatories were inadequate and in constant use. They were never cleaned or washed. The stench of the toilets and the foul odour of sweat and filth were unbearable. Prisoners were confined in their cells for eighteen hours. I whiled away the time by reciting from memory endless verses in Sanskrit, Pali, Sinhala, Tamil and English. Others sang Sinhala folk songs. Clever conversations were carried on in verse. The Burgher and Malay jailers or the Punjabi and Marathi soldiers and their superior officers from tea and rubber plantations had no idea that we were actually sharing information and experiences and preparing for more organized action to agitate for freedom.

One morning, to a spell-bound audience of prisoners, I composed *ex tempore* a poem in the Sinhala tradition of "Poetry on one's feet": ,

We languish behind bars as common criminals
Bereft of dignity, deprived of comfort,
Denigrated as scum and brutalized at will.
What crimes have we committed? We wish to know.

Liberty's offsprings with a history so long
Our inner selves crave the right to Freedom.
We hold our heads high with a culture so refined
Expressed in stone, in verse and lofty prose,
In values sublime and gentle ways
As sons and daughters of saintly Buddha.
Is that a crime in your laws imperial?

What galls you, O mighty men of arms,
With gunboats backing your sweet, evasive words?

640

What makes you feel safe in your borrowed mansions
When the men of action of a nation are locked
In mockery of your self-acclaimed justice?
Our patience? Silence? Force of non-violence?

Winning as you say your war nearer home
With futile sacrifice of lives so precious,
You fear yet the mob that roams in the streets
Of towns of an island so far removed.
You fear still more the words **we** *wield,*
For the power to condone your continuing domination
Or to cry "Enough" and bring the empire to its knees
Is ours, my friends, as the right is ours.

In months, maybe years, we shall breathe once more
The Jasmine scented air that sweeps the Kandy Lake.
The sun will greet us over the wilds of Upper Garden.
The nation will note the sacrifices we made
In the name of a future in basking rays of Freedom.
"Thank you," our jailers and their masters outside.
Into a crucible have you put us and the heat is right
Moulded into fighters for liberty we shall leave
The squalor and the odour of the prison cells.

"Thank you," we say with hearts of gratitude,
"No friend of the nation could ever do better."

I had warned them in advance not to applaud or to show any emotion. The fellow prisoners found solace and hope in the words I put into this poem. Soon we learnt to recite it together whenever frustration overwhelmed us. We called it our battle song.

When after eighteen hours of confinement in our cells, we were let out for exercise, we recited the sonorous verses *ad nauseam* to the utter exasperation of our jailers, most of whom were Malays, Marathis or Punjabis.

Months passed. The dreary cells seemed better lit; the bunk beds were not as hard; the foul odour was a thing of the past; and even the rice with saltless gravy was palatable. How very adaptable the human being is!

Our families were not allowed to see us. We had no news from outside. We missed our families and friends. In their place a new family had evolved and the camaraderie among us was our life line.

641

I was, however, more fortunate. Harcourt continued to be compassionate. He was really grateful for what Moon-Beam and Timothy had done to him. He would bring me news of Slim-Jewel and the family. He would bring for me from her some little delicacies: an oil cake or two, a few green gram balls or an egg hopper with pepper-roasted fish. Once he brought me a parcel of string hoppers with the usual accompaniments. It was a rainy day and his trench coat had a large enough pocket to hold this banquet. To enable me to eat it without being detected, he had himself locked in the cell. He leaned on the door until I ate the string hoppers greedily in the dark.

"There's something I want tell you, Valour-Lion. But I had no opportunity so far. It's something very serious," he said as he squashed the banana leaf and the newspaper in which the food was wrapped and stuffed then into his pocket.

"After your arrest, your house was searched on a warrant issued by the magistrate. They took all the papers you had in your study. What I hear is that three Mudaliyars in Colombo had gone through them and written a report. It is rumoured to be your death warrant. What did you have?"

I was perplexed. Was he telling me or asking me? I thought for a while. He resumed,

"I don't believe that you kept files on every important Britsh official to have served in the Island and saved crucial papers on their lapses, public statements and the like. How did you plan to use all that information?"

He paused for a while and added with a laugh, "Haul them as criminals if Germans win the war?"

I ignored the last comment and was about to explain how these papers came to my hand and the archival value they would have to students of the nation's history. But the guard informed that Harcourt was urgently needed by his commanding officer. All I could tell him was to apprise Timothy of everything he knows about these files.

"Timothy knows everything. If necessary he will contact Autumn-Moon whose father started the files," I said as Harcourt curtly turned about and left the cell.

A week later, Harcourt came again. He handed me a bar of chocolate.

"Your lawyer cousin is looking after your interests. Timothy says the case looks good," he said briskly and walked away.

This was the first intimation that a case would be involved. What would be the charges? Sedition? Treason? Conspiracy? Spying? I spent many a sleepless night, mentally turning every page and recalling the

642

contents of every document. Who were the three Mudaliyars? What experience did they have in archives and historical documentation? Would a trained archivist or documentalist review the files before indicting me? There were only questions. I had no answers. I felt lonelier than ever before. If only I could meet Slim-Jewel for a few minutes? If only I could tell her what needed to be done.

A few days later, Harcourt paid me a visit and I told him about the importance of meeting Slim-Jewel.

"I cannot promise you, Valour-Lion. You are no longer on preventive detention. You are a suspect awaiting indictment and trial."

"How come? I was not presented in court?"

Harcourt gave me a wry smile.

"They have no time for such niceties."

Before he left he gave me four bits of information. Homeless Dharmapala was in house arrest in Calcutta and he was barred from coming to the the Island. His brother, the doctor, detained in Jaffna, had died of cholera. A deputation of influential political leaders had gone to London to take the issue with the Government in London. Don Baron was released and was actively engaged in getting the other leaders released.

"Try to get to him, Valour-Lion," was his final advice. "How?" I asked myself as I surveyed the windowless tiny cell which was my home for eighteen hours of the day!

I had no visit from Harcourt for two weeks. My imagination ran riot. Every time some movement inside the prison was sensed, I expected to see the kind planter being led in as a prisoner for being an accomplice of a proven seditionist! I could not ask any one. As a Buddhist, I had no omnipresent, omniscient and omnipotent God to pray to. I wished I had. All I could do was to make a fervent wish for his safety and security. I was almost beyond all hope when the Prison Superintendent had me led to his office.

Sallow-cheeked with sunken eyes but yet very personable, Slim-Jewel stood as I entered the room. I motioned her to sit down and I sat on the chair by her, as shown by the Superintendent.

"This is a very rare concession made to a prisoner in times of Martial Law. You have ten minutes and I am afraid you have to talk in my presence."

There were a hundred things I wanted to ask her. Already a couple of minutes had gone in our effort to curb the onset of tears. With deliberate effort, I told her what had to be done.

"Tell Autumn-Moon that I will not be released even if the Martial Law is rescinded. I am to be charged for sedition, spying, treason or

643

conspiracy or all on the basis of the historical documentation I inherited from Uncle Victor. Entail the support of Don Baron. He may argue my case in courts. One of you must meet Stanley Williams."

"One minute more," said the Prison official.

"Tell Stanley that the files must be seen by him if he really wants his Government to do justice. I am convinced there is nothing incriminating in them."

The jailer led me out of the Office and Slim-Jewel was still standing by the open door when I turned back for a last look.

Relieved that I could communicate with Slim-Jewel, I stretched out on the bunker bed and snoozed. It began as a pleasant dream.

We were both younger. We had gone to Sangha-Gem-Field for a family occasion. I was driving our car and Slim-Jewel was teasing me showing the place I had planned to build a house for her and have a family of many children. Then something happened. She shrieked.

I got up with a shudder. Similar nightmares woke me up several times in the night. In all she shrieked and I got up.

I tried to sleep every time with the hope that I would know why she shrieked. I was a nervous wreck by morning.

He had never come this early to see me. Even before the guard unceremoniously shoved in a slice of bread with a tin can of plain tea, Harcourt was at my door.

"I do not know how to begin," he said, after staring at me for several minutes. "I think there is only one way. Let me be blunt."

He cleared his throat.

"Your wife came here last evening?"

"Yes. Thank you very must for arranging it."

"Valour-Lion, I wish I did not."

Slowly in measured words he told me what happened from the moment Slim-Jewel left the Prison.

"Her car was parked in the school premises. She was walking with the driver. He was there to accompany her to the car. They happened to be right at the intersection in front of the entrance to the King's Pavilion."

"Please tell me what happened," I was impatient.

"All right. All right. The Governor had come and there was a heavy guard at the entrance. Because the Governor was there, some people gathered at the gate with petitions. The guards lost their nerve and sprayed rose water."

"What do you mean, lieutenant?" I asked impatiently.

"I am very sorry, Valour-Lion. Recently the Governor told the Legislative Council that the riots were subdued by spraying rose water. And the expression has become an euphemism for shooting. As I was saying. the soldiers started shooting into the air. Your wife was hit in the head by a ricocheting bullet. She was rushed to hospital. Timothy was contacted. The operation went off well."

I grasped Harcourt's hands. He tightened the grip.

"I am sorry, Valour-Lion. My heartfelt condolences." He held my hands for a long time in genuine compassion.

"When did she die?" I asked minutes later.

"This morning when Moon-Beam and Timothy and their children were by her bed-side."

"Was she conscious?"

What Harcourt told me baffled me at the beginning. But later I had to concede that Slim-Jewel was a woman of extraordinary mental and physical resources. She had regained consciousness in early hours of the morning and expressed a wish to see the family. That was how every one was there. She was lucid. She had told them what I had told her. Her last words had been,

"Get in touch with Don Baron and Stanley Williams. They will get your Father out of this mess."

The mission accomplished, she had closed her eyes. With a radiating smile on her face, she had breathed her last.

It was a solace to have all these details. I was grateful to Harcourt. I needed one more favour from him. I asked him without hesitation. He has so far proved to be a friend.

"Yes, Valour-Lion. I cannot promise. But I will go as far as I can."

I wanted my fellow prisoners to know my sad plight. I began in verse but all I could form was a measly few lines:

"An errant bullet from a soldier's gun,
Shattering my heart to a million pieces,
Takes an angel to her abode in heaven
And the sun, the moon and the stars with her"

I choked on the last line. I cried shamelessly. In my lonely cell I hit my head on the ground. Words of consolation came from a hundred voices. I wish there was a kind hand which I could grasp in this hour of utter grief and loneliness.

645

When we were let out of cells, the fellow prisoners expressed their sympathies in different ways. Some hugged me. Some saluted me with clasped hands. Others shook hands. Some spoke. Some only expressed their grief in silence. In whatever way they did it, it was clear that each offered me solace. I was touched by the gesture of the Superintendent and the Jailers. In their own way, they shared my grief.

IX

The faith I placed in Harcourt was more than justified. Not only did he get permission for me to attend the funeral but made arrangements to accompany me. He had gone as far as he could. I was not to be shackled or handcuffed. But I had to be in the drab unbleached prison garment, made uglier with an all-over design of the symbol of Government ownership - three exclamation marks sharing a single dot. Now that the brightest spark of my life was gone, it did not matter how I looked. A kind jailer found me a pair of sandals.

We drove in an army vehicle through deserted streets. We were at the cemetery ahead of the cortege. I expected to see only a handful of family members. I thought that somebody had been thoughtful and permitted the people to assemble in the cemetery in large numbers. All societies and organizations in which we had served were present. They displayed their banners. Each slogan paid a tribute to Slim-Jewel, who was acclaimed as a mother to all.

All eyes were on me - a pitiful emaciated figure in oversize prison clothes. They had seen me smartly dressed in my grey slacks and Rugby blazer, the most fashionable Western dress, in the robes of a senior monk, in the elegant official garb of a Mudaliyar, in the white national dress of Homeless' design and in the simple home wear of a sarong and undershirt. For all I could infer from the sincerity and affection with which I was greeted by them, I must have been in princely robes.

The cortege entered. The casket was taken out of the chariot by Timothy and Autumn-Moon and handed over to pall-bearers from each organization, who actually carried it on their shoulders a few yards before another set stepped forward to do the same honours. Moon-Beam and the children embraced me and led me to where the monks had gathered for the last rites. My brother, the Chief Monk of the Royal Monastery of Sangha-Gem-Field, was there to lead the ceremony.

"How is all this possible?" I asked Timothy.

"Martial Law is no more. It was lifted this morning"

"Why am I in prison clothes?" I asked Harcourt who stood by my side.

"They have not finished with you," he said.

When he found that I had bought his explanation, he added,

"Two things. The order to release prisoners has yet to be issued. But in your case, you may have to vindicate yourself in a trial,"

The ceremony lasted less than half an hour. There were no speeches or eulogies. It was a solemn occasion, not to be marred in any way. At the request of the people the casket was opened and the mourners passed by with their hands clasped in veneration.

I stood on a side looking at a face I had seen in many a mood but never without compassion and subtle humour. I shall never see it again, I said to myself and wished that her journey in the sorrowful cycle of life and death would end with the highest bliss of Nibbana.

The more I recalled the teachings of the Buddha on the impermanence of existence, the more I was able to cope with the bereavement. How the wheel of worldly reality changed: profit and loss, fame and infamy, insult and praise, happiness and sorrow! "A mind touched by the realities of the world and still unshaken, that is the highest blessing."

With both my hands on my chin covering my mouth and nose, I entered into deep meditation as I gazed on the flames, lit by Autumn-Moon and Timothy, reaching the top of the pyre. "Impermanent are all conditioned phenomena."

I entered the Prison to be welcomed with my own song to which they added the solitary verse on Slim-Jewel's death. My fellow prisoners had been told of the end of the hundred day reign of terror. There was joy in their voices. Someone tried to be humorous and began singing,

> *Home for supper*
> *Home for supper*
> *There's the bell*
> *There's the bell*
> *Bacon and potatoes*
> *Ding dang ......*

No one joined him and he stopped abruptly. Even in their hour of infinite joy, they deferred to my grief. What a sense of solidarity! What an achievement in identification!

> *"Thank you," we say with hearts of gratitude,*
> *"No friend of the nation could ever do better."*

By noon the next day, half the detainees were released. Before the week was out there was only a handful left and they were to be indicted. It was for the courts to decide whether these prisoners were to be released. I was in that category.

648

Saturday afternoon, I had unexpected visitors. Autumn-Moon and Timothy came up to my cell with a bag full of clean clothes.

"Am I being released?"

"Not quite. The Big Boss wants to see us," said Autumn-Moon.

"The Governor is in Kandy. He has a meeting with the three of us in an hour," paraphrased Timothy.

They had brought me a Western dress suit complete with tie, coat, socks and shoes and also a simple national dress in pure white cotton with an embroidered shawl and sandals. I chose the latter not only out of renewed nationalistic sentiments but more because my scrawny body would be lost in Western clothes. I preferred not to look a scare-crow.

We walked to the King's Pavilion which was only a couple of hundred yards from the prison. Timothy showed me the spot where Slim-Jewel was shot. I stood there for a minute in silent meditation. In my mind I forgave the man whose bullet killed her. I also forgave the bungling bureaucrats whose fear psychosis alone led to heinous acts of inhumanity. That prepared me mentally to meet the Governor from whom I had expected a much better deal not for me but the whole nation. He was a profound admirer of the culture of our people!

We were expected at the gate. Prison guards were relieved by a posse of soldiers who led us to the door of the King's Pavilion. I had been there on many occasions. On the left from the door was the gigantic dining table. The bemedalled, khaki-clad top brass of the military were already seated on the right of the table. Civilians sat on the left. The Superintendent of Police sat with the civilians to the left of the Government Agent. H. L. Dowbiggin, the Inspector General of Police was to the right of the Brigadier commanding the armed forces. Three kitchen chairs were arranged in a row at the foot of the table for the three of us.

"Take your seats. The Prisoner in the centre and his advocate and doctor on either side." bellowed Dowbiggin.

If it was meant to be an added insult, so be it, I thought. But we did not have to sit down. The Governor walked in with Stanley Williams and J. G. Frazer, the Government Agent of Colombo.

The well-ensconced top brass were in a quandary. All stood and awaited the Governor to have them reseated. This he did deftly. He had the army and police officers to move down two seats and had Stanley and Frazer to sit on his right. He cleared the first three seats to his left and asked me to sit on his left, facing Stanley. Autumn-Moon and Timothy sat next to me. A. G. Frazer, the Principal of Trinity College, and two members of the King's House staff sat on our side of the table. The three kitchen chairs drew a stare from the Governor.

"Whose idea was this?" he asked.

No one replied but discomfiture was written on the face of the Brigadier. An orderly was summoned to remove the chairs.

"I am told, Gentlemen," commenced the Governor," that of the hundreds of people who were taken into preventive custody during Martial Law, Mudaliyar Valour-Lion is not to be released as there are criminal charges against him. Can one of you tell me what they are?"

Dowbiggin signalled the Superintendent of Police to speak.

"On instructions received from headquarters, his house in Royal Spout was searched. All the files and papers recovered were sent to Colombo."

"You have no idea as to what they contained?"

"No, Your Excellency."

"Who has?"

The silence was long and deafening. Dowbiggin began leafing through a thick file. It was perhaps the first time he had seen the file and he was looking for something that he could not identify quickly.

Autumn-Moon asked for permission to speak and the Governor was gracious,

"The files were handed over to three Interpreter-Mudaliyars and on the basis of their reports a submission was made to the Attorney General for advice. If you hand the file over to me I will be able to identify the reports, the submission and Attorney General's reply. Or else, may I present to your Excellency officially certified copies which I have obtained to prepare for my cousin's defence?"

The official bench, if that was the description for those on the Governor's right, was amazed.

The Governor wanted the copies. Autumn-Moon handed over his file where each was flagged with clear notation.

While the Governor read the copies, the Inspector General succeeded in his search and found the originals. They were proffered to the Governor, who waved them away. Second discomfiture for the official bench!

"Let me see. The Attorney General's advice is that the papers taken from Mudaliyar Valour-Lion's house should be re-examined by one or more competent lawyers to ascertain whether they would stand the scrutiny of the courts. Have you done that, Dowbiggin?"

"Not to my knowledge, Sir. But it will be done before presenting the indictment."

"When? How long do you think it would take?"

"I will initiate action when I return to headquarters. It may take a few months. Six at the most."

"In the meantime, you want him to be in remand. Didn't you have your hundred days."

The Governor turned to the Army Commander.

"Brigadier, you know anything about this?"

"Only what I was told, Sir."

"What would that be?"

The Brigadier, if at all, made Dowbiggin look a villain.

"I was asked to deal with the prisoner summarily. To take him before a Court Martial with a charge of sedition. But I was cautious. Since Henry Pedris was summarily dealt with and shot, I have been very cautious. Even the military top brass have a conscience."

"Enough of that." cut in the Governor. "What was your advice."

"I told the Inspector general that my men would act only if the prisoner directly or indirectly was involved in breaking the peace."

What he unfolded was an inept plot which was incompetently handled by untried provocateurs. Its designers found my request to Lieutenant Charles Harcourt to get Slim-Jewel to see me a convenient entry point. Her visit to the prison, the timing of her departure, the milling crowd of petitioners at the gate of the King's Pavilion, the presence of the military and the shooting were no accidents. But what went wrong was that Slim-Jewel who was to be drawn into a situation of open protest was accidentally shot. Her death changed everything and the lifting of Martial Law within hours put halt to any conspiracy in the brewing.

"Is this true, Dowbiggin?"

"Sir, it could be. My whole Department and I as its leader had only one policy. That was to teach the agitators a lesson that they would take centuries to forget so that the British Rule shall go on undisturbed for ever. We had to stop these nobodies trying to be somebodies. We relied heavily on the military. Yes, we took their advice on many occasions."

"Your Excellency," drawled the Brigadier. "Now that peace has returned, we will be the villains. That is the unenviable lot of the armed services. But let me go on record for the sake of my men who risked their lives in restoring law and order."

"What are your casualties, Brigadier?" asked the Governor.

"No deaths, Sir. But a few injuries, not necessarily attributable to enemy attacks."

"Any European civilians?"

"None either, Sir."

"All right. Continue."

"When Your Excellency told the Legislative Council that the riots were put down by sprinkling rose water, we took it to mean that you condoned our methods and wanted more action. We are sorry if we read you wrong. But that is it."

If what the military commander wanted was to make the Governor feel a bit uncomfortable, he did succeed. Sir Charles took a while to regain his composure. He addressed the offical bench:

"Gentlemen, let us return to the charges against Mudaliyar Valour-Lion. Am I right in understanding that none of you know what the contents of the files are?"

"I do, Sir," said Stanley Williams.

"No, Stanley. I mean excluding you and me."

That was the final discomfiture for the official bench.

The deafening silence on its part was broken by the Governor who called upon Stanley Williams to speak.

It was a well prepared masterly presentation. He highlighted the adverse comments in the report of the three Mudaliyars. He analyzed the Police submission to the Attorney General. He picked up for detailed examination two of the files which were said to be the most damaging to me: the file on Governor Robert Brownrigg and one of the dossiers on the financial policies of the Colony.

"Sir, what the three Mudaliyars have said is that the information contained in them, if known widely, would bring discredit and disrepute to His Majesty's Government. So my criteria have been: By whom were these documents written? Were they already published? Were they secret documents purloined by the collector? What was the intention of having them neatly categorized and filed?"

He proceeded to explain that none of the papers were stolen or obtained fraudulently. They were either official papers already made public documents by His Majesty's Stationery Office in London or published material in the official records of the Legislative Council or the House of Commons and journals and newspapers. The motive, he said, is quite clearly historical.

"My recommendation is that Mudaliyar Valour-Lion be requested to bequeath these documents to the national archives for the benefit of future historians."

In the meantime, Dowbiggin had recovered enough self-confidence to raise a question.

"Has the Deputy Colonial Secretary read the reference to provocative titles in the inner covers of the files?"

652

Timothy asked for the floor and explained how the comments in the inner covers came to be.

"They were meant to be eye-catching and not provocative. Both my father-in-law and I think that some day the history of the British Rule will have to be written under such chapter headings?"

"I saw them. I had not known my fellow oriental scholar to be a witty man," said the Governor.

Government Agent Frazer said to Principal Frazer in a stage whisper, "This bugger has all the aces."

Even the Governor was amused.

Tea was served in the drawing room. The Governor touched me on the shoulder and led me to the sofa on which he sat.

"I have sent you my condolences on your wife's tragic death. I remember her very well. She was such a charming and intelligent woman. She knew some of the intricate details of the Margosa Rite which others had not known. Her death is a tragedy. I can empathize with you, Mudaliyar. I lost my two sons tragically only weeks before the riots commenced."

I was deeply touched by his sincerity. I thanked him profusely. In doing so, I expressed my most grateful appreciation of every step he was taking to salvage my lost dignity. He called Timothy and Autumn-Moon to join our circle. He continued to speak of his sorrows and regrets, his disappointments and apprehensions. The intimacy in which he received us sent a message to the military top brass and the Police.He accorded to me and my family the respect he had always shown to us. On his own, he recalled our first meeting in England when he was student of the pioneering Pali and Buddhist scholar, Professor T. W. Rhys Davids.

"Your father-in-law was quite a young man and he was already a scholar with an international reputation. He was held out to us an a role model," the Governor told Timothy.

When the meeting was reconvened, the Governor resumed his business-like posture.

"Gentlemen, What is your recommendation?"

The Brigadier motioned Dowbiggin to speak.

"Sir, if you are satisfied that the contents of his files are not seditious, you may exercise the Crown's privilege and pardon him," he said without much deliberation.

Autumn-Moon stood up to speak. But the Governor requested him to sit down and turned to the official bench.

"I give you time to think and this the best you can come up with? No one wonder in a hundred days you have brought more disrepute to His Majesty's Government than any seditionist could ever do."

He was angry. But all in uniform were perplexed. Frazer the Government Agent spoke up.

"We are sorry, Your Excellency, we did not consult among ourselves. If we had, I would have pointed to the military and the Police that a pardon is given only to a person already convicted. It is an act of mercy exercised by the Crown in consideration of some attenuating circumstances."

"Exactly, Sir," said Autumn-Moon patting the right hand of his neighbour.

"You are right, Frazer. What is the next step that has to be taken?"

Stanley sought to answer that query.

"Sir, he was detained on the orders of a Magistrate. What needs to be done by the Police is to present him before a Magistrate and seek his release on grounds that there was no evidence to indict him."

"With all those incriminating files?" shouted the Brigadier.

"Which only His Excellency and the Deputy Colonial Secretary had read. They found nothing incriminating," blurted Autumn-Moon.

At that precise moment, a monkey from the Upper Garden Forest jumped from the window-sill to the Brigadier's shoulder and took away his topee, exposing a sun-burnt, spotted scalp. It provided comic relief to an otherwise tense occasion. Even I could not hold back a little laughter at his ultimate discomfiture.

"That will be done tomorrow morning - the first thing," said Dowbiggin more as an order to the Superintendent of Police.

"That would not be necessary," said Stanley Williams. "The Magistrate is ready to come as soon as I send word."

"Meeting adjourned," the Governor said. The official bench left without a word of apology or adieu. Frazers and Stanley remained behind to have another round of tea with us and the Governor.

"All's well that ends well," said Frazer the Principal.

"But not for many men," the Governor added. His face showed vividly the pain of mind he was going through. "Not for Mrs. Valour-Lion? How can we say that about the people who were dealt with summarily? The ones shot on sight?"

"But, Sir, you were ...." said the Government Agent Frazer.

The Governor interrupted him.

"in charge. Yes. I was the top dog. The people in London knew the situation better than I did. I heard only what those around me wanted me to hear. Maybe, it is all my fault. I am not cut out to be manipulating

654

and controlling people. I am a Treasury man and not a political animal. I am only good with money and in making financial decisions."

"And rendering into beautiful English the Buddha's Pali," I added to convey my sincere appreciation.

"You may be correct, Mudaliyar. I will get back to my books."

The Magistrate arrived with the Court Secretary and the records. I was affirmed. The Superintendent made the statement as drafted by Stanley. In five minutes, I was a free man.

The Superintendent of Police walked with me, Autumn-Moon and Timothy to the Buddhist School where their cars were parked. I asked him to thank the policemen responsible for rushing Slim-Jewel to the hospital.

He shook hands with me and said,

"Thank you, Mudaliyar, for not telling the Governor and the top brass that I could have prevented this whole dismal period of history in your beautiful country if only my officers took you seriously and got me to reroute the carol chariot."

"We believe in Karma. It had to happen this way."

X

It was easy to talk about Karma to an outsider. But it brought no solace. Timothy decided that I should go to his place. What a joyous reunion it was, especially for Moon-Beam and the children! Autumn-Moon gave a vivid account of the meeting with the Governor at the King's Pavilion. The children were enthralled by the way he magnified and portrayed the discomfitures of the military and Police top brass.The episode of the monkey and the Brigadier's topee sent them to hilarious laughter.

Suddenly back in civilization, I thought to myself what I needed most. There was little doubt about priorities. It had to be a good shower at the Royal Spout. Before nightfall, my wish was fulfilled. I was too excited to sleep. We sat round the dinner table and talked until cocks began to crow.

That day the things happened so quickly, I had no idea about what I should do next. Only one thing suppressed the pain caused by the death of Slim-Jewel. That was meditation.

"I wish I could go to a forest hermitage and meditate," I said.

"Not a bad idea, Father. But before you retire to the forest give me and Moon-Beam a chance to bring you back to good health. In three or four months, you will be perfectly hail and hearty and a forest hermitage would do no harm." said Timothy.

"Exactly," agreed Moon-Beam.

"That also gives you enough time to clear your mind. That is really what you should do," said Autumn-Moon.

"Let us sleep a bit," suggested Moon-Beam.

"No,Jewel. I will have another cup of tea, read the day's newspaper and go in the morning to join my Freezer Club at the spout."

"That's fine with me. I want to take Golden Jewel to clean the house a bit."

Thus commenced my new routine. Freezer Club at dawn. Three heavy meals. Vitamins and exercise. A nap. And as many hours as possible in deep meditation on the futility of pursuing vain desire.

For all intents and purposes I was a recluse. I had no intention to get back to the kind of work that I had done with Slim-Jewel. No associations. No meetings, No speeches. Not even correspondence, other than with Homeless Dharmapala and Don Baron.

Don Baron had received from someone a copy of my poem. He expressed his admiration for my insight.

656

"We are determined to fight for nothing short of Independence," he wrote. "Let this war end. We want to organize ourselves into a Ceylon National Congress on the lines of the Indian National Congress. You have to be a leading light in it."

My reply was simple.

"I am blind without my eyes. I am a cripple without my limbs. Of what use am I to you? Without my beloved Slim-Jewel I am a living corpse. You will have in Timothy a devoted representative of the next generation. I am sure that Autumn-Moon, too, will be with you very soon."

I also replied to a letter from Homeless, who was incarcerated in his own home in Calcutta. He was sick and infirm, pleading his innocence, declaring his loyalty to the British throne and imploring for his release. He longed to see the shores of the Island. I hoped that I could get something done for him through Stanley.

The more I regained my health the longer I could meditate and with greater vigour. Meditation became the be all and end all of my life. Even the children respected my need for silence.

When the schools closed for the December vacation, I felt that I had to give back to them the freedom of childhood. The freedom to play, to laugh and to quarrel. I spelled out my plans. Both Timothy and Moon-Beam agreed.

We drove to Sangha-Gem-Field on a Sunday morning. At a simple ceremony presided over by my brother, I was ordained a monk and given higher ordination simultaneously. I sat at the end table just ahead of the novices - the most junior of monks with higher ordination. It was an emotionally charged movement.

I recalled the circumstances under which I was ordained a novice when my Uncle the Chief Monk was felled by a stroke. Then I was pining for Slim-Jewel who was lost to me on account of superstition. The higher ordination brought back memories of the Siamese prince with whom I shared the ceremony. What a loyal friend he had been right up to his death. It is to support the widowed and abused Slim-Jewel that I cast aside the robe and sought employment with the Government. Slim-Jewel, being killed by an inept soldier serving the same Government, I had returned to monkhood. This time the purpose was clear.

A month or so at the Sangha-Gem-Field monastery was necessary to get ready the basic requirements for my next phase of life. The quiet life in the village with lonely spots in the jungle by the river to while away one's time in meditation served as a perfect transition.

It was a motorcade of four or five vehicles that left the Sangha-Gem-Field Monastery on the evening of the last day of 1915. Don Baron was on his way to England to agitate for justice and the right of self-determination of the people of the Island. I was on a similar journey to struggle for liberation. Mine certainly was selfish.

I was in a car with four senior monks. We travelled overnight through tantalizingly winding roads and reached by dawn the plain of Hundred Thousand Rice Fields. A monk who was familiar with the area pointed out places which figured in the Island's previous attempts in freeing itself from foreign yoke: where Gamini the Disobedient, in the second century before Christ, led his army northwards to oust the South Indian adventurer, who had been in control of the northern region for forty-four years; where Victory-Arm the Great campaigned in the eleventh century to free the country from the Cola Empire of South India; and where the rebels of 1817-1818 rose against the power of the British Empire. Curiously, I had lost interest in history. I could have said so much to enlighten my travelling companions. But I saw no point. Some kind of intellectual apathy was creeping into me.

After our morning ablutions by the Great Sand River and a frugal breakfast, we paid homage to the Buddha at the sacred shrine of Earth-Plain. It was reputed to be the first ever Buddhist monument to be established in the country. We drove southwards along the river.

The uneven cart track through the verdant bush had a charm of its own. Speed was out of the question not only because of the condition of the road but also the constant fear that the next bend would bring us to the midst of a herd of elephants. Deer and elk spied on us warily. Peahens hardly budged from the road until we were very close to them. An occasional peacock danced with its lustrous blue and gold feathers spread as a fan.

The first car stopped by a tree and those in it pointed to a leopard sleeping on a branch. A couple of bears crossed the cart track briskly and ran to the river. Watching them on their frolicking progress, we saw the most glorious sight of a herd of elephants bathing in the river. There could have been at least twenty. They lay like giant rocks all over river bed. The young ones - some hardly three feet high - were surrounded by the herd. The rustling noise we heard under the car turned out to be a ten-foot python who too was making for the river. It was an unending display of the wealth of wild life. It lasted the whole day.

As the dusk set in, we reached our destination, Great Monastery of Tissa. All that marked this historic monument, built in the second century before Christ, was a brick mound covered with lush vegetation. It was no longer the gleaming white pagoda which was seen for miles in the days of the national hero, Gamini the Disobedient.

After a whole day on the road, we were tired. The lonely monk who had made it his mission to restore the shrine to its pristine glory gave us herbal tea and invited the monks to share his cell. The rest of the group slept under the margosa trees in the compound of the pagoda. Moon-Beam's kids were thrilled.

The next morning, before dawn, we scrambled into four cadjan-thatched carts and proceeded to the Celestial Peak Forest Hermitage. The road was primitive and not motorable. Even the carts could move only very slowly. Once again, we were in the midst of wild life. Buffaloes grazed unmindful of our intrusion. Birds from as far as Russian Siberia had come there to spend the winter. Ducks and cranes and a rare flamingo watched us as we passed.

Occasionally, a flock of frightened white stork would rise into the sky before us and hover about making a plaintive cry. Crocodiles basked in the sunshine, letting birds pick their teeth. Deer and elk were plentiful. Monkeys had no fear of the carts. They carried on their morning palavers seated on their haunches in perfect circles. Some would hang with one hand on the cart roof and demand food.

A comb of bananas handed to one would recreate a Rugby scrimmage on the side of the road. An elephant eating leaves from a wayside tree moved a few feet to let us pass and returned to its feast. The observant carters knew exactly where to spot the nature's endless display of rich diversity. It was a world of fantasy. This was soon to be my world.

A long shed in the clearing of the forest marked the end of the cart track. A rustic signpost asked visitors to be silent and to behave in a manner conducive to the sanctity of the Forest Hermitage where monks were in meditation.

The shed was divided into three parts. The kitchen, with built-in hearths was spacious. Next to it was an equally commodious room where shelves lined each wall. More than half the shed comprised sleeping areas marked for men and women. I was curious and a carter explained.

"At least fifty monks are in deep meditation here," he said. "Their lay supporters come from all parts of the country. An association makes sure that some one is responsible for each day. It is our day today because the Chief Monk of Sangha-Gem-Field has had the day assigned to him. Usually they come on the eve of the assigned day, camp out here, cook the meals and wait for the monks. Around ten the monks come with their begging bowls."

"What happens if the person to whom a day is assigned is prevented from coming?"

"Anyone coming here has to leave their vehicles at The Great Monastery Tissa and take our carts. If any day due to whatever reason a party does not appear, we come here with at least rice and coconut salad. Once there was a hurricane and the rains lasted four days. Ten of us walked through the rain each carrying food for five monks."

The children followed the conversation with great interest.

"You will not starve, Grandpa," said the elder.

"If you do, you can always come to our home," said the younger.

While the lay people got busy cooking food for the monks, the four monks decided to explore the place. Since the inauguration of the Forest Monastery about a decade or so ago, the hill was out of bounds for the laity. But there was no restriction to monks.

The original monastery was founded in the second century before Christ. It is said to have housed twelve thousand monks. The site was breathtaking. Natural caves on the rocky outcrops had been dug into spacious residences for monks. The ubiquitous drip-ledges carved above each to prevent water from dripping into the residential area indicated that every cave had been deployed for some purpose or another. There had been other buildings too. Many a pagoda lay in ruin. Extensive foundations showed that the monastic complex had chapter houses and shrines.

To all intents and purposes it was a deserted city. The slightest noise of an insect, the chirping of a bird and even the breaking of a twig as an elephant, a bear or a monkey moved by, was heard. We were enthralled by the quietude. Our attention was drawn to the ravine by soft footsteps on pebbles. What a glorious sight it was!

The monks all clad in dark brown robes were wending their way to the alms hall. With the right hand they held a yellowish umbrella to ward off the sun and with the left they carried, covered by the edge of the robe, a begging bowl. We hurried down the hill to be at the shed ahead of them. We had been apprised of the practice and had brought our begging bowls. We joined them at the end of the line to receive the food that Timothy and Moon-Beam with the rest of the party offered us. It was a re-enactment of the age-old practice of begging for food.

It was a special day as I had come to join the community. The monks therefore decided to have their meal in the compound of the shed. A few queries about the number of rainy seasons since higher

660

ordination enabled us to find our places. My brother - the Chief Monk - was, of course, the most senior and I was about ten places from the bottom. Those after me were young novices who had devoted themselves to meditation before proceeding to formal education or higher ordination. We sat cross-legged on the ground in a hollow square. My brother was requested to perform the merit-offering ceremony. The Abbot spoke a few words and they were specially meant for my family.

"Venerable Pure-Wisdom, we welcome you as a devotee of the Buddha. We are a community dedicated to meditation. We have renounced all worldly comforts. We live in caves. Once a day we come here to beg for our food. We accept whatever is given to us and we return to our caves to partake of it. Other than this brief moment of our encounter with the donors of our requisites, we have no communication with the world outside: no visitors, no books and newspapers, no letters and messages. When Pure-Wisdom climbs the hill with us, he renounces everything. He ceases to be in your world. You cease to be in his world. He lives for one purpose and one purpose only - to realize the end of all suffering. But the merit he gains by his complete devotion his own liberation from the miserable cycle of birth and death will be shared by all of you."

Moon-Beam sobbed and tears rolled down her cheek. The children embraced her to comfort her. Timothy drew near them and took all three in his protective arms. It was with the greatest effort that I controlled my own tears.

Without further ceremony, the meditating monks rose and walked up the ravine to their caves. I was clad exactly as they were in brown robes and I knew my place in the order of precedence. I left my sandals behind as they were bare-footed. I dared not look at anyone who accompanied me from Sangha-Gem-Field. Their tears were too much to bear up. The cutting, smarting, burning sensation of my soft soles as they touched the hot, sharp gravel on the pathway was all that I was conscious of.

I was given a cave close to that of the Abbot, whose name was Wisdom-Flag. It faced due south. The glare created by midday sun dazzling on the blue ocean only a few miles away was off set by a cooling breeze that came from the same direction. Unless some slash and burn cultivators were in the forest below, there were no human habitations on this longitude to my south. Literally I was at the end of the world.

Wisdom-Flag summoned me at four. A flowering shrub called Hendrikka opened its variegated blossoms at this hour. It told the

661

clockless society that the sunset was exactly two hours away. It was to brief me. But he had little to tell me on the technique of meditation.

"Practice now what you read and taught others all this while," he said. "We leave it to you to meditate on the futility of the human body or on sensations. The Buddha's Great Sermon on the Four Foundations of Mindfulness is our guide. Start with mindful breathing. Progress at your own pace. We discuss our progress every day at sunset. Share with us your experiences as we would ours with you. You will live in the midst of dangerous snakes, ferocious wild beasts and annoying insects. Practice loving kindness toward them. They will never harm you."

When I returned to my cave, a senior monk more or less of my age was seated outside. He beckoned me to sit in front of him.

"Friend," he called me in Pali. "There a few things which you must know of our life in the monastery. It is regulated by the stock - that hollowed out log hanging vertically on that branch - which will be beaten at stipulated hours."

He pointed it to me. It was a polished, cylindrical log of satin wood, hollowed out like a drum and was about three feet long. Two holes pieced at the bottom end held horizontally a club also of satin wood. When beaten with the club, the drum-like log produced a vibrating boom which was heard hundreds of yards away. My colleague ensured that I understood what it was and what function it served.

"You will be woken by it at four in the morning. You get up and meditate until the next signal. Then you walk down to the lake, do your ablutions, bathe if you wish, wash your robe and any other clothes and walk back to your cave. We do not go to the lake alone. Animals always defer to us when we are in a group. They sense whether you love them, hate them or fear them. Always have kind thoughts for them. Always think for yourself, 'It's a misguided human of another life who is a denizen of the forest now.' Every minute we have to ourselves we meditate. Meditate for an hour seated under a tree or in your cell. For another hour do walking meditation on the promenade in front of you cave."

He pointed out to me the eighteen foot walk which monks might have used two thousand years ago.

"At ten, the stock will announce the time to go begging for our alms. We receive the offerings in our begging bowl and walk back. The Chief Monk will stay behind to deliver the Thanks-giving Sermon and return after us. We partake of our only meal of the day in our caves. We may rest or resume meditation. At four the blossoming Hendrikka will indicate the time for a herbal drink. Take your can to the caves of the novices and someone will serve you a drink. Back to meditation until the stock announces the assembly in front of the Chief Monk's cave. He must have told you what we do at this meeting."

"Yes, he did,"

"After the meeting you are on your own either to meditate late into the night or to sleep."

He persuaded me to meditate on sensations.

"Sensations - pleasant, unpleasant and neither pleasant nor unpleasant - race through our entire psycho-physical system like the strong winds that raise waves on the surface of the ocean. Be aware of them. Be mindful of them. Identify the character of each sensation, its origin, its progress and its passing. Do it diligently and patiently."

His explanation of meditation on sensations as a means of attaining mental tranquility was clear and detailed. He paraphrased passages of the Buddhist Canon which I could recall from memory. I wished I had realized earlier the practical implications of the Buddha's teachings.

All my life, my preoccupation had been with the intellectual minutea which passed off as scholarship. The inner essence of the Buddha's admonitions awaited discovery and application. I saw what the future held for me. I asked myself whether I was capable of fulfilling the new obligation. Would I face up to the physical and psychological challenge? Yes, I said to myself, thanks to the hundred days in prison.

"Thank you," we say with hearts of gratitude,
"No friend of the nation could ever do better."

I kept to the day's schedule. A delectable herbal drink made of a yellow wild flower was served by a novice. It was consumed by the community of monks in silence. I was curious to know their names and their backgrounds. But that was not to be. The monks dispersed as though they were summoned back to some very urgent task. I returned to my cave and sat down to meditate.

The folded robe which served as a cushion was too thin for comfort. I could not sit crosslegged for more than ten minutes at a time. My span of attention was even shorter. There were far too many things in my mind which bothered me. At one point, I must have dozed. I saw as in real life the smiling face of Slim-Jewel peering through the window of a prison cell. It was no doubt a dream because my cell had no window.

At the assembly of the community at dusk, I listened to the experiences of different meditators. The Chief Monk listened to each account with deep attention. At the end, he made his observations.

"Brethren, we will not be here if our task was easy. The control of the mind - the cultivation of the mind - is by far the most difficult thing to achieve. Had not our Buddha admonished us, 'The mind is ever in motion, fickle, difficult to be guarded and difficult to be restrained?' You and you alone know what progress you have made. The mind plays its own games on the indolent and the unheedful. The boundary between deep meditation and self-hypnosis is as thin and sharp as the razor's edge. I have only your words to go on. How much of it is fantasy or hallucination? How much is indicative of a becalmed mind? I will be meeting individually those who may still need guidance. When the stock is next beaten, please recite aloud the Discourse on Loving Kindness whether you retire for the night or continue to meditate. May all beings be well and happy."

We responded to him in the Pali equivalent of "Amen:" "Sadhu! Sadhu! Sadhu!" It was like saying good, fine or well thrice.

I was detained for instruction.

"It will take a week or two before you get used to our life with the barest minimum. If you need sandals to walk about, there is absolutely no objection. If you need a cushion to sit on, we can improvise one. Remember the first principle of the Buddha: we follow a path between self-indulgence and self-mortification. Your span of attention will improve as you go on. Diligence - that is the key. Perseverance - that is the fuel. When the key is in place and there is no dearth of fuel, your car will go wherever you want."

I marvelled at the Chief Monk's parable of the motor car.

He smiled and continued,

"Have you climbed the holy mountain to worship the footprint of the Buddha?"

"Yes, Venerable Sir. I climbed it several times."

"Then you know what what I mean."

With that I was dismissed.

I sat on the same thin cushion of folded robes. I felt it softer. My legs obeyed me better. I developed mindfulness on inhalation and exhalation. As I proceeded, my ears became gradually deaf to the tumultuous croaking of frogs in the lake and the high-pitched droning of the cicadas. But I was not sleeping for I heard clearly the stock and the melodious chanting of the Discourse on Loving Kindness which reverberated over the hill. I joined them with as clear and loud a voice I could command:

Thus should be done by the purposefully skilled
To reach the goal of Perfect Peace.
He should be able, upright and truly honest,
Courteous, mild and modest.

Contented, an easy guest,
No busybody but free of affection,
Restrained in senses, mature in outlook,
Bluster-free and detached from households.

May he not commit even a trivial thing
Which the wise in another would censure
"May all beings be happy and safe.
May they all have happy minds.

Whatsoever life exists -
Weak or strong without exception,
Long and huge,
Medium, short, atom-sized or large,

Seen or unseen,
Living nearby or far away,
Born or seeking to be born -
May all beings have a happy mind.

May not one deceive another,
May not one insult another,
Through anger or ill-will.
May no one wish harm to each other.

Just as a mother, with her own life,
Would save her only child - her son,
So should be radiated to all beings
A thought of boundless love.

Suffuse the whole world alike
With a thought of boundless friendship.
With neither enmity nor rivalry,
Above, below and across without obstruction.

Standing, walking, sitting or reclining
As long as one stays awake,
May this mindfulness be firmly held

Here is called the Sublime State.

Free from heresy, in virtue steeped,
Gaining true insight
With greed for sensual delights subdued
Never again shall one return to a womb.

Contemplating the sweet words of advice of the Buddha, I reclined on the reed-mat on the dry floor of the cave. In minutes I was in deep, dreamless sleep.

At the first stroke of the stock, I was up. Without much effort I developed mindfulness on inhalation and exhalation and sustained it for quite some time. I was so engrossed that I had not noticed the young novice who stood at the door of the cave. When I relaxed and turned around, he told me that he had come to help me to get down to the lake. He took me there.

Though the sun had not yet arisen, there was enough light to walk without tripping on protruding stones or coming too close to a snake. The head of a reptile emerged from a hole by the road. I took it to be a snake but the novice said that it was more like a young iguana. He took me to the rock where tin cans were kept, took one, filled it with water from the lake and showed the general area where I could relieve myself. Before leaving me to fend for myself, the novice told me,

"Come very cautiously so as not to trample on any crocodiles on your way to the lake. If there are any animals still round the lake, wait a little while more. They will withdraw as the sun comes up. If there is a herd of elephants, you have nothing to fear. But if the tailless rogue elephant is seen hanging around, don't disturb it."

By the time I emerged from the bush, a few more monks had come to the lake. There were no wild animals around it. We dipped in the cool and refreshing water, shaved one another's head and returned clean and invigorated. I had passed the most difficult test. Now that I learned to handle the morning's preparation for the day, I felt buoyant. I resumed my meditation and made some progress in developing mindfulness on the sensations I felt. I was determined not to give up. "Diligence is the key; Perseverance is the fuel."

At the signal, I joined the line of monks descending to the alms hall, received food in my begging bowl, returned to the cave, ate it after a brief moment of contemplation and drank some water from a pitcher which a novice had thoughtfully replenished. I stretched out to rest for a while. I reviewed how I had fared in the first twenty-four hours and felt quite satisfied.

While it was yet not clear to me why I had chosen this course, I was convinced that I could do it. And I did it. Day by day the routine became lighter. Physical discomforts vanished. The mind was responding to the demands made of it. Tranquility prevailed. The sheer joy of a mind free of worry and anxiety, remorse and repentance was worth any price. The Chief Monk was pleased.

"Pure-Wisdom, few have made as much progress in so short a time. Continue. Be diligent. Persevere. You have still a long way to go."

XI

Days passed and there was no calendar to keep track of them. Full moon and new moon marked the days when the monks with higher ordination gathered in the ruins of a chapter house and performed the Sabbath confessional ceremony. And that was all that the community had to know.

I did not know what that particular day was. I walked down with the rest to beg for alms. What a surprise it was to find Moon-Beam and Timothy, the children and my brother the Chief Monk and almost all the people who came to the hermitage with me. As on that day, the monks ate in the shed and the usual rites were observed. The visiting Chief Monk was asked to give the Thanksgiving Sermon. How far removed I was from things worldly! Until he intimated the reason for their having this particular date assigned to them, I did not recollect that it was my fifty-eighth birthday. Every time they come with alms in the future, I would know that it was my birthday.

Wisdom-Flag allowed me to spend some time with the family.

"You are not doing badly in spite of the rough life," said Timothy.

"To tell you the truth, you have a healthy glow. The life in the hermitage is positively doing you some good," added Moon-Beam.

To be so given a clean bill of health by two doctors was very encouraging.

"The real reason for my well-being, you may have no way to judge," I said." Meditation is perhaps the best tranquilizer. I wish I had known of it earlier."

"We are glad that you took time to know it. Otherwise we could have lost a loving and devoted Father too early", said Moon-Beam.

For a brief moment a scene from the fast flashed in my mind's eye. Slim-Jewel and I were on the lake bund in Kandy with Moon-Beam and Middle Banda buying balloons. It was so vivid. We were having fun with the seller who was making all kinds of queer shapes with long red balloons.

I had to blink to get the vision off my eyes. "Be mindful, Monk," I admonished myself in silence. "Your attachments are yet to be severed."

"We came to take you back if you found the place disagreeable," said Timothy.

"That will not be necessary, son."

"Any time you change your mind, you have only to tell one of these carters. The Chief Monk of the Great Tissa Monastery will contact us.

We are telling Venerable Wisdom-Flag to let us know through the same channels if you need any assistance."

I was thankful for their solicitude and hoped that it would be a long time before such an emergency arose.

They left with ample time to cross the forest before the elephants and bears could get on the road. I climbed back to the cave of the novice who had herbal drinks ready.

In spite of my determination, I was unable to get my mind back on focus. It reverted to the family. I missed the children whom I had not seen for a long time. I wondered how Middle Banda and Rose and Vickie and Beckie and their children were getting on. How I longed to see them. I explained my plight at the assembly that evening.

"Admonish yourself, Monk. Attachment to the family is a primary hindrance to the Path of Purification," was all that the Chief Monk would tell me.

For a week I shunned all company. I did not go for my meals. A novice brought me my share. Such purposeful action seemed to be effective. I returned to my normal schedule of meditation. A crisis was met and overcome. A lesson was learnt.

Never again would I allow myself to be overwhelmed by any thought of my past. Of course, it was not easy to rub the slate clean. The past was full of people I loved and people who loved me. I felt concerned about them. I was proud of them. I longed to see them again. I mourned for the departed ones. All I could do with the utmost effort was not to dwell too long on thoughts that would engender attachment. As advised, I counselled myself at every moment when I was distracted from my meditation.

As time went on things did improve. Three things happened without my even noticing.

I lost altogether the fear of wild life. The leopard who spent most of its time on a branch of the satin tree in front of my cave gave both me and the Chief Monk a sense of protection. Elephants passed in front of the cave at night and their silhouettes were framed against the moonlight as in a shadow play. Monkeys were bold enough to enter my cave when I was asleep or meditating. The crocodiles took no notice of me when I passed them on my way to the lake. A cobra disturbed by my rustling footsteps opened its hood, gazed at me for a full minute and slid into the grass. A bear swaggered behind me for a few hundred yards before climbing a cliff to attack a bee hive.

I came to accept the violence of the forest as ineluctable. It would be idle to save a single frog from the jaws of a rat snake. The shrieking

669

fawn, being wrapped around and crushed before being swallowed whole and alive by a python, was beyond assistance. So was the buffalo whose leg had been chewed by a hungry crocodile. My heart bled for the prey. But there was nothing else that I or anyone else could do. Yet my thoughts of Loving Kindness went to them. I wished that their future existences be more meaningful and conducive to their eventual cessation of all suffering.

The second change was that I had adjusted to the life of the hermitage and its routine. No longer did I miss my tiled bathroom with ceramic commode and enamel-coated metal bath. A dip in the cool lake became the equivalent of the spout with my Freezer Club cronies. The soles of my feet toughened and the hot sand was no longer a problem. I could sit cross-legged for long hours. Meditation became a source of tranquility and delight. The chanting of the Discourse on Loving Kindness as the last community activity for the day lulled me to sleep. One needed much more than a comfortable bed and a soft pillow to have a good night's undisturbed, dreamless sleep and I had them all.

The last of the happenings was baffling. As all others in the forest community, I lost track of time. Days and weeks ceased to count. The fortnight became the shortest unit of time. Twice a month as dictated by the moon we met to recite the Rules of Discipline and perform the fortnightly confessional ceremony. The year was marked by special events. For three months as the heat of the hottest season was waning we observed the Rainy Season Lent, even if there was hardly any rain. At the end of the Lent, crowds brought us robes and held in the shed the time-honoured ceremony of the "Difficult Robe" - difficult, as it had to be deserved by three months of discipline. As time passed, we participated in the ceremonies mechanically. But we counted each Lent because that determined our seniority.

When I entered the community, I was once again a neophyte. The Lent periods completed in my first term as a monk were not counted. I was a monk with higher ordination but without a single Lent to my credit. I had one other reminder that a year had passed in my life. The family never failed to appear with alms on the Fourth of February to mark my birthday. Yet I had forgotten most of the things that happened on these special occasions. Progress in meditation was all that counted - it developed a veritable one-track mind. What we tried to achieve was perfect concentration leading eventually to the realization of the true nature of existence.

I recall, however, my sixty-ninth birthday - that is, the fourth of February, 1927. Three were missing from the family that had made the arduous trip regularly. The two children of Timothy and Moon-Beam had been sent to England for their studies. My brother the Chief Monk was not there because he had passed away three months ago. Wisdom-Flag asked me to officiate in the ceremony that the family held to mark the third month of his death. They had planned to have it with my participation. My sermon on death as an object of meditation surprised me. I called it a divine messenger sent to convince us of the ineluctable impermanence of all phenomena.

Death had been stalking our little community. The hard life, the frugal meals and the absence of micronutrients made the frail monks ready victims of disease. Whereas there were at least forty monks between me and Venerable Wisdom-Flag when I came to the hermitage, in 1927 there were about twenty . When a virulent epidemic of malaria swept the country in 1934, the community lost over half its members. Fifteen died of malaria and ten sought the comfort and security of their parents or relatives. Only two returned when the crisis was over.

Among the dead was Wisdom-Flag. I was about ten behind the new Chief Monk. The reputation of the community attracted new recruits. By 1940, there were over eighty monks and I was the second in seniority. At eighty-two, I was fortunate to be sound in all faculties and physically strong. I had lost a few teeth. My skin was sallow and wrinkled. My distant vision was slightly blurry and the hearing in one ear diminished. I climbed the hill without panting and attended to my bodily needs without assistance. I continued to meditate long hours, alternating sitting with walking meditation.

At every visit on my birthday, Timothy would give me a physical examination, much against my wishes. He was usually pleased with the results.

"Good peasant stock, Venerable Father," he would say by way of explaining my robust health.

He also attended to the sick and the weak. He would distribute medicine and vitamins to them. The novices would be told about the use and storage of various pills and powders. They were specially instructed to see that every one of us had a tablet of quinine every day.

Some drastic changes were observed in the next two years. More often than not the carters for the Great Monastery Tissa brought us alms. The hastily improvised food consisted of millet paste, boiled jak and breadfruit. We were also disturbed quite often by low flying aeroplanes.

The only explanation for the changes that we could glean from the brief remarks of carters was that there was a major war in the world.

671

They called it the Second World War. Apparently, I thought, the war during which I entered the forest monastery was the First World War.

The rules pertaining to the thirty-two kinds of irrelevant or futile talk prevented us from pursuing further the world situation whose adverse effects had reached as far as our tiny forest community in a faraway corner of a remote Island.

"If the war comes to our country, we will not be able even to bring this food," one of the carters had told a novice.

The Chief Monk Lotus-Lustre once asked me,

"Pure-Wisdom, if our supporters are prevented from maintaining us with our requisites, what should we do?"

"What will you do personally in such an eventuality, Venerable Sir?"

"I could go back to my temple in the village and tide over the difficult time."

"That may be the solution for everyone," I suggested.

No action, however, was called for. The more we got used to the rustic food that was being served to us, the more we were convinced that we could continue in the hermitage. One thing was, however, disturbing. For two whole years we had had no new recruits.

"Life outside must be very difficult," Lotus-Lustre said at the end of an evening assembly and called upon us to chant texts from the Book of Protection to ensure world peace and the well being of all people. It became a regular practice.

I had already passed twenty-eight Lents of the Rainy Season and my eighty-seventh birthday was fast approaching. Mentally I was alert. Meditation came easily. I reached a remarkably high degree of concentration in a very short time. My memory, specially of the books I have read and the events of the past, was perfect. Little details I had begun to forget. On several days, I had gone a second or a third time to the novice to get my herbal drink and the tablet of quinine. At an evening assembly, I could not recall the name of the presiding Chief Monk and I was embarrassed.

On the eve of my birthday, a novice had to help me up the hill as I was dragging my right leg.

The Chief Monk, though senior to me by twenty Lents, was not yet seventy. He came to my cave in the morning of the Fourth of February 1945 and chanted benedictory stanzas to bless me on my birthday. Before taking leave of me, he said,

"Pure-Wisdom, Time has come for you to be wiser, not braver. When your daughter and her husband come today, please go with them

672

and find out if you need medical attention. Do not tarry here until you are disabled. You have the warning signs. You may still have a mission to accomplish."

"What other mission could I have, Venerable Sir? At my age? In my present state of deteriorating health?"

"We never know, Pure-Wisdom. Maybe, your mission now is to let future generations know of your life and times, to share your insights and values and to set the record straight."

"What record would that be, Venerable Sir?"

"The record of our nation's recent march to liberty. We are still not free. But we will soon be. Yes, Pure-Wisdom. *We will be free at last.*"

XII

I needed assistance to walk down to the shed. I had my arms round the necks of two novices and propelled forward with my left leg, dragging behind me my disobedient right leg.

"Since when?" asked Timothy who came up the hill to meet me half way.

The Chief Monk who was ahead of me answered because nothing audible enough to comprehend came from my lips however hard I tried.

What happened after I saw Timothy I do not know. Often I try to recall this moment and my otherwise sharp memory becomes a closed book. I remember when I woke up.

I was in an airy room, on a bed with a comfortable mattress, white sheets, soft pillows, a snow-white canopy and mosquito nets. On a bedside table was a vase with red and yellow roses. By it was a dimmed night lamp.

"Where am I? How long have I been here? How did I get here?" the questions proliferated. But I had no answers. I coughed lightly and Slim-Jewel emerged from darkness and raised the wick of the night lamp.

I was not dreaming and it was not Slim-Jewel. The nurse lifted the mosquito net and observed me carefully.

"How do you feel, Venerable Sir?" she asked me.

"I feel all right but I cannot move my right leg and arm."

"You were very lucky, Venerable sir, You had two doctors by your side when you got the stroke."

From what she told me I could piece out what had happened. I was in the paying ward of the Kandy Hospital. I was under heavy medication when I was admitted and I had slept at least fourteen hours. Most of it was drug-induced. I felt thirsty. The nurse gave me a sip or two of water.

"You are very lucky again, Venerable Sir," the nurse said. "Few regain their speech so soon after a stroke."

"Maybe it was not a stroke?" I ventured.

The more I thought about what the nurse told me, the more I was convinced that I still had a mission to accomplish. I was impatient for Timothy or Moon-Beam to visit me.

They were there by my bed within minutes of my wish.

"We are all very lucky, Father, to be where we were at the right time" said Timothy jubilantly. "If you are speaking as well as the nurse tells me, you are on the way to recovery. A little more rest and some effort on your part, you will be as good as before."

Moon-Beam, who looked every inch a faithful replica of Slim-Jewel, confirmed her husband's optimism.

"You have to get well soon, Father," she added. "You have a book to write."

"That is a good project to set your mind on, Father," said Timothy.

I had to get well. I had yet a mission to accomplish.

Within a few days I was able to limp out of bed and hop to a chair near the window. The physiotherapist came every morning. He taught me to walk again. I rotated a wheel with my right hand for hours. I held on to the window bars and did sit-ups. All that was difficult, even to a healthy man of eighty-seven. For one with a stroke whose last twenty-nine years had been in the perfect seclusion of a forest hermitage, it was murder. But I would not give up: I had a mission to accomplish; I had a book to write.

As I regained the strength of my leg and arm, my attention came to be focused on my hand: I had to learn to write. I was once again a kindergartner trying to gain control of the finer muscles. I trained both hands. In case! Moon-Beam was impressed.

"What an inspiration, Father. You never give up."

Quite unconsciously I said.

"I have to write this book, Moon-Beam."

After six weeks in hospital, I was discharged.The house at Royal Spout had been remodelled for my use. The wing I occupied had all the makings of a temple. The library had been redesigned with much thought. Half of it contained books neatly arranged in shelves. On the other side, laid on tables were my archives. Prominently displayed within my arm's reach were the files which would have sent me to prison for many years, if not for the friendship of Stanley Williams and the prudence and sense of justice of Sir Robert Chalmers.

The other wing housed a staff of six or seven to attend to my needs. A wheel-chair enabled me to be mobile indoors and outdoors. A thoughtfully laid path took me among flowers. A brand new car, a Vauxhall Wyvern - more stylish and spacious than the Ford Model-T - was in the car porch and a driver in a white uniform was at my service.

Three more amenities were within reach from my wheel-chair. A telephone was on my bedside stool. In the living room was a radio set.

675

An Underwood typewriter was placed on a low table in my study with a typist's chair in front of it.

With all these changes and amenities, my new residence was indeed a far cry from the cave in the forest monastery which had been my home for twenty-nine years.

Getting used to the telephone with my impaired speech was a challenge. Soon I mastered a few tricks like speaking slowly and spelling words which were distorted by the lisp. My callers were very sympathetic indeed. Timothy and Moon-Beam telephoned me several times a day and the children too would call once a while from England to ask about "Grandpa's days in the bush." They always had a new question. Autumn-Moon called me regularly every Sunday. Wickie and Beckie phoned from Illinois to give the good news that they were planning to spend the Summer Vacation with me.

"Father, we have a project in hand," Beckie said with great excitement. "We have some funding to document the real Rip van Winkle. So we will there by mid-June."

The call was brief and the line only passably clear. But the enthusiasm in their voices were striking. When Timothy and Moon-Beam dropped in that evening I told them of the phone call.

"Beckie and Wickie are going to Holland to write a book on a real Rip van Winkle and then they are coming here."

Both of them burst out laughing and Timothy controlled himself enough to say,

"Father, you are the *real* Rip van Winkle. Washington Irving's character slept for twenty years and found how much the world had changed. You cut yourself away from the world for almost thirty years. Vickie has convinced a Foundation that your story would be more dramatic. He seriously thinks your experience might suggest some methodological approach to the study of contemporary history."

I was amused that an American Foundation was funding my son and his wife to come all the way from the United States just to write a book on me.

The radio was the greatest solace. When the weather was good the reception was excellent. As I listened to programmes in all three languages - Sinhala, Tamil and English - there was always something informative and interesting. Sermons by eloquent monks were my favourite. Most of the preachers whom I adored came from the Diamond Monastery of a southern suburb of Colombo. Its Chief Monk Diamond-Wisdom was matchless. Remarkable were his disciples who had short names like Narada, Khema, and Soma.

676

Frequently heard in both English and Sinhala in religious as well as other programmes was another of my favourites. Young George Percival Wrestler-Diadem had, in deference to the campaign of Homeless Dharmapala , changed his first names into national names while retaining the same initials. His was superb eloquence, enhanced by erudition and tempered by a remarkable sense of humour. I never missed his weekly programme "Brain Trust."

The more I found myself not merely comfortable but in the lap of luxury, the more I felt guilty that I had become a burden to my children. One day I had to ask them,

"All these amenities must have cost you a packet, Timothy?

"It is all your money, Father. Your pension has grown to a princely sum. So were the proceeds from the sale of your household effects and two cars. And when you are ready to start on your book, we can engage a couple of stenographers to work with you" replied Moon-Beam.

That explained the presence of the typewriter. Tears welled in my eyes.

"What have I done to deserve you as my children?" I asked.

"We told you in England, Father. When we promoted you from Little Father to Father."

For the next six months, it was a single-minded struggle. I was determined to get well. I was never alone. My visitors were mainly the young men aspiring for a political future in an independent Sri Lanka. To them I was a living link with the already legendary figures of our recent history: the scholar-monks of undaunted courage, specially Venerable Gunananda and Venerable Sumangala; Colonel Olcott, the White Messiah; Homeless Dharmapala , the national conscience; and Don Baron Jayatilaka , the flagship of the nation's progress to freedom.

Among them were the new leaders who were actually running important departments of the Government. On D. S., the youngest of the Senanayaka Brothers, had fallen the political mantle of Don Baron. Not only was he the undisputed leader of the national political caucus but an effective Minister of Agriculture and Lands. The regeneration of the ancient system of irrigation and opening new land for cultivation was his obsession. His personality was captivating. Always dressed in the best Saville Row suits, imported from England, he was an inveterate Anglophile. He once brought with him Sir Ivor Jennings, the Vice-chancellor of the University of Ceylon - a Cambridge don, whose dream was to plant its replica in the verdant basin of the Great Sand River just outside Kandy.

677

Solomon West Ridgeway Dias Bandaranaike , an Oxford graduate with a silver tongue, was an impressive leader. Clad in white national dress, he upheld non-violence as the strategy for regaining the nation's independence. Not only had he drawn much inspiration from contemporary Indian leaders like Mahatma Gandhi, Sirdar Patel, Rajendra Prasad and Pandit Jawaharlal Nehru but he appeared in meetings with a spinning wheel in imitation of Gandhi. What he had achieved in the fields of Local Government and Health had endeared him to the people. That he had his ear to the ground was my impression after our very first meeting.

I also had a brief visit from the Minister of Education who was popularly called by his initials C. W. W. He had already made the legislative provisions to make education from the kindergarten to and including the University free of tuition fees, and was building high schools in rural areas.

Every such visitor reconfirmed my faith in the national leadership. Already with a very limited form of Self-rule, the real problems of the country were being addressed.

I was glad that I survived the ordeal of my self-imposed exile into the forest and was now able to witness the realization of dreams that I shared with men like Olcott, Homeless and Don Baron. It was well worth living for and returning to civilization.

My friends and acquaintances from the past were few. The price of longevity is loneliness! Homeless had passed away in 1933 in India. I was moved to hear that his last years were as an ordained monk. Don Baron had the privilege of representing the Island in the cradle of its culture. It appeared to be more than a coincidence that he too passed away in India less than an year ago.

Stanley Williams and his family had decided to settle down in the hill country after retirement. Almost as old as I was, he was still active writing and speaking on national laws, customs and taboos. He came to the Planter's Library once a while to take out books and he made it a point to spend a couple of hours with me. We reminisced on the crucial events which we had experienced together.

"Tell me when you begin the book. I will read it for you," he promised.

Erstwhile friends who were back in England and elsewhere were informed by Stanley about "my return from the bush." That Christmas brought a number of cards and gifts from all over the world. I was back again - a part of that charmed circle of oriental scholars.

678

Among the gifts was a book sent with the author's compliments: *BUDDHA'S TEACHINGS being the Sutta-Nipata or Discourse-Collection* by Lord Chalmers, Harvard Oriental Series, Volume Number 37, Harvard University Press, Cambridge, Massachusetts, 1931. A note accompanying it said,

> " *At the request of the author we have held this book for you until we could find your address. We are glad to send it to you to the address furnished by Mr. Stanley Williams of City-Light*"

I was deeply touched by the gesture of Baron Chalmers. He had remembered me when he published his most beautiful translation in verse of the oldest anthology of Buddhist poetry.

I recalled his face as he bid me farewell thirty years ago. His face had the unmistakable glow of a man who was at peace with himself with the thought that he had at last done the right thing. I hoped he was still among the living so that I could convey to him my thanks and respects.

I had not begun to count days or to rely on a calender. On this somewhat unusual day, I had a steady stream of visitors from early morning. Timothy and Moon-Beam came with milk and milk-rice to offer their wishes for a happy New Year. Others brought all kinds of gifts.

It was the first day of January 1946. I was not quite conscious of the significance of this day until the prelates of the Flower Garden and Horse Peak Monasteries came to see me after the morning service at the Temple of the Sacred Tooth. It was exactly thirty years from my entry to the forest hermitage.

The prelates blessed me and in their sermons made special reference to Slim-Jewel. After thirty years she was being remembered with affection. One of them said that her death by the bullet of an unknown foreign soldier was one of the many sacrifices that the nation had made in its struggle for freedom.

A little ceremony to offer merit to her according to the Buddhist tradition ended with the pouring of water while the appropriate verses were being chanted by the monks. Then I had to approach the prelates so that they could tie a holy thread on my wrist.

It was a miracle and I have yet no explanation for what happened. Was it the magic of the benediction? Or months of tender care and medication? Or my unwavering resolution not to accept defeat? Or the inner resources I had marshalled over twenty-nine years of strenuous meditation? Or the obsession that I should get well soon to write the book which everyone was expecting me to begin?

I raised myself from the wheel chair involuntarily, walked up to the prelates and offered my right arm for one of them to tie the holy thread. I was steady on my feet. I felt as hail and hearty as I always felt in the forest hermitage.

My visitors were amazed. Timothy approached me to be in readiness if I lost my balance. But that precaution was unnecessary. I kept standing until the prelates left. I saw them into their cars. Then I walked among my family, friends and acquaintances.

I savoured my newly won freedom from immobility. I walked to the garden, picked a trayful of jasmine flowers and went into the shrine room to pay my homage to the Great Teacher, The Buddha.

Never again did I need a wheel-chair.

XIII

That very night, I began to work on my book. Thirty years of recent history beginning with the riots on May 1915 had to be first explored. The politician in the family was a great help. He had continued the archives. The perusal of neatly filed press cuttings were supplemented by hours of discussions.

Timothy's own life has become the tale of the growing political awareness of the nation. When I withdrew from the scene, he filled the gap created by both me and Slim-Jewel in the Central Province and worked in cooperation with Albert Land-Frontier. Don Baron encouraged Timothy to be an active member of the Ceylon National Congress, which rapidly grew in power and influence and became the rallying point for the rising leadership of the nation.

While its stalwarts including Don Baron were in and out of England agitating for a better deal for the nationals, Timothy with an equally zealous band of younger men and women guarded the home front. He was able to get Autumn-Moon to take an active interest in national issues.

Entering politics with impeccable reputations as two of the finest professionals in their respective fields, they won instant recognition. Both acquired fluency in Sinhala and were much sought-after speakers. Senanayaka Brothers befriended them and F.R., in particular, associated them in taking the cry for political reform to the masses. From writing memoranda, passing resolutions and appealing to the goodness of the powers that be in England, the national politicians had begun to mobilize the nation to take over the responsibility of governing itself.

The post-riot period had seen a renewed cry for the transfer of power to the people by extending the principle of electing members to the Legislative Council. It was re-emphasized that the Council should have an unofficial majority and that the members should be elected on a territorial and not a communal basis.

Seeing the advantage of the imperial policy of "Divide and Rule," the Administration, however, persisted with communal representation. They went even further and made the ratio of elected to electors so unrealistic as to make the majority community's representation grossly inadequate and disproportionate.

Timothy explained to me the rapid changes that took place in the twenties. I was impressed with the flexibility of the Governor, Sir

William Manning, who implemented changes in the Legislative Council in 1921 and 1924.

He was also responsible for the completion of several long-term projects like the extension of the railway across the central massif to the capital of the remotest Province of the Island in 1924 and the opening of the University College of Colombo, affiliated to the University of London, in 1921.

Homeless Dharmapala continued to be kept under close guard in Calcutta even after the riots were over. But his interest in the march of the nation toward political and cultural liberation continued unabated.

In 1922 he issued a message to the young men of the country. It became instantly a national manifesto for collective action. His influence persisted in the political plane even though he was more and more interested in the propagation of Buddhism abroad.

Don Baron became the President of the Ceylon National Congress in 1923. The following year, he was elected from the Colombo District as a member of the Legislative Council. His charisma and ability had singled him out to be *the* emerging leader of the nation. The next set of constitutional reforms gave him the opportunity for which he prepared himself most arduously ever since he came under the influence of Colonel Olcott.

In 1927 a Royal Commission was appointed by the British Government in London under the chairmanship of Lord Donoughmore to report upon the whole system of government of the country. Both Autumn-Moon and Timothy had mobilized associations and individuals to support the claim of the Island for a greater measure of Self-rule. The commissioners were impressed with the political maturity of the population. Accordingly, they recommended a significant measure of self-determination in the day-to-day administration of the country.

Donoughmore Commission had also put an end to the abominable practice of electing legislators on a communal basis. Instead was introduced universal adult franchise which meant that every man and woman over the age of twenty-five years were empowered to vote.

The Legislative Council was replaced by a State Council which was modelled on the County Council of London. Its territorially elected fifty members elected a Speaker and formed themselves into seven executive committees of seven members each. Each had a subject assigned to it and the chairman became the Minister of that subject. The Executive Council of the Governor was replaced by the Board of Ministers which consisted of the seven Ministers and three Officers of the State (namely, Chief Secretary, Financial Secretary and the Attorney General).

Autumn-Moon briefed me on the controversies over the acceptance of the reforms. A communal touch was added to them in that Tamils in politics rejected *en masse* the new constitution and boycotted the State Council when it was eventually established in 1931.

Don Baron, I was told, was not altogether pleased with the reforms. But he was pragmatic enough to argue that it was wiser to accept half a loaf rather than wait for the whole loaf. He was the Vice-President of the Legislative Council. With the new constitution, he was elected the Leader of the House of the State Council, the Minister of Home Affairs and the Vice-Chairman of the Board of Ministers.

That was as high as a national could have aspired to rise in politics without the declaration of full independence.

Timothy had placed on my desk a full set of the Ordinances passed by the State Council. The very list of subjects was impressive. The real problems of the country were being dealt with and the solutions were astoundingly relevant. Priority had been given to health, education, transport, roads and communications, national archives and the safeguarding of antiquities and archaeological monuments. C. W. W. had told me of his Education Committee of 1942. I read its report and the regulations pertaining to free and widely accessible education which resulted from its recommendations.

To complete my grasp of the recent historical developments, I read the concise book *A History of Ceylon* by Ray Blaze, a teacher of Dutch descent in a school in Kandy, who was among the young men who had visited me since my return from the Forest Hermitage. I noted with interest his conclusion:

> *More than once has the loyalty of the Ceylonese been publicly referred to in the highest terms; and in concluding this sketch of our Island's history we may consider if indeed we have not cause to be loyal. Under British rule we enjoy almost every advantage which an Englishman enjoys in England. We have peace, protection of person and property, the fullest freedom and equal laws. We have numerous schools which prepare us for our work in life. Every profession is open to us, every trade and occupation is free for all. Natives of Ceylon have risen and can rise to very high positions in the service of the Government. The post, the telegraph and the steamer have brought us into communication with every part of the world. The literature of Britain, the arts and sciences,*

the highest ideals of Christian life and thought, and every
civilizing influence that makes for peace, comfort and happiness,
have all been placed within our reach. We belong to an empire
vast in extent, rich in noble traditions, powerful beyond its rivals,
and governed, under the King, ***by statesmen who are not only***
prompt to advance its best interests, but sincerely anxious to
promote the welfare of all its members. *It will be our own fault if*
we do not use the advantages we have to prove that we are not
unworthy of them. (Emphasis mine)

This was an assessment made half way in the life of the first State
Council. How correct he was in the confidence placed on the new
leaders!

I was, however, very pleased that the campaign for further political
reforms had not been abandoned. Another Royal Commission had been
sent to propose constitutional changes. Chaired by Lord Soulbury, it
was studying the proposals submitted by the national leadership led by
the youngest Senanayaka Brother, D. S. A greater measure of Self-rule
with perhaps some reservation with regards to foreign relations and
defence was imminent, said both Timothy and Autumn-Moon.

Thus assured that full independence was around the corner, I sat
down to write the story of my times. I was not sure whether my own life
and career would be of any interest to readers. After all what had I to
show for eighty-eight years of my life?

A childhood of bad memories simply because my birth
coincided with a land-slide which impoverished my family?

An undeserving beneficiary of the kindness of strangers?

A loser to credulity and superstition of rustic relatives?

A reluctant monk who tried to make the best of a bad bargain
and benefited from the sanctity that people attached to the yellow
robe of the Buddha?

A late bloomer who achieved his childhood dreams and
ambitions only decades later?

A renegade who devoted the best years of his life to serve as a
mercenary the very same foreign regime from which he once
hoped to save his Motherland's religion and culture?

684

A man who negated the promises he had made to such men of noble principles and devotion as Colonel Henry Steel Olcott and Homeless Dharmapala ?

A miserable creature who helplessly spent a hundred days in jail and indirectly brought about the death of the person whom he loved most dearly?

A coward who withdrew from action and retired to a forest hermitage for twenty-nine years to gain his own salvation?

A failure there too, who returned to civilization with little to show for those long years of renunciation?

Thus I reviewed every aspect of my life and career and came to the conclusion that it was not worth the paper on which I would write it.

I would, instead, write a history of the Island from 1848 to, I hoped, 1948 and would call it **"The Tale of a Tortuous Century."** As a child I had been brought up on the legends of courage and bravery, treachery and deception surrounding the rebellion of 1848. From my teen-age I had had a series of overwhelming experiences which questioned the prevailing biases and prejudices of both the rulers and the ruled.

So I began:

The hundred years from the Rebellion of 1848 has verily to be described as a tortuous century in the history of this Island. It began with the second abortive attempt of a nation which had never before had their country as a whole dominated by a foreign power.

On and on went the first two chapters duly documented with copious footnotes. It was like the days in Calcutta when I wrote my dissertation. There was something which looked incongruous. I wanted to consult Timothy and Moon-Beam whom I knew would give me straight answers.

It was Moon-Beam who came with her comments first.

"Father, Will you get offended if I tell you the truth?"

"Never, Jewel, Never. I want to hear only the truth from my children."

685

"Then I will tell you. This is pedantic drivel that anyone in the University can write. It is dry, uninspiring and devoid of life."

"Jewel, tell me frankly what do you expect?"

"Your life, experiences, insights and your unbiased personal reactions to things that have happened in this country in your life time."

I told her why I had decided against being personal. I told her exactly how I felt that my life was any thing but spectacular.

"From my childhood to my last fiasco of twenty-nine years spent in a jungle cave, I have done the wrong thing at the wrong time."

I spelled out my burgeoning list of negatives.

"Father, this requires a whole day and Timothy and if possible Uncle Autumn-Moon must be with us. You really need to revise the low esteem that you have of yourself."

Three against one, I hardly had a chance. To them I was a hero and they took pains to explain why they thought so.

"Why do you think that the Blakes and later Kenneth Saunders went out of the way to turn your childhood around and give you all the opportunities to make you who you are?" asked Moon-Beam.

"Would the world have known what a treasure the manuscript library of Sangha-Gem-Field contained, if you had not become a monk there? Do you know what you did to that sleepy village by the river?" asked Timothy.

"Why do you think that Venerable Sumangala, Venerable Gunananda, Colonel Olcott, Uncle Homeless, Uncle Don Baron and a host of others of the same calibre took you into confidence and involved you in the work they did for the national reawakening?" queried Autumn-Moon.

I had no answers to these and many other questions they asked to convince me that I had a life worthy of being recounted.

"Take even what you call your fiasco of twenty-nine years. This summer, Vickie and Beckie are coming all the way from America to write a book on it at the expense of someone who thinks that your memoirs are worth investing in," pointed out Autumn-Moon.

The last argument came from Moon-Beam.

"Father, can you think of any person who would sacrifice his esteem and reputation as an highly venerated monk, take a questionable Government job to help his childhood love in her hour of grief, bring up her child and two children from a socially discarded woman as his own and give the world three wonderful families? See what each of them have done to make the world a better place than they found."

686

She paused for a while and looked lovingly at her husband and uncle.

"Father, Is it not simply wonderful that you have a son-in-law who is playing an important role in the formation of the nation? And he is getting his equally talented Uncle Autumn-Moon to collaborate with him. Is this not all your doing, your guidance, your example, your inspiration?"

I was overwhelmed. I recalled the night in England when the three children and their kids elevated me from being Little Father to Father. I had to concede.

"All right. I will see if I really can write my own story."

I began to write in earnest an autobiography. I had no model to go on. In a rich literature in three languages - Pali, Sanskrit and Sinhala - produced over two millennia, not a single autobiography was to be found. That was not surprising since some of the major works were anonymous. Such was the spirit of self-effacement. Times had changed and here I was piecing together my memories because those who loved me the most and were the closest to me wanted my life to be written. It took a little time to convince myself that it was not my vanity which prompted me to agree with them.

Once I began to dictate to the two stenographers who took turns with short-hand and typing, my task became very simple. Thoughts rushed and long-lost memories surfaced. In less than two weeks, I had dictated the first draft of the what I called the first book on "All too Short a Childhood." Typed in five copies, I had it read by Moon-Beam, Timothy, Autumn-Moon and the ageing historian of Kandy, Mr. Stream-Spout.

Were they all pleased? Not exactly. Stream-Spout wanted a little more on the background, geographical and historical.

"Venerable Sir, bring your story to life by giving your reader a clearer idea of where and when you were. Tell us of the changes you saw taking place in your childhood. You were a child in a remote village untouched by foreign influence until thirty odd years before your birth," he said.

My family agreed with him and added,

"There is another way to bring the story to life. Recall the conversations you had with your family, the Chief Monk, the Abbot of Bo-Tree-Plain Temple, the Blakes and so forth," said the two men.

"Father, please tell us more about your Little Father. He seems to have been your first mentor - the one who led you to all others," said Moon-Beam.

It was a wonderful feeling. Revision was out of the question. The changes they asked for were basic. I dictated an altogether new version. I did not have the patience to wait for their comments. Ideas were flowing with such rapidity that I began to work on the second book on my Little Father. I called it "Mentorless Meandering." It was over in two months. Copies went to my four readers and I relaxed. That was a mistake. Or was it providential?

Events of the next few months kept me distracted. The Constitution recommended by the Soulbury Commission was adopted and General Elections were announced. There was much excitement. I had no clue, until Timothy explained to me, what elections had meant to the people since they were empowered to vote fifteen years ago.

"Since the introduction of universal franchise," he said, "the people took all elections very seriously. Participation was usually high and the feverish campaigns engrossed their attention for months. A carnival-like atmosphere prevailed. All enjoyed the fun."

To enable illiterate voters to identify the candidates the ballot boxes were of different colours. Candidates used the colour assigned to them in every possible way: flags, decorations, posters, pamphlets, flyers, the sarees of their female supporters and so forth. Processions of children carrying pennants of each candidate's colour crisscrossed the town or village. Supporters had paper streamers and illuminations outside their homes. Music, songs, theatrical performances, puppet shows - all formed a part of the campaign, and of course political meetings, where some speakers became recognized magnets to draw crowds. Voting was in secrecy. But the external manifestation of support was glaringly public."

So enthusiastically did others join in supplementing what each thought was characteristically significant in our elections, that I felt a little left out. While all this political awakening was taking place in the country, I was away in the forest hermitage.

I looked forward to the forthcoming elections. To the extent possible at my age and my secluded status as a monk, I followed the changes taking place in the political scene. The evolution of political parties interested me as I had been aware of the way the Tory and the Labour parties worked in Britain. I had also been impressed with the activities of the Indian National Congress under the leadership of the Theosophist Annie Bessant. I had little knowledge of the Ceylon National Congress other than it had been a rallying point for national politicians to channel their demands for constitutional reform.

Agitation for Self-rule and eventually independence had been nonviolent. None of the gruesome incidents which marred the struggle in the Indian mainland, like kidnappings, murders and mass killings, had taken place in the Island.

"Independence is near at hand and we would have won it without shedding a drop of blood," was the boast of the Ceylon National Congress.

D. S. Senanayaka formed the United National Party more or less transforming the Congress into an operational political party on the model of the British Conservative Party. My impression that it was the first of its kind in the Island was soon corrected by my family political caucus. It now included Moon-Beam, who had retired from Government Service and was free to work with her husband.

According to them the Marxist Leftist Movement had given rise to at least two major parties almost two decades ago. One was the Communist Party which had among its leaders some really remarkable intellectuals like Dr. S. A. Wickremasinghe and his British wife and Pieter Keuneman and Hedi, his Hungarian wife. Each one of them was a fine speaker. I was taken to the Temple Square on the day they had a party meeting at the Buddhist School. Seated in the office of the Headmaster, I followed their exposes of the Island's needs and problems and the solutions they offered from the point of view of Communism.

I had occasion similarly to hear several of the Trotskyite leaders of Lanka Equal Society Party, popularly known by its acronym, LSSP. Autumn-Moon, whose sympathies appeared to be with this group, arranged for a number of its leaders to visit me. That day, I was thrilled to receive Dr. N. M. Perera, the political scientist; Dr. Colvin R. de Silva, the lawyer-historian; Leslie and Vivian Gunawardene, a formidable husband and wife team; and Philip and Robert Gunawardene, two most volatile brothers in politics - anything but two peas in a pod. They wanted to know of my relations with Colonel Olcott, Homeless Dharmapala and Don Baron.

After they left, I asked Timothy what the difference was between the two groups.

"Very simple, Father. Both uphold Karl Marx, the Communists according to the Gospels of Engel and Lenin and the LSSPs according to the Gospel of Trotsky. But their impact on our national politics is fantastic. If Uncle Homeless was alive, he would have found them continuing his work of raising the awareness of the people of their problems."

The election fever was mounting and I directed my attention to the news over the radio and the newspapers. I hardly returned to my manuscript and the two stenographers did nothing more than attend to my correspondence. But all this changed when Vickie and Beckie came with a veritable mountain of luggage.

Beckie came charging in and would have hugged me if Moon-Beam did not stop her.

"Father, Father, We are going to make a film on you." she announced with much excitement.

So it was. From the very next morning, the stage was set for the film. I sat on a dais appropriately decorated with coconut flowers and tender leaves, under the glare of spot lights. Vickie cranked the camera and Beckie asked me questions.

"What are you really doing?" I asked them at the end of the first day. I was excited but physically exhausted.

"We are getting a few comments on your life and we will film in location the places you mention. Then we come to your life in the forest hermitage. Again you answer our questions. When we have your story, we go to the hermitage and film in location.When we return to America, the technicians will do the mixing of images with words. Voila, the life and times of our incomparable Father."

I was confident that the film would be well done. They had engaged as their adviser a young man whom I had admired in his youth. Since my encounter with the radio, I had never missed any of his programmes. I used to call him GPM. Now he was the Professor of Pali of the University of Ceylon of which Sir Ivor Jennings was the Vice-Chancellor. Professor Wrestler-Diadem was not only an erudite scholar but an indefatigable activist. In the eyes of the people he was the spiritual successor to Colonel Olcott, Homeless Dharmapala and Sir Don Baron Jayatilaka .

"Now that our task here is virtually accomplished, I plan to mobilize the Buddhists of the world," He told me when he came with Vickie and Beckie. "We do need a World Fellowship of Buddhists."

I wished him success. I knew that he could do it.

Moon-Beam, as usual, was solicitous. She took control of the schedule and ensured that I was not overly extended. Before long neither the lights nor Beckie's questions were a problem. I had become a professional actor, teased Beckie.

While Vickie and Beckie went to film the various places in the Island to be incorporated in the film, I followed the news of the Indian Subcontinent.

The partition of India into two sovereign states resulted in bloodshed. India and Pakistan engaged themselves in a pitched battle for the princely state of Kashmir, the scenic haven of tourists. Incredible border violence claimed the lives of millions of innocents who were uprooted from their ancestral homes.

Inhumanity to humanity manifested itself in the most unimaginable acts of cruelty. A taught wire at the neck level tied to pillars of a railway bridge decapitated or pushed into the river every man, woman or child who rode on the roof of the last train from India to Pakistan. Men killed wives, mothers and sisters to save them from the dishonour of being ravished and violated by infuriated ethnic extremists. Hundreds of thousands of people left the border area as refugees to settle in shanty towns in the country of their choice. Some were fortunate to exile themselves abroad.

What happened to the gentle people of the land of seers, saints and founders of religion?

Amidst the insanity of violence and the cacophony of allegations and counter-allegations was heard the voice of that great giant of Nonviolence - Mohandas Karamchand Gandhi - popularly known as Mahatma Gandhi. He used once again a weapon whose efficacy was proved many times. He went on a fast unto death demanding an end to inter-communal violence.

The world looked on with amazement. No one stepped forward to end the senseless killings. I was extremely dispirited.

Some temporary relief and distraction was provided by a surprise visit by Rose and Middle Banda. They had been invited to the ceremony marking the Independence of Burma. It was to be on the fourth of January 1948, a month before ours.

During his long years in the judiciary of this Buddhist nation, Middle Banda had befriended many of the new leaders. He admired in particular the Major General Aung San and Thakin Nu. Rose had many friends and thousands of students. They looked forward to meeting as many of them as possible. It had been a long time since Rose first and Middle Banda a few months later left Burma unceremoniously in the wake of Japanese occupation.

"It is a divided land, Father," Middle Banda told me. "I have no idea how they will fuse themselves into one nation. Besides, two major wars - one when the Japanese came in and the other when they were ousted - have left the country with far too many weapons of destruction."

"You seem to be diffident about Burma's future?"

"To some extent, Father. But I still hope that the leaders will do their best."

They left for Burma on the day after Christmas. Once again, I focused on the bad news from India and Pakistan. But the worst was yet to come.

I was listening to the news broadcast directly from London by the British Broadcasting Corporation. The English Service of Radio Ceylon relayed the programme and the reception was excellent.

Suddenly, I heard the voice of the new Prime Minister of India, Pandit Jawaharlal Nehru. He choked and had to gain control of himself before he continued. The Father of the Nation had succumbed to the bullets of an assassin who shot him point blank at the evening prayer meeting, he said. George Bernard Shaw paid a tribute to Gandhi, saying in the process,

"It is too dangerous to be too good."

Hardly a week before our own independence, the architect of the nonviolent transition to independence of four new nations of the region lay a victim of a fanatical Hindu radical. The crime which Gandhi had committed in the eyes of the assassin was that he preached harmony, tolerance, coexistence and peace. All he wished was that Hindus and Muslims would live in amity.

Gandhi's sudden death was a poignant reminder of my own mortality. Repeatedly I told myself that our fair Island would have an easier passage to independence. At the end I believed it.

I looked forward to the fourth of February. I decided to work on my book. This time I was determined to finish it. I did succeed.

Thus ends my account of my life and times up to the very day I resumed writing it.

> *May the rains fall in proper season*
> *Causing an abundant harvest*
> *May the world be prosperous*
> *And the rulers righteous.* [*]

---

[*] A Buddhist benediction used widely in South and Southeast Asia.

EPILOGUE

An year has gone by since I embarked on my third attempt. My mission has been accomplished. Though in a mundane sense, I could express my satisfaction only in the words of the Buddha's saintly disciples who reached liberation from the cycle of birth and death:

Katakicco - Done is my task

Katam karaniyam - Done is what had to be done

Ohitabharo - Lifted from me is the burden

Timothy was happy and Moon-Beam was relieved when I handed to them the corrected final version in Five Books. Stanley could not keep to his promise of reading my draft in its entirety. Ill-health kept him confined to his cottage on a hill slope enjoying an everlasting English spring. Our local historian Stream-Spout succumbed to a heart attack and he could peruse only the first three books. Finally I was left with Timothy, Moon-Beam and Autumn-Moon who have been my most faithful readers and most ardent critics.

I was hardly sure of surviving the ordeal, compounded further by having to help Vickie and Beckie to write a book on my life in the forest hermitage, in addition to completing the film. Perhaps my inner resources came from three decades of meditation in the forest hermitage. At least this is my friends' explanation for my limitless nervous energy. They dubbed me "indestructible."

At my age everything has to be savoured in leisurely mindfullness.

A year of independence of a nation whose dire vicissitudes I had personally experienced is a rare treat. It has to be enjoyed with the intensity that a starving beggar reserves for his first square meal.

My age and monkhood deprived me being present when ceremonies marked the transition of the Island from a Colony to a Dominion. I had to visualize them as I listened intently to the imaginative descriptions of gifted radio commentators.

I had a mental image of the nation's long-lamented discomfiture of the second of March 1815. I hoped that it would be reversed. I strained my ears to hear *"The moment has come for the Union Jack to be lowered and the Lion Flag to be raised in its place."*

It proved to be only my wishful thinking. I was greatly disappointed when the Lion Flag was raised even while the Union Jack was securely in place and the King of England, renamed for our purposes "His Majesty George the Sixth, the King of Ceylon," was recognized as the sovereign.

I could not hide my disappointment. I told Timothy,

"This is a sell-out. It would never have happened if Homeless Dharmapala was living and Don Baron was at the helm of affairs."

"No, Father. You are definitely over-reacting. These symbols hardly matter. Now our elected representatives of the Parliament will make our laws and no one has the power of veto them. That is what is important. Just imagine, Father, we have the power and the authority *now* to change both the King and the Flag. All we have to do, if we really want, is to become a republic and quit that nebulous union of nations called the British Commonwealth - just as Burma did."

He was right and my spirits rose high again. I had him drive me to the University Park in the eastern suburb of Kandy to witness the arrival of Duke of Gloucester and our own national leaders. I rushed back to the Royal Spout not to miss the broadcast of the proceedings of the ceremony of laying a foundation stone by the Duke.

Through the radio and the press, supplemented by a vivid imagination based on my own experiences, I kept abreast of the national transformation. What was going on in the Island boosted my optimism.

In contrast, news from the neighbouring nations has been dismal and disappointing.

How lucky we have been in our little haven of peace? Our worst fears of communal tensions seemed to be a thing of the past. The new Government was representative of all ethnic, linguistic and cultural specificities of the nation. "G. G.," the once-dreaded campaigner for "Fifty-Fifty", became a loyal member of the Cabinet. With that ended his agitation that fifty percent of nation's assets and opportunities had to reserved for the Tamil-speaking minority.

"We will make Lanka the Switzerland of the East," announced the young Minister of Finance. I recalled Timothy making the same remark when he chose the political platform in preference, or rather in addition, to the scalpel and the operating theatre.

"This country shall overflow with milk and honey," declared the rest of the Government.

Young and vigorous enthusiasts had their hands on the helm of the state.

Now that my book has been finished, I am bound to find more time to study my Motherland's progress for my own delectation. For how long? It does not matter.

With the ninety-first birthday dawning tomorrow my future is already behind me. But not so the future of my Motherland! Not so the bright and prosperous future which we now have the freedom to mould!

> *Free at last from foreign yoke*
> *My wish for you, Mother Lanka,*
> *Is wisdom to serve humanity,*
> *As you have always done,*
> *With faith and courage*
> *Compassion and truth.*
>
> *Yours is a record of love supreme*
> *For in your bosom have prospered*
> *Sinhala and Tamil, Moor and Burgher*
> *Each speaking their own mother tongue*
> *Professing in peace their chosen faith*
> *And building cultures on par with one another.*
>
> *Beckoned here by recent rulers*
> *Are guests who may soon not have*
> *A home to return as good as this Isle.*
> *Not a melting pot or a crucible*
> *Where diversity loses its richness*
> *But a quilt of the finest fabric*
> *Whose hues and shapes add glamour and beauty.*
>
> *These wondrous traits of your charm and glory*
> *Are the promise of a future as bright as the past.*
> *Inspire us, your children diverse,*
> *To work in unity to enhance your fame*
> *As the home of tolerance,*
> *The fountain of harmony,*
> *And a paradise for all,*
> *Where the words of the Buddha prevail*
> *With those of the Vedas, the Koran and the Bible.*

With this *Ode to Mother Lanka* I conclude. But have my sentiments got the better of me? Perhaps!

My concerns lurk.

Will the people be willing and ready to make sacrifices for preservation of sovereignty and maintenance of peace?

696

Will they strive to eliminate bigotry and prejudice with a view to creating a nation where plurality and diversity would be strengths?

Will the baton of leadership pass in order to brothers-in-arms, as in a relay race? Or, will unwarranted squabbles rob them of their idealism?

Will the leaders of the future be righteous and just?

Or will they succumb to the temptation of reserving power and position for one's own family and thereby disrupt unity and solidarity?

Will contenders for power, in frustration and desperation, seek to "divide and rule" and pander to base sentiments of race, language and religion?

Will the Buddhist Sangha rise above parochial interests and guide the new nation to peace and harmony with the benign teachings of the Buddha as their guide?

Or will my worthy brethren seek to be[*]

END

---

[*] With this involuntary bold line which tore the paper and scratched the desk ends the manuscript. At six thirty in the morning on the fourth of February 1949, Dr. Moon-Beam de Lanarolle went into the study of Venerable Pure-Wisdom with a cup of tea to offer him her respects and greetings on his ninety-first birthday. She found him slouching on the unfinished last page. Under the weight of his body the pen was broken in two. He had been dead for at least an hour, she estimated. Dr. Timothy de Lanarolle confirmed that his death had been peaceful and instantaneous resulting from a massive heart attack. - Editor/Translator.

NAMES OF PERSONS AND PLACES

Being the story of the march of the British Colony Ceylon to its independence in 1948, it centres on the lives and careers of a number of important personalities:

Anagarika (Homeless) DHARMAPALA = Don David Hevavitharana, Olcott's protege, who rose in prominence as a national leader and played a major role in the national and religious revival of the Colony and the propagation of Buddhism in India and the West;

Colonel Henry Steel OLCOTT of Orange, New Jersey, USA, the founder-president of the Theosophical Society, who embraced Buddhism in Sri Lanka and came to be known as "The White Buddhist";

Don Baron JAYATILAKA, (later Sir), another of Olcott's proteges who excelled as an educator, scholar and statesman and rose to the highest political positions available to a national in his days in the British administration;

Piyadasa SIRISENA, a protege of Anagarika Dharmapala and a pioneering novelist who used the novel and poetry to urge for national liberation;

Madame Helena Petrovna BLAVATSKY, Olcott's collaborator in the Theosophical Movement and the Corresponding Secretary of the Theosophical Society;

SENANAYAKA Brothers = D. C.., F. R. and D. S. Senanayaka, the last of whom the Right Honorable Don Stephen Senanayake P.C. became the first Prime Minister of Independent Sri Lanka;

Venerable GUNANANDA of Scribe's Garden in Bonito-Plain = Venerable Balapitiye Mohottiwatte (Migettuwatte) Gunananda, the leading orator in Buddhist-Christian controversies of 1860s and 1870s; and

Venerable SUMANGALA of Learning-Sword = Venerable Hikkaduwe Siri Sumangala Nayaka Thera = the pioneering scholar-monk;

The proliferation of such highly Sanskritized Sinhala names has been found to impede foreign readers. After a careful consideration of several options, it was decided that as many names of persons and places should be loosely translated into English.. This procedure has been in vogue since the Pali Buddhist Canon was first translated a hundred years ago and is quite common in renderings and adaptations of literary works of East Asia (e.g. Fragrant Mountain; Little Flower Drum).

Thus the narrator *Hanguranketa Vimalajnana* and his paternal uncle *Bopitiye Vimalabuddhi* become **PURE-WISDOM of Sangha-Gem-Field** and **PURE-INTELLECT of Bo-tree Plain**.

Their family name *Vikramasinha* is rendered as **VALOUR-LION**
The heroine of the story **SLIM-JEWEL** stands for *Heen-Menike.*
The ubiquitous personal name **BANDA** for men of the hilly region is retained while the distinguishing epithets like Tiny, Little, Big and Middle are translated.

All of their family and unnamed monks of various monasteries are fictional. So are the officials of the British Administration.

But **LORD CHALMERS** was really the Governor of Ceylon in the fateful days of the 1915 riots.

The model for the Siamese princely monk **NOBLE SON OF WISDOM** (= *Jnanavarorasa*) was Prince Prisadong who was in Sri Lanka as a monk under similar conditions.

The Kings of Kandy and the perpetrators and victims of the 1818 and 1848 rebellions are historical. Similarly, **the following are among the other scholar-monks** whose manyfold contribution to the national and Buddhist revival has been widely recognized:

Betel-Village = Venerable Bulatgama Dhammalankara Siri Sumanatissa Thera

Golden-Lustre of Mine-Garden = Venerable Patahavatte Siri Suvannajoti

Mango-Tree-Plain = Venerable Ambagahapitiye Nanavimalatissa Mahanayaka Thera

Pleasant-Gem-Tissa of Orange Island = Venerable Dodanduve Siri Piyaratanatissa Nayaka Thera

Sand-Village = Venerable Veligama Siri Sumangala Nayaka Thera

Subhuti of Curse-Sword = Venerable Vaskaduve Siri Subhuti Mahanayaka Thera

Equally important in the country's history are pioneering Oriental Scholars like **Viggo Fausboll, T. W. Rhys Davids, Herman Oldenberg, Rheinhold Rost** and **Wilhelm Geiger** and other national leaders: like **Dawn-Mountain** = Sir Ponnambalam Arunachalam, Dr. W. A, de Silva, Albert Godamunne **(Land-Frontier)** who figure as active members of the Temperance and political movements.

Reverend Father Augustine Berrewaerts, his school and its headmaster Walter J. Pieris as well as the scholar padres Gogerley and Spencer Hardy are real, whereas Reverend Kenneth J. Saunders of a slightly later period is the model for the character of the same name. The Blakes represent typical missionaries of their days.

Place-names and incidents associated with them are real. **Learning-Awakening** and **Learning-Adornment Colleges** are Vidyodaya and Vidyalankara Pirivenas, the prestigious seats of Buddhist higher learning. Better known places like Kandy, Colombo, Galle, Panadura, Anuradhapura,

Sigiriya (Lion-Rock), Polonnaruva are left untranslated. Others like Black-Ford (Kalutara), Ford-Village (Totagamuva) Sword-Taking or -Unsheathing (Kadugannava), Statue-Plain (Pilimatalava), Look-out (Balana) Palace-Hill (Maligakanda)are used to give the reader a flavour of the local names.

About the Author

Ananda W.P. Guruge, national and international civil servant, scholar, diplomat and academic, is by far the most competent authority on Sri Lanka to tell the authentic story of the nation's achievements and failures, trials and tribulations, aspirations and frustrations. An author of over 35 books and 120 research papers and a popular international speaker on Asian history and culture with special reference to Buddhism and Hinduism, Dr. Guruge attempts for the second time to use fiction to present his insights on his country's history in a form more accessible to the general public.

Dr. Guruge served the government of his country in the early years of its evolution as an independent nation and pursued an international career in UNESCO in France, India and Thailand. His multi-channeled career culminated in diplomatic appointments from 1985 to 1994 as Sri Lanka's Ambassador to France, UNESCO and USA with non-resident accreditation to Spain, Mexico and Algeria.

Currently a resident of USA, he is a Senior Special Adviser to the Director-General of UNESCO and the Dean of Academic Affairs and Director of Religious Studies of Hsi Lai University in Rosemead, California and a adjunct professor of Buddhism and Hinduism in the California State University, Fullerton. He is proficient in English, French, Sinhala, Tamil and Hindi besides the classical oriental languages Sanskrit, Pali and Prakrit.

utter dhana epa - don't touch !
6 ගීබ - Sarah

Printed in the United States
841100001B

9 781585 001361